SOMEONE TO LOVE

Praise for Jenny Frame

Wooing the Farmer

"This book, like all of Jenny Frame's, is just one major swoon."
—*Les Rêveur*

"This is the book we Axedale fanatics have been waiting for…Jenny Frame writes the most amazing characters and this whole series is a masterpiece. But where she excels is in writing butch lesbians. Every time I read a Jenny Frame book I think it's the best ever, but time and again she surprises me. She has surpassed herself with *Wooing the Farmer*."—*Kitty Kat's Book Review Blog*

Royal Court

"The author creates two very relatable characters…Quincy's quietude and mental torture are offset by Holly's openness and lust for life. Holly's determination and tenacity in trying to reach Quincy are total wish-fulfilment of a person like that. The chemistry and attraction is excellently built."—*Best Lesbian Erotica*

"[A] butch/femme romance that packs a punch."—*Les Rêveur*

Royal Court "was a fun, light-hearted book with a very endearing romance."—*Leanne Chew, Librarian, Parnell Library (Auckland, NZ)*

"There were unbelievably hot sex scenes as I have come to expect and look forward to in Jenny Frame's books. Passions slowly rise until you feel the characters may burst!…Royal Court is wonderful and I highly recommend it."—*Kitty Kat's Book Review Blog*

Hunger for You

Byron and Amelia "are guaranteed to get the reader all hot and bothered. Jenny Frame writes brilliant love scenes in all of her books and makes me believe the characters crave each other."
—*Kitty Kat's Book Review Blog*

"I loved this book. Paranormal stuff like vampires and werewolves are my go-to sins. This book had literally everything I needed:

chemistry between the leads, hot love scenes (phew), drama, angst, romance (oh my, the romance) and strong supporting characters."
—*The Reading Doc*

Charming the Vicar

"Chances are, you've never read or become captivated by a romance like *Charming the Vicar*. While books featuring people of the cloth aren't unusual, Bridget is no ordinary vicar—a lesbian with a history of kink...Surrounded by mostly supportive villagers, Bridget and Finn balance love and faith in a story that affirms both can exist for anyone, regardless of sexual identity."—*RT Book Reviews*

"The sex scenes were some of the sexiest, most intimate and quite frankly, sensual I have read in a while. Jenny Frame had me hooked and I reread a few scenes because I felt like I needed to experience the intense intimacy between Finn and Bridget again. The devotion they showed to one another during these sex scenes but also in the intimate moments was gripping and for lack of a better word, carnal."—*Les Rêveur*

"The sexual chemistry between [Finn and Bridge] is unbelievably hot. It is sexy, lustful and with more than a hint of kink. The scenes between them are highly erotic—and not just the sex scenes. The tension is ramped up so well that I felt the characters would explode if they did not get relief!...An excellent book set in the most wonderful village—a place I hope to return to very soon!"—*Kitty Kat's Book Reviews*

"This is Frame's best character work to date. They are layered and flawed and yet relatable. Frame really pushed herself with *Charming The Vicar* and it totally paid off...I also appreciate that even though she regularly writes butch/femme characters, no two pairings are the same."—*The Lesbian Review*

Unexpected

Jenny Frame "has this beautiful way of writing a phenomenally hot scene while incorporating the love and tenderness between the couple."—*Les Rêveur*

"If you enjoy contemporary romances, *Unexpected* is a great choice. The character work is excellent, the plotting and pacing are well done, and it's a just a sweet, warm read...Definitely pick this book up when you're looking for your next comfort read, because it's sure to put a smile on your face by the time you get to that happy ending."—*Curve*

"*Unexpected* by Jenny Frame is a charming butch/femme romance that is perfect for anyone who wants to feel the magic of overcoming adversity and finding true love. I love the way Jenny Frame writes. I have yet to discover an author who writes like her. Her voice is strong and unique and gives a freshness to the lesbian fiction sector."—*The Lesbian Review*

Royal Rebel

"Frame's stories are easy to follow and really engaging. She stands head and shoulders above a number of the romance authors and it's easy to see why she is quickly making a name for herself in lesfic romance."—*The Lesbian Review*

Courting the Countess

"I love Frame's romances. They are well paced, filled with beautiful character moments and a wonderful set of side characters who ultimately end up winning your heart...I love Jenny Frame's butch/femme dynamic; she gets it so right for a romance." —*The Lesbian Review*

"I loved, loved, loved this book. I didn't expect to get so involved in the story but I couldn't help but fall in love with Annie and Harry... The love scenes were beautifully written and very sexy. I found the whole book romantic and ultimately joyful and I had a lump in my throat on more than one occasion. A wonderful book that certainly stirred my emotions."—*Kitty Kat's Book Reviews*

"*Courting The Countess* has an historical feel in a present day world, a thought provoking tale filled with raw emotions throughout. [Frame] has a magical way of pulling you in, making you feel every emotion her characters experience."—*Lunar Rainbow Reviewz*

"I didn't want to put the book down and I didn't. Harry and Annie are two amazingly written characters that bring life to the pages as they find love and adventures in Harry's home. This is a great read, and you will enjoy it immensely if you give it a try!"
—*Fantastic Book Reviews*

A Royal Romance

"*A Royal Romance* was a guilty pleasure read for me. It was just fun to see the relationship develop between George and Bea, to see George's life as queen and Bea's as a commoner. It was also refreshing to see that both of their families were encouraging, even when Bea doubted that things could work between them because of their class differences...*A Royal Romance* left me wanting a sequel, and romances don't usually do that to me."
—*Leeanna.ME Mostly a Book Blog*

Blood of the Pack

"[A] solid entry into the expanding Lesfic urban fantasy/ paranormal romance genre. I look forward in seeing more from the Wolfgang County series."—*Colleen Corgel, Librarian, Queens Public Library*

Soul of the Pack

"I enjoy the way Jenny Frame writes. Her characters are perfectly suited to one another, never the same, and the stories are always fun and unique...there is something special about her urban fantasy worlds. She maximises the butch/femme dynamic and creates pack dynamics which work so well with those."—*The Lesbian Review*

Heart of the Pack

"A really well written love story that incidentally involves changers as well as humans."—*Inked Rainbow Reads*

By the Author

A Royal Romance

Courting the Countess

Dapper

Royal Rebel

Unexpected

Hunger For You

Charming the Vicar

Royal Court

Wooing the Farmer

Someone to Love

Wolfgang County Series

Heart of the Pack

Soul of the Pack

Blood of the Pack

Visit us at www.boldstrokesbooks.com

SOMEONE TO LOVE

by
Jenny Frame

2019

SOMEONE TO LOVE

ISBN 13: 978-1-63555-468-7

This Trade Paperback Original Is Published By
Bold Strokes Books, Inc.
P.O. Box 249
Valley Falls, NY 12185

First Edition: December 2019

Credits
Editor: Ruth Sternglantz
Production Design: Stacia Seaman
Cover Design by Sheri (hindsightgraphics@gmail.com)

Acknowledgments

Thank you to Rad and all the staff at Bold Strokes Books for your hard work and dedication.

Huge thanks as always to my editor, Ruth. Your infinite patience and guidance are greatly appreciated.

Thank you to my family for their support in everything I do.

Lou, without you I'd be even more unorganized than I already am. Thank you for your help and unwavering support.

Finally, thanks to my Barney Boy for always keeping me company and lying by my side. xx

For Lou.
My dreams never came true until the day I met you.

PROLOGUE

A shes to ashes, dust to dust, in sure and certain hope—"
Eight-year-old Davina Trent tuned out the vicar and looked around the graveside, panic growing in her chest. What was happening? What were they doing here? This was wrong. Everyone said her mama had gone to heaven, but she hadn't. The last time Davina saw her mother, she was sitting up in bed reading her a story. She had been ill, but she would get better. Now everyone said she was dead. It couldn't be true.

Davina looked at the faces around the grave—stern, solemn looking men and women, some with a tear in their eye, but most just staring into the ground where they had lowered her mother's coffin.

This was wrong. Her mama was not dead. The panic turned to anger and she shouted, "My mama is *not* dead."

Everyone looked at her, and her father gave her a deadly stare, the one that she feared, so she turned and ran across the graveyard, tears streaming down her face. Davina found a large old oak and hid behind it.

She touched a bandaged wound above her eyebrow and took out a picture of her mother, then said through her tears, "Mama, I don't believe them. Come back for me. Don't leave me with him."

Davina heard footsteps, and then her nanny was suddenly upon her.

"Davina Trent, stand up and stop making a spectacle of yourself," Nanny Wilson said. "What would your mama think of you?" She pulled Davina up and brushed down her clothes. "Look at the state of you."

Davina couldn't stop the tears from falling down her cheeks. This was all wrong and she didn't understand. There was a crunch of gravel and her father appeared at her nanny's side.

"I'm so sorry about this, Mr. Trent," Nanny Wilson said.

William Trent looked at her and said firmly, "Pull yourself together, Davina. People are watching."

"Mama isn't gone, Papa. Don't leave her here," Davina said through her tears.

William didn't respond to her. He turned to Nanny and said, "Take her straight home—she'll just cause a scene at the wake."

"Yes, Mr. Trent. Will you be home after the wake, sir?"

"No, I'm going to the office. I have work to do."

Davina watched him walk away and felt her heart hurting so badly. She broke free from her nanny and ran.

CHAPTER ONE

Davina Trent smiled smugly at the computer screen in front of her. The Osbourne divorce deal was done, and Trent got exactly what she'd set out to get. As a family lawyer, Trent dealt primarily with divorces, and she often wondered why on earth people got married in the first place. The first flush of married bliss in the rich always ended up here—in the London offices of Trent, Trent, and Masters—and making her a wealthy woman.

She sat back in her leather armchair and said to herself, "Marriage is good for business."

Trent looked around the large office that had once been her father's. It had changed little since he'd started working for his own father, many years ago. Her gaze trailed over the familiar oak bookcases filled with legal books, the antique furniture and old, valuable paintings, and the drinks cabinet across from her desk.

She had wondered many times if she should move to more modern offices, which would suit her style much better, but then again, the demographic of her clients was such that *they* lived in a world where musty paintings and antique furniture were the norm, so she always concluded this suited them better. She drew clients from the upper echelons of English society. The aristocracy, rich businessmen and women, foreign diplomats, and the odd celebrity kept her in business, wealthy, and in the sharpest of suits and the best of champagne.

Since taking over the top job from her father fifteen years ago, she had added some junior partners and expanded the size and scope of the firm. Her professional life couldn't be going better.

Trent's mobile beeped with a text. She checked the screen—it was from her closest friend, Rebecca Harper. *Lunch on Saturday at 1 o'clock. Don't try and wriggle out of it again. We miss you. Becca x*

Trent got up and walked over to the window and looked out at all the people coming and going. Business was going well, but her personal life not as much. Becca was the only woman she had ever loved, and she had let her slip through her fingers. Becca had wanted a family and that had filled Trent with terror.

They'd gone their separate ways, and soon Becca had her son Jake. But Trent had never quite let go of her love for Becca, and until about a year ago, somewhere in the back of her mind she'd thought they might get back together one day. Then Dale McGuire came along and gave Becca the love and family Becca had always wanted.

At first Trent tried to turn Becca against Dale, but as time went on she realized what a good, honourable person Dale was. They called a truce and became friends, and Becca insisted they all become one big, unusual family unit.

Becca invited her to dinner and lunch often, but lately Trent had used excuses to get out of the visits. Watching Becca and Dale with their perfect happy family reminded Trent that she had let go the one woman she had trusted, and she didn't think she could find that with someone again.

Trent saw a chauffeured car pull up outside and her next client get out. Lady Claudia Osbourne was a beautiful woman in her mid-fifties. She understood her sex appeal and used it to get what she wanted. She'd gotten a title and now a handsome divorce settlement from Lord Osbourne.

Claudia saw her at the window and waved. Trent smiled back and walked to her desk. Claudia had tried to seduce her all through the divorce process. Trent found the older woman attractive, but she wasn't some aristocratic old duffer, ready to give Claudia what she wanted because of her smiles and compliments. No, Trent had a solid rule. Never get involved with a client while on the case. But despite Trent trying to keep her distance, Claudia didn't give up.

Trent's office phone buzzed. She picked it up and her secretary said, "Lady Osbourne to see you, Trent."

"Show her in, India," Trent replied. She quickly straightened her tie and put her suit jacket on over her waistcoat.

The door opened and Lady Osbourne glided in. Today Claudia was dressed in a red dress that clung to her body. She had a fantastic figure and large full breasts—fake, no doubt, as a lot of Lady Osbourne was, but still extremely attractive.

"Darling Trent." Claudia gave her a kiss on each cheek, then lingered and breathed in her ear, "So good to see you."

The voice and the closeness of her breath, along with the smell of her perfume, turned Trent on. She hadn't slept with anyone in a month, highly unusual for her. Since Rebecca's wedding, at which she gave her away to Dale, Trent had tried to lose herself in sex, but it made the empty feeling inside her worse, so much so that she'd given up on her usual wine bars and went home each night after working late.

But maybe it was time to distract herself again. After all, she would be finished with Claudia's divorce case after today's meeting, and she wouldn't be breaking her golden rule. But that wasn't what she really wanted for herself, not any more.

"Good to see you too, Lady Osbourne." Trent escorted her to the seat.

"I've told you before—call me Claudia." She sat back and crossed her legs seductively.

"Drink?" Trent offered.

"I'm always ready for a drink, but"—Claudia took a cigarette case from her designer handbag—"it depends on whether we have anything to celebrate, darling."

Trent grinned and took a bottle of Krug champagne from the fridge beside the drinks cabinet. "I think you'll want to celebrate." She took two champagne flutes from her cabinet and came over to sit on the desk.

Claudia put a cigarette to her lips. She was the kind of woman who expected a light to be forthcoming from whoever was around her.

Trent didn't like cigarettes herself but kept a lighter on her desk for the odd cigar she enjoyed and offered to her clients. She lit the lighter, and Claudia touched the cigarette between her red lips, which matched her deep red nails, to the flame. She blew out a cloud of smoke.

"Thank you. Let's pop that Krug before it gets warm, darling."

"Of course." Trent poured out the glasses and handed one to Claudia.

She took a sip and said, "Hmm, a very good year."

Trent sat on the edge of the desk beside her and smiled. "I only give the best, Lady Osbourne."

Claudia ran a teasing fingernail down Trent's thigh, lighting a need inside her. "I'm quite sure. Now tell me what my dear husband has agreed to."

Trent pulled a file from the other side of the desk. "See for yourself."

Claudia gazed at the file and her eyes lit up. "That's more than you thought you could get, Trent. *Ten* million?"

Trent grinned, feeling the buzz of the win against Lord Osbourne's lawyer. "Let's just say that your stepchildren were worried about their inheritance. He doesn't have too many years left, and I suggested what we would be entitled to if he...passed on while still married. The ancestral home, et cetera."

"You are a genius. What about the house in Mayfair?"

Trent raised her glass and took a sip. "You've got the whole bag of tricks—plus you get five hundred thousand a year for the length of your life."

Claudia stood up and leaned in close to her lips. "Darling, you are a treasure." Then she kissed her softly before saying, "I'm having a divorce party tonight. Will you come?"

Like a predator, Claudia had been hunting her down since their first meeting. Trent hadn't been actively pursued by an older woman before—normally she did the chasing. Although she was flattered, she felt slightly uncomfortable at the relentlessness of the pursuit. She thought about her invitation from Becca, the hurt that still lived somewhere inside her. This was what she needed to banish the lonely feeling that was growing with each passing day. Maybe she should just go to the party for an hour or so.

"I'll be there, Lady Claudia."

❖

Wendy Darling looked up at the dark London sky as she rode in the taxi she'd gotten at the airport. She hoped the grey skies weren't an omen for the future. She hadn't been back to London for five years, but nothing seemed to be different.

The taxi driver looked in the mirror and said, "Just back from a holiday, sweetheart?"

"No, I was working abroad for five years." Wendy smiled.

"That's a long time from home. Where did you work?"

"All over—France, America, Canada, and Australia as a nanny, and then I taught English in Tokyo, Shanghai, Seoul, and Mumbai."

The taxi driver smiled. "You sound like a clever girl. I bet you're glad to be back home."

Home? Would it feel like home again? Wendy had left Britain, her bad memories, and a broken heart behind her, and she was frightened they would come back to haunt her now that she was back.

She'd thought long and hard about coming home. She didn't have family drawing her home. Her mother and father couldn't have cared less where she was, and her work history meant Wendy could have walked into any job abroad, but there had been a yearning to come home growing inside her for a year or more.

She wanted to finish what she'd started and not let any pain she had five years ago stop her.

"Yes, I'm ready for a new challenge," Wendy said to the driver.

Five minutes later he pulled into the car park of a block of flats. She handed over the fare and got out. The driver helped her with her large rucksack, guitar case, and duty-free bags.

Her whole life was in these bags. Not too much to show for her twenty-six years. She never thought her life would turn out like this. All Wendy ever wanted was to be a teacher, have a stable home, and a family to love. Instead she had become a traveller, moving from job to job, and living a nomadic life.

Wendy put on her rucksack and carried her guitar case up to the small block of flats. Her friend Kira had offered her a bed until she got on her feet. They'd met at university and become the best of friends.

She buzzed her flat and said, "Ki, it's me."

Wendy heard a scream of excitement over the intercom. "You're here! Get up here now, boho girl. I want to hug the life right out of you, sweetie."

Wendy laughed. "I'm coming."

Kira was one of the only friends Wendy had kept up with while she was travelling. They video-called each other at least once a week and shared all their news and problems. Kira called her *boho girl* because travelling through all the different countries had left her with a bohemian hipster style.

Wendy's highlighted blond hair hung loose under a large brimmed hat, two braids hanging down at the side. The many leather and beaded bracelets adorning her wrists were picked up at local markets as she travelled from country to country. On her wrists, hands, and feet were henna tattoos in intricate patterns, a vestige of her latest travels through India before heading home.

She was in so many ways a different woman than had left London five years ago—she hoped she had lost the innocence and naivety that had led to her broken heart, and that she was a more confident, strong woman.

The thing was, despite how much she had pushed the old Wendy deep down into her soul, she was there—the girl who wanted a home, wanted someone to love her and to make a family with. The only problem with that was she didn't think she would ever trust anyone again, not after Bailey'd destroyed her heart.

Wendy walked into the foyer area of the flats and was faced with two lifts. She looked down at her hands filled with bags and her guitar and felt weighed down by her backpack. She sighed. "Bloody lifts."

She'd been uncomfortable in lifts since she was a little girl. She did what she could to avoid them, but if forced to by the height of a building she was visiting, she had a tried and tested method. Close her eyes, cover her ears, and hum. Fortunately this building didn't have many floors, so she decided to climb them herself.

By this stage in her life, Wendy was well used to climbing stairs—a lot of stairs, but it was a daunting task. "Come on, Wendy."

She climbed the stairs to Kira's flat and finally arrived at her front door where her friend Kira was already waiting with her hands on her hips. "You still don't like lifts?"

"Not especially, Ki," Wendy said.

Kira had the biggest smile and opened her arms wide. "Come here, sweetie."

Wendy dropped her bags and went into her friend's arms. "It's so good to see you, Ki."

Kira stepped back and smiled, "You too." She lifted Wendy's arm and looked at her henna tattoos. "Dee, you look like you've just come from Glastonbury."

"I'll take that as a compliment. You look as beautiful as ever, Ki," Wendy said.

Wendy wasn't exaggerating. She had always admired Kira's beauty. Her warm brown skin and almond shaped, hazel eyes were gorgeous, and her petite figure and delicate bone structure only added to her beauty. All through university, Kira had never been short of a date, but like Wendy, she hadn't found the one.

"Are you going to invite me in?" Wendy asked.

Kira lifted Wendy's guitar case and said, "Come in and let's get the kettle on. I'm sure you've missed good old British tea."

Kira made the tea and brought it and some biscuits through to the living room. It was a comfortable small flat, with a tiny kitchen and two bedrooms, and handy for Kira's job at the local school, where she was a teacher.

She handed Wendy a cup and flounced down on the sofa. "So, you're back at last. I sometimes wondered if you ever would. You were only meant to be away for a year."

Wendy took a sip of tea. "I was making really good money, more than I could here, so it made sense when I had debts to pay off. Besides, the lifestyle in America and Australia was so good."

"So why now?" Kira asked.

Wendy pulled her feet up on the couch and sat cross-legged. "I'd made more than enough money to pay my debts"—Wendy looked down into her teacup—"and I felt like my heart had enough time to heal. Besides, I'm a lot stronger. It's time to pick up where I left off."

"I saw her, you know," Kira said softly.

Wendy immediately felt that familiar knot of tension when her ex-fiancée's name was mentioned. No matter how much stronger Wendy was now or how much she had matured, she didn't think she'd ever lose that sense of panic that she had the day she found out her ex, Bailey, had left her.

"When did you see her?" Wendy asked.

"About four months ago. I was out at a club with one of the other teachers from school. I spotted her by the side of the bar. I wasn't sure at first because the years haven't treated her well. It looks like she has been drinking like a fish since she left you."

Bailey had always liked to drink, any excuse really, and that was something Wendy had thought she could help her with. She'd been young and naive.

"Did she see you?" Wendy asked.

"Too right, she saw me. I marched right up to her and said, *Where is my friend's money?*"

Wendy put her hand to her mouth. "You didn't, did you?"

"I did," Kira said. "You worked two jobs at night, after classes, to save up for your wedding to that piece of crap, and not only does she cheat on you, but she empties your bank account and runs. I'm not letting her off by just glaring at her across the dance floor."

Wendy had worked hard for her money and was proud that she could save up the thousands it would cost for her dream wedding. Then in one day it was gone, and Bailey had destroyed all Wendy's hard work—and her heart.

She tried not to think about that day, as it made her shudder, but most nights when she closed her eyes she ran the movie in her head. She thought five years and travelling the world would diminish the memory, the pain, the embarrassment and shame of being taken for a ride, but it hadn't seemed to.

Wendy wasn't going to let Kira know that, though. "Thank you for defending my honour, Ki, but it's in the past. I've paid off my debts and I'm ready to restart my life where I left off."

"Quite right, sweetie. I know why you left university, but teaching is in your blood. You were the best in our year," Kira said.

Wendy gave an embarrassed smile. "I don't know about that, but it's time to take my life back, and that means finishing my teaching degree. Although I'm going to feel ancient compared to all those in my year. I never imagined I'd be a mature student."

Kira laughed. "A sexy mature student. You'll have the younger women running after you."

Wendy rolled her eyes. "Hardly. Besides, I don't think I'm going to be ready to go out with anybody, anytime soon—if ever."

"I don't believe that for a second," Kira said. "I'm convinced that there is someone for everyone. You used to be a romantic like me, Dee. Don't let that scumbag Bailey change what you are."

Wendy put down her tea and sighed. "She did change me, Ki. That's the problem. Things I used to love became less important. I let myself be overwhelmed with her personality, and the years I've spent away have been about getting the old Wendy back. I have in so many ways, but that last part—the romantic, giving faith and trust over to another person—I don't think I ever will get that part of me back."

Kira smiled and said, "Well, I'll keep the faith for you. So, when does uni start?"

"Five months. I've got myself on the books of a nanny agency, so I should find work until then."

"You can stay as long as you need—you know that. It'll be like old times when we shared our uni flat together," Kira said.

"I can't wait."

❖

Trent walked up the steps to Lady Osbourne's Mayfair mansion, a house that Trent had secured for Claudia by using her tough negotiating skills. Trent got a buzz from every win she got, and this divorce settlement was clearly a big win.

She straightened her tie and adjusted the gift box she was carrying—a celebratory bottle of champagne—then rang the doorbell.

The door was opened a few seconds later and she heard the sounds of loud music, laughter, and chatter, coming from inside the house. A grey-haired butler opened the door and said with a sneer, "Good evening, name please?"

Trent didn't like the way he was looking at her. Usually those looks were because of her style. Some people couldn't get over a masculine woman in a suit, but it was who she was, and had always been.

"Trent, to see Lady Claudia."

Recognition spread across his face. "Ah, Ms. Trent. Do come in."

She was led into the vast entrance hall. The floor was marble, and the walls were hung with museum-quality paintings, yet another win from her divorce deal.

The hall was full of people enjoying the party, which spread into the two rooms either side of the hall. There were half-dressed men and women standing with drinks and canapé trays, and one younger waitress approached her and offered her a drink. She took it and said, "Thank you," while not taking her eyes off the bodies on display.

Trent's lustful thoughts were interrupted by a loud feminine voice. "Darling, you made it."

She turned around and saw Lady Osbourne approach her in a gorgeous tight-fitting black cocktail dress. Her body's reaction told her it was too long since she'd had sex.

"Lady Osbourne, thank you for inviting me." Trent handed her the gift box. "A little something to mark your divorce day."

"You know it's Claudia, darling, and thank you for the gift. It's sweet of you." Claudia handed her butler the box and said, "Put this somewhere safe, James." Then Claudia took her hand and pulled her into the throng of the party. "Everyone, this is Trent, my brilliant divorce lawyer. If it wasn't for Trent, then there would be no divorce party here tonight. Three cheers for Trent. Hip, hip, hooray."

Trent was highly embarrassed at being the centre of attention all of a sudden. Most of the partygoers were women, but there were a few men dotted about here and there. They lifted their glasses and joined in with the cheers.

"Claudia, you're making me blush," Trent said.

Claudia laughed and said, "Oh, I do hope so. Come, let me show you around the house you won for me."

Claudia took her hand and led her through the throng of the party and up the grand staircase. When they reached the top of the stairs they saw a couple disappear into one of the bedrooms.

Claudia leaned in to her and said in a low voice, "Looks like they have gotten started early."

Trent was hit with a memory of doing exactly the same thing with Becca Harper when they were first getting together. She gulped hard trying to banish the emotion of the memory. Becca had understood her past and her emotional issues, and Trent trusted her like she hadn't anyone else in her life, before or since. If only she had been ready for the family that Becca wanted.

Now when she pictured Becca, Dale was always standing beside her. As much as she had come to like and admire Dale, it still hurt to know Becca was not hers any more.

The scent of Claudia's perfume brought her back to the present. Claudia was someone to lose herself in.

She trailed her fingers down Trent's tie and lingered on her belt buckle. "Why not start with my bedroom?"

Claudia grinned and took her hand and pulled her down the hall. She followed like a lamb, not a word that would normally be used as a description of her. She was a ruthless divorce lawyer, confident, dominant, but now she was nursing a broken heart. So for the first time in her life she was susceptible to being led.

Claudia opened a door. "Come in, dear Trent."

To Trent's surprise the bedroom was really old-fashioned looking. The walls and carpet were drab, and the room was decorated in dark wood furniture, including a four-poster bed that looked like it had come directly from an ancient castle.

Claudia must have noticed the way in which she was looking around because she said, "Please don't judge me, darling. This was my husband's room."

"You slept in separate bedrooms?" Trent said.

Claudia began to slip Trent's jacket off.

"Oh yes, I encouraged it. He could barely raise a smile, far less anything else," Claudia said while undoing Trent's tie. "He's sending a removal company to pick up his dusty old furniture." Claudia began to give her jaw little teasing kisses.

There were warning bells going off inside her mind. This wasn't a good idea. "Claudia…" Trent started.

But Claudia turned around and said, "Unzip me."

Trent unzipped her dress slowly and revealed the sexiest black lingerie with stockings and suspenders. Trent's excitement started to mute those warning bells. She loved stockings and garters and she didn't often sleep with a woman who wore them.

The dress dropped and Claudia kicked it away. She turned to face Trent, took her hands and placed them on her hips. "Not bad for a woman in her fifties, eh?"

Even though Trent knew not much was real on Claudia's body, she still wanted to lose herself in it. Trent pulled Claudia to her and said, "You look great."

She then kissed her and ran her hands up and down Claudia's body before unclipping her bra and letting it drop to the floor. The kiss had no passion, no feeling, and tasted of stale cigarettes, so Trent pulled away, but she wanted this, needed this to make her feel better. She cupped Claudia's breasts and squeezed.

Claudia led her back to the bed and pulled her on top of her. Trent cringed inside. This was a bad idea, but when she closed her eyes, she saw herself walking Becca down the aisle at her wedding. Trent hated dealing with feelings, and she wanted to cover over those feelings, even just for a short time.

She opened her eyes and saw Claudia grinning like the cat who got the cream. "Come on, darling, make me come."

Trent's heart started to race. This would make her feel better. She pushed two fingers inside.

Claudia gasped. "More, darling."

She added a third and then positioned herself on Claudia's thigh. Trent didn't draw it out. She thrust until Claudia tightened around her fingers and her own orgasm came with a whimper.

The rush of the muted orgasm was gone in a second, and she looked down at Claudia still groaning and coming down from her orgasm. And in that moment she had never felt so empty and alone.

Chapter Two

Trent attempted to get dressed straight away, but Claudia pulled her back into the bed. She rested her head on Trent's shoulder and stroked her fingernails across Trent's stomach. "I've always had a thing for alpha females, powerful women, but men I find are much easier to manipulate, and it gets boring. But as soon as I saw you, Trent, I knew I wanted you. There was someone once who I couldn't dominate, who made me feel like I was not in control, and you reminded me of them."

Trent said nothing, but her mind was full of thoughts. She lay staring at the ceiling, feeling stressed and uncomfortable. Sleeping with Claudia was not the answer to the echoing sadness inside her. Claudia had pursued her and got her exactly where she wanted.

Trent wasn't used to that and didn't like it. She needed to get out of here without offending a very lucrative client. *I should never have broken my golden rule.*

"You feel tense, darling," Claudia said and started to pepper kisses on her jaw and cheek. "Let me make you feel better."

Claudia began to reach her hand under the covers, but Trent sat up quickly. "I'm sorry, Claudia, I—"

"What is it?" Claudia said.

Before she had time to come up with a plausible excuse, Trent's phone rang on the bedside table. Saved by the bell.

"Excuse me," Trent said.

Claudia sighed audibly as Trent sat up and got her phone. Trent was surprised by the caller ID. It was her own lawyer—that was strange.

She answered it quickly. "Jasper? Is everything all right?"

Trent could feel Claudia's fingers stroking her back and so edged forward away from her touch.

"Sorry to phone you so late, Trent, but I have some bad news. Your cousin David was killed in a car accident this evening."

Trent stood up quickly. "Jesus, David...what happened?"

David and she had played together often when they were children and saw each other at family events, but she hadn't seen or heard from him since she was godmother to his first child. He had been the black sheep of the family, leaving university and joining a band instead of entering a good solid profession.

Jasper cleared his throat nervously. "Apparently he had gone to pick up his kids from a babysitter after a show. He was in a band, I believe?"

"Yes, that's right. He has a second child? He never told me," Trent said.

She saw Claudia get up and put on a silky dressing gown then light a cigarette.

"That's right, a six-year-old boy, the girl is eleven. They were involved in a head-on collision. David was killed instantly, but the children are okay, apart from bumps and grazes."

Trent started to pace up and down. "What about his wife?"

"She died three years ago, apparently. The police just contacted me. The hospital couldn't get a hold of any family, but apparently his solicitor knew about you and got in touch. The mother was estranged from her family since she was a teenager, and as far as David's legal papers go, you are the next of kin."

Trent ran her hand through her hair. "What do you need me to do?"

"Identify the body at the St. Giles Hospital. The children are being looked after there by a social worker, if you could speak to her too."

"Of course. I'll go straight there," Trent said.

"Thanks, Trent. I'll be back in touch about his papers, et cetera," Jasper said.

Trent ended the call and let out a breath.

"Bad news?" Claudia asked.

Trent started to pull her clothes on quickly. "My cousin David was killed in a car accident yesterday. I'm his nearest relative, so I have to go and identify the body."

Claudia walked over and slipped her arms around the back of Trent's waist. "I'm sorry to hear that. Can we meet tomorrow night again? I have more celebrating to do."

Trent just wanted to get out of there. Now dressed in her shirt and trousers, she pulled away from Claudia and picked up her tie and wallet.

Claudia wasn't exactly full of sympathy. Maybe her ex-husband and children were right about her. She was cold and heartless.

"I doubt it, I'll have a funeral to arrange by the looks of it. I'll call you." Trent had no intention of calling. "Goodbye, Lady Claudia," Trent said.

"For now, Trent," Claudia said as she walked out the door.

❖

Trent hurried into the A&E department of St. Giles Hospital and found it still full of people, even in the early hours of the morning. She waited in line at the desk, looking at her watch and tapping her foot anxiously.

Finally, she got to the head of the queue and a harassed looking receptionist said, "Yes?"

"I got a call to come and identify the body of my cousin, David Trent. I think he was brought in yesterday."

"Name?" the receptionist said.

"Trent, Davina Trent," she said in a quieter voice. Trent had always hated her first name.

The receptionist tapped the keyboard in front of her. As she waited, the noise of the casualty department increased. A young mother tried to calm her crying child, who was obviously in a lot of pain.

The sound triggered a memory in her of having a virus as a child, and even though her mother was very sick by that time, she took Trent in her arms and rocked her all through the night. The next time Trent was ill, her mother was dead, and her father and nanny let her cry all night, never once trying to comfort her. Nanny didn't believe in mollycoddling, and her father was disinterested.

"Ms. Trent?"

Trent realized she had gotten lost in her thoughts. She shook herself and said, "Sorry?"

"If you take a seat, I'll have someone take you over to the mortuary."

Trent didn't want to take a seat. Her mind was whirling with all sorts of thoughts. She would have to organize the funeral, and there was no other family but her it seemed, so she'd have to find out who his friends were and get the word out, or there would be no one at his funeral except her and his children.

The children, Trent thought, and her stomach twisted into a nervous knot as she remembered attending her own mother's funeral. It would probably be best if they didn't come. She didn't think she would ever forgive her father for forcing her to attend her mother's burial.

Then there was the guardianship of the children, but she supposed David's solicitor and social services would sort that out. She was sure David made provisions for them in his will.

A hospital orderly approached and said, "Ms. Trent, I'll escort you to the mortuary."

She followed him out of the A&E and walked over to a foreboding dull grey building on the other side of the car park. This building could only be the mortuary.

Trent's heart started to pound in her chest. She hated everything to do with death. Despite her confident personality, death and funerals made fear strike her heart. It had been her father's idea that she should see the body of her mother as it lay waiting for the undertakers, claiming to her nanny it would build strength of character. Nothing would ever take the image of her mother's lifeless body from her brain. She had shaken and shaken her mother's body, thinking that she would wake up, until she was dragged away in hysterics.

They reached the door and Trent shivered. *Stay in control, stay in control.*

She was guided to the second floor where a woman with a caring face was waiting for her by a set of double doors.

"Davina Trent?"

"Yes, that's me," Trent said.

"My name's Jane. I'm so sorry for your loss."

"Thank you. Is he in there?" Trent asked.

Jane's sympathetic look became more serious. "I just want to warn you that Mr. Trent's car crash was very violent, and it will be distressing to view his body. If you feel you can't do it, we can contact his doctor—"

"No," Trent said quickly, "I haven't seen my cousin for a long time, and I think it's my duty to do this for him."

"Okay, then we'll go in, and I'll get you to fill in the paperwork. If you'll follow me."

Trent's heartbeat got even faster. She took some deep breaths and followed Jane.

❖

Trent leaned over a toilet in the ladies' and tried to calm her stomach. After seeing the condition of her cousin's body, she'd walked back over to A&E in shock, then felt her stomach starting to churn. To see her childhood playmate in such a state was horrifying. She quickly ran for the ladies' toilets and got the usual looks, stares, and whispers from the women already in there. Her masculine appearance always made people look at her with accusation in their eyes, but she didn't have time to worry about that. She burst into the toilet and vomited a few times.

When her stomach started to settle, she took some toilet tissue and cleaned herself up, and swallowed the bitter, acidic taste in her mouth. She leaned her head against the cubicle wall and closed her eyes. This was not like her, reacting so emotionally to difficult times that came up through life.

Trent was always the strong one. She had learned from an early age to keep emotions well under lock and key, or she would receive punishment. That attitude gained her a tough reputation in university and made her a tough negotiator in the law. When Becca Harper had her whole life ripped away from her, she was the white knight coming to rescue her. Trent had handled everything, coolly and calmly, but this was different somehow.

After a few deep breaths she walked out to the sink area, washed her hands, and splashed some water on her face. She wandered out in the waiting area and sat down. Trent just needed to gather her thoughts before she enquired about the children and went home.

"Ms. Trent?"

Trent looked up to find a woman holding a folder. "Yes." Trent stood up.

"I'm Marjorie Swale, the social worker called out to handle Mr. Trent's children's case."

"Oh yes, pleased to meet you. How are the children?" Trent felt bad that she couldn't even remember their names.

"Physically it's just bumps and bruises. It's an absolute miracle they survived—so the police say."

Trent nodded. "Yes, I saw Mr. Trent's body. It is extremely lucky they survived."

"Yes, the girl, Alice, is in deep shock, not talking, and hiding away inside herself. She had a view of the front seat of the car, whereas the younger boy didn't."

After seeing David's body for herself, she couldn't imagine a child seeing that. "My lawyer said she was about eleven—is that right? I haven't seen David in years."

"Yes, eleven, and the boy Noah is six. He doesn't understand as yet that his father is gone. Follow me and I'll take you to them."

Trent didn't want this, to get any further involved, but Marjorie set off at a fast walk, so she had no other choice but to follow. They came to a curtained-off area and Marjorie pulled the drape back to reveal a little dark-haired girl with cuts and bruises, on a hospital gurney, hugging her legs. On the floor was a little boy playing with a toy dinosaur with one of the nurses.

"Alice? Noah? This is your cousin Trent," Marjorie said.

The little girl looked up with haunted eyes. Trent's mouth dried up, and she could hear the thudding of her heart in her ears. She had seen that haunted look before, in the mirror every day when she was a little girl. Trent panicked. She didn't want to acknowledge those feelings or let them even an inch out of the place she kept them locked away.

I need to get out of here.

Alice put her head down, but the boy, Noah, walked over to her.

"You look like my daddy," Noah said.

That was it. She couldn't handle this, and she turned around and walked away quickly, panic filling her body. When she reached the waiting room she felt a hand on her shoulder.

"Ms. Trent? Is everything all right?" Marjorie said.

Trent stopped and took a few breaths, rebuilding the cracks in her walls.

"Ms. Trent, I know it's been a shock, but those children need you."

"Need me? Why?" Trent asked.

"You're their next of kin. The mother had been estranged from her family long before she and David met. I mean, we'll make enquiries, but we hoped they could go home with you."

"Me?" Trent squeaked.

"It's you or they'll be taken into care, and we try to avoid that whenever we possibly can," Marjorie said.

"Oh no," Trent said with firm determination, "that is not happening. I will of course support them financially until their father's will is sorted out, but it is not possible for them to live with me. I run a busy solicitors' office and I live in a dockside penthouse, not suitable for young children."

"You want me to take them into the care system?" Marjorie's words had a hint of anger.

"It's the only possibility," Trent said coldly. "I'll be in touch about the will and David's funeral."

Trent turned around and walked quickly out of the A&E doors into the cool fresh air. Alice's troubled eyes floated across her mind.

Walk away, Trent told herself, and she did.

CHAPTER THREE

You're not applying for this, are you, Dee?"

Wendy was polishing the TV screen for what felt like the fiftieth time in the last few days. She stopped and turned around. Kira was holding the application form she had picked up yesterday from the local supermarket.

"Yeah, I thought I would. I phoned the nanny agency yesterday afternoon, and there's still no sign of a job."

Kira came over and sat on the edge of the couch. "But you've got savings, haven't you? This kind of nine-to-five will drive you mad after travelling for so long."

Wendy sighed and came to sit on the couch. "Yes, I've got savings, but I'm so bored when you're out at work. There's only so many times I can clean the flat, and it's months until I can start my uni course."

Kira looked around the room. "Yeah, my place has never been so clean in all its life, but have some patience—I'm sure a nanny post will turn up."

"Hmm," Wendy replied.

Kira snapped her fingers. "I know—why don't you start that children's book you always talked about writing? It was always your dream."

Wendy snorted. "That's pie in the sky. It's never going to happen."

"Well, it won't if you don't try. Remember the stories you used to make up for the children at the after-school club you worked in at uni?"

Wendy was full of children's stories. Nearly every cuddly toy she saw conjured up a story in her mind, and in fact the travel blog she had written while she globetrotted was called *Travels with My Teddy.*

Imagination, making up stories and songs, was the way she'd coped with family life when she was younger. Her parents were distant, unemotional people, and Wendy was the complete opposite. She craved affection, and her imaginary characters gave her comfort.

"I don't know. I've never written them down before. I'd feel silly," Wendy said.

Kira smiled. "Good, everyone should be silly every so often."

❖

Trent pulled into a lay-by a few hundred yards from Becca's vicarage, in the isolated village of Plumton, and turned off the engine. She wanted to gather her thoughts before arriving at her friend's house.

She let out a long breath and let her head fall back against the headrest. Since walking away from the children at the hospital, she'd hardly slept or eaten. She was racked with guilt, and every time she closed her eyes she saw Alice's eyes and recognized the pain in them.

Trent's brain tried its best to rationalize her decision. She was in no position to look after children. She had work, late nights—but most of all, there was fear. Today's Sunday lunch at Becca's was the last thing she needed. To be surrounded with the most loving of families would just remind her of what she was not doing for Alice and Noah, but she couldn't make any more excuses to Becca.

She scrubbed her face and started the car up. Better to get this over with.

Trent drove along to the entrance to the vicarage and pulled into the driveway. It was like a different house since Dale had fixed it up both on the outside and inside. It had gone from a cheap run-down house to one worth a lot of money. She parked and saw Dale with Jake by her side and little Gracie, the ten-month-old, sitting on her back in a carrier. Dale and Becca had brought chickens, ducks, and goats to the land at the side of the vicarage, and they were in the chicken enclosure giving them food.

Again guilt twisted her guts. Why did Dale find it so easy to be with kids and play with them? If Dale had been in her shoes, the kids would have come straight home with her from the hospital, she wouldn't have gone running scared.

Jake spotted her and started to run over to the car. Both Dale and Becca had helped her repair her relationship with Jake. For the longest time she'd resented his place in Becca's life and hadn't been as friendly as she should have been, but now she realized she and Becca had simply wanted different things in life. And in any case, Dale was the right partner for Becca. She'd accepted that, not that it still didn't hurt a little bit.

Trent got out of the car and Jake hugged her. This was so different to how things used to be between them. He was a forgiving boy.

"Hi, Trent. We're feeding the ducks and chickens."

"So I see. They are lucky to have you to look after them," Trent said.

She always felt slightly awkward when talking one-on-one with Jake, but she was getting better and had made an effort to engage with him. It didn't come naturally to her like it did for Dale. She'd never been around children since she was one, so it took effort.

Trent thought of Noah and his eagerness to engage with her because she had a family resemblance to his dad. She prayed they had found a decent foster home.

Dale approached, smiling. "All right, mate. We havnae seen you for ages. Becca's missed you."

"Uh…yes, my workload's been busy recently," Trent lied.

Dale lifted Gracie's hand and said, "Wave to Trent, wee yin."

"Hi," Grace said in her sweet baby voice.

Gracie was a beautiful child and so like Becca, Trent thought. She reached out and stroked Gracie's cheek. "What a pretty girl you are, Grace."

Then a thought flashed across her mind. This could have been her life. She pulled back, feeling uncomfortable all of a sudden. She tried to picture herself in Dale's shoes, with Jake and Gracie, but she couldn't shift Dale from the picture in her mind. This was Dale's family.

You look like my daddy. Noah's words to her simmered inside her, and then the guilt set in.

Jake took her hand and said, "Come in, and get dinner. Mummy's made a big roast chicken and roast totties—that means potatoes in Glasgow, Trent."

Trent and Dale chuckled. Jake had a habit of picking up words from Dale's Glasgow dialect, but in his very proper middle class accent they sounded adorable.

"Aye," Dale said, ruffling his hair, "and homemade apple pie and ice cream. Let's get going, wee man."

❖

As Dale fed Gracie apple pie, Becca watched Trent staring into her bowl, her mind somewhere else. Becca could tell since Trent arrived that something was wrong. She had lived with her long enough to know the signs. Trent had a dominant, confident personality, and when she went quiet and subdued, Becca knew she was struggling with her emotions.

Usually Trent was well practised at keeping her emotions under wraps. Emotions were weakness to her, but occasionally something would happen that sent her into her home office and into her head.

When Trent's father died, the emotions she had kept bottled up since she was a child were hard for her to handle. From what Trent had told her, he had scarred her emotionally, and his death made the anger threaten to burst out. Becca remembered the night it did. She had tried to talk to Trent about the emotional distance between them. They had a blazing row, and all Trent's anger poured out. The evening ended with Becca holding Trent as she cried. Becca suspected that none of Trent's other friends knew Trent had that side to her, the one that wanted to be loved and cared for like her mother had done.

Becca couldn't be that emotional safe harbour for Trent any more. She only wished Trent could meet the person who would love her, the way she'd found Dale. Becca looked up and got Dale's attention. "Why don't you take the kids out to see the goats, and we'll clear up here."

Dale smiled and winked. "No problem, hen."

Becca still got a shiver down her spine when Dale winked and smiled. She was adorable and sexy as hell at the same time.

Trent looked up when Jake, Dale, and Gracie went outside. "Sorry, I was miles away. The apple pie was great, Becca."

"Thanks. Why don't I make a cup of tea and we can chat?"

"Sure," Trent said with a hint of suspicion in her voice.

Once Becca made the tea she brought over the cups to the table. "So, what's been happening with you?"

Trent took a sip of tea and then said, "David passed away."

Becca was taken by surprise by that answer. "Your cousin David?"

"Yes, he was killed in a collision with a lorry on the motorway," Trent said.

"Oh my God! How did you find out?" Becca asked.

"My lawyer called. The police and the hospital were trying to get hold of his next of kin. Apparently, that's me. His wife died a few years ago. He didn't have any other family and neither did she. I had to go to the hospital to identify his body. It was quite a violent death…"

Becca saw Trent gulp down her emotion. She covered Trent's hand with hers. "I'm so sorry, Trent. That must have been a hard thing to do."

Trent had gotten her emotions under better control. "Yes, well. It was the least I could do. The last time I saw him was at his daughter's christening. I was godmother, if you remember."

"That's right. He had a little girl."

Trent nodded. She knew the question was going to come about the children. "Alice, she's eleven, and there's a boy—Noah. He's six. They were in the car when it crashed but survived without any bad injuries, miraculously."

"Dear God, those poor babies," Becca said. Becca's description of the children as babies made her feel worse. "What's happening with the children?" Becca asked.

Trent closed her eyes momentarily. *Here we go.* "They don't have any other relatives apart from me. Their mother was estranged from her family and no one's heard of them in years."

"So..." Becca hesitated. "What are you going to do?"

Trent had been on the phone constantly for the last few days, organizing the funeral, consulting with lawyers. "He left no money. David was a jobbing musician, so I'll support them financially of course. I've contacted several boarding schools to see if they can take them. I think it's the best solution."

Becca's eyes went wide. "Trent, you can't pack them off to boarding school, not after what they've been through."

"What would you have me do? I'm trying my best," Trent said sharply.

"They need family, Trent. They need you—plus, they're too young to send off to boarding school. Think of the six-year-old. He's still a baby."

Guilt enveloped Trent. "I was sent to boarding school at that age and it didn't do me any harm."

Becca raised a questioning eyebrow. "Really?"

Trent had a memory of her first night away from home at boarding school, and she could remember the fear and panic even now. Becca always could read her emotions and thoughts.

"I'm a busy lawyer, and you know I never wanted children."

Becca frowned. "Yes, I know only too well."

Trent rubbed her forehead. "I'm sorry. I shouldn't have said that. I can't do it, Becca. You know I can't."

"I don't believe that. I know you can, but even if you send them to boarding school, bring them home to you in the holidays."

"I don't know about that. Maybe. In any case, the boarding school I like can't take any more students for months."

"Wait," Becca said, "so where are they now?"

"In foster care," Trent admitted.

Becca shook her head. "Trent, you can't leave those children in foster care for six months until the school can take them. Have you any idea what foster care is like? Those two kids are traumatized."

"I assumed they'd be better off in a foster family," Trent said.

"Foster carers are in high demand. They're probably in a children's home at this very moment, and there's no guarantee that they'll be kept together."

Trent was lost for words. "I had no idea, Becca." She got up from the table and walked over to the kitchen window. Trent gazed at Dale with Gracie up on her shoulders and Jake standing close by her side. Dale was so open with the children and appeared to have a natural affinity with them, something Trent never had or wanted.

Childhood was a time that she didn't want to revisit or be reminded of, but then she tried to imagine Jake and Gracie alone, without their parents. The thought was horrendous.

Becca walked up to the window too and looked out in silence for a few seconds, before saying, "Couldn't you get a nanny, Trent? It's only six months, if you insist that they go to boarding school."

Trent let out a long breath. She couldn't live with the consequences of her actions and the memory of the kids in that hospital room, whether it was convenient for her or not.

"I'll bring them home to me—I am Alice's godmother after all—but I need a nanny to look after them, 24/7."

Becca hugged her from the side. "It's the right thing to do. There's a good nanny agency one of the mothers at Jake's school uses. I'll get you the number."

❖

Becca woke up and immediately felt Dale wasn't there. She looked at the clock on the bedside table and read three o'clock in the morning. She got up and walked onto the stair landing. She heard Dale before she saw her. She was singing one of her goofy Scottish children's songs.

She crept up to the door of Gracie's bedroom and peeked around the open doorway. Dale was standing in just boxers and T-shirt, singing softly with Gracie in her arms. Dale looked absolutely adorable and Becca just stood there and listened to her.

"Ye canny shove yer grannie aff a bus. Ye canny shove yer grannie aff a bus. Ye canny shove yer grannie, cause she's yer mammie's mammie. Ye canny shove yer grannie aff a bus."

Becca crept in so as not to wake Gracie and pressed herself against Dale's back. "I hope you're not planning to push Granny Sadie off a bus?"

"Nah, she'd kill me," Dale said with a smile.

Becca stroked Gracie's soft brown hair. "Was she crying?"

"No, but I couldnae sleep," Dale said.

After Trent went home, Becca had told Dale about Trent's cousin and the children left without parents.

"Why couldn't you sleep, darling?" Becca asked.

Dale brushed her lips over Gracie's forehead and then placed her in her cot. They both stood at the side of the cot, and Dale put her arm around Becca's middle.

"I kept thinking about those two kids. They just lost their da and they're in foster care, and I worried if that could ever happen to our two if something happened to us."

Becca turned into her arms. "That won't happen to Gracie and Jake. You know I've left instructions in my will that if anything happens to me, you are to get both kids."

"I know that, but what if something happens to both of us? It's possible, and we don't have any family—well, I don't have any family that's interested in me."

Becca stroked Dale's cheek. "You really are worried about this, aren't you?"

Dale took Becca's hand and kissed it softly. "When my ma died, I was seventeen, but I still felt so alone in the world. Imagine if that was Jake and Gracie."

"Dale, it would be extremely unlikely that both of us would die, but if that were the case I'd like to think Val and Sammy would take them. Why don't we ask them, and then change our wills to make it official?"

Dale suddenly felt so much better. "Yeah, I think we should. They'd have a safe, happy life with Val, Sammy, and Mia."

"Good, now any more worries I can smooth out?" Becca asked.

Dale cupped Becca's face and kissed her softly. "I'm okay, thanks to you. How do you think Trent will cope?"

"We'll support her. Trent has some issues, but she'll do the right thing, I know," Becca said.

"What was her family like?" Dale said.

"Not great. Her mother died when she was a child. She won't admit it, but she has so many unresolved issues from her mother's death."

"And her da?"

Becca sighed and gripped Dale's hand. "He was my father's lawyer. That's how we met. He sent Trent around to look after me, protect me from the press that descended on our home after my mother committed suicide."

Becca's father, a pain specialist, had been involved in the biggest drug fraud the country had ever seen, and when things were at their bleakest, Becca's mother took her own life.

"I met with her father a lot during those times, and all I can say is they had an extremely dysfunctional relationship, to say the least. He wasn't a nice man, and I felt sorry for Trent. He was hard on her and didn't behave like a parent at all."

"Hmm," Dale said. "It seems like we all have our issues with our parents. Maybe this is a chance for Trent to deal with some of her issues, just like I did when Jake came into my life?"

Becca leaned her head on Dale and gazed at a contented looking Gracie. "I hope so. I don't know if Trent's ready to face her old family issues yet, but we'll be there to support her if she needs us. Let's leave Gracie to sleep."

CHAPTER FOUR

It turned out to be a little more complicated than Trent calling social services and telling them she'd take the children. One week later, with the help of her secretary, she was still jumping through hoops to satisfy the standards that social services had given her.

There was a home visit where she'd had to assure them that she would be hiring a full-time nanny, since Trent worked, and promised to fit new locks on the balcony doors so the children couldn't get out there.

Trent had been so busy organizing everything she would need to have children in the house that she hadn't had time to dwell on what day-to-day life would be like. But now the day had arrived that she was to pick up the children, and reality was starting to set in. It was bad enough that she would have no privacy from the children, but she would also have the nanny staying in her penthouse too. It was going to be a difficult six months, but in the long run, she knew she was doing the right thing.

Her phone beeped with a message. It was from Lady Claudia and she didn't open it. She had given Trent a few calls this week, but she'd brushed her off since she had the funeral and so many other things to do.

The funeral went off without a hitch. A lot of David's musician friends came, and Becca came to support Trent. Alice and Noah weren't there. The children's social worker thought it might be good for them to say goodbye to their father but left the decision to Trent. Trent said no. She wasn't going to put them through what she did when she lost her mother.

There was a knock at her office door and India walked in.

"Trent, I've confirmed the nanny interviews for tomorrow. There's five so far from the agency, but if one of those isn't suitable, they can set up more."

"Okay, what about the seats for my car that social services insist I have?" Trent asked.

"They're being delivered here by lunchtime."

"Thanks. Anything else?"

India looked down at her pad and tapped her pen against her lips. "Mr. Anderson wanted an update on his wife's response to his divorce petition."

Trent sighed. Her work was getting so backlogged because of her personal problems. That was unprofessional, but hopefully once the nanny was in place, she could just leave her to get on with taking care of the kids.

"I'll give him a call."

❖

A few hours later she was driving back to her apartment overlooking the Thames, with Alice and Noah in the back seat. It was surreal and nothing like she thought her life would ever turn out, but it would only be six months out of her life. She kept telling herself that. The children's places at boarding school were secured, and she didn't have the guilt eating away at her any more. She was doing the right thing.

Trent looked into the mirror and saw Alice staring silently out the car window, as she had been silent the whole time. Noah, on the other hand, jabbered constantly, telling Trent about things he saw out the window, all that had happened since they last saw her at the hospital, and all about his toy dinosaur.

"Trent? Are we nearly at our forever home?" Noah asked.

The mention of *forever* gave her a sense of panic. "Remember, the lady talked to you about this, Noah. You're staying with me for six months until you go and stay at a new school."

"How long is six months, Trent?"

Trent shifted uncomfortably in her seat. "A few months after Christmas."

She cringed when she realized she'd have a Christmas with the kids. Christmas was about drinks parties, going out to restaurants, going on skiing holidays—adult things, all to help her forget what a bad time Christmas was for her growing up. What would she be expected to do with kids?

Trent sighed and thought to herself, *Nanny can take care of that. Don't panic.*

They finally arrived at Trent's riverside building. She parked in her designated place in the car park underneath the building and said before getting out, "Stay there a minute and I'll get your bags."

She got out and opened the boot to her Audi sports car. There wasn't much room for luggage in these cars, but the kids only came with one bag each. It wasn't much for two kids that age to have one bag of clothes and a few toys. Their social worker had told her that they went to David's rented flat for some of the children's things, and there was very little. He lived from gig to gig, it seemed.

She supposed she would have to get Nanny to get them some fresh clothes. Trent put the bags over her shoulders and shut the boot. It was funny—every time she said the word *nanny* to herself, she had a ripple of fear shoot through her. Her own nanny had left a lasting effect on her.

Trent shook the thought away and went to Noah's side of the car and unbuckled him from his seat.

"Do you live in a car park, Trent?" Noah asked.

"No, this is where we park the car—my flat is above here. We'll take the lift."

The car park attendant walked over and said, "Can I help you with any bags or anything, Ms. Trent?"

"No, Jack, but thank you. I'm having my cousin's children to stay for a while, and I will be employing a nanny, so I would be grateful if you could assign me another parking space for her," Trent said.

"Of course. We do have a few extra at the moment. I'll get that organized for you."

Once Jack walked off, Trent went around to open the door for Alice. She held out her hand to help the girl down, but Alice just slid out herself, holding on to her teddy bear. Trent felt hopeless—she couldn't even give comfort to her own goddaughter.

There was something in Alice's quiet grief and pain that made Trent uncomfortable and meant the limited words she said to Alice were awkward and difficult. "The lift is across there. Just stick beside me because there could be cars coming and going."

Trent held on to Noah's hand tightly but just kept an eye on Alice as she walked a pace behind her. She led them into the lift and touched her key fob to the panel, then pressed the button for the top floor. If it wasn't for Noah jabbering away insistently, then the lift ride would have been silent as Trent and Alice said nothing.

The doors opened and Trent led them to her front door and opened it up. "This is where you'll be staying for a few months."

Noah walked right into the middle of Trent's large open-plan living room and twirled in a circle. "Whoa. This is big, Ali. Bigger than Daddy's flat."

Trent looked at Alice, who scanned the whole room, then put her head down into her teddy again. Trent had no idea what she should say to her and didn't want the responsibility. After she chose a nanny tomorrow, then she could give this pressure to someone else.

Noah ran for the glass balcony doors.

"Noah, don't," Trent said sharply.

He didn't listen and tried the handle on the door. Trent hurried over and pulled him away. "No, you are never to go near this door, okay?"

Noah's expression fell from his usual smiley face, and he ran over to Alice, who held him in her arms protectively.

Trent let out a frustrated breath. She walked back over and Alice looked her in the eye for the first time since the hospital. Alice was her little brother's protector—that was obvious.

Trent held up her hands in apology. She hadn't meant to come over so harshly. Clearly she was failing with these kids already.

"Listen, I'm sorry. There are some rules we need to go over. You are never to go near the balcony. We are very high up and it's dangerous. The door will always be locked, but just in case, I don't want you near it, okay?"

Noah nodded. "Sorry, Trent."

"That's okay." Trent pointed to the open-plan kitchen and said, "Help yourself to anything in the kitchen—juice, snacks—but we'll be having a nanny start work soon, so I'm sure they will get you anything you need. I'll show you your rooms."

Trent led them down the short corridor to the bedrooms. She stopped next to one door and opened it. "This my office. Rule number two—don't go in my office. I'm a lawyer and I have important files and computer equipment in there."

"What's a lawyer, Trent?" Noah asked.

Trent was shocked when Alice said, "She breaks up families, Noah."

She had no idea how to respond to that. Alice must have googled her name, and that was her own impression of what a family lawyer did.

Trent gulped hard. This was not going well. She decided not to respond and led them to their bedrooms. "These are your bedrooms."

She handed Alice her bag. "Unpack your things and get settled in."

Noah ran into Alice's room and jumped on the double bed. "It's huge, Ali."

"Your room is next door, Noah," Trent said. Noah stopped jumping on the bed and went quiet. "What's wrong?"

Alice sat on the bed beside Noah. She kept looking down as she said, "We've always shared a room."

"Well, now you'll have some space. Both rooms are the same—I know they aren't decorated for children, but they are very comfortable. I'll let you settle."

Trent hurried back into the living room. She needed a drink. Forgetting her drinks cabinet had been moved, she walked over to the table bedside the balcony. She loved to get a drink and sit out on the balcony of an evening.

When she remembered her drinks were now housed in a high cupboard in the kitchen, she pulled down her bottle of malt whiskey and poured out a glass, frustration growing in her chest. Moving her drinks was just one of the many concessions she was forced to make by social services.

Social services instructed Trent that she couldn't have drinks on display with young children about, and her cutlery drawer and other kitchen cabinets now had child locks on them. Of course she forgot every time she went to get something from them. Her adult penthouse— where she gave cocktail parties, entertained women, and worked on her clients' cases—had now turned into Fort Knox.

Trent took a gulp of whiskey, leaned against the kitchen worktop, and closed her eyes. How was she going to survive this?

She opened up her eyes and saw Noah and Alice standing there, watching her. She'd never even heard them approach. Their sad faces said they were screaming out for reassurance, but Trent didn't know what to do or say. Her mind was blank.

All Trent could think of was to distract them. "Let me show you the TV and how to get the channels you'll like."

She led them over to the large, comfortable couch. The TV was on the wall opposite.

"It's like the cinema, Ali," Noah said.

Trent put it on and showed Alice the menu system. "Look—there's all the children's channels."

Noah jumped up and down on the seat. "You got the Disney Channel, Trent!"

Trent thanked God she had thought of getting the children's channels added to her TV package. She was sure it would keep them well occupied and let her get on with her own business.

She handed the controller to Alice, who looked her up and down silently. She felt Alice knew she hadn't wanted them there, and it made things feel extremely awkward between them.

"You two enjoy the TV. I'm just going to work on my laptop there, okay? I'll get you both a drink."

Trent went to the fridge and got some orange juice. She prayed she could find a suitable nanny tomorrow. The children had only been here a short time, and Trent already felt trapped by the responsibility.

❖

Wendy sat at the kitchen table with her iPad and studied the job details the nanny agency emailed. It was a live-in position, which solved her housing problem. She looked up when she heard a key in the door.

Kira walked in and said jokingly, "Hi, honey, I'm home."

Wendy laughed. "Don't get comfortable having me as your housewife, I've got a job interview. Besides, you're not my type." Wendy got up to make Kira a cup of tea.

Kira laughed and put her bags on the table. "True. So you got an interview?"

"Yeah, it's a live-in post too. It's a single woman with two kids. One eleven, one six."

"Sounds good. Where is the job?" Kira asked.

Wendy gave Kira her tea and sat back down. "It's one of those posh blocks of flats overlooking the Thames."

Kira took a sip of tea and said, "Oh, single woman with money. Sounds good. What's her name?"

Wendy checked her email again and said, "Davina Trent, it says."

Kira screwed up her eyes trying to think. "I know that name. Davina Trent, Davina Trent…" Then Kira snapped her fingers. "I know, she's that divorce lawyer. She does all the rich people's divorces.

Do you remember, last year that famous sixties singer—erm…Joe Donald—divorced the glamour model with the boobs?"

"Yeah, I remember. Funny how you remember the boobs," Wendy joked.

"Oh, shut up. Yeah, Davina Trent was the lady with the boobs' lawyer. Only married a year, and she got a hundred million in settlement. It was all over the news."

"Interesting. She must be really good at her job, I suppose," Wendy said.

Kira took Wendy's iPad and said, "Let's google her." A moment later she said, "Wow. I might not be your type, but rich boob lawyer will be—look."

Kira turned the iPad around and Wendy saw Davina Trent in all her delicious butch glory, standing beside her famous client addressing the media. She looked like an older woman too, going by the silver streaks through her hair. Over the last few years, Wendy had developed a secret fantasy about older women, and the suit only made Davina Trent look more distinguished and mature.

"Wow is right. Looks a bit stiff, though, and suave, too suave. Anyway, I doubt I'll get the job. I bet she'd want one of those nannies in a tweed suit and a bun in her hair."

"Nah," Kira said, "I think she'd like some eye candy to come home to."

Wendy stuck out her tongue at her friend. "Stop it."

❖

"Where are they now?" Becca asked Trent over the phone.

Trent sat down on the couch and looked around at the trail of destruction these two little people had wrought on her beautiful penthouse. There were half-empty glasses of juice, crisp packets, and pizza boxes all over her glass coffee table.

Trent sighed and put her hand down and recoiled. There was some sticky substance on her beautiful leather couch, and crumbs everywhere.

"In their bedrooms, getting ready for bed. There are crumbs everywhere, Becca. How can two kids make so many crumbs?"

Becca laughed. "Kids are messy, Trent. They can't help it. You know I'll help you however I can. Bring them out to the vicarage. Jake and Gracie would love to play with them."

"Maybe."

That would mean letting them into her family, and she didn't know if she wanted to let them get too close.

"I'm interviewing nannies tomorrow, so she'll be in charge soon," Trent said.

"Don't just pick the most attractive woman, like you usually do. Pick one that interacts with the children and gets on with them," Becca said with an edge to her voice.

"I don't always do that," Trent replied.

"Your secretary looks like she walked off a Paris catwalk."

"India is very efficient, actually," Trent said sharply. Although she had noticed her secretary's looks first at the interview.

"I'm sure. Just remember what those two poor children have been through," Becca warned.

"I will. I promise." Trent heard Noah crying. "Something's wrong with Noah. I better go, Becca. Thanks for calling."

"I'm always at the end of a phone if you need me. I'll always care about you, Trent. You know that."

Trent gulped away the emotion she felt at that moment, as she was reminded again what she had lost. If this had happened while she was still with Becca, Becca would have gathered Alice and Noah up and mothered them the way she never could or wanted to.

"Thanks, Becca. Goodnight." Trent hung up and walked to the children's bedrooms. Alice's was empty, so she opened the door to Noah's. Noah was in his pyjamas on top of the bed, being held by his sister.

"What's wrong?"

"He misses Dad," Alice said.

The siblings were so different. Noah laughed, cried, showed his emotions so easily, and Alice wore her sadness like a blanket and hid behind it.

"Daddy always gave me bed biscuits," Noah said through his tears.

"Bed biscuits? What's that?" Trent asked Alice.

"Dad gave us biscuits and warm milk before bed. Noah can't sleep without it," Alice said.

"Okay, don't cry, Noah. I'll see what I can do."

Trent hurried to the kitchen and got the milk out of the fridge. She poured it into two glasses and put them in the microwave. How long was she supposed to heat them for?

She ran her hand through her hair and pressed the timer for five minutes. Her mobile rang and she saw it was the client she was meant to call back, Mr. Anderson. He had completely slipped her mind.

"Mr. Anderson—"

"Where the hell have you been, Trent? Your secretary said you'd call me back this afternoon."

"I'm sorry, Mr. Anderson, but the good news is I spoke to your wife's lawyer yesterday, and they're ready to deal. I'm having a meeting with my opposite number on Monday afternoon. I'll give you a call after that."

"Okay, try and get this thing hurried up, Trent. I need out of this marriage quickly," Mr. Anderson said.

Trent heard a bang behind her that made her jump. She spun around and saw through the glass door on the microwave that the glass of milk was half empty. She pulled open the microwave door, and the smell of burnt milk hit her in the face. The liquid poured out of the microwave onto the kitchen counter.

"Jesus," Trent said under her breath.

She grabbed kitchen roll and tried to stem the flow of liquid, but it was now dripping onto the floor.

"What did you say, Trent?"

Trent had to get off the phone. "Sorry, I'll call you on Monday. I have to go."

She hung up the phone and stuffed kitchen roll into the microwave.

"Jesus Christ," Trent shouted.

She threw some onto the floor and mopped with her foot while wiping up the microwave. Trent was so angry. She couldn't even take a basic business call without the chaos ensuing. If this had been a few days ago, she would have made that call this afternoon and be out wining and dining somewhere.

"I'll be lucky if I've got a business left by the time these kids go to boarding school."

CHAPTER FIVE

Wendy got out of the taxi, carrying her guitar case. She thought she'd bring it, as a song might break the ice with the children, if she got that far in the interview. Wendy paid the taxi driver and looked up at the very tall apartment building.

"Oh God. Please say she lives on the first few floors," Wendy said.

The email with the interview details said she was to give her name to a concierge at the reception. She walked up to the front door and it opened automatically. There was an older gentleman sitting behind a desk in a wine-coloured uniform with peaked cap.

Wow, this is posh.

"Can I help you, miss?"

The surprised look that he gave her suggested that he didn't see many women who looked like her in front of his desk.

"Yes, I'm Wendy Darling. I have an appointment with Ms. Trent," Wendy said.

The man looked down at a clipboard on his desk and said, "Ah, yes. That's right." He walked around the desk. "My name's Victor. You need a fob to use the lifts. I'll take you over."

"What floor is she on?" Wendy asked.

"Ms. Trent is on the top, ten floors up."

Wendy sighed internally. "Actually, I'd rather take the stairs. I'm not great with lifts."

Victor screwed up his eyes. "Really? Oh, well, if you insist."

He led her over to a door at the back of reception, beyond his desk. He held open the door and she walked through. She looked up, and all she could see was floor after floor continuing up into the building.

"Good luck with your interview, Ms. Darling," Victor said.

"Thanks."

Wendy took the first few steps. Looked like she'd be getting fit, then.

❖

Trent sat at her office desk listening to her latest interviewee and growing ever more frustrated. This was the fourth interview today, and none had been suitable. Either too young, too inexperienced, or—like this one—too outdated. Mrs. Cod reminded her so much of her own nanny, who had scared her beyond belief. She was a nanny lifted out of the past with bun in her hair, tweed jacket and skirt, and bony, sharp features.

Mrs. Cod had spent the last five minutes explaining what she wouldn't do.

"I don't clean, or any other kind of housekeeping. I retire to my own room when you return from work, and I go to sleep early, so I don't like to be disturbed."

As Mrs. Cod rattled on, all Trent could think about was getting her out of her flat. The problem was there was only one more interview after this, and Trent was getting desperate. She assumed that she'd pick one of the many candidates the agency sent.

But if this last candidate didn't work out, then it would be a disaster. Trent would either have to work from home or take the children into the office and let India take care of them while she worked. Both options were disastrous.

"Ms. Trent?" Mrs. Cod said.

Trent realized she had gotten lost in her own panicked thoughts. "Sorry, Mrs. Cod?"

"Is that acceptable to you?"

"Well, I have a few more people to see, and then I'll let you know." Trent got up and opened the office door for her.

Mrs. Cod picked up her handbag and said, "Please make it before twelve tomorrow because I have other interviews to attend."

The bloody cheek of the woman. "Yes, of course." Trent ushered her through the living area. Alice and Noah were on the couch watching cartoons, and Mrs. Cod just walked right past them. She'd done the same thing on the way in. In fact, every one of her interviewees had done that. Not a great omen for a childcare provider. Even with her limited experience, she knew that wasn't right.

Once she got Mrs. Cod safely out the door, she walked over to the couch. "Everything all right? You need anything?"

Alice shook her head and Noah said, "Nuh-uh."

"Okay, just one more interview to go." Trent looked at her watch. "In fact, Ms. Darling should be here now."

Trent made herself a cup of tea and waited and waited, until the last interviewee was now twenty minutes late. Trent paced up and down, getting angrier by the second. If this woman was late, then it didn't bode well for her efficiency as a nanny.

Finally, the doorbell rang. She marched over and opened the door and without looking said, "You're twenty minutes late."

When she did look she was quite lost for words. Ms. Darling was leaning against the door frame, gasping for breath. "Yeah, I'm sorry…"

As annoyed as Trent was, she couldn't stop her eyes from taking in everything about Ms. Darling. She looked like she had arrived straight from a summer music festival. She wore a straw hat that sat upon sun-bleached golden hair, with a few braided strands hanging down, framing her beautiful face. And she was beautiful, in a girly, innocent looking way, nothing like the sophisticated women Trent normally met.

Her look could best be described as hipster. She wore a shift dress that came to mid-thigh, allowing Trent to see plenty of leg. Trent purposely shook herself out of her appraising gaze, remembered how annoyed she was, and noticed the henna tattoo on Ms. Darling's arm.

What kind of hippy was this woman?

"Sorry I'm late, Ms. Trent. I don't like lifts much, and I didn't realize you were so high up. I'm Wendy, by the way."

Wendy stuck out her hand and when Trent took it she felt a glowing warmth seep into hers.

"Pleased to meet you—wait, why don't you like lifts? You walked up ten flights?" Trent asked.

"Yeah, I'm used to it. I've got a kind of claustrophobic thing. Keeps me fit, though. Can I come in?" Wendy said enthusiastically.

Trent was a little lost for words, and she was never lost for words. She had been angry, but now a few short sentences later and she was showing Wendy in meekly. It was then that she noticed the guitar case. Why did she bring that?

Wendy stopped and spun around slowly, taking in the room. "Wow, great place you have here, Ms. Trent."

The spin made her shift dress float up and Trent's gaze lowered.

God, Becca would say I chose her for her looks. Wait, she hadn't given her the job yet.

"Call me Trent."

Then Wendy spotted the children looking at her quizzically. She turned to Trent and said, "Can I go and say hello?"

"Of course, go ahead," Trent said. None of the others had done that.

Wendy went over, put her guitar case on the floor, and immediately went down onto her knees in front of the kids.

"Hi, I'm Wendy. What's your names?"

Trent looked on quizzically. Going down to the children's level seemed to have an effect on Noah and Alice. Noah hugged her immediately and, to her surprise, Alice did too. People like Wendy, Becca, and Dale appeared to have a natural affinity with children, like she had missed some sort of class to show her how it was done.

"What's in there?" Noah asked, pointing to the guitar case.

"That's my guitar. I might show it to you later, but I have to go and talk to Ms. Trent first, okay?"

Trent felt a funny sensation as Wendy came back over to her. It was as if the room was lighter, and Trent's knowing worry about her responsibility for the children lessened. Wendy had come in like a whirlwind and blown away some of the dark feelings hanging heavily between her and the children.

"Follow me, Wendy," Trent said.

Wendy tapped her fingers on the arms of the chair while Trent silently looked over her résumé. She hated silences. Still it gave her a chance to look over the infamous Davina Trent.

Trent appeared every inch the tough alpha personality the media made her out to be. Sharp, short haircut, and even in her home wearing suit trousers, crisp shirt, and waistcoat. Kira was right—Trent was her cup of tea. Wendy had always gone for the boyish, butch type, but she had never met anyone like Trent before. She was more used to the surfer-skateboarder type, not the dapper kind.

Wendy's eyes focused on the pen tapping on Trent's bottom lip as she read, and she caught herself sighing wistfully. Trent had an intriguing kind of masculinity, which was softened at the edges just right. Her eyes were sparkling blue and her handsome face only made more attractive by the streaks of silver through her hair.

I wonder how old she is? The thought of a posh, suave, older woman made her stomach flip in a way it hadn't in forever. She'd never been with an older woman, despite her secret fantasy. Her first and only love had been slightly younger than her in age, but hugely younger in maturity, and Wendy always felt like she had to be the adult in the relationship.

Wendy had never allowed herself to think about love or a relationship again. She'd had a few flings as she travelled around the world, but nothing stomach-flipping worthy, just sex. *Pull yourself together, Wendy.* This was a job, but at least she'd have something nice to look at while she worked.

Finally, Trent sat back in her seat and simply gave Wendy a firm gaze. She presumed that was the same look she gave in court and used to intimidate other lawyers.

"So, Wendy Darling. Interesting name," Trent said.

"Yeah my dad thought it would be funny, which is strange because he never displayed much of a sense of humour." Wendy laughed. She faltered when Trent didn't even smile. Oh, great. Another person with a personality bypass, just like Mum and Dad.

Trent said eventually, "You have extremely good references, and an excellent résumé, Wendy."

"Thank you," Wendy said.

Trent kept leaving big pauses between her questions and those blue eyes continued staring straight at her. Wendy wondered how on earth Trent managed to be a parent to two kids and be so bloody uptight.

Trent leaned forward on the desk and clasped her hands. "I did wonder one thing, though. It says here you were at teacher training college and left in your last year. That could show a lack of commitment."

Wendy frowned. "Nothing could be further from the truth, Trent. A personal matter came up that meant I had to leave, but I'm going back to complete my degree. That's why this job suits me. My course doesn't start till next summer, and the agency said you only needed a nanny short term."

"That's right," Trent said.

Trent tapped her pen on the résumé, which Wendy noticed had various notes scribbled over it.

"Tell me, why is it important for you to finish your teaching degree?"

Wendy wasn't expecting that question, and it gave her pause. She looked down at the desk because she feared her eyes would betray too much emotion. As much as her heart had healed from the circumstances that made her leave university, the emotions were still lurking there, and along with pain and anger, there was also the embarrassment of being taken in by someone and played like a fool.

She answered as honestly as she could. "Teaching was my dream. I love children and I love teaching them through play, imagination, and nurture. So many children go through their formative years without the proper nurturing they deserve. I'm passionate about it and want to make a difference in the lives of the children I teach." Wendy looked up. "Why I had to give that up wasn't my fault, but now I feel able to put myself first and become the person I want to be."

"Hmm," Trent said, "I understand dreams, but I can't imagine dealing with children all day. It's bad enough dealing with lawyers."

Wendy couldn't understand how on earth someone could have two children and take that attitude. "Don't you like children? You have two beautiful—"

"Oh, good God, they're not mine," Trent said quickly. "Didn't anyone tell you?"

"No, I assumed they were yours."

"They are my cousin's two children. He was killed in a car accident a few weeks ago, and I was his and the children's next of kin," Trent said.

"Oh, I'm terribly sorry. Poor babies."

"Yes, well, they were in the car and were incredibly lucky to survive. So it was me or foster care."

"It's so lucky they have you, then," Wendy said.

A serious, almost panicked look came over Trent's face. "I can't take care of children. I'm a busy lawyer, plus I'm not a children person. No, I'm sending them to boarding school, but I can't get them places for six months, and that's why I need a nanny."

Wendy couldn't believe it. "Boarding school? But Noah is only six."

"That's really none of your concern. It is the only option. Besides, I was sent to boarding school at six."

And it showed, Wendy thought. Ms. Trent couldn't be that cold, could she? She took the kids in, after all.

"Your duties would be the twenty-four-hour care of the children. As I said, I'm very busy, and my work has been sorely neglected the past few weeks."

Wendy might lose her chance at this job but she couldn't stop herself from saying what was on her mind. "So you basically want to hand all responsibility to me?"

Trent's jaws clenched in tension. "I'm doing the best I can for them, Ms. Darling. They have a very comfortable home, will want for nothing, and will be given the best of educations so they can make the best of their lives. That's all I can do. I need to get on with my work and life, so that is why I'm willing to pay very well for a nanny to take up that caring role. Is that something you could do?"

Wendy could see in her mind's eye all the steel walls Trent had built around herself, but she remembered one thing from when she was greeting the children. When she hugged Alice, Wendy looked up and saw Trent watching and biting her lip with tension. Something about that small hug triggered emotion in this stiff, tough lawyer. Maybe she could help build some bridges between her and the children.

"Yes, it is something I could do," Wendy said.

She saw relief on Trent's face. "When could you start? I have work on Monday and lots to catch up on."

"I could pack tonight and start tomorrow."

"Excellent. I'll pick you up tomorrow." Trent held out her hand and Wendy shook it.

"Great." She'd done it. A good paying job, both short term and providing a roof over her head.

CHAPTER SIX

The next day Trent and the children picked up Wendy and drove her back to the apartment. Wendy chose to sit in the back seat of the car with the children, which Trent thought was strange, but when she looked into the driver's mirror she saw Wendy holding both Alice and Noah's hands.

That was quick, Trent thought. How did she bond so quickly?

But she supposed that was Wendy's job, and she could breathe a sigh of relief that now her only responsibility was financial. As they drove, Trent couldn't help but glance in the mirror and watch the interaction between Wendy and the children. Alice was still as quiet as ever, but Wendy kept engaging her in the conversation she was having with Noah, who was a chatterbox as always.

Wendy laughed at something Noah had said, and Trent gazed a little too long at her, before realizing the light had turned red. She braked quickly.

She saw terror in Alice's eyes when she looked to the back seat. "I'm sorry about that."

Wendy soon distracted her, but Trent kicked herself for being drawn in by Wendy's good looks. Trent was surrounded by beautiful women most days, between her secretary, her clients, and her group of friends, but Wendy was so different, and so…young.

All the women she knew were well put together, but Wendy was undone, so natural, so carefree, in her dress and personality. Today, instead of a straw hat, Wendy wore a red headscarf with hummingbirds on it, fifties style, holding her hair from her face.

She chuckled to herself at what her own childhood nanny would think of Wendy. They couldn't be more different. Trent pulled into the car park and said, "Here we are."

"Home sweet home," Wendy said to the children.

Trent shuddered. *No, this is my life, my world.* She got out quickly and got the bags, then looked around the back of the car just as Wendy was climbing out of the car door, giving her an eyeful of Wendy's pert bottom in tight jeans.

God, Becca would definitely say she'd hired her for her looks.

Wendy helped the children out and joined her at the back of the car.

"Right, let's go," Trent said. "I'll take the bags, if you hold on to Alice and Noah."

"I…" Wendy stammered.

"What?" Trent asked.

Wendy indicated with her eyes over to the lift area. "I'll take the stairs."

Trent sighed. "Wendy, you can't take the stairs all the time. What about when you're coming and going with the children?" *Tell me I haven't picked the wrong nanny.* "This lift has never broken down and I've lived here for five years."

Alice tugged Wendy's hand and said, "Are you scared?"

Wendy couldn't show Alice irrational fear, when Alice had so many legitimate fears.

"No, no. I'm fine," Wendy said.

They walked to the lift area, Wendy's heart beating faster and her mouth drying up. The lift doors opened. Alice, Noah, and Trent walked in. Trent held out her hand to her and said, "You'll be fine. I promise."

"Wendy, you come with us?" Noah said.

"I sure will." Wendy put on her most confident air. "I like to sing songs while I'm travelling in a lift. Do you two know the 'Baby Shark' song?"

"Yay," both kids said happily.

"Baby shark?" Trent said.

"We'll teach you, won't we, kids?"

Distraction. Exactly what Wendy needed.

❖

Wendy hung up the last of the clothes in the wardrobe and then slid her empty bags under the bed. By the time they had got back, it was the children's bedtime. Trent offered to get them into bed while she got settled in.

Her bedroom was really comfortable with windows that gave her a great view over the Thames. Wendy had mostly worked in large homes before, not penthouse apartments, so she had never had to use a lift before.

It was uncomfortable, but she did it, and the bewildered look on Trent's face and her subsequent laughter as they sang did a lot to distract from Wendy's discomfort.

Luckily for her, the lift was extremely modern and had a video screen down to the concierge at reception, nothing like the steel coffin she had been trapped in as a child.

Trent had asked Wendy to join her in the living area once she was unpacked. So she walked out of her room, past the children's rooms, and found Trent working on her laptop at the dining table by the kitchen area with a glass of wine.

"Wendy, come and sit down. I've a few things I need to go over with you," Trent said.

She sat at the table and Trent stood. "Drink?"

"Uh, not while I'm on duty," Wendy said.

"You're not on duty till tomorrow morning. Have a glass," Trent said.

"All right. Thank you."

Trent got Wendy a glass and the bottle from the fridge. "Here you are."

Wendy took a sip and the cold liquid tingled pleasantly in her mouth.

Trent picked up a notepad where she had written a long list. "Okay, first thing is school. I've had my secretary find out about local schools for the children, but as it's midterm, it could take anything from six weeks or more to get them in."

"That may be a blessing in disguise," Wendy said. "Going straight back to school after such a trauma might be too much for them."

"Hmm," was all Trent said.

Surely she must have thought of that. These children would need a lot of help.

"So in the meantime—"

"I can help them with reading and writing, while they are at home with me. Don't worry," Wendy said.

Trent took a sip of wine and gazed at her. Was her boss trying to unnerve her?

"Thank you. Now, I've written down the alarm code, and the number to my credit card. I'll order you another card, but use this for now for food shopping and anything the children or the house needs. I have an account with the local supermarket, so you can have food delivered."

"Thanks, is there anything else Alice and Noah need immediately?" Wendy asked.

"Clothes—they brought very little with them. Their father David didn't have much. He was a musician and lived from one gig to another, I think."

"Okay, clothes, no problem. Is there anything else?" Wendy asked.

Trent pushed a set of keys across the table. "Take my spare set of keys to the flat. The fob on it is for the lifts and the car park—oh, and there's a gym and pool that you are free to use. I'll have my secretary hire a car for you tomorrow, something with lots of room."

"Thank you," Wendy said. "Are Alice and Noah going to see a counsellor or child psychologist?"

Trent sat back in her chair. "The social worker did mention it, but there's a long waiting list apparently."

"Don't you think they should? They've just come through an unimaginable horror."

"Private psychologist, you mean?" Trent said.

Wendy nodded. "I think it would really help prepare them for what's ahead, leaving here and going to boarding school."

Trent thought it was a great idea. She was providing them with everything they needed, care, emotional support, without having the responsibility herself. She didn't need to feel guilty about anything any more. She could go to work and enjoy her private life knowing that her responsibilities were being met by other people.

"Good idea. Can you organize that for me?" Trent said.

"Yeah, I have a friend who is a school counsellor—she can give me a few names," Wendy said.

Trent looked down her list. "Well, that's everything I wanted to talk to you about. They're all yours now."

What a sense of relief it was to hand the children over to the nanny. She felt free, less constrained. Trent heard one of the bedroom doors open, and Noah walked out to the living area, dragging his blanket behind him and looking unsure.

"What is it, Noah?" Wendy asked.

"I can hear Ali having bad dreams. She's scared."

"I'll go," Wendy said straight away and got up and gathered Noah into her arms. "Come on, poppet, let's go back to bed."

❖

Trent finished dealing with her last email and shut her laptop. She rubbed her face and thanked God that there would now be some sanity back in her life. Wendy was a little different and not exactly who she had in mind as a nanny, but she did appear to have a natural affinity for Alice and Noah.

Trent had now met all her obligations and done everything she was required to do. Now it was over to Wendy.

She got up and put the wine glasses in the sink, then headed to her bedroom. She stopped as she approached Alice's bedroom. The door was ajar and she could hear voices.

Trent looked in. Wendy had Alice in her arms, rocking and trying to soothe her. Alice was crying and said, "I'm scared. I miss my dad, we have no one to love us any more. Trent hates us and doesn't want us."

Those words hurt Trent. The emotion surprised her and she didn't know what to do with it. Wendy looked around and saw her standing there. Trent gulped and hurried to her bedroom and slammed the door.

She walked over to the mirrored wardrobe and started to undress quickly. A million thoughts raced around her mind, and then her gaze was drawn to the mirror, to a scar just above her eyebrow. It was a reminder of how much you could get hurt if you let yourself care and love.

In her mind she heard her father's voice. *Shut the door. Hands out.*

Trent could still feel the fear of being sent to her father's study as a child. He was a terrifying man, the only one of two people she had ever feared, the other being her nanny.

Her mind wanted to play the movie of what happened next but she shook it off. "Don't go there. Be strong," Trent told herself.

Why did the look in Alice's eyes disturb her so much? Why did Noah's need for affection scare her so much?

Stop. She wouldn't be reminded of the past by the children. They had a nanny now. She would go to work and dine out, and not have to worry about what she should say or do. She just didn't have the skills for that. She shook her head. She might not have *those* skills, but she was very proficient in providing, and in having the wherewithal to pay others to make up for her own shortfalls.

❖

"So? How is it with the dishy lawyer?"

Wendy lay back on her back while talking to Kira on her mobile.

"It's weird. The kids are only with her because she's their next of kin. I've never seen someone so distant and guarded towards children before."

"A total grouch, then?" Kira said.

"That's what's strange. A couple of times I've seen something in her eyes, a need, a longing, when I've been hugging the kids..." Wendy sighed. "I don't know, maybe I'm imagining it, but I think there's something underneath trying to get out."

"And you're the Mary Poppins to do it?" Kira joked.

"Oh, stop it. Well, whatever it is, these children need love and help, especially Alice, the little girl. She saw everything when her dad was killed," Wendy said.

"Poor little thing."

Wendy sat up on her bed. "That's what I wanted to ask you, Kira. Could you phone John and ask if he could recommend a private psychologist?"

John was a friend of Kira's who worked as a counsellor for local education.

"Yes, I can do."

"Thanks, Kira."

Wendy said her goodbyes to Kira and then went out to the hall to check on the children one more time. Noah was fast asleep, but when she peeked in Alice's bedroom, she was sitting on the floor, clutching her teddy bear tightly.

She walked straight in and Alice jumped up to grasp onto her. "Bad dreams?"

Alice just nodded.

"Let's get back into bed and I'll sleep beside you, okay? I'll chase those bad dreams away."

Alice slipped back under the covers and Wendy joined her. She opened the music app on her phone and pressed play on a lullaby playlist she had, then held Alice.

"Listen to the music, Alice, and let your mind drift. I'm right here holding you," Wendy whispered.

Five minutes later Alice was fast asleep.

❖

Trent awoke to sound blaring from outside her bedroom. For a second she forgot her flat wasn't her own any more, and then it hit her and the feeling of anxiety and resentment began again to gather pace inside her.

She sat up and looked at the time. It was six in the morning. Why would children be up and about at this time? Normally Trent would wander through to the kitchen, make a coffee, and sit on the balcony, browsing the morning newspapers on her iPad. It was her precious quiet time before meeting clients and attending court during the day.

Trent scratched fingers through her hair in frustration. Last night she thought giving up her responsibilities would make her feel better, but the opposite happened, in fact. As she lay in bed last night, thoughts and fears circled in her mind, memories she had thought she had banished a long time ago.

We have no one to love us any more. Trent hates us and doesn't want us. Surprisingly Alice's words affected her somewhere inside, unlocking thoughts and emotions she didn't want to ever face again.

"Go out there, get your coffee, then go to work early," Trent said to herself.

She put on her dressing gown and walked out into the new morning. The TV was showing a loud children's show. Her breath caught when she turned her gaze to the kitchen. Wendy was by the cooker making something in a frying pan, dressed only in pyjama shorts and a matching T-shirt, and fluffy slippers. Her blond hair wasn't held back by the headscarf she had on yesterday. It was soft, flowing, and a bit wild as it bounced around while Wendy sang and danced as she cooked.

Trent felt that familiar tingle in her stomach she always got when she was attracted to someone, then a sense of panic because it was her nanny. Her employee. The children's much younger nanny. Wendy's résumé gave her age as twenty-six, and she was just about to turn forty. Far too young for her.

Why did she have to pick someone so attractive? Of course, Wendy was very far from her usual type, so she could hardly be blamed.

Alice and Noah were sitting at the kitchen island watching Wendy intently, with not a glance at the loud TV show behind them. Wendy turned around and gave her a huge smile.

"Good morning, Trent. Come and join us. I'm making pancakes."

Noah quickly turned and jumped off his chair. "Trent!"

Noah ran to her and threw his arms around her legs. "We're having pancakes!"

Trent froze and didn't know what to do or say. Wendy rescued her by saying, "Come on, Noah, your pancakes are getting cold."

Thankfully he ran off with the promise of food. Trent didn't know how to react to that kind of affection, and even if she did she wouldn't want to encourage any kind of closeness or bond, because they would just expect more in return and she wasn't capable.

She would just get coffee and get back to the bedroom. First she hurried over to the fridge and got a bottle of water for herself.

"Pull up a chair, Trent," Wendy said. "There's lots of pancakes for everyone."

"No, thank you. I'll just have coffee," Trent said.

Wendy held up the plate piled high with pancakes. "You have to try these. They're genuine American pancakes. I got the recipe from a diner cook while I was working in America."

Why did Wendy have to be so happy and smiley at this time in the morning? Were all teachers and childcare providers like this? Her nanny certainly wasn't.

"No, thank you," Trent said again.

Wendy put the plate of pancakes down and intercepted Trent, reaching for her coffee mug. She seemed determined to get Trent to take part in a family breakfast. "Well, I'll make your coffee, then. Sit down."

Trent gave her an incredulous look. "This is a professional coffee machine. You wouldn't know how to use it."

Wendy brushed her aside and grabbed the cup. "Oh, please, I've worked as a barista as I travelled."

"Is there anything you didn't do?" Trent snapped.

"Not really. What kind do you want?"

"Black Americano," Trent replied.

As Wendy busied herself with the machine she said, "Kids, let's sing the song about pancakes we learned." Wendy started to sing, "Mix a pancake, stir a pancake, pop it in the pan. Fry the pancake, toss the pancake, catch it if you can—"

Wendy could only hear Noah's voice joining in. Alice always seemed to go quiet in Trent's company. That was something she had to work on. It didn't matter if Trent thought she was getting rid of the children to boarding school. They would be back here in the holidays, with another nanny, no doubt, but Alice, Noah, and Trent had to have some understanding of each other, or it would hurt the children.

As Wendy waited on the coffee dripping from the machine, she and Noah repeated the song. She turned her head and saw Trent looking extremely uncomfortable, staring at the floor, while Alice stared at her plate of pancakes. She had so much work to do.

Wendy had been in many different kinds of families as she travelled the world. Some parents were extremely loving but had little time because they were working people, some were distant, and some tried their best to juggle their careers and parenthood.

Trent was different. She thought at first Trent just wasn't a kid person, and there was nothing wrong with that, but she had spotted some emotional looks and glances that suggested there was something deeper going on inside Trent. She had to give her best shot at finding out what that was.

Wendy finished with the coffee and handed it to Trent. "Here you go. I hope you like it."

Trent sniffed the cup and then took a tentative sip. "Mmm, nice. You've obviously been to barista school."

Wendy was buoyed by an actual compliment from Trent. "I told you. I picked up lots of new skills as I travelled." She ended with a wink.

"I'm sure," Trent replied suggestively.

Cheeky, thought Wendy. She turned to Alice and Noah and said, "We'll need to come up with a coffee song for Trent, won't we."

"Yes, yes," Noah said and clapped his hands.

Trent rolled her eyes. "Please don't. I'm going to get dressed. Thank you for the coffee."

Trent walked away to her bedroom and shut the door.

About forty minutes later Trent emerged fully dressed with her briefcase in hand. She was walking straight to the door without saying goodbye. Noah scrambled down from the chair and ran after her. Wendy had to stop Trent before she hurt the children's feelings.

Wendy said, "Is there anything in particular you'd like for dinner tonight?"

Trent stopped by the door and said, "I won't be home this evening. I have a dinner date."

Wendy folded her arms in frustration. Trent needed to accept her life had changed, whether she liked it or not. These children needed love, a parental influence to make them feel safe. Wendy had her work cut out for her.

CHAPTER SEVEN

After a long morning at court with a client, Trent walked back into her law office. She ignored India, who was trying to get her attention, and walked past her and straight in her private office.

India followed her in. "Trent, there's messages for you on your desk. Can I order you something for lunch?"

Trent only half heard her. Her mind was somewhere else, as it had been for most of the morning. The guilt that she had thought would be gone now that she was doing the right thing was back. Noah had run after her this morning but she'd walked out the door, and she kept repeating it over and over in her mind.

"Trent? Do you want lunch?" India asked again.

"What? No. I'm not hungry," Trent replied.

"Okay, your next appointment isn't for another hour," India said.

"Thank you."

As soon as India left the office, Trent was on her feet pouring a drink. She didn't often drink during the day, unless it was a celebratory bottle of champagne with a client, but today she felt the need for alcohol to quiet her mind. She had been distracted all through court this morning, and her client had noticed. It was unprofessional.

She just couldn't get the image of Noah running after her, desperate for some parental attention, out of her mind. Alice hadn't even moved from her seat. She already knew that Trent was pushing them away. Trent even lied about a dinner date just so she didn't have to go home.

She sat down and rubbed her forehead. Her behaviour reminded her of how she used to ignore and sideline Jake, Becca and Dale's son, but she had made great strides in opening up to him.

Dale would never have walked away.

"You are not their parent," Trent told herself.

She was trying to keep her distance and not get involved—she had to protect herself and her way of life. Trent had done her best, after all. They had a nanny, food, shelter. What more could they want?

In her heart, she knew the answer to that question because it was what she had wanted as a child. When her thoughts started to drift back to her childhood, she finished the drink in one go and pulled out her iPhone.

"No, I'm not going back there. I'm not letting myself go there."

Trent's finger hovered over Becca's contact details. Becca would know what to say—she understood her. Trent shook her head. Becca wasn't her safe place any more, and she had to stop running to her.

Then as she gazed at her phone a call came in from Lady Claudia. "Claudia? Sorry I haven't returned your calls. Things have been hectic. Dinner? Tonight?"

Should she? Claudia made her feel like an insect with a chameleon standing over her, ready to strike, but maybe this way would be better. She was scared of the emotions she had to face at home.

"I'd love to. What time?"

❖

Wendy and the children had had a productive day so far. After breakfast they did some reading, then went to the shops, and she found travelling in the lift easier than she expected with the help of the children and a good song for distraction.

Once they were back home and had lunch, Wendy got out the drawing materials they had bought—pencils, crayons, pens, and paper—and encouraged Alice and Noah to do some drawing and artwork.

Wendy joined in, sitting on the couch at the coffee table, and had an idea. If she got the children to draw a picture for Trent, it might tug at Trent's heartstrings and at the very least encourage dialogue between them.

When she asked the children to draw for Trent, Alice coloured the paper black and shouted, "I don't want to draw anything for Trent. She doesn't want us here."

"That's not true, Alice. She just has difficulty showing it. She's never lived with children before."

Wendy prayed that was true because if not, it was going to be so difficult for Alice to cope with her grief.

"She hates us!" Alice shouted, then ripped up her paper and ran to her bedroom.

Wendy let out a sigh and pulled Noah into a hug.

"Trent wants us?" Noah said.

"Let's tidy up and maybe get a snack, okay?"

Noah smiled. "Yeah!"

He was easily distracted, but Alice would be far more difficult. Wendy knew what feeling unwanted was like. Her own parents made it clear from an early age that she was unexpected and inconvenient. Luckily, she had two fantastic grandparents who filled in the gaps in her heart.

Alice and Noah had no one else.

❖

Music played softly in the background of the elegant and exclusive restaurant. Trent and Lady Claudia had just started their first course, but the conversation had been limited.

Claudia lifted her glass of wine to her lips and sipped. "You seem distracted, Trent. First you don't return my calls, then pay me little attention when I finally see you."

"I'm sorry, Claudia. I have a lot on my mind."

Trent had been hoping for distraction, but the longer the day went on, the more her emotions and thoughts churned inside her.

"Is it the sprogs that have been forced upon you?" Claudia asked.

The term *sprog* jarred inside Trent. She had used the dismissive term herself to Becca at one time and she'd reacted angrily to it then. Now she was on the receiving end, and Trent could see why it annoyed Becca.

"Things have been difficult, and the adjustment to living with me has been strained so far, so I am a little distracted," Trent said.

She refilled Claudia's wine glass.

Claudia said, "It was bad enough for me living with stepchildren for a year, but they were at least adults. My ex-husband adored them—I just saw them as a pack of spoiled brats. Young children would be even worse. Why not just pack them off to boarding school?"

That was exactly what Trent was doing, but coming from Claudia's mouth, it sounded so much harsher.

"They are going to boarding school, but I can't get them places for some months, so they have to stay with me."

"How awful," Claudia said.

Claudia was beginning to annoy Trent with her responses. "I have a nanny now, so it will be fine."

"Oh, dear." Claudia slipped her hand over Trent's and squeezed. "I hope not an attractive nanny who's going to distract you from me?"

Trent noted the slightly possessive connotation to Claudia's reply and she didn't like it.

It had been a mistake to sleep with Claudia. She had been pursued relentlessly and let herself be caught. So unlike her, but her hurt, lonely feelings induced by Becca had made her ripe for the picking.

"My rule is to never mix business with pleasure, Claudia. Besides, I'm sure your other lovers keep you well entertained."

"But I've so enjoyed my time with you, darling. It's so liberating being with another woman, and something I want to explore more."

The waiter came at exactly the right time to clear away the first course. Claudia said to the young man, "Bring me a bottle of champagne, darling. I feel like bubbles."

"Yes, Your Ladyship."

Trent looked at her watch. Alice and Noah would be going to bed around about now. Then she remembered Wendy wouldn't know about Noah's bed biscuits and milk. She had forgotten to tell her.

She stood up and said to Claudia, "Would you excuse me for a moment? I need to make a phone call."

"Make it quick, Trent. I'm starting to feel neglected." Claudia sighed.

❖

Wendy couldn't help but smile as she talked to Trent on the phone. "Yes, I'll make sure they get them. Thanks for letting me know."

She hung up the phone and clenched her fist. "Yes, I knew it."

That one phone call confirmed her thoughts. Trent did care. She'd cut into an evening dinner date to let her know about Noah and his bed biscuits. Not the healthiest, but the sentiment was what mattered.

Trent hid her emotions deep down inside, but now Wendy knew she had something to work with. She would bring this family together before she left her post, and she wouldn't give up.

Wendy got the milk and biscuits and made her way back to the children's bedrooms.

Alice was lying on Noah's bed, hugging her teddy and holding Noah's hand. It had been a difficult and emotional day with Alice. Drawing had been Wendy's idea to bring Alice's thoughts and feelings out into a picture, but she obviously wasn't ready to even contemplate her feelings.

The problem was when Alice was angry and upset, it reminded Noah that his daddy was gone. So Wendy had two upset children for most of the afternoon.

She walked in with the tray of milk and biscuits. "Look what I've got. Trent phoned home specially to tell me you liked bed biscuits."

Alice looked up surprised, and Noah bounced on the bed with excitement. "Bed biscuits! Bed biscuits!"

"We'll eat these, get your teeth brushed, then a story, okay?"

❖

Claudia tried to push Trent into the bathroom stall and loosen her tie. Trent stopped Claudia's hands from going any further. "Claudia, I really don't feel like it tonight. I have an early morning in court. I think I'll just head home."

Claudia dropped her hands in surprise. "No? You're saying *no*? It's those brats, isn't it? You've not been yourself all evening."

Trent was angry now and feeling defensive of Alice and Noah. "Don't call them that, Claudia. Their father has just been killed—their whole life's been turned upside down."

"And yours with it, darling. Once they're off to boarding school, life will be back to normal."

"Goodnight, Lady Claudia."

Trent stuffed her tie in her suit pocket and left. She caught a taxi, and as she made her way home, she thought about what Claudia had said. Life might go back to normal, but Trent was unconvinced whether it ever would. She was going to have a connection to Alice and Noah her whole life, no matter if they were at boarding school the majority of the year or not, and in any case, was her way of life normal? Lots of nightlife, sex if she wanted it, but no partner to come home to.

The taxi stopped outside her apartment building. She paid the fare and looked up to her penthouse flat. Her mind was busy with thoughts, and if she was honest, she was scared of going up after the way she'd left this morning.

Trent turned around and made her way down to the walkway that ran along the river. She leaned on the barrier and listened to the sound of the water through the darkness.

The feeling of something missing in her life just wouldn't go away since Becca and Dale's wedding. She was going to be forty in a few weeks' time. Was this what she wanted to be doing forever? Going for dinner and drinks and sleeping with people she would see for a few dates at a time?

Trent hadn't had a serious relationship since Becca. She had never found anyone she trusted like Becca. But maybe life was giving her a chance to do something good for two little people who had nobody. They said life began at forty. She was a bit late to the party, but she still had time. Perhaps if she made an effort that could be true.

The only trouble was, she didn't have the first clue about children. She had made strides with Jake, but this was different—this was living with them, making conversation, taking part in meals and play. Then she remembered the pretty Wendy, dancing in her pyjamas this morning. Like for Dale McGuire, it all came so easily to Wendy. Maybe she could let Wendy Darling be her guide?

Wendy rushed into Alice's room and switched on the light. The sound of her screams awoke Wendy from dozing on her bed.

She pulled Alice into her arms. She was shaking with fear and convulsing with tears. Wendy had never had to deal with a child who was so grief-stricken and frightened before, but she just used her instincts, held Alice tight, and rocked her rhythmically.

"Shh…shh…it's okay. I'm with you, Alice."

"I keep seeing it," Alice said.

Wendy pulled back a bit from her. "What do you see?"

"My dad in the front seat of the car. I can't remember nice memories of my dad. When I try to think about him, all I can see is him covered in blood and his face and head—" Alice put her hands over her ears and rocked back and forth. "It's in my head, it's in my head."

This was a full-blown meltdown and Wendy had to do something quickly. She gently placed her hands over Alice's and said, "Alice, look at me. Look at me, please, and I'll help you. Trust me."

It didn't happen straight away, but after a while Wendy felt Alice's hands under hers relax and fall away. Wendy cradled her despondent face and said, "Look at me, Alice."

Alice looked at her with tear-filled eyes.

"Now breathe with me," Wendy said.

After a few minutes, Alice's breathing calmed.

"Good girl, good girl. Now I want you to tell me the happiest memory with your dad."

"I can't, I can only see blood and—"

"You can. Keep looking in my eyes and think hard." Wendy could see the strain it was causing Alice. "Find it, even if you can only see it faded in your mind. Find it and tell me."

"When I was little, my dad picked me up from nursery early because my mum was in hospital having Noah. We went to a balloon shop, and I got to choose some balloons to take for my new brother. We took them into a hospital room, and my mum was sitting up in bed with Noah. I gave him the balloons."

"What do you remember feeling?" Wendy asked.

"Happy and excited. I really wanted a brother. Mum was smiling and Dad was too. He put his arm around Mum."

This was the part she hoped would help Alice. "Okay, now shut your eyes and imagine the bad memory of the accident on a TV screen. We'll call that channel one. Can you see that in your head?"

Alice nodded, her lip trembling.

"Now I want you to picture the good, happy memory on the screen—that'll be channel two, okay?"

"Uh-huh," Alice replied.

"Imagine it as bright and colourful and happy as you can. Can you see it?" Wendy asked.

"Yes."

"Okay, open your eyes."

Wendy got up and sat on the bed. She beckoned Alice up to her, and Wendy put her arm around her. "Now every time your bad memories come into your head, I want you to close your eyes, point your remote control at the TV screen in your head, and change the channel to number two. Can you do that for me?"

Alice gave her the tiniest of smiles. "I'll try."

Wendy kissed her forehead. "It'll take practice—those bad thoughts will try to worm their way in—but if you keep trying, you can do it."

Alice threw her arms around Wendy. "Thanks, Wendy. Will you stay until I fall asleep?"

"Of course I will."

That was one crisis averted. Now she had to find a way for Alice and Noah to bond with Trent. That should be easy. *Not.*

❖

Trent unlocked the door and put her case down on the kitchen island. The place was very tidy, but some subtle things were different and made her flat seem less empty and lonely. There were some toys that Wendy must have bought today, piled tidily in a storage box in the living room area, Wendy's guitar leaning against the wall, and a piano keyboard sitting on the dining table.

She must play piano too. Talented girl.

It was strange, but only yesterday she would have sworn she would panic at these signs of the children taking over the flat, but Trent had to admit she had a warm feeling not coming home to a dark empty flat.

The last time she had ever had a glimpse of this feeling was coming home from work and finding Becca cooking her dinner. That was such a long time ago.

Trent sighed and walked over to the fridge to get a bottle of water. She stopped in her tracks when she saw two pictures stuck to the fridge door. One was a childlike picture of her apartment building with four figures standing at the bottom, and Trent's, Wendy's, Alice's, and Noah's names underneath.

The picture was bright with a large sun painted in one corner. Even if Wendy hadn't printed Noah's name on the paper, Trent would have known it was his. Noah was a bright, smiley child and didn't yet feel the full force of losing his father. The picture made her smile. Even though she had tried her best to ignore him this morning, he still included her in his picture.

She turned her gaze to the picture next to it and felt guilt and sadness at Alice's picture. It had the figures of Wendy, Noah, and Alice, and the sky above them was nothing but black.

Trent was hit with memories of drawing countless pictures like this when she lost her mother, and the confusion and loneliness her mother's death brought. She wasn't in the picture, and it was hardly surprising since she was pushing Alice and Noah away just like her own father had done, but she didn't know how to rectify it.

Trent grabbed a bottle of water from the fridge and walked to the bedrooms to see if everyone was settled. As it had been the night before, Alice's room's door was open. She peeked in and saw Alice sleeping in Wendy's arms, and she had also dropped off to sleep.

She felt her heart thud at the gentle maternal care Wendy was giving Alice. Trent knew without a doubt she had picked the right nanny.

Alice had obviously had a bad night, and now she felt even guiltier for going out tonight. That was something her father had done. Did she want to be him?

Wendy must have heard her because she moved and opened her eyes. She gazed at Trent, but Trent didn't know what to say, so she retreated back to the kitchen and put the kettle on.

After a few seconds she heard Wendy's voice behind her. "Hi, did you have a good evening?"

"Yes," Trent lied. "Would you like a cup of tea?"

"That would be nice." Wendy stretched and her short pyjama T-shirt rode up, giving Trent a look at her body. It was funny—Claudia had been all over Trent, kissing her and trying to seduce her into bed, and her body felt nothing, but a glimpse at Wendy's midriff made Trent feel that all too familiar tightening in her stomach.

Wendy's body was so different from Claudia's. Where Claudia prized her ultra-thin angular body, Wendy had a softer, curvaceous figure, and Trent much preferred it.

She gave herself a shake and got a second cup from the cupboard. Trent couldn't think like that.

Wendy popped up on the stool at the kitchen island while Trent poured the tea. Trent handed Wendy a cup and sat beside her.

"Sorry if I woke you when I checked on Alice," Trent said.

"That's okay. I shouldn't have fallen asleep there, but she had some bad nightmares again and was inconsolable."

Trent nodded and tapped her fingers on her cup nervously. Wendy realized that even though Trent was extremely confident, this situation, having children and a nanny in her house, made her nervous and unsure how to react. It was out of her comfort zone.

"Did Noah settle down to sleep after his bed biscuits?"

Wendy smiled. "He did. I was so glad you called. Alice had a difficult day, and that makes Noah remember his dad, and then he gets upset, so it was really important to have his bedtime routine."

"I should have thought about it earlier." Trent stared down into her teacup and said, "And Alice? How was she tonight?"

Wendy sighed. "She had bad nightmares. I heard her screaming, and I ran through to her as quickly as I could. Once I got her calmed down enough, she talked quite a bit. She can't get the image of her dad after the accident out of her head. She says it's there every time she shuts her eyes. I taught her a technique to try to manage the memories, but even an adult would struggle to control them—for a child it's even worse."

"The social worker did say she saw some of his body," Trent said.

"She saw everything, saw it happen, and was there waiting for help for a while with him before the ambulance came."

"Jesus," Trent said.

"It's going to take a lot of work with a therapist to help Alice."

Trent rubbed a scar just above her eyebrow. Wendy had noticed her doing this a few times when she appeared tense.

"Has your friend given you any names of therapists yet?" Trent said.

"Yes, one locally who works out of her home, and one who has offices in Harley Street, so she's quite expensive."

Trent looked up and said firmly, "The one in Harley Street—give me her number, and I'll have my secretary book an appointment for her. I want only the best for Alice, for them both. I know what it's like to lose a parent. My mother died when I was very young."

Wendy caught her breath. Was this the same woman who walked out of the flat without looking back this morning? She was so much more open, more concerned.

"I'm sorry, Trent. Maybe you could talk to Alice about it? Show her you came through the same thing?"

Trent looked horrified. "No, no, I couldn't do that. Let her talk to the professional. I saw you bought some toys?"

Suddenly Wendy was worried she had done the wrong thing. "Yes, I hope that was okay. You did say to get what they needed—I have all the receipts."

"Of course it's okay. Get them whatever they need or want—don't worry about the cost," Trent said firmly.

Something in Wendy's mind flagged a warning. Trent was using money to show care. That seemed to be the only way Trent knew how to emotionally communicate, but still it was a step forward from this morning. Maybe Wendy would be able to knit this unexpected family together after all.

Chapter Eight

Becca sat at the kitchen table at her laptop poring over the internet as she had been much of the last few hours. She heard tires on the gravel driveway out at the front of the house. She looked at her watch and saw it was two o'clock. Far too early for Dale to be home, but a minute later Dale walked through the kitchen door.

"Hey, hen."

Becca sat back and smiled as Dale took off her work boots. "Did you run away from work today?"

"Nah, there wasn't much on, so I gave myself an afternoon off. One of the perks of being your own boss is being able to delegate so you can see more of your family."

She could see Dale had been for a haircut on her way home. Dale was like a teenage boy about her hair and loved Becca to notice it, like it, and make a fuss over her, but Becca loved to tease her a bit and pretend she didn't see it.

"As long as Sammy and Val don't mind," Becca said.

Dale walked around the table and kissed her tenderly on the lips. "Nah, business is good and we're all doing well." She stood back and preened like a peacock waiting for the validation she always wanted from Becca. "So, you notice anything different?" Dale said.

Becca folded her arms and pretended to think. "Erm…new shade of lipstick?"

"Oh, aye, that's exactly what it is. Come on."

Becca broke and giggled. "Your hair is lovely."

Dale smoothed her hand over her precisely waxed hair. "Bloody outstanding, isn't it?"

Dale's hair was a barometer of fashion trends. Since Becca met her, it had evolved from short and messy on top to this much more precise and sharp haircut. Dale had a friend who owned her own barber's and who kept Dale's precious hair looking good.

"So tell me, what's this called?" Becca asked.

Dale grabbed a drink from the fridge and sat at the kitchen table. "Undercut on the sides, with a hard parting and comb-over. Cool, eh?"

Becca presumed the line shaved in her hair was the hard parting. "You make more fuss than me about haircuts, darling."

Dale winked at her. "Well, I've got to look good for my posh girl. Is my wee yin sleeping?"

"She is, so don't wake her," Becca warned.

"I wouldnae dare. Are you working?" Dale indicated towards the laptop.

As a freelance photographer, Becca was able to pick and choose her jobs, and she worked mostly from home. When she had to go out on site, either Dale would take time off or Granny Sadie next door would babysit.

"No, I finished up my last job this morning. I've been trying to think what I could get Trent for her birthday at the end of the month. She's going to be forty."

"Oh, aye, I forgot she was going to be old," Dale joked and laughed.

"No jokes. I'm catching up with her," Becca said.

Dale took her hand and said in that sexy voice of hers, "Don't worry, babe. I love being married to a sexy older woman. I'll be your toy boy."

Becca snorted. "You're too old to be a toy boy, darling. I'm only a few years older than you."

Dale smoothed her hand over her hair and said, "But I'm like twenty-one in spirit years."

"Spirit years?" Becca questioned. "That's a new one. So any ideas what we could get Trent? She's been really generous to us since Gracie was born—helping you adopt Gracie quickly, managing all our paperwork, helping you with buying that site for the new garage..."

With business going well, Dale had started work on a new branch of McGuire's Motors. Becca sometimes still pinched herself when she thought about how far they had come since she'd met Dale. Now she didn't need to worry about leaking roofs, dishwashers breaking down, and central heating going haywire. Now Jake, Gracie, and Becca could plan for a bright future.

"Hmm, I suppose you are right," Dale said. She had seen a different side to Trent since the day Becca had been rushed to hospital and Gracie was born. They had gone from enemies, to frenemies, and now friends. All because they had Becca's interest in common, and because Becca insisted they be this one big unusual family along with Dale's best friends, Sammy, Val, and their daughter Mia.

Dale knew Trent still had some feelings for Becca, but she had never once put a toe out of line in that regard, and Dale knew she wouldn't. Trent had admitted that Dale was right for Becca and she was glad Becca found her.

"You know, when I first met Trent, I thought she was a pompous dick," Dale said.

"And now?" Becca furrowed her eyebrows.

She smiled at Becca and said, "She's still pompous and acts like she's got a stick up her—" Dale caught herself and thought of Jake's mantra passed to him by his mother—*Use positivity with your words.* Becca did not like bad language, so Dale mentally corrected herself before she said the wrong word and got told off. "Backside, stick up her backside, but she's not a dick."

"Well, that's a ringing endorsement, if ever I heard one," Becca said.

"You know what I mean, hen."

"I do." Becca smiled and turned her attention back to her laptop.

Dale took a swig of juice and noticed the two jars of jalapeños on the table, one red and one green. Becca had been ravenous for jalapeños when she was pregnant with Gracie but had calmed down since.

Dale pointed to the jars. "You're not pregnant again, are you?"

Becca gave her an incredulous look. "Now that would be miraculous. I just felt like them on my sandwich today."

Becca sighed loudly. "What can I get Trent? I mean, what do you get someone who has everything?"

Dale shrugged. "I don't know. I mean, I'm easy to buy for. A new Xbox or PlayStation game and I'm happy, but Trent would probably want something boring."

Becca shook her head. "You're one of the cleverest people I know and gave Jake your intelligence, but sometimes I think part of your brain stopped maturing at thirteen."

Dale laughed. "I'm young at heart, and that's why you love me, posh girl."

She got a thrill when Becca gave her a sexy little smile in response and giggled like a schoolgirl.

"Maybe." Becca then said, "It's a big birthday, and she doesn't have any family, so we need to mark it in some special way. When you were young, what did you want in your life by the time you were in your forties?"

Dale knew straight away. "Since I was really small, I only wanted four things when I was a grown-up, not to be rich or famous like other kids wanted. I wanted a cool car, a belter of a missus—"

Becca interrupted her. "A *what* of a missus?"

Dale chuckled. Even now they'd been married for a year and a half, she could still outfox Becca with some Scottish words.

"A belter of a missus. Belter means the best, the most beautiful, the classiest, the most amazing, that kind of thing."

Becca grinned. "And do you have a belter of a missus?"

Dale took Becca's hand and kissed it. "Oh, aye. A bloody belter, hen."

"So we've got the cool car and the missus chalked off—what are the other two things you always wanted?"

"A house with a garden, and a dog," Dale said.

"Well, you got the house and the garden, and we have a menagerie of animals out there, but why didn't you say you'd like a dog?"

"I thought you'd think it was too much, like you would end up having to look after it."

The truth was Dale was worried about putting too much pressure on Becca after Gracie was born. She very nearly died having their baby, and it had taken a lot out of her wife physically. Becca was everything to her, and she never wanted to put too much pressure on her so soon.

They had the goats and chickens, but Dale and Jake took care of them morning and evening. But a dog would need 24/7 care.

"You were trying to protect me again, weren't you? I'm not going to break, you know," Becca said sharply.

"Come here, babe." Dale beckoned her over to sit on her lap.

Becca did and wrapped her hands around Dale's neck. She scratched her fingernails down the nape of Dale's neck, along Dale's newly shorn hairline.

"I just thought it would be a bit much for you with Gracie and a new puppy running around."

"I could manage. I think the children would like to grow up with a dog, and it can be quite a big empty house when you and Jake aren't here," Becca told Dale.

Dale started to get excited. "You mean we can actually get one? You think it would be okay?"

"Yes," Becca said, "it would be nice to add to our little zoo of animals, and I want you to have all four things you wished for when you were little."

"Brilliant! Jake's going to love it. You see, babe? You are a belter." Dale grinned.

Becca leaned in and kissed her teasingly. "And you and your hair are so sexy. We have a few hours before Jake gets home, and Gracie is fast asleep."

Dale stood up with Becca in her arms. She didn't need to be told twice. "Oh yeah, babe."

She kissed Becca as she carried her to the kitchen door and nudged it open. She was so ready for Becca. All Becca had to do was look at her, and Dale wanted her, and that heavy beat started inside her.

When they got to the bottom of the stairs, Becca said, "Wait— we were talking about Trent's birthday present. You distracted me with your boyish good looks."

Dale did not want to talk about Trent or her present at this moment in time. "We'll adopt her a donkey or something. We can talk about it later. Now I just want to kiss your beautiful body all over."

"Get to it, then, toy boy," Becca joked and smacked her on the behind.

Dale carried her upstairs and into their bedroom. They kissed feverishly as Dale lowered her to the floor. Becca hurriedly pulled off Dale's T-shirt and pulled at her belt.

This was one of the reasons Dale loved Becca—how passionate she was. Dale never thought having sex with just one woman would be exciting, but with Becca it was more than exciting. She craved Becca, and luckily for her, Becca enjoyed the sexual aspect of their life just as much.

Becca pulled back from the kiss and said quickly, "I need to turn on the baby monitor. Get undressed."

Dale didn't need to be asked twice. She pulled at her jeans while moving to the bed and nearly tripped as she did.

"Shit, I nearly fell to my untimely death there."

Becca laughed as she took off her clothes quickly. "A slight exaggeration, my darling."

Dale's eyes were drawn to Becca's breasts as Becca took her bra off. She couldn't wait to get her lips on them.

Becca slipped under the covers and Dale said, "Do you want me to…" She was referring to the strap-on they both loved, in the wardrobe.

"No time, just get in here. I'm wet and I need you," Becca said with a saucy smile.

Dale grinned. "It must be the haircut that's turning you on."

She joined her wife under the covers and groaned when her body touched Becca's. Becca opened her legs and Dale slipped in between. Becca pulled her down into a kiss and scratched her fingers down the back of her hairline.

I knew it was the haircut, Dale thought. She could feel Becca's wetness against her own sex and Dale's hips thrust against it quite naturally. "You are wet, babe."

When Dale went to move her hand down to touch her, Becca wrapped her legs around Dale's hips and said, "No, just like this, darling."

Dale nodded and moved her hand to squeeze Becca's breast. Sometimes Becca wanted them as close as they could be and moving together. Dale was happy to give Becca whatever she wanted and she loved the feel of her wife's legs wrapped around her.

She thrust slowly at first, enjoying the sensation of being so close. She started to thrust faster when Becca scratched her nails up and down her back.

"I can feel you," Becca moaned. "So close."

Dale rested her forehead against Becca's. Her sex was throbbing and all she could think about was coming.

"Yeah, babe. I'm gonna come quick." She groaned.

Becca wrapped her hands around Dale's neck. "Me too. Faster, darling."

Dale ground her sex into Becca's and steadily upped her pace and pushed her face into Becca's neck. She was trying her best to make it last as long as Becca needed, but then she felt Becca's legs tighten around her and her fingers grasped her hair.

"Now, darling, now."

"Fuck, yes," Dale shouted as she thrust wildly and let her orgasm take her over.

"I love you, I love you," Becca said as she came.

Dale's orgasm exploded over her sex and spread like wildfire all over her body. "Fuck."

They held each other as their breathing calmed. Dale lifted her head and smiled down at Becca. "We're good at that," Dale said with a grin.

Becca laughed and pulled her into a deep, wet kiss. "*You* are so good at that."

"I don't like to brag," Dale joked.

"Oh, you do." Becca dug her nails into her buttocks and breathed, "Again."

Dale grinned and began to grind her hips again.

"I love you."

❖

"This place is gorgeous, Dee." Kira walked over to the balcony of the penthouse and looked out. Kira's school was on their October break, giving her a chance to visit Wendy's new digs.

"It's not bad, is it?" Wendy checked on Alice and Noah as she passed the couch. They were engrossed in a Disney movie.

"Not bad, that's an understatement," Kira said.

Wendy pointed to the kitchen and said, "Let me get us coffee and then we can have a chat."

Kira smiled. "Sounds good. Did I see an expensive looking espresso machine in there?"

"You did. Cappuccino with an extra shot?" Wendy said.

"You remembered!" Kira said.

"Of course, we drank enough of them at uni to fill the English Channel. I'll just be a few minutes."

Wendy quickly checked the casserole she had cooking in the oven. Tonight was the first time Trent was going to share dinner with her and the kids, and she was determined to make it go smoothly. She knew Trent was uptight and nervous about it—sharing a table with two kids wasn't her usual type of dinner date. So she wanted to make it perfect.

The casserole still had time to go, so she shut the oven door and went to make the coffee. Wendy brought two mugs over to the dining table and handed one to Kira.

"Thanks. Mmm, this looks good." Kira took a sip. "Delicious. So, beautiful house, nice kids, gorgeous but scary lawyer—you've got it all. What's the scary lawyer like?"

Wendy gave a quick glance over to the children and made sure their attention was on the TV.

"Complicated. She doesn't know how to relate to the children at the moment, but I've seen potential in her. I'm going to knit this little family together."

Kira laughed softly. "Why do you always feel the need to mend every family you work for? You're channelling Mary Poppins again."

Wendy took a sip of coffee and sat it down. "You know why. I don't want these families I care about to be like mine. I know how that ends."

"Grabbing on to the first person who shows they care about you, even if they'd cheat on you and steal your money?" Kira said.

"Exactly. These children are going to be connected to Trent for a long time, and they've been through so much. They need someone to love them," Wendy said.

"What if that someone doesn't or can't?" Kira asked.

Wendy said confidently, "She will. She just needs a bit of guidance before I go back to uni."

"If anyone can, it would be you, Dee." Kira closed her eyes and sniffed the air. "Is that amazing smell dinner?"

"Yes, it's the first dinner Trent is going to share with us," Wendy said.

"Well, good luck with that." Kira raised the cup to her mouth and said, "How are you dealing with the lift?"

"Really well. It's an ultra-modern thing with a video screen, so I don't feel alone, and the kids help me with their singing."

Kira chuckled the said, "Did you contact one of the psychologists for Alice?"

Wendy nodded. "Trent insisted on the expensive Harley Street doctor. She starts next week."

Just then she heard Noah shout, "No, Ali," and saw Alice running away to her room.

She got up immediately and hurried over to a crying Noah. "What's wrong, sweetheart?"

He grasped on to her and said, "The mummy in the film died."

Wendy put her head back and sighed. What an idiot she had been. She should have thought more deeply about what film to put on. She was going to have to vet every film and TV show from now on.

Kira was now by her side. "Kira? Could you look after Noah for me? I need to talk to Alice."

"Of course. Hey, Noah? You want to show me your favourite toys?" Kira said.

Noah nodded and went to her. He was so much easier to placate as he didn't comprehend fully that his dad was gone for good.

Seeing he was happy to go with Kira, Wendy hurried to Alice's bedroom. Music was pounding loudly behind the door. Wendy opened the door and turned down the volume on the radio Alice had playing. Alice was sitting up against the wall with her arms hiding her head.

"Alice, I'm sorry. I should have checked out the film storyline before I put it on. Come here."

"No. Go away!" Alice shouted. Then Alice started to flail her arms to stop Wendy holding her, but Wendy caught her arms and pulled her close. Alice stopped struggling, went limp, and convulsed in tears.

It broke her heart to see Alice so upset, and all she could do was try to comfort her. Comfort was all she had to offer, but it made her even more determined to help Trent relate to these kids.

"Alice, I'm here, I'm here." Wendy rubbed her back.

Alice muffled a sentence into her chest.

Wendy pushed Alice forward slightly. "What did you say, Alice?"

"We won't have you for long. We'll be on our own soon again."

Wendy took a tissue from her pocket and wiped Alice's tears. "You won't be—Trent is your family."

"No, she won't be with us," Alice said through fresh tears.

Wendy took her hand. "Alice, I want you to listen to me. Adults aren't perfect. They have issues and fears too. I think Trent would like to be able to talk and play with you, but she doesn't know how."

"How can you not know how?" Alice asked.

Wendy handed her a fresh tissue for her tears, then picked up Alice's hair brush. "Let me tell you a story, and I'll fix your hair."

"Can I have little braids like yours?" Alice asked.

Wendy smiled. "Yes, no problem."

She started to drag the brush slowly through Alice's hair, and as she did, Wendy saw the little girl's shoulders drop and relax. It was a trick she had picked up from her grandma. When she was upset, Grandma would brush and braid her hair in different styles, while they talked. It was the personal attention, the feeling of the brush on her scalp, almost like getting a head massage.

"What's your story, Wendy?"

"When I was a little girl, I wasn't close to my parents. They had busy jobs, and I came along late in their lives. Mum and Dad aren't children people—"

"Like Trent?" Alice interjected.

Wendy thought about her mum and dad and the way Trent had called home to make sure Noah had his proper bedtime routine. Her parents wouldn't have done that. Trent had more potential.

"Hmm, I don't think so, but keep listening. I would come home from school and let myself in, because they were both at work. When they got home, we heated up microwave meals and ate in separate rooms. If all I had was them, then I wouldn't know how normal families worked or how to show love. I don't know all the details, but I think Trent had a difficult, lonely childhood, and that had an effect on her."

"So how are you different, Wendy?" Alice asked.

Wendy put down the brush and started on the little braids. "I had one saving grace, in fact two, a grandma and grandpa who were the most loving people in the world. My grandma used to do my hair like this, and we watched old romantic films together. My grandpa was a fantastic musician and taught me the piano and the guitar."

"My dad was a great musician," Alice said.

Wendy gave her a kiss on the cheek. "I bet he was."

She twisted the first braid and used an elastic hairband to hold it in place, then started on the second. "What I'm trying to say is that I might have had difficulty relating to children and being in a family if it wasn't for my grandparents. I don't think Trent had anyone like that growing up. I might be wrong, but that's my hunch, so I want you to do me a favour."

Wendy tied off the second braid and Alice turned to face her. "What favour?"

"Give Trent a chance to learn. Can you do that?" Wendy asked.

Alice looked down at the bed and stayed silent.

"Trent's going to have dinner with us tonight and says she will do as often as she can, but it will be tricky for her at first. She won't know what to say or do, so give her a chance. She'll make mistakes, but I'm sure there's a woman who feels very deeply underneath that gruff exterior."

"How do you know?" Alice was a tough sell.

"I'm good at reading people." She didn't say that there was certain vulnerability and fear in Trent's eyes. That was for Wendy to know. "So what do you say? Will you do it for me?"

Alice nodded. "Okay."

"Great, now why don't you have a lie-down before dinner. Take my iPhone and listen to an audiobook or some calming music, not the loud stuff on the radio."

Alice showed interest when Wendy said *audiobook*. "You have audiobooks? I love books."

Wendy opened up her audiobook app. She had most of the children's classics and some for older children like Harry Potter. She used them a lot in her job as a nanny for children who had trouble sleeping.

Wendy stroked Alice's hair and said, "Books are places you can visit in your imagination when real life is difficult, I always think."

Alice scrolled through the books and stopped on *Peter Pan*, then gave her a half smile. "You're in this one, Wendy."

Wendy laughed softly. "When I was a little girl, I wished that Wendy Darling and Peter Pan would fly me off to Neverland."

Wendy scrolled further down and stopped on *Alice's Adventures in Wonderland*. "Why don't you start with this one. You're in that story."

"Okay. If you think so." Alice got her earbuds from her bedside table and plugged them in to the iPhone. "Wendy, who are these people? I didn't mean to go into your pictures—I just hit the wrong button."

Wendy looked at the phone quickly and smiled. It was her photo album named *My Families*. She opened the album and pages of family photos were displayed on the screen. "These are all the families I've been nanny for. All the families I've helped. I started this little tradition of taking a photo before I leave, and it led to this full album."

Alice leaned her head to the side and regarded her quizzically. "Are you here to help us?"

Wendy smiled. That was her goal, to bring families together, and she wasn't going to let this unusual one flounder.

"Yes, I'm here to help."

Alice smiled and put her earbuds in. "Call me Ali, Wendy. My dad did."

"I will, thank you."

Wendy got up off the bed and left Alice to her audiobook. Maybe the film upsetting Alice wasn't so bad after all. It got them talking, and Alice was much happier after this chat than before.

Now to make dinner a success.

❖

Trent was stuck in traffic, but she wasn't too upset about that. She was nervous about having dinner with Wendy and the children, so the longer the traffic jam, the longer she could postpone it.

She looked around the large Mercedes people carrier her secretary had leased for her and was quite satisfied with it. Trent picked it up after work and was pleasantly surprised at the car. The very phrase *people carrier* had made her shudder in the past because it was everything that made her feel uneasy. Wife, family, home, 2.4 children.

Dale had bought one of these for her family, and even though she still had her sports car in the garage, it felt like you had to give up part of yourself, part of your personality, to have a family. But it was as luxurious as her sports car and had a fantastic engine on it. It would certainly be safe and comfortable for Wendy, Alice, and Noah. And she wanted them to be comfortable—she might not be a kid person like Dale, but she would be good at providing everything they needed.

Trent's mobile rang, hooked up to the car's Bluetooth. It was Lady Claudia again. She had been texting and phoning since Trent walked out on dinner the other night, and Trent had ignored her.

She just wanted to let her go, but she couldn't ignore her forever. Lady Claudia was a big name in socialite circles, and those circles were the bulk of her clientele. She had to find a way to brush her off without causing offence.

She accepted the call and said, "Hello?"

"Well, hello. You are a hard woman to get hold of."

"I'm sorry, Lady Claudia, I've been extremely busy at work and at home," Trent said.

"Hmm, well I just wanted to apologize for the way dinner ended the other night. I didn't mean to offend you."

The traffic jam started to move at last. "Don't worry about it. My life is upside down at the moment, and losing my cousin in such a violent way was difficult."

"I understand completely." Claudia started to laugh. "The thought of you trying to handle children is just too funny for words, but I want to remind you that your old life will be waiting for you when they've gone to boarding school, and so will I. In the meantime, you have a nanny—use her, and we can still go out."

Life would be waiting for her? Is that what life really was? Wining and dining with shallow, pompous rich people and coming home to a dark penthouse? Did she want to be doing that when she was fifty, sixty?

"I'll need to get back to you, Lady Claudia. I have a call coming in from home," Trent lied.

"Very well, but I'll be expecting a call soon. Goodbye."

Trent let out a sigh of relief when Claudia hung up the phone. Claudia made her uneasy, and she wished she had never slept with her. Claudia reminded her of what she had said to Wendy and the children and her plans for them. It made the guilt she carried rear its head.

She looked at the car phone display and had the urge to call home. She had no idea of what to say but felt like she should.

The phone had voice controls, and so before she could change her mind she said, "Phone home."

Just saying those two words gave her an unfamiliar tingle in her stomach. The phone rang a few times and then Wendy answered.

"Hello? Davina Trent's residence."

Trent would need to tell her to cut out the Davina. "Hi, it's Trent. I'm running a little late. I picked up the car for you and the children on my way home, but traffic is horrendous."

"That's okay—we can wait for you. I made a casserole for dinner, and I can just heat that up when you get here."

Damn. She'd hoped they might go ahead with dinner and she would get away with delaying her first awkward mealtime.

"If you insist. How are Alice and Noah?" Trent asked.

"All right. Noah is doing well. Alice had a wobble earlier, but we talked things through, and she felt better. She's lying down just now and listening to an audiobook on my iPhone."

"Okay, good. I won't be long then. See you soon."

"Bye, Trent," Wendy said.

Trent said, "End call," and the phone obliged.

Now she was even more terrified. They were waiting for her. What would she say when she walked in the door? What would Wendy say? What would Noah do?

She had the urge to turn the car around and run away, but something stopped her. She pictured Alice's sad face and the look in her eyes, then gazed at her reflection in the rear-view mirror and touched the scar above her eyebrow. Trent couldn't run when she knew how Alice felt right now, and she knew because she had been in Alice's position as a child.

Trent couldn't dismiss Alice and Noah as she had been. She had to try her best for them.

❖

Trent's nerves grew as she rode up in the lift to her penthouse. There was a warm home with good children and a beautiful nanny up there waiting. It shouldn't be scary and would not be to a normal person.

The lift came to a stop, and Trent walked down the short corridor to her front door. She stood there staring at it, trying to find the courage to walk in. She put her key into the lock but didn't turn it and held on to her case and the bag of sweets she had picked up at the local shop.

Trent thought that if she had something to hand over, it would ease her way. "Come on, Trent," she told herself. She was never afraid of a packed courtroom or the toughest of judges, but this was daunting.

Trent took a breath and unlocked and opened the door. When she walked in, she was hit with warmth and the delicious smell of dinner. That unknown tingle was back again.

Wendy was at the cooker and Noah appeared to be drawing at the island in the kitchen.

She walked a few steps in, and Wendy looked up and gave her a happy, sweet smile. "Hi there."

Noah spotted her and got down from his chair and ran over to her, throwing his arms around her legs. "Hi, Trent. We made dinner for you," he said happily.

Trent was tense being cuddled like that but managed to stroke the top of his head. "Thank you. I am hungry." She was lost for what to say next, then remembered the sweets she had bought. "I…um…bought you something. Come over to the kitchen."

Wendy was waiting for her. "Dinner is ready when you are—oh, and I put a bottle of wine in the fridge for you."

"Thank you," Trent said. What was this growing tingly feeling? Wendy's preparing dinner and anticipating her needs intensified it.

"What did you buy, Trent?" Noah said.

Trent took out a big tub of chocolates and one full of jelly sweets. "I bought you these sweets. I hope you like them."

"Yes, thanks," Noah said.

Wendy gave her a pointed look. Did she not approve?

"Can I have some now?" Noah asked.

Wendy immediately intervened. "None till after dinner, Noah. Go and wash your hands. We'll be eating shortly."

Trent cleared her throat and pulled out the car keys from her pocket. "These are your keys for the car I leased. It's a Mercedes people carrier. Lots of room for the children and shopping bags. I hope you'll be happy with it."

"It'll be perfect, although I'll be a little nervous driving such an expensive car."

"Don't worry," Trent said. "I'm sure you're a careful driver. I'll just go and put my case in my office, and then I'll come back for dinner."

Wendy smiled and Trent had the urge to run her fingers through those little braids in her hair, which hung free from the blue headscarf Wendy was wearing today. The little braids made her appear whimsical, sweet, and soft.

Trent shook off the unusual feeling and walked along the corridor past the bedrooms. She stopped at Alice's room and peeked in. Alice was lying down with earbuds in, but her eyes were wide open and she looked at Trent. She didn't know what to say or do, so she waved her hand to Alice, smiled, and hurried further along the corridor to her office.

She shut the door quickly and took a few deep breaths. Her body was a maelstrom of emotions right now, and she didn't know what to do with them.

Wendy finished dishing out her beef casserole, mashed potatoes, and vegetables and took a seat. Trent lifted the bottle of wine and said, "Would you like some wine, Wendy?"

Wendy smiled. "That would be nice. Thank you."

Once it was poured, Wendy took a sip and watched Trent with interest. Her body was full of tension, but she was trying hard not to show it.

Trent began to eat and said, "This is delicious."

"I'm sure you're used to much better in the restaurants you go to."

Trent looked her in the eye and said, "No, I'm not. This is wonderful. I haven't had home-cooked meals in a long time."

Wendy wondered if Trent had ever had a long-term girlfriend or if she simply liked the single life. She was fascinated to know.

The table went quiet after that. Noah was wolfing down his food, Alice was quietly eating her meal, and Trent was doing similar. She had to get family conversation going.

"Noah? Alice? Trent? At mealtimes I like everyone to tell us about their day," Wendy said.

Trent snapped her head up and looked even more tense. But

talking was the only way to get Trent to build bridges and connections with these kids.

"Why don't you start, Noah?" Wendy said. She knew Noah would be full of things to tell Trent. He was the easiest to start with.

"After breakfast we went for a walk down at the water. Me, Ali, Wendy, and my dinosaur," Noah said.

Wendy smiled, "That's right—we walked along the river, and tell Trent what we saw."

Noah gave Trent a big smile. "Ducks and swans!"

"Isn't that nice, Trent?" Wendy said.

This felt like a peace conference with Wendy as the negotiator, bringing both sides together.

Trent still looked tense but replied, "Yes, I've never gone along the river walkway very far."

Wendy finished eating her mouthful of food and said, "You'll have to come with us one time."

She looked at Alice next, but she appeared unsure of herself so she went to Trent. "How was your day, Trent?"

"Me?" Trent said nervously.

"Yes, you must have been busy today," Wendy said.

Trent put down her cutlery and lifted her glass of wine. After a long sip, she said, "I was in court this morning, then saw some clients this afternoon."

"What does a lawyer do, Trent?" Noah asked.

Then Alice said out of the blue, "Breaks up marriages."

Wendy looked up at Trent and saw her retreating back into herself. She had to fix this. "That's not the case, Alice. Sometimes marriages don't work out, and people need to decide who gets what, in a fair way. Trent helps them with that." That was an oversimplification and put Trent's work in the best of lights. Divorces were rarely as civilized as that, but Wendy wanted the children to see Trent in the best light. After all, she was their only hope.

When she looked up Trent mouthed the words *thank you* and gave her an open smile, so different from the dismissive way she'd left home yesterday morning.

I knew you had potential. I'm going to make you three into a family.

CHAPTER NINE

The next two weeks went okay for Trent. She was having to get used to clutter around the flat, noise, the songs Wendy sang for every activity the children did, and dinner and conversation every night. She was using the one question Wendy had given her—*How was your day?*—every night, but without Wendy to hold the conversation together, she would be lost after that.

Alice didn't speak to her much. Noah, on the other hand, made things easy. Trent simply coming home was exciting enough for him, which she didn't quite understand. He was naturally good-natured, but Wendy told her he talked about her looking like his daddy a lot. That had been the first thing he said to her at the hospital and one of the things that made her flee that night.

That still scared her, but she did want to be able to hold a conversation with the kids when they met up in school holidays. Trent had found taking home treats after work was an easy way to ease her way with the children, even though Wendy had asked her not to any more, as she liked to keep sugary sweets to a minimum. But she couldn't just arrive home with nothing. It wasn't enough just to be herself.

Friday came along, and Trent was facing a whole weekend where she would be in much greater contact with Alice and Noah. Last weekend she had managed to get away with spending most of her time in her office since she had court to prepare for on Monday, and Wendy didn't take her day off on Sunday, just to help out.

But this weekend Wendy was not only taking her day off but going out for the day, so Trent would be alone with her charges a lot. As the week progressed, she was getting more and more anxious about it. She needed something to occupy them and hopefully something they would enjoy.

She thought of Jake, and Sammy and Val's daughter, Mia, and

what they liked to do, and it came to her—computer games. It was perfect. Kids loved games, and video games would keep them busy and quiet, at the same time as buying some goodwill, Trent hoped.

The only problem was she had no idea what to buy. A quick phone call to Dale and they made plans to meet up on Friday afternoon to look at gaming systems.

Trent asked her secretary to keep her afternoon free on Friday so that she could leave early. She packed up her briefcase and got a taxi along to the shopping centre nearest her office. Trent walked in through the sliding doors and was immediately aware of the noise of schoolchildren excited for their weekend ahead, busy mothers and fathers pushing prams, and crying children.

She wasn't used to this kind of shopping. Hers was normally done online or in the exclusive department stores and boutiques London had to offer. This was chaotic.

There was a board by the escalator with directions to all the shops. She looked down the list until she saw the name Gaming World. The shop was located on the second floor, so she made her way up. As she came off the escalator, she saw Dale waiting by the door of the games shop, looking at her iPhone and completely oblivious to the group of young women across at the coffee kiosk, gazing at her and giggling like a bunch of schoolgirls.

What was it that women found so intriguing about Dale, Trent wondered. Then, as she got closer, she noticed Dale's new haircut. What the hell had she done to her hair?

Never in a million years could she have imagined Becca would end up finding love with someone like Dale, but Dale loved her and took care of her like Trent couldn't, so she was glad Becca had her, even though a small part of her still hurt.

Dale spotted her and walked over to meet her. "All right, mate?"

Trent shook her hand. "Yes, I'm fine. How are Becca and the children?"

Dale's face came to life, and she beamed with smiles at the mention of her children. "They're doing great. How are Alice and Noah? They must have gone through hell since their dad died. I lost my mum at eighteen and my world collapsed around me, so I can't imagine what it would be like to have that happen at such a young age."

Dale's words brought the pain Alice and Noah must be feeling into sharp focus, and Trent remembered the pain that she herself had felt when her mother died.

"They're doing okay. Alice is feeling it most. She's old enough to understand exactly what happened," Trent said.

Dale put her hand on Trent's shoulder. "You know Becca and I will be here for you and help however we can."

"Thank you. I appreciate it," Trent said.

Dale cocked her head in the direction of the gaming shop and said, "Let's put smiles on their faces, then."

Wendy strummed her guitar to finish the song she had been singing with Alice and Noah. She had set up the keyboard for Alice and taught her one piano chord for their song, and Noah was on the tambourine. She was a great believer in using music and song to help children cooperate and express emotions.

She heard a key in the door and looked at her watch. Trent wasn't due home this early.

"Who's that?" Alice said nervously.

Alice was so jumpy and anxious about everything. Wendy was sure she was suffering from post-traumatic stress. The sooner she got to the psychologist the better.

Wendy put down her guitar and said, "It'll be okay, honey. I'm here."

Just as she was getting up, Trent walked through the door with someone. Alice immediately hurried to Wendy's side and cuddled into her arms for reassurance, and Noah followed suit.

Trent and her companion were holding a lot of bags. Bags from a gaming store.

Wendy sighed internally. It looked like Trent had moved on from sweets and chocolates to toys and games. She put on her best smile and went to greet their guest. Alice and Noah stayed behind.

"Hi, Trent. You're home early," Wendy said.

"Yes, I finished early today so I could go and meet my friend. Wendy, this is Dale," Trent said.

"Pleased to meet you, Dale." Wendy offered her hand and Dale put her bags down.

"Aye, you too. Trent was telling me what a good help you've been to her," Dale said.

Dale was gorgeous in a boyish, James Dean kind of way, and her Scottish accent was just charming.

"Oh, I'm just doing my job. Where in Scotland are you from?" Wendy asked.

"Glasgow. I came up to London when I was seventeen," Dale said.

Wendy glanced down to Dale's hand and saw a thick wedding band there. No surprise she was taken, Wendy thought. "I've been to lots of music festivals in Scotland. The Scots really know how to enjoy a concert."

Dale grinned. "Aye, way plenty of drink."

Wendy laughed. "Well, yes, there was plenty of that too." She turned to Trent, whose eyes were narrowed and serious. What was Trent thinking? "What did you buy, Trent?"

Trent pulled a box out of one of the bags. "A games console. Dale helped me choose it."

Noah squealed when he heard that and ran over to Trent. "You bought us Nintendo, Trent?"

Trent showed him the box. "Yes, I thought you would like to play with it over the weekend. My friend Dale is going to connect it all for you."

Noah threw his arms around Trent's legs. "Thank you so much!"

Something stirred in Trent's heart to see how happy she had made Noah, and she wanted more. Alice stood in the background as always and said nothing. What could she do to get the same reaction from her?

Wendy turned to Alice and said, "Say thank you to Trent, Ali."

"Thank you, Trent," Alice replied.

Trent nodded. "You're welcome. Dale, can you set it up for them?"

"Aye, nae problem." She took Noah's hand and said, "Let's get this thing going, so you can play Mario Party, eh?"

Noah jumped up and down excitedly. "Yeah."

When Dale reached Alice she dropped to one knee and said, "Hi, you must be Alice. It's nice to meet you."

Alice cracked a smile and then laughed when Dale told her a silly joke. Dale had just met her and got more of a response from her than Trent had in the whole time she had known her.

Trent didn't like the feelings that were stirring inside her.

❖

Wendy was preparing dinner in the kitchen while Dale was setting up the games console with the kids. Trent stood behind the sofa, quite apart from them, silently watching.

Dale had Noah and Alice in the palm of her hand. In fact, Wendy hadn't heard Alice laugh so much since she'd met her.

Wendy put her tray of vegetables in the oven and washed her hands. When she turned around she couldn't take her eyes off Trent's lonely figure. How could someone with such a confident personality look so forlorn? She looked quite sweet, actually.

Trent appeared as though she felt left out. She was supposed to be the hero bringing home the exciting gift, and now the kids' attention was all on Dale, who just happened to be a natural with kids.

She was drawn to go and stand with her. "Dinner's prepared for later. Will Dale be staying?"

Trent crossed her arms defensively. "No, she has to get back home to her own family." She turned her head and looked at Wendy. "She is married, you know," Trent said a little sharply.

That was a weird reaction. Trent seemed to be jealous of the attention Dale was getting.

"Yes, I did know. I spotted the wedding ring on her finger earlier," Wendy said.

"It didn't stop you flirting with her. Dale's married to my best friend."

Wendy was taken aback. Where was this coming from? Was it just the attention Dale was getting, or was there something else bothering her?

Wendy whispered, "I wasn't flirting. I was exchanging pleasantries. You know, that thing normal people do? Besides, I think I'm professional enough not to flirt with my employer's friend."

She could see anger and annoyance in Trent's eyes. Trent held her gaze for a few seconds, then turned back to Dale and the kids. By this time Alice was sitting right next to Dale and Noah was on her knee.

Wendy heard Trent sigh with annoyance. "Dale, I'm just going to answer some important emails. I'll be back out soon."

"Aye, nae probs, mate. We've nearly got everything done," Dale said.

Trent marched away and Wendy heard her shut her office door loudly. Alice looked back to her and Wendy gave her a reassuring smile.

There was an emotionally confused person hiding under that tough shell, Wendy thought.

❖

Later that evening, Trent was finishing up some work in her office. She closed up her laptop and sat back in her seat. She could hear Wendy singing with Noah in the bathroom. It sounded like the brushing your teeth song, which she was beginning to know by heart. Wendy had a song for everything. She imagined what her nanny would think of Wendy's approach. Her head would probably explode. Nanny Wilson didn't need songs—she had threats of violence and psychological terror to get what she wanted.

Trent swung around in her office chair and gazed out of her window at the evening gloom settling down on the dockside apartment and it mirrored her mood. She was depressed. What was meant to be a nice gesture today had made her face some unpleasant feelings.

Dale had been her usual good-natured self and endeared herself to both the kids and Wendy. Trent didn't know how she did it. She could charm a woman at a drinks party or a bar, but two kids and their nanny, that was foreign to her.

As she stood back and watched the attention Alice and Noah were giving Dale, she had to admit she felt jealous. They were *her* family and Wendy was *her* nanny.

She couldn't understand why she was feeling so possessive and envious all of a sudden.

It really irked her when she thought Wendy was flirting with Dale. Why did Dale impress and charm all the women in her life?

Wendy is not a woman in your life, Trent chastised herself.

Her head and chest were a mish-mash of feelings. Before the children came into her world, life rarely confused her and feelings were not complicated.

She cringed at what she'd said, accusing Wendy of flirting. Apart from when the children were around, Wendy hadn't spoken to her since. Trent had to make an effort with Alice and Noah and Wendy. Wendy was an amazing nanny and she wouldn't be lucky a second time.

Trent wanted a drink, so she got up to leave the sanctuary of her office. She spotted her iPad sitting on the edge of the desk and wondered if Alice would like to use it. Alice had been stealing Wendy's iPhone to listen to audiobooks and play games a lot, so maybe she could let Alice use her iPad until she could buy one for her.

She imagined the smile she would get, like Noah today, if she came home with bags from the Apple Store. Trent felt a wave of excitement at that thought.

Yes that was what she'd do.

She picked up her iPad and left the office. She could hear Wendy in Noah's bedroom, so she walked along to Alice's door and knocked.

"Alice? Can I come in?"

"If you want," Alice said in a low voice.

Trent walked in and found Alice sitting on her bed playing with Wendy's phone. When Alice looked up she could feel the gulf and tension between them.

She had to speak first. "Did you enjoy the Nintendo?"

Alice didn't smile but said, "Yes, it was fun."

There was an awkward silence and Trent tried to think what she would have wanted someone to say to her when she lost her mother, but all she felt was pain in her chest and her mouth dry up. She couldn't go there.

Then she remembered the iPad. "I saw how much you liked Wendy's iPhone and I wondered if you'd like to use my iPad?" Trent walked over to the bed and held it out. Alice eyed it, looking unsure of herself. "You can read, listen to audiobooks, go on the net, play games, whatever you want."

Alice took it from her and said, "Thank you. I won't break it."

"I know you'll be careful. Buy any games you want—the app store is linked to my card."

Alice appeared to be surprised at this turn of events and unsure how to respond. Trent wasn't too sure either so she said, "I'll say goodnight then."

"Night, Trent," Alice replied.

Then Trent left and hurried to pour out a drink. Her heart was pounding in her chest. She had never been nervous talking to anyone before, but one little girl made her so.

❖

Despite having been completely pissed off with Trent over the flirting accusation, Wendy still wanted to finish the weekend itinerary she had started yesterday. She had dealt with emotionally distant parents before and giving them structured events helped them focus and reconnect.

Trent's case was a little more extreme, but she was determined to make a difference and leave this family in a better place than where she found them. Wendy pressed *print* and went into Trent's office after knocking, to pick up her printed itinerary.

"Now the tricky part," Wendy said to herself.

Wendy walked into the living area and found Trent nursing a drink with the lights dimmed and some soft music playing. She felt a flutter in her chest. *She looks adorable and gorgeous.* Wait. Did she just think that? She was annoyed with her.

Wendy shook herself and walked over to the couch. "Trent, can I have a word with you?"

Trent, who had been staring into space, took a big intake of breath and said, "Of course, sit down. Do you want a drink?"

Wendy sat. "No thank you."

"I gave Alice my iPad to use," Trent said out of the blue.

"You did?"

Trent nodded. "I thought since she uses your iPhone all the time, she would like it. Most kids her age have all those things. I'll order her an iPad and iPhone online."

"No, wait." Wendy sighed in exasperation.

"What is it?" Trent asked.

Wendy put down her paper and held her hands tightly under her chin, considering whether to say what she was bursting to say.

"Can I speak freely?" Wendy asked.

Trent looked at her quizzically. "Of course, we're not in the army."

"I know, but you're my employer and could give me the sack if you don't like what I say."

"I won't sack you over you giving me your opinion on something. The kids love you already, and this flat wouldn't run without you. I'm tough—I can take it, Ms. Darling."

Wendy had to come out and say it. "You can't just buy Alice and Noah presents to show them affection."

Trent furrowed her eyebrows. "Are you saying I'm trying to buy their affection?"

"Not in a bad way, but you bought the games console today and now you're planning an iPhone and an iPad? I mean, Christmas is in a few months' time. You'll have nothing left to buy them."

Trent gulped down her drink and got up to pour another. She hadn't told Wendy she had started to make plans to go skiing at Christmas. She didn't think she could go through a family Christmas. Too many bad memories.

She tried to curb her anger and annoyance. After all, she had promised Wendy she could speak freely, and Trent hadn't behaved well when Dale was here.

"It's not about buying anything. I'm providing. That's what I do. Any relationship I've ever been in, I provide. They see a nice coat they like, shoes, a beautiful piece of jewellery, I buy it. That's just who I am, so if these children need things, I provide them."

Wendy looked at her silently, then said, "I think more than any games console or iPad, Ali and Noah would like a hug or just to talk and listen to them."

Trent sat back down and stared into her glass. "I don't know if I can. This is the best I can do."

"I don't think so," Wendy replied.

After a few seconds of silence Trent said, "I'm sorry for earlier—accusing you of flirting. It was childish."

"That's okay," Wendy said.

Trent met her eyes. "It's not, but I was feeling sorry for myself, I suppose. Dale can just walk into a room and immediately have everyone onside. The kids, and you. I envy her that."

"You said Dale was your friend. Where did you meet her? You look like you move in different circles," Wendy said.

"I mentioned that she was married to my best friend, Becca? Well Becca is my ex-partner."

"Oh, I see," Wendy replied.

Trent snapped her head around. "What do you mean, *I see*?"

Wendy shrugged. "Just that those relationships can be difficult."

Trent nodded. "Yes, I suppose."

"How long were you together? If you don't mind me asking?" Wendy asked.

If this had been anyone else like Claudia, she would have minded. Trent was a very private person, but something about Wendy made her feel at ease, and safe.

"Seven years. We have been split up for about twelve, though," Trent told her.

"Becca is a big part of your life, then?"

Trent nodded. She became fascinated with the two blond braids hanging down the side of Wendy's face. She had the biggest urge to touch them.

"Trent?"

She had been so busy daydreaming, Trent didn't hear Wendy's follow-up question. "Sorry, Wendy. What did you say?"

"I said, did you get on with Dale straight away?" Wendy asked.

Trent chuckled. "Oh no. In fact, I tried to break them up, but over time I realized Dale gave Becca everything I couldn't, and then Becca was determined to make us all this big extended happy family."

"But you hadn't quite let go yet, had you?" Wendy asked.

Trent wasn't ready to answer that, so she picked up the piece of paper Wendy had brought through and said, "What's this?"

Wendy held her gaze for a few seconds and Trent was sure she wasn't going to let the last question go.

"I made an itinerary for your first Sunday alone with Ali and Noah. You don't have to stick with it. I just thought it might be helpful."

Trent cleared her throat nervously. "I actually thought the games system would keep them busy."

Wendy narrowed her eyes. "You can't leave them in front of a TV all day."

Having the reality of her inner thoughts and plans repeated to Trent made her realize how bad it sounded, similar to when Lady Claudia advised her to pack the children off to boarding school.

"I suppose not," Trent blustered. "I thought they would be happier than spending time with me."

Wendy appeared as if she was choosing her words carefully. "Earlier you said that you envied the way your friend Dale could naturally have a rapport with the kids." Wendy turned around to face her straight on. "If you want to develop that relationship with them, you have to spend quality time doing activities with them. Just living in the same house won't develop that affinity."

Trent nodded. "I suppose you're right."

Wendy gave her the biggest smile and then winked. "Of course I am."

Trent's stomach fluttered and clenched at the sight of that cheeky wink. Oh no. They were not going down that path, Trent warned her body.

Suddenly Becca's warning about choosing an attractive nanny resonated. She couldn't afford that kind of complication in her life at the moment.

She got back to the business at hand and scanned the paper. "Item one, breakfast—cereal. Item two, take out frozen meals for dinner. Wait, what frozen meals?" Trent asked.

"I'm going to make dinner and freeze it, so all you have to do on Sunday is take them out, defrost, and put in the oven," Wendy explained.

"I should be able to manage that." Trent smiled and she was

sure she saw a blush on Wendy's cheeks. So she was cute as well. Trent sighed inwardly and went back to the Sunday itinerary. "Item three, drive or take the Tube to either the Natural History Museum, the Science Museum, or the Tower of London. Hmm, I think I know which one Noah would choose." Trent was trying to remain calm but the thought of being responsible for the children all day was daunting, to say the least.

Wendy smiled. "I know, he loves dinosaurs. I would have said London Zoo but I think we'd need to go together. It's a big place."

Trent loved the idea of Wendy coming with them. She wished Wendy was coming with her on Sunday.

"Okay," Trent said.

Wendy apparently saw the tension on her face because she said, "Don't worry. You'll do fine. Just keep your eyes on Noah. He gets so excited when he sees something, and runs off."

Now Trent felt even more nervous.

"So what are you going to do with your day off? See your parents?" Trent asked.

Wendy gave a hollow laugh. "Eh, no. We're not close. I'm going to music practice with my band."

Now that was something she wasn't expecting to hear. "You play in a band?"

"I haven't for a long time. My friends and I formed the group when I was at university. We played festivals and pubs, we even went to the Edinburgh Festival one year, but then I started nannying abroad. When they heard I was back, they asked me to play again," Wendy said.

Trent smiled. "I'd love to hear you sometime."

"I don't think you would. It's a folk music band, and besides, I'm very rusty. Too used to singing children's songs. Which I know irritate you beyond belief."

"Oh, I don't know. They're growing on me."

They held each other's gaze, and the words held more meaning than Trent could understand for the moment.

Wendy stood and said, "Goodnight then, Trent."

"Goodnight, Wendy, and thanks for this." Trent held up the paper.

"Of course." Wendy smiled. "I'm here to help you."

Trent watched Wendy walk away and couldn't help admiring the roll of her hips in her tight, ripped jeans, and she felt a tightening in her chest. Wendy was nothing like the usual women she went for. Her type of woman usually wore a cocktail dress, not henna tattoos, beads, and braids in their hair, but Wendy was beautifully different and, she was beginning to realize, shone with goodness.

Chapter Ten

On Sunday Wendy rode the Tube to her band rehearsal. She checked her watch constantly. This was Trent's first day alone with the children and she was nervous. She wanted this to work for them.

Alice hadn't been too enthusiastic to spend the day with Trent, but Noah was happy, as usual. It was only through these kinds of outings that Trent would build a relationship with Alice. They were both so uncomfortable around each other, but she hoped they could make a breakthrough soon.

Wendy walked them down to the Tube station and then they went their separate ways. Alice would hardly let go of her hand when she left, and she felt bad as her train pulled away and she saw Noah holding Trent's hand and Alice standing awkwardly beside her. Maybe she should have gone with them? Wendy's stop came, and she picked up her guitar and made her way up and out of the station. Despite her worries about Trent and the kids, she was excited. The band was meeting in a friend's bar to rehearse, and she couldn't wait to get back into it again. Music had always been a big part of her life, and she'd missed it terribly when she was out of the country.

A few minutes later she arrived at the Red Lion Pub. Despite its traditional name, the Red Lion was a popular gay pub and during the day served excellent pub food.

She walked in and got some admiring looks from the lunchtime crowd. Kira, who played the flute in the band, had said to meet them in the pub's function room. She walked up to the bar and got a bottle of water before heading to the back room.

When Wendy walked in the members of the band were sitting on the edge of the stage—Kira, River, who played drums, bongos, and the traditional Celtic bodhrán, and Skye, who played mandolin.

"Hey, you bunch of hippies," Wendy said.

"Dee," Skye shouted and rushed over to meet her, with River following behind.

Skye and River were brother and sister and stereotypical New Agers. Both wore their hair in dreadlocks. River had a beard, and Skye had henna tattoos.

Skye wrapped her arms around Wendy. "So glad you came home, wanderer."

Wendy could smell the scent of incense and the unmistakable smell of marijuana on Skye's loose-fitting T-shirt.

"It's so nice to see you both again," Wendy said.

Skye pulled back and cupped Wendy's face. "I—we missed you so much."

"We really did," River added, holding his arms out for a hug.

Skye held on to her a little too long, and Wendy worried that Skye still had a crush on her. They'd had a drunken kiss after Bailey left her and Wendy was an emotional mess, and there had been an awkwardness for a while. She hoped things would be easier now time had passed.

River pushed his sister out of the way and said, "My turn. Come here."

He spun her around in a circle. Kira came over and said, "Put her down, River. We're here to play music."

❖

Trent held Noah's hand tightly as they walked around the Natural History Museum, and Noah held his toy dinosaur tightly.

Alice was the only one walking alone. Trent had tried to hold her hand and engage with her a few times, but to no avail. So she just kept her eye on her as best she could.

Suddenly Noah shouted, "T-Rex!" He went to bolt off and Trent grabbed the back of his jacket.

"I told you not to run off, Noah. Hold my hand. We all go together," Trent said firmly. She looked back and Alice was dragging even further behind. "Alice, please stay with us. We're going to see the T-Rex next. That'll be nice, won't it?" Alice looked up at her moodily but said nothing. "Let's go."

They looked all around the large dinosaur, and Trent lifted Noah up when he wanted to see the display board. She looked over her shoulder to check on Alice and didn't see her. Trent put Noah down quickly and looked all around her. Alice was nowhere to be seen. Fear and panic entered every cell in Trent's body.

"Alice? Alice?" Trent shouted.

"Where's Ali, Trent?" Noah said worriedly.

She stroked his head, trying to appear calmer than she felt. She couldn't lose Alice on their first day out.

With no sign of her, Trent hurried over to a security guard. "Excuse me, I can't find my goddaughter. I'm her guardian."

The man was immediately on alert. "Can you give me a description? I'll radio all the guards."

While he was talking into his radio, she said to Noah, "Stay with this nice man until I find Alice. Okay?"

"Uh-huh," he replied, clutching his dinosaur like a teddy bear.

Trent looked everywhere and was getting more panicked and anxious with every second. She knew what kind of people frequented family visitor attractions like this, and the thought of anyone getting hold of Alice made her terrified.

After ten minutes, one of the guards came to find her.

"We've found her, Ms. Trent."

"Oh, thank God. Where was she?" Trent felt relief like she never had before.

"Hiding behind a large fossil rock in another exhibition room. We have her at the security office. Follow me."

She was led into the security room and saw Alice sitting on a seat with her head down. Noah ran to her.

"We found Ali."

"Yes, good boy, Noah." Trent needed to speak to Alice.

Trent asked the security guard if he'd take Noah out for a moment and he happily obliged.

Trent sat down beside Alice and let out a breath. "You gave me the fright of my life, Alice. I thought we'd lost you."

Alice looked at her with a mixture of anger, resentment, and confusion. "It's *Ali*—you don't even know that. Everyone calls me Ali."

"Ali, okay. Why did you run from us?"

"Why do you care?" Alice snapped.

"Of course I care, Ali. If your intention was to give me a scare, then you did," Trent said firmly. That feeling of helplessness and panic was something new and she didn't want to repeat it.

"I don't want to spend the day looking around at stupid old bones, pretending everything's all right, when my dad is dead. I saw him dead right in front of me. We have no family now."

Alice convulsed in tears. Trent's heart raced. What should she do?

"You have me." Trent tried to wrap her arm around her shoulder, but Alice pushed her away.

"No we don't. We're only here today because it's Wendy's day off and she told you to take us," Alice said with disdain.

She was technically correct. If Wendy hadn't been off today, Trent would probably be in her office working, but she had genuinely enjoyed herself until Alice ran. Watching Noah's excitement and wonder at the sight of the dinosaurs was a new and wonderful thing. She was reminded of the time her mother took her to see an Egyptian exhibit at the British Museum. There was no nanny, no father, just her and her mama, laughing and enjoying themselves. Trent's mother was so different outside the tight constricts of their family home and watchful eye of her father.

"Ali, I—"

"No!" Alice snapped. "You're sending us away. I hated foster care. It was scary, and Noah cried all the time."

Alice was obviously equating boarding school with foster care. She needed to explain and tried to remember how Dale and Wendy had spoken to the kids. She got down on her knees in front of Alice.

"Ali, listen. I'm not sending you and Noah away because you're bad or I don't like you. I'm single and I've never had children. I don't think I could be what you need as a full-time parent—that's why I thought it best. Boarding school isn't like foster care. It's a safe place where people will look after you every day and night. You will have everything you could ever want. I will always make sure of that."

Alice's eyes filled with tears. "You can't bring my dad back or replace him."

"I don't want to replace him. I never could." Trent sighed. How could she explain her feelings when she didn't understand them herself? Seeing Dale with the kids made her envious, and the past few days Trent had allowed herself to think about how nice it would be to have Alice and Noah look at her the way Jake and Grace looked at Dale.

But how could she bridge this gulf between Alice and herself? Then she thought of the only other time she had opened up her heart and asked someone to trust her—it was Becca.

When Becca's mother committed suicide, and her world collapsed around her, Trent found Becca on the floor of her family home, on the verge of emotional collapse.

Trent offered Becca her hand and asked her to trust in her, because she was all that Becca had.

"Ali, we've not had the best of starts, and I know it's been my fault, but I want to make this better." Trent held out her open hand, looked Alice in the eyes and said, "I'm asking you to trust me and allow me to do better. I'm going to make mistakes. I've never had children live with me, didn't think I would ever want to, but I want to try to make this work. So? Will you give me that chance?"

Alice eyed her hand carefully, while biting her lip nervously. She finally put her small hand in Trent's and said, "Wendy said we should give you a chance, so I will."

Trent felt a surge of emotion like she didn't anticipate. She closed her hand around Alice's and had a flash of her mother doing the same thing and giving her that big, beaming smiling face that she always had when Father wasn't around.

Trent had to gulp down the growing emotions that were swirling around inside her. She had kept these thoughts and memories locked up so tightly that they were flooding out at the first chink in her armour.

"Thank you, Ali. I'll try to do better, but please don't run away again," Trent said.

"I won't," Ali replied.

Trent smiled. "Let's go and get your little brother, then."

Trent started to walk out the door, and she felt Alice's hand slip into hers. Trent looked down at Alice and smiled. In that one little moment she realized how special it was to be given that trust from Alice, and she was determined to keep earning that trust.

❖

Wendy used her fob to get into Trent's apartment building. Victor the attendant came over from his desk to greet her. She had gotten to know him in the last few weeks, as she came and went with the kids.

"Evening, Wendy. Did you have a good day off?"

Wendy smiled at the older man as he took her guitar case to carry it for her. "Yes, it was fun. Did Ms. Trent and the children get back home okay?"

"Oh yes, laden down with toy dinosaurs and the like," Victor said.

Wendy shook her head. More gifts? Despite Wendy's warning Trent was clearly still trying to build emotional bridges with money and not heeding her warning. At least they were home in one piece, she supposed.

"I better get up and see how they got on today," Wendy said.

She started to head for the stairs. She had lots of time to walk up.

Victor said, "Let me ride on the lift with you—it's too many stairs."

"I think I'll just stick to the stairs, Victor. Thanks."

Victor pursed his lips. "At least let me take your guitar up for you."

"Okay, thanks." Wendy handed her guitar case to Victor and walked through the door to the stairway.

By the time she got to the top of the stairs, she felt like crawling to the front door of Trent's flat, but she dragged herself there upright and unlocked the door. When she walked in she found Noah bouncing around on the couch, holding toy dinosaurs, with the TV blaring. Alice was sitting at the kitchen island with Trent's iPad, and Trent was piling pizza boxes in a rubbish bag. Noah squealed when he saw Wendy and rushed to hug her.

"Wendy, we saw loads of cool dinos," Noah said.

She hugged him and said, "I can't wait to hear all about it."

Wendy spotted her guitar leaning against the wall. Victor must have dropped it off and went back downstairs.

"Hi, Wendy, did you have a good day with your friends?" Trent asked.

She walked over to the kitchen area and put down her bag. "Yes, I had a good day. We were a bit rusty after all these years, but we'll get better." Wendy pointed at the pizza boxes and said, "What happened to your homemade dinner?"

Trent turned her gaze to the freezer and said sheepishly, "I forgot to take them out this morning, and we were hungry so…"

Wendy shook her head. "I bet you've eaten more pizza since these two came to live with you than you have the whole of your life."

"Quite so. It's convenient for children," Trent said. Trent picked up some empty ice cream tubs and threw them in the bin bag.

"Did they polish off these two tubs of ice cream too?" Wendy frowned and put her keys down on the kitchen countertop.

Trent nodded. "Yes, they seemed to enjoy it."

Wendy came closer to Trent and said in a low voice, "Of course they enjoyed it, and now that's why Noah is jumping around like a jack-in-the-box. I need to teach you to cook some emergency meals for when I'm not here."

She then turned to Alice, who was quiet as usual. "Did you have a good day, Ali?"

Then something strange occurred. Alice and Trent exchanged a look, and when Trent opened her mouth to answer, Alice said quickly, "It was good. We had fun."

There was a story here she was missing. Alice was covering for something.

"I'm glad. Why don't you finish clearing up and I'll bathe Noah?" Wendy said.

"But it's your day off," Trent said.

Wendy smiled. "I don't mind."

That smile made Trent's stomach tighten. "Thanks, Wendy."

When Wendy walked off to get Noah, Trent berated herself. No, no. Not the nanny. *Get those thoughts out of your head right away.*

She realized then that Alice was watching her intently.

"Are you okay, Trent?"

"Absolutely fine. Why don't you go to your room and listen to your book? I'll get cleaned up here."

"Okay."

After getting cleaned up and dripping some pizza sauce on the sleeve of her shirt, Trent went to her office. She was writing some bullet points about a case on her whiteboard when she heard a knock on her door. "Come in."

Wendy came in. She had changed into a little strappy top that drew her eyes, and one of her headscarves that held back her beautiful blond hair and reminded Trent of a 1950s housewife. Of course, Wendy wore it ironically, but it was sexy nonetheless.

"Can I have a word?" Wendy said.

"Of course, sit down."

Wendy sat, and as Trent passed on the way to her desk, she saw a beautiful colourful butterfly tattoo on Wendy's shoulder. She had to stop herself from running her fingers over it. When she sat down she crossed her legs. She tried to get the image of brushing her lips over it out of her head.

"Something wrong?" Wendy asked. She had clearly noticed how uncomfortable Trent was as she shifted around in her seat.

"What did you want to talk about?" Trent asked, trying to divert Wendy's attention away from her.

"Oh yes, well, I wondered if something happened today," Wendy asked.

"What makes you say that?"

Wendy leaned forward and tapped her nails on the desk, drawing Trent's eyes to them. "It seemed like you and Alice were covering for something," Wendy said.

Trent had to come clean. "Okay, I was going to tell you, but Alice stopped me."

"What happened?"

Trent sighed, and just as she was about to speak her mobile rang. It was sitting in the middle of the desk and Claudia's name flashed up on the screen. She stared at it, willing it to stop, but it didn't.

"Aren't you going to answer?" Wendy asked.

Trent hit the decline button. "No, I can't deal with her just now."

"A girlfriend?" Wendy asked.

"No. Anyway, I kept a firm hold of Noah, but Alice wouldn't hold my hand. She didn't want to be there at all and just trailed behind us. Then I looked back and she was gone. I looked for her everywhere I could in the last exhibit we were in, and then I alerted the security and they started a search."

Wendy's eyes went wide.

"I know," Trent said. "You don't have to tell me. I never felt panic like it. I lost her, my own family, and I lost her."

"How did you find her?" Wendy asked.

"One of the guards found her hiding behind a big display of fossil rocks. She ran from me."

Wendy looked angry and worried at the same time. She stood up suddenly. "I'm going to have a strong word with her."

Trent got up quickly and walked around the desk to stop Wendy. "No, don't. Sit down. I talked to her, just like you advised me to," Trent said.

Wendy sat back down slowly. It heartened Trent that after only a short time, Wendy cared for the children already. So different from her own nanny.

"You did?"

Trent nodded. "Ali had the idea that boarding school was like me sending her into care. I explained that it wasn't like that. It was an expensive place with everything that they would need, and I admitted that I hadn't been the most welcoming. I promised I would try harder if she would give me a chance."

Wendy jumped up and unexpectedly threw her arms around Trent and hugged her. "Oh, well done. You've taken the first step. I'm proud of you."

No sooner had she received the unexpected hug that set off sparks all over her body than Wendy backed away quickly and seemed quite embarrassed.

"I'm sorry. That wasn't appropriate."

"It's all right—"

"No," Wendy interrupted her, "I'm an emotional person and sometimes emotions overtake me. It's something I'm working on."

Even though Trent was a master at suppressing emotions, it was sad to hear someone as kind and caring as Wendy was trying to do the same.

"You shouldn't do that. I admire that in you," Trent said.

Wendy gazed at her silently and the blush on her cheeks made Trent wonder what she was thinking.

"Anyway," Wendy said, "it's not appropriate to hug your boss."

"I suppose," Trent agreed reluctantly.

Wendy's big smile was back. "But I'm happy you made some progress in your relationship with Ali."

"Yes, you were right, of course. I'm going to be connected to them as long as they need me, so it makes sense to make an effort."

Wendy's eyes fixed on her sleeve. "What happened?"

Trent lifted her arm and remembered about the pizza sauce. "Oh, that? I got it on me when I was clearing up."

Wendy took a step to her and undid her top button. "Take it off. I'll soak it."

Trent covered Wendy's hands on her shirt. "It's okay. I'll buy a new one."

"It's an expensive shirt. You can't just throw it—Oh, I'm doing it again." Wendy dropped her hands quickly and pushed one of her braids behind her ear sheepishly.

Trent decided to save her blushes and unbuttoned her shirt, leaving her in her white T-shirt. She handed it to Wendy and said, "If you can save it, then I'd be grateful."

"If you're sure. I'll give it a go." Wendy took the shirt and walked out of the office.

Trent touched her fingers to her jaw, where Wendy's cheek had touched, and closed her eyes. She could still smell Wendy's perfume and her mind started to wander.

"No, no. She's your nanny remember? Remember? Your much, much younger nanny." Trent felt there was a memory just out of grasp. Something about her nanny. Trent shook off the feeling and went back to her whiteboard.

CHAPTER ELEVEN

As the next few weeks passed, Trent got more and more used to having Alice, Noah, and Wendy in her life. In fact, she found herself making excuses to phone home in the afternoon and trying not to stay late at work. Coming home to a warm home was something she hadn't experienced since Becca left her, and even that was quite different to the barely controlled chaos that two children brought.

A thought struck her. This was what Becca had wanted to bring to their relationship all those years ago—warmth, and family. When Becca made it clear that she wanted a baby, their relationship broke up because Trent wouldn't even consider it. She couldn't understand the need to add to their relationship. Was this what Becca wanted to add?

Trent leaned back in her office chair and turned towards the window. Her life had changed so much since the last time she'd gazed out of that window, wondering what was missing from her life. Her social life was non-existent but it didn't seem to matter that much. She was actually enjoying dinner at home and learning a different set of social skills than she was used to.

She had always been charming and an expert at small talk, but talking with children was a completely different beast. Trent couldn't even draw from her own childhood—she had always felt more comfortable with adults as far back as she could remember. But she was getting better with Noah and Alice.

Alice was still extremely quiet and had terrible nightmares, but she was giving Trent a chance, and she had started visiting the child psychologist, so they were hopeful that would help. Noah had grown even more attached to Trent. She pretended to find it tiresome, but it was actually nice to feel wanted for something other than her money or her notoriety.

Trent was shaken from her thoughts by her phone beeping with a text message. She picked it up and read, *Trent, make a decision about your birthday celebrations, or I will plan you the biggest surprise party with cake, clowns, and pony rides. You know I would. Becca x*

Trent chuckled. "Oh, I know you would."

Becca had been bugging her about doing something for her birthday for weeks. She thought if she delayed long enough, it would be too late to do anything, but Becca wasn't kidding.

She thought about what would be the easiest and least fuss. "I've got it." She typed back, *Dinner at mine. Bring the kids to meet Alice and Noah, and ask Sammy and Val. I'll ask Wendy my nanny to help me organize it. Will that do, bossy? x*

The text came back seconds later: *Perfect. I can't wait to meet her. x*

"That's one thing sorted out." Trent had been itching to call home and now she had the excuse. She picked up the phone and dialled. Wendy answered after quite a few rings.

"Trent residence," Wendy said.

"Hello, it's me. How are things today?" Trent asked.

"Oh, hi," Wendy said brightly, "it's music time."

Trent could hear the tambourine in the background and felt a smile creep up her face. She gave her cheek a soft slap and thought, *Stop it. You're getting too soft.*

Wendy sang at every opportunity, but each afternoon she had a time set aside for music and both children really looked forward to it.

"What are you singing today?" Trent said.

"Songs for the fireworks tonight. You haven't forgotten? Will you still be able to come?"

Shit. Trent had forgotten. It was November fifth, Fireworks Night, and they were going to an organized display at London's Victoria Park. Wendy planned it as her first night out together with the children. There were going to be food stalls, fairground rides, and entertainers.

Just as she was about to answer, there was a knock at her office door. "Could you hang on a second, Wendy?"

"No problem."

Trent pressed the hold button and said, "Come in."

India walked in holding a suit carrier on a hanger. The awards dinner, Trent remembered.

"Your dinner suit's been delivered for the awards dinner tonight." India hung up the carrier on the coat hook on the back of the office door.

The annual family law awards dinner was the biggest night of the year in her field. Recognition by one's peers was the highest accolade, and her father had won an award, and tonight she was nominated for the second time. This time she was expected to win.

"Thank you, India."

Trent rubbed her forehead anxiously. What was she going to say to Wendy and the children? She had been making progress and building a relationship with Alice and Noah, and a friendship with Wendy—was she going to let them down on their first big family night out together?

But if she was a no-show at the awards, it would show a complete disregard for her colleagues, and she already had a difficult relationship with some of the other firms due to her reputation and tough negotiating style.

She couldn't miss this.

Trent took a breath and took Wendy off hold. "Wendy?"

"I'm here."

"Wendy, about tonight—" Trent's guilt made her stumble over the sentence.

"You're not coming, are you." Wendy sounded disappointed.

"No, I'm sorry. I forgot about a work thing. I'm going to be late back. Get the children whatever they want, make sure they have a good time, and I'll reimburse you."

"Of course I will. That's my job." Wendy's voice had gone from happy and enthusiastic to monotone.

Trent felt like the biggest arsehole in the world. "Thank you. See you tomorrow morning, then. I'll be late back."

"Bye." Wendy hung up.

Trent put the phone down and guilt churned in her stomach. She stood up angrily and walked over to her suit carrier. She unzipped it a few inches and saw the black tie hanging loosely.

Under normal circumstances, she would have had this night in the forefront of her mind, have a date to go with and a hotel suite booked for afterwards, but her life was anything but normal now. This night had slipped her mind.

"Why should I feel guilty? This is my job, my livelihood." Her chance to achieve the award her father won at an earlier age than him, Trent added silently.

I've turned my world upside down for them. They'll probably have a better time without me.

But that was difficult to make herself believe. Alice and Noah had been jabbering about Fireworks Night at breakfast. It was the most excited she had seen Alice since coming to live with her.

Trent sighed and shook her head. There'd be other Guy Fawkes Nights to go to. This was important for her career, and the children would just have to understand.

❖

Wendy pulled Noah's jumper over his head and encouraged him to push his hands through the sleeves, but Noah had lost his usual excitement and zeal. After she told Alice and Noah that Trent would be working, a gloom had descended over the flat.

Wendy was angry at Trent. The worst thing someone could do when they were trying to build a relationship with a child was to let them down. She had worked so hard since she arrived to get them to this point.

A work thing? More likely a date.

Did Trent genuinely forget or was she trying to get out of this night out?

Wendy didn't know, but even if this work thing was important, Trent had to remember beforehand and not build up the children's hopes.

She smiled and gave Noah a kiss on the cheek. "Cheer up, little man. We're going to have fun no matter what."

Wendy stood up and said, "We'll get tasty things to eat from the food stalls, and there's games, and a big bonfire. We'll have fun."

Noah nodded sadly.

She stroked his head. "I'll just go and see if your sister's ready."

It was sad to see Noah's little disappointed face. Noah had decided to transfer all of his love and hero worship from his dad to Trent when they first met, no matter how much Trent didn't want it. She just wished Trent could see how disappointed he was.

Wendy walked to Alice's bedroom and found her sitting on her bed with her earbuds in, blocking out the world. Another angry and disappointed child.

She couldn't blame them. There was a part of Wendy that was looking forward to spending the evening with Trent. Watching her progress and her tentative steps to making a relationship with Alice and Noah was sweet.

It was kind of endearing that this successful lawyer, who tore people to shreds in court, was flummoxed by a hug and a kiss from two little people. Not to mention that she was incredibly good-looking, in a stiff, chiselled kind of way.

But work obviously came first.

Wendy took off Alice's earbuds. "You're supposed to be getting your warm clothes and shoes on, Ali."

Alice scowled. "I don't want to go. It's just a stupid fireworks display."

Wendy put her hands on her hips and looked directly at Alice. "You didn't think that when we were singing songs about it earlier today."

Alice said nothing and Wendy answered her own question. "Is it because Trent isn't coming?"

"No," Alice said a little too quickly.

"We'll still have a fun time, Ali. Come on. Get your things on."

Wendy heard the front door open and close. Trent wasn't coming home till late. So who was that?

"Who is that?" Alice said fearfully.

Wendy put her finger to her lips. "I'll look."

She carefully looked around the door and was relieved to see Trent standing by the kitchen counter.

She walked down the hall. "You gave me the fright of my life. Did you come home to get changed for your *work thing*," Wendy said sarcastically.

Trent just smiled at her jibe. "No, I cancelled my *work thing*. I've got a fireworks display to go to."

Noah, who had followed her into the living area, ran and jumped into Trent's arms. "You're coming with us?"

Wendy watched Trent give him a hug without the awkwardness she usually saw.

"Yes, I am." Trent looked into Wendy's eyes and said, "Work can wait."

Wendy felt a joy and excitement in her chest and stomach. That should not be happening. It was good for the kids, after all, not her.

❖

Trent got a quick change, and she and Wendy took two now very excited children to the Tube station. The Tube was packed with other commuters going to the fireworks display. When they got to the station, Wendy said, "You hold on to Alice—I'll take Noah. Keep a tight grip."

"I will," Trent said. "I've learned my lesson."

After getting off the Tube, they followed the long line of people going in the same direction. There was a big crowd inside the park and lots more going in the gates alongside them. Alice was holding Wendy's hand and Noah was stuck to Trent, who said to Wendy, "It's really busy."

Wendy nodded and stopped them once they got into the park and directed her words to Alice and Noah.

"This is a really busy place, so you have to make sure you hold our hands and keep close, okay? If you see a ride or a stall you want to see, tell us, and we'll go together. No running off. Promise?"

"Promise," Alice and Noah said in unison.

They walked on to the area with the fairground rides and game and food stalls. Trent was surprised by the squeals of happy children and adults. It wasn't like anything else she'd been to before.

"What will we go on first?" Trent asked.

"How about the big wheel? We can all stay together then," Wendy suggested.

Trent nodded and the kids jumped in excitement. As they waited in line, Trent said, "Why don't we get something to eat after this, and then we can buy dessert and eat it while we watch the fireworks?"

Wendy and the children were wreathed in smiles. This wasn't scary, Trent thought. Making these three smile made her feel happy, and she wanted much, much more of this feeling.

As it turned out, they enjoyed themselves so much on the big wheel they decided to go on a few more rides before they ate. Trent had taken them on the waltzers alone, as Wendy could never stand the dizzying feeling. It gave her a good opportunity to take some lovely pictures of the three. She took a whole raft of photos, and her heart melted at one of them that captured each one smiling brightly. Perfect. Trent had grown so much in this last month, and even if she didn't know it herself, Wendy was confident she would be a good parent.

Then a sadness came over her, as she reminded herself that she would have to leave these three eventually. Just then, Trent looked at her from the ride and smiled. Wendy felt a powerful thud in her heart. *No, no, don't do this. Don't be falling for your employer.*

She took a few pictures with Trent's phone and saw lots and lots of texts and Twitter notifications popping up, all saying, *Congratulations!* She wondered what that was about.

As promised, Trent bought them food from the stalls, and once they were finished they took their dessert of fresh doughnuts, cookies, candy floss, and toffee apples to the display area.

Trent handed out the treats, keeping the toffee apple for herself.

"I haven't seen a toffee apple in years," Wendy said.

"It's my first time. I always wanted to try one." It was a traditional Fireworks Night and Halloween children's treat, one she'd never had but had seen other children have.

Alice tugged on her jacket. "When does it start, Trent?"

Trent looked at her watch. "Any minute now."

"Stay close, both of you. It's getting busier," Wendy added.

Trent remembered she wanted to ask about her birthday dinner. "Wendy, it's my birthday in a few weeks' time, and my friends insist I have a celebration. If we have a dinner party at the flat, would you help me organize it? I'll get a caterer, of course."

Wendy smiled. "I'd love to. Don't get a caterer, though—I'll be happy to make the food."

"Are you sure? I didn't want to put you to any trouble."

Wendy leaned in and whispered to Trent, "It would be my pleasure."

Trent shivered. Wendy was so sexy, even when she wasn't trying to be.

Then the first of the fireworks shot into the air to mark the start of the display. This was a great day, Trent thought.

❖

Wendy came out from Noah's bedroom and peeked into Alice's room. What she saw there made her heart flutter. Trent was sitting propped up against the side of the bed, holding Alice's hand. They had both dropped off to sleep, exhausted from the night of high emotion. The first few fireworks had been okay, but then the big bangs started and Alice didn't react well. She covered her ears and screamed as her mind took her back to the night of the accident.

Much to her surprise and delight, it was Trent who leapt into action, taking Alice to the side and calming her down. After that, they got a taxi home.

Wendy couldn't believe this was the same person who'd hired her a month ago, but Alice and Noah were slowly burrowing their way into Trent's heart, and again her own heart fluttered at the thought.

No—no fluttering, Wendy chastised herself. When she had been travelling, she'd had a few lovers but was very careful not to get her heart involved. Her heart hadn't fluttered like this since Bailey.

Wendy gave herself a shake. *Stop it. You have a job to do.*

She crept in and touched Trent's shoulder. Trent's eyes sprang open and Wendy said, "Shh, she's asleep now. Let's leave her to rest."

Trent nodded and carefully let go of Alice's hand. Wendy led her out of the bedroom and shut the door. Trent rubbed her eyes.

"Do you want a cup of tea?" Wendy said. "You look exhausted."

"That would be nice."

Trent followed Wendy to the kitchen and leaned against the counter. She stretched and scrubbed her face in her hands. "I've got to be in court first thing. That'll be fun," Trent joked.

Wendy looked back and saw Trent smile. She smiled a lot more these days. "Do you regret coming?"

Trent furrowed her eyebrows. "What? No. I loved it. I've never been to a fireworks display before."

Wendy turned around in surprise. "You're kidding?"

"No. Or had a toffee apple—I loved that. It's not something my nanny would have taken me to. My mother, if she had lived, might have done but—"

Wendy handed her a cup of tea and said, "You had a nanny? Was she anything like me?"

Trent rubbed the scar above her eyebrow. Wendy had seen her do that a few times in stressful or awkward circumstances.

Trent chuckled at Wendy's question. "Nothing like you, Ms. Darling. Picture your typical Victorian nanny, and that came pretty close to mine."

"Well, I'm glad you were there. It would have been so difficult to handle Alice on my own with Noah too," Wendy said. "I should have realized that the loud bangs might trigger her panic attacks."

"Don't be silly. I should have thought about it too. We were just trying to give the kids a normal night out."

Wendy took a step towards Trent and cradled her teacup in her hands. "You were very good with her."

Trent shrugged. "I'm not good with games and spontaneous fun, but I understand the fear. I had to deal with my mother's death, and it wasn't nearly as traumatic and violent as my cousin's. I'd like her to learn to handle the anxiety better than I could."

Wendy wanted to ask more and go deeper but she sensed it was a sensitive area, and she didn't want to frighten Trent away. Plus, she was desperate to ask about what she had seen on Trent's phone while she took pictures of her and the kids.

The beeps from Trent's phone that had gone off constantly earlier had slowed but still came in every so often. Trent looked at her phone and placed it face down on the counter.

"Bloody phones. Never shut up, do they?" Trent joked.

This was Wendy's opportunity. She looked into her tea and tapped her fingers on the side of her cup. "I hope you won't mind me asking but—"

"But what?" Trent asked.

"When I was taking your picture earlier, you were getting a lot of tweets congratulating you on something. I wasn't prying—they just flashed up on the screen."

"Oh, that." Trent put her cup down on the counter and crossed her arms. "It's a bit embarrassing, really."

"You don't have to tell me if you don't want to," Wendy said.

"It'll all come out in the wash over the next week anyway. I won an award at the family law awards dinner tonight."

Wendy gasped. "Was that the *work thing* you were going to tonight?"

Trent nodded. "With everything that has happened in the last month, I genuinely forgot about it. Then my suit was delivered from the tailor's while I was on the phone with you."

"You gave up your awards ceremony to come to a fireworks display?" Wendy asked.

Trent shrugged. "I promised I would go, and I didn't want to jeopardize the trust I've built with them."

Wendy was totally surprised that Trent would do that. Miss out on something so important, for Alice and Noah.

"If you had explained, we would have understood. I know how important your work is to you," Wendy said.

Trent picked up her phone and scrolled through her Twitter account. She had been tweeted a lot of pictures from the evening by friends and colleges. Trent found the one she was looking for and showed the picture to Wendy.

"That's my friend Regan picking up the award for me. We were at university together."

"Wow, Lawyer of the Year? That's amazing. I'm so sorry you missed out on that," Wendy said.

"I wanted that award for years. My father won it and told me a woman wouldn't win it. I wanted to prove him wrong," Trent said.

Wendy's head snapped up quickly. "He said that?"

Trent nodded. "I think that's why I worked so hard all these years, to prove him wrong. He didn't win it till he was much older."

Wendy held up her hand. "Wait there." Then she hurried off to rummage in her handbag on the coffee table.

"What are you doing?"

"Aha," Wendy said and came hurrying back over with what looked like a spool of stickers.

"What is this?" Trent asked.

Wendy stepped close to Trent with a big happy smile. "I use these with the kids, to make them feel special." Wendy looked into Trent's eyes. "I want to make you feel special."

Trent's heart thudded. She would love Wendy to make her feel special.

Wendy took off a sticker and placed it on the left hand side of Trent's chest. She looked down and saw it was a big thumbs-up sign, with the words *Well Done!* on it.

"A huge well done, Lawyer of the Year," Wendy said.

Before Wendy could take her hand away, Trent grasped it and held it to her chest. "You are such a kind, caring woman, Wendy. I don't know how I would have coped without you."

Wendy took a step closer and said, "Call me Dee. All my friends do."

Trent was sure her chest was going to burst. Wendy being so close made her stomach tighten. *I want her.* Her body wasn't listening to sense.

"Thank you." Trent couldn't stop herself from reaching out to touch one of Wendy's braids that hung down the side of her face. "Dee, I—"

Before Trent could finish her sentence, Alice screamed at the top of her voice and they ran to the bedroom.

Chapter Twelve

The next morning, Trent hurriedly threw on her clothes. She had slept in, something she never did, but she and Wendy had been up most of the night with Alice. Although Alice was improving her relationship with Trent, her panic attacks were getting worse. Every time she closed her little eyes, she could see the accident in more detail.

Trent looked at the time. "Bloody hell." She stuffed her shirt in her trousers as she spoke to her phone and said, "Call India."

Calling India, it replied.

India answered quickly. "Trent, Trent, and Masters. How may I help you?"

"India, it's me. I'm running really late. I need to go straight to the court. Can you have Tristan meet me there with my laptop? I left it on my desk. I need the file on it for my case this morning."

"Of course, Trent. He'll be right over."

"Thanks, bye."

She hung up and stuffed her phone in her pocket, then grabbed her jacket and bag and hurried out of her bedroom.

Wendy lifted up a plate of toast and said, "At least have some toast before you go."

"No time." Trent kissed Alice and Noah on the head as she passed the kitchen island, then without thinking kissed Wendy on the cheek and froze. "I'm so sorry—I didn't mean that. That was extremely inappropriate." What the hell was she doing?

Trent hurried out the door not wanting to look back. She heard Wendy shouting her name, but she just kept going.

❖

Wendy finished clearing up after lunch and walked over to the couch. Noah was sleeping on one side and Alice was sitting quietly with her iPad. Last night had been fun, emotional, and exhausting, and it had taken its toll on Alice and Noah.

Trent had asked her to try to get an extra appointment for Alice with her psychologist as soon as possible, but she could only give her this Saturday morning, when Wendy had a dentist appointment. She hoped that Trent could take her, because Alice really needed it.

Wendy sat down and lifted her arm to offer Alice a hug. Alice cuddled into her side and said quickly, "I don't want to talk."

She was a scared little girl and as much as she needed to talk, Wendy felt some distraction would probably do better after a highly emotional night.

"I wasn't going to ask you to talk. No, it's Trent's birthday next week, and she's asked me to organize it—that's why I brought my pad and pen over. I thought we could plan it together and look up what we need on the iPad."

Alice gave her a little smile. "Okay, what age is she going to be?"

"Forty." And ever so sexy. Trent's salt-and-pepper hair only made her sexier. It had been a strange twenty-four hours. She had known there was a heat simmering between them since she started working for Trent, but yesterday was the first time Wendy felt it was more than simple attraction.

First, seeing her dealing with Alice so tenderly, then when she had put the sticker on her chest, her heart had ached to kiss Trent's lips. And this morning Trent had kissed her goodbye. It had just been a mistake as Trent hurried out the door, but it felt so right. Her heart was threatening to wake up, and that was dangerous.

Wendy had followed her heart with Bailey and found herself used, stolen from, and up to her eyes in debt. If Trent did reciprocate her feelings, then it was just physically, because she quite obviously didn't do relationships. Besides, she was her boss. *Get a grip of yourself, Dee.*

"Trent's invited her friends and their kids to dinner here. It'll be fun for you to meet some new kids," Wendy said.

Alice didn't say anything.

Wendy leaned over and kissed Alice. "Don't worry. I think they're around your age. You'll be fine."

"Will you be there?" Alice asked.

Wendy smiled. "Of course. Trent's asked me to cook the food and I'll serve it, so I'll be around for you."

"Okay, we need balloons," Alice said.

Wendy squeezed the little girl. "That's the spirit. So those big balloons that say forty on them—we'll get lots, and put them all around the room to remind Trent how old she is, eh?"

Alice giggled. "Yeah, oh, and normal balloons for the little kids to play with. Noah loves balloons."

Wendy wrote down *balloons* on her notepad. "Good thinking. What next?"

They made a long list of things that would probably embarrass Trent, but Alice had a lot of fun coming up with ideas.

"What about a cake, Dee?"

The doorbell rang and Wendy stood up. "Yes, we need something funny to go on top. Give me a sec—Trent said her award might get delivered today."

Wendy opened the door and was surprised to find three delivery people, two men and one woman, holding boxes and something big under a thick plastic cover.

"Can I help you?"

"Delivery, miss. There's a card with it," one of the delivery people said.

She took the card and opened the envelope. There was a picture of a baby grand piano on the front and inside it said, *To Wendy Darling, Alice, and Noah—for music time.*

❖

Trent felt like hell as she rode the lift up to her flat. She was exhausted, had been aggravated by her client today, and had paperwork up to the ceiling to get through before coming home. Just over a month ago she would top off a stressful day by going for drinks and dinner, and meeting someone to spend the night with, but now that was the last thing on her mind.

She hoped the piano had arrived and that it would shift focus from this morning, a diversion like the games console. The thought of her mistaken kiss had stayed with her all day, distracting her from her work and her client.

Why did she kiss Wendy on the way out? She had been telling herself that it was understandable considering she was in such a rush, not thinking clearly, and—

Trent couldn't really finish that thought. She had been in a rush lots of times but had never kissed Wendy. Her head was a mish-mash of feelings and confusion. It was bad enough that she was starting to care deeply about her two new family members, but now she was intensely attracted to her twenty-something nanny.

Trent shook herself. Her conduct, her thoughts—was she taking advantage, being predatory? Was she treating Wendy like Claudia was treating her?

When the kids were off to boarding school and Wendy was gone, the flat would be empty again. These feelings she was developing would hurt her, because everyone she had loved had left her and it would happen again.

That thought gave her an intense feeling of sadness. She was getting used to the noise and hustle-bustle of her home. The lift door opened and she walked to her front door, determined to ignore the memory of the kiss this morning, and to harden her heart.

She took out her door keys, and a noise stopped her as she was about to put them in the lock. It was piano music, and Wendy and the children were singing along. She closed her eyes and felt her heart ache. Then she was hit with a memory, something she hadn't thought of in years.

When she was a little girl, Trent had sung along with her mother as she played songs from her favourite musicals. She loved listening to her mother singing, and watching her smile, because her mother never did when her father was around. Then, as they were singing, her father stormed into the drawing room, slammed the piano shut, and shouted at them for making too much noise. He'd ruined it—he always ruined it.

Trent smacked herself on the head and said, "Stop thinking."

Since Alice and Noah had arrived, Trent had been thinking about her past constantly and she didn't like it.

Just go in and go straight to your office.

She unlocked the door and walked in. All her plans for going straight to her office and not getting involved were dispensed with when she saw three smiling faces sitting at the new piano. Her heartache was back with a vengeance.

It was the perfect family scene. Now Trent understood why Dale gave up her single life. In this little moment she saw happiness, family, and love, the things she had craved as a child and never gotten.

She stood there motionless, trying to process everything, when Noah came running over.

"You got us a piano, Trent."

Trent dropped her bags and lifted him into her arms. "You like it?" Alice followed him and took her hand. "We love it."

Trent kissed them both. "Glad you like it."

They walked over to the piano and Wendy said, "It's beautiful."

"I thought maybe Alice could learn to play, if you could teach her," Trent said.

Wendy didn't have her headscarf on today and her hair hung loose around her shoulders. Beautiful.

Wendy got up and said, "We thought we'd make your favourite dinner since you got us this for music time, and to celebrate your award."

❖

Later that evening Trent walked into Alice's bedroom to check if she was settled. Alice smiled when she saw her, which was a new thing, and it made Trent happy.

"Are you okay, Ali?"

Alice nodded. "Yeah, I'm just reading my book on your iPad."

"Good. Have you had a better day?" Trent asked.

Alice shrugged, "Yeah. The piano was really exciting. Do you really think Wendy will teach me?"

Trent sat on her bed. "I'm sure. What did Wendy say when she saw the piano?"

Alice smiled. "She was so happy and excited."

"That's good. I want to make her happy." Trent realized how that sounded and added, "Because she's helped us so much."

"You smile a lot when Wendy is with us," Alice said.

Trent was a little taken by surprise, not by the fact that Wendy made her smile, because she did, but because Alice had noticed.

"Do I?"

Alice nodded. "She's really pretty, isn't she?"

"She is."

"You know, she has pictures of all the families she's looked after on her phone? She likes to help them be a family and remember them," Alice said.

"Does she? Well, she is very caring. I'll let you get on with your book. Night, Ali." Trent leaned down and kissed her.

Trent walked out of the bedroom and into the living area. The lights were low and the sound of light piano music filled the room.

Trent just gazed at Wendy, taking in the beautiful moment that this was. Wendy looked up and smiled.

"Hi," Wendy said.

Trent didn't know what to say. Her tongue was dry and not working. Then she said, "Would you like some wine?"

"That would be nice."

Trent poured two glasses of wine and brought them over to the piano. She handed one to Wendy and sat beside her on the piano stool.

"You play well."

Wendy took a sip of wine and placed the glass down on the floor. "It's not all children's songs and folk music. I like classical sometimes too."

"I never thought it was. There's nothing you can't do, Wendy Darling. You sprinkle your magic dust and anything is possible," Trent said.

Wendy laughed. "Is that what you think I do?"

Trent took a drink and put her glass down. "Alice told me about your photos. The album of families you've put back together."

Wendy lowered her head, feeling a little embarrassed. "Oh yeah."

"It must be important to you. I mean, nannying doesn't seem just a job to you," Trent said.

Wendy began to play again as she spoke. "It wasn't at first. I started travelling and I always loved working with kids, so nannying seemed like a good idea."

"Then what happened?" Trent asked.

To Wendy's surprise, Trent started to play alongside her. She played too?

"I worked with families that were struggling because of parents working hard and having no time and kids acting out because of it, and I wanted to make things better if I could. I didn't want them to be like my family."

"*Your* family...I always assumed you had a great, loving family because you're so good with children."

Did she really want to talk about this? If she wanted Trent to open up, then yes. Trent was doing well with the kids, but she was holding back a big part of herself, almost like she was scared to let them fully in.

"My parents were scientists. They worked for a drugs company. I was an unexpected inconvenience. Mum and Dad never wanted children, and in fact I don't know why they were married. You know, I never saw them give each other a peck on the lips? They were more like lab partners. Anyway, I would come home from school and we'd all eat dinner in different rooms."

"I know how that feels," Trent piped up.

Wendy was encouraged. Telling her story was getting Trent to think of hers.

"But I had two saving graces, my grandma and grandpa on my dad's side. I don't know how my dad ended up an emotionless, socially awkward person because they were the most loving people you could find. I stayed with them as much as I could. It broke my heart when they passed away."

Wendy's voice cracked on that last sentence, and Trent covered Wendy's hand on the keys. "That's why you want to mend families."

"When I was young, I always wished that Peter Pan would come and rescue me, like he did for my namesake. It was my favourite book, and I used to have dreams I would escape to Neverland. It never happened, though. I didn't want the children I looked after to feel like that, so I helped and counselled the family as much as I could."

Everything had gotten intimate all of a sudden. The room was lit only by the lamp in the corner, giving the room a romantic feel, and the touch of Trent's fingers as they came close on the piano keyboard was sending electricity all over her body. This was not the hard, emotionless lawyer that Kira and the press talked about.

"You haven't met your Peter, Wendy Darling?" Trent covered Wendy's hand on the keyboard and the music stopped, but her heart beat like a drum. *You*, her heart answered, but she knew not to trust her heart. Love brought nothing but hurt.

"Anyway, it wasn't all bad," Wendy said, trying to tone down the intense atmosphere. "I was lucky to have Grandma and Grandpa. Other children have no one."

❖

Trent didn't let go of Wendy's hand. She didn't want to. Since Wendy had come into her life, everything that was black and white was now in colour, and every unshakable rule she had didn't seem to matter any more. Was she really falling for Wendy?

But she was so much younger than Trent, and to make things more extreme, Wendy was going to be a university student before long. She wished she had Becca to talk to, the only other woman who had made her heart ache.

"Who taught you to play?" Wendy asked.

"My nanny beat it into me. I haven't played in a long, long time."

Wendy brought her hand to her mouth. "Your nanny *hit* you?"

Trent's stomach started to roil. This was something she never talked about. It made her feel hurt and weak.

"Yes, both she and my father. My mother, on the other hand, was the gentlest, kindest woman you could meet. Father was a terrifying man. It was only when I grew older and stronger than him that he couldn't push me around any more. It's sad, but the day he died was the first time I felt truly free."

"I understand."

Wendy turned in her seat and Trent flinched when Wendy touched her fingers to the scar above her eyebrow.

"How did you get this?"

Wendy's touch was tender, gentle, and Trent didn't want it to stop. She didn't want to think about how she got the scar. She wanted to study Wendy's beautiful face, and she found herself getting closer and closer to her lips. She wanted to feel Wendy's lips, to taste them, but all of a sudden Wendy pulled back and jumped up from the seat.

"I'm sorry. I've done it again, being too hands-on and touchy-feely. I shouldn't be invading your space and touching your scar."

Trent stood up and reached for her hand. "No, you don't have to be sorry. I feel—" She was about to say she wanted Wendy to touch her, that she could feel something growing between them, when Wendy stopped her and put her hand up between them.

"No, it's not right for me to do that. You're my boss and it's not appropriate. I'm sorry for being overfamiliar and making you uncomfortable. It won't happen again. It wouldn't be good for the children to see me so familiar with you. They'd be confused."

Wendy said it in such a way that Trent felt she was telling her there could be nothing between them, without hurting her feelings.

Who was she trying to kid? Of course a young, free-spirited woman like Wendy wasn't interested in an older, bad-tempered person like her. Wendy probably got this kind of attention all the time in her nannying jobs.

"Of course, of course, you're right," Trent stuttered. "I'll leave you to it, and I'll be in my office."

❖

Trent hurried off to her office and shut the door quickly. She slapped herself on the forehead. "What the hell are doing, you idiot? You don't seduce the nanny."

Then the memory that had eluded her lately came crashing into her mind. When her mother was quite ill with cancer, and was getting distressed by the pain, she had ran from her bedside to find some help and found Nanny Wilson and her father William in a heated clinch.

They broke apart when they heard her gasp, and she ran. It was after that things got a lot worse.

Trent was in shock at the new memory. How could her father have an affair while her mother was lying in bed, ill and dying? She felt tears come to her eyes, tears for her mother's betrayal by her father. Had her mother known about it? She hoped not.

She went over to her desk and sat down, trying to calm herself. She shouldn't have been shocked—cheating and betrayal were the stock-in-trade of divorce lawyers. When her clients told her their stories, it never bothered her one jot, even as emotion overcame them in her London office.

But putting her own mother in their shoes made her see the real pain and distress betrayal could cause. In her own personal life, she had never cheated on anyone, despite her reputation for enjoying the company of women. Trent had never cheated on Becca, never even thought about it. Becca had been all she needed.

Since they broke up, Trent had always been up front with the women she met—she didn't want a relationship. She'd thought her heart wouldn't ever want to love again after Becca, but Wendy was making it wake from its slumber.

But Wendy had made things quite clear out there. Their relationship would have to remain professional.

CHAPTER THIRTEEN

On Saturday Trent took Alice to her child psychologist appointment while Wendy went to a dental appointment. Both she and Wendy didn't think it wise to take Noah along to the appointment, so Wendy had arranged for Kira to look after Noah at her flat.

Trent parked outside Kira's block of flats and got Noah out of his car seat.

"I won't be long, Ali," Trent said.

She held Noah's hand and they walked to the front door of the flat, Noah holding tightly to his new favourite dinosaur that Trent had bought him. Kira was waiting for them with a big smile and open arms for Noah.

"Hello again, Noah," Kira said.

She hugged him as warmly as Wendy did. Trent had expected Wendy's friend to look like her, straight from a summer folk festival, but Kira dressed more like the sophisticated lawyers she mixed with every day. She was very good looking but not in the way that made Trent's heart race like Wendy did.

Kira offered her hand. "Hi, I'm Kira."

"Nice to meet you. It's very good of you to look after Noah for me. We were in a bit of a bind with Wendy's dentist appointment when it was."

Kira stroked Noah's head. "Don't worry about it. I'm happy to spend more time with this cute boy."

"Thank you," Trent said.

She crouched down, as she had learned to do, and spoke to Noah face to face. "I'm going to take Ali to the doctor now, but Wendy will pick you up from here soon, and I'll see you later."

"Okay." Noah threw his arms around her neck and hugged her.

She was starting to get used to hugs and kisses and it was actually nice to be missed.

"Be a good boy, okay?" Trent said.

"Uh-huh, bye, Trent."

Trent walked back to the car and got in. She looked back and saw Ali was looking tense. Wendy had said that Ali clammed up when they went to see the doctor.

"Ali? Do you want to sit in the front with me?" Trent said.

Alice nodded vigorously, got out of the car, and jumped into the front seat. She sat quietly and Trent was unsure what to say. The silence was awkward.

Why am I not better at this?

"Shall I put on some music?"

Alice nodded but said nothing.

"You pick the station, then. Show me what kind of music you like," Trent said.

She picked a pop station and Trent forced herself to smile. It was the kind of noisy music she imagined Dale enjoying.

"Sounds good, let's go."

They arrived at the car park just a few minute's walk from Harley Street. Trent parked and turned off the engine, then looked at her watch.

"We're here in plenty of time. Are you ready?" Trent asked.

"I don't want to go," Alice said and started to cry.

Oh no. How was she going to handle this without Wendy? She took Alice's hand. "Don't upset yourself. Why don't you want to go? Is the doctor not nice to you?"

"She's nice, but she makes me talk. I don't want to talk. I don't want to remember what happened to Dad."

Alice was getting really upset and was in danger of going into a full-on panic attack, and now Trent was starting to panic. She had to get Alice into the appointment.

Then it came to her. Negotiation. Trent's career was built on negotiation, and that was something she could understand. She got a packet of tissues out of the glovebox. "Look at me, Ali."

She did and the girl's tear-stained face broke her heart. She knew exactly how Alice felt, and it wasn't pleasant to remember. She wiped Alice's tears and said, "Take big breaths for me and we'll talk about it. Breathe with me."

Alice breathed along with her, calming with each breath. Trent was surprised by her intense feelings of protectiveness. These children were worming their way into her heart.

When Alice was calmer, Trent said, "Listen, I'll make you a deal. If you go to see the doctor today, and give it one last try, I won't make you go back if you don't want to. We'll find another way."

"Do you promise?"

Trent had an idea. She took a small notepad and pen from the centre console of the car.

"Why don't we do this. I'm a lawyer, I deal in contracts, and I see to it that people follow contracts to the letter. Why don't we write out a contract and we both sign it?"

Alice wiped her eyes and gave her a small smile. "Okay."

Wendy trudged up the stairs to Kira's flat, laden down with bags. She had taken the opportunity of having no children with her to pick up some things for Trent's birthday dinner. The kids had made a list of items, and Wendy wanted to make it special. It would be a chance for them to bond even more.

She couldn't stop thinking about Trent and Alice, worried how they were both getting on together. Alice's appointment with the psychologist was always a stressful and emotional day for the little girl, and she hoped Trent was handling it okay.

Trent was coming on leaps and bounds with the children. The change in her had been remarkable, but there was still so much of Trent she was hiding inside, and going by the stories about her father and nanny, she wasn't surprised. Her childhood had bred a woman who prized emotional control, strength, and showing care through money, presents, and taking care of people financially.

Then there was her own heart that seemed determined to fall for the troubled lawyer, despite the harm that love had brought to her life in the past. Wendy stopped at Kira's door and tried to catch her breath. "No, I can't." She knocked on the door before using her key and stepped into the flat. "Knock, knock, it's me," Wendy said.

"Wendy!" Noah shouted and ran over from the couch to hug her.

Kira followed him and took some of her bags. "You've been busy."

"It's things for Trent's birthday next weekend." Wendy looked down to Noah. "We want it to be special, don't we, little man?"

"Uh-huh. You get balloons?" Noah asked.

"Lots."

Kira gave her a questioning look then said, "Noah, I'll bring you some juice. Why don't you finish watching your cartoons?"

"Okay."

He ran off, and Wendy went to the kitchen table and put her bags on the floor. Once Kira returned from giving Noah his juice, Kira asked, "Tea?"

"That would be lovely. Thanks for looking after Noah," Wendy said as she took a seat.

Kira got out two cups and switched on the kettle. "It's no trouble at all. He's a great boy. So, what's this about Trent's birthday?"

"She asked me to organize a dinner party for her fortieth birthday. She didn't want anything, but her friends persuaded her."

Kira poured the tea and said, "Are you going?"

"What? No. I'm just doing the cooking and organizing. Look…" Wendy rummaged through her bags and pulled out a canvas picture and a photo of the children in a nice silver frame. "The canvas is for her home office. I got the shop to fit all the nice photos of her and the children I've taken, and the smaller frame is for her office. So she has pictures of the children in each place."

Kira raised an eyebrow. "And what are they for?"

Wendy gave her an incredulous look. "They're a gift for her birthday from me and the kids."

"From you and the kids."

"What?" Wendy said, "You said that as if it had some significance."

Kira shrugged. "It seems as if you're close to her, that's all. I mean making so much effort for her party and giving her a gift. She is your employer."

Wendy was starting to feel a bit defensive. "It's for the children, Ki. I'm trying to bring them together. I don't want to leave them without helping them make bonds that will last. Trent is Alice and Noah's only hope for family."

"And that's all?" Kira asked.

"Of course it is. You must have seen how far Trent has come from the way I first described her?"

"I did see the way she talked to Noah when she brought him, but you have to remember that she's a ruthless lawyer with a vicious reputation. There's a reason why people pay fortunes to hire her."

Wendy didn't like that description of Trent. "That's work, and besides, she's changing." She whispered so that Noah wouldn't hear. "Trent didn't want to be in the same room as the kids at the start, and now she's spending every Sunday with them on her own and taking Alice to see her psychologist—besides...she had a horrible childhood, Ki. She's damaged."

Kira placed her fingers on her forehead and shook her head. "Damaged? Now I know you're into her."

"I am not into her, Ki. She's my boss. Besides, why do you say *damaged* like that?"

"Ki, every woman you've ever had the hots for was damaged. You have this Mary Poppins syndrome where you want to fix everyone. Every family you've worked for you've tried to fix too. Remember, I've seen your family photo album on your phone."

Wendy was feeling exposed. That's not what she did, was it? "I just try to help the families I'm with, and I don't have the hots for damaged women."

"Oh, please, Dee. You know you do. You're a sucker for a hard luck story. Remember, I know the women you dated at uni, and then Bailey came along with the best hard-luck damaged story going. You fell for it hook, line, and sinker."

"She had a lot of problems, yes, but—"

Ki leaned forward and took Wendy's hand. "Every time you nearly saw the light and were going to break up with her, she came up with a new set of problems to hook you in."

Wendy saw that was true with hindsight, but things were different now, weren't they?

"Maybe in the past, but I went away from home to heal and change. I haven't, and I will never let anyone back into my heart, but this is different. I'm helping a family, not Trent. We've talked a lot after the kids have gone to bed, and it's been nice to make such a difference in a family."

"Evening chats? Was there wine?" Kira asked.

"Wine? Yes, she offered me a glass or two. What difference does that make?"

"It's part of the seduction. You know how people have a thing about nannies. First comes wine, then the sympathy stories, my wife doesn't understand me, my mummy and daddy didn't understand me. You know this—besides she's a lot older than you," Kira said.

Kira said that like it was a problem, but Wendy liked that about Trent. The thought of being with an older woman attracted her. She wouldn't have to feel the pressure of being the grown-up all the time. But was Kira right? Was she being seduced?

She thought back to sitting at the piano with Trent. They'd talked, and the feelings Trent expressed were raw—she couldn't be faking them. But Kira was right. Trent was a very different person in her work life and a tough negotiator. Was she being negotiated into bed? If she hadn't gotten up from the piano when she did, they would have kissed.

Wendy closed her eyes and mentally kicked herself. She thought after being away, living and learning, that she wasn't such a pushover. Obviously she needed to be on her guard.

Wendy sighed and opened her eyes. "Okay, Ki, I hear you. I am attracted to her, I admit, but I've heard what you've said and I'll be careful."

"It's just because I love you, Dee. I don't want you to be taken for a ride again the way Bailey did," Kira said.

"I promised myself that I wouldn't let anyone into my heart again, and I won't."

Kira frowned. "That's not what I'm asking for, Dee. I want you to meet someone nice and have the family you've always wanted. I know that's part of your dream. Family, teaching, writing children's books— just choose wisely. No damaged people for you to put back together."

Wendy thought about the excitement she felt when Trent spent time with her and the children and how her heart ached when Trent was open and showed her feelings. It was too dangerous, and it had to stop.

"I can't trust myself, Dee."

❖

Trent finished flicking through the year-old car magazine in the doctor's waiting room and sighed. You would think that with the fortune they charged you here, they could buy some up-to-date magazines.

She put it back on the coffee table in front of her. The décor in this doctor's waiting room was similar to her lawyer's office. Old oak furniture with green leather seats, expensive paintings, and the secretary's desk in the corner looked as if it was taken from an English country house.

Trent made a mental note to ask India to make sure they always had up-to-date magazines in her office from now on. It occurred to Trent that both she and the good doctor here catered to the same clientele.

The doctor's secretary, an older woman, must have seen her

fidgeting, because she came over and asked, "Would you like another coffee, Ms. Trent?"

"No, thank you."

She looked at her watch. Alice had been in there with Dr. Trevino for forty minutes so far. Trent wasn't frustrated because she was bored waiting, but she was anxious for Alice being in there alone without her. It was a new and strange sensation to feel so protective over a child.

Just as she was about to stand up and pace, the office door opened and Alice emerged with Dr. Trevino, her cheeks tear-stained.

Trent stood up immediately and held out her arms, and Alice ran to her.

Trent was on alert. What had this woman said to Ali?

"Ms. Trent? May I have a word?" Dr. Trevino said.

"Of course."

Trent bent down and said, "Stay here. I won't be a moment."

On the walk back to the car park, Trent tried to digest everything the doctor had said. Alice wasn't making progress. Dr. Trevino explained that Alice felt out of control without the strong parental figure her father was. She felt responsible for Noah and that was too much on her young shoulders. Alice wouldn't deal emotionally with the post-traumatic stress until she had that strong parental figure behind her as a safety net.

Trent had no choice. She had to do something, or this little girl was going to have far more emotional problems as an adult than she did.

When they got into the car, Alice lifted the contract they had signed. "You said I didn't have to go back, and I don't want to."

What could she do? Leave this to Wendy to sort out? No, she couldn't do that. Dr. Trevino said that Alice needed a strong parental figure, and despite her trepidation, that was what she had to be.

"I will always honour a contract, and if that's what you want, I won't make you come back, but let's take a drive first, maybe—" Trent racked her brain. "Maybe get an ice cream?"

"Ice cream?"

"Yes, that would be a nice treat before we go home, wouldn't it?"

Alice nodded. She looked unsure at this turn of events.

"I think there's an ice cream parlour in Fortnum & Mason—"

"McDonald's."

"McDonald's?" Trent said with surprise. "The hamburger place?"

Alice nodded vigorously. "It's my favourite. Daddy used to take us there."

Trent was dubious about a hamburger shop's ice cream, but if that was what Alice wanted…"Okay, McDonald's it is." Trent spoke to her satnav. It pulled up the nearest McDonald's drive-through, and they made their way there.

It was an experience for Trent. She had never negotiated a drive-through before, and Alice had to instruct her at each stage.

They parked and Alice handed her one of the ice creams.

"So this is your favourite?" Trent asked.

"Uh-huh." Alice licked her ice cream. "It's soft."

Trent hesitantly took a taste. She was pleasantly surprised. "Not bad."

There was a silence while Trent thought about how to talk to Alice. Strong, steady, parental figure, Dr. Trevino said, but that was easier said than done.

She remembered some advice Wendy had given her near the beginning of their time together, and that was to share her own story of grief. Could she do that?

"Ali? I know you don't want to talk—I understand it."

"How can you understand?" Alice said a little sharply.

Tell her, Trent mentally nudged herself. "I lost a parent as a child too."

Alice looked surprised. "You did?"

Trent hesitated. She had to do this for Ali.

"Yes, I was eight years old when my mother died. She had cancer, but I didn't know that at the time. I thought she was in bed for a long time because she was ill and would get better. My father was a gruff, frightening man, and he never told me anything. He was more concerned with his business and—"

She wasn't going to explain to Alice about her nanny and her father.

Alice had stopped eating her ice cream and was listening intently.

"Then one day she wasn't in her room any more. She was just gone and I didn't understand."

"Were you scared?" Alice asked.

This was so new, admitting to these feelings, but she didn't have to worry about Alice's judgement the way she would with an adult. Plus, Alice understood her pain.

"Yes, terrified. I didn't believe she was dead. I thought all the adults around me were lying. Even at the funeral, I kept demanding to know where she was. I thought it was all one big lie."

"What happened?"

Trent touched her scar. "I was punished, and I learned not to talk about it. As I grew older, I accepted what had happened to her, but my resentment and bottled-up grief made me shut down my emotions and have difficulty relating to people. I've only realized that recently, and I'm nearly forty."

It felt so good to say this out loud.

Alice looked out the car door silently. "You think that will happen to me?"

"I hope not, but I want you to know that things are different for you. I had no one to lean on. You have me, and I promise you will have me as long as I live, Ali. I'm your godmother. That means I took an oath before God to look after you."

Trent held out her hand in offer to Alice. Alice took it and said, "I want to talk."

❖

Wendy looked at the clock for what felt like the hundredth time. She was in the kitchen having just finished preparing Saturday night dinner, and Noah was drawing at the coffee table in the living area.

It was long after Trent and Alice should have been home, and Wendy was worried. She had already sent two texts and gotten nothing back. She didn't want to phone and give Trent the impression she didn't trust her alone, so she waited and waited.

What if Alice ran off? She was so vulnerable when she went to her therapist. Finally her phone beeped and she grabbed it off the counter.

We're on our way. We stopped for ice cream and had a talk. Ali is exhausted.

Wendy pushed her braids behind her ears nervously. She was worried about how Trent had managed their talk. Was Alice exhausted because she was upset?

She walked over to Noah and said, "Hugs, Noah?"

He didn't need to be asked twice. She hugged him tightly and tried to calm her worry.

"Will Ali be home soon?" Noah asked.

"Very soon, sweetheart." She kissed his head.

Wendy always cared for the children in her care—she had a lot of love to give—but Alice and Noah were different. She was truly falling in love with them. It probably wasn't professional how much she cared, but they had no mother and no father and they needed her. It was going to be so hard leaving them when it came time to go back to university.

Wendy waited and waited for Trent and Alice to return. She sat with Noah as he watched TV. Then the doorbell rang.

She got up quickly and hurried to the door. When Wendy opened it up she found an ashen faced Trent holding a sleeping Alice. She could tell by Alice's puffy eyes that she had been crying.

"What happened?"

"We went for an ice cream and had a talk." Trent indicated with her head down to Noah who had appeared at her side. "I'll tell you later."

"Is Ali okay?" Noah asked worriedly.

"Ali's fine," Trent said, "just tired, that's all."

Wendy ushered them in. "Let's put her to bed."

Trent carried Alice through to her bedroom and laid her down. "I'll let you get her undressed," Trent said to Wendy.

Then she was off like a shot. Wendy's heart broke looking at Alice's tear-stained face. She must have made a breakthrough with Dr. Trevino.

Once she had Alice settled, she said to Noah, "Why don't you watch TV in your room for a while, Noah. I'll give you a shout when dinner's ready."

"Okay," Noah said and ran to his bedroom.

Wendy wouldn't normally encourage him to watch so much TV, especially on his own, but she wanted to talk to Trent alone.

She walked from the bedroom to the family room and saw Trent standing on the balcony with a glass of whiskey, just staring out in space. The doors to the balcony had never been open since she and the children arrived. There was a key, but she knew that the social workers had demanded locks be fitted and the key kept in a safe place.

Wendy walked over to the doors of the balcony and gulped. She couldn't go any further—she was afraid of heights. "Trent? Can you tell me what happened?"

Trent looked around and Wendy saw tears in her eyes. It took her by complete surprise. Her heart made her take a step out onto the balcony and take Trent's hands.

"Could you stand by the door and tell me? I'm afraid of heights," Wendy said.

Trent nodded, finished her drink quickly, and moved inside the doors. Wendy didn't let go of Trent's hands and had to stop herself from hugging her.

"Tell me what happened," Wendy said softly. She didn't want to spook Trent.

"The doctor asked to talk to me. She said that she was getting nowhere with Ali, and that Ali needed to feel safe. Needed to have the strong parental figure, like her dad, standing with her, before she would ever open up."

"You," Wendy said.

"Yes. I had to think on my feet as to how I could get through to her—then I remembered your advice to tell her about losing my mother. So I took her to McDonald's for an ice cream, and I told her."

Trent started to tell Wendy the same story. She felt safe with Wendy and now that she had shared it with Alice, the words came a lot easier.

"There were things I didn't tell Alice, like how I got this." Trent pointed to her scar.

Wendy took a step closer. "Do you want to tell me?"

Trent looked into Wendy's eyes and didn't hesitate. "Yes. Part of the memory I didn't know until recently. I had been sitting with my mother and she started to struggle with her breathing. I ran downstairs and burst into my father's office, which was a big no-no, and found him in a compromising position with my nanny."

Wendy gasped. "While your mother—"

"Lay dying upstairs, yes. I froze, confused and terrified. My father was a frightening man. He grabbed me and wanted to punish me for bursting into his office."

Trent was no longer present. She was a bystander as her mind rolled back the years to that memory.

She watched tears roll down her own face as a child as her father demanded she hold out her hands. Then he took the birch that hung by a leather strap on a hook on his office wall. Her younger self shook with fear while Nanny Wilson watched coldly behind her father.

"You must never tell anyone about this, and never barge into my office again, do you understand?"

Trent's stomach churned as he struck the birch down onto her younger self's hands. It was harder, she remembered, than any of his other punishments, presumably because of what she had interrupted. It became so hard and violent that Trent pushed her father and ran as fast as her legs could carry her.

Trent was back with Wendy. "I ran right into the sill of his office door, knocked myself out, and woke up with this head injury. All these years I only just remembered being punished but not what for. Having Alice and Noah here brought all these memories flooding back."

Wendy reached out and touched her fingers lightly on her scar. Trent jumped at first, then felt heat spread all over body. She liked this comfort.

"You poor thing. I'm so sorry you had to go through that," Wendy said.

Trent covered Wendy's hand with hers. "It's nothing to what Alice has gone through."

"What did she tell you?" Wendy asked.

Trent recounted Alice's story in graphic detail, and as she did Wendy got closer and rested her head on Trent's chest.

"I don't care if this isn't appropriate," Wendy said.

Trent wrapped her arms around Wendy and held her close. "Me either."

They held each other like that while Trent finished Alice's story. "She was trapped, and she had David's blood all over her. It sounds like something from a nightmare."

Wendy pulled back from her with tears in her eyes. "We have to look after them."

Trent nodded and wiped Wendy's tears away with her thumb. "You and me. I don't know what I'd do without you, Wendy."

She couldn't help but lean into Wendy and kiss her lips. After a second Wendy responded to her kiss and opened her mouth enough for Trent to trace the tip of her tongue along Wendy's lips and dip inside her mouth.

Trent was lost in the kiss, as if all her hurt and pain from today was eased by Wendy's tender lips. She lowered her hands to Wendy's buttocks and pulled her to her pelvis. Her sex was wet and her clit pounding harder than she could remember in a long time.

Wendy moaned into her mouth and then pushed her back saying, "No, Trent."

Trent stopped immediately as the spell was broken. "Wendy?"

"We can't do this. We're both very emotional, it's understandable, but it's not right."

It wasn't right? It felt right and that was all Trent cared about. "Wendy, it doesn't matter what's right—"

"It does," Wendy said sharply. "You're my boss and the children could see us. Let's forget this happened, okay?"

Trent knew she couldn't forget about it. But she didn't want to scare Wendy off. She wasn't going to be the boss who made unwanted advances.

"Okay. If that's what you want," Trent said.

"It is. I'm proud of you for getting through to Alice. I'll just go and check on dinner," Wendy said.

Dinner? The way Trent's body was feeling she would need alcohol and lots of it to numb her aching want.

CHAPTER FOURTEEN

All through dinner, there was a tension between Trent and Wendy. Wendy could have slapped herself for kissing Trent only hours after having her heart to heart with Kira and promising she wouldn't fall for Trent's vulnerability.

That's what Trent was showing when Wendy listened to her story. Seeing such a commanding woman showing hurt and vulnerability was exactly what made Wendy reciprocate Trent's kiss. She couldn't fight it, and yet she must.

Wendy looked up from her plate of food and found Trent gazing at her. She flicked her eyes away quickly and concentrated on what Noah was talking about. Maybe she had come back to Britain too soon? Maybe she hadn't healed as much as she thought she had?

One thing was for certain, one kiss from Trent was so much more thrilling than any of the lovers she had while out of the country. Trent was ridiculously sexy, and Wendy could have controlled herself if she had stayed her moody, gruff self, but she was changing and growing beautifully, which made her irresistible to Wendy.

They had to talk. Annoyingly Trent made herself even more attractive after dinner. Alice was glued to her now that they had shared something so emotional. Trent was becoming her strong parental figure, just as the doctor had suggested.

At bedtime Alice insisted Trent escort her to bed, and the pair held hands until the girl fell asleep. As Wendy passed the bedroom she thought that it was so much easier to resist the distant Trent.

After settling Noah, Wendy went to her room to wait until she could talk to Trent. About nine o'clock, Wendy knocked on Trent's office door. When she walked in, Trent jumped up from her seat and looked upset. "Let me talk—let me talk before you hand in your notice."

"Hand in my notice? I—" Wendy said with confusion.

Trent walked around the desk and pulled out a chair for Wendy. "Please sit and let me talk for a moment."

Wendy was confused. Trent looked genuinely panicked and ran her hand through her short salt and pepper hair.

"I want to apologize for kissing you earlier," Trent said. "I realize how it must look to you. I'm your employer, I'm fourteen years older than you, in a position of power, and I made advances towards you. Before you consider leaving, please know that I was in an emotional state earlier and that I felt there was something growing between us recently."

"I kissed you back," Wendy said.

Trent stopped pacing and sat back in her office chair. "But you might have felt obliged because I'm in a position of power. I don't want something I've done to make you leave us. The kids need you so much, and things have gotten so much better with you around."

Wendy raised an eyebrow. "Believe me, Trent. No one would make me feel obliged to kiss them. Besides, I'm not going to leave my job. I love the kids and I love living here. I just wanted to talk about it."

Trent gulped and clasped her hands in front of her. "Okay, talk to me. I'm ready."

How could she put this into words without looking like an idiot? On the one hand she wanted to rip that highly starched shirt off Trent and kiss her everywhere, and on the other her heart was terrified at the strength of her feelings.

"I think it's clear there is some attraction between us, and when we kissed…it felt good, but I can never let it be more than that."

Wendy assumed suggesting more, like a relationship, would frighten off a perennial bachelor like Trent, but instead Trent asked, "Why? Why not more. A young woman like you should want to find love."

"Because in love I make poor choices and get hurt. I can't trust myself," Wendy said.

"What do you mean?"

Telling her truth out loud, and to someone other than Kira, was daunting.

"The reason I gave up university and left the country was because I had my heart and life broken by someone who said they loved me. I am never going to let that happen again."

"What idiot broke your heart?" Trent asked.

Wendy smiled at Trent's assessment of her ex. "Bailey. We were together at university for two years. She worked on the janitorial staff there. We met, she charmed me, gave me her sad story—which, my friend Kira reminds me, I always fall for—and I was hooked."

Trent frowned. "What did she do?"

Wendy sighed. "Probably more than I'll ever know about. But we were engaged. I always wanted to be married and have a family. Something secure, love that was real. I know in hindsight that I was trying to make the family my parents didn't give me. Anyway, we got engaged, and I began working two jobs to save up for our wedding and first home."

Trent watched as Wendy twisted one of her braids around her finger, something she had noticed Wendy doing in times of stress. She had a feeling about where this was going. Trent had heard enough relationship tales of woe in her office to recognize a relationship disaster waiting to happen.

Wendy continued, "Bailey always had troubles with money. She drank a lot, and I had to bail her out of debt time and time again. My friends warned me about that and that she wasn't always faithful, but you know how it is when you put your head in the sand. I didn't want to know. Plus I was working so hard I didn't have time to notice. I had enough saved up for a deposit for a flat and I was so proud of myself..."

Wendy went quiet. Trent could feel her anger bubbling up because she knew what was coming. It clearly still hurt Wendy after all this time.

"You can tell me, Dee," Trent said.

"I came home one night to find a note saying Bailey had met someone else and couldn't go through with the wedding. At first all I felt was pain and hurt, but then the next morning I started to think about all the deposits I'd made for the wedding which I would lose. I checked my bank accounts and all my savings had been cleared out, and my credit card was maxed out. Bailey had been using it all that time. Now she was gone, my money was gone, and I was up to my eyes in debt."

"Fucking bitch," Trent said.

"I couldn't afford to stay at uni and pay off my debts, and I vowed to pay off every last one."

"That's when you went abroad, for nannying jobs?" Trent asked.

Wendy nodded. "I came back home when I had paid off all my debts and I thought my heart had healed. I promised myself never to let myself get hurt again."

"You think I'd hurt you?" Trent asked.

"Not intentionally, but look at us—we're from different worlds. You're this rich, hotshot lawyer, who mixes with celebrities and aristocracy, and I'm a hipster nanny with tattoos, who plays in a folk band."

Trent let out a long breath and got up and walked to the window. The more she thought about this, the more she wanted Wendy, but Wendy clearly didn't trust her.

She turned around to face Wendy. "Normally the rich part would win me some points."

Wendy smiled. "Not with me."

That response just made Trent want her more. "But—"

"No, Trent. I work for you. It's not right. Our affection for the children has brought us together, but they will go to boarding school and I'll go back to university. Then you'll want your life back."

The thought of life going back to what it was filled Trent with dread, but clearly Wendy wanted an out, so she would give her one.

"You're right, of course, and I don't want to make you feel uncomfortable while you're here. Let's forget this and pour all our energies into the children."

"Thank you," Wendy said.

❖

The next week went by quickly. After Wendy's talk with Trent, she had kept her distance. Wendy had to admit that she missed their late night chats with wine, but Kira had said talks with wine were dangerous, and she had to keep that emotional distance or she knew she'd fall deeper for Trent.

But today was different. It was Trent's birthday, and she wanted the children to enjoy the day, and for Trent to feel appreciated.

Alice and Noah had gotten up early and were helping Wendy make Trent breakfast in bed. They were both excited about today. It was amazing how far both Trent and the children had come. Trent still had a lot to learn about having a family, but at least now she wanted one, even if it would be part time when they went to boarding school, and that's what mattered.

"Okay, eggs ready. How's that toast coming?" Wendy spooned the fried eggs onto the plate beside the bacon and sausages.

"Nearly ready," Alice said.

The kids had seen these toast cutters when they were out one day and insisted on buying them. So now Trent was going to get her breakfast along with star, dinosaur, and happy face shaped toast.

Alice lifted the plate of toast over and added it to the breakfast tray.

"Great job, you two. Okay, Noah, you carry the presents, I'll get the tray with coffee, and Ali, you carry the orange juice."

They walked to Trent's bedroom, and Noah said, "Trent is going to love my dinosaur toast best."

Wendy smiled at him. Noah was such a sweet boy. "Ali, can you knock?"

She did and Trent's voice said, "Come in."

Ali opened the door for Wendy and they walked in to find Trent sitting on the edge of her bed.

"Okay kids, after three. One, two, three."

They all began to sing "Happy Birthday," just like they'd practised. Trent looked slightly embarrassed with a sweet pink tinge to her cheeks.

It was nice to make someone so clever and accomplished blush, Wendy concluded. When they finished singing, Wendy said, "The kids have made you breakfast in bed for your birthday."

"That's very nice of you both," Trent said.

Trent was clearly out of her comfort zone but was handling this new kind of attention well.

"We made dinosaur toast for you," Noah said while scrabbling up onto the bed.

Trent helped him up and said, "Dinosaur toast? Well, that is special."

Trent looked at Wendy quickly and winked at her. Wendy's stomach clenched. *Stop being so sweetly sexy, Trent,* Wendy shouted inside her head.

Alice put the juice on Trent's bedside table and got on the bed too. Trent was doing really well. Wendy doubted she'd had two kids on her bed before.

Trent put her an arm around each of the children and hugged them. She was trying her best to be good for Alice and Noah. She wasn't good at celebrating her own birthday, and when she was with Becca she had always tried to play it down, much to Becca's annoyance.

She had always been better at giving than receiving. She loved spoiling the ones she loved but felt awkward when it was reciprocated. But she did realize this was more about what Alice and Noah needed rather than her, so she played along as best she could.

"Open your presents, Trent," Alice said as she gave her a sweet smile.

Trent would never have thought how hard she would fall in love with these two children. To see Alice smile made her melt inside. Alice still had nightmares and the haunted look in her eyes, but much less than it had been.

Wendy put the breakfast tray on the dressing table and said, "Hurry up, then, before Trent's food gets cold."

Noah handed her three wrapped gifts. She opened the smallest one and found a coffee mug with the phrase *This is what an awesome lawyer looks like* and arrows pointing up.

Trent chuckled and Alice said, "It's for your coffee at your office."

"I love it." Trent gave them each a kiss.

"These other two are from all of us," Wendy said.

"Okay, I'm feeling really spoiled," Trent said as she ripped open the paper.

The first one was a canvas with pictures of her and the children. They looked like a normal happy family in it, and Trent felt the emotion rise up into her chest.

"I've never seen these pictures before," Trent said to Wendy.

"I took them on my own phone at the fireworks display. They were such nice pictures, that I thought they should be framed."

She held Wendy's gaze and had to gulp down the emotion that was rising in her throat. This was all Wendy. She was the most thoughtful, sweetest, kindest woman in the world, and Trent's heart was crying out for her.

"That one's for home. Open the other," Wendy said.

The smaller one was a picture frame with another wonderful picture of the three of them.

"That one is for your desk at work," Wendy said.

The sentiment meant so much to Trent. Wendy thought of everything and was making her life what she never thought she could have. How was she going to let her go when she left next year? In fact, how was she going to get through the day without telling Wendy that she was falling for her?

❖

Trent spent a nice day with Wendy and the children. Wendy was busy cooking and Trent washed all the glasses and prepared the drinks table.

Later she was banished to her bedroom while Wendy and the kids decorated the flat for their guests. She didn't quite know what to do with herself as she waited. It was so strange having the attention on her. She always did the gift giving and spoiling of others, and it was difficult to feel comfortable being on the other end. She picked up the photo frame Wendy had given her.

It was a perfect picture except for one thing—someone was missing. Wendy should have been in it and made the picture complete.

She thought of Becca and what she would make of Trent wanting to make these three her family. She hadn't been ready when Becca wanted a family, but maybe she was ready now. Could she handle this life indefinitely?

Eventually a knock came at her door and she heard Noah's voice say, "You can come out now, Trent."

She opened the door and saw Noah jumping with excitement. "Come and see what we've done for you."

Trent took his hand and was led out to the family area. Wendy and Alice were waiting with huge smiles on their faces. In each corner of the room were large helium balloons in the shape of four and zero. On the floor were lots of normal-sized balloons and inflatables of a large champagne bottle, and on the walls hung Happy Birthday banners.

The dining table was set beautifully with more helium balloons fixed to the middle of the table, and the smell of delicious food from the kitchen was mouth-watering.

Trent had never felt so touched. She walked over to Wendy and Alice with Noah and said, "You did all this for me?"

Wendy gave her a dazzling smile. "We wanted to make this a special day for you."

Trent's emotions and heart hadn't been used as much in years. "It really is."

She opened up her arms wide and invited Noah, Alice, and Wendy into a group hug. Wendy hesitated for a moment, then walked into her arms. Alice and Noah hugged her tightly, and Trent pressed her nose into Wendy's hair and closed her eyes. She felt Wendy's fingertips stroke the short hairs at the base of her neck. This moment was perfect. She never wanted it to end, but when it did and Wendy pulled away, Trent said, "This is the best birthday I've ever had."

Wendy smiled. "It's not over yet."

"Trent," Alice said, "come and look at the table. I made place cards."

She lifted Noah up into her arms and let herself be dragged over to the table. Next to her dining table was a smaller table, she assumed for the children to sit at.

"Look, Trent." Alice picked up a handful of shiny, coloured number forties that were spread all over the tablecloth. "These were my idea."

"They are very nice, Ali. Thank you." Trent gave Alice a kiss on the cheek and let Noah down.

"You like it, Trent?" Noah said.

"Yes, I don't think I've ever had a nicer birthday."

When the two kids wandered off to the kids' table, Trent noticed there were only five places set out at the adult table. She checked the name cards at each place. Becca, Dale, Val, Sammy, and herself.

Trent walked over to the kitchen where Wendy was fussing around the oven.

"Dee? There's only five places set at the adult table," Trent said.

Wendy turned around and had a brief look of panic on her face. "What? That's right, isn't it? Rebecca, Dale, Val, Sammy, and you?"

"You're forgetting your place," Trent said.

Wendy furrowed her eyebrows. "My place? What do you mean?"

"Your place at my birthday dinner. Next to me," Trent said.

"I have no place. I'm your nanny, a member of staff, cook for the evening. I'll be serving you and keeping an eye on the kids so your friends can enjoy your birthday."

Trent walked around the kitchen island so she could speak in private to Wendy. "When I asked you to organize a birthday dinner for me and my friends, I meant for you to come too. You're part of the family."

Wendy checked to see that the kids weren't watching. "Trent, I'm your kids' nanny. How would it look to your friends for the staff to sit down with you?"

Her description of herself as staff angered Trent. She took Wendy's hand. "You are not staff. You are so much more than that."

Wendy pulled her hand away. "I can't be more than that, Trent. You know that."

"I wouldn't have asked for dinner if I'd thought you wouldn't come and celebrate my birthday."

Wendy sighed with exasperation. "You know it's not about that."

"No, it's about the fact that we have feelings for each other that won't go away," Trent said sharply. "I'm not some pimply youth at university who is going to steal your money and break your heart." Wendy stopped dead and Trent could have kicked herself. She'd hurt Wendy's feelings. "I'm sorry—I shouldn't have said that."

Wendy put down her spoon and said in a low voice, "I'm going to get changed for your guests coming."

"I'm sorry, Dee," Trent said, but she just walked off.

Trent smacked herself on the forehead. Now she had upset Wendy.

"It's no wonder I'm single," Trent said before Noah dragged her off to play with the balloons.

About twenty minutes later Wendy emerged from her bedroom with a lacy navy blue minidress on. Trent forgot to breathe. "Wendy, you look beautiful."

"I don't always look like I'm going to a festival, you know," Wendy said.

Trent sighed. "I know. I don't mean you don't look beautiful normally, because you do. I just meant you look particularly beautiful tonight."

Wendy checked the oven. "I need to fit in with your friends."

Chapter Fifteen

Wendy was making last minute dinner preparations in the kitchen while Trent mixed with her guests. She enjoyed meeting Becca and putting a face to the only woman Trent had loved. She was a lovely woman and Wendy could see why Trent and Dale had fallen for her.

She looked over to the piano, where Alice was sitting on the piano stool with Mia deep in conversation and looking at Mia's iPhone. It was nice that Alice had another younger girl to talk to.

Noah, on the other hand, was stuck like glue to Jake. They were playing with the games console, and Noah was jumping up and down on the couch with excitement. Close to them Dale, Sammy, and Trent stood talking in a group. Dale was as happy and charming as the first time she'd met her, and Sammy equally nice. They all had been pleased to meet her and weren't treating her like staff, but as a new friend.

Wendy heard a voice behind her say, "Can we help you with anything?"

She turned around and saw a smiling Becca and Val. On first impressions both seemed open and friendly.

"Erm...I'm just about ready. But you could help me take the dishes over to the table."

"Gladly," Becca said.

Wendy took the chicken out of the oven and Val said, "That smells gorgeous."

"Thanks, it's my grandmother's old recipe."

"Let me take it over for you." Val took the chicken on its tray over to the table. The smell drew the children and Dale and Sammy over.

"Mummy!" Gracie toddled over and wanted to be picked up. Becca lifted her into her arms and kissed her.

Wendy smiled and took her little hand. "Hi, Gracie. Are you hungry?"

"Uh-huh," the little girl replied.

"She's a beautiful girl, Becca," Wendy said.

"Thank you. She is, but she's a handful. Luckily I've got Dale to help." Becca leaned in and said, "I wanted the chance to speak to you alone."

"Sure, go ahead," Wendy said.

Becca placed her hand on Wendy's arm and smiled softly. "I wanted to thank you for what you've done for Trent and the children. Trent was in a dark place when this huge responsibility was placed on her shoulders. She's never been good with children, but to see her interact with Alice and Noah the way she is tonight is like night and day to the Trent that took on this responsibility."

Wendy was pleased Becca had noticed the change in Trent. "I knew when I came to work here that Trent had potential, a desire to become closer to Alice and Noah. She just needed some encouragement, and I just helped her along." Wendy gazed over to Trent and found she was looking straight at her. "She feels so deeply about things and is so kind and can be really gentle, especially with Alice."

Becca gave her a knowing smile. "I know you did more than that, Wendy, so thank you."

Wendy felt her cheeks burn. She was sure Becca had noticed. "I'd better get this food on the table before it gets cold. If you could take the roast potatoes, Becca, that would be a great help."

❖

Trent was so full. The meal Wendy made was delicious, and even better, Wendy had relented and set a place for herself, so Trent had her next to her all meal. It was everything she wanted wrapped up in an evening.

All her friends were chatting around the dining table. Dale was holding court, telling them another story of how she nearly got expelled at school by filling the teachers' biscuit tin with maggots, which drew consternation from Becca, Val, and Wendy, but laughter from the children.

It constantly amazed Trent how Dale managed to become a successful business owner, going by all her school stories. As they listened, Trent reached under the table and took Wendy's hand.

Wendy looked at her quickly and Trent squeezed her hand. "Thank you for a wonderful birthday, and thanks for sitting with me. It meant the world to me."

"You're welcome, but there's more to come." She stood up and said, "Kids? Who wants to help me with the cake?"

They jumped up excitedly and ran to the kitchen.

Once Wendy was gone, Becca came over and plonked herself down next to her. "Are you having a nice birthday, then?"

Trent smiled. "It's been great, and thanks for your present. It's really something special."

Dale and Becca got her a special vintage bottle of champagne for her collection.

"You're welcome. Maybe you can open it at your fiftieth."

Trent chuckled. "Let me get used to being forty first, Becs."

"So? What's going on between you and Wendy?" Becca asked.

"What? Becca, what do you mean?" Trent said.

"You two have been gazing at each other all night. There's an electricity between you."

Trent said, "It's complicated."

"Isn't it always? She's a lovely woman," Becca said, "although I see you went against my advice of not just choosing the most attractive nanny."

"You've met her—you've got to say I picked the right woman for the job," Trent argued.

Becca smiled. "You have a point. So why is it complicated?"

"I have strong feelings for her. I think she does too, but I'm forty, she's twenty-six, and I'm her employer."

"Does she think the age gap is a problem?"

"I don't think so—but I'm not sure. Wendy had some bad experiences with a relationship, so she's wary of another one."

"Trent, if there is something there, don't let fear make her slip through your fingers."

The lights went off all of a sudden, and everyone took their phones out to film the large birthday cake covered in candles Wendy and the children carried over.

Everyone started to sing "Happy Birthday," but Trent couldn't take her eyes off the woman carrying the cake.

❖

Trent excused herself after the cake cutting and went to the bathroom. She splashed water on her face and looked at herself in the mirror. It was difficult for her to have so much attention on her, but Alice and Noah had enjoyed it so much that it was worth it. If it made them happy she was happy, something Trent never thought she'd think or say.

Then there was Wendy. Beautiful, kind, loving, perfect Wendy. Every time she looked at her, the feelings she was harbouring got stronger, and Becca had noticed. Becca warned her not to let Wendy slip through her fingers if she had feelings for her, but Wendy had made it clear on the day they kissed that she wouldn't and couldn't take things further.

How was she going to cope when Wendy left them to go back to university?

Trent let out a breath, dried her face, and went back out to her guests. Dale was standing with Sammy chatting beside the couch while the kids played the games console. "Hey, mate. You have a good birthday?"

"It's been great, thanks, and thank you for your gift."

"Aye, I wanted to adopt a donkey for you, but Becca would nae go for it." Dale winked after her comment and Trent chuckled.

"I'm sure you did."

Sammy, who was already in her forties, said, "Don't worry about the big 4-0. Life just keeps getting better once you get used to it."

"Well, I have Alice and Noah to worry about now," Trent said, "so life is probably going to get busier and more interesting."

"Is there something going on with you and Wendy?" Dale asked. "There's heavy tension with you two. Like sparks going everywhere."

"I—" She looked for Wendy and didn't see her. "Becca? Where did Wendy go?"

"She's gone down to your car. Noah's left one of his dinosaurs there," Becca said.

Trent sighed. "I better go and get her, or she'll be forever climbing the stairs. Wendy isn't too great with lifts. Alice? Keep an eye on Noah. I'm just going to get Wendy."

Trent walked out of the flat and got the lift down to the parking garage. When the doors opened, she found Wendy walking back from her car, dinosaur in hand.

"What are you doing here?" Wendy asked.

"I've come to get you and accompany you on the lift. I know you won't go in it without someone being with you."

"Okay, but I've got a system with the kids. We sing a song."

Trent raised an eyebrow. "Are you serious?"

"Do you want me to get in the lift or not?" Wendy said.

Trent held up her arms. "Okay, okay. We'll do it your way."

When Trent pressed the button for the lift, Wendy's nerves started.

The lift arrived and the doors opened. Trent stepped in and held her hand out. "You'll be fine. Come on, the party is waiting for us."

She took a deep breath and walked in. "You remember 'Baby Shark.'"

"I'm sure you'll remind me," Trent said.

Wendy started to sing, and she prodded Trent to sing along. She could feel the lift moving smoothly. This was okay. Seconds later there was a shudder and the lift stopped. Wendy didn't want to open her eyes. She could feel something was wrong.

Trent tapped her on the shoulder and she opened her eyes. She could see the lift panel was flashing and Trent said, "I don't want to alarm you but—"

Trent didn't get a chance to finish her sentence. Wendy went straight into full-blown panic. "Oh God, oh God. We're trapped."

Trent took her hand and led her over to the lift panel. "We're not trapped. We'll be out soon. Look, I've pressed the button. This is an expensive, well-protected apartment building. Someone will be with us in a jiffy."

Just then the intercom on the panel came to life and Wendy jumped.

"Hello? Is everyone all right?" the voice came from it.

"Hi, this is Davina Trent from the penthouse. The lift has stopped suddenly."

"We're checking on the problem now and sending someone to your location. How many are there in the lift?"

"Myself and one other, but my friend is very distressed, so if you could be as quick as possible," Trent said.

"Of course, Ms. Trent. We'll be with you as soon as we can."

"You see?" Trent squeezed her shaking hands. "It's all under control."

Wendy looked around, and the lift walls seemed to be closing in on them. "It's getting smaller. The walls—I feel sick."

Trent pulled her into her arms and her breathing started to calm. She pressed her face into Trent's neck and she calmed even more. The smell of her neck, the scent of her cologne, was wonderful.

"You make me feel safe, Peter," Wendy said.

That one word blew her away. Wendy had described always wanting Peter Pan to whisk her away from an unhappy home life. Trent would gladly be Wendy's Peter.

Trent rubbed her back soothingly. "That makes me happy. I want you to feel safe with me."

Wendy shivered when Trent traced her fingers across her back.

Wendy said, "Can we just sit down?"

"Of course."

They sat against the wall of the lift. Wendy's hands still shook, so Trent held her hand. "I'm with you. We'll be okay."

"Alice and Noah will be worried about us," Wendy said.

"Don't worry, Becca will look after them."

Wendy nodded. She'd had a pang of jealousy when she had seen Trent speaking to Becca while she got the cake ready. Why she was thinking of that when she was in the middle of being trapped in a lift, she didn't know.

"Jake and Mia are nice kids, and Gracie is adorable," Wendy said.

"They are, and I think Noah and Alice loved them. It's nice for them to have some friends to play with."

There was a silence while a question about Becca burned in her head. Under normal circumstances she wouldn't have brought it up, but her emotions were raw at the moment.

"I asked you a question one time and you never answered me."

Trent turned to her. "Oh? What question was that?"

"Are you over Becca? Have you let her go? I saw you talking really quietly together." As soon as Wendy asked it, she felt like a complete idiot. "I'm sorry. I'm your kids' nanny. It's none of my business."

Trent cupped her face and Wendy felt tingles travel all over body. "I was telling her that I was falling for my much younger nanny, and that I didn't think she would give me a chance. So I think you could say that I'm over her. I'll always love her as a friend—we were a big part of each other's lives—but she has Dale now."

Wendy was gobsmacked. "You—you said you were falling for me?"

Trent nodded, then leaned in to kiss her, but at that exact moment the lift shuddered into life and a voice came through the speaker.

"We have the problem fixed, Ms. Trent. You'll be on your floor in a few seconds."

The moment was gone.

CHAPTER SIXTEEN

Trent hugged Becca goodbye, and Becca said, "Remember, if this is what you want, don't let her slip away from you."

"Easier said than done, but I'll think about what you said." Trent kissed her on the cheek.

Becca took Dale's hand and started to walk away. She turned back and said, "Think about Christmas too."

"I will."

Becca and Dale were taking Jake and Gracie to Lapland for Christmas, since Sammy and Val and Mia were going to stay with Val's family in Wales. Becca had suggested that she, Wendy, Alice, and Noah come with them.

Trent had long since given up her idea of going on a skiing trip and leaving the children with Wendy, but going to Lapland for the ultimate family holiday was another kind of pressure altogether.

Trent shut and locked the door. When she turned around Wendy came into the living area.

"They all gone?" Wendy asked.

"Yes. They're all staying at a local hotel for the night," Trent said.

There was a heavy silence. Things had felt awkward ever since they got out of the lift, and Trent was beginning to regret admitting that she was falling for Wendy, and probably Wendy was regretting calling her Peter. Everything seemed so open and raw in the lift. She'd wanted Wendy to know she cared deeply about her, but now it was just awkward.

Wendy brushed her hands down her dress. "The kids went out like a light."

Trent nodded. "They looked exhausted."

"Well, I better get cleaned up," Wendy said.

Trent looked around at the mess. She didn't think her penthouse apartment had ever been so messy, but it was good messy. It showed that she was living at last.

"Why don't we leave it till the morning, and I'll help you clean up?"

Wendy smiled. "Sounds good. I'll just put the leftovers in the fridge. You go on to bed."

"Okay." Were they really going to just ignore what happened?

Trent took a breath to say something, but Wendy was already busy. Maybe she had freaked Wendy out.

She headed for her bedroom and shut her door.

Wendy paced back and forth in the kitchen trying to figure out whether to listen to her head or her heart. Tonight had been difficult—having to face the fact that she wanted Trent, and getting stuck in the lift—but then Trent made it better. She calmed her fears. She had been the Peter to her Wendy.

"She said she was falling for me."

When she'd finally come home to the UK, Wendy didn't think she was going to walk into the life of a woman who made her heart want to love again. Wendy's head told her this was all too perfect. She could hear Kira's voice in her head, warning about the perfect children who needed her, the damaged, sexy, older woman who needed her—

"And the family I need." Wendy leaned against the kitchen counter and groaned in frustration. "Just go to bed."

She walked up the hall, peeping in Alice's and Noah's bedrooms as she went. She arrived at her door, and her hand hesitated on the handle. She looked over to Trent's door and it was pulling her like a siren's song.

Go to bed, Wendy told herself. *Go now.*

But her feet didn't obey, and she found herself in front of Trent's door. Wendy took a breath and knocked.

Trent came to the door. "Wendy? What's wrong?"

Oh my God, this was not right. "Nothing, I just wanted to say happy birthday, and I hope you've had a good day."

Trent flashed a smile that melted her insides. "I had the best day, and it's thanks to you and the kids. You want to come in for a minute?"

Wendy walked in and Trent indicated for her to sit on the bed. "No, I'll stand if that's okay. I want to talk."

Trent sat and said, "Whatever makes you comfortable."

Wendy began to pace again. "I wanted to talk about what happened in the lift."

Trent put a hand up. "Listen, I'm sorry if—"

"No, I need to talk. I wanted to tell you why I'm kind of scared of lifts. That sounds stupid, I know, but there's a point to this." Wendy rubbed her forehead. "I'm rambling now."

"Ramble as much as you want Wendy…Darling."

The beat Trent left between her names made Wendy want to jump on her right now. But she had to get it together.

"When I was eight, I got trapped in a lift for three hours with my mother. The lights were off, and we were in blackness."

"I'm sorry—that must have been awful as a child. It would be at any age," Trent said.

Wendy nodded. "My mum was terrified of lifts and was in a terrible state, as was I. It felt like we were going to suffocate to death in there. The point is, my mum didn't make me feel safe, but today when we were trapped, *you* made me feel safe. You took control and gave me this wall of reassurance, and I liked it."

"I'm glad I make you feel that way," Trent said.

Wendy sighed. "What you said when we were in there? Will you finish it?"

"You mean what I was going to say?" Trent asked.

"I'm not putting this very well." Wendy thought for a second and then said, "You keep asking me if our age difference is a problem, but it's the opposite. It's one of the first things that attracted me to you. I've always been with people younger, in years or maturity. I've always had to be the adult in the relationship, making sure things got done, bills got paid, made the decisions. Bailey couldn't make a decision if her life depended on it, but you are different and it's exciting and daunting all at once."

Trent stood up. "What exactly are you asking me to do?"

"I'm scared of what I feel, what I want, and I need someone to take that responsibility, that control, to make my heart feel safe."

Trent took the few last steps towards Wendy. She caressed Wendy's face with her fingertips, and Wendy shivered. "What if you break my heart?"

Trent whispered, "You don't have to worry. I'm Peter, and I will take really good care of it. I'm going to kiss you now."

Every cell in Wendy's body was electrified and hungry. She was giving up control of her fears and letting Trent take control and it was intoxicating.

Trent leaned in and hovered over Wendy's lips, then instead of kissing them, brushed her lips over Wendy's nose and cheek and finally kissed her neck. Wendy groaned at the touch of Trent's lips on her neck. She didn't get the kiss she was expecting and wanting, and it made her desire all the more desperate.

She groaned and grasped for Trent's neck. "Kiss me, please?"

Trent slowly ran her fingers up and down her sides and whispered into her neck, "I'll take care of you, trust me."

Wendy couldn't help but moan and dig her nails into Trent's strong neck. She was wet and had an aching need to be filled. Handing over responsibility to Trent was liberating and new, and she wanted Trent to touch her everywhere.

Trent finally came to her lips, and just as she was about to touch lips she whispered, "You're safe."

When Trent's lips kissed her, she almost melted against the door. The kiss was tender and slow. She opened her lips and let in Trent's tongue, which touched hers and then ran along her bottom lip.

Wendy grasped Trent's free hand and put it to her breast. Oh God. Nothing had ever felt like this.

She started to undo Trent's shirt buttons frantically, but Trent stopped her and she pulled back from the kiss.

Wendy pleaded, "I need you inside me."

Trent took her hand and said, "Come to bed."

She led Wendy over to the bed. Trent wanted nothing more than to feel Wendy beneath her while she thrust her fingers into her, but this was about trying to make Wendy feel safe and showing her that this meant something.

Trent took off her own shirt and T-shirt and threw them to the side. Wendy reached out and traced her fingers over Trent's muscled shoulders and chest and brushed over her hard nipples.

"I love your body," Wendy said.

Trent took a step closer and unzipped Wendy's dress while keeping her eyes focused on Wendy's.

The dress dropped and Wendy pushed Trent's hands onto her lace covered breasts. "Feel me. I want you to touch me so badly," Wendy said.

Trent couldn't wait to see Wendy's beautiful breasts. She undid the clip and threw the bra to the side. She ran her hands over Wendy's breasts, taking in every inch. Wendy's body was beautiful and soft, and Trent couldn't believe she was being allowed to touch her.

Trent kissed her and ran her fingers down between her breasts and down past her taut stomach. "You're so beautiful," Trent said.

Wendy kissed her more frantically and Trent got caught up in the passion. She quickly took off her trousers and underwear and lifted Wendy so that her legs wrapped around her hips. Wendy gasped.

Trent laid her down on the bed and pulled off her lacy panties.

Trent lay over Wendy and began to kiss and gently bite her breasts. "Oh God, I'm so wet. Please go inside."

Trent leaned over and kissed Wendy while she allowed herself to thrust her sex into her lover's. Wendy was right. She could feel how wet Wendy was, and she groaned into Wendy's kiss.

Trent couldn't remember the last time she'd been so hungry for sex, to touch someone else's body.

"You do want it, don't you?" Trent said.

Wendy wrapped her arms around Trent's neck and her legs around her hips. She undulated her hips into Trent's sex, encouraging her. "I want you to make me come."

Trent was throbbing with desire just touching Wendy's beautiful body, and she wanted to be inside her making her come.

"I promised you that I'd take care of you, Wendy Darling."

Trent reached down and squeezed Wendy's soaking wet sex. She felt her lover dig her nails into her back as she moaned. She loved that.

Trent's fingers slipped easily into Wendy's wetness. She split her fingers and rubbed the outside of Wendy's clit a few times, making Wendy thrust her hips and groan, "Yes, like that."

She had to be inside Wendy. Trent moved her fingers down and teased Wendy's opening, doing everything gently and making Wendy feel taken care of and safe.

"Inside, Trent. I need it," Wendy said breathily.

She slipped one finger in, then two, making Wendy gasp in pleasure. Wendy pulled Trent down to kiss her and said desperately, "Just fuck me. I need it so badly."

Trent nearly came at that remark. Wendy was not all sweetness and light. She clearly loved sex and to be naughty. Trent stroked a braid away from her face. "You're a naughty girl, Wendy Darling."

"Yes," Wendy said.

Trent kissed Wendy while she started to thrust, while her thumb teased her clit.

"Yes, baby, deeper," Wendy whispered through passion.

She thrust deeper and moaned at her lover opening up to her. She could feel the slight fluttering of Wendy's sex. Trent looked down into Wendy's eyes. "I can feel you're going to come soon."

"Uh-huh," was all Wendy could say while she thrust herself against Trent's fingers. Suddenly she groaned and held on to Trent's neck tightly. "It's going to be too much, I can't…"

"You can. Look at me."

She did and repeated, "It's too much. I can't let go."

"I've got you." Trent slowed her thrusts and instead swirled her fingers more gently. "You can let go. I'll keep you safe."

Wendy nodded and held on to her tightly. Trent started thrusting her fingers fast into Wendy's wet sex.

"You need to come badly, don't you?" Trent asked.

"Yes, yes, now."

She hastened her thrusts and felt the walls of her lover's sex tumble into orgasm.

Wendy squeezed her neck so hard while obviously trying to stifle her scream, in case the kids heard anything. Then her arms went limp and Trent felt her start to shake.

❖

Wendy tried to control her breathing and she clutched her hand to her chest.

"Are you, all right, Dee?" Trent asked while stroking her cheek.

"I don't know." She couldn't help it when tears started to fall from her eyes. The emotion, the tenderness had been all too much for her, and all she wanted was to show Trent what she had unleashed from her heart. "I'm fine, I just need to touch you."

She moved to turn Trent onto her back. Trent let her, and Wendy straddled her stomach as she kissed her passionately. Wendy hadn't felt this kind of passion with anyone she had slept with since Bailey. She hadn't thought she had it in her any more, but she was wrong.

Trent grasped her buttocks and pulled Wendy to her groin, and they both began a rocking motion. Wendy started to pull away from Trent's kiss, grasped her lip between her teeth, and lightly bit it.

"You are a naughty girl." Trent groaned.

Wendy smiled. "We'll see."

She kissed her way down Trent's body and spent time kissing around her navel and stomach. Wendy could feel Trent's hips moving and thrusting into nothing.

"Jesus, I love the feel of your hair," Trent said hungrily.

Wendy noticed her hair was brushing Trent's inner thighs. Interesting.

She kissed her way down to Trent's sex, making sure her hair dragged slowly over the area. Trent's moans encouraged her that she was doing the right thing.

Trent sat up and said, "Suck it."

When Wendy ran her tongue around her clit, Trent grasped her two braids and held them, encouraging Wendy to get on with it, and she did, sucking Trent right into her mouth.

"Oh yes, good girl." Trent held her hair and thrust her hips faster.

Wendy loved hearing those words and feeling so free to give Trent this, after so long burying her needs and emotions.

Trent suddenly went stiff, grasped her hair tightly, and came with a low guttural moan. "Fuck."

Trent relaxed her hold on Wendy and she crawled back up Trent's body. They kissed and Trent said, "You are the most beautiful woman in the world."

"I'm not beautiful. I'm a hippy who you would be embarrassed to take to one of your fancy lawyer events."

Trent frowned. "Don't ever say that. I love…who you are. Besides, I don't let just anyone put me on my back."

Wendy chuckled. "Too used to being on top, eh?" She traced her fingers along the scar above Trent's eyebrow. "Don't worry. I like you to be the butch top you are—I just needed to show you how I felt."

"Why were you trembling and upset after you came, Dee? I didn't do anything you didn't like, did I?"

Wendy shook her head. "No, you couldn't. I didn't realize how much emotion and hurt I still had inside. I thought I had conquered it, but it was still in there, and the way you touched me, the way I was able to let go, it all came out."

"You must have had lovers since you split up with your ex," Trent said.

"I've had a few. It was just physical but this—" Wendy realized she had said too much. She wasn't ready to talk about feelings, so she kissed Trent and hoped she wouldn't ask any more.

❖

Trent woke up and saw Wendy standing by the window in her shirt. It was funny—normally after she'd had sex with someone, she'd try to think about how to get out the door. She contrasted the feeling in her heart with how she'd felt after sleeping with Lady Claudia. She'd wanted out even before it started. It had been such a mistake.

Wendy looked so sexy in her shirt, but going by the tension she could feel in the air, a remark like that wouldn't go down well.

"Dee? Are you all right?" Trent asked.

Wendy turned around. "Hi. I don't know if I'm all right, to be honest."

She was regretting it already, Trent thought. She sat up in bed and tried to build up the steely armour around her heart, but it wasn't working. Wendy had destroyed it.

"Look, Dee, if you think you've made a mistake, if you're looking for a way out—"

"No. It's not that." Wendy walked back over to the bed and sat. "Honestly, it's not that. I'm scared. I promised myself that even though I had feelings for you, I would stay strong, because I can't trust my emotions. I've never felt this way since Bailey."

"I'm not going to abscond with your life savings," Trent joked.

Wendy smiled. "I don't think it would be worth your while. It's not about that, it's…she broke my heart. You haven't been in a relationship for years, and maybe…Anyway, you're a divorce lawyer. You know how difficult relationships are."

Trent sighed and took her hand. "I could say that I would never do that to you. I could tell you that I've never cheated on anyone in my life, but I know that hurt young woman inside your head won't listen straight away, and you're right about my work. It's given me a pretty dim view of long-term relationships, but then I saw how happy Dale and Becca were. Did you know, I gave Becca away at their wedding?"

Wendy shook her head and slid closer. "No, was that hard for you?"

Trent remembered walking down the aisle holding Becca and her heart hurting a little when she saw Dale waiting for her.

"Somewhat, but it also made me realize that there was something missing from my life. Despite all the drinks parties and wine bars of an evening, I felt more alone than I ever had. I wanted more, but I didn't know how that was going to change. Then two children came running into my life, with you not far behind them."

Wendy cupped Trent's cheek. "I was lost and lonely too. I didn't just come back from abroad to finish uni. I was lonely. I lived and worked with all these families, and all I wanted was what they had. But you broke up with Becca because she wanted a family. Now you have an instant one, and you're doing really well, but if we take this further maybe it'll be too much."

"It's scary for both of us. I never imagined myself with a family like my friends', but despite all the difficulties, I've loved having the children here, and you have made my heart come to life again."

"Everything's happened so quickly," Wendy said.

Trent thought for a moment, then had an idea. "It has been fast due to the circumstances, and we've missed out all the normal dating things. How about we start at the beginning? We go on dates and see if these emotions feel right, and build trust?"

Wendy smiled. "Yes, that makes me feel so much better."

"And"—Trent sighed—"I can't believe I'm going to say this. We don't end up back here until you're ready."

"That's a perfect idea, Peter." Wendy kissed Trent's lips and it developed into a long, slow kiss. Wendy pulled back breathlessly. "When does this no-sex thing start?"

Trent looked at her bedside clock. It read half past four in the morning. "Seven o'clock?"

Wendy giggled. "Yes, plenty of time."

Trent pulled Wendy on top of her. "Come here, Wendy Darling."

CHAPTER SEVENTEEN

November had rolled into December, and Alice and Noah were starting the local school today. Trent was nervous about letting them go. They would be out without her protection, and that was difficult for her to handle. Officially they would be there until the summer holidays, then would be enrolled in boarding school, but going by how anxious she felt now, Trent had no idea how she would let them go, a thought that would take time for her to come to terms with.

Trent had purposely kept her morning free so she could go with the children to school.

They were standing outside the school gate. Children were shouting, laughing, and running around, while lots of parents stood in groups, more interested in talking to each other than watching their kids.

Wendy was trying to button up Noah's school blazer while Alice stood quietly beside Trent, holding her hand with a vice-like grip.

"Noah, stay still so I can button your jacket," Wendy said.

"I'm too excited." Noah seemed to be the only one looking forward to school.

Trent looked at Alice and saw tears in her eyes. "Hey, what's wrong, Ali? Don't cry."

"I don't want to go to school. I want to stay at home with Wendy."

Trent crouched down and gave her a hug. "I know it's scary when you don't know anyone, Ali, but you'll make friends. I promise. And I'll get in trouble if I don't send you to school."

Wendy piped in, "And we don't want that, do we?"

Alice shook her head.

"Besides," Wendy said, "it's December, so you'll be doing lots of projects for Christmas. Artwork, school nativity play, learning Christmas songs—it'll be great."

"Will you walk in with me?" Alice asked Trent.

"Of course I will. I'll take you both to the school office and let them know you're here." Trent had made the school aware of Alice's problems, and they promised to be very careful with her.

Trent stood up and said to Wendy, "Are you coming with us?"

Wendy said, "Why don't you take them in, and I'll wait for you at the car?"

Trent was the kids' strong parental figure, and Wendy thought she should do this by herself. She gave both kids hugs and walked away.

She got back to the car and turned on the radio. Just as she saw Trent come around the corner and walk towards the car, the big love song of the moment started playing. Her heart fluttered. Trent was utterly gorgeous, and in that moment she regretted their pledge to go slow.

Trent was more kind and loving than she gave herself credit for, and when she talked so lovingly to Alice at the gate, Wendy realized she was falling in love.

Despite their pledge to have dates and build the trust they had in each other, their dates consisted of watching a movie together and cuddling up on the couch, as they couldn't leave the children alone. Wendy loved the simple movie nights, but Trent, from what she had told her about her past, liked going out for dinner, for drinks at wine bars, generally very social things, and Wendy worried she might get bored.

Trent got into the car and let out a breath.

"Everything all right?" Wendy asked.

"That was one of the hardest things I've ever had to do."

"What happened?"

"The school secretary welcomed them and said she would take them to class, if I would like to leave. I could see how anxious Ali was, and I had to walk away."

Wendy's heart fluttered even more. "You really do love these kids, don't you."

Trent turned to her and smiled. "I never thought I'd ever say this, but I really do. They need someone and I want to be that someone."

Wendy couldn't help but lean over and kiss Trent tenderly. Trent smiled again. "What did I do to deserve that?"

"For being you, Peter."

Trent grinned. The term of endearment meant a lot to Trent. If Wendy thought of her that way, she was privileged.

Trent had started reading *Peter Pan* to Noah and Alice. She was intrigued by Wendy's love for the story and had never read it as a child. Fairy tales weren't encouraged by her nanny, but she was beginning to understand why Wendy liked it so much.

"Wendy, there's something I wanted to talk to you about."

Wendy looked worried. "Is it something we should be talking about in front of the school?"

"It's nothing bad, I hope. I know we haven't had the chance to be alone much and to get to know each other like we planned. The kids are always with us, and the closest thing we have to a date is watching a film together. At your age you want to be out enjoying life, and I'm wondering if what we have together is holding you back?"

"You're worrying about *that*?" Wendy started to laugh.

"Yes, why is it funny?"

"Before you got back to the car, I was worried that you missed your social life, dinners out at nice restaurants, wine bars—I thought watching movies with me was holding *you* back," Wendy said.

Trent cupped her cheek. "Never ever think that. I enjoy dinner with you and the kids and then having you in my arms on the couch as we watch whatever is on TV. I'm happy."

"Then we should both stop worrying and enjoy our time together."

The only thing Trent regretted was saying they should wait before ending up back in bed together. She wanted Wendy so much, and every night when she closed her eyes, all she could think of was making love to Wendy.

It was frustrating, but she wanted to make Wendy—and her heart—feel safe and comfortable with her.

"Now that we have that sorted out, I wanted to ask you something. Becca and Dale are going to Lapland to spend Christmas with their kids. It's a Christmas magic experience—you stay in a log cabin, do Christmas activities, and meet the real Santa Claus."

Trent winked at her last statement and Wendy laughed. "That sounds so sweet."

"Yes, Becca asked us to go. I thought it might be a good idea to take the kids' minds off their dad. I think Christmas is going to be hardest for them."

"I think that's a wonderful idea. Every kid dreams of going to visit Santa."

"I never had a magical Christmas. I hated it and was always jealous of how excited my school friends got about it. So I'd like to make it magical for them. Alice and Noah deserve it so much after what they've been through."

"Sounds perfect," Wendy said.

Wendy didn't seem to realize she was invited. "Would you come with us, Dee? I know you're entitled to your holiday away from us, and I don't want to press—"

Before Trent could finish her sentence, Wendy had thrown her arms around her. "I'd love to. It'll be magical, romantic."

"That's what I thought—we could spend time exploring our feelings. There will be lots for the kids to do."

Wendy kissed her and then gasped. "We've got barely three weeks to get everything we need—warm winter clothes, presents to take with us for them."

"Yes, it's going to be a rush, but I think it'll put smiles on the kids' faces, and that's what makes me happy," Trent said.

"You are sweet." Wendy giggled.

Trent furrowed her eyebrows and made her voice gruff. "I am not. I'm a ruthless lawyer."

"Not to me." Wendy grasped Trent's tie lightly. "I'm picturing an open fire and a large rug. So romantic."

Trent would make sure the cabin had those two things when she booked. She liked the sound of that. "I'm sure it will be."

CHAPTER EIGHTEEN

Preparation for the trip to Lapland had been fraught and stressful. Most of it was left to Wendy, since Trent's work schedule was less flexible. Alice and Noah were overjoyed when they found out and were looking forward to Christmas instead of dreading it. No doubt they would have some wobbles of emotion when the special days arrived.

They were leaving this morning, 23rd December, and returning on the 27th. Wendy was sure they would have a good time when they got there, but the stress of organizing two kids was getting to both her and Trent.

There were already two bags at the front door, and Trent was trudging back and forth to the bedrooms to get the rest, grousing and muttering as she went.

She'd been in a bad mood since she got up this morning and it was beginning to annoy Wendy.

"It feels likes there's lead weights in these cases," Trent muttered.

Wendy marched over to Trent and said, "They are heavy because you insisted the children get every present under the sun. Need I remind you that *I* got all the presents and the clothes, shopping in busy shops at the busiest time of the year. All you have to do is bring them out to the lift and get them into the car. So stop sniping at me."

"I'm not sniping. I just wish you could all be a bit more organized. The car I booked to the airport has already been waiting for fifteen minutes downstairs. We're going to be late."

"What is your problem? You've been in a bad mood since you got up."

"I have not. There's nothing wrong with me," Trent said defensively.

Wendy covered her face with her hands in frustration. This was their first fight since they became more than friends, and Wendy realized Trent was as stubborn as a mule.

"Just take the bags downstairs to the car, I'll round up Alice and Noah, and we can start our magical family holiday," Wendy snapped.

"Fine," Trent replied and walked off with two suitcases out to the lift.

Just as Wendy was about to go and get the kids, the house phone rang. She walked over to the kitchen and answered, "Hello, Trent residence."

"Good morning, could I speak to Trent, please?"

"We're actually just about to leave the house for a Christmas holiday. She's taking the luggage out to the car. Can I take a message?"

"Who am I talking to?" the voice said more sharply.

"I'm the nanny. May I take a message?"

"Tell her Claudia called. I'm sure she'll call me the first moment she can." Then without any niceties, the caller called Claudia hung up.

Strange. Wasn't that the name that kept calling Trent, that she ignored?

Trent stood up and leaned over the seats in front of her. Alice and Noah were engrossed in the movie playing in front of them, as was Jake across the aisle. Wendy had popped to the bathroom leaving her on her own.

"Awrite, mate?" She heard Dale's distinctive voice say. She turned around and Dale said, "Is it all right if I sit with you? The missus is talking to Wendy."

"Of course. I'm glad she's getting on well with Becca," Trent said.

Dale sat, stretched out her long frame, and crossed her ankles. "Aye, I hear you've got a thing going on." Dale smiled and winked at her.

She could be infuriating at times, especially this time, when Trent didn't want it to be a *thing*. She wanted it to be a relationship.

"We're seeing each other and taking it slow. Dee has issues about relationships and—" Trent paused and then rubbed the scar above her eyebrow. "What the hell am I talking about? *I* have issues with relationships—well, you know that."

"Well, it looks like you're doing good to me. Those two kids love you, and if that lassie is into you, then you're a lucky bastard. She's a belter," Dale said, smiling.

"What? Belter?" Trent asked with dismay.

"A smashing bird, a brilliant, gorgeous woman," Dale explained with exasperation. "I would have thought belter was self-explanatory."

Trent shook her head and smiled. "Not really. Sometimes I think you're making half of these Scottish words up to confuse me."

"Nah, seriously, she's really nice. Not how I pictured your type though. You're so...stiff."

"I said the same thing about you when you came into Becca's life," Trent said smugly.

Dale laughed. "Aye, and the rest."

Trent sighed. "I get the impression her friend has warned her off me."

Last night Wendy had gone to her room to talk to her friend Kira. Trent hadn't tried to listen but when she went to her office she overheard Wendy's side of the conversation.

"You don't know her, Ki. She's not like that and—No, she's not taking advantage of me, and age doesn't matter...Ki, please trust me, I can handle this. I promise I'll not jump into anything, and I know I've got my whole life in front of me."

"Her friend only knows me from my reputation, you see—"

"And what a reputation," Dale joked.

"Well, quite true, but that's work. This is—"

"Love?"

Trent nodded. "Yes, on my part, but they think I'm some sort of Lothario, as if I'm sleeping with the much younger nanny for the kick of it. Her friend may be right, but it's not even as if there've been lots of kicks."

Dale raised an eyebrow. "No?"

"Just one kick, and then we decided to go slow and get to know each other better."

Dale leaned in and whispered so the kids wouldn't hear. "That's why you look like a grumpy bastard."

Trent gave her a stare. "Is your wife not looking for you?"

"I'm only taking the piss," Dale said.

"Every so often I'm reminded of our age difference—the music we like, our politics, views on the world—and I'm worried that maybe her friend is right." Trent sighed.

"Age is nothing—don't worry about it. As long as it's what you both want. Besides, you're doing a good thing with the kids, seriously. Bringing Alice and Noah to Lapland for Christmas. Taking their mind off not having their da. Plus a lovely girl to spend your time with? Like I said, you're doing good, man."

"The terrifying thing is that she thinks I'm the experienced one, the wiser head to negotiate all these issues we have, but I'm not ashamed to say I'm terrified. Instant family, instant partner."

Trent jumped when she heard someone clear their throat. It was Wendy. "Dale? Becca would like to see you."

"Better go, my chain's being yanked back. See you later, mate," Dale said.

How much did Wendy hear? "Hi, did you have a nice chat?" Trent asked.

"Yes, you?" Wendy said.

The tone in Wendy's voice made Trent sure she'd heard her. Great.

"Just so this is clear, you came in on the end of a conversation. I was not complaining about having an instant family and partner. I might be a lot older than you, but I get scared too."

"Why are you scared?"

"I've never done a family Christmas. All this kid stuff that Dale will make amazing for her kids? Mine—I mean, Alice and Noah—will just have me. The only experience I have with Christmas is a drinks party at the Duke of Westminster's London mansion every year."

Wendy silenced her with a kiss. "It's not a competition. Ali and Noah love you. They'll have a great time with their new friends."

"I heard you on the phone with Kira last night. I didn't mean to listen but you were speaking quite loudly."

"Ah, that's why you've been in a terrible mood since this morning."

"Look, I don't know what your friend is telling you, but I'm not pressuring you into anything. We haven't even slept together again. I promised you could trust me."

"I know you're not. I said that to her. Kira doesn't know you—I do, and I know what I want."

"What's that?" Trent asked.

"You, and tonight we are going to have a night to ourselves. Becca's offered to take Ali and Noah for dinner and a sleepover." Wendy pointed at Trent's heart. "We are going to get to know each other alone, and then the next few days are family time. What do you think?"

A smile erupted on Trent's face. "That's the best idea you've ever had, Wendy Darling."

"Thank you, Peter. Oh—did you call back your friend Claudia before we left?"

Trent's smile faltered and she turned her attention to outside the plane window. "She's not my friend."

❖

They arrived in Rovaniemi Airport in Lapland. It was a mammoth task to get a gaggle of excitable children and many suitcases to the front of the airport, where the travel company's cars were waiting for them.

Wendy enjoyed the comical expression on Trent's face when their drivers and tour guide were dressed as elves and in full character for the children. Dale, of course, was straight into the spirit of the thing, as usual. The two families got into the two cars and set off for Santa's cabins.

Wendy could feel Trent's tension. It had to be strange for someone like Trent to go from a single life of adult activities and conversation to being driven to a cabin in Lapland by two elves driving a people carrier. But that was one of the reasons she was falling in love with Trent. She was willing to put her two young cousins ahead of herself. She had such a kind heart, which no one who had heard her reputation as a lawyer would believe.

Ali held on to Trent's hand and Noah would barely stop talking.

"Santa's elves are driving us to Santa!"

Wendy, who was sitting beside Noah, added, "Yes, it's magical, isn't it?"

Ali, who had been quiet said, "Dad would have loved this."

Wendy looked to Trent, who nodded. Trent put her arm around Alice and said, "He will be so happy knowing that you are here to enjoy it. David wouldn't want you to be sad, Ali."

She nodded and laid her head on Trent's chest.

Wendy couldn't stop smiling. Trent was doing everything exactly right. She was so proud of her.

Alice soon became distracted by the snowy landscape. There was something about snow that excited children. She didn't understand it, although she could see how beautiful it was.

The cars finally pulled into a small car park beside a large rustic wooded building. The girl elf in the passenger seat turned around and said, "Okay, girls and boys, we just need you to sign Santa's guestbook at the reception building, and then we'll transport you to your cabins."

"By car? I don't see any roads," Trent asked.

The elf smiled. "No, by Santa's reindeer."

Wendy gasped and pointed as three large sleighs, pulled by reindeer, arrived at the front of the wooden reception building.

Alice and Noah started to squeal. "There's Santa's reindeer!"

"Oh my God," Trent said as she shook her head.

CHAPTER NINETEEN

The wooden cabin was surrounded by snowy wilderness. Trent had to admit it was truly breathtaking. Alice, Noah, and Jake immediately went out to play in the snow, while the adults unpacked. The two cabins were just a few hundred yards apart, good for allowing the children to play together.

Pleasingly, the large cabin did have a wood-burning fireplace, just like Wendy had hoped. It was picture-perfect. Trent was watching the kids out the window as they started making a snowman.

She felt Wendy's presence behind her and shivered when she put her palm on her back.

"Here's some coffee."

"Thanks."

"Are you still mad?" Wendy asked.

When they had gotten out of the car at reception, she had been smacked in the head by a large snowball thrown by Dale. She wasn't best pleased.

"No, I'm just happy to see Ali and Noah happy." Trent put her arm around Wendy.

They were very slowly building up their intimacy together, especially since they took so much care not to let Alice and Noah see. Wendy had suggested it wouldn't be wise to let the kids get their hopes up that the two people they loved would be together.

"You just have to get her back. We'll ambush her with snowballs at the earliest opportunity."

Trent sighed. "I'm not well-versed in snow etiquette or snowball fights—I never really did that kind of thing as a child. I was moulded into an adult at a very early age."

Just then they saw Dale walking across the snowy landscape to join the children. "I don't have the skills Dale has."

"Listen, I know you're nervous about making this a nice Christmas for them, but it's going to be great. I promise I'll help you make it great."

"What were your Christmases like as a child?" Trent asked.

Wendy smiled. "I went to stay with my grandparents, thank God. Mum and Dad weren't interested. I got an envelope of money for Christmas from them, but Grandpa and Grandma made it special. What did you and Becca do at Christmas?"

Trent smiled. "A completely adult Christmas. We did the whole drinks party circuit with our group of friends, and then we went on a skiing holiday to Switzerland. It was on our last Christmas holiday that things started to go wrong."

"How do you mean?" Wendy asked.

"Becca hadn't been herself for a while. You know the story about her father?"

"Yeah, I doubt there's many people that don't. It was in the newspapers for years, it seemed like."

"Yes, well, her father had tried to commit suicide in prison, and emotionally things were difficult for her."

"Did he die?"

Trent shook her head. "No, not that time, but it started a need in Becca for more, for a family like she never had. I see now that this is what she wanted. Family, Santa Claus, making things magical for your children—not skiing—but I wasn't even near the right place for that. I withdrew in terror from what she wanted, and eventually we broke up. She found the right person for her, as hard as that was for me."

"From my talks with her, Becca seems to really care for you," Wendy said.

Trent pulled Wendy closer. "Yes, I know she does. She could have cut me out of her life after she got together with Dale. I mean, I wasn't the nicest when Dale came into the picture, but she insisted on making me part of their extended family. I suppose we share a lot of history together." Trent started to chuckle. "I bet she never thought we'd be going to Lapland together on the ultimate family holiday."

"Life is a journey. We adapt and change along the way. You maybe weren't ready back then, but you are now. Trent, you don't give yourself enough credit. You made the breakthrough with Ali—not me, not the doctor. Follow your instincts, and they won't take you far wrong."

"Maybe, but only because you give me confidence and reassurance." Trent kissed her softly. "So, what is our itinerary, Wendy Darling?"

"Well, Peter…" Wendy went to the coffee table and picked up the welcome booklet. "A Christmas tree and decorations will be delivered tomorrow by Santa's elves at ten o'clock, and then after we can decorate it together, with hot chocolate."

"They do really think of everything. And then?"

"Uh…a husky ride to visit Santa's Grotto, then back here to toast marshmallows in front of the fire, and eggnog for the adults. I did say we'd have Becca, Dale, and the kids here tomorrow night for dinner."

Trent turned to Wendy and said seriously, "You do know you're not here as nanny and cook for the rest of us? I could order a meal from the hotel restaurant to be delivered, just like tonight."

Wendy placed her hands on Trent's chest. "What am I here as?"

Trent wasn't quite sure if she had the bottle to tell the truth. She took a moment and replied, "You're here as part of the family, my lover, if you'll have me."

Wendy didn't answer her straight away, and so Trent took that as a bad sign. "I mean girlfriend or—I mean, just because I say *lover* doesn't mean I expect anything in that department if you don't want to."

Wendy silenced her with a kiss. "Shut up. Why do you think I've organized this night alone together?" She pulled away from the kiss quickly. "The kids are coming back."

Trent pointed to her lips. "Can I get another one of these later?"

Wendy grinned. "If you play your cards right, Peter."

❖

Wendy watched as Trent tied up Noah's and Ali's scarves. She thought Trent was more anxious about them going to stay with Dale and Becca than the children were. It was sweet. Dale had arrived to take them over to their cabin.

"Remember, Ali, if you feel nervous or have any bad dreams, I'll come and get you straight away."

Dale put an arm around Alice. "She'll be fine. We're gonna have fun. Come on."

Alice hugged Trent tightly and gave her a kiss.

"Let's go, little guy, princess girl," Dale said.

"Bye, Trent, bye, Wendy," Noah said.

"Bye."

When the door shut, Wendy slipped into Trent's arms. "So what are your plans? After dinner should we toast some marshmallows by the fire?" Wendy grinned.

"Well, we could do that, or we could drink the champagne I ordered in the hot tub."

Wendy gasped. "There's a hot tub? You never told me that."

"Only the best of cabins for us. It was meant to be a surprise. I thought it would be romantic," Trent said.

Wendy moved in on Trent's lips. "That pales the fireplace into insignificance."

They kissed and Wendy wished they could fast-forward to the hot tub right that second. "Thank you for making this effort for us," Wendy said.

Trent stroked her fingers across Wendy's cheek. "I would do anything for you, Dee."

That comment made a huge impact on Wendy. No matter what Kira tried to tell her, she knew Trent was serious about her.

❖

Trent held Wendy's hand across the dinner table. The meal, the candles, the music were perfect.

"You know how much you being here means to me?" Trent said.

"I think I do." Wendy smiled.

"It means the children are part of the package," Trent said.

Wendy frowned. "Do you think that puts me off? Peter Pan says, *To die will be an awfully big adventure*, but I think to live a life with you will be an awfully big adventure."

"I hope so, but we won't have many times to be alone like this," Trent said.

"That's what families are like, and what I've always wanted. Why don't we start our own little adventure?"

Trent grinned. "The hot tub?"

Wendy gave a sly smile and nodded. "You go and get it going, and I'll get changed into something…more appropriate."

Trent's heart and clit started to beat at the same time. "Hurry."

Wendy hurried off to her room and Trent blew out the candles, locked up the doors, and went out to start up the hot tub. Luckily it didn't face Dale and Becca's cabin, so they had complete privacy.

Trent then changed into shorts and a T-shirt and headed back out with the champagne, ice bucket, and glasses. She poured two glasses and set them on the side. She slipped into the warm water and pulled off her T-shirt. As she was waiting on Wendy, Trent took a drink of her champagne and took in the landscape. It was a magical scene, to be surrounded by thick snow as far as the eye could see, and thick pine forest with snow-covered branches.

As she looked around she thought, if this was what Wendy really wanted, maybe she should think about making some serious decisions. Yes, it was time to get serious with life.

"It's like a Christmas card."

Trent jumped. "What is?" She hadn't even heard Wendy approach. She looked up and said, "Jesus, you are gorgeous."

Wendy had on a bikini. The top didn't cover a lot of her breasts, and the bottoms were held together by a knot.

Suddenly Wendy looked bashful. "Are you sure? I haven't had much experience with these things."

From their brief discussion of these matters, Trent had gathered that Wendy was turned on by her being the older dominant woman, and that suited Trent just fine.

"Come here and I'll show you how perfect it is."

Wendy slipped into the water. "This feels amazing."

"It's even better if you come and sit here." Trent pulled her onto her lap, facing outwards so she could see the scenery, then handed her a glass of champagne. "Take a drink and look out at this beautiful scene."

"It's magical," Wendy said with awe in her voice.

Trent held on to her hips underwater and had to stop herself from thrusting her hips into Wendy. They weren't there yet, but Trent was. She was throbbing, and her sex would have been wet even without the water, but she had to make this special for Wendy.

Trent ran her fingers up and down Wendy's back a few times before stopping by the string that held the top on.

"I don't think you need this, do you?"

"No," Wendy said.

Trent undid the string and Wendy pulled off the top. As it floated away, she turned around and sat facing Trent, in her lap.

The sight of Wendy's breasts, nipples hard and dripping with water, was almost enough to make her come on the spot.

"I love your breasts." She grasped them both and brushed the nipples with her thumbs.

Wendy pursed her lips and hummed in pleasure. "Hmm, kiss me."

Trent kissed her soft and slow, her tongue tasting and dancing with Wendy's. She loved the feel of Wendy's breasts. They were soft and real. Trent pulled away from her lips and placed kisses on Wendy's wet, dripping breasts. "I need to taste these now."

She kissed all around them but when she traced her tongue around Wendy's nipple, she felt Wendy's hips jerk.

"You like that?" Trent asked.

"Yeah, they're very sensitive."

That was all Trent needed to hear. She couldn't wait to suck Wendy's wet nipple into her mouth.

Wendy moaned and held her arms tightly around Trent's neck. Every time Trent would change from licking to sucking and back again, Wendy's arms tightened, and she moaned and thrust her hips.

Trent bet she would love to come here in the hot tub, so she pulled the ties on the sides and took the bottoms off.

Wendy grinned and grasped Trent's hand and tried to push it to her sex. Trent didn't let her, as she guessed saying no would turn her on.

"No, I don't think so," Trent said while grasping her buttocks under the water.

Trent knew she was right to say no by the movement of Wendy's hips. She looked at Wendy's blissed-out face. Her eyes were closed, and her hair was now wet, with her little braids hanging around her face. She was the most beautiful woman Trent had ever seen.

Wendy opened her eyes and saw Trent gazing at her, her eyes full of want and mischief. Trent was such a good lover. She seemed to sense exactly what Wendy craved and she was so generous.

"I always fantasized about someone like you," Wendy said.

"What did a naughty girl like you fantasize about?"

"An older, dominant butch, that—like I said before—I didn't need to look after, or take the lead for. She would just know what I needed. There was always so much pressure on me to take the lead and look after Bailey. She had the maturity of a child."

"Let's not talk about her. You're mine now," Trent said.

"Yes," Wendy breathed. She loved that proprietary statement. It was so hot.

Trent pulled her close and whispered, "You're going to come."

"Yes."

Trent kissed her breast again a few times before taking her nipple in her mouth.

The pleasure was painfully exquisite for Wendy. The electric jolt of pleasure travelled directly to her clit. She only got relief from the ache when Trent palmed her sex and gently squeezed.

She shivered at the cool air wafting across her shoulders and said, "Oh yeah, please?" when Trent traced her fingers around her clit. Wendy was praying she would go inside, and she did. Wendy groaned and stilled momentarily.

Trent let her nipple go with a pop and sat back against the tub. "Show me how much you want to come."

Trent's confidence was intoxicating. She felt like she would do anything she told her. Wendy rested her hands on the edge of the tub, just behind Trent's shoulders, and started to undulate her hips on Trent's fingers. The sensation of the water was exciting, as if she was floating to an orgasm, and she could see Trent's eyes glued on her breasts bobbing in and out of the water.

It felt so good to be desired. She wanted to be desired, wanted, loved, everything rolled into one.

She felt the pressure building in her sex. "I'm going to come soon."

Trent pulled her closer and helped her by thrusting her fingers. "Come, I'll keep you safe."

Those words *I'll keep you safe* were as intoxicating as any others Trent could say to her.

She stilled and held Trent tightly, and let her orgasm wave over her like the water around them.

"I've got you, darling," Trent said as Wendy's breathing calmed.

Wendy laughed softly, "Darling?"

"My Wendy Darling." Trent smiled.

"That was so good." Wendy kissed Trent on the lips.

Trent kissed her back feverishly. She was taut, wound up, and ready to burst.

"You need to come," Wendy said.

Trent licked the water droplets from Wendy's lips. "I want to come while I'm inside you."

Wendy grinned. "Is that why you looked a bit sheepish when our bags went through the scanner at the airport?"

Trent said, "Perhaps, but I'll not use it if you don't like it, of course."

Wendy was starting to get excited already. She leaned into Trent's ear and whispered, "Tell me I'll like it."

It was Trent's turn to groan. After a few seconds she said forcefully, "You'll like it. Let's go to bed and mess up the sheets."

CHAPTER TWENTY

Trent exited the en suite with her strap-on held down by her black jockey shorts. The hard length of her strap-on exactly matched how ready she was after watching Wendy come for her in the hot tub. This had been one of the best nights of her life so far, and it wasn't even finished.

Wendy was standing in front of the mirror, brushing her hair. Behind her was a super king sleigh bed. Wendy was naked, her skin still red from the hot water, and droplets of water still dripped down her skin. The sight of her younger lover waiting for her, ready for her, still wet from the hot tub made her hunger, want, need like she hadn't done since she was a much younger woman. She had always had a high sex drive, but as she had grown older, her desperate need for sex had diminished, but now with Wendy, it was as if her soul was being reborn.

She was drawn over to Wendy and her eyes and hands were drawn to her lover's buttocks. Trent pushed her hips into Wendy's buttocks so Wendy could feel the hardness. Wendy immediately turned around and placed one arm around her neck, while with the other she softly scratched her nails around Trent's breasts and nipples, and down her stomach.

"Do you have any idea how sexy you look?"

"I saw where you were looking." Wendy smiled and moved her hand down to gasp Trent's bulge.

"Here?" Trent pinched her bum cheek.

"Yeah," Wendy squeaked.

"It does look good enough to eat." Trent's arousal was growing by the second with Wendy rubbing her strap-on through her jockey shorts.

Wendy whispered, "You've given me so much. This is all for you." She lowered onto her knees and kissed all over Trent's bulge.

"Jesus." Looking down and watching Wendy kiss her there was beginning to make her feel like she had the control of a teenage boy. She softly grasped Wendy's hair. "Come up here. I need to come, and I want to do it when I'm inside you."

When Wendy stood, Trent kissed her passionately and manoeuvred her onto the bed. She kissed and squeezed her breast while she pulled her strap-on from the waistband of her underwear.

She rubbed it up and down her lover's wetness. "Are you okay?"

"Yes, just put it in me."

The rawness of Wendy's request took her by surprise and doubled her hunger. She eased in the tip and realized her lover probably wasn't used to using one. Being the first to give her pleasure in this way was also a turn-on, because no matter what Wendy said about this being about her, she would always be concerned about giving Wendy pleasure before herself.

She eased her strap-on in an inch at a time, being mindful of any tension in Wendy's face or gasps. Trent was nearly all the way in—she just needed Wendy to relax.

"Dee? Look at me?"

She did and Trent leaned in to give her the softest of kisses. "Relax for me—just trust me and relax." Trust always seemed to be the magic word with Wendy. She felt her immediately relax and her strap-on moved easily all the way in.

"Is that okay?" Trent asked her.

"Yes, it feels so full."

"Good." Trent started with tiny thrusts until she was moving smoothly in and out. "Jesus, you feel so good." Trent groaned.

Wendy was rolling her hips right along with her. "Yeah, it feels good."

Trent wanted Wendy to enjoy every second of this experience and not race to the end simply for her sake. She slowed her pace and alternated between circling her hips and long deliberate thrusts.

Soon both of them were desperate and racing to the edge. Trent felt Wendy's legs wrap tight behind her hips, locking them closely together, but Trent wanted them to be even closer.

She asked Wendy to relax her legs, and then lifted them over each shoulder, allowing her to be closer and thrust deeper. Trent couldn't stop herself from starting to come when Wendy's legs trembled and Wendy came with a low guttural moan. Trent's hips thrust erratically as she followed her over the edge.

Trent collapsed onto Wendy, and Wendy held her tightly until their breathing calmed. Then their mouths came together in soft low kisses.

Wendy pulled back and stroked Trent's brow. "That was amazing."

"It really was," Trent agreed.

Trent felt like she would burst if she didn't say what was in her heart. She placed her hand on Wendy's heart and said, "Wendy Darling, I love you to Neverland and back."

Wendy look stunned and gulped a few times. "Peter, I—"

Just then Trent's mobile began to ring. Trent sighed and reached for it on the bedside table.

It was Becca. She sat up immediately, worried about Alice and Noah. "Becca?"

Wendy sat up and placed a hand on her back.

"No, don't worry about it, I'll be right over." Trent hung up.

"What's wrong?"

Trent rubbed her face. "Ali had a nightmare and won't calm down. I'm sorry."

"Why are you sorry?"

"Because this was our first night alone, but I have to take care of her. I will always have to put them first," Trent said.

Wendy smiled and kissed her cheek. "That is the sweetest thing you've ever said. Of course they come first, on you go."

CHAPTER TWENTY-ONE

The next morning, after everyone had a lie in, Wendy cooked breakfast and then they waited on the arrival of the tree and decorations. Alice was stuck like glue to Trent after last night, but Noah stood at the window as lookout for their decorations.

Finally the decorations arrived. Wendy cleared up breakfast while Trent and the kids got the tree ready to decorate. She looked out the kitchen window and was awed by the snowy landscape. This place really seemed to have a magic that transported you into a world where anything was possible—Santa Claus, elves, flying reindeer, happy ever after with a well-known ruthless divorce lawyer...

Wendy wasn't as scared of the future here. This felt like a family holiday, and a family she was part of.

But what scared her was what Trent had said last night. Trent said she loved her, and even though Wendy knew she loved Trent, there was a part of her heart that made her hesitate, the last part of her that remembered how badly she was hurt before and how devastated she would be if she was hurt again.

She picked up Trent's mobile so she could wipe the table and noticed it had two missed calls.

She was distracted when Trent shouted, "Dee? We're ready to start, are you?"

"One minute, you guys." There were two more things to do to make the day special. She hurried and got the special item from her bag in the bedroom and went back to the living area. She beckoned Trent over. "You have a few missed calls on your mobile."

"Do I? I'll check later."

Trent seemed evasive for some reason, but she let it go. "When I get the music going, give them this," Wendy said.

She handed over a clear glass bauble with a picture of Alice, Noah, and David, their dad. Underneath the picture was glitter and etched on the front it said *Daddy, Always in Our Hearts*. Trent looked touched.

"This is beautiful. When did you get this made?"

"Before we left. I thought it would be nice to make their dad part of Christmas. Even though we are trying to take their minds off their grief, it's important that they remember him."

Trent gazed at her lovingly and reached out to caress her cheek. "You truly are the kindest, most beautiful woman I know."

"Trent," Noah shouted and they stepped apart.

"I'll get the music."

Wendy hooked up her iPhone to the Bluetooth speakers, and the Christmas songs started to play.

Trent kneeled down by the foot of the tree and handed Alice the bauble. "This is the first bauble we're going to put on the tree. Wend—"

Wendy cut her off. "Trent had this idea and had it made for you both. Isn't it special?"

Trent gave Wendy a confused look. "But…"

Alice leapt from her seated position and wrapped her arms around Trent, then Noah followed.

Trent mouthed, "Why did you say that?"

Wendy just smiled in response and Trent realized what she was doing. Making her look like the hero to boost her bond with Alice and Noah.

"Thank you, Trent. We love you." Trent gave in to Wendy and let herself enjoy the hug.

"You're welcome. I want you to know we will always remember your dad. His will be the first decoration on our tree every year," Trent said.

Alice pulled back and just looked at her, then said, "Will we always have Christmas with you?"

"Yes." Trent kissed them both. "I know we had a rough start, but we've managed to get along together, and this is as good a time as any to tell you."

Wendy looked at her quizzically. "What?"

"Before I left home, I asked my lawyer to set the wheels in motion so I could get full custody of you both, and eventually adopt you." Trent held her breath waiting for the reaction.

"We stay with you in our forever home?"

Trent nodded. "What do you think?"

"What about boarding school?" Alice asked.

"No, I'll enrol you both in a local private school. I want to see you every day, not just in the holidays."

Both kids squealed and jumped on her excitedly. Trent squeezed them tightly.

Wendy had the biggest smile on her face. "Thank you. You've made them really happy."

Trent closed her eyes and felt the love these two precious kids were giving her. She opened her eyes and looked up at Wendy. "I love you all."

Trent wanted Wendy to be a part of their family. She was ready for this, but was Wendy? Maybe she wanted to enjoy her youth, dating women of her own age. She had said that older women were a turn-on for her, but making Trent her partner and getting an instant family was a very different thing.

Not only had she started the proceedings for custody, but she'd also started to look for a family home, not a penthouse flat, for them to settle down. It was going to be a surprise for the kids, and she hoped Wendy might want to settle with them.

They spent the next few hours laughing and joking while they decorated the tree until it was finally time to switch on the lights.

"Okay, Noah. You can have the honours," Trent said. "Press the button."

"This one?" Noah pointed.

Alice put her arm around him. "Press it, Noah."

He did, and they all gasped as the multicoloured lights twinkled. When they had been decorating, the choice of clear lights or multicoloured ones had been a hotly contested debate between Trent and Wendy, but of course Trent followed Wendy's lead and it had worked out beautifully, as always.

"You were right about the multicoloured lights, Dee."

"I know." Wendy grinned. "All the different colours are much better for a kids' tree."

Trent squeezed Alice's shoulder. "What do you think, Ali?"

Alice walked closer to the tree and touched the bauble with her dad's picture in it, then turned to look at Trent. She smiled with such openness and with such emotion that Trent felt her take that final piece of her heart she was holding back.

"I love it," Alice said. Trent felt Noah hug her legs and so she put her arm around him. "My dad will love it."

In this moment, standing next to Wendy and with two children smiling up at her, Trent felt what had been missing in her life. Now she just had to convince Wendy that they belonged together, and the picture would be complete.

CHAPTER TWENTY-TWO

It was Christmas Eve, and Trent, Dale, and all the kids were going on a husky ride to Santa's Grotto. Wendy and Becca were staying behind with Gracie to make a buffet dinner. Gracie was too young for the husky ride.

Becca kissed Dale and Jake and said, "You make sure Jake is safe in that thing. They go very fast."

"Don't worry, hen. I'll take care of him."

Trent then said, "I can't believe we're going on a husky ride to Santa's Grotto. If my colleagues hear about this, my reputation as a tough negotiator will be gone."

Wendy chuckled. "No one outside these four walls need ever know. Now remember, magic doesn't just happen—you need to make it happen."

Wendy had been telling Trent this all day, when she was complaining about the husky ride. This part with Santa was the main event, the experience that would make Santa alive in their minds, and it was up to Trent.

After they left, Wendy said, "I think we deserve a glass of wine."

"Yes, please."

Becca sat Gracie at the kitchen table with her favourite Disney movie on an iPad. Wendy took two bottles of wine out of the drinks fridge and said, "White or sparkling rosé?"

"Oh, sparkling, I think. It is Christmas Eve, after all."

Wendy poured them out two glasses and said, "Isn't it nice that the elves provided us with wine and lots of it?"

Becca laughed. "They knew we'd be stressed out with a gaggle of kids at Christmas. So how did things go last night?"

Wendy could feel the heat of a blush on her cheeks. "It was really special. Thanks for looking after the children."

"Don't mention it. I am only sorry your night was cut short. Alice has really bad nightmares, but it's not surprising," Becca said.

"They've gotten a lot better recently. It was probably being away from Trent. Trent is her rock."

Becca smiled and shook her head. "I never thought I'd see Trent changing her life like this. I'm so proud of her."

"Yes, me too. The kids were so happy to find out they were staying with Trent," Wendy said.

"It'll be the best thing she ever does. So, are you together officially?"

"Not yet, but she told me she loved me last night."

Becca hugged her. "That's so wonderful."

"I'm finding it hard to let go of that final piece of my heart. I've been so hurt before," Wendy said.

"You can trust her, Wendy. Trent never gave me cause to distrust her, and the way she looks at you is plain to see. She loves you."

"I just need some more time. We better get this food cooked before they come back starving."

❖

Trent had to admit, rushing through the wintery forest on a dog sleigh was exhilarating. She kept a firm hold on Noah and Alice, but they seemed to be loving it. The ten minute ride was slowing down. Dale and Jake's sleigh was in front of them, and when they came to a stop, Dale shouted, "Woo-hoo! That was amazing. We beat you, Trent."

"She's such a show-off," Trent said to Alice and Noah. "Why don't we teach her a lesson?"

"Yay!" Noah said.

After they were helped out of the sleigh, Trent gathered up a snowball and threw it at Dale. It hit her square on the back of the head. "Bull's-eye!" Trent shouted.

"You got her, "Alice said excitedly.

Dale turned around slowly and glared at Trent, but then the corners of her mouth lifted into a sly smile. "Snowball fight!" Dale shouted.

Dale, Jake, Trent, Alice, and Noah started a full-blown snowball fight. They laughed and giggled throughout. Trent had never done anything like this before. It was so unlike her, but she loved it.

The fight ended when a rather serious elf admonished them and said Santa was waiting for them. So they calmed and walked up a cleared path into the forest. In a clearing they came upon a cute little cottage.

Dale leaned over and said, "You know, in other circumstances, a cottage like this in the middle of the forest would be in a horror movie."

Trent laughed and they approached the door. The elf leading them said for one child to knock. Dale told Alice to go ahead.

The door opened and a lady dressed as Mrs. Claus answered with a big smile. "Hello, children."

After some milk and cookies they were taken through to Santa. Trent had to admit that he looked like the perfect Santa. Alice held on to Trent's hand tightly while Jake and Noah went first.

When it came to Alice's turn, she hesitated. They hadn't talked about it, but Alice was probably too old to truly believe in Santa, though she was entering into the spirit.

"Hello, little girl, your name is Alice, isn't it?" Santa said.

"Yes."

"What would you like for Christmas, Alice?"

Alice looked to her and then back to Santa. Trent was worried she'd ask for her dad back. That was one piece of magic no one could perform.

Instead she said, "I'd like my dad in heaven to know how happy we are with Trent, and how much we love her."

If there was any speck of hardness left in Trent's heart, it truly melted then and there.

❖

"I'll treasure that moment forever."

Wendy was lying with her head on Trent's chest while Trent told her what had happened at the grotto.

They came home and enjoyed the evening with their friends, and then after the children went to bed, they put out the presents. Then they went to Trent's room and couldn't help but make love.

"You see," Wendy said, "you have to make the magic happen. That was a special moment."

"It was. I'm very lucky."

Wendy kissed Trent's lips and said, "I better go back to my room before the kids find us in the morning." Wendy got up and started to put on her clothes.

Trent sat up in bed. "Why don't we just tell them? I don't want to be apart from you."

Wendy sighed. "What would we tell them? We're dating to see how it goes and figure out how we feel? You can't do that with children, especially these two who have been through so much emotionally."

Trent got out of bed and pulled on her jeans and a T-shirt. "I know what I want. I want you, Dee. I love you."

Wendy was silent and started to get dressed. "Give me a chance. I'm old enough to know what I want. I want you and the children to be a family."

"Maybe *you're* not ready for a family. You're young—maybe you want to live a bit first."

"Would you stop with the age thing? It's nothing to do with that. I've been ready for a family since I was sixteen years old. The truth is, I love you and I'm frightened," Wendy said. "I don't think I could survive another broken heart. I need time. The kids knowing would just add pressure. We probably shouldn't have done this," Wendy said. "Is that all right?"

Trent walked around the bed to Wendy. "Everything is all right, now I know you love me."

They kissed softly and then Trent's door opened. It was Alice, who gasped and ran away.

"Shit," Trent said.

"Go and get her. Just be honest with her," Wendy said.

"Okay."

Trent put on shoes and walked into the living area. Through the window she saw Alice standing on the deck of the porch. She grabbed a fur blanket from the couch and went outside.

"Ali? Come inside."

Trent wrapped the blanket around her and said again, "Please come inside. We'll talk and I'll tell you the truth."

Alice was silent when she walked back in but she was shivering.

"Sit down on the couch and I'll start the fire to warm you up."

Making fire was a new skill for Trent and it took her several attempts before it caught light. "I bet Dale does it first time," Trent said under her breath.

Trent went back to Alice and sat beside her. She looked like she had retreated into her shell again.

"Alice, I know what you saw between Wendy and me, and I think we should talk about it."

"Don't want to talk," Alice muttered.

How should she do this? Wendy said the truth, so that's what she would do.

"Now, Ali, I told you last night that you and Noah were going to stay with me. A forever home and family. I don't want to start our family life with misunderstandings and bottled-up feelings."

"Fine," Alice snapped.

Trent let out a long breath. "Okay, well, Wendy and I have been getting closer over the last few weeks. We have feelings for each other, but we're just trying to work out what we are to each other."

"In your bedroom?" Alice said with anger.

"Why does that make you angry, Ali? You love Wendy," Trent said.

"I do, but we just got you, and now you're going to love someone else."

Suddenly it dawned on Trent what the problem was. "Ali, I do love Wendy, but that love in no way takes away from my love for you and Noah—it only makes it better. I'd love to make a family with you two and Wendy, but Wendy has had her heart broken, and she's being careful."

"Why didn't you tell us?" Alice had a softer tone in her voice.

"Wendy didn't want you to feel bad if we didn't work out, and it became awkward with her being your nanny."

Alice started to cry and threw her arms around Trent. "I thought you wouldn't want us if you had Wendy. I'm sorry I ran away."

Trent squeezed her tightly and kissed her head. "Of course I want you and Noah, and no matter what happens with Wendy and me, I will love you and keep you safe. We can even write out a contract if you want," Trent joked.

Alice giggled. "I believe you, and I love Wendy. We have to make her part of our family."

"Let's see how it goes. Adult relationships are complicated," Trent said.

"But you can make her believe," Alice said.

Trent pointed to the Christmas tree. "Look, Santa's been. We better get you back to bed. Noah will be up at the crack of dawn to open gifts."

❖

Wendy yawned and brought out two cups of coffee for herself and Trent. She sat down and laid her head on Trent's shoulder. "Christmas morning is tiring."

"But so much fun," Trent said happily.

Who would have thought Trent would throw herself into Christmas like this. She had a video camera set up on the other side of their tree to capture this moment forever.

"You got them so much—you'll spoil them," Wendy said.

"It's what I like to do, I'm a giver." Trent winked and Wendy laughed.

"True."

Alice came over when she unwrapped her iPhone and iPad and hugged Trent.

"Thank you, Trent."

Trent cupped her cheek. "Anything to see a smile on your face."

Then Noah ran over and jumped on Wendy's lap. "Xbox, I got an Xbox from Santa."

"You did?" Wendy turned to Trent. "Why did Santa think that Noah needed another games system?"

Trent grinned. "I believe Santa said that Jake had one, so Noah needed one. They can play their games together now."

Trent was still competitive with Dale—it was funny. Then Trent's mobile rang, and she grabbed it from the coffee table quickly.

"Who's calling you on Christmas Day?" Wendy asked.

"It's business, I need to take this. Excuse me."

Trent left the room and Wendy felt a bit annoyed. She thought Trent had left the workaholic side of her behind.

Five minutes later, Trent came back into the room with a strained look upon her face.

"Everything all right?"

Trent clapped her hands together. "Yes. Ali? Can you bring me that present?"

She pointed to a large square present, perfectly wrapped. Alice brought it over and Trent came to sit beside her again.

"This is for you, from me and the children."

Wendy clasped her hand to her chest. "Oh, thank you. I wasn't expecting anything."

"Well you should, because you are special to us."

"Open it, Wendy," Alice said, full of smiles.

She unwrapped the present and found a black velvet box with *Cartier* printed in gold on the top.

She looked up at Trent. "What have you done?"

"I knew you weren't a regular jewellery person, but I wanted you to have something special, and when I saw this, I knew it was perfect."

Wendy opened up the box and saw a gold necklace with three thick loops, two gold, one silver, each encrusted with small diamonds. She was stunned.

"We wanted something to make you think of us. The two gold hoops are Alice and Noah, and the silver one is me. You can keep us close to your heart, wherever you are."

Wendy was in shock.

"You like what Santa brought, Wendy?" Noah asked.

Wendy couldn't stop the tears from dropping from her eyes. She knew that this was it for her. No more being afraid.

"I love it, and I love all of you. I'm not going to be frightened any more, Trent. I want all three of you as my family."

The three of them engulfed her in a hug. "We love you," Alice said.

Wendy looked in Trent's eyes. "I love you and I'm yours."

CHAPTER TWENTY-THREE

I said to him, forget it. I want to have fun. I'm not going to become some stuffy old viscount's wife and pop out an heir and a spare at my age—I want to live a bit first."

The door to Trent's office was ajar and she couldn't help but pick up on India's telephone conversation.

It was late Friday afternoon on a wet, gloomy January day. The excitement of Christmas in Lapland had ebbed away for Trent. Now she was back to reality, and worries and uncertainties had beset her, backed up by what she had just heard India say about her boyfriend.

She clicked the screen on her computer and brought up the details of the property she had put in an offer for before the holidays. Wendy had been annoyed at her secretiveness around phone calls and messages while they were in Lapland, but at the time Trent thought it was all worth it. Now in the harsh light of day, she wondered if she was doing the right thing.

She looked over at the outfit hanging on her bathroom door. Wendy had picked out jeans and a jacket from her wardrobe and bought her an appropriate T-shirt to wear with them. Her clothes were meant to make her fit in with those attending Wendy's show tonight.

Her band was playing their first gig since they got back together, and Becca and Dale were looking after the children so they could enjoy the night together. Wendy said she could wear what she wanted, but Trent didn't want to stand out and embarrass her.

The outfit, along with this night at a pub venue, was yet another reminder of their age gap, and that was what was niggling away at her. Before she went away with Wendy and the kids, and she'd set the ball in motion to adopt Alice and Noah, she had been secretly viewing properties, trying to find that perfect family home for them all.

She felt the kids deserved security, a forever home that they knew would always be theirs and a garden for them to play in. But here she was buying a house to set up a family home, a settled family home where she hoped they might get married and be a family, but Wendy wasn't at that stage in her life.

Wendy was playing gigs and going back to university, still enjoying her youth. India was around the same age as Wendy, and she had just confirmed all her fears were legitimate. Wendy seemed happy, but maybe what Trent had to offer was too much.

Trent's mobile rang. "Hello?"

It was her lawyer. The bid for the house had been accepted and life was about to change. She was happy for herself and the children but could Wendy be a part of that?

She heard the front door open and the sound of heels marching towards her office. India could be heard saying, "Please wait here, Lady Claudia, and I'll see if Trent is available."

Oh no. That was all she needed. Wendy was to meet her here before they made their way to the pub where her band were playing.

Lady Claudia came marching straight in and India said, "I'm sorry, Trent. I couldn't stop her."

Trent held up a hand. "That's all right. If you could just shut the door on the way out."

"I've found you at last, darling. Your secretary let me in," Claudia said.

"How can I help you, Lady Claudia?" Trent said.

Claudia frowned and took a few steps towards her. "Why *Lady* Claudia all of a sudden?" She ran her nails down Trent's lapel. "It wasn't so formal when you were sleeping with me."

Trent cringed at the remark. What had she been thinking, sleeping with her client, even if their business was completed? It was a stupid, unprofessional mistake and she was paying for it now.

"What is it that you want—I have an appointment to keep," Trent said.

"Why have you been ignoring my calls?" Claudia had an angry tone to her voice now.

"I was on holiday over Christmas," Trent said.

"Oh, that's right. Your little family trip to Lapland."

"How did you know where I was?" Trent was starting to get really irritated now.

Claudia sat on the edge of her desk. "I have my sources. Imagine my astonishment to hear that you, dear Trent, were on the most family-orientated holiday you could get. That's not you."

Trent was annoyed about the presumption of her character. "There are only two people in the world who truly know me, and you, Lady Claudia, are not one of them. So don't try to presume what my thoughts and wishes might be."

"Touchy, aren't you? You've really changed since those brats came into your life."

"Don't call them that," Trent snapped. She had to restrain herself from bodily throwing her out the door.

"Hit a nerve, have I?" She giggled.

Trent shook her head. "You have my attention now. What is it you want from me?"

Claudia obviously thought she was getting somewhere. She sidled towards her and reached her hand out to touch Trent's cheek.

"You, my darling. I want you."

Trent grasped her hand to stop it. "I'm seeing someone."

Claudia looked as if she had just stabbed her in the stomach. "How could you?"

Trent could not understand Claudia's anger. They had slept together once and had dinner once.

"What is this about, Claudia? We slept together once. You've had many lovers, many husbands—you can't be jealous because I met someone."

"You got me the biggest payoff I've ever had from any man. I am rich, thanks to you, and I don't need to fake interest or pretend to laugh at the jokes of old creaking men. I'm independent, I'm rich—people need to laugh at my jokes now." Claudia ran her hand over Trent's shoulder and down to her waist. "You were my chance to live again, Trent. You were the road I could have taken when I was a much younger woman and didn't."

"You were always interested in women?" Trent asked.

"The only person I have ever loved was a woman"—Claudia studied her face—"and you remind me of her so much. I walked away from her for my first husband, and I've lived with that pain ever since."

"Then go and find her. I'm not her, and I'm not on the market," Trent said firmly. Claudia's clambering touch and possessiveness were making her skin crawl.

"She's no longer with us. As soon as I met you for my first appointment, I knew you were my second chance."

Trent was starting to get exasperated. "I'm forty years old, Claudia. I'm too old to be your toy boy. Walk into any gay bar in London, and you'll find plenty of women who will laugh at your jokes."

Claudia's face turned to thunder in seconds. "Who is this woman you're seeing? Your pretty secretary?"

"No, and it's none of your business," Trent said.

"Your nanny?" Claudia guessed.

Trent's hesitation gave her away.

"She's a child. No surprise you were attracted to her," Claudia spat. "You get to an age where you want to feel young again, so you ditch the older woman and take up with someone half your age," Claudia said angrily.

"You were never mine to ditch, and I'm not with her because of her age. I'm in love with her."

It was a new experience declaring her love out loud, but nice all the same.

"You love her? You love her?"

Trent was now starting to realize that Claudia's ex-husband might have been right about her. Luckily he'd gotten disentangled from her.

"Please leave now," Trent said.

The hurt look on Claudia's face turned to a sly grin. "What goes around comes around, darling. Just remember—you are in my position now, you are the older woman in your so-called relationship. How long before your young nanny is pining for someone her own age?"

"Get out," Trent said.

Claudia laughed. "You know I'm right."

Wendy finished tuning her guitar and rested it against the guitar stand. The bar was starting to get busier. They should have a good crowd tonight. She gazed over to the bar and saw the lonely looking figure of Trent standing alone and nursing a drink. Trent had been quiet ever since they met up at her office.

This was meant to be a special night for them. It meant a lot to Wendy to show Trent her band and her music, but also to have a date night since the children were staying over at Becca's.

She'd tried to talk to Trent on the way over, but she said nothing was wrong. How could they have any problems after the way they'd committed to each other on holiday?

She touched the necklace Trent had given her and heard her bandmate Skye say, "Is it true?"

"Is what true?" Wendy asked.

"Kira says you're with her now." Skye pointed over towards Trent, who saw them looking.

"Yes, I am. I'm in love with her."

"Are you out of your mind? What has she done to you? Seduced you when you're feeling vulnerable?"

"I'm not vulnerable. What do you mean?" Wendy asked.

"You've been vulnerable ever since Bailey. She's a ruthless divorce lawyer, Dee—she's moved in on you like a predator. A much younger nanny was probably all her dreams come true."

Wendy was furious. She had been aware of Skye's crush on her, but this was ridiculous.

"You know nothing about our relationship, so keep your opinions to yourself, Skye."

"She probably just wants you as a mum for her kids."

Wendy jumped down from the stage and turned to Skye. "Don't talk to me unless it's about music or the band."

She made her way through the growing crowd. Wendy needed to touch Trent. She stepped into her arms. "I love you."

Trent felt a little stiff. "And I love you."

Wendy pulled back. "I want to talk later when we get home. There's something worrying you, and I don't want you to say there isn't because there is."

Trent went to speak but Wendy silenced her. "No, I don't want to hear there isn't. I told you. I have to go now, but we'll talk later."

Wendy walked off in a determined fashion. She was a strong woman—Trent had to admit that. Maybe she was worrying too much? Then she looked around at the other bar patrons, with long hair, beards, tattoos, and assorted piercings, and she felt the gap between them as wide as ever.

A voice beside her said, "I'm Skye."

"Hello, you're in the band?" Trent said.

"Yes, and I'm one of Wendy's closest friends. I want a word with you."

❖

Trent couldn't have been prouder of Wendy than while watching her perform. She felt such a rush of love, and it brought some clarity to her confused thoughts, especially after the words of her so-called friend, Skye.

She was sure much of what Skye said was nonsense. She sounded like a jealous crush, but the words she used—predatory, pressurizing Wendy—were triggering to Trent. She could see how their relationship could be painted to look. Had she been predatory? Maybe Lady Claudia was right—maybe they were exactly the same.

She knew in that moment that she loved Wendy enough to let her go, as heartbreaking and painful as that was.

They drove back home in relative silence, which was unusual for them. When they entered the lift, Wendy grasped her hand as usual, and sang her silly little song. It would destroy her, letting this perfect woman go, but some things were more important than her heart. Wendy was.

Trent unlocked the door and Wendy said, "Right, let's sit on the couch and sort out whatever cloud has been hanging over us since we got back."

"Let me just put my briefcase in my office." And delay the inevitable.

She walked into her office and sat down at her desk, putting her head in her hands.

"As I thought, delaying tactics." Wendy sat down in front of her desk. "What is the problem? We couldn't be more in love, but since we came back from Lapland, you've been on a downer."

Trent clasped her hands together. "Not a downer, just a realization of what was right."

Wendy furrowed her brow. "What do you mean? This isn't about the kids, is it?"

"No, no. They are my life now and always will be. No, the realization is this—I'm too old for you, Dee."

"What are you talking about? Has Skye been talking to you at the bar?"

"She did have a few jealous words for me, but I had already formed that opinion."

"Formed that opinion? Formed that opinion? You're not in court now, so stop giving me that stoic crap." Wendy stood up and started to pace. "You're *older*, not too old."

"Dee, you're a young woman with the world at your feet. You should be with someone your own age."

Wendy slapped her hands down on the table. "And how well did that work out for me the last time? I got cheated on, up to my eyes in debt, and having to leave university. I wanted someone who was ready for the things I was. Bailey clearly wasn't, and neither would Skye be, as much as she thinks she is. I want a partner and children. Our stages in life and wants mesh perfectly."

Trent hadn't thought of it that way, but then she remembered what Wendy had said the first time they were intimate.

"That's not what other people will think, and do you remember what you said to me when you came to my room on my birthday?"

"I said lots of things—remind me?"

Trent grasped Wendy's hand. "You said you couldn't trust your heart, so you wanted me to take the lead, take care of you. How do you know you can trust it now?"

"Because I trust you, which is more than can be said for you. Fine, call it all off, break your heart, break my heart, all because you don't trust me, and you're worried about what other people will think."

Wendy slammed the door on her way out, then the door to her own bedroom. Trent covered her head with her hands. How could someone be so lucky as to fall in love with two wonderful women in her life, and not get to be with either one.

She picked up the brochure for the new home she'd bought, screwed it up into a ball, and threw it against the wall.

CHAPTER TWENTY-FOUR

Trent became aware of a voice. It was Wendy, but was it a dream? She slowly began to wake up and felt intense pain in her neck. She had fallen asleep at her desk and felt like hell.

The crumpled-up house brochure was now flattened out and sitting in front of her, as was Wendy. She was sitting on the other side of her desk in her nightdress, and her eyes were puffy from a night of crying, she suspected.

"What's that?" Wendy asked.

Trent stretched, trying to ease the discomfort in her neck. "A house I've bought."

"You bought a house? Without even talking to me about it? Is that what all those secret phone calls were about?"

Trent nodded. "It was meant to be a surprise. I wanted to buy a family home for the children and for you. I was going to do it all properly, ask you to marry me and all that."

"Are you still going to ask me?" Wendy said.

"No, I don't think it would be right. Besides, after last night—"

"Take me to see this house."

"Why?" Trent asked.

"Because despite the fact that sometimes I like you to take responsibility for us, from time to time, I do still know my own mind, and I will not be told what's best for me. I want to see the home you bought for us, and I do mean *us*, Peter."

The warm light of day, and furiousness of Wendy's determination, thawed the cold worry that had been building up in her heart.

"If you're sure. I'd need to call and see if I can get the keys," Trent said.

Wendy smiled and walked around the desk. She leaned over and whispered, "I'm sure."

Then Wendy kissed her teasingly, shattering any ice still left in her heart.

❖

Trent turned the car into a leafy street of super-expensive terraced houses. She parked on a numbered space outside one of the houses and turned off the ignition.

She rubbed her hands together nervously and kept staring ahead. She let out a breath and said, "I'm forty years old, set in my ways, grumpy, a workaholic, and I have no right to have the love of a young woman like you."

Wendy tried to reply, but Trent looked at her and held her hand up to silence her. "No, I need to say this. I lost one woman because I never opened up, and I'm not going to let that happen again."

Wendy could feel her hands start to shake. She wanted to hold Trent in her arms now. After the emotion of last night, to have Trent hopefully give them a chance was everything. To hell with what her friends would think.

"Okay, tell me."

Trent took her hand and cradled it softly. "As I said last night, at your age you should be out at clubs, dancing the night away, going to music festivals, and listening to music that I would call noise, not sitting on the couch with me of an evening, like an old married couple. I don't know why you were attracted to me, but you were, and I've treasured getting to know you and earning your trust. I know what trust is to you. You came into my world like Mary Poppins and did everything in your power to help me build a relationship with Alice and Noah. I love them like my own children, something I'd never thought I'd have or be capable of."

Wendy couldn't stop the tears welling up in her eyes, "You were always capable of it, Peter. You just needed some guidance and someone to love."

Trent brushed one of Wendy's braids off her face. "You are that someone, Wendy Darling. I love you, and you were right last night in everything you said. If we are happy with our differences, then who cares what people think, as long as you swear to me you've never felt pressured or obligated to be with me…in that way."

"Never, I've been attracted to you since we first met. You being older than me isn't a bad thing. It's perfect for us."

She watched Trent take the keys they had picked up out of her pocket. "I wanted to show you and the kids that I wanted a family, a future with you all. When we were in Lapland, I called my estate agent to instruct him to find some properties for me to look at. Not a penthouse bachelor pad like my flat, a family home. This was the one I thought was perfect."

"Aren't there people living in it?"

Trent smiled. "No, it's unoccupied. It's just been decorated and furnished for sale. Would you like to see it?"

"Yes, please."

They both got out of the car, and Wendy looked up at the architecture of the white stone terraced home. There was a pretty archway over the front door, and a black wrought iron gate, and matching fences between this and the other identical houses along the street.

"What are you thinking, Dee?" Trent asked.

"It looks just like the house in *Peter Pan*."

"That's why I liked it."

Wendy leaned over and whispered to Trent, "Take me to Neverland, Peter."

❖

Trent watched Wendy walk slowly around the large drawing room, her footsteps echoing on the wooden floor. She had been quiet, taking everything in since they walked into the house.

"What do you think?"

Wendy held her arms out and twirled in a circle. "It's so big, but beautiful."

"I hoped you'd like it. There's so much more to show you. Follow me to the kitchen," Trent said.

They walked down the spacious hallway and came to a wooden spiral staircase, heading to the lower floor. Wendy ran her hand along the wooden banister as they walked down. "There's no lift to worry about."

"No, just stairs. It's all been recently remodelled. I hope you'll like the kitchen. I think it's truly something."

They got to the bottom of the stairs and stepped into the room. Wendy clasped her hand to her mouth. The kitchen space ran nearly the whole length of the bottom floor with stone floors, a new ultra-modern kitchen, and French doors out onto a patio area.

Wendy was just taking it all in, so Trent said, "This is what really sold it to me. I thought it would be great for the kids. We could be cooking while the kids sit at the kitchen table at the other end of the room, or in the summer the French doors could be open, letting them play outside."

Wendy turned to her, smiling. "*We* could be cooking?"

"Well, you, but I'm willing to start learning. I just didn't want it to seem as if it would be your job."

"This is so perfect," Wendy said. "I just can't…It's overwhelming."

Trent took her hand and said, "Let's look at the bedrooms. I think Alice and Noah will be really comfortable here."

Wendy followed Trent up two sets of stairs. This place was huge. Wendy loved it and what Trent had planned for them, but moving here, making this her home, would change the dynamic of their relationship. Things couldn't stay the same.

They looked around what would be the children's rooms, and then Trent led her to the master bedroom. It was sumptuous and big, more than enough room for the super king size bed the sellers had set it out with, with walk-in dressing rooms and an en suite bathroom.

Wendy walked over to the window and looked out over the gardens.

"So can you see yourself living here?" Trent asked.

She turned back to Trent and said, "You do know how expensive this area of London is."

"Very aware, but what does that matter if we make this our forever family home? Alice and Noah are always talking about a forever home, and I thought this place was right for it."

"Things will need to change," Wendy said.

"I know. I want you to marry me, everything that goes with a forever home."

Wendy thought about all the implications, what Kira and her friends would say. It was a lot to consider, but she knew what her heart wanted.

"If we're going to do this, I have to quit my job. I can't be your employee. We can't start out our life together as employer and employee."

"Whatever you need to do."

Wendy smiled and wrapped her arms around Trent's neck. "I do."

Trent let out a sigh of relief. "You could have anyone, you know. Are you sure you want to hitch your wagon to a forty-year-old divorce lawyer?"

Wendy leaned in close to her lips and said, "You're forgetting I've got a thing for older women."

EPILOGUE

The normally serious London courtroom was alive with laughter and excitement. After getting married and moving into their new home a few months ago, Trent and Wendy were in front of a judge, finalizing the adoption of Alice and Noah. Although both still had their moments of grief and trauma, Alice in particular, they had settled in at their new school and were happy.

This was the day they had been looking forward to, even more than the wedding of their two new parents, because today meant they had found their forever home officially.

Trent and Wendy were about to sign the adoption papers at a table in front of the judge, and behind them sat their family and friends. Becca, Dale, Sammy, Val, and Kira, who had slowly come around to the fact that her friend loved the ruthless divorce lawyer Davina Trent.

Trent had Alice next to her and Noah was sitting on Wendy's knee. Trent signed and passed the paper to Wendy, who looked at her and smiled. "Are you ready for this, Peter?"

"I never would have been without you," Trent said.

Wendy signed and their lawyer took it up to the judge to do her part. Judge Castillo was an old work acquaintance of Trent's, and she was happy to have someone she knew in charge on this special day.

The judge looked up from the bench and said, "Alice? Noah? Come on up here."

Alice looked at Trent nervously. "Go on. The judge wants to see you."

She took Noah's hand and walked up behind the judge's bench.

"Come closer," Judge Castillo said. She opened up her arms and each child sat on a knee. "When I sign here, it'll make Trent and Wendy your mums. Will that make you happy?"

"Yes, yes," Noah said, bouncing excitedly.

Trent thought it was so nice that she was taking the time to make this a special day for Alice and Noah.

She glanced to the side and saw her boho hipster girl with braids, who she loved so much, beaming up at the children. To outsiders they looked like an odd couple—she in her sharp, boring suits, and Wendy in her short flowery sundress, with her three ringed necklace representing their family, and her leather wrist straps and bangles—but they worked. So well, that their first few months of marriage had been perfect.

Trent took Wendy's hand and rubbed her thumb over Wendy's engagement and wedding rings. It always filled her heart with happiness to see them there. She looked down at her own hand, with its wedding band.

This was a life she'd never imagined, and that made it all the more exciting because she had no idea what was coming next. Yes, life was going to be an adventure now that she had someone to love.

Trent turned back and saw Becca sitting behind them holding a wriggling Gracie. Things had changed and moved forward so much, and now Becca wasn't the woman she'd let slip through her fingers. She was family.

Becca smiled and gave her a wink. It was an amazing comfort to have that feeling of family support behind her. It was strange because neither she, Wendy, Becca, or Dale had blood relations as part of their lives, but they had forged this family of choice that was so much more secure. She hoped both her mother and David were looking down on them with happy smiles.

Trent felt a nudge from Wendy. "She's signed it. We're a family."

Wendy grasped her face and kissed it. "We did it."

"Come on up and join us," Judge Castillo said.

She and Wendy walked up and joined the judge, Alice, and Noah.

"We're a family," Alice said.

Trent hugged and kissed them both. "A forever family."

"I'm really yours?" Noah asked.

"Yes, forever," Wendy said.

"Let's get some pictures of this happy moment." The judge waved up Becca.

Becca gave Gracie to Dale and picked up her camera. She got in position, and Wendy and Trent stood on either side of the judge. The children stood in front holding the adoption certificate.

"Say cheese," Becca said.

"Cheese!" they all replied.

Once Becca had taken a few pictures, she said to the judge, "Can I get a few family shots?"

"Of course. The more the merrier. Up you all come."

Dale, Jake, Gracie, Sammy, Val, and Mia all made their way to the judge's bench.

While Becca was getting everyone in position, Wendy said to Trent, "Are you happy?"

Trent turned to her and looked deeply into her eyes. "Happy, proud, lucky. How will you feel when we come to your graduation in a few months as a family?"

Wendy had completed her teaching degree and would hopefully be starting work in a school shortly thereafter. She also had some publishers interested in her children's book series, *Travels with My Teddy.*

Trent was proud of Wendy. She had juggled study and writing with looking after the kids and preparing for the wedding. Trent thought she was a superwoman.

"I'll feel like I've finally become who I was meant to be," Wendy said. "This is all I've ever wanted. To be married with children and have a happy secure home. You've given it to me."

Trent shook her head and kissed her softly. "We gave it to each other. I love you to Neverland and back, Wendy."

Wendy smiled sweetly. "I love you too, Peter."

Dale interrupted them. "Save those kisses for later, Trent. My missus is ready to take the picture."

Becca had the camera set up on a tripod. She set the delay and came hurrying over to join the picture.

Their family pictures were getting larger, and that was just perfect, because everyone needed someone to love.

"Say cheese!"

"Cheese!"

About the Author

Jenny Frame is from the small town of Motherwell in Scotland, where she lives with her partner, Lou, and their well-loved and very spoiled dog.

She has a diverse range of qualifications, including a BA in public management and a diploma in acting and performance. Nowadays, she likes to put her creative energies into writing rather than treading the boards.

When not writing or reading, Jenny loves cheering on her local football team, cooking, and spending time with her family.

Jenny can be contacted at www.jennyframe.com.

Books Available From Bold Strokes Books

Face Off by PJ Trebelhorn. Hockey player Savannah Wells rarely spends more than a night with any one woman, but when photographer Madison Scott buys the house next door, she's forced to rethink what she expects out of life. (978-1-63555-480-9)

Hot Ice by Aurora Rey, Elle Spencer, and Erin Zak. Can falling in love melt the hearts of the iciest ice queens? Join Aurora Rey, Elle Spencer, and Erin Zak to find out! A contemporary romance novella collection. (978-1-63555-513-4)

Line of Duty by VK Powell. Dr. Dylan Carlyle's professional and personal life is turned upside down when a tragic event at Fairview Station pits her against ambitious, handsome police officer Finley Masters. ((978-1-63555-486-1)

London Undone by Nan Higgins. London Craft reinvents her life after reading a childhood letter to her future self and, in doing so, finds the love she truly wants. (978-1-63555-562-2)

Lunar Eclipse by Gun Brooke. Moon De Cruz lives alone on an uninhabited planet after being shipwrecked in space. Her life changes forever when Captain Beaux Lestarion's arrival threatens the planet and Moon's freedom. (978-1-63555-460-1)

One Small Step by MA Binfield. In this contemporary romance, Iris and Cam discover the meaning of taking chances and following your heart, even if it means getting hurt. (978-1-63555-596-7)

Shadows of a Dream by Nicole Disney. Rainn has the talent to take her rock band all the way, but falling in love is a powerful distraction, and her new girlfriend's meth addiction might just take them both down. 978-1-63555-598-1)

Someone to Love by Jenny Frame. When Davina Trent is given an unexpected family, can she let nanny Wendy Darling teach her to open her heart to the children and to Wendy? (978-1-63555-468-7)

Uncharted by Robyn Nyx. As Rayne Marcellus and Chase Stinsen track the legendary Golden Trinity, they must learn to put their differences aside and depend on one another to survive. (978-1-63555-325-3)

Where We Are by Annie McDonald. A sensual account of two women who discover a way to walk on the same path together with the help of an Indigenous tale, a Canadian art movement, and the mysterious appearance of dimes. (978-1-63555-581-3)

A Moment in Time by Lisa Moreau. A longstanding family feud separates two women who unexpectedly fall in love at an antique clock shop in a small Louisiana town. (978-1-63555-419-9)

Aspen in Moonlight by Kelly Wacker. When art historian Melissa Warren meets Sula Johansen, director of a local bear conservancy, she discovers that love can come in unexpected and unusual forms. (978-1-63555-470-0)

Back to September by Melissa Brayden. Small bookshop owner Hannah Shepard and famous romance novelist Parker Bristow maneuver the landscape of their two very different worlds to find out if love can win out in the end. (978-1-63555-576-9)

Changing Course by Brey Willows. When the woman of her dreams falls from the sky, intergalactic space captain Jessa Arbelle had better be ready to catch her. (978-1-63555-335-2)

Cost of Honor by Radclyffe. First Daughter Blair Powell and Homeland Security Director Cameron Roberts face adversity when their enemies stop at nothing to prevent President Andrew Powell's reelection. Book 11 in the Honor series. (978-1-63555-582-0)

Fearless by Tina Michele. Determined to overcome her debilitating fear through exposure therapy, Laura Carter all but fails before she's even begun until dolphin trainer Jillian Marshall dedicates herself to helping Laura defeat the nightmares of her past. (978-1-63555-495-3)

Not Dead Enough by J.M. Redmann. In the tenth book of the Micky Knight mystery series, a woman who may or may not be dead drags Micky into a messy con game. (978-1-63555-543-1)

Muslims and Jews
in France

Muslims and Jews
in France

History of a Conflict

Maud S. Mandel

P PRINCETON UNIVERSITY PRESS
Princeton and Oxford

Published by Princeton University Press, 41 William Street, Princeton,
    New Jersey 08540
In the United Kingdom: Princeton University Press, 6 Oxford Street,
    Woodstock, Oxfordshire OX20 1TW

press.princeton.edu

Library of Congress Cataloging-in-Publication Data

Mandel, Maud, 1967– author.
    Muslims and Jews in France : history of a conflict / Maud S. Mandel.
        pages cm
    Includes bibliographical references and index.
    ISBN 978-0-691-12581-7 (alk. paper)
    1. Muslims—France—Social conditions—20th century. 2. Muslims—France—
Social conditions—21st century. 3. Jews—France—Social conditions—20th century.
4. Jews—France—Social conditions—21st century. 5. Muslims—Cultural assimilation—
France. 6. Jews—Cultural assimilation—France. 7. Social integration—France. 8. France—
Ethnic relations. I. Title.
    DC34.5.M87M36 2014
    305.6′970944–dc23   2013020112

British Library Cataloging-in-Publication Data is available

This book has been composed in Minion

Printed on acid-free paper ∞

Printed in the United States of America

10 9 8 7 6 5 4 3 2 1

For my family

CONTENTS

ACKNOWLEDGMENTS

As all authors, I owe a tremendous intellectual debt to the many people and institutions that have guided and supported me as this book project has evolved. The deeply gifted scholars with whom I have worked at Brown University both in the Program in Judaic Studies and the Department of History have profoundly shaped the way I write and think. While space limitations prevent me from naming the many colleagues who have offered feedback throughout this process, I would like to thank in particular Omer Bartov, Lynn Davidman, Carolyn Dean, Calvin Goldscheider, Mary Gluck, Elliott Gorn, and Michael Steinberg for guidance at critical stages in the writing process. In addition, Ethan Pollock and Robert Self read almost every chapter of this book. These two insightful and creative scholars have not only helped me improve the manuscript but have also made the process far more enjoyable. Deborah Cohen's feedback and, additionally, her sustained friendship gave me confidence when I needed it most.

Also at Brown, I have had the opportunity to interact with a group of intelligent, articulate, and dynamic undergraduate and graduate students, several of whom have aided in the research of this book. For their tremendous help in this capacity, I would like to thank Flannery Berg, David Beyer, Kathryn Boonstra, Kelly Colvin, Rebecca Russo, David Rudin, Stephen Wicken, and Audrey von Maluski.

Several colleagues at other institutions have been extremely supportive over the many years that I have been working on this project and sometimes long before. Phyllis Cohen Albert, Leora Auslander, Vicki Caron, Todd Endelman, Nancy Green, Robin Judd, and Aron Rodrigue have invited me to present work in progress, and/or written letters of recommendation and encouraged me along the way. I was extremely lucky to become acquainted with Ethan Katz shortly after I had begun my research and as he was embarking on his own study of Muslims and Jews in France. An exceptionally generous colleague with boundless energy, Ethan has offered extensive feedback on written work, shared source material, and joined me in several collective endeavors. This fruitful partnership has been one of the most rewarding aspects of this project. Cécile Vidal continues to offer me a home away from home in France and a stunning model of intellectual rigor that I have sought to emulate; she will forever be a source of my profound admiration and affection.

Numerous institutions have made this book possible. At Brown University, the Cogut Center for the Humanities, the Pembroke Center for Teaching and Research on Women, and the Watson Institute for International Studies all provided aid for the initial stages of this project. I would also like to thank the American Council of Learned Societies, the American Philosophical Association, the American Historical Association, the Memorial Foundation for Jewish Culture, and the National Endowment for the Humanities for their crucial aid.

How does one thank the "inner core" adequately for all the help and love they provided? Words fail. Barrett Mandel, Ruth Mandel, and Jeff Lucker not only supplied the TLC on which I have come to depend, but they moved to Paris for stretches of time to help care for my young children and gave me the precious gift of time to carry out my research and writing. My children, Lev and Ava Simon, do not remember a moment when I was not working on this book. Although their presence meant there were long stretches when I was unable to work on it, their love sustained me throughout. Steve Simon has not only been at my side for all endeavors since long before this book began, he also shared a home office with me as I wrote the pages that follow. Indeed, he sits at his own desk a few feet away as I write these very sentences, unaware of my efforts to find words to express my gratitude. But he knows. I dedicate this book to the people who make up this paragraph. It takes a family.

Muslims and Jews
in France

Introduction

In autumn 2000, Muslim-Jewish relations in France captured national attention following a dramatic spike in anti-Jewish violence. Largely the work of Muslim youth from the country's most disadvantaged sectors, the violence raised alarms over rising antisemitism and emerging ethno-religious conflict in France. Periodic moments of dramatic bloodshed such as the 2006 torture and murder of twenty-three-year-old Ilan Halimi, and Mohammed Merah's March 2012 shooting of a rabbi and three children at Ozar Hatorah, a Jewish school in Toulouse, have kept such fears alive, while studies of increasing French Jewish intolerance toward "Arabs" suggest that relations between France's two largest ethno-religious minorities have been forever damaged.[1]

Explanations for the discord have ranged widely. According to some, anti-Jewish attacks have been encouraged by the media's "methodical stigmatization" of Israel and an intensifying anti-Jewish bias in France.[2] Most others, however, have focused on a timeless Muslim Judophobia rooted in the conflict between Islam and Judaism, a ubiquitous European antisemitism that has penetrated Arab culture, or the combustible fusion of radical Islam and anti-Zionism.[3] For still others, the conflict is entirely contemporary: either a by-product of the Arab-Israeli conflict or an expression of the frustrations of disenfranchised French Muslim youth and an increasingly ethnically enclosed Jewish minority.[4] While often diametrically and even angrily opposed to one another, the overall tone of all these analyses is that Muslims and Jews in France are on an explosive collision course.[5]

I envisioned this book as a challenge to that assumption. Polarization, I believed, was a gross simplification of the much richer and more varied range of Muslim-Jewish relations in France. I therefore began my research most drawn to the cultural and historical connections linking these two populations, of which there are many. Indeed, France houses the largest Jewish and Muslim populations living side by side outside of Israel (current estimates number 4,000,000–6,000,000 Muslims and 500,000–600,000 Jews), thanks to the many in both communities who left North Africa following decolonization.[6] Sharing certain linguistic and cultural traditions and a common experience of displacement, these newcomers also experienced similar pressures to assimilate while also often feeling rejected by the nation seeking to integrate them.[7] These multifaceted cultural, linguistic, residential, and historical connections meant that

Muslim-Jewish relations in France were never defined solely as a bitter war over Palestine and Israel, Islam and Judaism, or any other set of binary divisions.

Conflict, nevertheless, dominates the archival record of Muslim-Jewish relations in postwar France. Indeed even if such relations have been multiple and variegated, it was the episodic interethnic political disagreements—whether over French policies in the Middle East and North Africa or over domestic issues related to minority integration in France—that most often caught the attention of a diverse range of social actors, including international Jewish representatives, anti-Zionist Algerian nationalists, French police, Jewish student activists, and second generation Muslim anti-racist organizers. In following these sources, this book thus evolved from a straightforward challenge to narratives of Jewish-Muslim conflict into an examination of how such narratives emerged and in time helped produce the very conflicts they purported to recount.

The result is a study of the evolution and political meaning of conflict. It traces the process through which "Jew" and "Muslim" became political symbols, even as actual Jews and Muslims rarely clashed. Indeed, the very terms "Jew" and "Muslim" hide as much as they reveal, because they cluster various national and ethnic origins under broad religious categories that imply homogeneity and communal identifications in place of the profound heterogeneity that characterizes each population. As I argue throughout these pages, however, heterogeneity is largely irrelevant to the hardening of the political binary *Muslim-Jewish*. Beginning with the birth of Israel and North African anti-colonial warfare and continuing through the failed efforts of the 1980s anti-racist campaigns to bridge ethno-political divisions between activists in France, episodic moments of Muslim-Jewish conflict cemented a narrative of polarization.[8] This book asks why this narrative has proven so powerful and enduring.

Central to this account is France. While global developments, particularly in the Middle East, created fault lines around which activists began to mobilize, the nature of this mobilization (i.e., who was involved), the political rhetoric employed, and the success or lack thereof of their appeal emerged from French political transformations—especially the decolonization of North Africa, the 1968 student uprisings, and the 1980s experiments in multiculturalism. Moreover, the impact of Middle Eastern war was never straightforward. As one relocated Algerian Jew told a researcher in the early 1990s, "When we say 'the Arabs,' I feel hatred, but those are Middle Eastern Arabs. I am not talking about the Arabs who live [in France], because they don't do us any harm. They work, they earn their living, they have children and families like us, *à la française*. That's fine. If we could live together and get on well as we used to back there, it would be perfect. But the problem in Israel is still not solved. So since I've known the Israeli problem, I am anti-Arab, but not against the Arabs of France."[9] As such a remark suggests, focusing *solely* on the Middle East in an effort to understand Muslim-Jewish politics in France misses key aspects of the story.[10] The goal here, then, is not to remove the Middle East from the equation; indeed, the repercussions of conflict between Israel and its neighbors will be a central analytic thread throughout. Rather I will underscore the way global dynamics, both in the Middle East and in French North Africa, *came together* with national and even local factors to shape Muslim-Jewish relations in postcolonial France.

This focus on the postcolonial is far from incidental. From the standpoint of demography alone, decolonization was monumental in the historical trajectories of France's Muslim and Jewish populations.[11] Not only were one million French citizens "repatriated" as a direct outcome of the violence (including many Muslims and Jews), but the dramatic growth of the metropolitan economy meant tens of thousands of former colonial subjects also came to France as immigrants.[12] While Algerian Muslims had begun arriving in the early nineteenth century, their numbers grew from 130,000 in 1930 to over 600,000 by 1965 in a "veritable hemorrhaging of Algeria to France."[13] By 1982 the number had grown to more than 800,000, while Moroccan and Tunisian Muslim populations had grown to 440,000 and 190,000, respectively.[14] Jewish immigration brought 240,000 new arrivals to France between 1944 and 1979, more than half from Algeria and the rest from Morocco and Tunisia.[15] These newcomers more than doubled France's Jewish population, forever transforming its socioeconomic, cultural, political and religious contours and creating new and visible subgroups within a population primarily made up of those with roots in France since before the French Revolution and those who had migrated from war-torn Eastern Europe.[16]

While similar origins and settlement patterns at times forged bonds between different kinds of migrants from North Africa, the juridical and social inequities embedded in French colonization policies and the vastly different levels of Muslim and Jewish communal development in the metropole created sharply divergent integration processes.[17] Beginning with the invasion of Algeria in 1830, colonial administrators, scholars, and legislators constructed categories for understanding North African society that emphasized regional, ethnic, religious, social, and economic divisions over indigenous unity.[18] Jews, in these constructions, were often held to be more intelligent and "assimilable" than the Muslims among who they lived. In Algeria, where such thinking took legal form, the 1870 Crémieux Decree granted French citizenship to all Algerian Jews, juridically cutting them off from most Algerian Muslim subjects.[19] In Tunisia and Morocco, which remained nominally under Muslim control throughout the colonial period, no mass naturalizations occurred. Nevertheless, the "Frenchification" of local Jewish populations took place through more informal administrative practices and the schools of the *Alliance israélite universelle*, meaning Jews had greater opportunities to acculturate to European social and cultural norms than the Muslim populations amidst which they lived, and this contributed to the formation of new social hierarchies.[20] Although the post–World War II French government granted citizenship to Algerian Muslims in an effort to diminish support for the growing independence struggle, those in France continued to face systematic discrimination, particularly after 1954 when the outbreak of FLN (Front de libération nationale) armed protest transformed Algerian Muslims into "the central and even unique symbol of 'the enemy within.'"[21] France's decision to recognize the French citizenship of Jewish Algerians in the war's final negotiations at the very moment when Muslim Algerian French citizens were permantly excluded enfolded Jews into the wider "European" family.[22] Jews fleeing newly independent Algeria thus benefited from all the subsidies and aid available to repatriating citizens, while Muslims from Morocco, Tunisia, and particularly Algeria faced administrative structures that distinguished them from other incoming migrants.[23] For example, while most arriving Tunisian and Moroccan Jews did not share the benefits of citizenship like their Algerian co-religionists, they reported that authorities "bent over backward" to help them obtain French nationality while doing nothing to aid Muslim newcomers.[24]

These inequities had profound economic, cultural, and political consequences in 1960s France, among which were sharply divergent processes of Muslim-Jewish integration. Arriving Jews thus joined a long-rooted French Jewish community, which although deeply undermined by Vichy legislation during World War II, had been engaged by the mid-1950s in a decade-long rebuilding process that had given rise to a highly developed communal infrastructure.[25] While encounters between incoming Jews and those already settled in France were never smooth, the new arrivals benefited from institutional structures geared to facilitating their integration and a communal leadership determined to defend Jewish interests, particularly when Jewish lives were understood to be endangered.[26] Arriving Muslims not only had no equivalent infrastructure in place, but also the organizations that sought to speak for them were profoundly distrusted by French authorities as sources of political instability.[27]

The combined impact of this asymmetrical integration and communal development process was that compared to their Muslim counterparts, French Jewish spokesmen had a far more developed apparatus with which to articulate a group politics and greater access to national and local officials for promoting the causes important to them. Thus while this book seeks to trace Muslim-Jewish political exchange, it does not proceed as an equal tale of two halves. The divergent histories of Muslims and Jews in France's colonial project and the more integrated position of Jews in the metropole necessarily gave the organized French Jewish community more opportunities to shape public discourse and greater access to the hallways of power. In addition, they cast a longer shadow, leaving a larger body of French language sources behind. Indeed, if many of the Jews and Muslims under study spoke Arabic, the public sphere in which they interacted was conducted primarily in French—another arena in which Jews were better schooled.[28]

We should be careful, however, not to assume that the relative ease of Jewish integration into post–World War II France meant they could dictate the terms of that integration. Although by the early twenty-first century, Jews proved more economically mobile, better educated, and professionally better placed than the general population and certainly than French Muslims, the organized community was often criticized for failing to defend Jewish interests successfully (however they were defined in a given moment), particularly with regard to foreign policy around Israel.[29] Dramatic moments of anti-Jewish hostility, such as the October 1980 explosion at the rue Copernic synagogue or the May 1990 desecration of the Jewish cemetery in Carpentras were also raw reminders of Jewish leaders' ongoing inability to use their social capital to end violence and bigotry against them. Moreover, whatever the asymmetry between the stature of Jewish and Muslim spokesmen, respectively, the latter were neither passive nor without political agency, also seeking to influence political culture in France on matters of concern to themselves and their Jewish interlocutors.

The following pages, then, explain when and why certain voices predominated over others and how the combined result created a political landscape so often understood as inevitably polarized. Each of the six main chapters addresses a moment in which Muslim-Jewish conflict became a matter of concern whether to French police charged with maintaining social order, to media sources, or to a wide array of self-appointed communal spokesmen. Beginning in 1948 when war in the Middle East caused minor unrest in the city of Marseille, chapter 1 traces the way in which disagreements over Israel became a way to debate inequities in French minority policies at home and in North Africa. Chapter 2 builds on the link between French colonial policies and Muslim-Jewish relations in the metropole by tracing how decolonization throughout North Africa changed the way a diverse set of social actors, including French colonial administrators, international Jewish spokesmen, and a wide range of indigenous nationalist groups conceptualized Jewish belonging throughout the region. The process, I argue, led to the emergence of the "North African Jew," a category to which no individual ascribed but that worked rhetorically to unite the diverse Moroccan, Tunisian, and Algerian Jewish populations into a collective often understood to be in conflict with "North Africans," "Muslims," or "Arabs." Chapter 3 then examines how these new ways of conceptualizing Muslim-Jewish interactions, and the longer term inequities built into French colonial and minority polices, shaped integration into the metropole in the late 1950s and early 1960s.

In these chapters, and in those that follow on the impact of the 1967 Arab-Israeli War, the 1968 student uprisings in France, and the effort to establish a multiethnic anti-racist campaign in 1980s France, I look closely at the way

Muslim-Jewish conflict unfolded—who participated and why—and I examine how rather isolated episodes of conflict created new binary frameworks often despite the intentions of those involved. Chapter 4 thus considers the impact in France of the 1967 Arab-Israeli War showing that while conflict between France's large Muslim and Jewish populations was, in fact, quite rare, the story of two polarized ethno-religious political units hardened as new political actors, particularly university students, began to use the French campus as a space in which to engage matters of foreign policy. Student uprisings in France in 1968, the subject of chapter 5, then brought the story of Muslim-Jewish polarization to France's national conversation as student radicals began to link the occupation of Palestinian territories evermore fully to leftist politics at home. While many Jewish and Muslim leftists worked together in these endeavors, highly visible moments of discord, such as a riot in the Parisian immigrant neighborhood of Belleville in June 1968 and ongoing conflictual encounters between Muslim and Jewish university students, continued to fuel perceptions of polarization. Indeed, paradoxically, even those who emphasized the cultural connections and shared histories binding Muslims and Jews contributed to this process, since in seeking to counter more polarizing rhetoric, they unwittingly legitimized the boundaries of political discourse as it was taking shape: to deny Muslim-Jewish polarization was to acknowledge the problem, thereby reinforcing the very categories they were seeking to dismantle.

It was not until the 1980s, however, when a new generation of Muslim and Jewish French nationals came of age, that polarization emerged as the central motif for understanding Muslim-Jewish relations. During that decade, a surge of anti-minority violence gave rise to large and widely celebrated anti-racist campaigns that brought Muslim and Jewish youth together in a common struggle. Born in the period following François Mitterand's 1981 election to the presidency on a pro–immigrant rights and decentralization platform, the anti-racist coalition took advantage of the political establishment's unprecedented willingness to recognize the nation's cultural and linguistic diversity. Within a few years, however, growing electoral support for Jean Marie Le Pen's anti-immigrant and nationalist political agenda and a mounting fear of international terrorism meant that officials from across the political spectrum began adopting a more conservative discourse toward religious and cultural difference. "Integration" rather than the "right to be different" once again became the watchword of the day.[30] This mounting conservatism, while mostly directed at France's Muslim population, could conflate the nation's religious minorities,[31] and some Jewish figures began backing away from public connections to Muslims.[32] Meanwhile, some Muslim activists, who had seen value in underscoring a common anti-racist agenda, began reasserting the particular nature of their own community's struggle.

By decade's end, the much-celebrated efforts at cross-ethnic cooperation had given way to distrust and bitterness; interethnic conflict was henceforth presumed. During the 1991 Gulf War, for example, journalists, government officials, and religious leaders predicted widespread Muslim-Jewish conflict in response to unfolding events in the Middle East. The fact that such fears never materialized is one of the paradoxes at the heart of this book. Indeed, whatever their links to the Middle East (and such ties were never homogeneous or frozen in time), Muslims and Jews related to each other *also* as former residents of French North Africa, immigrants competing for limited resources, employers and employees, victims of racist aggression, religious minorities in a secularizing state, and citizens. These multiple and complex interactions were often lost, however, as a narrative of polarization took root, thereby helping to erase them.

The Dilemmas of Terminology

Writing of "Muslims" and "Jews" creates two distinct but overlapping problems for the historian. First, these terms risk collapsing significant diversity under essentializing labels, and second, they seemingly privilege ethno-religious over ethno-political categories of analysis. I will address each of these problems in turn.

As the wide-ranging scholarship on Jews and Muslims in France has made clear, neither population formed an organized or homogeneous body in ethnic, national, religious, social, economic, or political terms. The post–World War II Jewish population included citizens with roots in France prior to the French Revolution as well as large numbers of immigrants or newly minted citizens from Central and Eastern Europe, North Africa, and the Levant. Although a handful of important organizations claimed to speak for all French Jews, the population held a wide range of views on national minority policies, war in the Middle East, racism in France, religious practice, and everything else.[33] Nor was France's Muslim population any more unified, made up as it was of migrants from Algeria, Tunisia, Morocco, Egypt, West Africa, Syria, and Lebanon.[34] In the 1990s, sub-Saharan African, Bosnian, and Central Asian Muslims also came to France.[35] Not surprisingly in a migration this large and spanning numerous decades, national, religious, ethnic, cultural and socioeconomic diversity was the rule.[36]

If recent work has stressed this heterogeneity, however, it has also underscored a certain "community of experience."[37] In the words of Jonathan Laurence and Justin Vaïsse: "Despite their ethnic and national diversity, what Muslims in France increasingly do have in common is their 'lived experience,' which includes the bitterness of exclusion as well as successful efforts to integrate."[38] Scholarship on French Jews has also begun emphasizing bridges linking the diverse Jewish collective. Dominique Schnapper, Chantal Bordes-Benayoun, and Freddy Raphaël, for example, have stressed a social homogenization process from the 1970s to the 1990s. While refusing to use the language of "community," given ongoing French discomfort with recognizing ethno-religious political groupings, they stress how shared experiences of democratic life and economic homogenization have diminished prior differences among Jews.[39]

The existence of communities of experience reminds us that overarching terms like "Jew" or "Muslim" reflect a certain—if partial—lived reality. Moreover, despite the constructed nature of collectives based around these terms and the fact that some who might be considered Jews or Muslims would object to being classified primarily as such, we should not deny their power to shape historical outcomes. As Joyce Dalsheim argues,

> [T]he ways in which we order, divide, and categorize our socio-political world are not innocent. . . . These divisions have very real outcomes, including the constitution of categories of identity, religion, and politics, the delimitation of the contours of action and debate in the present, and the construction of boundaries within which we might imagine possible futures. The narratives that emerge through these divisions become familiar to us, taking the form of common knowledge upon which we base our judgments and take action in the world.[40]

To site but one example of this process: According to Naomi Davidson, beginning in the early twentieth century, French politicians, colonial administrators, intellectuals, and urban planners elaborated a notion of "*Islam français*" that functioned as an essential and eternal marker of difference in French society. While Islam français posited certain compatibilities between French secular republicanism and Islam, it also articulated a "reductionist, totalizing religio-cultural category 'Muslim'" that served to racialize religious difference. Nor was this articulation of an Islam français simply a discursive move, as it became the primary administrative medium through which the French state interacted with Muslim residents in the metropole.[41] This process gathered steam with the decolonization of Algeria. As Todd Shepard has shown, French juridical and bureaucratic practices at the end of the Algerian War of Independence divided "Muslims" from "Europeans," as eight million of the former were stripped of their French citizenship and several hundred thousand non-Muslims—many of whom had never lived in Europe—were claimed as "French."[42] The media then reified these divisions.

As such scholarship has made clear, socially constructed categories had legal, administrative, and cultural implications for those categorized as "Muslims" whether they embraced the label or not. Likewise, if post–World War II

French authorities rejected Vichy legal distinctions, "Jews" never disappeared into a neutral public sphere. Indeed, governmental archives abound with references to "Jews" and the "Jewish community," and self-appointed spokesmen and media outlets repeatedly confirmed the boundaries of such a collective regardless of individual ascription. The categories "Muslim" and "Jew" thus had social meaning for those inside and outside of the "communities" collapsed therein. Muslim-Jewish political conflict evolved in and helped define this discursive space. Assertions of polarization—whatever the reality on the ground— helped legitimate social understandings of group belonging. To understand the evolution of polarization, therefore, is also to understand the way categories calcify, obscuring and flattening the social complexity therein.

Recognition of calcifying political categories raises the second dilemma that the terms "Jew" and "Muslim" create for the historian. As scholarship on both has made clear, the meaning of these terms has changed over time as understandings of the groups they represent have shifted. French Jews were thus known as "israélites" from the time of the French Revolution until the middle of the twentieth century, a construction that emphasized Jewish religious affiliations over ethnic or racial identifications so as not to challenge categories of belonging within the French nation. Nazi and Vichy racializing practices coupled with the nationalizing claims of the Zionist movement challenged such constructions of Jewishness. By the mid-twentieth century, the term "juif" had replaced "israélite" in spoken French and even for most French Jews, who, while rejecting Nazi racial categories, nevertheless emerged from World War II with a reinvigorated sense of ethnic identification.[43]

The term "musulman" has had a similarly complex history in France. Indeed, despite the emerging historiographical consensus that the category "Muslim" has been more powerful in colonial and post-colonial French history than previously recognized, it is also true that until the 1970s, French authorities often used the terms "Musulmans," "Algériens," "Nord-Africains," "Arabes," "Musulmanes nord-africains," and "indigènes" interchangeably, a lexical confusion that reflected colonial conflations of geographic, religious, ethnic, and legal categories.[44] In the sources upon which this book is drawn, and particularly those from the 1940s through the 1970s, Algerian, Moroccan, and Tunisian Muslim migrants in France were most typically—although never exclusively—referred to as "Arabes," a category that at least some adopted for themselves as part of wider political struggles that sought to link Muslim North Africans with Arab national liberation struggles.[45] It was only in the late 1970s, after the Iranian Revolution spurred fears of spreading Muslim fundamentalism and as French society became increasingly aware of a generation of French-born children of North African immigrants living on the edges of national, social, and cultural life, that media outlets and the wider public began to speak more consistently of musulmans.[46]

Despite this relatively recent development, I have opted to use the term "Muslim" even when analyzing citations that refer directly to Arabes, Nord Africaines, or Algériens. This choice should not be understood to imply that for the migrants themselves religion was more important than ethnic, racial, or national identification, nor does it suggest that theology lay at the heart of evolving Muslim-Jewish relations.[47] Rather, the term works to distinguish Algerian, Tunisian, and Moroccan Muslim migrants from Jews and Christians coming from the same regions (since all were, in fact, Algerians, Tunisians, or Moroccans) and is preferable to the term "Arab," which not only glosses over the varying national and ethnic origins of the migrants collapsed therein but also reflects assumptions about their political allegiances and foreign status that this book seeks to challenge. Put differently, whatever the limitations of the term "Muslim," it shifts the focus away from the Israeli-Palestinian conflict and re-centers our gaze on France, the context in which this term has come to stand in for at least two generations of French-born citizens pushed to the national margins.

Geography and Politics: Harmony and Conflict in One French City

To tell a French story is often to tell a Parisian story, and this book is no exception. Not only does the highly centralized nature of state bureaucracy and cultural production in France focus attention on the nation's capital, but Paris houses the country's largest Muslim and Jewish populations and their most visible institutional structures. Insofar as there have been signs of Muslim-Jewish conflict, they have often been in Parisian immigrant neighborhoods, whether in Belleville in 1968 and 1973 or Sarcelles in 2000. Anti-racist demonstrations have famously ended their marches at the Place de la République and the Place de la Bastille.

If Paris stands at the heart of this study, however, it is in a second French city where de-colonization and Middle Eastern war had their most profound impact. As France's largest port and its gateway to the Mediterranean, Marseille had a front-row seat to the various crises in North Africa and the Middle East. French soldiers departed from this city for Algeria, tanks and guns were shipped to Israel from her ports, "repatriates" fleeing newly emerging independent North African states sought refuge in her neighborhoods, and colonial soldiers and laborers all poured into Marseille in search of exit or work, respectively. While most departed again, the city's identity as a center of transit profoundly marked its political, social, and cultural development and shaped the way Muslims and Jews interacted therein.

Decolonization was particularly unsettling for Marseille. Not only did the city serve as the main arrival point for most of the 1.5 million "returning" French nationals from 1954 to 1964, but its population also grew from 650,000 to 900,000 by 1975 (a 40 percent increase).[48] Although Marseille had attracted large numbers of immigrants before (nearly one quarter of the city's population before diminishing significantly during World War II), those arriving in tandem with France's withdrawal from North Africa transported shared cultural memories of trauma and rupture with them to their new city. Approximately 100,000 French Algerian settlers (*pieds-noirs*) shared the space with large numbers of mostly Algerian Muslim immigrants also fleeing economic and political upheaval, whose numbers grew from 10,000 in 1949 to 35,860 in 1968, and 50,000 by 1974.[49]

The Jewish population also grew dramatically. With a surviving remnant of 4,000–5,000 at the end of World War II, migrations from Egypt, Tunisia, Morocco, and Algeria brought the Jewish population to between 12,000 and 15,000 by 1955.[50] In 1962, with the full-scale Jewish flight from Algeria, the numbers soared, reaching approximately 65,000 by the 1970s, the largest Jewish population in France after Paris.[51]

The encounter between Muslims and Jews in Marseille reflected the specificities of this ethnically heterogeneous postwar urban landscape. Three factors in particular made Marseille distinctive. The first was the port, which as the city's major economic engine, served as a highly visible indication of France's link to the Mediterranean. Carrying migrants, arms, and soldiers to and from the city center, Marseille's port created sites of conflict for those with vested interest in French actions in the Middle East and North Africa.[52]

Second was the visible diversity of Marseille's landscape in a period when other French cities were directing immigrant laborers to the urban periphery.[53] Like all French cities, Marseille experienced an acute postwar housing crisis that posed problems for settling tens of thousands of incoming migrants. Most were pushed into the most squalid residential quarters near the city's industrial and harbor districts (14th, 15th, and 16th *arrondissements*) and in the industrial suburbs (9th arrondissement). Built out of planks and corrugated iron and without electricity, running water, or adequate transport, these slums (*bidonvilles*) were a world apart from Marseille's urban core.[54] Unlike other French cities where a similar process took place, however, downtown Marseille also saw new arrivals move into the overcrowded unventilated apartments in the 1st and 2nd arrondissements. Centrally located between the Old Port and the main train station, these immigrant neighborhoods abutted the Hôtel de Ville (city hall), the Bourse (chamber of commerce and industry), and the Canebière, the city's main commercial district. Symbolically cutting the city's northern industrial sectors from its middle-class and upper-middle-class neighborhoods to the south, the Old Port was the heart of commercial Marseille.[55] No matter where one lived in the city, all residents spent time in or passed through this area regularly, bringing the city's mixed ethnic life into public view and giving it a cosmopolitan flavor.[56]

These mixed neighborhoods—marked by an immigrant-centered commercial culture—provided opportunities for Muslim-Jewish interactions. If by 1975, Muslim immigrants made up 35 percent of the population of the Belsunce area, for example, numerous Jews conducted business in the neighborhood's commercial streets, and Jewish merchants—particularly jewelers—continued to populate the rue d'Aix and the neighboring markets on the rue Sainte Barbe.[57] While such neighborhoods were not unique to Marseille (Belleville, in Paris, for example, was similarly integrated),[58] the acute nature of the housing crisis meant that incoming repatriates and immigrants often lived for years in the same areas. As one anthropologist described the neighborhood around the porte d'Aix in 1972: "Jews, Arabs, Blacks, Italians, French of modest means . . . all live together. It's their complementarity that permeates the area."[59] Although wealthier repatriates—Jews among them—moved out as soon as was economically feasible, ethnic intermingling continued to mark Marseille's urban development, as those remaining in the commercial districts continued to work in a sophisticated economic trading zone that linked the central port regions of the city with secondary markets in other parts of the city.[60]

The third factor that made Marseille distinct was its relatively stable political landscape. Dominated by one figure, Marseille's postwar political life was linked directly with socialist Gaston Defferre. Mayor for thirty-three years (1944–45; 1953–86), Defferre controlled the city's political establishment, the local socialist party, and the major center-left newspaper Le Provençal (which he cofounded following the Liberation). Nationally visible due to his long-standing participation in the National Assembly (1945–58, 1962–86), Senate (1959–62), ministerial positions, and bid for the presidency, Defferre maintained unchallenged control over Marseille's political establishment, a position he used to confront national political figures when it suited him. Defferre felt particularly strongly about Israel. A vocal advocate for the young state, he used his position to speak out in its defense and worked closely with the local Jewish leadership to create links between Marseille and Israel. When war broke out in the Middle East in 1967 and 1973, much of Marseille's response as well as the way Muslim-Jewish relations unfolded were a product of the climate he created.

Due to the three factors described above, Muslim-Jewish relations in Marseille were clearly distinct from that in other French cities. The focus on the southern port city, however, serves more than as a counterpoint to generalizations derived from Paris, because Marseille can be understood as the space in which all the major factors influencing Muslim-Jewish conflict in France—decolonization, Middle Eastern politics, and French minority politics—came together in their most combustible form. As such, it serves less as a case study and more as the physical meeting point of all this book's central themes. And yet, despite its potentially explosive interethnic landscape, Muslims and Jews in Marseille also have a history of harmonious and even convivial exchange. As one Jewish cab driver remarked to a journalist in 2005, "I'm a Jew, my neighbors, they're Arabs, we understand each other fine."[61] Although the city experienced some of the most heightened fears of polarization during the 1991 Gulf War, widespread conflict did not break out; likewise in the post-2000 period when Muslim-Jewish relations garnered so much popular attention in France, relations in Marseille remained largely calm. A focus on Marseille thus captures the way fears of growing Muslim-Jewish conflict could take on a life of their own, divorced from the more variegated social landscape.

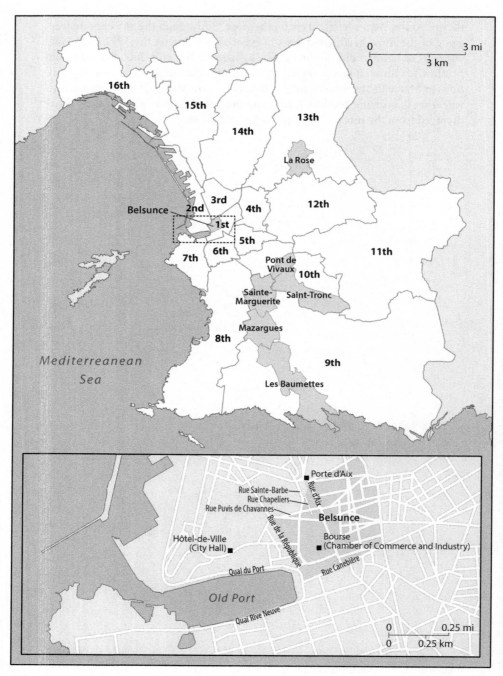

City of Marseille by arrondissement. Inset: 1st and 2nd arrondissements.

Colonial Policies, Middle Eastern War, and City Spaces

Marseille in 1948

In June 1948, North African Muslim dockworkers in Marseille refused to load freight onto boats transporting Jews or arms to the Middle East. As one official reported, "They consider Marseille to be one of the principle supply bases for the state of Israel."[1] Others complained that complaisant French officials were turning a blind eye to the thousands of Jewish migrants traveling through the city en route to Israel who, upon arrival, sent their passports to their co-religionists in Morocco and Tunisia for re-use.[2]

As such comments suggest, the 1948 war over the declaration of Israeli independence had repercussions in France. The war coincided with the growth of North African anti-colonial movements in the metropole, which at times criticized British and Jewish control of Palestine as a symbol of wider European efforts to dominate the Arab world, and the growth of Jewish nationalism in the aftermath of the Holocaust. These elements gave the struggle between Israel and her neighbors a powerful local resonance. Interestingly, however, while Paris held much larger Muslim and Jewish populations, that city saw few of the tensions evident in Marseille in the same period. Rather, animosities in Marseille were linked to charged city spaces and specific sites associated with Jewish migration, including the port and transit camps that housed large numbers of refugees en route to Palestine. The former gave the distant war a local immediacy; the latter highlighted contradictions in French policies toward its Jewish and Muslim populations. Indeed, a focus on these tumultuous months in Marseille makes clear the degree to which local clashes over Palestine were as much about wider questions related to French minority policies at home and in North Africa as they were about war in the Middle East. Put differently, for the demonstrating dockworkers cited above, France's willingness to condone the passage of Jewish people and arms through its port became part of a criticism of France's relationship to its Muslim subjects and citizens writ large and of the inequalities built into French colonial policies. That criticism was about Israel and Palestine to be sure, but it was also, in equal measure, about France.

As France's largest port and its gateway to the Mediterranean, Marseille saw a significant transient population of twenty thousand Jews travel through the city between March 1946 and May 1948 en route to Palestine.[3] To facilitate the migration, Jewish welfare and Zionist organizations established local offices, transforming Marseille into one of the most vibrant and politicized Jewish institutional landscapes in postwar Europe. The same period saw anti-colonial activities expand in the city as well, as approximately ten thousand Algerian Muslims took advantage of migration reforms to settle in the area.[4] Promised the same rights as all French citizens by the law of 20 September 1947, these impoverished, mostly male laborers nevertheless suffered from discrimination and heavy police surveillance.[5] In response, Marseille saw the establishment of several Algerian nationalist organizations, some of which promoted pan-Arab and pro-Palestinian causes as part of their wider anti-colonial agenda.[6]

Animosities in Marseille in spring 1948 emerged from the combustible encounter between these Jewish and pan-Arab nationalists over who would be victorious in Palestine. Equally divisive, however, was the way *French* policies in the Middle East seemed to favor one minority over the other. Disagreements among policymakers marked French approaches to the Palestine issue, reflecting fears of spreading pan-Arab nationalism, on the one hand, and postwar discomfort over further limiting Jewish movement, on the other.[7] The Ministry of Foreign Affairs, anxious to keep North Africa stable in the face of mounting Arab nationalism, saw Palestine as a tinderbox capable of exploding in unpredictable ways.[8] In the words of one official: "One cannot forget that there is no Jewish problem in France; [however] a Muslim problem is emerging which does not allow us to participate in a settlement to the feud that . . . violently antagonizes the Arab states. It is to be feared that once the Palestinian affair is settled, the Arab League will turn its attention toward 'the Liberation of their North African brothers.'"[9] The irony that a "Muslim problem" had so rapidly erased France's "Jewish problem" seems to have escaped notice; clearly, however, concern that Arab nationalism could spread to North Africa and endanger French rule encouraged some authorities to prioritize appeasement of Muslim subjects and citizens over their Jewish counterparts.

Such an outlook meant that despite sympathy for Jewish victims of Nazism, North African policymakers cautioned against allowing migration to Palestine, which, it was feared, would galvanize Arab nationalism throughout the Maghreb.[10] As one official wrote in 1947, "One cannot underestimate the disadvantages, notably in North Africa, of being on poor terms with England on the one hand and with the Arab countries on the other regarding the Palestinian matter."[11] Such thinking caused considerable French equivocation around the November 1947 United Nations partition plan for Palestine, as the government first supported and then withdrew support for the plan.[12] Likewise, authorities held off for nearly a year before granting Israel recognition after its declaration the following May, in part due to warnings from the major Tunisian, Moroccan, and Algerian nationalist movements, Neo Destour, Istiqlal, and the MTLD, over France's pro-Zionist and anti-Arab policies.[13]

Yet if those foreign ministry officials focused on North Africa were worried about the impact of supporting Zionist aims in Palestine, not all French policy-makers shared such perspectives. Many in the government, particularly those in the Ministry of the Interior, were sympathetic toward the plight of Jewish survivors, disgruntled with British efforts to oust France from the Middle East, and committed to a political liberalism that mandated tolerance for Zionism.[14] Such beliefs, as well as a concern that North African Jewish migrants might come to France if Israel was forbidden, encouraged many to turn a blind eye to refugee movements. As a result, thousands of illegal Jewish refugees traveled though French ports between 1946 and 1948, mostly through Marseille.[15] This choice transformed Jewish outmigration into a symbol of French duplicity and a source of considerable bitterness in North Africa.[16] Algerian Muslim spokesmen thus complained to diplomatic officials over French complicity in migration schemes, and French officials recorded significant discontent in Morocco over the same issue.[17]

In Marseille, the gathering point for Jewish clandestine migration to Palestine, such anger was compounded by frustrations that French officials seemed to be favoring Jewish refugees over newly minted French Algerian Muslim citizens. Conflicts around war in the Middle East thus became an opportunity for politically active Muslims and Jews to negotiate their relationship with the French state, as the former established new parameters for political participation in the aftermath of the Holocaust by pushing the French government to support Israel, and the latter tested the limitations on a citizenship that never made good on its promises.

Palestine and Postwar Muslim-Jewish Politics in France

Before turning to clashes in Marseille related to the 1948 war in the Middle East, it is important to understand the relatively circumscribed ways in which the Palestine issue shaped interethnic relations elsewhere in France both prior to and during the 1948 war. While the burgeoning Algerian Muslim nationalist movement in France, and certain segments from within the Jewish population, particularly newly arriving immigrants from Eastern Europe, displayed growing interest in their co-religionists in the Middle East well before World War II, clashes between them were rare given the relatively restrained public activism in both populations and their limited contact with each other. As in Marseille, however, when conflicts *did* emerge, they were often entangled in wider questions related to French minority policies at home and in North Africa. Put differently, disagreements over Palestine were rarely ever *only* about Palestine. Rather, such conflicts became one way that Muslim and Jewish nationalists negotiated their relationship with the wider polity in a period when both Jews and Algerian Muslim residents were experiencing radical changes in their political status.

By the late 1930s, France's Jewish population numbered 300,000, and was made up largely of Eastern European immigrant families and French-born Jewish citizens.[18] The Muslim population, which had begun growing significantly during World War I, hitting a peak of nearly 140,000 in 1937, was comprised largely of young seasonal workers from Algeria.[19] Differing in culture, language, place of origin, and status in the polity, members of the two populations had little contact with one another. Moreover, those Muslims and Jews who did interact regularly had far more that united than divided them. Indeed, among the 150,000 Jewish immigrants who came to France before and after World War I were 35,000 Jews from North Africa and the Levant.[20] Having more in common with other North Africans than with East European or French Jews, these new arrivals often lived in similar neighborhoods as incoming Muslims, where cafes, stores, kosher butcher shops (Muslims sometimes purchased ritually slaughtered meat), and markets brought together those with a common North African background.

Insofar as Palestine *did* emerge as a source of interethnic tensions, it was often entangled with the wider issues of French colonial and minority policies, in which both Muslims and Jews had a significant stake in the tumultuous period preceding and following World War II.[21] As Ethan Katz has recently shown, the contours of Muslim-Jewish relations in France were established in these years.[22] World War I, which brought colonial soldiers and laborers to the metropole in unprecedented numbers and which forever changed the European and Middle Eastern landscape, introduced new debates on the future of Palestine, French colonial policies, and the status of immigrants, establishing the parameters of Muslim-Jewish interactions in France for the next several decades. The interwar growth of both populations, coupled with debates over fascism, mounting xenophobia, and the emerging Algerian crisis, ensured that such interactions could be charged.

World War II radically transformed the hierarchies that had previously shaped the parameters of interethnic relations. French Jews were stripped of a wide range of rights, as Nazi officials sought to win Muslim allegiances with promises of increased autonomy and possible independence. For colonial subjects seeking to better their sociocultural status, the new racialized discourse provided one way to curry favor with the authorities, and helps explain the marked hostility toward Jews that emerged from France's Muslim population even as some helped Jewish friends and neighbors to hide. With the return of republican rule, however, and the abolition of Vichy's antisemitic policies, Jews returned to their former status in the polity while North African Muslim struggles for political recognition began to intensify.[23] General de Gaulle's decision to sign the Roosevelt-Churchill Atlantic Charter in September 1942 committed France in principle to the right of self-determination, giving politically active Muslim nationalists hope that once the war was over, France would be forced to make concessions with regard to its colonial holdings. For the leaders of the Provisional Government and the IVth Republic, however, maintaining France's colonial territories was essential to reestablishing the nation's strength and vitality. Rather than dismantling the empire, therefore, political leaders instituted a series of reforms that reaffirmed France's commitment to colonial rule while removing some of its worst political abuses.[24] Beginning with the ordinance of 7 March 1944 that abolished special penal statutes for Muslim subjects and offered citizenship to those who met certain criteria and gave up their rights to native or Muslim courts (about sixty thousand), subsequent statutes and ordinances, particularly that of 20 September 1947, broadened voting rights, extended citizenship to all Algerian Muslims, and dismantled travel restrictions between France and Algeria, opening the door to significant emigration.[25] The post-1944 reforms promised more rights than were granted, however, establishing unequal political representation for Algerian Muslim citizens. Moreover, legislative transformations did little to change practices of exclusion either in Algeria or in the metropole.[26] Violent repression of a mounting nationalist momentum in Algeria, most notably in the 8 March 1945 massacre at Sétif, proved an additional reminder that Algerian Muslim citizens were citizens of a different order.

Given the tremendous disruptions of the war and the concomitant transformations in political status, most Jews and Muslims had far more to worry about in the years immediately following World War II than developments in Palestine. Among Jews, support for Zionism had certainly grown after an initial period of profound wariness at the end of the nineteenth century, while Muslims too saw a growing interest in Palestine among key sectors of the pro-independence movements. A primary focus on the struggle for national independence, however, kept Muslim attentions focused elsewhere, while Jews—traditionally reticent to voice a visible ethnic politics in France and primarily consumed with rebuilding their disrupted communities—kept much of their pro-Zionist activism behind the scenes. As a result, Muslim-Jewish conflict around the Palestine issue was rare.

For French Jews, interest in Zionism had begun to increase with the 1930s refugee crisis in Central and Eastern Europe, which pushed many Jewish immigrants to France; such Zionist activism intensified following the expropriations, mass arrests, and deportations of the Second World War.[27] East European Jewish immigrants, already more sympathetic to Zionist ideology and disproportionately targeted by the war's antisemitic persecutions, also became the movement's most ardent supporters, as did new refugees—often en route to Palestine—who held small but regular pro-Zionist rallies in Yiddish.[28] In this context, French Jewish organizations began cautiously voicing support for Jewish nationalism, most notably in the declarations of the newly formed

Conseil représentatif des israélites de France (CRIF), which brought together leaders of the native French Jewish establishment and immigrant Jews of Zionist, Communist, and Bundist affiliation. While political disagreements undermined the CRIF's initial unity, and representatives of the traditionally anti-Zionist Jewish left continued to criticize Jewish nationalism, the new organization remained steadfast in its support of Palestine as a home for Jewish refugees.[29] Zionism now had the mainstream institutional legitimacy it had lacked. As one French official noted, even those "in the circles most removed from Zionism generally support the energetic attitude of Zionists of all tendencies and of Jewish patriots who call for the creation of an independent Jewish state in Palestine."[30] Likewise, the president of the Consistoire, the primary Jewish religious body and a former bastion of anti-Zionism, reported in spring 1945 that while "before the war, Zionism held no attraction for French Jews who, above all, sought to mark their belonging to the French community," the recent persecutions had created new solidarity.[31] Such increased support for Zionism did not, however, translate into widespread public activism, and few French Jews considered migrating to Israel after 1948.[32]

In late 1940s France, the growing if muted support for Zionism among French Jews was mirrored by a mounting interest in the Palestinian question among Algerian Muslim nationalists. Nevertheless, the issue did not become a central social or political question for most Muslim immigrants. Living on the margins of their host nation and absorbed with the daily tasks of providing for themselves and the families they had left behind, most did not involve themselves in the domestic or international controversies of the day.[33] As one Marseille police official noted in 1949 describing local North African populations, "The Muslims are apolitical. They rarely take an interest in the nation's political life, and only a tiny minority, insignificant one might say, is affiliated with the parties."[34] Although a highly politicized sector of Algerian Muslim activists did emerge during the late 1940s and early 1950s, their efforts focused intensely on Algerian independence.[35] Insofar as the Palestinian issue made headway, it did so through Messali Hadj's Parti du peuple algérien (PPA), which expressed profound sympathy for Palestinian struggles. Denouncing Jewish colonization of Palestine as an extension of European imperialism against Muslims, the PPA placed Zionism at the heart of its support of the Arab fight against domination.[36] Disagreement among Algerian Muslim migrants in France, however— between those who viewed Algeria as an integral part of the Arab world and those in the majority Berber population who stressed an Algerian Algeria over an Arab or Muslim Algeria—kept support for an Arab Palestine second to other concerns.[37]

Muted public activism around the question of Palestine meant that there was little Muslim-Jewish interaction around this issue in the 1940s. When Palestine *did* emerge as a source of tension, it was often enmeshed with the wider issues of French colonial and minority policies characterizing the period. For example, in October 1944, 200–300 Muslim protestors shouted anti-Zionist slogans during a meeting of the Organisation sioniste de France (OSF) in Paris.[38] The debates that day, while ostensibly about the future of Palestine, became a forum for establishing political legitimacy in France. Joseph Fischer, the OSF's secretary general, responded to the demonstrators by accusing them of harboring pro-German sentiments and undermining national harmony. In a context in which France was rebuilding from Nazi occupation and in which Jews were reclaiming their citizenship after years of debilitating exclusionary legislation, this linkage of Muslims to the enemy worked to cast them as outsiders at a moment when Jews were asserting their Frenchness. The protestors were equally quick to draw on war symbolism. According to one circulating flyer, "these people who suffered the most from deportation and forced expropriations have brutally changed face; from the persecuted that they were, they have become persecutors, deporting and expropriating an innocent and peaceful people on a very large scale." Protesters cautioned the French government that supporting Zionist aspirations would anger millions of Arabs in the empire who "consider Palestine the most beautiful and most sacred part of their *patrie* and who are ready to defend it against all imperialist efforts no matter their origin."[39]

The accusations of racism, national destabilization, and anti-imperialism flying around the room suggest that debates around Palestine were inextricably linked to key questions shaping France's broader political landscape in the postwar years. Fischer's accusation of pro-German sympathies among the Muslim demonstrators (implicitly underscoring Jewish loyalty to the republic) and the protestors' counterclaim that supporting Zionist aspirations would enrage France's Muslim subjects, allowed both to proclaim their place in the nation. Debates over Palestine thus became one way for Muslim and Jewish activists to claim their political legitimacy in France.

Such assertions also accompanied direct efforts to influence French policies in the Middle East. Here, though, French Jews' deep roots in the Republic, reclaimed after the years of Vichy persecution, provided them with greater access to the centers of French diplomatic power than was true for Muslim supporters of Arab Palestine.[40] Indeed, while Zionists and friends of the movement often worked from within the political establishment, Arab interests were represented by ambassadors and diplomats from abroad.[41] These efforts rarely overlapped, and interlocutors of the two "sides" had little contact. Moreover, while Zionists had significant organizational representation in France, those supporting Palestinian Arab interests did not have the same institutional strength, a fact that was a matter of commentary in the Arab world. The Egyptian newspaper, *Al Afif*, for example called France "the main center of Zionist political activity" and bemoaned the inability of Arab representatives to challenge Zionist influence.[42] Thus while the Association des amis de la palestine arabe in Paris protested to the Ministry of Foreign Affairs that the 1947 partition plan in Palestine would result in a "politics of division" between Arabs and Jews, and the ambassador of Egypt and the archbishop of Galilee argued that support for partition would threaten French interests in North Africa and the Middle East, they did so from outside the French political establishment.[43] Supporters of Jewish interests in Palestine, in contrast, used their connections in government circles to push for Jewish migration and later for partition.[44] In May 1945, for example, when a pan-Arab demonstration in Paris invited sympathetic French politicians to speak in opposition to Zionism, CRIF officials were concerned enough to petition foreign ministry authorities to support Jewish settlement in Palestine.[45] Likewise, during the 1947 UN debate over the partition of Palestine, various prominent Jewish politicians, such as René Cassin, René Mayer, Daniel Mayer, and Léon Blum, worked behind the scenes to obtain official French support, despite warnings from diplomats and foreign ministry officials over compromising national interests in the Arab world.[46]

Once the United Nations had voted on partition and the British began to withdraw, such activism increased. In January 1948, for example, the Fédération des sociétés juives de France (FSJF), the umbrella organization for East European Jewish immigrants in France, invited its participant organizations to register volunteers for the Jewish fighting forces in Palestine.[47] Likewise, Algerian Muslim nationalist circles solicited funds and recruited volunteers for combat, with the PPA providing anyone interested with a passport to Belgium from where they would be transported to Palestine.[48] While neither effort yielded significant results, passions were mounting. On 13 April 1948, at a meeting of the Comité hébreu de la libération nationale, for example, two hundred "Arab" protestors occupied the chairs until police emptied the premises.[49]

As the numbers of protestors suggests, however, the Palestine issue hardly galvanized North African Muslim populations in France. While Jewish residents in Paris welcomed Israel's declaration of independence on 18 May 1948 with great enthusiasm, and thirty thousand flocked to the Vel d'Hiv to celebrate, such passion did not translate into discord with local Muslim workers.[50] Although Jewish anti-racist organizations called for the immediate cessation of hostilities and for "Arab-Jewish cooperation," such appeals were directed to the Middle East rather than to Paris where 1948 came and went with little interethnic unrest.[51]

Marseille in 1948: Urban Space, Colonial Politics, and the Arab-Israeli Conflict

Unlike in Paris, officials in Marseille predicted a general Muslim-Jewish standoff around the 1948 Arab-Israeli conflict. A close examination, however, makes clear that conflict was quite limited and focused on specific, highly charged sites—the port from which armaments and refugees departed; the cinemas in immigrant neighborhoods where newsreels relayed information from the war zone; and camps where Jewish and Muslim migrants cohabited. The nature of these sites should not surprise, as they displayed directly France's contradictory policies with regard to the newly declared state of Israel—refusing, on the one hand, to recognize the new nation out of fear of alienating Muslim subjects in the empire, while on the other allowing arms and refugees to travel to Israel through French ports.

Post–World War II Marseille was a center of international transit for thousands, serving as a portal for the conflicts of the wider French empire. Five years of bombardment, pillaging, and occupation had destroyed nine kilometers of docks (out of twenty-five) and thousands of buildings, and caused massive demographic dislocation.[52] To facilitate reconstruction, the Provisional Government concentrated initial resources on rebuilding the port and central rail lines. With the reestablishment of regular maritime relations, crucial supplies and people were able to travel to the city while those trapped in Europe began to leave. By the late 1940s, then, Marseille served as a key transit site for liberated French soldiers, prisoners of war, survivors of labor brigades, returning deportees, Jewish refugees, displaced colonial soldiers, immigrant laborers, Syrian exiles fleeing the first wave of decolonization, "repatriating" Armenians, and North African Jews en route to Palestine.[53]

For most, Marseille was a stopping point on a journey elsewhere.[54] Even a several-week sojourn in the city, however, brought many voyagers into contact with one another. An acute postwar housing crisis and an enormous transient population led local authorities to settle tens of thousands of migrants in transit camps on the city's periphery.[55] Distanced both physically and culturally from the city center, thousands of East European (and to a lesser extent Moroccan and Tunisian) Jews awaited departure for Palestine from these camps; similar camps housed North African Muslim soldiers and laborers trapped in France during the war and awaiting repatriation.[56] Incoming Algerian Muslims, fleeing difficult economic conditions and surging inflation at home and seeking opportunities in the expanding postwar metropolitan economy, often moved into the same areas. In the largest such camp, Grand Arénas, many of these Muslims and Jewish refugees actually cohabited, albeit in separate barracks. Others resided in the crowded streets of the city's traditional immigrant neighborhoods or near the factories that employed them on the city's outskirts. Centrally located between the Old Port and the main train station, the city's first and second districts had earned the moniker *quartier arabe* due to the large numbers of Algerian Muslims who had settled there. The neighborhood was, however, mixed, and a number of Jewish agencies opened offices there to facilitate refugee movement from the train station, just north of the quarter, to the port on its western edge.[57]

The combination of postwar housing shortages and port life thus brought significant visibility to Jewish migratory movements in the very neighborhoods where Algerian Muslim laborers were heavily concentrated, focusing local attention on the distant Middle Eastern conflict and underscoring the French government's willingness to support the Israeli side in the conflict despite equivocation by the Foreign Ministry. Already during the Exodus Affair of July 1947, when the French government allowed 4,515 European Jews to sail from its shores to Palestine, Algeria's Arabic-language press accused the government of being "propagandists for Zionism not only in France but also in North Africa."[58] As tensions emerged in Marseille around the Palestine issue, anti-Zionist hostility was also often directed at the French. Like arguments at the Zionist rally in Paris in October 1944, those in 1948 Marseille reflected a postwar moment in which Muslim and Jewish subjects of the French empire were renegotiating their position within the polity and in which the Jewish victims of Vichy were rebuilding from a period of significant dislocation and loss. Tensions often reflected these negotiations of status, born during the war itself and far from settled in its immediate aftermath.

As noted earlier, the racial politics of the Nazi and Vichy years stripped Jews of their place in French society while providing Muslims with new opportunities to promote their communal self-interest. In Marseille, the largest city of the Unoccupied Zone and free from Nazi occupation until November 1942, the port and railroad had linked Switzerland with Spain, attracting large numbers of fleeing Jews. By 1941, fifteen thousand Jews lived in the city, a quarter to a half of whom were of North African and Mediterranean origin.[59] The city also housed France's second largest Muslim population, also numbering approximately fifteen thousand, as well as a large apparatus for administering North African and Muslim affairs.[60] Common origins and immigrant commercial life brought the two populations into regular contact. When war broke out, a few Muslims protected Jewish acquaintances, and some North African Jews relied on their knowledge of Arabic to "pass" as Muslims. At other times, however, Muslims denounced their Jewish neighbors. As the Service of Algerian Affairs of Marseille reported in December 1941, "Hardly a [Muslim] conversation in Marseille takes place without complaints expressed against the Jews," a state of affairs the report attributed to the success of German propaganda in convincing Algerian Muslims that Jews were manipulating French colonial control of their homeland.[61] Indeed, Nazi propagandists emphasized links between Jews and the European imperialist project as part of their campaign to win support in North Africa. Such efforts seem to have yielded results in France when coupled with the anti-Semitic context of the Vichy years and decades of Muslim nationalist rhetoric regarding Jewish colonial designs in Palestine. At the very least, World War II strengthened discursive links between Jews and European colonialism in certain strands of North African nationalist rhetoric.[62]

With the war's end and the restoration of Jewish citizenship, the Provisional Government quickly repudiated the racist politics of its predecessors, but Vichy's downfall did not end questions about the place of ethnic and religious minorities within the polity. Although Jewish citizens quickly regained all the rights of which they had been stripped, officials downplayed the specificity of their war losses, making restitution difficult.[63] For severely weakened Jewish communities, such as the one in Marseille, rebuilding was a slow and arduous process. Dramatically depleted due to deportations and dislocations, the local Jewish population had dropped from 18,000 to 4,000–5,000 by 1945.[64] With no infrastructure in place, those who remained had significant difficulty reconstituting a robust communal structure. These problems were exacerbated by the heterogeneous nature of the Jewish population, which was made up of native Jews with long-term regional roots, North African and other Mediterranean Jews who had arrived in the century's first decades, and Central and Eastern European refugees. Jewish dispersion throughout the city also impeded communal development.[65] As one returning Jewish POW described:

> [A]ll the persons of a certain age who had responsibilities had been deported. . . . Thus we find ourselves in the months of June and July in Marseille . . . with a community that could be deemed nonexistent in terms of leadership. The Chief Rabbi of Marseille is all alone. . . . [T]here is no money, and the new president of the Consistoire, Monsieur Fedia Cassin . . . paid from his own pocket the entire reconstruction of the community, all of the organization, the staff of the Consistory and the rabbis.[66]

The influx of thousands of illegal Jewish refugees in 1946 and 1947 exacerbated the sense of crisis. Although many officials turned a blind eye to their movements, others were less sanguine, particularly in Marseille where such migration created new social tensions. Thus if the war's end had reestablished Jewish citizenship, it was several years before those in Marseille felt secure.

Algerian Muslims, who made up the majority of Marseille's Muslim population in the late 1940s, found themselves in an even more tenuous position, since while French Jews may have continued to feel insecure in the decade following World War II, the government had, in fact, restored to them the rights of which they had been stripped. For Algerian Muslims, in contrast, the end of the Second World War raised anew the question of French colonial control in North Africa at a moment when both Britain and France were seeking to reconcile the victory of democracy in Europe with their desire to justify ongoing control of their empires.[67] As we have seen, the result was a series of political and economic reforms that culminated in the 1947 Statute of Algeria granting—among other things—citizenship to Algerian Muslim men in mainland France and establishing unregulated migration between France and Algeria. Employment, settlement, and policing practices, however, continued to discriminate against them, helping to explain why incoming Algerian Muslims were interned until 1946 in transit camps under military supervision.[68] That year, the Ministry of Interior reminded local authorities that practices that "appear to establish distinctions among the French" could no longer be tolerated.[69] Discrimination nevertheless continued: The caution was reiterated in 1947, demonstrating that legal equality had not translated fully into administrative practice.[70]

Nor did many Algerian Muslims take advantage of the full range of new rights available to them. Working to stay solvent in a context where housing shortages and a struggling postwar labor market made their position precarious, in the late 1940s, only one thousand Algerian Muslims had registered on electoral rolls.[71] While some joined the Confédération générale du travail (CGT), such affiliations seem to have reflected a hope of assuring work rather than a commitment to participating in French political life.[72] Insofar as Algerian Muslims in Marseille expressed their political engagement with France, they did so as elsewhere in the country by participating in the burgeoning nationalist movement. In 1945 the Parti du peuple algérien created four federations in France, one of which was in Marseille.[73] In 1946, after its leaders had been arrested and the party reconstituted as the Mouvement pour le triomphe des libertés démocratiques (MTLD), its charismatic leader, Messali Hadj, received an enthusiastic welcome in Marseille.[74] Over the next several years, the pro-independence movement spread.[75] Although city officials sought to counter its appeal by improving living and working conditions and relaunching prewar discussions on the construction of a mosque and welcome center, political frustrations continued to mount.[76] At the annual 1 May 1950 Labor Day Parade, for example, several hundred Algerian Muslims followed behind the CGT calling for the abolition of colonialism.[77] Eight days later, the MTLD organized a commemoration of the Sétif massacre.[78] While police believed a handful of Muslim elites were provoking their co-religionists who were concerned primarily with material issues, anti-French rhetoric was clearly on the rise.[79]

Pro-Palestinian activism, while hardly widespread among Algerian Muslims in the 1940s, increased as part of this wider nationalist movement. Most notably, the MTLD-PPA—which as we saw above condemned Zionism as part of its larger anti-colonial vision—promoted Palestinian rights. In December 1947, for example, copies of its newspaper, L'Emigré, circulated in the city's North African quarters. Given a ban against the publication, we can assume its diffusion was limited. Nevertheless, a glance at the paper points to the centrality of anti-Zionism in the movement's rhetoric. While the first article stressed the nationalist movement's commitment to creating a state for all Algerians irrespective of race or religion, the second, entitled, "The Arab States and the Palestinian Question," railed against Zionism. Although "the Arab states hope that the Jewish communities in their countries will not suffer," the authors insisted, they would fight Zionism's outrages "by all means at their disposition."[80] Such rhetoric came to Marseille in other forms as well. In a wide-ranging speech at the Cinema Colibri on 5 May 1950, for example, Larbi Bouhali, the secretary general of the Algerian communist party, called for (among other things) the suppression of colonialism, the banning of the atomic bomb, and support for the Palestinian people.[81] Pro-Palestinian appeals were not unique to Marseille.

It was in Marseille, however, that pro-Palestinian Muslims and pro-Zionist Jews began confronting each other thanks to certain characteristics distinctive of the city. In particular, Maresille's close proximity to North Africa and the Middle East, its position as a leading port city with thousands of Jewish and Muslim transits, and its city spaces all brought the two into contact with each other and drew attention to the contradictions in French policy regarding the intensifying struggle for Palestine.

The first Zionist and pro-Palestinian activities in Marseille in May and June 1948 were focused on France's role, or lack thereof, in the conflict. On 6 May 1948, for example, fifteen hundred Zionist activists gathered to promote the Jewish struggle, raise funds for arms and supplies, and criticize French neutral-ity in the conflict.[82] Early June saw Muslim dockworkers protest when trade union leaders tried to enforce this neutrality by telling members not to load a ship sailing for Syria, one of the belligerents in the conflict.[83] It was only later in June, however, when tensions began to mount. According to police accounts, anti-Jewish hostility became evident when "Arab circles" that had initially been optimistic about eliminating the Jewish state began fearing the reverse would occur.[84] Such interpretations, however, overlooked the primary trigger for mounting hostilities—riots in the Moroccan town of Oujda on 7 June during which five Jews were killed and another fifteen injured. That evening during further rioting in the nearby mining town of Djérada, thirty-seven more Jews were murdered. These events, which others have covered ably and at length, need not be revisited here.[85] Of central concern for our purposes, however, is the riots' origins, which were directly related to Moroccan nationalist efforts to win adherents to the anti-French cause and which channeled anger against French officials for turning a blind eye to Jewish migrations from Morocco to Palestine into energy for the nationalist movement. Most work on the riots has overlooked Jewish migration to Palestine as a spark for local animosity, em-phasizing only that agents of the Moroccan nationalist movement, Istiqlal, fo-mented the violence in an effort to channel anti-Zionist sentiment into support for their movement.[86] Contemporary observers offered similar impressions. Alphonse Juin, for example, the French resident general, stressed Istiqlal's in-volvement: "Disjointed and dormant for a year, [Istiqlal] found in anti-Zionism a means of re-building strength and cohesion by exploiting a widely shared sentiment among Muslims. After having organized a boycott, they provoked the riots with the secret hope that we would respond violently thereby strength-ening their propaganda."[87]

Many Moroccan Jews seconded the notion that the riots had been pre-planned. The president of the Jewish community in Oujda, for example, noted: "For about a month, tendentious rumors circulated among the Muslim popula-tion; they accused Jews of allegedly placing a bomb in the new Medina. These false rumors were spread to create agitation. Jews were molested, insulted in the streets, calls for boycotts circulated."[88] The stress on nationalist agitation allowed locals to blame outsiders for disrupting a generally peaceful social landscape. According to a local Jewish school director, for example, "one wonders how such acts could take place in a city where Jews and Arabs have always lived on such good terms."[89] The answer, agreed many, was Moroccan nationalism, which had used the Palestine issue for its own ends.[90]

While these arguments make clear how anti-colonialism and anti-Zionism became further entangled in Morocco in 1948, they overlook the specific role of Jewish migration in intensifying passions. A border town between Morocco and Algeria, Oujda not only attracted "propaganda agents of all ideological stripes," but it also served as a transit point for young Zionists en route to Palestine.[91] It was this fact, above all else, that allowed Moroccan nationalists to use the anti-Zionist criticism as a way to forward their anti-French agendas. Already in the weeks prior to the riot, Jewish outmigration from Oujda had angered local Istiqlal representatives who had organized patrols to prevent suspicious passengers from departing. In a region that had been galvanized by massive strikes (particularly in Djérada), tensions were high.[92] According to the regional head, M. Brunel, the riot began when a Jewish barber attempted to cross the border from Morocco to Algeria, en route to Palestine with explosives.[93] In his account, while the war had enflamed passions everywhere, what "overheated" the local atmosphere was "the clandestine passage over the border of a large number of young Zionists from all regions of Morocco trying to get to Palestine via Algeria."[94] Juin too stressed the intersections of geography, anger over Jewish migration, and nationalist-inspired efforts to rile the population. Claiming that the proximity of the Algerian border was one crucial factor in the rioting, he noted "the clandestine departure of Jews for Palestine ignited the anger already inflamed by professional agitators."[95] Similarly, the French Ministry of Foreign Affairs believed Jewish migration to be a significant irritant: "It is characteristic that those in this region near to the Algerian border consider all Jews who depart as combatants for Israel."[96] Anti-Zionism, then, however present in an abstract sense in 1948 Morocco, only became a source of violent local conflict when Jewish Moroccans started leaving to fight in Palestine. In this sense, the transnational mobilization of certain Jews provoked a transnational countermobilization on the part of some Moroccan Muslims, entangling the anti-colonial movement with the anti-Zionist movement in tangible ways.

I have focused at length on the riot in Oujda and its causes because it was this event and not the 1948 war in Palestine, as such, that first brought passions to a head in Marseille. Indeed, local police reports on interethnic conflict all date from 9 June or after. For Jewish and Muslim observers in Marseille—many with family and friends in North Africa—the riots suggested that the war between Israel and its Arab neighbors was spreading to their *own* communities. Marseille's North African Muslim dockworkers thus accused Jews of starting the Moroccan riots and vowed revenge.[97] Meanwhile Marseille's Jewish leadership organized a day of mourning, arguing that recent events were the "logical conclusion of the tension in North Africa between Muslims and Jews."[98] As such rhetoric suggests, Muslim and Jewish political discourse in Marseille was intimately connected with North African politics, leading local French authorities to fear that rioting would spread to the metropole. They thus increased protection around all Jewish institutions accordingly, warning that given "the sudden and violent excesses to which [Muslim laborers] are accustomed," conflict was a distinct possibility and that further departures to Palestine should be curtailed until spirits had calmed.[99]

The biases evident in such assertions and the acknowledgment that Jewish migration through French ports was a trigger for North African Muslim nationalist politics remind us that French officials were not bystanders in an ongoing drama between Muslims and Jews, but were, in fact, helping to shape the context in which conflict was emerging. Indeed, the first near confrontation between Jewish and Muslim residents in Marseille focused primarily on the way the war in Palestine was underscoring inequalities between them in France. On 10 June at the cinema on rue Canebière (directly abutting Marseille's immigrant districts), Algerian Muslim spectators complained of biased newsreels. While Jewish attendees clapped exuberantly at portrayals of heroic Israeli combatants and the valiant Zionist struggle, Muslims criticized a general silence on the Arab struggle, which—when covered—presented Arab soldiers as rebels. While no violence broke out, Algerian Muslim attendees complained that foreign-born Jews had no business taunting French Muslims.[100]

This assertion of "Frenchness" in contradistinction to the "foreignness" of Jewish refugees was a fascinating attempt to assert Algerian Muslim's status as citizens at a moment when many authorities still treated them as immigrants. To the frustration of many, in summer 1948, officials monitored the comings and goings of North African Muslims even more so than that of Jewish refugees, arguing that a growing Muslim presence was problematic at a moment when so many refugees were also traveling through the city en route to Israel.[101] That Jewish refugees enjoyed greater recognition than Algerian-born Muslim French citizens proved galling to the latter who also complained angrily when French Jewish politicians used their position to support the Zionist struggle against the Arabs.[102] For them, Jewish inclusion (so recently returned) in contradistinction to their own marginalization was an ongoing source of irritation, and for us, such motivations serve as a reminder of how inequities in political access can stoke interethnic clashes.

Such frustrations were also clear in Muslim responses to the transfer of arms and immigrants to Palestine through Marseille's ports with the apparent acquiescence of French officials. By the end of World War II, Marseille had become a visible center of Zionist activity, as Jewish welfare agencies flocked there to support the transient refugee population.[103] Keren Kayemet LeIsrael (KKL), for example, one of the fund-raising arms of the Zionist movement whose activities had been suspended under Vichy, quickly reestablished a presence, raising funds to buy land in Palestine and aiding clandestine migration.[104] Arms made their way through the city, mainly via the efforts of the Zionist paramilitary group, Ha'Irgun HaTzva'i HaLe'umi BeEretz Yisra'el, or the Irgun, which established a local branch in spring 1947.[105] Jewish agencies from Great Britain and the United States created local affiliates to help clandestine refugees find housing, resources, medical aid, and temporary employment, and the communist organization, Union des juifs pour la résistance et l'entraide (UJRE), opened centers to tend to refugee needs. Most visibly, the Fédération des sociétés juives de France, the umbrella association uniting the myriad Eastern European Jewish compatriotic organizations into one cooperative, opened offices on 24 rue des Convalescents, near the train station and in the heart of what was already called the "Arab quarter."[106] Under the direction of Frédéric Thau, the FSJF became the primary intercessor between the municipal government and the Jewish Agency (the body responsible for organizing migration to Palestine/Israel), establishing an active if financially precarious network to provide food, legal aid, child care, and employment to Jewish refugees.[107] Relying on the good will of local authorities, it also ran several regional refugee camps (the largest in Trets, Pélissanne, and La Ciotat) as well as two welcome centers in Marseille (Roucas-Blanc and Caillols).

With the declaration of Israeli independence, clandestine migration operations moved into the open, and Marseille's ports began "packing them in from all sides."[108] While the FSJF continued to facilitate refugee care, Israeli and international Jewish agencies now openly participated in receiving, housing, and feeding migrants, establishing fourteen camps in the Marseille region for those en route to Israel, two of which the French government owned but made available to the Jewish Agency (Grand Arénas and St. Chamas) and twelve of which the American Joint Distribution Committee rented or purchased for the FSJF and the Jewish Agency. The former generally served as welcome and transit centers while the latter (often run by religious and secular youth movements) housed those between the ages of sixteen and eighteen for three to six months as they studied agricultural techniques, elementary Hebrew, and Jewish history before embarking for Israel.[109]

May and June 1948 were the "coming out" of this Jewish migration program, causing resentment for Algerian Muslim activists who saw Jewish fortunes reverse so successfully while their own deteriorated. The anger, not surprisingly, was focused on the two sites where such activities were most visible. The first was the port, the symbolic "door" to France for both populations and a visible reminder of the munitions, supplies, and bodies traveling to Palestine. For Algerian Muslim laborers—many of whom worked on the docks—the port was a site of war, and activists threatened to sabotage ships they feared were supplying Jewish fighters.[110] Conflict around port activities intensified on 11 June when the *Altalena*, an Irgun-owned ship, sailed from the Port-de-Bouc—thirty miles from Marseille—loaded with one thousand Jewish volunteers and stockpiles of weapons. Although Irgun agents attempted to maintain secrecy around the operation, hiding such a large vessel proved impossible. Given the heightened tensions in Marseille, word of the *Altalena*'s departure caused considerable consternation, particularly since the ship—originally scheduled to sail in early June—did not depart until 11 June, the first day of the truce between Arab and Israeli forces in Palestine. Calling a dockworker strike, the Syndicat des ouvriers musulmans de Port-de-Bouc refused to load the ship,[111] while Muslim protesters in Marseille threatened sabotage, and local nationalists called for Arab unity.[112] Fearing the consequences of significant unrest to the well-being of the already distrusted Algerian Muslim laboring population, Marseille's Muslim communal leaders implored their compatriots to remain calm while appealing to French authorities to prevent infractions of the truce.[113] Meanwhile, Jews from Marseille traveled to Port-de-Bouc to load the ship while the FSJF and Jewish student groups called for donations of binoculars, sleeping bags, backpacks, and other objects to aid Jewish combatants.[114]

A second site of conflict in June 1948 was the refugee and labor camps on the city's periphery in which Jewish refugees and Algerian Muslim transients often resided. For Algerian Muslims, angry that local Jews had established "a veritable framework for aiding their co-religionists in Palestine," Marseille's refugee centers appeared to be military schools that used the cover of their agricultural and educational facilities to train Jewish recruits. For such critics, Jewish transients were not needy refugees but "soldiers who would soon be fighting Arab armies," while the FSJF's refugee center was an arms-smuggling hub, as evidenced by the comings and goings of trucks between midnight and 4:00 A.M. and the armed guard at the door.[115] Spying on these camps became one expression of Algerian Muslim anger, as were PPA calls for volunteers to fight in Palestine or to donate funds to supply Arab armies. The PPA also criticized the opening of a consulate in Marseille to facilitate Jewish immigration. While the Office palestinien d'immigration had in fact already functioned for two years as a quasi-clandestine body, its transformation into the Office d'immigration de l'État d'Israël in May 1948 made Jewish migratory activities highly visible, angering PPA adherents.[116]

In spite of these simmering tensions, the only incidents of interethnic violence (and these rather mute) broke out in June 1948 in the Grand Arénas transit camp. Constructed by the French government in 1939 to hold prisoners of war, by 1946 Grand Arénas sheltered thousands of displaced persons and immigrant laborers. In June 1948, Vietnamese migrants and four hundred Jewish refugees (the latter funded and cared for by the Jewish Agency) shared the camp with several dozen Algerian Muslim laborers who resided in barracks operated by the Ministry of Labor. Living side by side with no barrier between them, Muslim and Jewish migrants largely ignored each other, and the camp experienced no disruptions in May 1948 despite daily combat exercises by the camp's Jewish inhabitants. In mid-June, however, when two Muslim workers wandered separately into the Jewish barracks while hunting for their own, tensions mounted. While the first was "unceremoniously" dismissed, the second was detained for the morning and forced to work in the Jewish canteen, raising passions in the Muslim barracks.[117] Two weeks later another lost Muslim laborer wandered into the Jewish camp and was roughed up after insulting several residents. Shortly thereafter, two or three seemingly drunk Jewish residents entered the Muslim barracks where they attacked the French guard.[118] The next few days brought similar small-scale harassments leading Mohamed Talmoudi, president of the Association des Musulmans algériens, to request separation of camp residents.[119] No separation occurred.[120] By late October, a labor ministry official was still lamenting the problems caused by the presence of Jewish and Arab elements in the camp, warning that "serious incidents" might result.[121]

Despite such concerns and the charged environment around Jewish refugee camps, however, summer 1948 saw no serious violence between Marseille's Muslim and Jewish migrant populations. With the exception of the few incidents described above, daily police reports indicated peaceful intercommunal relations throughout the charged days of June *even* in mixed residential areas like Grand Arénas.[122] With the war's second ceasefire from 18 July to 15 October, tensions continued to dissipate.[123] If police continued to document Muslim support for "their Arab brothers in Palestine" well into 1949, the previous summer's passions had cooled.[124] Tellingly, however, if "slogans of 'Arab victors throwing Jews in the sea' have given way bit by bit to peaceful and amicable understandings between Jews and Arabs," what remained was profound resentment over French complaisance to Jewish departures for Palestine. Indeed, ongoing anger and frustration over the Arab defeat was henceforth channeled almost entirely toward French policymakers who it was believed had favored the Zionists despite assertions to the contrary.[125]

That police continued to document Muslim resentment toward French support for Jewish migration is revealing. For many Muslims, Jewish migration was not only an indication that Middle Eastern war was locally relevant but it also signaled the inherent inequities facing Muslim migrants in France. Marseille's Zionist organizations seem to have understood these dynamics. Seeking to avoid igniting passions around migration, they maintained as low a profile as possible even after the previously clandestine Palestinian immigration office was allowed to move into the open.[126] Although the city's ports continued to be major sites of Jewish departures, a formal Israeli consulate did not open until July 1950. In the interim the FSJF continued to operate as a link between the French government and the Jewish Agency, but its officials conducted migrations with considerable discretion.[127] Moreover, the French government's decision to withhold formal recognition of Israel for several months created little protest among Marseille's otherwise vocal pro-Zionist organizations. Cognizant of the problems facing "a power whose influence extends over a vast Muslim empire," the Jewish leadership remained silent, and fewer than one hundred participants attended a meeting organized by the Jewish communist group, the UJRE, in November criticizing such policies.[128] Even members of the city's most ardently Zionist circles proved sensitive to the way their support for Israel could irritate local conditions. In May 1949, for example, the FSJF celebrated Israel's first anniversary. So as to avoid sparking controversy, organizers chose to show a film stressing Israel's efforts to incorporate Holocaust survivors rather than one on the recent war.[129] Such choices helped ensure that tensions that had mounted in Marseille in summer 1948 would diminish quickly in the war's aftermath.

The city's distinctive profile had nevertheless allowed conflict to emerge in ways that were atypical for France. The reasons, as we have seen, were threefold: First, although Marseille was a French city, its political culture was deeply affected by events in North Africa. Although the Mediterranean divided the colonies and protectorates from the metropole, the line was porous, meaning that anti-colonial, nationalist, and Zionist politics in North Africa had repercussions in Marseille. Second, the specific contours of Marseille's urban landscape brought Jews and Muslims together in ways that drew attention to France's willingness to support the Zionist side of the struggle even while claiming neutrality. Transit camps, the port, and even the Cinema Colibri, located on the edge of a mixed immigrant neighborhood, were shared spaces in which migrants of all kinds came together, making the issue of Jewish migration and the war in Palestine particularly visible. Third, World War II had raised vexing questions as to the place of both Jews and colonial subjects in the French polity, the repercussions of which lasted well into the postwar period. With Algerian Muslim citizenship so fragile and contested, and with Jewish citizenship having been so recently tested, the issue of French support for Palestine became a highly charged barometer of the country's fluctuating and contradictory commitments to some of its most insecure citizens. It was in Marseille's port and transit camps that these fluctuations and contradictions were most visible.

With the end of the 1948 war and France's formal recognition of Israel the next spring, whatever tensions had existed between largely transient Muslim and Jewish populations receded. While the MTLD-PPA continued to sympathize with the Palestinian plight, by the early 1950s most politically active North African Muslim migrants in France were focused on their own liberation struggles. For Jews, Israel was of more sustained interest. The Jewish press and mainstream institutional bodies focused heavily on strengthening Israel's economy and social structure and promoting political and cultural exchanges between France and Israel.[130] The depth of communal engagement, however, is hard to gauge. Many local activists complained of paltry numbers at pro-Israel events, and Israeli hopes that France would become the center of European Zionism gave way to understandings that most Jews continued to view France as their home despite the traumas of World War II.[131] Furthermore, prominent Jewish intellectuals, such as Raymond Aron, took issue with the notion of a unified Jewish people, expressing public discomfort at being seen as anything other than French.[132] If most French Jews looked favorably on Israel, their support was largely passive and private, expressed around dinner tables and as part of intercommunal dialogue. Even financial contributions to the new state, which increased throughout the 1950s, compared poorly to those from Great Britain, despite the smaller size of the latter's Jewish community.[133] Given the rather latent interest of most French Jews in Israel and the focus of Algerian Muslim migrants on North African politics and the struggles of daily life, by the late 1940s, Israeli statehood—never a major source of intercommunal tension—posed even fewer problems.

In two crucial respects, however, sources of tension in 1948 France extended beyond a narrow focus on war in Israel: first, by making clear that French commitment to its Muslim or Jewish subjects/citizens could be understood through its relationship to Palestine-Israel, and second by underscoring the way ethnic politics in French North Africa could influence Muslim-Jewish political discourse in the metropole. As French decolonization pushed ever larger numbers of North Africans (Muslims and Jews) to France, these dynamics intensified, a process to which we will now turn.

Decolonization and Migration

Constructing the North African Jew

The emigration of Moroccan and Tunisian Jews, already a source of tension in 1948 despite the small numbers, surged during French decolonization. Sixty-one thousand Moroccan Jews thus left for Israel between 1955 and the first half of 1956, as did 15,300 Tunisian Jews.[1] In addition, approximately 20,000 Algerian Jews departed from 1954 to 1961 (after which most others left), although their destination was almost always France where they held citizenship.[2] By 1984, North Africa, which had once housed 470,000 Jews, held 16,700.[3]

The complex push factors behind this migration, which coincided with France's violent withdrawal from the region, included poverty and economic upheaval, bloodshed, and fear of independence.[4] Yet if motivations were diverse, departures came to be understood as "Jewish" for many with a vested interest in the region. One key legacy of this process was the construction of the "North African Jew," a discursive category to which no individual ascribed as such, but that framed the diverse Moroccan, Tunisian, and Algerian Jewish populations into a collective often understood to be in conflict with "North Africans," "Muslims," or "Arabs."

This way of thinking emerged through three channels. The first was through French administrators charged with governing the nation's colonial territories and increasingly fearful of the threat that pan-Arab nationalism and Zionism posed to regional peace.[5] The reports and letters warning of this danger often imagined North Africa's diverse populations as two polarized cross-regional ethno-religious factions. While never the only way of conceptualizing ethnic relations in Morocco, Tunisia, and Algeria, local French officials regularly referred to North African Jews as a collective and hypothesized that developments in one country were likely to undermine Muslim-Jewish relations elsewhere. Certainly, as Todd Shepard has made clear, by the time of the 1962 negotiations between the FLN and the French, the latter had rejected distinctions between Jews and other "Europeans" thereby juridically sealing the "Frenchness" of Algeria's Jewish population and marking them off from Jews elsewhere in North Africa.[6] And yet this juridical move never fully erased competing conceptualizations of Jews as a distinct political unit increasingly at odds with the region's Muslim majority.

The endurance of this way of understanding Muslim-Jewish relations in North Africa came secondly from international Jewish organizations that began focusing on the region in the late 1940s as part of their wider post-Holocaust efforts to save Jewish life. Such interest had roots in the nineteenth century when the Alliance israélite universelle, established in Paris in 1860 to fight for Jewish political rights and modernization worldwide, established an educational network in Morocco and Tunisia.[7] The Alliance continued this work after World War II, while expanding its mandate to a range of juridical and social issues, particularly in Morocco.[8] The growing international Jewish philanthropic network, which reached its apogee after World War II in the American Jewish Joint Distribution Committee, initially showed little interest in North Africa given its post-Holocaust efforts to rebuild European Jewish communities. The struggle in Palestine, however, refocused the international Jewish gaze on Muslim lands, particularly on Iraq, Libya, and Syria where anti-Jewish violence spiked in response to the 1948 war. North Africa—removed as it was from both the site of the Holocaust's worst devastations and from the center of the Middle Eastern conflict—received less attention. Soon, however, both the size and poverty of the local Jewish population caught the attention of agencies focused on the Jewish future. While not always concerned with "North African Jews" as a whole—mitigating poverty, disease, and education in Morocco received the most sustained attention—the legacy of the recent devastation in Europe combined with the mounting conflict in other regions of the Middle East meant that Jewish life in Algeria, Tunisia, and Morocco was often interpreted in a much wider context.[9] Moreover, for those rebuilding Jewish life after World War II, local tensions were often viewed as an indication of likely future violence, a problem to be solved before the fact, often through migration to Israel. If for many international Jewish agencies a pro-Zionist agenda existed in tension with efforts to ensure minority rights in the emerging independent states of North Africa, meaning migration was never their sole priority, other expressly Zionist organizations sought actively to encourage Jewish departures, emphasizing their co-religionists' alienation and exclusion from the entire Arab world.[10]

A third source for the more homogenized image of the "North African Jew" came from indigenous nationalist movements. Here too, the crystallization of this category was never straightforward and, indeed, often contrary to the stated aims of the mainstream Algerian, Tunisian, and Moroccan nationalist parties whose leaders downplayed quarrels with local Jews in their efforts to build united national fronts. Thus, the FLN, Neo Destour, and Istiqlal, the major Algerian, Tunisian, and Moroccan independence movements, respectively, all declared Jews to be equal partners in the struggle against the French and integral members of their respective nations. All three movements, however, had spokesmen that blurred the lines between Jews and Zionists. Warning Jews that emigration, particularly to Israel, was a sign of disloyalty to their birth nations, nationalist rhetoric in all three countries helped establish new binaries around which those monitoring Jewish life took note.[11]

The combined voices of French colonial administrators, international Jewish organizations, and nationalist activists meant that by the end of the decolonization process there was a North African Jewish story to tell, a story that rendered less visible the diverse ways in which Jews and Muslims interacted on the ground or alternative political visions of Muslim-Jewish cooperation.[12] This chapter will trace the emergence of this story by looking closely at Jewish departures and the way a whole host of actors came to see particularistic meanings within them. While I will concentrate heavily on Algeria both because nearly 90 percent of that nation's Jewish population relocated to France and because recent scholarship has emphasized the "Frenchness" of these departures, a narrow focus on one country overlooks the way many of the political actors considered here came to see Jewish emigration as a sign of a broader Muslim-Jewish crisis.[13] While not the only way of understanding the impact of decolonization on North Africa's diverse Muslim and Jewish populations, this narrative proved powerful and enduring in subsequent decades in France.

Decolonization and the Renewal of Jewish Migration

In August 1954, just after the first anniversary of France's exile of Morocco's Sultan Muhammad V to Madagascar for his nationalist sympathies, seven Jews were killed in the town of Petitjean. Part of the wider violence associated with challenging French rule in the region, the murders reflected the escalating nature of the conflict. Indeed, although the French premier, Pierre Mendès-France, proposed granting greater autonomy for Tunisia and gradual internal reforms for Morocco in 1954, the early 1950s were characterized by widespread nationalist resistance and concomitant economic, political, and social breakdown.[14] Likewise, in Algeria, the outbreak of anti-French agitation in November 1954, ultimately pitting Front de liberation nationale terrorism against the French military's ruthless tactics, undermined the lives of many residents. In response, thousands of Muslims, Christians, and Jews left the region, often for France but also for Canada, South America, Israel, and elsewhere in Europe.

Jewish migration was very much a part of this wider collapse of colonial control and the social, economic, and cultural change that followed. In the eyes of many contemporaneous observers, however, these departures were all too Jewish. French officials, in particular, watched Jewish migration with profound ambivalence. Indeed, the 2,075 Jews who requested to leave Morocco after the murders in Petitjean, a dramatic increase from the 561 during the same period in 1953, appeared to Regency officials as misguided. In the opinion of Francis

Lacoste, Morocco's resident general, the ethnicity of the Petitjean victims was coincidental, terrorism rarely targeted Jews, and fears about their future were unwarranted.[15] In fall 1955, foreign ministry officials asserted that Jews had suffered comparatively fewer troubles than the wider European population.[16] Rather, they argued, it was migrations themselves that stirred animosity.

Such concerns first appeared in 1948 when French colonial officials began reporting strong opposition from Muslims in Algeria, Tunisia, and Morocco to immigration to Israel. Between 1948 and November 1951, approximately 46,000 Moroccan and Tunisian Jews had emigrated (after which Israeli selective immigration policies reduced numbers).[17] According to French military and diplomatic correspondence, these departures were highly provocative. In February 1949, for example, the Ministry of the Interior informed the Ministry of Foreign Affairs that "a massive exodus of Moroccan and Tunisian Jews to Palestine, even after hostilities between Jews and Arabs have ended, is likely to provoke serious discontentment among the Muslim populations we govern."[18] While France's ability to object to migrations to Israel, now legally recognized, had diminished, officials in the Foreign Ministry warned that "departures should not be so large as to irritate our Muslim subjects."[19] Throughout the spring, colonial administrators were thus told to provide "no encouragement" to migrating Jews.[20] Similarly, officials argued against awarding international refugee status to Moroccan Jews, insisting that the 1948 riots in Oujda and Djérada had been "absolutely localized." It was, they warned, migration itself— and not widespread anti-Jewish animosity—that had sparked Muslim anger.[21] As Alphonse Juin, the French resident general commented in April 1949 when commenting on a proposal by the French Jewish organization, the Alliance is-raélite universelle (AIU), to both rationalize Moroccan Jewish outmigration and improve the juridical position of those remaining, "It will be difficult to prevent the Sultan's subject from seeing Jewish émigrés as disloyal to the state to which they have belonged for time immemorial."[22]

As such fears suggest, migration to Israel—already considered a sign of French duplicity during the 1948 war—continued to irritate in its aftermath, and not only in Morocco.[23] In January 1949, for example, the Prefect in Alger complained that migrants traveling through the country "can lead to frictions and difficulties for which it is difficult to determine the repercussions."[24] Similarly, in the International Zone of Tangiers, which had seen no disturbances in 1948, the Minister Plenipotentiare reported growing anger to spreading Zionism and particularly emigration. During one incident, several hundred Jews, hoping to bid farewell to departing co-religionists, "invaded the docks" after breaking through police barriers. Muslim activists responded by publically condemning "Jewish provocations." In the minister's view, European Zionists were to blame for spreading propaganda and ignoring warnings of moderation.[25]

Because Jewish departure rates diminished in light of French caution, Israeli migration laws, and rumors of the poor conditions facing migrants upon arrival, hostility diminished somewhat after 1951.[26] Following Petitjean, however, concerns over the implications of departures resurfaced.[27] As the resident general in Rabat reported, "This movement is spreading to the North African Jewish communities more generally."[28] As his reference to the wider Maghreb make clear, while French officials were well aware that most migrants were coming from Morocco, and from the poorest sectors of the Moroccan Jewish population at that, many saw in the departures a wider peril: "Jews" spurred by "Zionists" were leaving, and "Muslims" were angry.[29] This problem, while at times framed in national or local terms, was often referred to in broader terms, and numerous reports spoke of "North African Jews" or "Muslims" when framing the conflict they understood to be emerging.[30]

International Jewish organizations, far more likely than French administrators to see Jews qua Jews as the targets of nationalist ire, also often framed North Africa as a single unit, particularly after Petitjean. The French Zionist newspaper, *La Terre retrouvée*, for example, asserted that, "the situation of Jews, drowning in a mass of Arab fanatics, is becoming more tragic by the day."[31] The Board of Deputies of British Jews, while focused specifically on Morocco, similarly likened the murder in Petitjean to violence in other Arab countries where "feeling against Jews has been stirred up" and worried that any future in which Moroccan nationalists held power would "bode ill for the fate of the Jews."[32]

Such framing of North African nationalism as dangerous for Jews—often in some future rendition that had yet to be articulated—was widespread in the early 1950s. The World Jewish Congress (WJC), founded in 1936 to improve the status of international Jewry, for example, remained nervous about how the shifting political situation in Morocco would affect Jewish life. Having welcomed Moroccan Jewish delegates to its November 1944 congress, the WJC was one of the first international Jewish organizations to pressure the French government to rethink Jewish legal status in its protectorate.[33] Events in Oujda in 1948 increased the WJC's sense of urgency.[34] As WJC delegate Sylvain Cahn Débra reported that month: "One can say without exaggeration that Moroccan Jews live in a kind of terror and are convinced that they must at all costs avoid giving the Arabs the slightest pretext for new serious incidents."[35] With its attention drawn to the region, the WJC established a section in Morocco in 1949, the head of which was Jacques Lazarus, a former member of the French resistance and the Hagana, and head of the Comité juif algérien d'études sociales (CJAES), which represented Algerian Jews to the French administration. Although Lazarus and WJC leaders assumed a future for Jews in Morocco, they insisted on the "urgent necessity of maintaining the French presence in North Africa."[36] By early 1954, WJC representatives had established a good working relationship with Istiqlal leaders in the hopes of ensuring protection for Jewish residents in a new Moroccan state.[37] Following Petitjean, however, the head of the WJC's international affairs bureau, Maurice Perlzweig, attributed Jewish safety to the French and accused Istiqlal of doing "absolutely nothing to purge anti-Jewish tendencies from Arab nationalism."[38] Meetings in March and June 1955 between WJC and Istiqlal representatives did little to assuage Perlzweig's concerns.[39] If later meetings proved more fruitful,[40] WJC leaders continued to fear that inexperience and lack of pragmatism within Istiqlal opened the door to religious fanaticism and xenophobia within the party.[41] The WJC's efforts to ensure a North African Jewish future and to prevent antagonizing the French or the nationalists over the emigration issue were thus tempered by attempts to promote Jewish departures, particularly from isolated areas.[42]

Migration, thus, which had been until then on the periphery (if never absent entirely) from Jewish political strategies in North Africa, began moving to the center. As Herb Katzki summarized, reflecting a general consensus among American Jewish Joint Distribution Committee (AJDC) leaders: "While some regard [events in Petitjean] as an isolated incident which will not be repeated, others fear it is a first step in what may be a concerted anti-Jewish program." Or according to another Joint colleague, "there is no doubt in anyone's mind that the days of Jews in Morocco are numbered, and that sooner or later, many will have to be moved out."[43] The Joint, like the WJC, had been drawn to Morocco in the late 1940s. Although already working in North Africa during the Vichy years, in 1947 the Joint established a small North African department in its Parisian headquarters. The 1948 violence in Oujda and Djérada increased interest dramatically. Herman Stein, employed in the Joint's Welfare Department in Paris, was subsequently given resources to help "Jewish victims of Arab hostility," as well as to provide feeding centers for infants and children, medical care, nurseries, summer camps, vocational training and education.[44] Aid increased again in 1949.[45] As one Joint official noted, "It is not too late for American Jewry to make amends for the many years that their eyes were shut to the crying needs of our sorely stricken North African brethren."[46]

As such comments suggest, growing aid was driven by the perception of a dangerous political context primarily in Morocco but throughout the region as well. As one Joint official lamented in October 1948: "These people are leaving Morocco for fear of their lives. The political situation there is very bad and they are almost entirely unprotected." According to this perspective, after the declaration of Israeli statehood, "the Arabs manifested their nationalist feeling very strongly. . . . [The French] find themselves powerless against them and now they make hardly any attempts to stop Arab acts of violence until they are completely out of hand."[47] By 1950 the Joint's representative for North Africa, Hélène Cazes-Benatar, was arguing that "there is the certain DANGER which menaces this Jewish minority of half a million souls, lost in a mass of about twenty million Arabs, whose scorn and hidden hostility towards the Jew has been transformed to open hate since the establishment of the State of Israel."[48] By spring 1955 such views were circulating widely. According to the AJDC's Moses Beckelman, "long range prospect for Jews in [North Africa was] not satisfactory" and "gradual emigration of substantial numbers of Jews" was essential.[49] Samuel Haber, who emphasized poverty rather than politics as the major factor behind Moroccan Jewish departures, nevertheless predicted that "time may be running out" and that only swift action could prevent disaster.[50] Even André Blumel, president of France's Zionist Federation who downplayed antisemitism among the Moroccan and Tunisian nationalist parties, Istiqlal and Neo Destour, nevertheless warned that widespread anti-Zionism made it "absolutely indispensible" to organize migration to Israel "if you really want to save the Jews."[51] So central was migration to organizational thinking that representatives expressed mystification at French opposition to such an obvious solution.[52]

Given that post–World War II Jewish organizational and philanthropic bodies had directed significant resources to resettling Holocaust survivors, it is not surprising that they saw relocation as the obvious solution in North Africa as well. Indeed, even the profoundly assimilationist French Jewish Alliance israélite universelle, while never abandoning its commitment to ensuring Jewish educational and political opportunities at home, began to advocate for orderly, selective migration to Israel—long rejected as antithetical to the AIU's project of ensuring Jewish emancipation in their home nations. Yet as Yaron Tsur has argued, the AIU leadership came out of the Second World War rethinking its assimilationist commitments. While more narrowly focused on easing poverty and discrimination in the Moroccan *mellah* than on "Arab" antisemitism, the AIU, like Jewish organizations, saw in migration one reasonable solution to a wider Jewish problem.[53]

Just as French colonial officials and Jewish agencies saw a specifically Jewish story in the political unrest and migration from North Africa in the early 1950s, so too did Moroccan, Tunisian, and Algerian nationalist activists. Here, the historical narrative is hardly straightforward, since all the major nationalist parties went out of their way to reach out to Jews and all had indigenous Jewish supporters who fought alongside their Muslim co-nationalists to dislodge the French and to establish independent states for all citizens regardless of faith or ethnicity.[54] However, as noted in the last chapter, the FLN, Neo Destour, and Istiqlal all warned the French Ministry of Foreign Affairs not to recognize Israel, called France's pro-Zionist policies anti-Arab, and warned their Jewish minorities to steer clear of Zionism. At times, these calls dangerously blurred the lines between Jews and Zionism, such as boycotts of Jewish businesses in Morocco or Istiqlal's instigation of the riots in Oujda and Djérada.[55] And while nationalist rhetoric was very careful not to target Jews qua Jews, Jewish émigrés were increasingly a source of frustration.

Interestingly, in the initial surge of Jewish departures after Petitjean, neither the sultan nor the Istiqlal spokesmen expressed any objections, perhaps due to French colonial administrators' efforts to restrain the migration wave.[56] Thus it was largely radio broadcasts from Egypt and Damascus that attacked Jewish migrants for leaving.[57] Very soon, however, local French officials began reporting growing tensions.[58] In June the leader of Istiqlal, Allal el Fasi, strongly denounced collusion between Zionist organizations and the French government and warned Moroccan Jews not to leave.[59] Istiqlal's Abderkader Benjelloun later insisted that el Fasi had been misunderstood, and the goal had not been to threaten Moroccan Jews but to encourage them to stay. Promising equal rights in an independent Morocco, he insisted that "emigration of Moroccan Jews to Israel is due in part to a lack of confidence in the future and we have the impression that it is being encouraged by unjustified propaganda."[60] Whether meant as threat or enticement, Istiqlal's discomfort with Jewish departures was palpable. As two Istiqlal officials, Omar Abdjellil and Abdelkhalek Torres, made clear, emigration and the transfer of capital to Israel was "double treason."[61] A similar ambivalence toward migration was evident in Neo Destour's pronouncements. Thus, in 1954 Neo Destour's Habib Bourguiba met with WJC representative Alexander Easterman, promising equal rights for all citizens be written into the Tunisian constitution while expressing profound ambivalence toward Israel. While several months later he made clear that Jewish Tunisians would have the same right to emigrate as all other Tunisians, he nevertheless asked that Jews be discreet so as to avoid provoking tensions.[62]

Independence in both Morocco and Tunisia dramatically changed the context once again, and thus lies outside this chapter's purview. As should be clear, however, while Jewish departures were certainly the response to a broad range of push-and-pull factors, including fear, lack of opportunity, poverty, anti-Jewish oppression, encouragement by some Jewish and Israeli officials, and Israel's relaxation of migration restrictions, the very fact that some Jews started to leave helped create the reality that so many feared. Namely, while migration may have been a response to hostility it also *sparked* hostility, making Jews seem more foreign. Whether migrants opted to go to Israel, to Paris, or elsewhere, their departures were often understood by French officials, Jewish observers, and Muslim nationalists to be a Jewish flight. Although this conclusion may seem unremarkable when discussing departures from Morocco and Tunisia, the historiography of Algerian Jewish migration has downplayed this component. Yet, as I will argue, in Algeria, too, a Jewish story emerged that—while often being submerged in the story of a wider European flight—nevertheless provided a powerful and enduring counternarrative for understanding Jewish departures from the region.

Migration and the Algerian War: A Jewish Story

While most Moroccan and Tunisian Jews went to Israel prior to 1967, nearly 76,000 went to France.[63] There they were met by nearly 140,000 Algerian Jews who left as part of a much wider flight of the 925,000 French, Spanish, Italian, Maltese, and Algerian Muslims (140,000 of the so-called Harkis who contributed to the French war effort and who subsequently fled to the metropole).[64] Recent assessments have concluded that because Jews were included in the wider category of French repatriates, their departure should be understood as "not a Jewish exodus but [a] *pied noir* exodus."[65] Yet if Jewish departures were similar in kind to others caught up in the process of decolonization, they were not identical in meaning. Although Algerian Jewish representatives insisted that their French citizenship entitled them to access to any protective legislation negotiated for Europeans, this juridical move never fully hid their concern over a distinctly Jewish fate. Both French *and* Jewish, their loyalty to the nation that had emancipated them and their concerns about living under Muslim control merged during decolonialization.[66]

To be sure, the Jewish population was not monolithic, and opinions about the Algerian Revolution ranged according to social status, age, economic milieu, geographic context, political formation, and relationship to France, meaning that some Jews supported or even joined the FLN's struggle, while others were committed members of the Communist party (which ultimately also supported independence), and still others fought with those defending Algérie française. Indeed, one Joint official who toured Algiers, Constantinople, and Oran in 1961 noted so much communal diversity that it was like visiting three distinct countries.[67] As I will argue, however, the organizations and individuals who spoke publicly for Algerian Jews, while on the one hand consistently insisting upon that diversity, on the other, saw more unified Jewish meanings in the unraveling of French North Africa.[68] Moreover, the presence of international Jewish agencies dedicated to encouraging emigration meant this issue was part of communal discussions from the outset of the Algerian crisis even when only small numbers of Jews had left. The combined result was that from early in the FLN's struggle, key figures were articulating particular dangers for Jews under Muslim rule, insisting on the importance of French control for maintaining communal life, speculating on the necessity of Jewish departure, and articulating "specific problems" that affected only them, "like it or not."[69]

Most depictions present the Algerian Jewish leadership as apolitical—loyal French citizens, who due to their sympathy with the Muslim plight and fears about endangering their delicate position, declared neutrality in the conflict.[70] While many disapproved of Muslim political subjugation and felt deeply attached to Algeria, they felt grateful to France for their improving social, economic, and civil status.[71] Stuck between a "rock and a hard place," as André Narboni, president of the Fédération sioniste d'Algérie, later commented, Algerian Jewish spokesmen sought to protect their citizenship without publically identifying with either side.[72] As the CJAES under Jacques Lazarus insisted after the outbreak of hostilities in November 1954, "The majority of this assembly declares itself in favor of caution: nothing must suggest that the Jews have taken a specific position in response to events."[73] Arguing in 1956 that Jews were not a political body but a set of individuals each with his or her own political affinities, the CJAES asserted that no organization could speak on behalf of a Jewish collectivity.[74]

Proclamations of neutrality did not, however, prevent key communal leaders from expressing unabashedly pro-French politics behind closed doors (while explaining the dangers of adopting "inopportune" positions too publicly).[75] As early as 1950—several years before the formal outbreak of war—Algerian Jewish representatives *already* reported that Muslim-Jewish cooperation was no longer possible, and that Jews would be "compelled to collaborate with France . . . to defend, when necessary, their lives and property."[76] Or as representatives of the major Algerian Jewish organizations informed a visiting American congressman in November 1954, "We are unanimous in underscoring the absolute necessity of maintaining a French presence for the future of North Africa's Jewish communities."[77] As in Morocco and Tunisia, such broad assessments were echoed by international Jewish observers, such as in the 1953 *American Jewish Yearbook*, which reported that although Algerian Jews supported reforms to raise Muslim residents' standard of living, they nevertheless "remain[ed] unanimously faithful to the principle of a French presence in North Africa."[78]

Such pro-French comments from both Algerian and international Jewish representatives mirrored those circulating throughout the wider settler population, while still mapping out distinctly *Jewish* political concerns as well.[79] For such observers, developments in post-independence Morocco and Tunisia—where emigration continued to be a touchstone issue—raised significant concerns about the Jewish future. In 1956 the new Moroccan government dismantled the Zionist organization charged with coordinating migration. Although individuals could still depart on their own, by 1957 all citizens, whether Jewish or Muslim, had difficulty obtaining a passport. The Tunisian government permitted emigration and—as in Morocco—initially incorporated Jews into its governing bureaucracy. But in both countries, increased identification with the wider Arab world and efforts to break down communal autonomy and to Arabize educational institutions promoted clandestine migration.[80] Given that refugees often stopped first in Algeria, their plight was particularly visible.[81] Stories on the Moroccan and Tunisian Jewish experience began filling the main Algerian Jewish paper, *Information juive*, and communal leaders made regular references to events throughout the Maghreb when speculating on their own future in Algeria.[82]

This message of Jewish particularity was reinforced by developments in the wider Middle East, most notably in November 1956 during the Suez crisis, when Nasser's nationalization of the canal sparked Franco-British-Israeli military intervention and significant anti-Jewish activities.[83] The forced departure of many Egyptian Jews led French foreign-ministry officials and reporters to speculate over deteriorating Muslim-Jewish relations throughout the Middle East and North Africa, including in Algeria where elements within the FLN maintained close links with Nasser.[84] Algerian Jewish representatives claimed otherwise.

Information juive thus proclaimed the strength of local Muslim-Jewish relations, and the CJAES insisted on Algerian Jewish distance from events in the Middle East. The very act of engaging in such discussions, however, if only to deny their relevance, reaffirmed a Jewish collectivity.

In the early years of the Algerian crisis, Lazarus, the CJAES, and the Joint also began tracking anti-Jewish violence in ways that defined a Jewish experience within the wider anti-colonial struggle.[85] One informant wrote to Lazarus, for example, of the two hundred Jews of M'Sila who had reportedly lived "on good terms" with their Muslim neighbors but whose fortunes changed in 1955 "when FLN agents took possession of the city." Within a year, a boycott of local businesses coupled with increasing social distance and violence led all but two of the town's Jews to depart.[86] Similarly, a May 1956 bomb in a Constantine café reportedly to punish Jewish cooperation with the French police and a counterattack by Jewish self-defense forces, promoted fears of targeted anti-Jewish activities.[87] By early 1957 Benjamin Heler, president of Algeria's Fédération des sociétés juives, was warning that a "very great physical danger" threatened all the "30,000 Jews in the hinterland of Algeria . . . [who] should be moved either into the cities on the coast or to France and other countries."[88] That summer, Jacques Attal reported to Lazarus that Jews in Bône were seeking French protection from the FLN.[89] As such statements suggest, public proclamations of Jewish "neutrality" coexisted with internal communal discussions underscoring the need for a strong French presence and even migration.

To suggest that communal leaders saw Jewish meanings in Algeria's fight for independence is not to suggest that all Algerian Jews agreed or that social reality always reflected these perceptions.[90] In July 1957, for example, after four grenades were thrown at Oran's Jewish quarter, a local informant insisted that violence had emerged when rebels were pushed into that part of the city, not from anti-Jewish sentiment.[91] In September 1958, after a bomb exploded during synagogue services in Boghari, the rabbi emphasized "the feelings of disgust, revulsion and even hate expressed by all, and particularly by Boghari's Muslims, due to the place where the attack was carried out."[92] Similarly, following a 1960 attack on the main synagogue in Algiers, Muslim residents offered sympathy and protection to their Jewish neighbors, and local Jewish leaders, including those directing the Algerian Zionist Federation, "admitted that there was no organized Moslem movement against the Jews."[93]

Even those who emphasized the enduring friendship between religious communities, however, acknowledged the *possibility* of interethnic clashes in order to dismiss them. In other words, the very claim that Jews and Muslims could live in harmony was always shadowed by its opposite, ultimately reenforcing notions of a distinctive Jewish experience within the independence struggle. Moreover, even those who saw Muslim-Jewish relations as stable, often stressed the importance of ongoing French control to ensure peaceful relations. In the words of Henri Chemouilli, an Algerian Jewish teacher writing in a French

Jewish magazine: "if relations between Jews and Arabs were excellent here and less strong there, they were, overall, good." Yet, "if France is defeated, then we would all, the Jews of Algeria and the Jews of France, bear the consequences."[94]

This sense that there was a Jewish dimension to the Algerian struggle meant that by the late 1950s, the question of departure—if not the act itself—was increasingly discussed in communal gatherings.[95] Most scholarship has focused on de Gaulle's visit to Algeria in 1960 and the desecration of the synagogue of Algiers as the moment when Jews began seriously considering leaving.[96] David Cohen argues, for example, that in 1956 "departure for the Hexagone had not crossed anyone's mind. The Jews envisioned living harmoniously in Algeria with both Christians and Muslims for many years."[97] Much evidence backs up this claim.[98] As Daniel Timsit, a Jewish medical student who joined the FLN, recounted of these years: "[Algerian Jews] did not think that they had to leave. . . . [T]hey did not consider themselves a particularly threatened community."[99] Similarly, Jean Bensimon—who later migrated to France—wrote that although Algerian independence seemed likely in 1954, he did not feel obliged to leave "a country that was mine."[100] Israeli and American Jewish representatives concurred after being rebuffed in efforts to encourage departure.[101] The director of Constantine's Service social de l'association consistoire israélite reported in 1956 that there was no interest in emigration planning, an observation that the chief rabbi in Bône shared.[102]

Such comments have, however, misled historians. True, most Jews were not standing on the docks in the 1950s. Emigration was nevertheless a topic of communal conversation, often driven by the Joint and other international organizations.[103] The very Jews in Constantine and Bône who refused to discuss rescue plans thus told their American and Israeli interlocutors that future emigration was a real possibility.[104] Likewise, the Joint's Stanley Abromovitch noted in June 1956 that talk of departure was the "topic of the day. People discuss this problem at home, in business, everywhere. It was the only subject I heard constantly." In his view—one he spread in his travels—an independent Algeria boded ill for Jews, who would lose civil service positions, businesses and customers. Security questions were also a concern: While "Arabs . . . have no interest in massacring the Jews," Abromovitch explained, "[t]his does not exclude the possibility of a pogrom. In a tense situation, the smallest spark may cause a conflagration. . . . At the present time, any incident may easily cause a panic, a flight from Algeria to France, and to a much lesser extent to Israel. . . . They see no future in Algeria and want to leave. They want to emigrate."[105]

As a Joint representative, it is not surprising that Abromovitch saw danger everywhere; international Jewish agencies, as we have seen, encouraged migration out of fear of future violence. Tellingly, however, the CJAES—the local body so vested in Jewish neutrality—also informed the AJDC and various French Jewish organizations in June 1956 that they should prepare for a large emergency migration to France, "even if it should . . . cause political repercussions either among the French or the Arabs." In their view, "the Jews . . . felt themselves in danger."[106] The following January, the CJAES established a commission to help those of modest means leave for the metropole.[107]

To say that emigration was the "topic of the day" does not contradict previous assertions that Jews hoped to stay. Indeed, this very same CJAES commission had not met by June presumably due to lack of candidates. What should be clear, though, is how essential French control was to the decision to remain. In 1956 most still believed "that the French will protect them; that France will remain in Algeria." As Abromovitch reported, "as long as France intends to stay . . . there will be a possibility to live in Algeria."[108] Given that faith in France's ability to withstand the FLN fluctuated, so did migration plans. In 1957, departures thus increased in conjunction with fears over security.[109] After de Gaulle returned to power in June 1958, security improved, the economy stabilized, and violence subsided, meaning that some who had previously left returned, and migration numbers dropped.[110] Violence and uncertainty surged again, however, after de Gaulle's 16 September 1959 promise to grant Algerian self-determination.[111] On Yom Kippur that October, a grenade in a synagogue killed the rabbi's granddaughter and wounded eleven others. Offering the mirror reflection of Boghari's rabbi a year previously, Rabbi Sellem of Bou Saada commented, "The Muslims express their condolences to us, blaming the so-called criminals and offering a lot of clap trap that makes us not believe them."[112] Or as the *American Jewish Yearbook* described the atmosphere that year, "Confronted by an apparently endless war and mindful of what had happened in Tunisia and Morocco, many Jewish families solved their personal problems by leaving Algeria for France or Israel. Others made preparations to leave if things got worse. In general, a wait-and-see attitude prevailed."[113] These fluctuations reflected hopes that France could renegotiate its colonial relationship in ways that would ensure safety for all; in the eyes of Jewish observers, however, they also demonstrated distinctly Jewish meanings. As one member of the CJAES board noted in June 1957, "one day or another we will be overwhelmed by the Arab world."[114]

Such perspectives shaped Jacques Lazarus's views of the political and economic risks facing Algerian Jews qua Jews, proclamations of their Frenchness notwithstanding. As he warned the WJC's Nehemiah Robinson in June 1957, "In addition to ethnic and religious [prejudices] can be added a nationalist prejudice based in race, meaning that increasingly Arabs buy from Arabs and go to Arab doctors and lawyers, even if, in certain cases, the services offered by Jews proves more advantageous."[115] Born in Alsace in 1920 and having joined the French resistance after escaping a deportation train during World War II, Lazarus's view was undoubtedly influenced by recent European events. In 1946 he moved to Algeria on behalf of the Jewish vocational agency, the Organization for Rehabilitation and Training (ORT). After marrying a woman from a prominent local family, he became active in Algerian Jewish politics, becoming general secretary of the CJAES in 1948 and, as we have seen, director of the WJC's North African division.[116]

Given this background, it is not surprising that Lazarus saw a Jewish story within Algeria's political chaos (he underlined Jewish names in dozens of newspaper articles of murders and terrorist attacks).[117] In 1957, before the UN's debate on the Algerian issue, Lazarus confidentially insisted to the WJC's Maurice Perlzweig that the organization must protest any challenge to France's hold on Algeria. While acknowledging the WJC's broader commitment to justice and equality, Lazarus held that it must support France "without reserve" because "the future of the Jewish collectivity in North Africa is predicated, in large measure, on the maintenance of the French presence in Algeria."[118] These were striking words from a man who had repeatedly asserted there *was no* Jewish collectivity! In fact, while Lazarus insisted that, "there is not a Jewish politics," he also believed that to be Jewish was "a political and not only a religious or social phenomenon."[119] This nuance means that he devoted his life to Jewish politics while claiming they did not exist.

This "Jewish politics" was deeply embedded by 1957. If Algerian Jewish spokesmen fought desperately to protect their citizenship by stressing their integration into French colonial society, the story of Jewish distinctiveness was equally potent and part of their assessment of future opportunities (or lack thereof) in North Africa as a whole.[120] Jewish emigration, while still not widespread, was intrinsically linked to this analysis and became all the more so as the war intensified.

The FLN and the Solidification of an Algerian Jewish Question

By the late 1950s, the FLN had also come to see a Jewish dimension within the wider independence struggle. To be sure, for most of those engaged in a broader struggle, the concerns of the Jewish minority were largely irrelevant. Nevertheless, Jews posed a problem for Algerian nationalists. As indigenous members of Algerian society, Jewish participation in the independence struggle was a potentially valuable way to grant legitimacy to the movement's claim that its struggle pitted oppressed colonial subjects against their imperial masters rather than Muslims against Christians or Arabs against Europeans.[121] Jewish support for the French made such efforts far more complicated.[122] Moreover, as Jews threw in their lot with the French, they did more than side with the despised colonial oppressors; rather, as an indigenous population, they, like the Muslim soldiers who fought with the French army and who were despised as traitors, had—in the eyes of many—committed treason.[123]

Such views were not preordained in 1954 when the FLN first rebelled. Nor did social reality necessarily reflect the increasingly polarizing rhetoric regarding the place of Jews in the Algerian nationalist struggle. As in all such movements, nationalist doctrine did not spread evenly to all social categories or regions, and many associated themselves with family, clan, ethnic group, or tribe over nation.[124] Muslim-Jewish relations "on the ground" reflected this diversity. Moreover, while FLN rhetoric toward Jews played a key role in defining who stood within and who outside the nation, this rhetoric was itself fluid, evolving in response to power struggles within the organization and growing awareness of the pro-French biases behind Jewish neutrality. Put differently, Jewish political discourse influenced nationalist attitudes and vice versa in a dynamic process that redefined how each saw the other.[125] Yet even a cursory glance at hardening FLN rhetoric shows the way nationalist political discourse, despite stressing Jewish Algerianness, actually pointed to their distinctiveness.

In its earliest incarnation, anti-colonial activists collapsed Jews into broader categories of the nation.[126] After the 1956 violence in Constantine, however, and CJAES declarations to the WJC of Jews' commitment to their French citizenship, FLN assertions of Jewish "Algerianness" coexisted with public recognition of their distinctive political status. During his April press conference acknowledging his collaboration with the FLN, for example, moderate Ferhat Abbas distinguished Jews from other Algerian nationals because they benefited from French nationality.[127] Two months later, the FLN asked Jews to join their struggle by similarly underscoring their differences from other Algerians: After having been raised on "cheap patriotism" and "respect for imperial grandeur," Jews now faced "the moment of choice and big decisions," while "for us, Algerians, the choice is made."[128]

With the FLN's recognition of Jewish particularity came a more targeted outreach to join the nationalist camp coupled with a sharp criticism of Jewish silence on colonial injustice. These two facets emerged mostly clearly at the Congrès de la Soummam in August 1956, where the FLN established its platform. Favoring a secular and democratic Algeria, the Congrès de la Soummam represented a moment when more moderate members of the FLN triumphed over those calling for a more religiously inflected political vision. The result, therefore, was a platform that temporarily created space for Jews within the movement.[129] This outreach, however, did not address Jews as Algerians like all others, but rather as those with questionable loyalties. The platform thus posited that while Jews had not gone "definitively into the enemy's camp," they had not chosen a side. The FLN also criticized the chief rabbi who, unlike the archbishop, had not spoken out against colonialism. A letter to Algerian Jewish leaders the following fall similarly criticized this silence. While recognizing that individual Jews supported the revolutionaries, the mainstream Jewish leadership needed "to solemnly confirm their belonging to the Algerian nation" in order to "dispel all misunderstandings and eradicate the seeds of hatred planted by French colonialism." Calling Jewish Algerians "sons of the nation," the FLN nevertheless underscored a growing frustration with Jewish silence.[130]

For the FLN, the 1956 declaration at the Congrès de la Soummam was a culminating point, both a concerted effort—in light of the violence in Constantine—to prove that the national movement was neither religiously fanatical nor an instrument of the Arab League, and to win over a small but influential constituency.[131] Reminding Jewish Algerians that a common indigenous heritage should unite them against the colonial regime, the FLN publicly rejected civil and juridical categories that established Jews as French. By stressing their particular choices, however, and critiquing their position on colonial injustice, the FLN also emphasized Jewish difference from other Algerians.

Such contradictions continued to influence FLN approaches throughout late 1950s.[132] Arguing before the United Nations, on the one hand, that independence in Morocco and Tunisia had brought full political, economic, and social inclusion for Jews, the FLN insisted that the same would be true in a future Algeria. Criticizing certain Jewish spokesmen, they lauded those who supported the nationalist movement and promised equality to all.[133] On the other hand, public invitations to come together were accompanied by more aggressive tactics; some wealthy Jews, for example, received threatening letters "requesting" their support for the nationalist cause, and violence against Jews and Jewish institutions increased.[134] Moreover, periodic pronouncements on Jews continued to stress both their integral position within the nation *and* their particularity. A November 1959 statement (published in February 1960 in *Le Monde*), for example, proclaimed, "You are an integral part of the Algerian people; you do not have to choose between France and Algeria but to become actual citizens of your real country," while noting the distinctive choice before Jews: "Do you want to exercise fully in this country . . . rights that nobody will ever challenge or will you accept living under a reign of contempt and to content yourselves with a citizenship conferred upon you by your oppressors." This recognition of Jewish choice echoed the 1956 declaration if ending somewhat more threateningly by encouraging Jews "to resolve any ambiguity that risks compromising our future relations."[135]

If similarities with the 1956 declaration were palpable, it was the threat to which Jewish leaders responded, underscoring how the give and take between FLN and Jewish spokesmen pushed both into more polarized camps. The CJAES thus publicly condemned the FLN's attempt to impose a collective status on all Jews. Even more upsetting to Jewish leaders, however, was that the FLN's statement appeared in *Le Monde* on the same page as an article asserting de Gaulle's support for a federated Algerian state with rights for Kabyles, Arabs, Chaouias, Mozabites, Jews, and French.[136] The coupling of nationalist assertions of Jews' "Algerianness" with an emerging political consensus that Jews were not French but a separate ethnic community sent the CJAES into overdrive.[137] Establishing that Jews were indistinguishable from other French citizens henceforth became the organization's main goal.

Paradoxically, however, all efforts to prove Jewish Frenchness ended up very much entangled with particularistic ethno-religious concerns. CJAES delegates, for example, asserted the *collective* importance of French citizenship to Algerian Jews, which—in their words—had been their "essential safeguard" (an ironic claim given the Vichy years). As Lazarus explained: "[T]he situation of our co-religionists in Arab countries having won independence, even neighbors like Morocco, should be a subject of interest and bitter reflection for us. How can we believe nationalist leaders who, once independence of their countries has been won, have been eager to forget—whatever the reason given—the solemn promises made regarding the total legal equality that would be granted to their Jewish citizens?"[138] Or as one French Jewish lawyer wrote to the Secrétariat d'état aux affaires algériennes, "Because of its atavistic anxiety and because of the attitude of the Arab world toward the Jewish world, the Jewish minority, fears a Holocaust by the European and Muslim communities."[139] In such missives, we see the reflex not only to assert a collective Jewish politics, but also to collapse Algerian Muslims into broader North African and Arab political categories.

Jewish efforts to protect their French citizenship flew in the face of FLN efforts to claim Jews as Algerians, and in June 1960, Ferhat Abbas warned of a growing alienation among Muslim Algerians.[140] While the FLN disavowed the destruction of Algier's central synagogue on 12 December and condemned antisemitism,[141] criticisms intensified against the "collusion" of some with the colonial regime, as well as "the wait-and-see attitude" of the communal leadership.[142] Such proclamations allowed FLN spokesmen to deny charges of antisemitism while still insisting that there was a price to pay for helping the French.[143] As a March 1961 FLN booklet threatened, the time for decision had come: "For a long time, we have understood and even excused our Jewish friends, deceived by colonial maneuverings, for the difficulty of resolving this division, this 'internal tearing,' this uncertainty. . . . Today, the Algerian people must know on what side its true children will fall."[144] Abdel Kader Chanderli, the United States' FLN representative, likewise warned American Jewish organizations that Jews' retention of French citizenship would be viewed as treason.[145]

Jewish citizenship was, then, a touchstone issue around which debates over loyalties played out. Paradoxically, however, as Jews insisted that they were French like all others and the FLN insisted that Jews were Algerian like all others, both ended up underscoring Jewish distinctiveness. Lazarus admitted this openly to Louis Joxe, Algerian-affairs minister, in March 1961 when he insisted that Jews were asking for no particular guarantees as Jews while still noting that they experienced "anxiety that was perhaps deeper than that of other elements in the population because of their Jewishness, the declarations of the FLN claiming them as Algerian in contempt of the right of auto-determination, and the excessiveness of independent Arab states, most recently Morocco."[146]

International Jewish organizations also underscored this particularity. As one AJDC official put it, "there is a real problem *which only the Jews face* and not the other French nationals in Algeria from who[m] French citizenship cannot be taken away. Under the circumstances, there is a far greater urge to have the Jews of Algeria leave the country before they are caught and trapped as are the Jews in Morocco."[147] Similarly, observers from the American Jewish Committee commented, "If, in an about to become independent Algeria, [Jews] positively dissociate themselves from the Algerian mass whose leaders consider them as Algerian, they may very well be considered as traitors. The attitude of Algerian Moslems toward them would, therefore, be different than to other Frenchmen for who[m] the act of remaining French would seem natural to the Algerians."[148] After visiting Algeria that spring, Max Lapides of the Joint's Geneva Office, described Jews as "surrounded . . . in a sea of Arabs. Today France and the Army afford them the necessary protection and bolster the dikes which keep the sea from all but drowning them." Traveling throughout the country, he spread word of Jewish dilemmas in all Muslim lands and stressed the importance of "tak[ing] positive action while the gates remained open."[149] In Algeria, as in Morocco and Tunisia, then, international Jewish agencies disseminated a "Jewish story" within the wider political chaos and encouraged emigration as a solution.

Unsurprisingly, such efforts angered Algerian nationalists, as Jewish migration once again became a political football. Although on 10 September 1957, Ferhat Abbas, hoping to win Israeli support in United Nations' deliberations over Algeria, promised that as equal citizens, Jews would have the right to emigrate, a spokesman of the Gouvernement provisoire de la république algérienne (GPRA), the political arm of the FLN formed in September 1958, later declared that the future Algerian government would not authorize such departures.[150] These contradictions reflected divisions in the FLN between a moderate group, including Benyoucef Benkhedda, Krim Belkacem, and Mohamed Boudiaf, who pushed for discreet relations with Israel as a means of distancing the Algerian revolution from Egypt, and a second group, headed by Ben Bella, that was close to Nasser and aggressively anti-Zionist.[151] Although the FLN made no formal statements regarding Jewish migration to Israel, particularly given the small numbers involved, Jewish Agency efforts to encourage departures irritated them.[152] In April 1961, Abdelkader Chanderli complained vigorously to AJC representatives over campaigns that "give the impression that the Jews in Algeria are in peril." Somewhat contradictorily, however, he made clear that any migration should take place before Algerian independence, since subsequent departures would reflect poorly on the new state.[153] The ambivalence evident in Chanderli's complaint continued to surface as Jewish migration accelerated, even when the final destination was France. As Henri Chemouilli described, "We didn't leave for Israel, you see, but our departure from Algeria was also a mark of our allegiances [in the minds of Algerian nationalists]."[154]

While limited sources make it difficult to ascertain the prevalence of such views, by the early 1960s there were certainly few illusions about Jewish loyalties. As one Algerian Muslim political leader told a reporter, "It must be said that the Jews have not always had a very favorable attitude toward us. They were fully engaged in support of French Algeria."[155] An exchange between the Muslim deputy from Bône, Abdelbaki Mosbah Chibi, and Jacques Lazarus provides further evidence of concern over Jewish loyalties.[156] Following the violence in Constantine, Chibi, known for his outreach to the Jewish community and his pronouncements on the necessity of Arab-Israeli collaboration, nevertheless expressed concern that Jews had instigated the violence.[157] Lazarus reassured him that no Jews had been involved and praised Muslim outreach in the aftermath. The good will between the men wavered, however, when Chibi requested public Jewish support for the Algerian republic, a gesture that would go a long way in repairing misunderstandings. Lazarus responded by reiterating the CJAES's neutrality and refusing any initiative likely to be misinterpreted.[158]

This exchange points to the way Jews remained outside both Algerian and French political collectivities despite assertions by various actors to the contrary. Indeed, paradoxically enough, proclamations of Jewish inclusion in these wider groups often served to underscore their distinctiveness, a process that became all the more evident in the last two years of the Algerian Revolution as migration numbers soared for all European setters. Even here, where Jewish behavior seemingly mirrored patterns of the wider settler population, distinctive Jewish patterns emerged, patterns that forced changes in FLN policies toward them and once again emphasized a Jewish story within the Algerian independence struggle.

Migration, Jewish Politics, and the Unraveling of French Algeria

In spring 1961, as the first Evian negotiations between the GPRA and the French government began to establish the terms of a cease-fire, the FLN changed its position regarding non-Muslims. Accepting Jews as part of the so-called European minority, the FLN applied the principle of self-determination, which had been so central to their own nationalist struggle, to the Jewish minority. As Krim Belkacem specified in July 1961, "They are indigenous, but we will not force anyone to take a stance one way or another."[159] This move, which French negotiators also promoted, meant that over the last year of the Algerian conflict, Jews "disappeared" juridically into the European majority.[160] Subsequent violence among counterrevolutionary paramilitary forces, the FLN, and the French army similarly deemphasized differences between Jews and non-Jews. As one Joint informant commented in October 1961, "[W]hen one leaves home in the morning, one is never sure of getting back alive and, if one does, of finding the apartment intact and the family safe and sound. This is true throughout the country . . . and applies to all—Moslems, Christians and Jews alike."[161]

And yet the very process that allowed Jews to blend into the pieds noirs population—seemingly detaching them from their particularistic identities—continued to hold powerful lessons about where Jewishness fit in the newly emerging North African political landscape. As one Joint official noted, "The underlying and basic Algerian nationalist feeling about Jews is . . . that they are, if not traitors to independent Algeria, at least collaborators. This sentiment comes through, and Jews feel it, despite any statements that Algerian nationalists may make, in their olive branch moments, that they wish and hope that Jews, like other Europeans, will stay."[162] Moreover, as violence against Jewish victims surged in 1961, the view that Algerian Muslims were Arabs in North African clothing, sworn enemies of the Jews, grew even more pervasive among those working to preserve Jewish life.[163] The failure of the initial Evian conferences further convinced Jews that they would soon become hostages of the Algerian government, since "in Arab countries, political and economic difficulties always translate into coercive measures against Jewish communities." As local French officials reported, "[T]he fear of later finding themselves in a tête-à-tête with the Muslims in an independent Algeria, in which all cohabitation was impossible" circulated widely.[164]

In addition, regional events continued to stoke fears of the dangers lurking in North African independence. Most notably, just as French/FLN negotiations were collapsing in summer 1961, Tunisia clashed violently with the French over the latter's ongoing presence at the Bizerte naval base. Subsequently, the nationalist press accused Jews of supporting the French as departures for Israel and France increased substantially again.[165] As one Joint observer commented on Algerian Jewish reactions to these events: "If even in moderate Tunisia, ruled by Western oriented Premier Habib Bourguiba, such things can happen, then there is no future for us anywhere in Moslem North Africa."[166] Or according to the AJC, "Jews particularly feel that there is no place for them in an independent Moslem state, citing Tunisia and Morocco as examples of what can happen to Jews in Moslem lands. They add that the situation will be much worse in Algeria where passions have been aroused to a pitch never felt in the neighboring countries."[167]

Many of these tensions came to a head in Oran in September 1961—on the morning of Rosh Hashanah—when a father en route to synagogue with his daughter was killed with another man. Jewish self-defense units retaliated, burning cars and shops and murdering local Muslim residents.[168] While the FLN warned Oran's Muslims not to be diverted into a war against the Jews, and the CJAES called for calm, anger and fear were palpable throughout the city.[169] A boycott of Jewish businesses followed, while commentators reported that "feelings between Jews and Moslems is even worse than between Moslems and the rest of the European population."[170] One angry depiction thus described Jews as "shouting slogans borrowed from the racist Europeans, and taking part in actions analogous to those of the ultra imperialists when they organized demonstrations and *ratonades*." By imitating "the blinding racial hatred of imperialist criminals and [throwing] themselves onto a suicidal path," local Jews had committed a kind of treason: "We deeply regret this disease that has infected the Jews, driving them to shout sordid and hostile slogans likely to cause hatred and provoke reactions contrary to their interests and to the peaceful coexistence of Algeria's communities. Furthermore, in acting this way, the Jews risk seriously compromising their future in our country."[171] While the murder was very likely carried out by the Organisation de l'armée secrète (OAS), the counterrevolutionary paramilitary group formed in February 1961 to protect French Algeria, such discourse contributed to the sense of a growing Jewish-Muslim polarization.[172]

For some Jews who found themselves in a "state of bewilderment and chaos" in fall 1961, previous ambivalence around migration dissolved.[173] In September alone, departures for France more than doubled.[174] As one official reporting on Jewish choices made clear: "fears over the attacks and aggravated relations between communities has transformed into panic in certain regions. Emigration seems the least harmful solution to many."[175] While many pieds noirs made a similar decision, this commonality masked the particular contours of the Jewish exodus.[176] Initial migrations thus brought out a greater percentage of Jews and reflected particularistic concerns.[177] As the chief rabbi noted to an American reporter, "[Y]ou Americans still believe Algeria should be independent because that's democracy! Your democracy—see what it does to us—the holy Torah in the mud, the house of God defiled."[178] In Constantine, where the 1956 violence and the destruction of the synagogue had left notable scars, street confrontations and assassinations of Jewish targets forced most families to remain indoors. By January 1962 only 8,000 of the city's 18,000 Jews remained. Life in Algiers and Oran seemed equally bleak; by January 1962 at least some were predicting, "Oran's 28,000 Jews will not be able to remain."[179]

Among those who stayed, sympathy for the OAS spiked considerably, although scholars disagree over the depth of Jewish support for the movement.[180] While most agree that Jews—like many in the "European" population—hoped the OAS would prevail, few, it is argued, openly supported the OAS due to its antisemitic leanings.[181] Thus if Jewish support was evident in Oran where Jewish commandos assassinated opponents and organized self-defense units,[182] generally speaking Jews were not enthusiastic supporters.[183] More recently, Todd Shepard has dissented, arguing that there was significant Jewish support for the OAS by early 1962 when press accounts and military officials took note of increasing anti-Muslim vigilantism among Jews and when government sources reported that those in Algiers and Oran in particular were abandoning their previously moderate politics.[184] Moreover, Jewish departures slowed down—evidence to Shepard of renewed hopes for French Algeria—while *Paris Match* charged the Israeli Irgun with training OAS commandos.[185]

Shepard's argument, and particularly his position on Jewish departures, challenges work that has emphasized Jewish panic and dislocation.[186] However, a variety of Jewish sources confirm his assessment. The American Jewish Committee (AJC), for example, reported in January that "the mass of the Jews are overwhelmingly pro-OAS or Algérie-Française or at the least for French presence in Algeria. Even those who are not pro OAS believe that such gains as have been wrenched from the FLN are due to the OAS intransigence."[187] Local Joint employees concurred, noting significant Jewish arrests for their OAS participation.[188] In addition, the French Jewish organization, CRIF, debated the risks of condemning OAS activities given their belief that the "vast majority of our Algerian co-religionnaires" supported the organization.[189]

Shepard errs, however, when he links the drop in departures too fully with support for the OAS. Intimidation may have had as much to do with this shift as OAS appeal, since the diminution in exit visa requests directly followed increased threats against emigration.[190] OAS posters announcing the murder of Moise Choukroun, vice president of the Cultuelle de Maison-Carée, for "desertion," thus provoked significant consternation among Jews planning to leave.[191] Another factor contributing to the reduced Jewish departures included the migration of most communal leaders by late 1961 due to fears of targeted assassination, leaving those remaining "without advisors."[192] This flight of visible leadership, it should be noted, was another sign of the particularity of Jewish migration at this stage, since among non-Jewish Europeans there was no similar loss of spokesmen.[193] By February, rumors of substantial assistance for those leaving Algeria for France and a belief that the French government was winning concessions during negotiations provided those remaining with hope that they still had time.[194] According to the Joint's M. Jordan in March, Algerian Jews believed they would have an extended period to adjust their affairs and were putting off immediate departure.[195]

As such evidence suggests, the diminution in Jewish departures in early 1962 was the result of a complex landscape. While support for the OAS grew and many hoped that France would hold on to Algeria, other factors, including lack of resources, loss of most communal leadership, and fear of reprisals also contributed.[196] Shepard is thus right to argue that in these months "departures . . . became *pied noir*, and no longer 'Israelite' 'Spanish' or of 'French origin.'" I would argue, however, that as departures became fully linked to the pied noirs destiny, they rendered invisible the Jewishness that was still shaping perceptions of future possibilities in an Algerian state.[197] As the AJC summarized, "The Jews in Algeria are today beset by the same passions and conflicts as all others in Algeria, with an additional set of difficulties arising out of conditions special to them."[198]

Arguments that suggest that repatriation pushed Algerian Jewish identity into the background, while magnifying allegiances to France, downplay the way departures reinforced notions of Jewish particularism.[199] This paradox was on full display in a meeting between Jean Morin (France's délégate général in Algeria), Jacques Lazarus, and Andre Narboni in February 1962 where the question of migrations was discussed. During the meeting, Morin offered the two men positions on a provisional body charged with carrying out the transition of power from French to Algerian hands. Both refused on the grounds that Algerian Jews did not need a representative, since they did not make up a political entity. And yet, if Jews had no "special status," they still had particularistic concerns. Thus as Lazarus and Narboni argued for the importance of facilitating migration to France for all citizens, they emphasized "the fundamental problem of relations between Israel and the Arab States with all that implies for Jews living in independent Arab countries," as a way of making clear that Jews could not remain in Algeria.[200] Here, then, claims of universal citizenship masked particularistic concerns that were also at play.

Moreover, a sense that Jews were still being negatively singled out, despite FLN concessions to treat Jews as Europeans, continued to influence Jewish political discourse.[201] In late spring 1962, for example, when FLN spokesman Abdelkader Chanderli threatened reprisals against Jews who participated in the OAS's "indiscriminate killing of Muslims," the Joint's Abe Karlikow remarked that "the FLN harbors *particular resentment* that Jews should thus have identified with the rest of the Europeans in Algeria, with some few exceptions, in support of the OAS." He pointed to a rise of kidnappings and executions in spring 1962 as well as to an FLN letter to Jewish leaders in Oran demanding 400,000,000 old francs (approximately $800,000) as evidence that anti-Jewish sentiment was intensifying.[202]

"Repatriation" reached its zenith in summer 1962 between the signing of the Evian accords in March and the declaration of Algerian independence in July with over half a million "Europeans" departing despite extensive protections promised to them. Jews, like others, fled in fear of reprisals, ongoing violence, economic upheaval, and uncertainty.[203]

Yet if their departure marked a "symbolic step in establishing their Frenchness," it also reconfirmed newly solidified "lessons" about the place of Jews in Muslim lands. As Jean Bensimon, a French soldier turned FLN supporter, noted, "When it was my turn to be threatened, I went to find refuge among my Algerian friends in the city's outskirts. I well understood from their cold welcome how futile it was to be between two sides [*entre deux bords*] and how impossible to reconcile the irreconcilable. I also knew that there was nothing else for me here.[204] Likewise, one Jewish communist who joined the FLN early in the war was infuriated to discover that he would not automatically attain Algerian citizenship: "For Jews there was a particular problem; the Jews were in Algeria before the Arabs! And now they would be asked to fill out forms to become Algerian citizens! That was unbearable because even Arabs or Muslims who had betrayed the cause or their country or their brothers were automatically

Algerians. And [Jews] had to fill out forms because . . ." When he complained, a fellow Algerian Muslim communist accused him of Zionist affiliations.[205]

Such comments remind us of the distinct dilemmas facing Jews as the Algerian crisis came to a head, and particularly as the more virulently anti-Israel Ahmed Ben Bella began to assert control within the FLN. As Bensimon asked,

> When Ben Bella says that he is "an Arab, an Arab and again an Arab," how can the other not detect a threat and why can I not write "I am a French Jew, a French Jew, and again a French Jew"? They would object that if the Jews were identified with an Algerian Algeria, Arabism would not frighten them any more than French Christianity. Perhaps, but didn't Tunisian Jews, for example, equally colonized and identified with Tunisian nationalism, feel like outsiders when the first article of the Tunisian constitution announced that the republic was Muslim and Islamic?

The position of Jews elsewhere in North Africa as well as fears over Algeria's deteriorating relationship with Israel—as more moderate GPRA members lost out to their opponents—reinforced fears that Jews could never be Algerians like all others.[206] Ben Bella's denunciation of Israel and his threat in April 1962 to send troops to fight the Jewish state exacerbated such fears.[207] "When Ben Bella promised to send one hundred thousand Algerian soldiers against Israel," continued Bensimon, "I wondered what Ben Bella and I, born on the same land, under the same sky, had in common."[208]

Such concerns merged with wider fears of retribution and upheaval to push four-fifths of Algerian Jews out of the country by October. Their decision to embrace their French citizenship led to what Benjamin Stora has called a "a double erasure of Algerian history, as if the war of independence and the departure of the 1960s had slowly but surely eroded all of Algeria's ancient Jewish heritage. In Jewish memories, Muslims seem to embody the negative representation of the 'other,' while the hostility of the Europeans has been minimized."[209] If such narratives were not the only way that departing Algerian Jews remembered the war, images of Muslim-Jewish discord remained prevalent. As Bensimon described, "Algerian nationalism seemed to threaten their Jewish selves as much as their French selves," a view that was perpetuated in communal discourse as subsequent migrations emptied North Africa of its Jewish populations.[210] These "lessons" coupled with those learned in 1948 about the way French policies in the Middle East indexed unequal power relations in the metropole created the discursive terrain on which Muslim and Jewish immigrants met in France.

3

Encounters in the Metropole

The Impact of Decolonization on Muslim-Jewish Life in France in the 1950s and 1960s

The lessons learned in North Africa from 1948 to 1962 had significant repercussions in France. First, for many French Jewish leaders preoccupied with rebuilding from the recent Nazi and Vichy persecutions, the Jewish meanings in French decolonization were all too clear. While those on the left expressed empathy for Muslim victims of French racism and called for Muslim-Jewish cooperation throughout the Algerian crisis, many of those representing major Jewish institutions or publications echoed fears that the "Arab world" had turned on its Jewish residents. As a result, distrust and animosity rather than commonalities and cooperation tended to dominate mainstream institutional representations of the "Arab world," a broad designation that often collapsed Muslim North Africans uncritically within it.

A comparison with Muslim institutions and periodicals in France in the same period is impossible given the far more developed Jewish communal structures in these decades and the greater number of sources they have left behind. However, this very imbalance points to the second major consequence of the decolonization process on Muslim-Jewish relations in France–the importation to the metropole of the profound juridical and social inequities embedded in colonial North Africa. As noted in the Introduction, thousands of Muslim and Jewish migrants came to France throughout the decolonization process. Importing similar cultural, linguistic, and even religious practices from Algeria, Tunisia, and Morocco, Muslim and Jewish migrants often shared a sense of displacement and common origins that facilitated bonds between them. However, differing relationships to the French state—many resulting from the legacy of French colonialism—were equally powerful in shaping mutual perceptions in the 1950s and early 1960s. Early encounters in the metropole must be understood, therefore, as intimately connected to the North African past and France's violent departure from the region.

An examination of migration and settlement in Marseille in the 1950s and early 1960s illustrates the impact of colonial legacies in shaping the contours of Muslim-Jewish relations in the metropole. While Paris remained the main pole of attraction for both, Marseille's close proximity to North Africa, its Mediterranean climate, and its expanding economy meant that the city attracted thousands of repatriates and immigrants in the 1950s and 1960s. Shared cultural frameworks and the common experiences of migration and displacement meant that Muslim and Jewish newcomers often had much in common, creating the basis for convivial exchange in the mixed immigrant neighborhoods where many initially settled.

Such commonalities did not, however, ensure similar processes of incorporation into French urban life. Differing relationships to the French state and levels of communal development meant that incoming Jews often not only had more resources available to them than Muslims arriving in the same period but also benefited from a local administration sympathetic to their concerns. Governed by socialist mayor Gaston Defferre—a vocal advocate of Israel with deep ties to the Jewish community—Marseille's political establishment embraced its Jewish minorities in ways that emphasized the inequities between Jews and Muslims evident in the colonial structure. Colonial legacies, then, had long-term consequences in the metropole.

French Jews and North African Decolonization

Given the diversity of French Jewish life, there was no unified communal perspective on French decolonization, North African nationalism, or the Algerian war. As the Algerian conflict intensified, conscriptions increased, and violence spread to the metropole, opposition to the war began to grow throughout many sectors of French society. French Jews, like other citizens, responded with the variety typical of a heterogeneous population. Nevertheless, the recent anti-Jewish persecution in Europe coupled with the birth of Israel and its complex relations with its Arab neighbors meant that French Jews, like the international Jewish agencies discussed in chapter 2, often saw Jewish meaning in France's disentanglement from its North African territories, meaning that was debated extensively in communal organizations and media outlets. While some called for dialogue and cooperation based on a shared Muslim-Jewish commitment to national self-determination and anti-racist struggles, others focused on Jewish victimization at the hands of "Arabs" and dismissed dialogue as impossible due to rising antisemitism in the Arab world. It was the latter perspective that came to dominate most mainstream communal discourse by the mid-1960s.

French Jewish interest in the "Jews of Arab lands" increased after World War II as part of the wider American and European Jewish focus on the issue. While the CRIF continued to rely on the AIU to take the lead on all North African projects, focusing primarily on European antisemitism and war restitutions, delegates nevertheless took interest in the region beginning in 1948.[1] Moroccan Zionist Paul Calamaro was thus invited to speak at a January meeting, and in

April, CRIF president Léon Meiss visited Morocco for an AIU school inauguration.[2] Following the riots in Oujda and Djérada, CRIF delegates protested to French authorities and called for restitution.[3] Likewise, the Fédération des sociétés juifs de France, the umbrella organization representing East European Jewish immigrants, introduced a new charge in November 1948 that called, among other things, for French Jewish aid to North Africa.[4] Both the FSJF and the CRIF also joined other organizations in protesting the persecution of Iraqi Jews from 1949 to 1951,[5] often comparing Iraq's policies to Hitler's.[6] Egyptian Jews similarly captured attention, first in 1948 when two hundred families sought asylum in France, and more consistently after "Operation Susannah" in July 1954, when a small network of Egyptian Jewish and Israeli spies firebombed several sites in Alexandria and Cairo.[7] It was following the Suez crisis, however, when thousands of Egyptian Jews fled, five thousand of whom sought shelter in France, that French Jewish organizations took greatest notice.[8] If the presence of these new Jewish refugees strained aid institutions still working to rebuild from the Holocaust, they also inspired empathy from those who shared a recent past of persecution.[9]

In response, anti-Arab discourse mounted, as audiences at pro-Israel rallies were warned to "remain on their guard before the Arab world" so that "the Arab cannot practice the verse in the Koran: 'If you cannot convince, exterminate.' "[10] Jewish publications were also saturated with comparisons of Nasser to Hitler.[11] According to the secretary general of the Association indépendante des anciens deportés et internés juifs: "Barely twelve years have elapsed since the destruction of the last barbed wire fences around the Nazi concentration camps stopped the tragic deportations in which six million of our own perished, when once again the nightmare of Nasser's deportations and concentration camps confronts our Egyptian brothers." Or as one speaker proclaimed at a December 1956 rally, thousands of Egyptian Jews were being "thrown into prisons, new Auschwitzes, now with Arab names."[12] While some commentators downplayed widespread Egyptian antisemitism, emphasizing instead the government's role in requisitions, arrests, and expulsions, headlines in the Jewish press, such as "The New Cairo, Mecca of Anti-Semitism," blurred such distinctions.[13] Baron Alain de Rothschild, president of the Consistoire, similarly drew parallels between the Holocaust and the persecution of Egyptian Jews: "We would betray the memory [of the six million martyrs massacred under Hitler] if, at this crucial moment, we did not declare our total solidarity with the members of a community threatened with complete and brutal annihilation."[14] Rhetorically linking European antisemitism with Arab nationalism, such pronouncements placed Jews in a politically antagonistic relationship with "Arabs," a perspective that solidified as the North African crisis accelerated.

Prior to the mid-1950s, French Jewish spokesmen had relatively little to say about their nation's policies in Morocco, Tunisia, and Algeria. In January 1948, for example, Léon Meiss echoed the CRIF's perennial discomfort with criticizing the government when he reminded delegates to be prudent in pronouncements on Maghrebian Jews.[15] While that organization did protest the 1948 riots in Morocco and while the AIU encouraged the French government to better conditions for Jews in the protectorate, such efforts were rare. In 1954, however, as Moroccan and Tunisian Jews began departing for the metropole, questions over how to respond became more acute.[16] On one side stood those who believed that North African Jewish life was in peril. As one CRIF member remarked in November, "As long as France remains, the situation for North African Jews will be bearable, but make no mistake about the meaning and import of current developments."[17] Many French Zionists also expressed skepticism over the Jewish future in an independent North Africa, with some underscoring the antisemitism of all Arab states—thereby asserting the "Arabness" of the region—and others warning that the anti-Israeli stance of North African nationalist leaders made migration to Israel essential.[18] On the other side stood the Zionist left, which rejected such analyses, as did a range of non-Zionist intellectuals and activists.[19] In August 1954, the Bund's French chapter thus argued that Zionists were exploiting the situation to encourage migration to Israel.[20] While in favor of helping Jews who desired to emigrate, Bund members also called for faith in Muslim promises of security, arguing that many indigenous Jews supported the independence struggle.[21]

This debate—between those arguing that Jews qua Jews were the target of Muslim animosity and those arguing that Muslims and Jews shared common aspirations—intensified in tandem with the Algerian conflict.[22] In fall 1955, for example, as demonstrators in several French cities protested an increase of troop contingents, the Union des étudiants juifs de France (UEJF)—the main body representing Jewish high school and university students—publicly condemned collective repression in Algeria and insisted that all French youth, and Jewish youth in particular, be spared participating in military occupations.[23] Their stance infuriated CRIF officials who had adopted a predictably cautious position on growing militarization in Algeria.[24] In their condemnation of French colonial policies, however, the Bund and the UEJF joined various prominent Jewish thinkers and leftist activists who criticized the army for its violent tactics and argued that it was unethical and hypocritical to support Israeli independence while rejecting the same for Morocco, Tunisia, and Algeria. Well-known Jewish intellectuals such as Jean Daniel, Pierre Vidal-Naquet, Claude Lanzman, and Wladimir Rabi wrote in favor of Algerian independence, condemned French torture tactics, and defended those unwilling to serve in the army. While not all rooted their political positions in their Jewishness, others very consciously made such links.[25] Rabi, for example, argued that FLN terrorism rarely targeted Jews and called for Jewish protests against Algerian Muslim mistreatment: "Others may allow themselves to be derelict. We do not have the right."[26] For Alain Geismar, the founder later of the Maoist, Gauche Prolétarienne, and eighteen at the time of the Algerian conflict, activism was very much a response to prior Jewish persecution. Stopped often by police due to his dark skin, Geismar recalled their excuses once realizing he was French: "Pardon us, we thought you were Algerian. Excuse us, we thought you were an Arab." Such racism, Geismar insisted, "is intolerable and can only remind us of Jews who were arrested fifteen years before."[27] Other French Jews signed petitions, worked as "suitcase carriers" transporting documents and funds for the FLN, or defended imprisoned Algerian militants in court. According to Janine Cahen, a twenty-nine-year-old Mulhouse teacher who worked as a suitcase carrier, "It is because I am Jewish that I aid the FLN; it must be made known that those who proclaim 'Algérie française' are the same as those who scrawl out 'Death to Jews.'"[28] Or as one Jewish activist declared somewhat hyperbolically, "Ninety percent of those who made up the underground network were Jews . . . maybe not ninety percent, but eighty-five percent."[29]

Even those most convinced of the righteousness of the Algerian cause, however, at times had trouble reconciling their Jewish commitments with their progressive politics. Such difficulties emerged clearly in the UEJF's efforts at interethnic dialogue, which while pursued with great enthusiasm in the late 1950s and early 1960s, also reflected significant ambivalence.[30] The organization, founded in Paris in 1945, sought to bring together Jewish students of all political, religious, and cultural orientations. With fifteen chapters in universities throughout France as well as several subsections in Paris, the UEJF attracted approximately 10 percent of the most highly engaged Jewish students (or about 2,500 people), many of whom believed deeply in pluralism and cross-cultural dialogue.[31] In March–April 1957, for example, the UEJF's organ, *Kadimah*, featured the essay, "Plea for a Certain Metropolitan Dialogue."[32] Written by René Kochmann, a frequent contributor, the article argued for improved communication between Jewish and Muslim students in France. Even this initial call for dialogue, however, was marked by a certain ambivalence, as Kochmann reflected on the naïveté of asking North African Muslim students to accept the independence of a Jewish state without asking the same for Algeria. Here, then, a desire for exchange was quickly shadowed by awareness that to engage in dialogue required putting Algerian Muslim needs ahead of French or Jewish national priorities.

According to Henri Atlan, an Algerian Jew who had come to Paris in 1949 to pursue his studies, and one of the movement's leaders, UEJF members in fact worried that dialogue with North African nationalists might conflict with their Jewish commitments. By defending "the values that seemed to be essential to our history and traditions . . . we appeared to be allying ourselves with Arab nationalism, which we had from the outset every reason to suspect of anti-Israelism and therefore of anti-Semitism." For Atlan such fears were unwarranted, since the UEJF was not seeking "to give up our identity in the name of a utopian universalism as those on the left are occasionally tempted to do, but to establish a dialogue based on a mutual comprehension of our hopes, differences, and needs."[33] *Kadimah* seemed to reflect this perspective. The June–July 1957 issue, for example, featured an article by the Algerian Muslim nationalist writer, Yacine Kateb, a proponent of Muslim-Jewish cooperation in Palestine, in addition to a transcript of a heated discussion following his presentation to *Kadimah*'s editors and students.[34] The exchange excited the journal's editors, who commented: "Usually, student conferences are raucous, violent, and impassioned [but] we all had the feeling that . . . something at once positive and intangible was created here."[35] And yet Kateb was the only prominent author in *Kadimah*'s pages to receive a lengthy explanatory note and rebuttal, which narrowed the scope of the dialogue by imposing an interpretation on his analysis.

Likewise, several attempts to bring together Jewish and Muslim students in France failed due to mutual distrust. As Albert Memmi, the Tunisian Jewish author, described of his participation in one such group in Paris: "Must I acknowledge that reticence was almost equal on both sides? That the non-Jews and the non-Arabs who were with us were full of goodwill but skeptical. In brief, we failed; we must acknowledge it because nobody expected it."[36] Such failures came, in part, because progressive politics was often directly at odds with group affiliations. Lionel Cohn captured this dilemma in winter 1960 in *Kadimah* when asserting that Jews were caught between the impossible choice of "their love for their Jewish brothers [and] their passion for justice." Drawing on Camus, he noted, "If I had to choose between my mother and justice, I would choose my mother."[37] In the interest of dialogue, *Kadimah* published a response by Mohammed Ben Bachir, an Algerian Muslim student in France, who argued that Algerian Jews were African and more welcome there than in France.[38] And yet UEJF editors published Ben Bachir's piece with numerous disclaimers, cutting out sections they believed to be inflammatory and insisting that his arguments were "baseline invalid." The UEJF commitment to dialogue was thus highly circumscribed despite its criticisms of French policies in Algeria and its commitment to the ideal of national self-determination and Muslim-Jewish exchange.

Given the difficulties of establishing dialogue among those most committed to the endeavor, it is not surprising that others proved even more skeptical. In a special edition of the popular Jewish monthly *L'Arche* entitled, "Is Israeli-Arab Peace Possible?," the editors seemingly committed themselves to such a good-faith exchange. The decision to devote an entire issue to the question, the editors explained, emerged from growing pressure from the Left " 'to open a dialogue,' 'to stretch out a hand,' " so as "not to avoid an objective confrontation with opposing theses." With this goal in mind, the editors posed a set of questions to specialists on North Africa and the Middle East about the possibility of peace between Israel and its neighbors. The questions reveal much about the framework from which certain mainstream French Jewish institutions approached the issue. Although ostensibly about peace in the Middle East, the first question focused on "Muslim anti-Semitism," asking if "such anti-Semitism was a constant of the historical tradition of Islam." While the subsequent questions returned to "Arabs" and the conflict in the Middle East, the issue had been firmly contextualized as part of a deeply rooted Muslim rejection of Jews.[39]

Despite the biased questions, *L'Arche* editors expressed shock and dismay that only the Parisian delegate of the Bureau arabe de presse et de publications responded to the dozens of requests sent to North African and Middle Eastern spokesmen. Lamenting the more than fifty unanswered letters, the editors denounced the refusal to discuss "a problem that presents so many analogies with their own." Those student activists who demurred on the grounds that they had nothing to add to the Arab League's pronouncements or because they were focused on their own independence struggles were condemned for their unwillingness "to be seen in the columns of a Jewish journal." The editors concluded darkly that Muslim-Jewish dialogue was impossible due to a "lack of viable interlocutors." "Make no mistake," they warned.

> This is not a "small matter" around the Israeli-Arab conflict, this is not a phenomenon on the "margins" of the major challenges that Islam faces today as it adapts to the modern world. This is, to the contrary, what the Anglo-Saxons call a "test case," a prime example. The way in which the Arabs learn to overcome their resentment towards the Jews will determine their aptitude for re-shaping their old Islamic societies and for adapting to the standards that govern the contemporary behavior of States and individuals."[40]

Here, then, "Arabs," whether Middle Eastern or North African—overtaken with an essentialist rejection of the Jew embedded in Islam—were presented as an existential threat to the Western world. Dialogue, framed as the debate between two equivalent "sides," failed because of one side's backwardness and bigotry. Of course, not all commentators described Muslim-Jewish relations this starkly. The same magazine published pieces that emphasized good relations between North African Muslim and Jewish residents or that downplayed anti-Jewish conspiracies.[41] More dire assessments, however, continued to gather steam.[42] By summer 1961, as Bizerte and the Algerian crisis pushed ever larger numbers of Tunisian and Algerian Jews to the metropole, depictions increasingly stressed anti-Jewish biases. One article, for example, cited a Tunisian Jewish man saying, "We no longer have any future in Tunisia; we do not dare to go out or to speak. It is as it was under Hitler."[43] Other articles, collected and circulated by the CRIF, also emphasized Muslim antisemitism. One story in the CRIF's "Note d'information," told of Dr. Ovadia who had fled Oran "threatened with death as a Jew." In his words, "If we do not immediately take appropriate action, we will see in Oran in the coming days the bloodiest pogrom in all of Jewish history."[44] Another editorialized that "only the willful or the partisan would ignore the anti-Semitism that has filtered down from the top to the bottom in the Arab nationalist world."[45] Still another spoke of Muslim students in Tlemcen who carved swastikas on school walls and forced Jewish students to kiss them.[46]

Such perceptions of increasing antisemitism spreading from the Middle East to North Africa were accompanied by a growing belief that many Algerian Jews supported French victory and even the OAS. Rumors of a Jewish chapter of the OAS began circulating in March 1961, leading to vigorous debates within the CRIF over whether to condemn OAS violence.[47] To do so, one member remarked, would cut off the CRIF from "our Algerian co-religionists, whose sympathies are leaning mostly toward the OAS." Or as another commented: "The large majority of Algerian Jews have adopted a position contrary to the official policies of the metropole. They very actively support a movement that symbolizes the Resistance."[48] While the left-leaning member associations rejected such assertions, arguing that Algerian Jewish opinion was diverse and that most opposed the OAS, and still others criticized the stoking of anti-Arab panic,[49] their opponents saw diminishing common ground between Jewish and Muslim North Africans.[50]

Such debates also circulated following the brutal police repression of Algerian anti-war demonstrators on 17 October 1961.[51] In the aftermath, several Jewish organizations held protests, making comparisons with antisemitic persecution in the 1940s. In this instance, however, parallels between Nazi/ Vichy oppression and contemporary events were used to underscore solidarities between Muslims and Jews. The UEJF, for example, declared itself unable to remain silent before "measures recalling those taken against us Jews by the Nazis under occupation." Its protest on 21 November condemned all forms of racism; called for the prosecution of those responsible; and demanded the reestablishment of peace in Algeria.[52] Likewise, the FSJF condemned silence, "as some did during the period when we were forced to wear the yellow star" and expressed its solidarity with the victims. The Jewish communist organization, Mouvement contre le racisme, l'antémitisme, et pour la paix (MRAP), formed after World War II to fight inequity in France, was equally vocal in its criticisms. As Rabbi Sirat, France's Jewish youth chaplain, commented during the MRAP's demonstration, "the poor treatment that the Algerians suffered touched me personally." Recalling the recent persecution of French Jews, he insisted, "We must do something so that it does not begin again."[53] The president of the Union des engagés volontaires et anciens combattants juifs, Isi Blum, urged the CRIF to speak out as representative of a people that had also suffered racial persecution.[54]

The CRIF's response to this appeal, however, points to diverging Jewish perspectives on the Algerian war and to difficulties in forging Muslim-Jewish alliances around areas of common concern. While the governing board condemned violence against Muslim Algerians, it expressly refused to compare recent events with antisemitism in the 1940s.[55] While in part reflecting the CRIF's traditional commitment to republican universalism, this decision also reflected pressure from the wider Jewish population, such as a November article by Algerian Jewish repatriates who insisted that Muslim immigrants deserved *no*

Jewish support having never taken a stand against antisemitic violence.[56] Thus while a progressive Jewish wing urged greater support for Algerian Muslims based on profound commonalities, the most prominent Jewish institutions refused to make such links, often presenting a far more dire perspective on Muslim-Jewish relations throughout North Africa.

Such debates persisted throughout the last year of the Algerian war. While those on the left continued to insist that "in an era when all men must choose only one loyalty," Algerian Jews had a moral duty to side with the FLN—culminating in a June 1962 collective appeal to Algerian Jews to remain in their country—for many others, the emptying out of North Africa's Jewish population provided evidence of the Jews' particular fate.[57] As M. Moch of CRIF remarked in January 1963, Algerian Jews had left for "for distinctive reasons," citing their flight in percentages larger than other Europeans as evidence.[58] Or as Gérard Israel asserted in *L'Arche*, "Algerian Jewish repatriates in France find themselves in a situation a bit different [than other repatriates] because they were rejected by an Algerian society of which they were, in some ways, the integral part."[59]

Such perspectives became a central trope in French Jewish discourse throughout the late 1950s and early 1960s as Jewish departures increased, seemingly confirming the dire predictions of those who had warned against mounting antisemitism. While calls for dialogue and cooperation were never fully extinguished, mainstream Jewish institutions increasingly portrayed Jews and Muslims as antagonists in a polarized political crisis in which the latter had been infected with the Arab League's propaganda.[60]

For most French Jews, however, "Arabs" remained an abstraction associated with the Middle East and North Africa, and few Jewish publications or organizations expressed any opinion about what, if anything, the growing Muslim population in France meant for Jewish life.[61] In the late 1960s, however, when events both at home and abroad finally drew Jewish attention to the local Muslim population, frameworks forged during decolonization established the parameters of communal discourse around the Muslim question. While those who had fought hard for Algerian independence continued to defend interethnic dialogue, their perspective was increasingly marginalized in mainstream Jewish circles.

Early Encounters in the Metropole

If the Jewish establishment proved largely oblivious to the potential communal implications of surging Muslim migration to France, arriving Moroccan, Tunisian, and Algerian Jews proved far more cognizant of this development. Sharing a sense of displacement and an overlapping cultural and linguistic heritage with Muslim North Africans, many Jews found comfort in the familiarity of the other. One Tunisian Jew, for example, capturing his sense of discomfort after arriving in France, described "Arabs, whose path I cross only by chance in certain neighborhoods of Paris and who, like me, have become immigrants," with a sense of having undergone a similar experience of displacement.[62] Moreover, France's postwar housing crisis meant that incoming Muslims and Jews sometimes settled in similar neighborhoods where common origins and similar challenges served as a social bridge. Within relatively short order, however, differing relationships to the French state and levels of communal development rooted in the colonial past highlighted stark contrasts.

Housing shortages sometimes led Muslims and Jews to settle in similar neighborhoods on the outskirts of large French cities. Although the government sought to distribute repatriates throughout the country so as to avoid overwhelming any one area, most Jews gravitated toward France's largest cities.[63] There, housing shortages and high prices sent many to newly constructed apartment projects on the urban periphery, some of which were initially reserved for repatriates, including in Sarcelles, Aulnay-sous-Bois, Bondy, and Créteil in the northern and eastern Parisian suburbs and Saint-Marguerite (9th), Saint-Tronc (10th), La Rose (13th), and Pont de Vivaux (10th) in Marseille. While few Moroccan and Tunisian Jews benefited from government subsidies, many moved to similar areas or to inexpensive neighborhoods within city limits, such as the traditionally East European Jewish neighborhoods of the 4th (Marais) and the 20th (Belleville) as well as the 12th, 18th, and 19th arrondissements in Paris or to the 1st and 2nd arrondissements in Marseille. These residential patterns meant that newly arriving Jews at times shared city spaces with North African Muslims who settled in similar areas, although economic differences and the repatriates' political status as citizens often gave them access to neighborhoods unavailable to Muslim migrants.[64]

The cafés, groceries, restaurants, schools, and streets in mixed neighborhoods became meeting spots for those with shared culinary, cultural, and linguistic practices. In the 1960s and 1970s, most Algerian, Moroccan, and Tunisian Jewish adults spoke Arabic, helping to forge bonds with other Arabic-speaking North Africans.[65] As one transplanted Algerian Jew made clear: "We are Berbers. We are from there and France is elsewhere [c'est un ailleurs]. We always lived there; my grandmother did not even know how to speak French. My parents' maternal language is Arabic. Me, I speak Arabic. I love Arab music. I am from there."[66] Neighborhood grocers sold to a mixed clientele raised on couscous, olive oil, and North African alcohol. Muslim and Jewish men played cards and smoked together in local cafés. Interactions in these neighborhoods were often friendly, rarely reflecting the wider political struggles taking place in the Maghreb or Middle East.[67]

If common origins and similar settlement patterns helped establish new forms of sociability, however, they could not mask divisions that influenced the integration of both into the French state.[68] In the 1950s, Muslims and Jews from Algeria came with French citizenship, as did some Jews from Morocco and Tunisia and Egypt. Equality on paper did not translate into equivalent access to French society, however, where distrust and fear of Muslims surged in response to a brutal war of decolonization.[69] Subsequently the decision to recognize the French citizenship of Jewish Algerians in the final war negotiations provided legal justification for excluding Muslims while opening the door to Jewish integration.[70] Algerian Jews thus benefited from the extensive housing subsidies, working papers, professional *reclassement* and medical and social security available to repatriating citizens.[71] In contrast, Moroccan, Tunisian, and particularly Algerian Muslims faced administrative structures that distinguished them even from other incoming migrants, including Jews from the same countries whose integration was often made easier by sympathetic French administrators.[72]

A focus on Marseille underscores the way in which shared cultural connections and a postwar housing crisis initially pushed Muslim and Jewish migrants together, while colonial legacies and differing relationships to the French state pulled them apart. Some aspects of Marseille's story are, of course, unique. The 40 percent increase in the city's population in the 1950s and 1960s as it welcomed French citizens expelled from Egypt, European settlers and functionaries from Tunisia and Morocco, North African laborers, and Algerian "repatriates," meant that at least statistically, Marseille was more affected by France's loss of its North African territories than other French cities.[73] Moreover, the leadership over several decades of Mayor Gaston Defferre gave the city unmatched political stability in which some groups fared better than others. Despite Marseille's particularities, however, the processes that pushed Muslims and Jews together and eventually pulled them apart mirrored those at work in other large French cities.

As in other cities, Marseille's Muslim and Jewish populations increased substantially. In 1951 alone, 195,000 Algerian Muslims passed through Marseille's port and airport, a number that grew to 210,000 the following year. While most did not remain due to the city's depressed economy, by 1953, approximately 15,000 Algerian Muslims had settled in the Bouches-du-Rhône, primarily in Marseille, a number that reached 24,000 by 1959.[74] This migration, largely male until 1950, was distinctive for the relatively large number of women and children that soon followed. Although Marseille housed 8–9 percent of France's North African population in the early 1950s, it sheltered 17 percent of all families. These relatively large numbers gave rise to particularly acute problems regarding housing, education, and social services but also provided more permanence to the migrant population.[75]

Like Muslims, Jews poured into Marseille in the 1950s primarily en route from Morocco and Tunisia to Israel.[76] At the peak of the decade's migration in October 1956, more than 35,000 Moroccan Jews passed through Grand Arénas, which continued to be controlled by the Jewish Agency and had become the major transit camp for those en route to Israel. Egyptian Jews fleeing the Suez crisis also passed through Marseille.[77] While most migrants only stayed a few days or weeks and left few traces of their presence, others remained, bringing Marseille's Jewish population to between 12,000 and 15,000 by 1955.[78]

France's postwar housing crisis, particularly acute in Marseille, meant that new arrivals often settled in mixed neighborhoods where similar backgrounds, overlapping struggles, and shared public spaces facilitated neighborly relations. Ironically, Grand Arénas itself became such a site, as those unable to depart rapidly due to medical or other concerns settled in for a longer sojourn. If, in 1948, the transit camp had served as a space to act out colonial political struggles for those passing through, by the 1950s, the camp and its surroundings had become a site of integration *into* the metropole. No longer transients, its permanent residents—whether Muslim or Jewish—sought to make a home for themselves in France, providing space for their cultural similarities rather than their political differences to emerge.

Such contacts were initially limited due to the Jewish Agency's efforts to isolate camp residents from the wider metropolitan area. Organizing Grand Arénas as a world unto itself, the Jewish Agency maintained its own staff, educational system, medical team, hospital, religious facility, and eating space. A clearly defined boundary marked its Jewish sections from the parts still populated primarily by Algerian Muslim workers. The latter faced dire conditions in the early 1950s. While often receiving aid from several private agencies, most notably the Association d'aide aux travailleurs d'outre-mer (ATOM), which received government subventions to ease the migrants' transition, needs surpassed resources.[79] "One word characterizes the material and moral condition in which the majority of North Africans in France reside," noted a 1952 report, "turmoil."[80] Living without electricity or plumbing in shantytowns known as bidonvilles or in hotels or worker hostels, most of the 36,000 families in Marseille that lacked adequate shelter in 1951 were Muslim laborers. According to estimates in 1953, 8,600 Muslim workers lived in insufficient housing, including overpopulated rooms, cellars, attics, and sheds.[81] The Algerian Muslims who lived in temporary barracks in and surrounding Grand Arénas thus resided alongside their Jewish neighbors without the resources available to the latter. According to one Jewish resident, "There was a camp for Jews and a camp—really a shantytown—in the other part of the barracks in which French generally of Muslim origin lived. In between was barbed wire. They were absolutely separate."[82]

Complete isolation, however, proved illusive as those Jewish residents who remained in the camp began establishing commercial relationships in the surrounding neighborhood, attending local cafés and cinemas, playing soccer in parks with neighborhood residents, and sometimes establishing friendships. Once Jewish migration through Grand Arénas began to diminish in the early 1960s, poor squatters—often Muslim laborers from Algeria—began moving into its blocks and barracks, increasing their numbers and the camp's diversity. Given that Marseille's housing crisis was not fully addressed until the 1970s, many lived in what became a kind of shantytown for years.

Despite the poverty and poor living conditions, residents remember the neighborhood as one in which people from contrasting backgrounds lived together in harmony. As one Algerian Muslim recalled, Jews and Muslims from the Maghreb connected around common origins: "We didn't know much about the Maghreb. . . . [A]nd we learned about our country through these people who were North African before they were Jews." For him, neighborhood relations were strong: "We never had communal or relational problems between us. . . . There was a solidarity that continues to this day. Me, I often get together with people from that epoch, Jews who did not leave for Israel."[83] Others stressed the neighborhood cafés, cinemas, and bars as sites of interaction and convivial exchanges. "When there was a party—a baptism in the small chapel on rue Vaucanson, a circumcision—everyone took advantage, both Jews and Arabs. . . . When there was an Arab wedding, a gypsy wedding, everyone went."[84]

While Grand Arénas may have been atypical, it was not unique thanks to a housing crisis that pushed poor Jews—and even those with considerably more resources—into the same urban areas as North African Muslims. Such settlement patterns were particularly notable in the traditional immigrant neighborhoods of the city center. On the rue Sainte-Barbe (1st and 2nd arrondissements), for example, Jews, Armenians, Greeks, Italians, Spanish, Algerians, and Moroccans lived together, and on the perpendicular, rue Puvis de Chavannes, "the determining characteristic" was the "lack of spatial segregation," with a Jewish fabric store, for example, next to a Tunisian restaurant. The adjacent rue des Chapeliers, held thirty-two North African Muslim businesses and twenty-seven Jewish, Armenian, Greek, and "European" shops.[85] According to one Muslim resident, "My mother and all the other women bought cloth at the fabric stores, Arab or not (Jewish or Armenian), but they all spoke Arabic."[86]

Here, then, shared linguistic and cultural heritages bridged other divisions and were even built into the cityscape in the immigrant commercial districts surrounding the Old Port and the train station, where those with North African roots could find food and goods from home. Indeed, unlike other large French cities, Marseille's visibly "North African" downtown, which cut the city's northern industrial sectors from its middle- and upper-middle-class neighborhoods to the south, created a centrally located space in which residents of all educational, economic, national, ethnic, and religious background could interact, providing those with North African roots a means through which to connect with their past and one another.[87]

Such interactions, as we saw above, were not unique to Marseille. Shared city spaces, such as Belleville or the Marais in Paris or in Sarcelles, just to the north, allowed Muslim and Jewish neighbors to interact regularly. Jewish entrepreneurs at times also employed Muslim workers. As one assessment of these encounters argued, "In these neighborhoods as in these small businesses, these small shops, these restaurants, relations between Jews and Muslims are mostly good: they are marked by a certain collusion [*connivence*] that comes from the 'land of the sun' that both left."[88]

As the class implications of Jewish bosses hiring Muslim employees suggests, however, common origins and a shared newcomer status could not erase all differences among those arriving in the 1950s. Thus while only 3 percent of incoming Jews lacked a primary education, most Muslims were not formally educated.[89] And while North African Jewish arrivals tended to represent a lower socioeconomic level than their largely middle-class French co-religionists, often dropping in economic status due to the migration itself, they nevertheless experienced rapid social mobility as they moved from artisanal, industrial, and commercial employment into salaried positions, the civil service, and the liberal professions, such as law or medicine.[90] Muslim migrants, in contrast, were most often employed in the most dangerous, difficult, and poorly paid sectors of the French economy, including the building trades, public works projects, industrial labor, mines, and cleaning services.[91] Moreover, observers comparing them in 1953 noted that while North African Jewish and Muslim communities had similar social structures, Jews as the "longer anchored element" were more "rooted and assimilated" and had "less difficulty" than Muslim workers.[92] Emile Touati, for example, writing in the French Jewish magazine, *L'Arche*, differentiated between Muslim and Jewish arrivals by noting Jews' greater knowledge of the French language and culture; their inclination to migrate as families; their plans to settle permanently in France; and their urban middle-class status versus the poor agricultural backgrounds of most Muslim immigrants.[93] Such differences, while varying among Jewish migrants from Tunisia, Morocco, and Algeria, and modifying as larger numbers of Muslim families established permanent roots, influenced initial opportunities.[94]

Incoming Muslim and Jewish migrants also encountered vastly different communal structures that influenced their social and economic integration. French Jews, scarred by the Holocaust and seeing in the new arrivals the hope for a more vibrant future, relied on AJDC aid to establish a network of old-age homes; child care and medical facilities; youth programs; scholarship funds; employment agencies; professional retraining bodies; cultural, religious, and educational programs; and financial assistance bodies.[95] Through these efforts, Jewish agencies aided fifty thousand new arrivals between 1954 and 1959 alone, primarily from Morocco, Tunisia, and Egypt.[96] Although facilities were often stretched to the breaking point and communal leaders bemoaned their inability to prevent newcomers "[from] living in truly terrible and degrading conditions,"[97] such aid provided a crucial safety net.[98] Other arriving Jews—primarily from Egypt and Algeria—held French citizenship, giving them access to national welfare programs, or came with sufficient resources to care for themselves. According to Marseille's chief rabbi, "the new arrivals generally do not show up at [the] same reception centers as Muslims."[99]

The very way Rabbi Salzer framed the issue points to the distinction between incoming Jews and Muslims in the 1950s. While impoverished Jewish refugees often required aid, others could fend for themselves, and those who *did* need help could take advantage of an institutional structure determined to help, guide, and support them. Muslims, in contrast, faced a more precarious situation. With nothing like the established communal infrastructure of France's Jewish population, the largely Algerian population that made up the Muslim labor force after World War II was constituted primarily of young, single, and highly mobile workers whose primary base remained in North Africa. Although technically French citizens, they lacked the philanthropic, religious, or social network that French Jews had built since World War II. In the words of one Jewish aid worker, "There is no Arab set up in French life to welcome a co-religionist."[100]

The 1950s surge in North African nationalism made the settlement of Muslim laborers even more fraught as they became trapped in the struggle between French authorities and the FLN. Marseille's Algerian Muslim population was too disorganized and transitory to engage in much political activism. Police nevertheless saw a mounting threat as early as 1951, insisting that the Kabyle population, the majority of the city's Algerian migrants, were "almost all anti-French nationalists" and had won over many of those previously believed to be pro-French, encouraging Algerian, Tunisian, and Moroccan Muslims—who had "previously formed distinct clans"—to unite around common aims.[101]

In 1954 such concerns intensified following the FLN's initial insurrection. By 1956, as troops and supplies began moving unceasingly through Marseille's port, travel restrictions cut Algerian Muslim workers off from their families. Meanwhile, the FLN, having established itself in the city through the networks that had supported Messali Hadj, sought supporters in cafés and lodging houses, particularly in the city center (Belsunce-Porte d'Aix).[102] While FLN activities were limited and police repression intense, the nationalist organization was able to carry out several strikes against the French and internal opponents, making police more nervous about a citywide insurrection.[103]

In this environment, surveillance of Muslim workers intensified, a shift evident in new urban development projects that allowed for more efficient policing. Although the postwar housing crisis had allowed some mixed Muslim-Jewish neighborhoods to emerge, these new policies encouraged greater social and economic segregation. In 1958, city officials thus began systematically demolishing migrant slums and moving residents to cités de transit as part of a larger process of improving urban hygiene and policing suspect populations. Constructed on vacant lots in the urban periphery and often lacking basic infrastructure or resources, these structures were meant to last for a year or two after which immigrants would move into the more permanent Habitations à loyer modéré (HLM), the public apartment blocks that made up the central component of the national housing plan. In practice, however, many cités de transit remained in place for two decades, allowing authorities to police Muslim workers during the Algerian conflict and beyond. The result was their structural isolation, including from incoming "repatriates" who had privileged access to the HLM structures.[104]

The contrasting living conditions of Muslims with incoming Jews, many of whom took advantage of housing for repatriated "Europeans," did not go unnoticed by the former. One Algerian Muslim in France since the early 1940s complained to the mayor of his many co-nationals waiting without adequate housing for years, "while the families of how many French Jews and other people departed from Egypt and elsewhere since 1957" were already lodged. "This practice is not only revolting for its injustice but particularly for its separatism and for all the hatreds it creates." As his comments suggest, at least some Muslims viewed the relative ease of Jewish settlement as a stinging reminder of their own second-class status and of ongoing French willingness to favor some citizens over others: "I believe that it is the obligation of a politician doubling as an administrator," he continued, "to ensure equality between all citizens . . . so that public services are really used by all and do not favor one fraction of the privileged."[105]

If by 1960 when this letter was written, the uneven settlement patterns facing Muslim and Jewish arrivals were already apparent to some, such distinctions became even sharper over the next few years as the Algerian crisis stripped citizenship from Muslim Algerians while re-affirming the Frenchness of Jewish Algerians. Given the initial chaos of such a large migration, the impact of this shift was not always evident. With time, however, the imprint of France's colonial legacy and the violent war that ended it became clear, shaping Muslim and Jewish economic and political fortunes in the metropole and their evolving relations with each other.

Algerian Independence, Repatriation, and City Politics

The "repatriation" crisis of 1961 and 1962 brought tens of thousands of former Algerian residents to Marseille. As part of this migration, the Jewish population surged, reaching approximately sixty-five thousand by the early 1970s. With twenty synagogues and over sixty rabbis or preachers, Marseille's Jewish community became the second largest in France.[106] Nor did North African independence do anything to stem the tide of Muslim arrivals fleeing political unrest and economic turmoil.[107] As Marseille's industrial and construction sectors developed, the population of primarily Algerian Muslim laborers rose to more than fifty thousand by 1974.[108] The enormous growth of both populations, however, did little to flatten the differences between them with regard to access to city resources. Rather such differences were exacerbated as thousands of Algerian Jews—all bearing French citizenship—arrived in Marseille.

The speed and intensity of the massive migration, particularly in June and July 1962, initially overwhelmed all municipal services, masking distinctions among those arriving in city ports. On 25 June alone, seven boats brought nine thousand "repatriates" to the city. "Marseille is asphyxiated," reported *Le Figaro* on 7 July, "and can no longer cope with the massive arrivals such as those of last week."[109] The series of building projects to replace housing destroyed during the war were still under construction in 1962.[110] Hotels were inundated quickly. In June, Marseille was so saturated that incoming families were being sent fifty miles away for one night's lodging.[111]

In this context, Algerian Jews—like all newcomers—faced significant challenges. Although receiving extensive aid from Jewish agencies, no institution could fully address the problems accompanying such a large and rapid migration.[112] Primarily civil servants, shopkeepers, and craftsmen, the new arrivals were often unprepared to work in France's industrial labor force. Government subsidies and job retraining aided some while civil servants were often reclassified, but it took several years for the dust to settle. Those who remained in Marseille were generally less well off than those who went to Lyon, Paris, Nice, or Strasbourg, making the initial years more challenging. As one noted, "We do not have enough money to consolidate communal structures as we should."[113] While most had found an economic foothold by the mid-1970s, as late as 1968, commentators were noting significant numbers of "idlers" [*oisifs*] among Marseille's Algerian Jewish population.[114]

Moreover, just because the organized Jewish community coordinated aid for incoming Algerian, Moroccan, and Tunisian Jews, their landing was not always soft. Indeed, Marseille's Jewish population, which was extremely diverse, was riddled with strife.[115] As one FSJU representative noted, it would be impossible to talk of Marseille as "*a* community." Rather, the city's Jewish population was made up of a "conglomerate of groups of various ethnical [*sic*] origins, scattered all over an area larger than the city of Paris."[116] This heterogeneity was reflected in congregational terms.[117] Thus, the previously settled largely Ashkenazi population controlled the main synagogue on rue Breteuil, while three small synagogues on the rue de la Dragon housed those from Turkey, Poland, and Constantine, respectively. Jews from Oran prayed primarily on the rue Saint Dominique while those from Tunisia and Morocco attended synagogue on the rue Montgrand. Such divisions dominated commercial life as well, and power struggles among the groups could be intense.[118] Not only did Marseille's Jewish population increase by 400 percent, but also North African Jews—with their own practices, levels of religiosity, and cultural traditions—quickly became the majority.[119] Although the settled Jewish population was smaller, it had little intention of turning over communal institutions to the newcomers.[120] As a result, tensions and personal animosities dominated communal politics for years, and commentators made dire predictions about Marseille's Jewish future given the name-calling and ugly rifts, such as when one Consistoire member accused his North African co-religionists of having "the mentality of Arabs."[121]

This "slur" is suggestive at multiple levels. Clearly pointing to the divisions and cultural conflicts that encumbered Marseille's Jewish population as it adjusted to its growth, the angry remark challenged the "Europeanness" of arriving North African Jews. While legal categories may have allowed the latter to assert their "Frenchness," the established Jewish leadership was not convinced, suggesting that juridical categories could not fully capture the reality of such a heterogeneous population.[122] In addition, and perhaps more relevant to this analysis, the remark reflected the negative associations with the term "Arab," which, as we have seen, circulated in communal discourse during and after the Algerian crisis.

Yet whatever divisions prevented the easy integration of Marseille's Jewish community, their position was far more assured than that of incoming Muslims, 140,000 of whom were so-called *harkis* and their families, the auxiliaries in the French army and others who had supported the French presence and who had fled with departing troops.[123] Rejected by the established Algerian Muslim population, harkis were often viewed as traitors.[124] Thus although 26,000 harkis arrived in Marseille in summer 1962 (6,000–9,000 of whom remained in the Bouches-du-Rhône), no representative "introduced himself to them at the port of arrival to welcome, guide, or advise them. They were alone before the administration that repatriated them."[125] For those arriving in Marseille's port, the difference was immediately apparent. As one Jewish representative working at the docks to direct arriving co-religionists to communal welfare agencies reported: "Our placard attracted many looks. Two young Tunisian Muslims, noting the blue Star of David [*Magen David bleu*], shrugged their shoulders."[126] Or as one Algerian Jewish author described the scene at Orly airport in Paris:

> [I]n a quarter of the airport, someone installs a small counter with stools. The seats are cramped and the signs touch each other. "Catholic Relief Services," "Jewish Social Services [FSJU]," "Students," "Algerian Gas and Electric," and others with more mysterious signs. Each comes to find his own. Only the Arabs have no right to any sign in particular. Having disengaged, they are part of our past, and as such we abandon them to the good heart of the Red Cross."[127]

As such comments suggest the French administration did little to welcome their former supplemental military forces. Initially opposed to their "repatriation" and worried that the harkis would transport subversive political affiliations to France and/or create conflict within the Algerian Muslim migrant population, French settlement policies isolated them, preventing them from living in apartments set aside for "European" repatriates, and placing them instead in military transit camps before moving them to cités de transit, *hameaux de forestage*, or subsidized housing units constructed for them on the urban periphery.[128]

Harkis were not, however, the only incoming Muslims to live isolated from other North African arrivals. The settlement patterns of most Muslims when compared to Jewish repatriates clearly demonstrates how different relationships with the French state influenced residential options. While many Jews settled into temporary housing wherever it was available, within relatively short order, they—like other pieds noirs—were able to relocate to new HLM housing projects, 30 percent of which were reserved for repatriates over five years.[129] Certain developments became magnets for pieds-noirs, and particularly Jews, including Roy d'Espagne, La Cravache (around Boulevard Michelet), La Rouvière, and Frais-Vallon. While Jews also settled in St. Marguerite (9th arrondissement), St. Tronc, Pont de Vivaux (10th arrondissement), La Rose (13th arrondissement), and streets around the main synagogue on rue Breteuil (6th arrondissement), as well as in the working class and commercial neighborhoods of the city center, few moved into the 14th, 15th and 16th arrondissements or the quartier des Baumettes in the 9th arrondissement where North African laborers were generally located.[130]

Settlement patterns for the latter became increasingly concentrated in the city's industrial periphery. In the 1960s and early 1970s, an expanding labor market combined with growing investment in the industrial and construction sectors led to property speculation in the city's outlying areas (90 percent of housing developments were built at least 5 km outside central Marseille in these years). At the same time, urban renewal programs sought to restore large areas of the city (such as the area around the train station), demolishing the poorest and most unsanitary residential sectors and pushing their populations to the large *cités*. Given that many of those in the demolished areas were Muslim North Africans, the program of Marseille's urban renovation became intimately linked to the problem of housing immigrants. The long-term impact was the socioeconomic division of Marseille between a poorly equipped northern industrial sector with a high concentration of immigrants and a well-equipped middle- and upper-class southern sector.[131]

The fate of Grand Arénas residents points to these shifts. Constructed as a temporary structure to deal with housing shortages and population overflow, the camp had fulfilled its purpose by the late 1960s. As Jewish migration diminished, the Jewish Agency removed its remaining population to the former military hospital in Montolivet. In 1973, as part of a wider urban development plan, Grand Arénas was razed and the remaining population moved elsewhere. If the friendly relations that emerged in this transitional space capture the way the city's infrastructure—so unprepared for the massive arrivals of the 1950s and early 1960s—created opportunities for interethnic contact, its demise points to the different opportunities available to Muslim and Jewish newcomers over time. Divided at arrival between "Europeans" and "Muslims," Jews were absorbed into the former, while Muslims became immigrants of a lower order.[132] These differences shaped more than housing, ultimately influencing schooling, economic opportunities, and levels of integration.

One area where such inequities were particularly visible was in the arena of city politics. Under the supervision of Mayor Gaston Defferre, Marseille's political establishment embraced its Jewish minority with remarkable intensity. Indeed, according to municipal records, beginning in the early 1960s, Mayor Defferre fostered "strong ties, almost emotional" with many of those representing communal life,[133] including Rolland Amsellem, a lawyer who held leadership positions in many local Jewish institutions, and Robert Safrani, a businessman, both of whom served as town councilors on Defferre's list.[134] In addition, Defferre went out of his way to support organized communal life, providing municipal space for religious activities when synagogues proved too cramped and supporting Jewish political activities. Whether his solicitousness was—as some suspected—a simple calculation that Jews represented "a non-negligible potential electorate" or a particular affinity for the community, his outreach was a source of commentary in the city.[135]

With regard to international affairs, Defferre also consistently sided with his Jewish constituents on matters about which they cared. Most importantly, he was a vocal supporter of Israel, lending his voice to the young state's struggle on numerous occasions. In June 1961, for example, Defferre called for the GPRA to distance itself from the Arab League's anti-Israel politics and to establish formal ties between the two countries, warning that a more aggressive course would diminish French and Jewish support for Algerian independence. Linking Algeria's ability to succeed as a "modern enterprising nation directed toward the future" with its willingness to let go of antagonisms toward Israel, Defferre expressed wariness at Algeria's readiness to govern, and unadulterated respect for the Jewish state.[136] In fact, Defferre's support for Algerian independence had solidified only late in the conflict due to his concern for the pieds noirs.[137] This stance coupled with his pro-Israeli politics won him friends among incoming Jews who found the city a comfortable space in which to express their Zionist affiliations.

Indeed, one of the notable political developments among Marseille's Jews in the 1960s was their vocal support for Israel.[138] If, in the 1950s, Zionist activists regularly complained that Marseille's Jews donated too little to pro-Israel causes and while only one thousand turned out for a May 1950 celebration of Israel's anniversary, the May 1962 celebrations drew thousands, making the southern port city one of France's most active Zionist centers in the early 1960s.[139] Defferre's public support for the Jewish state facilitated this development. After visiting in spring 1962, for example, Defferre published a three-part article entitled, "Impressions of Israel" in his newspaper, *Le Provençal*, calling the Jewish state "a future solution for the free world" and an example of "efficiency and democracy."[140] Establishing Marseille as a sister city of Haifa that year, Defferre also created numerous cultural connections between the two countries.[141] In August 1962, for example, he welcomed a leading Israeli folk group to the Hôtel de Ville.[142] Only one of numerous ongoing links between the municipality and the Jewish state, such efforts provided a politically sanctioned space in which Marseille's Jews could express their affections for Israel without fearing accusations of dual loyalty.[143]

Causing few evident tensions with Marseille's Muslim population prior to 1967, thereafter the combination of the outbreak of another war in the Middle East, vocal support for Israel, and the municipality's repeated willingness to take sides on a distant conflict, once again created tensions. As we will see in the next chapter, in 1967 as in 1948, the struggles between Israelis and Palestinians became an opportunity to express the local resentments that had been building since even before French decolonization.[144]

Even in the early 1960s, however, colonial legacies left their mark. In January 1962, the French Jewish commentator Rabi thus reported that Marseille's Jewish population "feels endangered in a majority Muslim milieu."[145] While a vast exaggeration of the city's demographics—Muslims were little more than half the city's foreign population that was itself less than 10 percent of its total population—Rabi's comment captures the powerful way in which the previous decade's focus on Jewish victimization at the hand of North African "Arabs" had begun to frame understandings of Muslim-Jewish relations in the new context even though relations on the ground were often cordial.[146] Indeed, whatever the daily reality, colonial legacies—both in the story of Jewish victimization at the hands of Muslims and in the inequities built into the colonial structure and transferred to the metropole—created the context in which Muslim-Jewish relations would evolve in France.

4

The 1967 War and the Forging
of Political Community

This chapter investigates how the 1967 war between Israel and its Arab neighbors influenced Muslim-Jewish relations in France. As will become clear, this conflict—which ended with Israel's occupation of significant Arab lands including the Gaza Strip and the West Bank—had little impact on daily interactions more fundamentally shaped by the colonial North African past and the French present than the Middle East. Nevertheless, the unprecedented mobilization of Jewish organizational life around Israel and efforts to create parallel affinities in the Muslim North African population around Palestine continued to shape political discourse in binary terms. The result was that while conflict between France's large Muslim and Jewish populations was rare, the story of two polarized ethno-religious political units hardened as new political actors, particularly university students, began to use French campuses as spaces in which to engage in discussions of foreign policy.

It is a truism of modern Jewish history that 1967 transformed Jewish identity throughout the Western world. France was no exception as Jews became politically visible in unprecedented ways, raising enormous sums, participating in vocal demonstrations, and even volunteering for Israeli military service. Our grasp of the "Zionization of French Jewry" is not matched, however, by an equally clear picture of Muslim political affiliations in France during the Middle East conflict.[1] This chapter will address this gap by tracing early efforts of FLN representatives, the Arab league, and Muslim student activists to encourage North African Muslim immigrant identification with the Palestinians. Such efforts, while less successful than Jewish efforts to assert the same with regard to Israel, increasingly made disagreements over outcomes in the Middle East relevant to minority politics in France.

In 1967, however, these disagreements rarely influenced life on the ground in French cities. In other words, although French Jewish political rhetoric continued to demonize Israel's Arab enemies, and those seeking to mobilize Muslim immigrants around the Palestinian cause harshly criticized Israel, such criticisms were generally directed at the Middle East rather than at each other. Indeed, France experienced little conflict during that summer's brief war, and in the rare examples in which discord did break out, once again mostly in

Marseille, the anger seemed, as in 1948, to reflect frustration at evident inequities in city politics since decolonization–this time expressed in the municipality's dramatically vocal pro-Zionist stance and ongoing willingness to favor one minority over another.

If, however, such tensions point to the way the colonial past continued to shape ethno-religious relations in contemporary France, clashes on French campuses indicate the way political struggles over the Middle East began to pit Jewish and Muslim activists against one another in new ways. Foreshadowing the significance of campus politics in shaping Muslim-Jewish encounters in the decade to come, summer 1967 saw new political actors come of age who began creating political coalitions around Israel and Palestine. These new alliances would have far-reaching consequences in 1968 and beyond.

The Impact of 1967 on Jewish Political Mobilization

With the Arab-Israeli war in 1967, Jewish commitment to Israel burst onto the public stage, as French Jews, traditionally reluctant to link their heritage with a visible ethnic politics, began "display[ing] a political activism which at times took prominent leaders of the Parisian community by surprise."[2] This transformation emerged for three key reasons. First was the shift in French policy away from its unambiguously pro-Israeli stance of the early 1960s.[3] Due to France's departure from North Africa and its evolving interests in the Middle East, by 1967 de Gaulle was cultivating alliances in the Arab world. These efforts coupled with a belief that Israeli actions in the weeks preceding the conflict were unnecessarily aggressive led de Gaulle to declare French neutrality and to impose an arms embargo on Israel.

Frightening French Jewish leaders who saw de Gaulle's move as a national repudiation of the Jewish state, many also accused the French media, traditionally supportive of Israel, of adopting a more critical tone and the French left of fostering anti-Israeli sentiment.[4] Given that national polls in June showed 56 percent of the French public supporting Israel as opposed to 2 percent supporting the Arab states, such fears were overstated. Indeed, by September, pro-Israel sentiment had surged to 68 percent versus 6 percent for their opponents.[5] Moreover, support for and criticisms of Israel during the 1967 war cannot be divided neatly into left and right.[6] Jewish organizations worked assiduously to represent all political affiliations at pro-Israel rallies to demonstrate cross-party support.[7] Nevertheless, both the French Communist and Socialist parties, which had both enthusiastically supported Israel following 1948, readjusted these positions somewhat after the 1967 war.[8] And even earlier, numerous Jewish leaders expressed fears that the "French left"—influenced by Soviet pressures and anticolonialist struggles—was hostile to Israel and Jews.[9] Thus despite the overwhelming pro-Israel sentiment expressed at all levels of society, French Jewish representatives feared a growing ambivalence in governing circles.[10] The impact of this perception should not be underestimated when thinking about the significance of 1967 on communal galvanization.[11] Indeed, the "Zionization" of French Jewry was less a newfound expression of pro-Israeli sentiment, which was already well entrenched by the mid-1950s, than a new willingness to pursue an ethnically infused Jewish politics even when it conflicted with France's international agenda.[12]

A second factor fueling this vocal politicization was the influx of North African Jews to France. These new arrivals were less self-conscious about expressing an ethnic politics than their French co-religionists. Having fought in their native lands to preserve their rights as newly independent Muslim states threw off French rule, they arrived in the metropole more politically militant than the local French Jewish communities and more viscerally connected to Israel.[13] Moreover, anti-Jewish hostility in Tunisia and Morocco in summer 1967 led several thousand more Jews to seek refuge in France despite government efforts in both countries to protect and reassure their Jewish minorities. Arriving with fresh stories of Muslim aggression, the newcomers provoked strong responses from those who had departed in previous waves, fueling agitation in France.[14] As the president of the CRIF described their impact on communal life: "North African Jews made us less inhibited. They pushed us to shout, to cry, to sing, to pour into the streets. They have no inferiority complex [aucun complexe]. And France watched this extroverted Judaism with curiosity."[15]

Thirdly, as Joan Wolf has demonstrated, French Jews perceived the 1967 war as an immediate threat to Jewish survival, reading events through the prism of World War II. As the Egyptian president Gamal Abdel Nasser repeatedly called for the annihilation of Israel, French Jews became consumed with "the threat to survival—of Israel, the Jewish people, and Judaism." Although the majority of France's Jewish population was North African and therefore distanced from the Holocaust's most extreme brutality, the postwar conflation of Muslim antisemitism with previous violence against Jews made such distinctions less meaningful. Communal discourse was thus saturated with Holocaust imagery, as the Jewish community, and particularly those who had come of age after World War II, sought to come to terms with their past.[16] Blurring the boundaries between Europe during World War II and Israel in 1967, for example, the newly formed Comité democrate socialiste pour le droit d'Israël warned, "The brothers and sons of the martyrs of the arrests in Paris, the Warsaw Ghetto, and the camps of Auschwitz and Treblinka are once again threatened by hate and death."[17] Or as Claude Lanzman proclaimed at a rally on 31 May, "If Israel was destroyed, it would be more serious than the Nazi Holocaust. For Israel is my freedom."[18] One man proposed that all Jews don a yellow star—the symbol of their oppression under the Nazis—as a sign of solidarity with the Jewish state.[19] For these Jews, Israel's war was their own.

The combination of the new political context, enlarged numbers, and fears of Israel's destruction, provided French Jews with new confidence to speak publicly as Jews.[20] By late May, mounting tensions between Israel and Egypt brought thousands of people—both Jewish and not—to meetings dedicated to alerting public opinion to the "grave situation facing Israel's frontier."[21] Thirty thousand Parisians, for example, demonstrated in front of the Israeli embassy on 31 May while another twenty thousand attended a rally at the Cirque d'Hiver the same day.[22] Similar demonstrations took place in many major provincial cities, including in Marseille, Lyon, and Toulouse.[23] All synagogues affiliated with the centralized consistorial system conducted prayers for Israel on 26 and 27 May.[24]

Jewish organizations also leaped into action in unprecedented ways, establishing, for instance, a Comité national de coordination on 26 May under the presidency of Guy de Rothschild (president of the two largest French Jewish philanthropic bodies) to express their "total solidarity" with Israel and to convey their "determination to participate with all the means at their disposal in Israel's struggle for existence."[25] This new body coordinated all aid for Israel, including rallying support among religious leaders, professors, and journalists; organizing demonstrations; intervening with elected officials at all levels of government; raising and centralizing funds; surveying press coverage; gathering medical supplies; and organizing volunteers for civil service in Israel.[26] Concern that too many demonstrations and financial appeals would wear out goodwill, the Comité de coordination also sought to prevent other organizations from taking their own initiatives, intervening, for example, in efforts to send packages to Israel outside their own control.[27] Such efforts, if somewhat heavy-handed, led to unprecedented coordination.[28]

By 4 June, when 1,200 delegates came together representing sixty Jewish communities and all French Jewish organizations, local committees had been established in five Parisian neighborhoods and in 39 towns and cities (a number that eventually grew to 130).[29] Speeches focused heavily on Israeli and French Jewish solidarity. Chief Rabbi Jacob Kaplan, for example, reminded attendees that, "Israel's crisis is our test,"[30] while André Neher declared, "Even yesterday, I confess, I regret, only a fraction of my being struggled for Israel. Today my entire being is with Israel. . . ." For Théo Klein, a lawyer and CRIF delegate, "French Jews had maintained a vague friendship for Israel. Brutally, their Jewish identity now leaps into their faces. They have learned that *their* freedom is at risk [*en cause*] in Akaba." Put even more starkly by Jacques Dreyfus, representative of Lyon's Comité de coordination: "Those who do not help Israel do not have the right to call themselves Jews."[31]

Such proclamations defined French Jews and Israelis as one—linked by religion and culture but also by *politics*. Critiquing their birth nation in unprecedented ways, Jewish leaders spoke against France's policies in the Middle East. Chief Rabbi Kaplan, for example, who had remained virtually silent throughout the Algerian crisis, publicly criticized the arms embargo.[32] Guy de Rothschild described French policies as "making us uncomfortable in our skin,"[33] while André Neher urged his co-religionists to challenge their government: "[T]his is the time to remember that in certain cases the sacred obligation of all citizens in a free country is to disagree with their nation's policies and to protest and to act based on that disagreement."[34] While mainstream French Jewish institutions had long worked to influence government policies behind the scenes, Jewish leaders had also parroted the republican ideal that Jews had no political identity qua Jews. The 1967 war challenged such perspectives. As Claude Kelman, vice president of the Comité de coordination, argued "[T]he steps that we are taking are the product of the adoption of a clear-cut position with no ambiguity or prevarication; we are acting as *Jews*, our reactions are Jewish reactions."[35]

This shift was more than symbolic. Indeed, an "irresistible need, an urge . . . to do something" penetrated Jewish communities.[36] As Adam Loss, the director of the Fonds social juif unifié described the sentiment: "I have never experienced anything as wrenching. Old women rushed to my office and begged me to take their last remaining jewels to send to Israel. All French Jews were desperate."[37] Fund-raising for Israel was particularly successful in this environment. Tapping into mounting fears for Israel's security, philanthropic outreach built on the widely circulating themes of Israel/Diaspora unity. According to one appeal, it was an obligation to aid a "state that struggles heroically for its own freedom that is also our own."[38] Or as another insisted, "the first thing that you can do and that you must do for yourself is to contribute financially to this sacred and vital struggle."[39] Such appeals stressed the value of symbolic sacrifice, urging potential donors to give up a month's salary, sell a piece of property, or transform vacation time into labor for Israel.[40] Pressure to donate was so intense that those who refused could face social ostracism or even more severe repercussions.[41]

Such efforts were enormously successful. By uniting all fund-raising under the Comité de coordination, halting all other philanthropic projects, and framing donations as a tax on those in the Diaspora "so that Israel can live," contributions reached fifteen million francs within one week of the campaign's launch.[42] Even when the war had ended, solicitations continued;[43] by July, more than fifty million francs had been raised from sixty thousand donations, a 50 percent increase in the numbers of individual contributors to pro-Israel causes and a sum greater than French Jews had ever raised for Israel.[44] According to one community official in Marseille, "The phenomenon of an awakening of consciousness has even moved peripheral Jewish populations, those whose numbers, means, and ways of expressing (or not) their Jewishness is unknown to us."[45]

Particularly affected by the pro-Israel campaign were Jewish youth born after World War II, who, coming of age in the late 1960s, found in Israel's struggle an answer to the Holocaust's legacy and a means of exploring their Jewish identities. In the preceding year, a survey of Jewish university students in Paris indicated that 90 percent considered their ethno-religious identity meaning-ful.[46] With the 1967 conflict, this identification became newly visible. As *L'Arche* declared triumphantly in a June headline, "Our Youth Rediscovers Its Soul."[47] Journalist Anne Sinclair documented the moment in the following terms: "I was nineteen and I affirmed my Jewishness at that precise moment because Israel's solitude seemed unbearable to me."[48] Similarly, Françoise Tenenbaum, seventeen years old in 1967, reported sneaking radios into school to follow war news: "It was my dream to go to Israel even though I didn't speak Hebrew."[49] As another young French Jewish woman remembers: "The war in 1967 was when I started to want to meet other Jews. I didn't know much about Israel, but the Six Day War had a very important impact on my life. My mother supported Israel, and in Paris I had friends who didn't talk to me at the time because I was Jewish. I was shocked. I realized then that I needed to start meeting more Jewish people."[50]

Drawing on such sentiments, the Comité de coordination established sections for university students and youth that encouraged them to "be among the thousands of young Jewish boys and girls who are going to help Israel during its difficult hours."[51] Likewise, pro-Israel youth movements challenged young Jews to prove their new loyalties with migration: As one opined: "After the public demonstrations and the slogans must come action."[52] Such appeals resonated to such a degree that the Israeli government created a civil service program to place volunteers in the hospitals, factories, and administrative positions previously occupied by soldiers, a program that brought 675 young French Jewish volunteers to Israel by 16 June.[53] While the end of the brief war brought this migration stream to a halt, many young Jews still left for Israel.[54] Thirty to forty departures a month in the early 1960s thus grew to 500 by 1969,[55] and between 1965 and 1971, 6,852 Jews made a similar move, substantially increasing the post–World War II numbers.[56] While many of the migrants were of North African origin, French Jewish spokesmen understood 1967 to be a turning point.[57] As Simon Sibony, a rabbi from Dijon, reflected: "In the past the community was indifferent to Israel. That changed after the Six Day war. It was an important moment for all the communities in France."[58] Government analysts concurred, asserting that the 1967 war had established a "new phenomenon: almost all French Jews are concerned by Israel's fate. Sensitivity toward Israel has become one of the components of French Judaism."[59]

The depth of this transformation is difficult to gauge. Many clearly believed that "French Judaism, which we previously deplored for its passivity, has come out of its lethargy."[60] In the words of one communal leader in Marseille, the Jewish population had "suddenly discovered unity—a dignity and a depth that only yesterday we were wondering how long it would take to achieve (if in-deed we ever could)."[61] Certainly many were elated with Israel's victory, and the Comité de coordination sought to transform the momentum into a broad pro-Israel movement.[62] As another Jewish organization declared, "The Eternal miraculously saved us, and now that we have been freed from the terrible threat are we going to take up our daily routines as if nothing happened?"[63] The FSJF likewise insisted that many of its members, "traumatized by June events . . . have realized their obligations to Israel and the Jewish community as a whole."[64]

Such assessments overstated the unity around Israel in June 1967. A vocal minority—particularly those affiliated with the Communist party—criticized Israel as the aggressor and for its occupation of newly conquered territories. Holding demonstrations or writing in the leftist press, they made clear that their Jewishness was irrelevant when assessing the crimes of an imperialist state.[65] Eastern European Jewish immigrant communities, long divided over Communism, were particularly polarized in summer 1967, as is clear from a perusal of the Parisian Yiddish dailies.[66] The Communist Naye Presse, mirroring Soviet pronouncements, adopted a critical stance toward Israel and accused its Zionist and Bundist rivals of working with neo-Nazis to create a second Auschwitz. For their part, the newspapers of the non-Communist Jewish left demanded that Jewish organizations remove all Communists from their rosters.[67] Other Jewish leftists reacted with shock to the vocal nationalism from their co-religionists. Daniel Cohn-Bendit, the soon-to-be-infamous student radical who led the May 1968 uprisings, described his shock that summer: "It was awful, all these nationalist and chauvinistic Jews. This was the first time that I experienced Jewish racism: exactly the same comments that the Germans make about the Turks today or the French about the North Africans. When I tried to explain that national unity in Israel would resolve nothing, I almost got beaten up. Nobody could open a discussion. My Jewish identity was broken."[68] Some of these Jewish leftists—many of whom had been actively engaged in the struggle to free Algeria—reached out to Muslim activists on the left. Representatives from the Jewish Communist group, MRAP, thus used the June crisis as an opportunity to connect with Arab workers and to assert their commitment to fighting anti-Arab racism.[69] Several Jewish leftists, notably Tony and Benny Lévy, founded the Comité des étudiants juifs antisionistes, which later established contact with Yasser Arafat.[70] Others published a petition in Le Monde on 15 June, proclaiming themselves "entirely in solidarity with the Arab people in their just struggle" and criticizing Israel for its "war of aggression and conquest."[71] These alliances proved essential in the emergence over the next few years of a pro-Palestinian movement in France.

For many Jews, however, the 1967 war had the opposite impact, pushing them away from those on the left with whom they shared years of political struggle. A number of prominent Jewish intellectuals thus made clear that they resented accusations of Israeli aggression and imperialism, while others— uncomfortable with Israeli policies toward Palestinians—sought to differentiate their unconditional support for the state of Israel from its policies.[72] Still others left the Communist party in anger over its criticisms of Israel.[73] Inside the CRIF, some argued that Communist member organizations should sign a statement critiquing the Soviet anti-Israel campaign and acknowledging Arab responsibility for hostilities.[74]

Such divisions over the war meant that pro-Israel energy necessarily dissipated when hostilities ended, leading some analysts to question the long-term impact on French Jewish life.[75] In 1968, for example, sociologist Sylvie Korcaz argued that commitment to Israel varied considerably and that charitable donations and willingness to move to the Jewish state had already decreased significantly.[76] Jewish leaders often agreed, as was clear at a meeting in Marseille that April in which participants questioned the depth of the war's transformation of French Jews.[77] Others disagreed, however, seeing in 1967 the moment that "caused many Jews living in France to find their way back to Judaism."[78] Whatever the extent of the long term transformation, 1967 was clearly a moment when Jews of different origins, political orientation, and level of religious practice came together to support a single issue, and when passive support for the Jewish state was transformed into a visible, combative stance on its behalf.

1967 among Muslim Migrants to France

At the very moment when French Jews found their political voice, Muslims were facing an increasingly hostile environment that made political mobilization far riskier. If the former felt betrayed by the government's neutrality and the arms embargo on Israel, they were nevertheless bolstered by the widespread public perception that Israel was the victim of unprovoked Arab aggression. For Muslims, in contrast, de Gaulle's policies could do little to assuage an increasingly precarious social context in which anti-Arab racism grew and in which media images portrayed Arabs as violent religious fanatics who had provoked the conflict.[79] According to historian Yvan Gastaut, the 1967 war played an important role in liberalizing racist discourse largely silenced since World War II, by refocusing it away from Jews and onto Arabs.[80] In particular, those still angry over French decolonization saw a renewed "Arab threat" in the making and rallied around Israel. Readers of the newspaper *Minute* or of *Aspects de la France*, for example read, "Arabs love war," or "with Arabs only one policy is possible that of the rod and kicks in the ass because [Arabs] only understand and respect force."[81] Such rhetoric was accompanied by physical attacks against several Muslim North Africans in Nice on 7 June and the harassment of others in Paris and the Midi.

Moreover, as we have seen, French Jews took advantage of a highly developed institutional structure put in place after World War II to create a centralized and efficient fund-raising and political apparatus. This infrastructure provided space for unprecedented political mobilization and collective ethnic expression. For incoming North African Muslims, the majority of France's Muslim population in 1967, few similar structures existed. While the Arab League, which had established an office in Paris in 1965, and the Union générale des étudiants palestiniens (UGEP), an outgrowth of the Palestinian Liberation Organization (PLO) founded the previous year, sought to bring attention to the Palestinian issue, Muslim activism around the issue remained relatively muted throughout May and June 1967 particularly when compared to the pro-Israel activities among French Jews.[82]

One key exception was the Amicale des Algériens en France, a social welfare organization for Algerian Muslim immigrants that worked tirelessly to inspire pro-Palestinian sentiment among its constituents.[83] If its failures underscore the divergent paths of Muslim and Jewish communal politics in 1960s France, the effort nevertheless initiated the use of the Palestinian issue as a tool for forging political cohesiveness among France's North African laboring population, a strategy that gathered significant steam over the next decade.

Created in November 1962, the Amicale took shape after the FLN's political bureau closed its local chapters and "comités de soutien," transforming them into a social welfare organization for Algerian Muslim nationals in France.[84] Financed by the FLN and charged with enforcing its policies in Europe, by 1967, the organization, now called the Amicale des Algériens en Europe (ADAE),[85] aspired to educate and unite Algerian Muslims abroad.[86] Boasting youth groups, sporting clubs, publications, religious institutions, and clubs throughout Europe, the ADAE claimed to have one-fifth of the Algerian Muslim migrant population in its ranks (French authorities called the number highly inflated; in their estimation, only 4,000 out of the approximately 500,000 Algerian Muslims in France had joined).[87]

French laws on foreign associations limited the ADAE's activities to the educational and cultural realm. Moreover, because officials feared the Amicale would spread FLN propaganda, the Ministries of Interior and Foreign Affairs denied it formal recognition, only "tolerating" its existence unofficially. Such a status compelled the Amicale to refrain from all political activism. Most ADAE campaigns thus focused on issues such as literacy, housing aid for large families, defense of Algerian Muslims threatened with expulsion, hospital visitations, religious and Arabic instruction, and efforts to solidify Franco-Algerian relations.[88]

With the mounting crisis of summer 1967, however, the ADAE changed course, manifesting ardent support for Arab nationalist movements and becoming a vocal supporter of the Palestinian cause. Adopting similar rhetorical strategies as Zionist activists who blurred distinctions between French Jews and Israeli citizens, the ADAE asserted direct links between French Algerian Muslims and the wider Arab world:

> Events in the Middle East have bereaved the entire Arab nation. From the Atlantic to the Persian Gulf, Arabs feel their flesh wounded. . . . The distance that separates us from the Orient does not alleviate the feelings of indignation that each one of us suffers in light of these sly maneuvers. Our

determination will tolerate no equivocation and no momentary setback will weaken it. *Each Algerian must feel Palestinian* and provide concrete support to the Arab cause.[89]

This solidarity, the ADAE insisted, should lead Algerian Muslim migrants to demonstrate, raise relief funds, mobilize military recruits, and boycott Israeli products.[90] The ADAE itself worked to promote such solidarity by circulating pamphlets and holding meetings to raise awareness of the ongoing struggle.[91] Moreover, the organization's journal, *L'Algérien en Europe*, devoted its June issues to the Middle East conflict. The cover of the 15 June edition, for example, pictured a determined soldier, masses of troops, and a tank captioned: "The National People's Army against Imperialist Aggression." Articles addressed Algerian support for the Palestinians, the history of "Zionist aggression," and support for Arab nationalism.[92] Future editions were concerned with similar matters.[93] Indeed, a survey of *L'Algérien en Europe* over several years makes clear that the Palestinian issue had become one of the ADAE's central concerns.

Moreover, like Zionist activists, ADAE officials, working with the Algerian consulate, encouraged their constituents to volunteer for military duty in Palestine. In Marseille, for example, 150 recruits signed up on 5 June due to Amicale urging.[94] Similar efforts took place in Paris, while the Prefect of Essone reported the recruitment of approximately thirty Algerian Muslims from that region.[95]

Why did the ADAE focus so heavily on the Palestinian issue? Most simply, as a representative of the Algerian political establishment, the ADAE reflected national priorities.[96] Algerian officials were early supporters of the Palestinian liberation movement. Yasser Arafat's older brother headed the Arab Maghreb Bureau at the Arab Higher Committee office in Cairo through which he met most of the FLN's leading members. Fatah delegates attended the Algerian independence ceremony in 1962, during which they gained permission to establish a Palestine Office in Algiers. Soon after, 400 Palestinian teachers were recruited for the expanding Algerian education system (a number that rapidly grew to 1000), and 150 Palestinians enrolled in Algerian universities. In summer 1964, the Algerian army also trained 100–200 Palestinians in guerrilla warfare, and President Ben Bella publicly railed against Palestinian suffering.[97] Likewise, in May the Union générale des travailleurs algériens (UGTA) announced a day of solidarity with Palestinians.[98] The coup in September 1965 that brought Houari Boumediene to power did little to minimize this support. In 1966 the Algerian military academy ran an advanced course for twenty Fatah trainees, and in March 1967, the FLN organ, *El Moudjahid*, began a ten-day special series that showcased the PLO and the Palestinian cause.[99] In June 1967, the Algerian president pledged to aid in the war against "Israel and imperialism."[100] Huge pro-Palestinian demonstrations were coupled with fund-raising efforts, blood banks, and military recruitments.[101] By 1968 Algeria had emerged as the second largest supplier of arms to Fatah, over China.

Such policies were rooted in Algeria's recent war against French domination and the country's anti-imperial philosophy. When the ADAE argued that "the enemy is still on Arab land," it recalled this long history of revolutionary struggle. Echoing the Algerian government's wider anti-colonial agenda, the ADAE insisted that "Israel is only the lowly executor; the secular arm is imperialism. Without the aid, protection and encouragement of imperialist and colonialist authorities, the Zionists would never have dared attack the Arab world."[102] Articles in *L'Algérien en Europe* similarly proclaimed, "Israel is not a state but an imperialist base planted in the heart of the Arab world."[103] The anti-imperialism that was deeply entrenched in FLN culture provided an obvious justification for supporting Palestinian self-rule; for the ADAE, linking anti-Zionism with the Algerian independence struggle was self-evident.[104]

Yet if the ADAE's pro-Palestinian stance reflected the Algerian government's priorities, such appeals also served a broader agenda—uniting Algerian Muslim nationals in France. In numerous calls to support Arab unity and protest racism, the ADAE presented itself as *the* voice of Algerian Muslims in France. *Algérien en Europe* was replete with calls not only to fight imperialism and Zionism but also to foster Arab unity in the face of Western hostility.[105] The adoption of the Palestinian cause was central to this endeavor. In summer 1967, as part of calls to support the Palestinians, for example, Algerian Muslim migrants were instructed to refrain from listening to Western radio programs and reading Western newspapers, considered arms of Zionist propaganda. Rather Radio Alger and particularly "our own news organ *L'Algérien en Europe*" should be their news source. As such directives suggest, the ADAE's work for Palestinians, while ideologically rooted, also reflected a larger effort to influence Muslim migrants' political allegiances. As its own writings made explicit: "For the Algerian émigré to mobilize at this juncture [summer 1967], means above all, to join the activities of the Amicale and to pay subscription fees regularly. Those who have not yet done so are obliged to do so; it is their duty to join our organization under fear of betraying the unity that must cement our struggle."[106] Here support for Palestine and membership in the ADAE were directly linked; to remain aloof, a form of betrayal.

Not surprisingly, French officials, traditionally averse to any immigrant activism, and particularly distrustful of the ADAE due to its ongoing links to the FLN, warned it and the Algerian embassy to cease all political activities.[107] By December, ADAE officials had agreed to limit their efforts to social and cultural work once again, and pro-Palestinian efforts diminished.[108] Governmental concern may, however, have been misplaced, since most evidence suggests that the pro-Palestinian campaign launched in summer 1967 enjoyed limited success among France's North African Muslim population. While *L'Algérien en Europe* asserted an overwhelming response to the 15 June 1967 edition with dozens of respondents asking how they could help the Palestinian cause, such responses were atypical.[109] The French Ministry of Interior thus reported in July that the

ADAE's fund-raising efforts only raised about 120,000 francs, a small sum when compared to the 5,000,000 French Jews raised during the same period. While police informants undoubtedly had an incomplete picture of the migrant community's financial contributions and while the vastly inferior capabilities of the Algerian Muslim working population cannot be easily compared to the middle-class and wealthier French Jewish population, it is still clear that many Algerian Muslim migrants did not find appeals for Palestine attractive enough to turn over hard-earned wages. Indeed, support for Palestine stands in stark contrast to the large sums such migrant communities contributed to Algerian independence efforts earlier in the decade.[110] While many of these "donations" had been made under pressure, similar processes were clearly at work in 1967. Furthermore, military recruitment efforts remained paltry. The thirty volunteers from Essone, for example, did not comply after receiving mobilization orders.[111] In fact, if anything, ADAE efforts to recruit supporters seem to have fostered resentment, as some Algerian Muslim merchants complained of feeling pressured to aid the war effort despite their own disinclination.[112]

As such evidence suggests, the ADAE's decision to use the Palestinian issue as a means of creating political solidarity among Algerian Muslim migrants remained limited. The ADAE never managed to attract most Algerian Muslims to its ranks precisely because the organization was perceived as too heavy-handed and because most of the new immigrants were, in fact, disinclined to take part in activist politics regardless of the cause.[113] As one police report noted: "Such efforts have failed to mobilize the Algerian masses in France to aid and support the Palestinian resistance. . . . [T]he Algerians, for the most part, are not concerned with the Palestinian matter."[114] While such assessments may overlook the degree to which the Palestinian issue surfaced around café tables or markets in Muslim neighborhoods, they accurately reflect the differing levels of political mobilization of French Muslim and Jewish populations during the 1967 war.

The Impact of 1967 on Muslim-Jewish Relations in France

Whatever the degree of political mobilization among Jews and Muslims, the 1967 war had few immediate repercussions for interethnic relations on the ground. Indeed, insofar as pro-Palestinian efforts took hold among Muslims, they generally focused on the conflict abroad without much consideration of Jewish efforts in France to influence public opinion. To the contrary, at the end of June, the *Algérien en Europe* underscored the problems with conflating an ethnic/racial category, Jews, with a political category, Israel.[115] Similarly, French Jewish activists directed their efforts overwhelmingly toward the Middle East and French international policy, rarely expressing interest in or even awareness of their Muslim neighbors. And insofar as they did speak of the surrounding Muslim population it was often to divide events in the Middle East from a wider condemnation of the Arab people. For example, Gerard Bismuth, representing Marseille's Comité de coordination de la jeunesse juive, underscored that his organization's quarrel was with Arab governments, "and not the Arab people, who without doubt desire peace like the Israelis."[116] Or, as a flyer from the mixed Muslim-Jewish neighborhood of Sarcelles reminds us, after calling on Jewish residents to attend a demonstration on 7 June 1967 to "stop genocide," their quarrel had no impact on the "friendship" and "esteem" they felt for "the Arab people." While condemning Israel's enemies for instigating a second Holocaust, meeting organizers also called for a rapid, peaceful, and constructive solution to the problem of Arab refugees "instead of nursing a hateful and negative attitude against them."[117]

It would nevertheless be a mistake to dismiss the impact of the 1967 war in negatively shaping interethnic relations. As this section will argue, if intercommunal relations in France remained generally calm, tensions mounted in two specific arenas. First, while Paris and other large cities experienced no unrest, Marseille showed signs of strain. These tensions, many believed, were the result of the city's ethnic mix, its proximity to the conflict, and its port, which brought the Middle Eastern conflict home. As *Le Monde* later reported, "Eighty-thousand Jews (the third largest population in Europe after London and Paris), thirty thousand Arab workers, longstanding links with the Middle East and Mediterranean countries, French bombs and tanks leaving from its port for Tripoli and Djedda: Marseille cannot help but feel more strongly than most the Israeli-Arab conflict."[118] However accurate, this analysis overlooked the way the Middle Eastern conflict brought already simmering postcolonial tensions to the fore as Mayor Defferre used Israel's war to link Jews evermore tightly with the municipality, highlighting their integration and Muslim marginality. Second, conflict between student activists began to increase as highly politicized sectors of the student body seized the Middle East crisis as a way to promote group belonging and cement loyalties. While still rare in 1967, these encounters laid the groundwork for greater interethnic strife the next year, after student radicals broadened the boundaries of French political discourse even further.

On 25 May 1967, Jewish political integration reached new heights in Marseille when Mayor Defferre and other local political figures joined Jewish leaders in establishing the Comité unifié de soutien à Israël. A silent demonstration on 31 May brought out 4,500 supporters (Jewish and non-Jewish) to "protest the Arab threat against Israel" and to demand French support.[119] Two days later, Defferre accepted the presidency of the Comité, stating his allegiances with no equivocation: "We at the Federation have chosen our camp. We are with Israel."[120] Subsequently, he campaigned actively in Paris and Marseille to raise funds for Israel's defense,[121] and under his leadership, the city sent large quantities of blood and medical supplies to Jewish soldiers.[122] Nor was Defferre Marseille's only public official backing Israel. As elsewhere in France, support came from a diverse range of political, intellectual, and cultural figures, many of whom participated in the demonstration on 31 May.[123] Both daily papers, *Le Provençal* (Defferre's socialist paper), and *Le Méridional–La France* (the center-right paper), insisted in similar terms on this wide-ranging support for the Jewish state.[124] As one headline read, "A Magnificent Display of Solidarity for Israel Animates Marseille's Population."[125] Only the Communist paper, *La Marseillaise*, refrained from discussing the pro-Israel rally on 25 May, instead publishing an editorial by René Andrieu criticizing Israel's Arab policies.[126] In response, numerous local Jews cut their affiliation with the Communist party.[127]

With their city and its leadership strongly behind them, then, Marseille's Jewish community felt less alienated by de Gaulle's declaration of French neutrality than their co-religionists elsewhere, particularly since Defferre's socialist and center-left coalition used its ardent support of Israel as a way to distance themselves from their Gaullist rivals.[128] As Defferre remarked, "if a broad public movement occurs in the country in the same frank way that I am arguing, the government will be compelled to reconsider its position as has been the case in other circumstances."[129] For local Jews, Defferre's stance reinforced the lines between them and their city. According to Charles Haddad, president of the local Zionist federation, "If the starting point for the government's policy reversal comes from Marseille, we would have another reason to be proud of the city that has adopted us."[130] And the Comité de soutien sought to do just that. Meeting on 3 June at the Hôtel de Ville, it adopted a highly critical motion against French neutrality, drawing local political lines around the Middle Eastern issue. While signatories included a handful of centrist politicians who opposed de Gaulle, the overwhelming majority were members of Defferre's Fédération de la gauche démocrate et socialiste (FGDS).[131]

Local Gaullists responded by arguing that the Comité soutien français Israël had become an offshoot of Defferre's party and was inciting war to attract Jewish voters.[132] Even a local Jewish organizer noted that while Defferre's adoption of such a clear pro-Israel position had been helpful, it "had the corollary of tying the Comité de solidarité français à Israel to [Defferre's] parliamentary agenda, making it a sort of Socialist subsection."[133] This link helped reinforce the alliance between Marseille and its Jewish population. On 7 June, for example, a gathering of young FGDS adherents met at the Cinéma Chavé under the aegis of the Comité de soutien pour Israel.[134] While attendees were primarily young Jews, the support of local political figures was evident.[135] Also vocally supporting Israel was the Section Marseille Provence du mouvement démocratique féminin, the president of which was also on the local FGDS executive committee. When the Centre de liaison et d'information, a club affiliated with the FGDS, declared its support for Israel, it did so on the basis of the "bonds of friendship that tie us to Marseille's Jewish community."[136] On 13 June, the Comité de soutien sponsored yet another pro-Israel demonstration at which more than two thousand attendees wildly applauded Defferre and during which a delegate from Haifa thanked Marseille's mayor for his tireless support.[137]

Over several weeks, such widespread and enthusiastic support for Israel began making the city's Muslim residents uncomfortable. In May and early June, neither tensions in the Middle East nor in the city's first pro-Israel demonstrations moved the North African Muslim population to action.[138] Recruitment efforts in the city's North African quarters, for example, largely failed. While rumors that the Algerian consulate was registering volunteers that brought in thirty men, the ADAE did not participate, and most North African migrants manifested little interest.[139] Once war broke out, however, the growing number of pro-Israel demonstrations began to "worry the Algerians a bit." In response, ADAE recruitment activities increased, and on 5 June, approximately 150 volunteered, while several others returned to Algeria. According to police, Muslims were "sensitized to Jewish reactions, particularly in Marseille where the demonstrations of solidarity for Israel preoccupy the Algerian masses. They seem to fear that the young element of the Jewish community might provoke incidents which, according to their gravity, could lead to a clash between Arabs and Jews."[140]

Such fears were undoubtedly fueled by Zionist propaganda that collapsed all Muslims into singular political categories. Betar, for example, printed tracts that accused "all Arab countries of one goal—exterminating the Jews in good and due form. . . . No Hitler is not dead, because he lives through these wretched creatures that he made."[141] While not all Jewish pronouncements were as extreme, others also blurred the boundaries between North African and Palestinian Arabs. In a strongly worded proclamation supporting Israel, for example, the Association des Juifs originaires d'Algérie (AJOA), founded in 1963 under the guidance of Jacques Lazarus to provide welfare and cultural services to incoming Jews, made striking parallels between the fate of Palestinians and Jews in Algeria.[142] Reminding readers that its membership was "almost entirely . . . Jewish refugees from an Arab country," it stressed their forced departure from a land where "they had lived for centuries," having to abandon property "of considerable value of which they were completely pillaged." While Algerian Jews had responded "neither with hate nor resentment toward Arabs," Palestinian refugees, in contrast, had "spent twenty years in idleness and vengeful excitement serving as an excuse for an imperialist and fundamentally racist expansionism leading to a new attempt at genocide."[143] Here then, a mere five years after Lazarus had stressed the "Frenchness" of Algerian Jewish departures, the "Jewish story" had emerged in full. Jews had fled Algeria not as French repatriates but as Jews fleeing Arab persecution—part of an even exchange for Palestinian refugees leaving Israel.

The political posturing of Marseille's Jews worried Muslim residents to such a degree that in certain bidonvilles, the latter organized surveillance teams to protect themselves against malevolent attacks they feared would be directed against them by their Jewish neighbors. The destruction of two small dwellings [*cabanons*] in Calade was thus attributed to Jews. Aggression, however, went in both directions. A Jewish welfare worker thus opted to leave her post after repeated harassment by Algerian Muslim militants, and Consistoire officials went so far as to request police protection for the synagogue on rue Breteuil. By month's end, Marseille's Muslim residents were purportedly suffering from a "deplorable" state of mind, "traumatized by the failures suffered by their brothers in the Middle East" and constantly listening to anti-Western diatribes on Radio-Alger; they "see enemies everywhere and are "easily provoked; their nationalism has been exacerbated."[144]

By the end of June, then, postcolonial tensions, simmering in the city since the early 1960s, had been reignited thanks to the municipality's investment in the Middle East conflict and seeming embrace of its Jewish minority, a process that continued long after the war had ended. If anything, Defferre's pro-Israel advocacy and support for Marseille's Jewish community increased in subsequent years.[145] Publicly condemning antisemitism in *Le Provençal*, he continued to use support for Jews as a way to differentiate himself from the Gaullist regime. Following de Gaulle's much criticized press conference in November 1967, for example, in which he labeled Jews an "elite people, sure of themselves and domineering," Defferre accused the French president of legitimizing discriminatory campaigns: "and we remember how those ended under Hitler's regime and during the second world war: in the death camps." While stopping short of accusing de Gaulle himself of antisemitism, Defferre used his own support for Jews and against antisemitism as a cudgel with which to beat the president; the hero of the Liberation had opened the door to the return of Nazi horrors.[146] For Marseille's Jews, who like their co-religionists throughout the country expressed profound dismay that such a long revered figure could abandon them, Defferre's public support was deeply reassuring.[147]

Defferre's support for Israel also remained steadfast. In spring 1968, for example, newspaper headlines celebrated Marseille as "Israel's door to Europe" after Defferre sought to increase Israeli exports to Marseille.[148] More interestingly, that February the Fédération sud de français rapatrié (FSFR) and the Comité de soutien à Israel organized a 1,000-person-strong protest of France's arms embargo against Israel at which Defferre spoke. This mix of pieds noirs and Jewish concerns reflected Marseille's post-1962 landscape in which former supporters of *Algérie française*, socialists, and Jews used the Arab-Israeli issue as a basis for creating local solidarities. For Defferre, peace with the pieds noirs was of ongoing importance given early missteps. In summer 1962, as thousands had poured into the city, and police worried about urban instability, Defferre told *Paris-Presse* that the repatriates must "leave Marseille quickly" and "readjust elsewhere."[149] Not forgiven five years later, he used the pro-Israel rally to announce the decision to erect a monument commemorating the departure of French colonial subjects.[150] A rally critiquing French Middle Eastern policy thus became a moment to forge local alliances between pieds noirs and Jews. The FSFR's general secretary, for example, commented that pieds noirs were not surprised by the anti-Israeli embargo having also been abandoned by de Gaulle, while another called for "a veritable union" between repatriates and Jews.[151]

How can we understand a political coupling criticized by the local Communist paper for bringing together "supporters of French Algeria, forgers incidentally of racism and anti-Semitism" with Socialists and Jews?[152] The answers are the same as those that brought the city's Muslim and Jewish populations into conflict in 1967, as divisions forged in the waning days of French colonial rule took on salience in the new context. While few Jews joined the many pied-noir associations established in Marseille following decolonization, their similar socioeconomic position, their support for French Algeria, and the difficulties of the initial years in Marseille encouraged political alliances between them.[153] As Wladimir Rabi wrote as early as 1962 of Jewish life in Marseille, "There is a symbiosis between Christian and Jewish repatriates."[154] If not necessarily "anti-Muslim" or "right wing," these alliances continued to prove useful in Marseille as a tool of political integration.[155] Support for Israel, which most pieds noirs and Jews shared with Marseille's political establishment, thus became a way of forging alliances that necessarily marginalized those more critical of Israeli activities.

If Muslim-Jewish tension in Marseille during the 1967 war point to the way the colonial past shaped ethno-religious relations in contemporary France, clashes on campuses foreshadowed the significance of leftist political activism in shaping Muslim-Jewish encounters in the coming decade. The first evidence of such tensions actually predated the 1967 war by a year when on 25 May 1966, the UGEP and the Association des étudiants musulmans nord-africains en France organized the first pro-Palestinian rally since Israel's founding.[156] Given the small size of the gathering—only one hundred people attended—it should be clear that the Palestinian question was hardly a galvanizing issue in the wider North African Muslim population, student or otherwise. Despite its small size, however, the demonstration was covered in the mainstream press (*Le Monde* published a story about the rally) and elicited angry responses from several Jewish organizations. Attended by, among others, the Middle Eastern historian Maxime Rodinson–the bête noir of the Jewish community due to his Jewish origins and readiness to attack Israeli policies–the event sought to "convince French public opinion of the unjustified and improper link made between the struggle against anti-Semitism and the Arab-Israeli conflict." If all speakers vigorously condemned antisemitism and the genocide of European Jews, they also all underscored the injustice of "repairing evil with evil" by making Palestinians pay for Nazi crimes. Stressing their opposition to Israel, speakers nevertheless insisted that they did not support "throwing the Jewish populations of Palestine into the sea." Rather—to the prolonged ovation of those in attendance—they called for the reestablishment of "age-old friendship of Jews and Arabs" while distinguishing legitimate political conflict from any religious or racial hostility. The Egyptian journalist Aly El Samman, for example, called on Arabs to become active participants in the fight against antisemitism by joining organizations such as MRAP; as such they would not only rebuild alliances with Jews but would weaken Zionism, which was itself an outgrowth of European antisemitism.[157]

Such arguments proved infuriating to Israel's Jewish supporters, who overlooked the demonstration's appeals for interethnic cooperation. In response, on 7 July 1966 various organizations, including the Fédération des sociétés juives de France, the Alliance France-Israël, the Amitiés France-Israël, and the Ligue internationale contre l'antisémitisme, held their own rally expressing their "indignation to see these students abuse French hospitality by publicly uttering extermination threats towards Israel, one of France's allies." By pointing to the students as "abusers of French hospitality" and underscoring the links between France and Israel, the protesters drew a symbolic line between their own citizenship and the foreignness of the students in question. The sin of the Muslim protestors was that they took part in activist politics in the first place, their specific politics being secondary. Protesting students were thus constructed as "outsiders" abusing French hospitality, not as fellow residents working within the polity to influence its direction.

Like much of the rhetoric surrounding the 1967 war a year later, the proclamation also invoked the Holocaust, "urging all true anti-racists, lovers of freedom and justice, not to accept fallacious arguments that classified Jews into categories, a method used by the Nazis with the tragic consequences that we all know."[158] Well before 1967 the Holocaust had become a reference for those on both sides of the Israeli/Palestinian debate.[159] While protestors at the Mutualité evoked the genocide in their self-defense strategies, the Jewish organizations railed against their right to do so. According to Michel Salomon who condemned the pro-Palestinian demonstration in L'Arche, it was both scandalous and intellectually and morally dishonest to compare Israelis with Nazis.

Salomon, like the Jewish protestors on 7 July, also focused on the foreignness of the pro-Palestinian demonstrators. Dismissing the demonstration as the first manifestation of the Arab League's efforts to win over the French population now that the Algerian war was over, Salomon accused the organization of establishing "a phantom Union générale des étudiants palestiniens en France, of which nobody has heard anything before." In this view, not only was a foreign power—the Arab League—promoting hatred in France, but also Middle Eastern and North African intellectuals were following suit. In Salomon's telling, then, the rally had been an ugly event: "For an observer mixed into the shouting crowd . . . there was a singular feeling of nausea that predominated, a nausea that overwhelmed even the disappointment at once again seeing the dimming of the possibility of a true dialogue between Jews and Arabs beyond demagoguery or hatred." Here, as during discussions of the Algerian war, Muslim participants—and particularly those from the Maghreb—were denounced for their unwillingness to engage in a good faith dialogue and for succumbing to the worst forms of bigotry. "Outsiders" from a "phantom" organization were manipulating minds and hearts. Calls to join the MRAP, rather than a sincere appeal to unite to fight bigotry, were a clever ploy manipulated by politically astute racists.[160] Such assertions meant that Salomon and other Jewish critics could withdraw from dialogue while claiming that the "other side" was to blame.

The MRAP, it should be noted, did not accept this characterization. In the association's view, Jews "firmly attached to Israel" and Arabs "whose patriotism cannot be doubted" had proven capable of joining forces in anti-racist struggles. According to Charles Palant, the secretary general, such encounters demonstrated that divisions created by the Middle Eastern conflict were surmountable. Indeed, the MRAP had held a symposium on the Middle Eastern conflict the year before during which "Jews and Arabs held an open dialogue with a remarkable spirit of truth and justice."[161] According to observers, the many hours of discussion were carried out "in a spirit of fraternity and mutual tolerance" and compromise prevailed.[162]

For others, however, the intermingling at universities of young people from different ethnic and religious backgrounds provided an opportunity to promote group solidarity. In November 1965, six months after the MRAP's celebration of Muslim-Jewish cooperation, the Israeli embassy in Paris hosted a meeting of the Union mondiale des étudiants juifs (UMEJ), which brought together eighty students from across Western Europe to discuss historical sources of opposition between Jews and Arabs; recent growth in Israel's Arab population; surveys on the number of Jewish students who had participated in conferences with Arabs; and methods with which to combat Arab propaganda.[163] Far from promoting the "spirit of fraternity and mutual tolerance" that dominated the MRAP's discussions, the UMEJ meeting focused on conflict and polarization. Speakers—including many representatives of the Israeli government—provided students with Israel's perspective on the conflict. While encouraging Jewish students to establish contact with Arab peers in European universities, these efforts were directed toward countering their propaganda.[164] Jewish attendees were thus trained to defend Israel in the emerging hotbed of university politics. As Michel Solomon wrote the subsequent July indicating communal concern with these spaces: "We have certainly had time these last years to accustom ourselves . . . to the aggressive positions adopted by Arab students on the subject of Israel."[165]

As tensions increased in spring 1967, student activists became evermore politicized. In early May 1967 at the Cité Universitaire—a set of dormitories in southern Paris designed to bring foreign students together to promote international harmony—Syrian students circulated anti-Zionist tracts to protest the planned showing of the film *Exodus*, leading the Minister of Education to cancel the film.[166] Either way, campaigns on university campuses to influence student opinion were beginning to spread. Then, on 20 May, the UGEP and the Association des étudiants musulmans nord-africains—which had brought together Palestinian and North African students a year earlier—organized a day of international solidarity with Palestinians against "Zionist imperialism."[167]

As one Algerian Muslim student noted later, "The Six Day War in 1967 was a turning point for us."[168] By June, Jewish sources were reporting worriedly about the intensification of "Arab student propaganda in diverse universities" that "endeavor to spread the myth of Israeli imperialism." The Comité étudiant inter-arabe, which united thirteen student groups, for example, denounced "Anglo-American collusion" with the Zionists and called for the Arab people's triumph over imperialism and Zionism."[169] Meanwhile in Aix a debate between an Arab and Israeli on the Middle East problem was canceled due to fears of mounting hostility among students.[170]

Muslim groups, it should be noted, were often careful about blurring the lines between Judaism and Zionism. In the inflammatory environment of campus politics, however, such nuances could be lost. At the University of Strasbourg, Arab students in the Comité anti-colonialiste, for example, contrasted Judaism and Zionism while insinuating that the latter was in the process of irreparably harming the former. In response, students from Union des étudiants juifs distributed their own tract, which argued that the circulation of such "base propaganda" was inappropriate in a university dedicated to dialogue.[171] Such statements overlooked the fact that Jewish propaganda was also pervasive. Universities in Marseille, for example, were papered with tracts comparing Nasser to Hitler and calling on Jewish students to prevent a second genocide.[172]

Indeed, despite calls for dialogue, Jewish youth organizations made it clear that they too had taken sides. The Comité de coordination de la jeunesse juive de France, for example, insisted that although French Jewish youth had sought to establish dialogue, they now had to stand with Israel: "Without renouncing the desire for such an opening, French Jewish youth, completely taken up with the current situation, want to leave no doubt about their obligation to participate in Israel's struggle and to safeguard its existence."[173] Similarly the UEJF stressed Jewish loyalty to Israel. Still maintaining its leftist leanings and its hopes for Muslim-Jewish dialogue, UEJF members distributed tracts decrying anti-Arab racism in France.[174] Nevertheless, at a UEJF demonstration at the Maison de la Mutualité on 20 May speakers insisted, "we will not tolerate an ambiguous attitude towards Israel among our friends" and promised that all Jewish youth, no matter what their affiliation, would "unite to fight for Israel."[175]

In emphasizing loyalty to Israel while rejecting racism at home, the UEJF was one of several youth organizations that began reconceptualizing the parameters of Muslim-Jewish relations in France, a process that linked developments in the Middle East evermore closely with the inequities in France. It would take the upheaval to French political culture in 1968, however, to raise these developments to a fever pitch, as radical activists—many of them Jewish—brought the Palestinian cause to a wider French audience and moved the Middle East from the margins to the center of Muslim-Jewish relations in France.

Palestine in France

Radical Politics and Hardening Ethnic Allegiances, 1968–72

In June 1968, almost one year to the day after the 1967 war, a riot in the Parisian immigrant neighborhood of Belleville between Muslim and Jewish residents took France by surprise. Capturing widespread media attention, many commentators feared the violence was evidence that transnational ethno-religious allegiances had inevitably begun to pit Muslims and Jews against each other. And yet the riot's origins were more complex than such assertions suggested coming, as they did, in the midst of the *événements* of May/June 1968. During those weeks, Anarchist, Trotskyist, and Maoist student groups initiated uprisings that led to the largest general strike in French history. This tumultuous environment not only created the riot's immediate context but also pushed the Israeli-Palestinian issue from the margins to the center of Muslim-Jewish relations in France. Indeed, few commentators at the time or subsequently have traced the powerful impact of late 1960s youth radicalism in making Middle Eastern conflict relevant to local Muslim-Jewish political discourse.[1] This context is crucial, however, for understanding how distant political struggles took on local meaning.

Protests and strikes in late 1960s France brought to mainstream attention issues previously on the social margins, including feminism, sexual freedom, gay rights, and anti-racism.[2] Anti-imperialism and third-worldism, both ideologically central to the New Left in France and elsewhere, also won wider public hearing as campus radicals gained national attention. France's "discovery" of the Palestinian problem was linked to these developments.

Ten months earlier, French campuses had emerged as sites of conflict for Muslims and Jews around this issue. For much of 1968, however, pro-Palestinian activities remained muted.[3] Radicals on the far left—particularly Trotskyists and Maoists on university campuses—began to change that dynamic. Differing in their strategies and ideological aims and distrustful of "bourgeois" national liberation struggles, various radical groups shared a blend of Marxism and third-worldism that translated into broad sympathy for anti-imperial struggles.[4] During 1968, support for Palestinians became fused with this anti-colonialism. Already in June 1967, the Maoist organization, Union des jeunes communistes marxistes leninistes, held the only pro-Palestinian demonstration in Paris (driven largely by Egyptian exiles Adel Rifaat—an Islamic convert of Jewish origin—and Bahgat El-Nadi, known by pen name Mahmoud Hussein). Interest intensified in March 1968 when Chinese and Vietnamese leftists threw their support behind the Palestine Liberation Organization and the Jordanian army in their battle against the Israel Defense Forces (IDF) in Karameh, Jordan. For French radicals, who drew inspiration from Chinese and Vietnamese revolutionaries, and particularly for Maoists who linked armed struggle and revolution, the Palestinian cause took on profound symbolic resonance. In the words of one Maoist poster that linked Palestinian, Algerian, and other revolutionary struggles: "Vietnam, Palestine, FLN, El Fatah: The same combat."[5]

University campuses, hotbeds of French radical culture, soon became key arenas for attacking the so-called American-Zionist imperial axis. In July 1967, the largest student union, the Union nationale des étudiants français (UNEF), condemned Israeli aggression and recognized Palestinian national rights.[6] During the 1968 uprisings, Arab nationalist and Zionist students constructed competing stands at the entrance of the occupied Sorbonne. Although the Occupation Committee removed both due to resulting tensions, the Palestinian issue had become linked to the anti-racism and anti-colonialism undergirding university discourse.[7]

External developments also facilitated interest in the Palestinian cause. Arab losses in the 1967 conflict pushed Palestinian nationalists to seek new allies. In particular, Yasser Arafat's, nascent organization Fatah, weakened by limited organizational abilities, the power of Israeli countermeasures, insufficient participation of the Palestinian masses, and the failures of Nasserism and the wider Arab world to defeat Israel, was soon forced into exile.[8] Turning abroad in a search for new supporters, Fatah focused on France where it was hoped that pro-Arab policies and a growing Muslim population would help foster sympathy.[9]

This chapter traces how French radicals, North African Muslim students, and Palestinian representatives created alliances that brought the Palestinian issue to French public attention and the way these alliances shaped Muslim-Jewish relations. Although Muslim immigrants were only marginally engaged with pro-Palestinian politics, the period beginning in 1968 with the student uprisings and ending in the early 1970s with the decline of radical politics had a decisive impact on Muslim-Jewish relations, particularly among students. The publicly visible and, at times, violent confrontations between Muslim and Jewish youth resulted in increasing polarization around Middle Eastern politics, as the Jewish community—already galvanized by the 1967 war—took notice, and as larger numbers of Muslim immigrants came to see themselves as having a stake in France's domestic and international affairs.

Yet for all its divisiveness, the tumultuous environment also created unexpected Muslim-Jewish alliances. Indeed, the very radicals who promoted

Palestinian interests and who worked with Muslim activists to fight racism were often Jewish. While rhetorically rejecting identity politics in favor of universal humanism, many understood their leftist commitments in particularistic terms, that is as a direct response to the history of anti-Jewish persecution. Many were in fact children of Holocaust survivors seeking to come to terms with their parents' past.[10] Their participation in pro-Palestinian struggles created bridges between Muslims and Jews at the very moment conflict between them was becoming more visible.

This cooperation reminds us that Jewish-Muslim polarization around the Middle East was not a predetermined outcome of ethnic transnational allegiances. Rather, when "polarization" did emerge, it did so as a product of the political space created by late 1960s French radical culture, which both made room for a new generation of Muslim activists who infused their pro-immigrant politics with the Palestinian issue and pushed politically active members of France's Jewish population—and particularly high school and university students—away from traditional affiliations on the left and toward a more combative politics. The result was a growing number of highly visible Muslim-Jewish conflicts that linked Jews with Israel and North African Muslims with Palestinians in increasingly rigid ways.

The Belleville Riots and the Changing Terrain of Muslim-Jewish Relations in France

On Sunday, 2 June 1968, three days before the anniversary of the outbreak of the 1967 Arab-Israeli war, two Tunisian immigrants, one Jewish and one Muslim, fought over a card game at a local café.[11] The fight soon escalated. Some blamed Jewish observers for breaking the café's windows when the Muslim loser refused to pay his debt. Others asserted that Muslim residents chased Jews with bottles and clubs. The result, however, was that over the next two days, forty to fifty Jewish- and Muslim-owned stores were ransacked and several people injured.[12] Before police finally quelled the unrest, Muslim participants had launched Molotov cocktails at the synagogue on rue Julien-Lacroix, where Jews had congregated for the holiday of Shavuot, and a self-defense squad of Jewish youth had set up barricades in the courtyard.[13]

What explains such violence in the previously harmonious neighborhood?[14] As the game preceding the riot suggests, convivial relations were the norm in Belleville as in other mixed immigrant neighborhoods.[15] The largely Tunisian Jewish and Algerian Muslim residents shared not only their North African origins and many cultural practices but also the struggles of all newcomers.[16] While congregating on differing streets, a vibrant market culture and some mixed apartment buildings brought residents together. Jewish employers, somewhat better off than local Muslim immigrants, hired the latter, sometimes

creating class tensions but also establishing neighborhood ties; cafés and groceries served a mixed clientele, and religious festivals saw the sharing of holiday
foods, a practice imported from North Africa. As one Jewish café owner asserted after the riot, "We are all brothers. We knew each other in Tunis and we
live together." Published in the magazine Le Jeune Afrique with a photograph
of two boys captioned, "Which is Jewish, which is Muslim," the article stressed
the common background and experiences of local residents.[17] Indeed, if ethnic
and religious practices distinguished the two populations, there was little in the
quarter's daily life to foreshadow the violence.

For many, the riot's proximity to the anniversary of the 1967 war was all the
explanation necessary. Local press reports, sensationalizing the violence, referred to the "Six Hour War."[18] As Ethan Katz has shown, while some communal
leaders downplayed the Middle East's impact on local Jewish-Muslim relations,
many were "ready to embrace the largely mythical view of the Belleville riots
as the signal of new Jewish-Muslim tensions that extended directly from those
in Israel-Palestine."[19] Although Muslim and Jewish political and religious leaders worked tirelessly to restore calm to the neighborhood,[20] both the Algerian
paper El Moudjahid and ADAE representatives blamed Zionist provocateurs,
while some Jewish spokesmen faulted Fatah and a circulating Arabic tract calling for "holy war."[21] After the riot, Albert Memmi declared that Arab colleagues
had warned him of an Arab League plan to provoke conflict, while Jean Simon,
vice president of a Zionist youth group, insisted that "Belleville resulted from
intensive Arab propaganda."[22] A resulting schisim in the UEJF ensued, as some
members broke away to found the Front des étudiants juifs (FEJ), a far-right
group dedicated to self-defense and fighting anti-Zionism.[23]

A monocausal focus on war in the Middle East, however, overlooked the
generally nonconflictual interethnic terrain in Belleville a year previously and
important international and domestic transformations in the ensuing months
that had changed the environment. Anti-Jewish riots in Tunisia in June 1967
had increased Belleville's Jewish population by several thousand, bringing to
the neighborhood new resentments against the "Arabs" who had destroyed the
Grande Synagogue in Tunis and ransacked the Jewish quarter. Although the
Tunisian government condemned the violence, departures to France and Israel,
which had slowed since the early 1960s, increased substantially; of 23,000 Jews
in Tunisia on the eve of the 1967 War, only 7,000–8,000 remained one year
later.[24] Those who settled in Belleville joined earlier migrants who saw in the
newcomers' arrival affirmation of their own decision to leave and a reminder of
lessons learned about "Arabs" during decolonization.[25] Such wounds were still
fresh a year later when the French environment became explosive. The UEJF
president, in Belleville during the riot, likened the ambience to a Jewish quarter
in Algeria, "a wave of panic mixed with some aggression and a general ten-
dency to entertain any kind of bunk [bobard] such as, 'there are 500 Arabs in
Barbès headed this way with machine guns.' "[26]

The riot also unfolded in the context of the political radicalism of May 1968. The massive protests and worker walkouts, in which many foreign students and laborers participated, transported radical politics from the universities to the streets.[27] Moreover, strikes that month left much of Belleville's working population aimless, as did the Jewish holiday that kept Jewish stores and cafés closed for two days. Even those disconnected from the student struggle were swept up in the surging radicalism. "An effervescence reigned," noted one Jewish student who helped establish a UEJF medical response unit. "Among the group in place were youth who felt somewhat marginal to the events of May 1968. They had a suppressed activism that they set off, believing it was permanent. It lasted from the 5th to the 15th of June. We believed we were living in highly revolutionary times. In hindsight, it seems a bit absurd."[28] The combustible combination of leftist radicalism, massive strikes, postcolonial politics, *and* Middle Eastern tensions explains tensions in Belleville in June 1968.

Whatever the link between the riot and Middle Eastern tensions, however, the former's impact was certainly to increase communal sensitivity to such a linkage. Indeed, two years later, when new disturbances in Belleville and the neighboring district left a sixty-year-old Algerian Jew dead (of a heart attack), several policemen wounded, twenty-eight mostly Jewish businesses vandalized, and thirty-three mostly North African Muslims arrested for defacing the rue de Tourtille synagogue, such linkages were assumed.[29] As in 1968, Jewish and Muslim leaders—such as Rabbi Couchena and the Algerian consul in Paris, Amor Benghezal—patrolled the neighborhood to stem the violence and called for calm. By 1970, however, the Middle East conflict played an even greater role in shaping perspectives on events. Rioters shouted "Vive Israël" and "Vive Palestine," respectively. The ADAE blamed "Jewish residents" and "Zionist provocateurs" and called for justice.[30] A letter from one reader to the *Algérien en Europe* blamed the riot on "Zionist merchants" and the "young Nazis of Betar," the far-right Zionist youth movement, and asserted that police had unfairly punished only Muslims.[31] Muslim student organizations argued that "Zionist propaganda" had been the riot's primary beneficiary and warned that anti-Arab racism and antisemitism would intensify as a result.[32]

Jewish organizations underscored Fatah's role in the violence.[33] While a CRIF statement to *Le Monde* on 21/22 June spoke somewhat vaguely of Jewish victimization at the hands of "provocateurs" (noting that only Jewish stores were attacked and only Muslims arrested),[34] internal CRIF disucssions noted police "certainty" that the incidents were "the work of certain Arab elements" working with Fatah's support. A pro-Palestinian rally held at the entrance to Belleville two days later, which, according to CRIF sources, was attended by a mix of French leftists and "Arab students," confirmed such fears.[35] The FEJ likewise condemned "Palestinian progressives and their leftist and Nazi allies," while Jean-Pierre Bloch, president of the Ligue internationale contre le racisme et l'antisémitisme blamed "provocateurs."[36]

Such accounts reflected growing fears that the Israeli-Palestinian crisis was destabilizing intercommunal relations in France. To understand these concerns, we must move away from Belleville to wider political developments in France after the 1968 student riots. While communal leaders were right to recognize the Palestinian-Israeli conflict as increasingly relevant to Muslim-Jewish relations in France, this development also had local origins.

Building Alliances: Pro-Palestinian Mobilization, 1968–70

This section will explore how Palestinians, largely invisible in France in 1967, became a subject of public concern and how Muslim student activists seized the Palestinian cause as their own. An alliance among three distinct groups of political actors allowed this dynamic to unfold: (1) Palestinian nationalists searching for new allies following Arab losses in 1967; (2) French far leftists seeking to win adherents among Muslim laborers in France via the Palestinian issue; and (3) North African Muslim student activists—already highly politicized in response to developments in their home nations and the radical environment on French campuses—who saw in the Palestinian issue a rallying cry for oppressed Muslims in France.[37] On campuses where these students were increasingly visible and where some Jewish students expressed a more vocal pro-Israel politics in response to the 1968 foment, conflict grew. Interestingly, however, it was often Jewish leftists, well represented in the *gauchistes* movement, who vocally supported Palestinian nationalism, reminding us that at the very moment when many commentators were coming to see Jewish-Muslim political polarization around the Middle East as an essential dividing line, it remained far from automatic.

In January 1969, Fatah representative Muhammad Abou Mayer arrived in Paris to foster international support for Palestinian nationalism. As part of his mission, Mayer and his subsequent replacement, Mahmoud Hamchari, a well-known Palestinian activist and Arafat's close collaborator, were charged with challenging Israel's hold on French sympathies. Establishing themselves as the primary Palestinian representatives among those organizing Muslim political life in France, such as the Arab League and the ADAE, Mayer and Hamchari produced numerous bulletins and tracts, organized public meetings, launched a French language newspaper, *Fedayin*, and forged alliances within the wider anti-colonial movement. Hamchari also established contact with the foreign ministry, regularizing his status, and introducing Palestinian diplomacy to France.[38]

Fatah focused on winning supporters within two overlapping arenas: universities and radical left-wing political organizations. Universities—already sites of pro-Palestinian activism during the student uprisings—remained a welcoming space thereafter.[39] In November 1968, for example, the Comité de liaison des étudiants arabes organized a week of meetings and lectures about Palestine at the university in the western Parisian suburb of Antony, and the next month, the Union générale des étudiants libanais de France held pro-Palestinian meetings on campuses in several large cities.[40] Once Fatah had established a Parisian office, it supported such efforts through the Union générale des étudiants de Palestine.[41] By February 1969, Fatah's student delegates had established alliances with various revolutionary groups known to support the Palestinian cause, such as the Jeunesse communiste révolutionnaire and the Fédération des étudiants révolutionnaires. Together, they established Comités d'action Palestine on many French campuses, including in Marseille and Paris (particularly Censier). These groups held demonstrations, teach-ins, and expositions, and collected funds, medical supplies, clothes, blood, and sometimes volunteers for Palestine.[42]

Creating such institutions was doubly useful to Fatah. First, the Comités d'action Palestine gave Fatah access to a wider audience. As police noted, "El Fatah relies on the zealousness of the 'friends of Palestine' to provide the Arab cause with openings to the general public as well as with a means of eventually putting pressure on the French government."[43] Second, the Comités gave Fatah access to leftist circles where they sought support from those who had backed Algerian independence. Indeed, gauchiste interest in the Palestinians was an early indication to Fatah representatives that the role Jews had historically played in French revolutionary circles would not necessarily be an obstacle.[44] In fact, as we will see, many Jewish leftists supported the Palestinian cause.

For gauchistes, Fatah's appeal was a complex blend of the ideological and the pragmatic. Ideologically, Fatah's arguments invoked long-standing commitments to anti-imperialism and third-worldism. In the various organizations committed to Palestinian liberation, such as the Comité de soutien aux luttes anti-impérialistes des peuples arabes, presided over by the Trotskyist journalist Daniel Guérin, or the Section française du mouvement contre le racisme anti-arabe (MCRA), anti-imperialism was the motivating concern.[45] As the Comité de soutien's journal, Résistance populaire, asserted in May 1968, the Palestinian struggle was a battle against imperialism, not the so-called Jewish nation.[46] Likewise, a January 1969 MCRA flyer called followers to "support the liberation struggle of the Palestinian people, victims—like the Vietnamese—of imperialism."[47]

Ideology worked in tandem, however, with pragmatic hopes among leftists that the Palestinian issue could serve as a bridge between North African immigrant workers and the gauchistes. Largely invisible to French media and social commentators since the end of the Algerian crisis, North African laborers attracted significant attention during the 1968 uprisings.[48] The riots, which broke out at the University of Nanterre, were adjacent to France's largest immigrant slum. Striking students visited the area, and various Maoist, anarchist, and Trotskyist groups, hoping to distinguish themselves from large leftist political parties that had little to say on immigrant rights, denounced the deplorable conditions. Seeking to promote proletarian solidarity and internationalism, they argued the West could not reverse bourgeois society alone; third-world radicalism—embodied in immigrant labor—would help spark the coming revolution. Slogans such as "French workers–immigrant workers, same combat," sought to initiate the necessary alliance.

To win supporters in the relatively closed world of France's foreign workforce, however, required new tactics. A wide range of Basque separatists, Spanish anarchists, American pacifists, and student nationalists, thus moved into the immigrant slums, signing up for Arabic classes, offering French literacy courses, encouraging strikes, and distributing tracts.[49] The focus on Palestinian nationalism was central to these efforts, as French radicals linked the struggle for immigrant rights to wider anti-imperial and anti-capitalist campaigns.[50] MCRA activists, for example, positioned themselves against three adversaries: (1) Zionism, (2) Gaullism, and (3) anti-Arab racism, which—in their view—had surpassed contemporary antisemitism in scope.[51] While devoting most columns to the Palestinian issue, *Résistance populaire* thus also condemned the treatment of Arab workers and called for solidarity between French and Arab laborers.[52] Such links were often explicit, such as at a 1971 rally to protest racism that ended with a slide show on Palestine or in posters that read, "Workers, the *fédayins* are also fighting for you."[53]

Maoist militants, particularly those associated with La Gauche prolétarienne (GP), a pro-Chinese revolutionary movement, were the most ardent backers of the Palestinian issue.[54] Of particular significance for our purposes, a number of GP members, including its two leaders, Alain Geismar and Pierre Victor (Benny Lévy), were Jewish. Indeed, gauchisme in general was marked by a small but highly visible Jewish presence. Three of the four most outspoken student leaders, Daniel Cohn-Bendit, Alain Krivine, and Alain Geismar were Jewish. Eleven of twelve of the Ligue communiste revolutionnaire's governing body were Jewish as was a similar proportion of those making up the Lutte ouvrière. Cohn-Bendit later commented that the French gauchiste leadership could have communicated in Yiddish.[55]

Jewish origins did not translate into specifically Jewish agendas, at least in ethnic terms. As descendants of Holocaust survivors or escapees, many radicals had dedicated themselves to fighting fascism, but for them, the war's lessons were universal. Neither hiding nor celebrating their ethno-religious origins, they believed that the answer to fascism and racism was social revolution.[56] Moreover, for many Jewish radicals, nationalism was an anathema, particularly after 1967 when images of occupying soldiers clashed with long-standing images of Jewish victims and resistors.[57] Maxime Rodinson, for example, a Middle Eastern scholar of Jewish origin, emerged as a vocal, leading critic of Zionism.[58] Emmanuel Lévyne, a rabbi whose father was killed in Auschwitz, condemned the "Israelization of the Parisian Jewish community," and authored *Judaïsme contre Sionisme*.[59] Journalist Ania Francos, whose family was also murdered during the Holocaust, maintained close relations with representatives of El Fatah. Supporting leftist causes in Cuba, South Africa, and Algeria, she wrote against Zionism and Israeli occupation. Professors with Trotskyite and Maoist leanings, like sociologist Catherine Lévy, joined the Comités Palestine asserting that to be a revolutionary meant fighting for the Palestinians, while Trotskyist Jean-Louis Weissberg visited a refugee camp affiliated with the Popular Democratic Front for the Liberation of Palestine (PDFLP) in December 1969 and proclaimed it an honor to be a Jew at the side of Palestinians.[60] Nor were all those on the anti-Zionist Jewish left intellectuals. Patrick Rabiaz, a French worker of Jewish origins, for example, justified his hunger strike in sympathy with North African Muslim protestors by comparing Zionist oppression against Palestinians with his own family's suffering in Nazi concentration camps.[61]

As these last two examples suggest, some Jewish radicals did link their politics to their Jewish origins or history while others proved reluctant to criticize Israel too aggressively. According to Yair Auron, the Palestinian cause received relatively muted support in France when compared to support for other leftist causes in part because of Jewish participation in radical groups. For example, in 1971 Toulouse, Maoists in the Comité permanent d'action pour la Palestine pushed out Trotskyists ostensibly over ideological clashes; local observers, however, believed it was the Jewish presence in the Trotskyist organization that had caused the rift.[62] For many Jewish radicals, however, anti-Zionism was a central component of their ideological makeup, and their support was used to prove the righteousness of the cause. One Maoist poster, for example, ended with, "Long live Fatah's Jewish combatants."[63]

Nowhere was the Jewish presence more visible than in the Gauche prolétarienne under Geismar and Levy. Benny Lévy (half brother of Muslim convert and leftist Adel Rifaat) had fled Egypt after the 1956 Suez crisis. As a university student in France, he entered the Union des étudiants communistes and then, in 1966, co-founded the Maoist Union des jeunesses communistes marxistes-léninistes. In response to the 1967 war, he and his brother Tony established the Comité des étudiants juifs antisionistes.[64] Alain Geismar, born in 1939 into a nonpracticing Alsatian Jewish family, faced racist violence at an early age. When the Algerian crisis broke out, Geismar experienced profound guilt over French atrocities, seeing in them parallels to Nazi tactics. He reached out to the FLN, launching his career in radical leftist struggles, a path that took him later to Maoism and anti-Zionism.[65]

Under Lévy and Geismar, the GP became infamous for its pro-Palestinian politics.[66] Establishing ties with Fatah's Parisian office, Geismar and Léo Lévy (Benny's wife) spent August 1969 in Jordan visiting Fatah's military branch, al-Assifa. Symbolically distancing the Maoist organization from links to the French Jewish establishment, in September, three hundred GP demonstrators scrawled anti-Zionist slogans on a Rothschild mansion and bank. This link between Jewish capital and Israeli imperialism was echoed a year later after "Black September" when Jordan's King Hussein responded to an attempted coup by killing and expelling thousands of Palestinians. Posters advertising a subsequent GP demonstration read, "The capitalist Rothschild oppresses the French people; the Zionist Rothschild oppresses the Palestinian people; the imperialist Rothschild oppresses the Jews world over." By linking capitalism, Zionism, and imperialism through the symbol of Rothschild and familiar anti-semitic stereotypes, Maoists made clear that Jewish participation did not influence the movement's allegiances.[67]

The GP's most significant contribution to pro-Palestinian politics in France, however, came in 1970 when it worked with Algerian, Tunisian, Moroccan, Syrian, and Lebanese Muslim students to found the Comité Palestine ouvrier Nanterre. Drawn to Maoist circles because of their commitment to social justice, their criticisms of their home governments, and their interest in pro-Arab causes, these Muslim student activists used the Comité Palestine to fuse the problems facing immigrant laborers in France with a pro-Palestinian agenda.[68]

As already noted, Muslim student interest in the Palestinian issue pre-dated Maoist encouragement. These sympathies intensified in 1968 as various student organizations, including the Union nationale des étudiants algériens, the Association des étudiants musulmans nord-africains, the Union générale des étudiants tunisiens, and the Union nationale des étudiants marocains, expressed increasingly progressive, pro-Arab, and anti-Zionist stances.[69] By 1970 the UGEP and the Parisian branch of the Croissant-rouge had moved into the Foyer des étudiants musulmans nord-africains and the Maison du Maroc at the Cité Universitaire.[70] Indeed, residents temporarily renamed it the Pavillon de la Palestine libre when Moroccan rebels who had sided with the Palestinians against Jordan during Black September escaped there.[71]

The Palestinian issue thus came to play a determinative role in the political evolution of a generation of North African student activists in France.[72] For many, this commitment found expression in the new Maoist Comités Palestine.[73] Linking the Palestinian revolution to the struggle "of all Arab peoples to liberate themselves from all forms of exploitation and imperial oppression," the Comités Palestine connected Algerian nationalists and Palestinians fighting Israel to immigrants in Paris. "In the working districts [of France] . . ." read one pamphlet, "we have organized meetings where for the first time since Algerian independence, 800 immigrant and French workers have come together to support the Palestinian revolution."[74] According to the tract's authors, Algerian Muslims should care about the Palestinian plight both because it mirrors their own struggle and because it is part of Arab efforts to free themselves from Western domination. In this way, the Palestinian cause was linked to anti-racist campaigns in France and to efforts to better working conditions.[75] As one Ministry of the Interior report noted, "As the committee mixes the very real complaints of the people in the neighborhood with those concerning the Palestinian issue, they make it necessary to accept or reject both issues in one block."[76]

The linking of these issues ultimately created tensions between gauchistes and their pro-Palestinian allies in France. Having relied on radicals to promote Palestinian interests, Fatah representatives and their allies in the ADAE soon worried that subversive politics could endanger the cause.[77] Hoping to build alliances with the French government and on record for praising de Gaulle's pro-Arab policies, the wider Palestinian political leadership began working "to neutralize the anti-Gaullism of their French friends."[78] Fatah representatives thus asked the UGEP to refrain from activities that could be perceived as antisemitic or too leftist and insisted in early 1969 that the Comités d'action Palestine remain focused on the Palestinian struggle and promoting Arab self-reliance.[79] Efforts to use North African immigrants for purely Marxist or revolutionary ends should be curtailed.[80] Such views corresponded with Fatah's ideological efforts to build a popular liberation movement based more closely on Algeria's anti-colonial nationalism than on the Chinese and Vietnamese "people's war," but they also reflected pragmatic concerns that the very people who had brought the Palestinian cause to a wider French public would alienate potential supporters.[81] UGEP leaders agreed, fearing French officials would reduce grants to Palestinian students.[82] At a November 1972 rally, the UGEP thus discouraged leftist participation so as to downplay links between Palestinian and gauchiste politics. Rather than calling for a Palestinian "revolution," they opted for the term "resistance" in the hopes of drawing more support.[83]

Fatah's rejection of gauchiste efforts to use the Palestinian conflict as an entrée into the Muslim émigré population suggests that "Arab unity," while a useful clarion call in the propaganda efforts described above, was as much a construct as "Jewish unity" in late 1960s France. Recognizing such divisions does not, however, undermine the significance of the initial relationship forged between Palestinian nationalists, French gauchistes, and Muslim student activists. This relationship not only brought the Palestinian question to France, but also opened the door to the particular blend of Maoism and Palestinian nationalism that drove the Comités Palestine into France's North African immigrant neighborhoods. For French leftists attracted to the movement, the move into North African immigrant neighborhoods was a major appeal. One Jewish student, for example, explained her attraction to the GP because its outreach was to "neither intellectuals nor students but primarily Arab laborers and Palestinians."[84] Ironically, the Maoist Comités Palestine may have been one of the few arenas where Muslims and Jews interacted outside of mixed immigrant neighborhoods like Belleville. While atypical, these collaborations make clear that disagreements around the Palestinian-Israeli issue were not the only option available to Muslims and Jews in late 1960s France. Yet in helping to legitimize the pro-Palestinian movement, these alliances paradoxically helped create the political landscape that was increasingly pushing Muslim and Jewish activists into opposing corners. Indeed, as we will soon see, although the Jews who joined these efforts typically did so on universalist terms that incorporated the Palestinian issue into wider leftist goals, they could not control the way those supporting Palestinian nationalism or Zionism began drawing ethnic boundaries around these political movements.

North African Muslim Immigrants and the Pro-Palestinian Movement

Before tracing the impact of pro-Palestinian activism on Muslim-Jewish relations, it is important to consider how deeply the pro-Palestinian agenda penetrated into France's Muslim immigrant populations. Did North African Muslim laborers rally around the issue? The short answer is that most did not; in the late 1960s and early 1970s, the period when leftist radicalism was at its peak, Muslim immigrant communities displayed little interest in the Palestinian cause despite the propaganda targeting them. If falling short of their primary goals, however, the efforts of French, Muslim, and Jewish radicals had long-term consequences forever fusing the Palestinian issue with the most important Muslim political body in the 1970s, the Mouvement des travailleurs arabes (MTA), and thereby institutionalizing an ethnically grounded connection between North African Muslims in France and the Palestinian issue.

North African Muslim immigrants became actively engaged with French domestic politics for the first time in the early 1970s. Growing numbers, particularly of women and children, made their permanence irrefutable, while heightened immigration restrictions, police repression, high unemployment, and expulsions increased tensions between immigrants and authorities.[85] The 1971 nationalization of Algerian oil/gas companies put stress on the Franco-Algerian relationship, leading to debates over immigration numbers and a spike in anti-Muslim aggression, including the murder of eight Algerian Muslims and the wounding of forty more in the first trimester of that year. In October, the concierge of a Parisian building argued with and then killed resident Djellali Ben Ali, an Algerian Muslim teenager, claiming simply that he "didn't like Arabs." In autumn 1973, another wave of racism broke out, exacerbated by the war in the Middle East and the oil crisis, after an Algerian Muslim immigrant stabbed a Marseille tram conductor.[86] The poor conditions and increasing hostility spawned large immigrant protests. Housing demonstrations, factory occupations, hunger strikes, and worker walkouts increased over the early 1970s and particularly in 1973.[87]

This new immigrant political mobilization continued to be infused with the Palestine issue, even after June 1972, when its most highly developed body, the Mouvement des travailleurs arabes, broke away from the Comités Palestine and the GP, arguing that even sympathetic French intellectuals could not fully understand the problems facing Muslim immigrants or their attachment to the Arab world.[88] While links to French gauchistes and the GP never fully dissipated, the Comités Palestines were disbanded as the MTA took form.[89]

The Palestinian issue nevertheless remained central to the MTA's agenda.[90] According to one founder, Mimoun Hallouss, "In the 1970s, the Palestinian struggle defined our activism. For us, there was a direct line between the Palestinian struggle and the Arab workers' struggle."[91] *Fedai*, the publication of the Comités Palestines, served as the MTA's organ, and militants continued to raise money and promote the Palestinian issue in neighborhoods and cafés, reflecting the organization's commitment to "Arabness" as the basis for its activism.[92] Despite such efforts, however, MTA militants shifted the *primary* focus elsewhere, reflecting Muslim immigrants' sensitization to political struggles in France proper. Improving housing, regularizing the status of illegal immigrants, increasing wages, improving factory conditions, and fighting racism were now of central concern. According to one MTA militant, Muslim immigrants often criticized the Palestine focus: "You speak to us only of Palestine, us who live in shit. Who is going to defend us?"[93]

Such comments reflect the limitations of the pro-Palestine campaign to reach France's Muslim laboring population. In July 1969, a half year after Fatah launched its campaign, the Ministry of the Interior reported that most Algerian Muslims workers were not all that concerned.[94] By April, the general assessment had not changed.[95] In Marseille, where one might have expected greater support given events in 1967, patterns were similar. Although the local GP became active in 1969, gauchistes had little success winning over North African Muslim adherents despite regular visits to slums, factories, and campuses.[96] In 1970, police reported, Algerian Muslims in Marseille "remained unmoved by Maoist propaganda" and were "impervious to all European political influences."[97]

Following Black September, interest in Palestinians increased as evidenced by larger sales of *Fedai* and attendance at public meetings. In October 1970, for example, six hundred North African Muslim workers and one hundred French and foreign workers attended a pro-Palestinian meeting in Paris. Elsewhere North African Muslims raised two thousand francs for a local Comité Palestine. Some even volunteered to fight with the *fedayin*. Activists in the Comités Palestine reported that if ten demonstrators marched with a Palestine flag in Barbès, residents would emerge in large numbers carrying their own flags.[98] Nevertheless, if in March 1971 French police worried that calls for revolution in Arab countries and particularly the Palestinian revolution "reinforced ideas of combat among Arab workers," by June they reported that the combined propaganda of all the pro-Palestinian organizations had not mobilized Algerian Muslims in France.[99]

In October 1970 new GP leadership came to Marseille from Paris, combining forces with politically energized immigrant organizations and giving new life to the pro-Palestinian movement.[100] March 1972 thus saw 200 demonstrators—primarily Tunisian and Algerian Muslims—protest Jordanian and Israel policies toward Palestinians.[101] That December, another 250 demonstrators—80 of whom were of North African or Middle Eastern origin—marched through Marseille with signs reading, "Halt to Zionist terrorism and anti-Arab racism" and "Long live the Palestinian revolution of workers and Arab students."[102] The formation of Marseille's MTA in summer 1972 undoubtedly influenced this process. According to police, however, "the appeal did not resonate, even in the largest North African quarters."[103]

French police, it should be noted, often portrayed foreign laborers as passive.[104] One 1971 report, for example, described Algerian Muslims as apolitical and isolated from their self-appointed representatives.[105] Likewise, the majority of Moroccan and Tunisian Muslims "were illiterate, without political ideas, and abstained from activism," displaying "evident neutrality" with regard to Arab/Palestinian nationalism.[106] The next month, the consensus was the same: "The majority of North African immigrants are virtually apolitical. They are uninterested even in events as spectacular as the Arab-Israeli conflict and the clashes of May 1968." Only students were sometimes vocal, police felt, and even they were fairly discreet.[107]

Such assessments ignored the way French neutrality on the Middle East conflict and aggressive policing of immigrant activism prevented North African Muslim laborers from supporting Palestinians publicly even if they felt so moved.[108] One pro-Palestinian meeting in October 1970, for example, was interrupted when police arrested fifty-one attendees.[109] In addition, Muslim immigrants must have been all too aware that Palestinians did not enjoy widespread public support. One example makes the point: In May 1971, Fatah and the UGEP worked with several French political figures to organize a week of pro-Palestinian activities.[110] Organizers were disappointed, however, with the low level of public interest. In contrast, a pro-Israel event in December was tremendously successful thanks to larger sums of money available to fund the event and the greater number of politicians and intellectuals who lent their support. According to the Ministry of the Interior, "this Week for Israel demonstrated the feeble impact of Palestinian organizations in France under Zionist influence."[111]

It is impossible to determine if the broader silence around the Palestinian cause among North African Muslim immigrants was a product of fear, self-protection, lack of affinity, or lack of interest in political activism more generally. Certainly militants in the Comités Palestine and MTA continued to claim significant support. The newspaper *Fedai*, for example, reported that foreign workers in a factory in Suresnes greeted one another daily with, "Palestine will vanquish."[112] Police, however, remained skeptical due in part to the complaints they received from Muslim informants about pro-Palestinian activities in their communities.[113] When the PFLP distributed tracts about its exploits against the

Israeli airline El Al, for example, some Muslims, particularly those employed by or with connections to Jews, gave copies to French police.[114] Others complained over Algerian militants' efforts to use financial incentives to enlist resistance soldiers.[115] Nevertheless, the combined efforts of North African, Middle Eastern, and gauchiste activists forever linked the Palestinian issue with local Muslim political development. The consequence was increasing confrontation with the most militant sectors of the Jewish population, themselves also radicalized by 1968 political upheaval.

Muslim-Jewish Conflict after 1968

Muslim student politicization around the Israeli-Palestinian issue was mirrored in France's Jewish student population. In 1970 there were approximately 170,000 Jewish youth in France, 5,000–6,000 of whom were enrolled in Parisian universities. While only 10 percent were affiliated with Jewish organizations, since 1967 many had begun displaying a greater interest in their Jewishness.[116] The year 1968 proved important in this process. As noted, many of those who took to the streets had families who had suffered during the Holocaust, and their engagement with the student movement often politicized these memories. While for some this process led to the embrace of radical leftist ideologies, for others it led to a newfound militancy around Israel.[117] Given the growing anti-Zionism on French campuses, conflict could be explosive. The growing animosity coupled with the 1968 Belleville riot—which as noted earlier brought out Jewish student activists—meant that what recently had seemed like a Middle Eastern problem now had local saliency.

While Jewish leftists numbered among the most vocal critics of Israel on French campuses, others—having become Israel's ardent supporters in June 1967—felt their post-1968 political radicalism challenged by their love for Israel.[118] The result was often a distancing from those further to the left. After the UNEF declared allegiance with the Palestinians, for example, one Jewish member tore up his membership card, telling writers for *L'Arche*, "Now it's finished. The UNEF has become a branch of the Arab League and Kuwait."[119] Or as another put it, "Pro-Israeli Jews found themselves rejected from the leftist paradise."[120]

For some young Jews, such as those who stayed affiliated with the UEJF, the late 1960s saw a complicated balancing act between Zionist engagement and a measured criticism of Israeli policies. Despite its stated pluralism, UEJF members were often to the left on the Algerian crisis and other issues. In 1968, however, the UEJF broke away from the anti-Zionist left, asserting Israel's right to exist and moving from "the search for dialogue . . . to the search for authenticity."[121] While acknowledging the Palestinians' right to national self-determination, the UEJF also declared Israel's occupation of its 1967 war gains legitimate, pending its Arab neighbors' formal recognition. According to one UEJF leader, the anti-Zionist climate on French campuses drove this vocal pro-Israel stance.[122] UEJF members thus challenged pro-Palestinian meetings on their campuses even as they opposed certain Israeli actions.[123] In May 1972, for example, Marseille's UEJF chapter publicly criticized Israel's Palestinian policies while warning of a "deep fracture in the student movement" over blurring anti-Zionism and antisemitism.[124] Such positions won them no friends. According to Marseille's UEJF president: his organization was "challenged by the *gauchistes* while also being rejected by the Jewish community."[125] Indeed, for the Front des étudiants juifs, the UEJF had not distanced itself sufficiently from the anti-Zionist left. Having broken away during the height of the 1968 Belleville crisis, FEJ leaders defined their group as *the* pro-Israel organization on French campuses. Criticizing the UEJF for cosigning petitions with the Comités Palestine, the FEJ became vocal supporters of Jews in the USSR and Arab lands and provided "protection" for Jewish university students under attack from political opponents.[126]

In casting French campuses as "dangerous" for Jews, the FEJ struck a chord. Many young Jews were, in fact, feeling singled out in the tense environment. Françoise Tenenbaum, a student at Paris's Jussieu campus, for example, described taking down anti-Israel posters in 1968.[127] Others felt greater unease. One student from Nice, for example, ripped down pro-Palestinian posters attacking Rothschild. Such words "of typically Nazi inspiration," she wrote, made "my heart miss a beat."[128] Propaganda of this nature often linked Israel, Jews, and the United States in a deadly bond. One PFLP poster, for example, depicted Uncle Sam's skull with Israeli defense minister Moshe Dayan in one eye (recognizable by his tell-tale eye-patch over one eye), two dead Arabs in his mouth, and four Jewish stars emblazoned across the blue stripe of his hat. This mix of anti-American, anti-Israeli, and antisemitic iconography implicated all Jews in the murder of Palestinians.[129] Likewise, ADAE spokesmen blamed "the Jews" for a December 1968 shooting that left two dead and three wounded in a Muslim-owned café in Aubervilliers, while the newspaper *El Moudjahid* accused "Zionist henchmen" and racist groups "nostalgic for the OAS" of several attacks against Algerian stores, cafés, and bars, including a brawl in a Parisian bar between Jewish and Muslim customers.[130] The FEJ vowed to protect young Jews against "the sudden virulence of a certain 'anti-Zionism'" and "increasingly violent attacks" by training members in paramilitary techniques.[131]

By 1969, then, many French campuses had small groups of Muslim, Jewish, and gauchiste militants committed to confrontational politics around the Middle East conflict. Their presence meant that no discussion of the Palestinian-Israeli conflict could go uncontested. In Marseille that May, for example, Jewish and Muslim leftists faced off at a pro-Palestinian event at the Faculté des Sciences. That June, the Comité pour la paix negocié au Moyen-Orient called off a Cité Universitaire debate on the Middle East in response to Maoist anti-Zionist threats.[132] The same month, Algerian and Moroccan Muslim gauchistes requested police protection for a pro-Palestinian event in response to threats of "Zionist sabotage."[133] On 4 December 1969 at "Sciences Po" in Paris, students and gauchistes had a brief but violent scuffle, and days later, four people were wounded when thirty Jewish students came armed with sticks to a screening of *La Palestine vaincra* at Censier.[134] When the FEJ protested anti-Jewish activities at Censier the next month, passions erupted once again. According to FEJ president Jacques Kupfer, some two hundred Maoists and Jewish leftists arrived with anti-Zionist tracts. Fistfights ensued to cries of "Palestine will overcome" and "Death to the Jews."[135] The FEJ responded to these "pogrom attempts" by threatening "to crush anti-Semitic vermin."[136] Such rhetoric had repercussions. In early June 1970, vandals ransacked the headquarters of the Union nationale des étudiants algériens and the Association des étudiants musulmans nord-africains, scrawling, "Israel will overcome" on the walls.[137] While no evidence tied the FEJ to this attack, the charged atmosphere was palpable.[138]

The diversity of Jewish responses to campus politics and the Israeli-Palestinian conflict is evident in these events. Indeed, university political culture cannot be understood as a dichotomous split between Jewish and Muslim "sides." While Jewish students often supported Israel, many supported the Palestinians, and neither "side" was united. Thus not only were Jewish leftists among those pitted *against* the FEJ, but also various organizations, including the UEJF, condemned FEJ violence.[139] Similarly, Mischmar—representing the Zionist left—denounced the aggression of both the pro-Palestinian movement and ultra-nationalist Jews.[140] In contrast, the student chapter of the Alliance France–Israël blamed events on "the anti-Semitic psychosis created at the heart of the university."[141] More moderately, the Comité d'entente de la jeunesse juive asked supporters of Israel's struggle for peace "to organize to defend their ideas and their right to speak in French universities."[142] As such rhetoric suggests, late 1960s campus life created and challenged alliances that ran counter to ethnic claims of solidarity. In a telling example, in March 1970, the UEJF complained that to counter Jewish student support for Palestinians on several campuses, the UEJF had established pro-Israel stands only to be thwarted by Jewish elements on the far right who had destroyed their propaganda![143] Jewish students clearly did not all stand on one "side" of the Israel issue nor did they agree on tactics.

A similar diversity was evident in the CRIF's responses to events at Censier. Whereas some sought to distance their organization from "a group of 'fascist' Jews that clashed with Palestinians," others countered that Jewish students had been "ambushed" in the anti-Israel campus environment. According to one, in a university steeped in pro-Fatah propaganda, "Jewish students are molested, terrorized and unable to express themselves. . . . That Jewish students wanted to react for once is essentially normal." Agreeing, another delegate remarked, "If Jews defended themselves, were they wrong?" Worried about taking sides in a divisive matter, CRIF delegates decided that the president, in his own name, should condemn all violence regardless of the source. Even this relatively bland option, however, was soon discarded.[144]

Notwithstanding the CRIF's indecisive response, the debate over Censier reveals the emerging focus on campuses as dangerous for Jews. As *L'Arche* reported, "It is certain that most young Jews are subjected to permanent aggression, sometimes surpassing the purely verbal."[145] For some CRIF representatives, the environment showcased a distinct new danger in French political culture. As one commented, "We are threatened by an anti-Semitic campaign coming from diverse Arab milieus. We must create defense committees ready to respond rapidly."[146] Such comments reflected the dramatic change in both Muslim political activism and Jewish communal perceptions since 1967, at which time "Arabs" had been a distant threat for French Jews worrying about Israel's future; by 1969, the threat had come home.

Significantly, however, CRIF officials did not collapse France's Muslim immigrant population into this equation. As one delegate noted after the second Belleville riot, "North African workers in Paris do not support the Palestinians; El Fatah's outreach has failed to touch them." Rather, they feared that anti-semitism in the guise of anti-Zionism was infecting French campuses and that their *own* co-religionists were helping to *create* tensions: "[I]f young Jews allow themselves to be provoked, Arab elements could change their attitude and there will be, alas, a confrontation. We must warn young Jews of this danger."[147] As such comments suggest, at least some CRIF officials worried that growing radicalism around the Palestinian issue would infect intercommunal relations and that Jewish radicalism could prove as dangerous to social relations as its Arab/Palestinian counterpart.

CRIF caution, however, could not stem the dramatic gestures of young radicals. In April 1971, for example, during a reception celebrating Syrian independence, a Jewish militant protested the oppression of Syrian Jews by releasing twenty mice and frogs among the three hundred attending dignitaries. An accompanying pamphlet sought to reclaim leftist politics for the Zionist movement: "Arab comrades . . . Do not allow your leaders to tarnish the name of Socialism; Do not allow them to make you believe that your enemy is the pacific Jewish people and their liberation movement, Zionism. Do not let them divert you from anti-capitalist and anti-imperialist struggles. Down with reactionary Arab leaders; For the immediate cessation of anti-Jewish persecutions. Long live the Socialist revolution in the Middle East!" Such efforts to unify Muslims and Jews around a reclaimed leftism gained little traction in the heated environment. Shortly thereafter, Louis Terrenoire, president of the Association de solidarité Franco-Arabe, the organization that had convened the celebration, received an anonymous death threat.[148] Angry Syrian students called for revenge at an upcoming pro-Israel rally. Conflict was forestalled only due to the UGEP's plea that sympathizers avoid giving their opponents more fodder. ADAE officials similarly instructed Algerians to avoid conflict while recommending that those living near large Jewish populations travel in groups and be prepared to respond to provocation. Such warnings show the degree to which passions had mounted, an observation that police informants and sporadic violence confirmed.[149] In January 1972, for example, ten Jewish teenagers burst into a pro-Palestinian event organized by the Comité d'action contre la guerre mondiale wounding a forty-year-old Algerian Muslim man in the ensuing skirmish.[150] That June, other young activists threatened the Syrian ambassador with the execution of three hundred diplomatic employees and their families if Jews remained trapped in his country.[151]

If such threats never materialized, the environment remained tense, particularly after the September 1972 Palestinian commando attack against Israeli athletes at the Munich Olympics. While a handful of far-left organizations defended the action on the grounds that Israelis were the "real terrorists," images of Jews murdered in Germany were widely condemned in France.[152] Unsurprisingly, Jewish organizations of all stripes denounced the violence.[153] The FEJ, however, launched a counterthreat, declaring it would "take the necessary steps" to ensure communal security.[154] Shortly thereafter, the organization began photographing visitors to the Syrian embassy.[155] After German officials freed three Palestinians who had participated in the killings, the UGEP complained of threats and called on adherents "to prevent themselves from being drawn into a conflict with no relevance on the European scene."[156]

By 1972, however, the Middle Eastern conflict *had* come to Europe, largely in the form of several dramatic Palestinian and Israeli commando attacks. In France, these included explosions at the Librairie Palestine and Hamchari's apartment, the murder of a Syrian journalist, a letter bomb to the former director of the UGEP, the violent disruption of the Conférence des jeunes d'Europe et des pays arabes, threatening letters to several North African and Middle Eastern dignitaries, and fourteen attacks from September through December against Jewish targets, including an explosion at the main synagogue in Marseille.[157]

Local Jewish and Muslim leaders understood the violence to come from outside France.[158] Thanks to years of radical politics around the Israeli-Palestinian struggle, however, distinctions between the "here" and the "there" were breaking down. In early 1973, for example, *L'Arche* speculated whether anger over Hamchari's murder and an impending visit of Israeli Prime Minister Golda Meir would instigate new anti-Zionist campaigns among leftists seeking to recruit North African Muslim immigrants.[159] The explosion of a bomb outside the Jewish Agency the night before Meir's arrival only added to a growing "psychosis" in the Jewish community.[160] Likewise, Jewish and Muslim spokesmen were increasingly blurring the lines between Israeli/Zionist/Jew and Muslim/Palestinian/Arab/North African when referring to one another. The magazine *L'Arche* thus defined the bomb at the Jewish Agency as an act of "Arab terrorism," marking all "Arabs" (the common term in the 1970s for Muslims from the

Middle East and North Africa) as potential aggressors.[161] At a UGEP rally after the Hamchari attack, one speaker denounced the intermingling of Jews in pro-Arab organizations, a particularly caustic remark given that Alain Geismar was one of the speakers. Others criticized the reception Zionists received within public agencies and their participation in police actions against Muslims.[162] The *Algérien en Europe* meanwhile, while rarely referring to Jews qua Jews and indeed often making positive mention of anti-Zionist Jews, blamed French Zionists for bolstering "anti-Arab hysteria" after the Munich affair and of creating a climate of insecurity around Muslims.[163] Such depictions angered French Jews, who, in turn, labeled the pro-Palestinian faction racist.[164]

By early 1973, then, well before the Arab-Israeli war that October, the Middle East conflict was being felt in France in ways unimaginable in 1967.[165] In February, when ten FEJ members attacked the offices of Iraqi and Syrian Arab Airways, throwing a bucket of animal blood and tracts demanding liberty for Jews at the frightened staff, they once again embodied this process. "We will not permit new imitators of Hitler to indulge in their murderous barbarism," read tracts agitators glued to the windows.[166] As we have seen, such linking of the Holocaust to the oppression of Jews in Arab lands echoed developments in Jewish politics from 1948 forward, intensifying in 1967. By 1973, however, radical youth culture in France provided space for a more confrontational politics. While marginal to the Jewish establishment, their mirroring in the Maoist-influenced North African student population created new divisions around the Israeli-Palestinian question.

Nowhere was this more evident than in Marseille, where the postcolonial tensions traced previously became entangled with the new politics around Israel in 1973. That August, a violent racist campaign broke out following the stabbing of a French tramcar driver, Emile Gerlache, by an unstable Algerian Muslim immigrant. Then, on 6 October, Israel went to war against a coalition of Arab states. In Marseille, these issues quickly became fused, as a more radicalized Muslim population drew parallels between the Palestinian situation and their own marginalization. While Jewish and Muslim leaders sought to avoid confrontations, the Israeli/Palestinian conflict began playing a bigger role in shaping dynamics between the two populations.

The Gerlache incident coincided with a period of recession and unemployment that undermined Marseille's already fragile economy and stoked xenophobic resentment.[167] "We have had enough," proclaimed a much-cited editorial in the right-wing newspaper *Le Méridional* after the murder. "Enough of Algerian thieves, enough of Algerian thugs, enough of Algerian troublemakers, enough of Algerian syphilitics, enough of Algerian rapists, enough of Algerian drug dealers, enough of Algerian crazies, enough of Algerian murderers."[168] Five thousand outraged demonstrators attended Gerlache's funeral, and right-wing extremists attacked immigrant shantytowns with rifle fire, killing eight North African Muslims over the next several weeks.[169]

Fearing for their lives, Muslim immigrants stayed inside when they could. The assassination on 28 August of Lounès Ladj by passing gunmen, however, launched a collective rebellion. Two thousand mourners attended the procession carrying his body to the port on 1 September. Two days later, an MTA call for a twenty-four-hour strike to protest racism brought out thousands more.[170] New organizations, such as the Comité des travailleurs algériens, were formed to take on the problems plaguing immigrant life.[171] A massive anti-racism rally on 7 September drew another two thousand to Marseille's streets, and on 14 September, the MTA sponsored the largest nationwide strike by North African Muslim workers to date.[172] Six days later, Algeria suspended migration to France.

Interestingly, neither the mounting racism nor the MTA's anti-racist campaign attracted much attention from France's established Jewish community. L'Arche never mentioned events in Marseille, and the CRIF's public statement notably distanced French Jews from the North African Muslim immigrant population: "Having experienced throughout its history the terrible effects of racism and hatred of the stranger, French Judaism recalls the fundamental biblical principles: 'Thou shall love thy neighbor as thyself and thou shall love the stranger.'"[173] This generic call for brotherhood, simultaneously underscoring the victim's foreignness and drawing no parallels to antisemitism, is particularly notable, since, by the 1980s, the joint struggle against racism served as one of the few bridges between two populations that had begun to see each other as adversaries. In 1973, however, these bridges had not yet been built. Insofar as French Jews took note of the Muslims around them, they focused on anti-Zionism or antisemitic tracts in Arabic.[174] As the president of the French chapter of Keren Kayemet LeIsrael insisted at a CRIF meeting in October while urging a boycott of Arab businesses in France, "You can no longer treat the people you have before you as those you must persuade but rather as those you must combat."[175] Such statements mark the distance that had been traveled since 1967 when French Jews saw "Arabs" as a threat to Israel and to Jews in the Middle East but paid scant attention to those around them.

It was in this charged environment that the October 1973 Arab-Israeli war broke out. As in 1967, France's organized Jewish community publicly defended Israel, raising even more money than had been true six years previously.[176] In Marseille, the Appel unifié juif de France collected nearly 2,500,000 francs, a million more than was raised for Jewish causes the previous year. On 8 October, two days after the outbreak of hostilities, five thousand paraded silently on the city's major thoroughfare, la Canebière, under the banner of the Comité de soutien à Israel. Mayor Defferre was once again in the lead, alongside elected officials from most municipalities and all the major Jewish organizations. As in 1967, only the Communist left remained silent.[177]

In 1973, however, Defferre's unadulterated support for the Jewish community—already an irritant six years previously—was all too evident to a politically energized Muslim population that felt marginalized by their city's surging racism. Already practiced at using the Palestinian issue to motivate the foreign workforce, local Muslim activists responded to events in the Middle East by organizing numerous demonstrations around both issues.[178] The municipality, however, refused them equal access to city streets. During the pro-Israel rally on 8 October, for example, police established a barrier around the immigrant quarter in Belsunce (which abutted the thoroughfare on which Jews were marching). Even though police had registered "no effervescence" in immigrant neighborhoods in response to pro-Israel demonstrations, local law enforcement sought to contain Muslim activism.[179] MTA representatives complained over this biased access to city space, particulary after authorities refused them the same thoroughfare for a pro-Palestinian demonstration on 13 October, instead restricting participants to the area around the Porte d'Aix.[180]

As in other cases of Muslim-Jewish conflict in France, the October 1973 tensions were largely confined to highly politicized groups. While police reported that the MTA's pro-Palestinian rhetoric was finding "a certain echo in the immigrant community,"[181] others pointed to the city's calm interethnic landscape. According to one article, Marseille's Muslim quarters "did not appear to have a different physiognomy than other days." The shared neighborhoods around rue d'Aix "where the jewelers, notably of Jewish origin, are numerous or in the neighboring souks on the rue Sainte Barbe," showed no perceptible change, "other than a few transistor radios stuck to the ears and tuned in to Radio-Alger."[182] The MTA carefully avoided turning attacks against Israel into broad denunciations of Jews, while Jewish leaders encouraged young activists to refrain from provocations.[183] Although Jewish youth handed out tracts, demonstrated, and recruited volunteers for Israel, they followed communal directives to avoid racist and anti-Muslim overtones.[184]

Activists nevertheless continued to make the Middle East a visible part of Marseille's ethno-religious landscape in 1973 and thereafter. In late October 1974, when the French foreign minister met with Yasser Arafat in Lebanon, French Jews were distraught.[185] In Marseille, Jewish organizations declared themselves "ready to do all in their power" to prevent the opening of a promised PLO liaison office in Paris.[186] Muslim activists were likewise highly mobilized to defend Palestinian interests, and on 7 November, both groups manifested their politics on city streets. Three hundred and fifty members of diverse Jewish organizations thus processed down la Canebière shouting, "Arafat assassin; Giscard accomplice,"[187] while the Comité Palestine held a counterdemonstration for North African Muslim laborers.[188] Although the small numbers indicate that Marseille's Muslim and Jewish populations had little interest in the Middle East, spotty evidence suggests tensions had deepened. On 5 November, for example, the vice president of Marseille's Consistoire complained to the prefect over France's rapprochement with the PLO, pointing to "a notable degradation in relations between Muslim immigrants and their Jewish employers" and warning that "clashes" could follow.[189]

While a single source does not provide enough evidence on which to base significant conclusions, it points to the way Marseille's ethno-political landscape had begun to fuse divisions over the Israeli-Palestinian issue with the already embedded postcolonial divisions that had shaped city life since the 1950s. As incoming Jews solidified and often bettered their economic position, Muslim immigrants became trapped in a cycle of poverty. These distinctions took on new political meaning by the early 1970s as the city that had embraced its Jewish residents and their pro-Israel agenda seemingly rejected its Muslim residents, many of whom had begun to see parallels between their own struggles and those of the Palestinians.

Conclusion

In 1975, renowned author Romain Gary published the prize-winning novel, *La Vie devant soi* under the pseudonym Émile Ajar. The novel, soon made into a movie starring Simone Signoret, depicts the relationship between an orphaned Muslim boy, Momo, and a dying Holocaust survivor and former prostitute, Madame Rosa, who runs a boardinghouse for the children of sex workers. Set in Belleville, the story unfolds in the multiethnic neighborhood so recently marked by violence. In Gary's Belleville, however, shared adversity unites those of diverse backgrounds. A former Senegalese boxing champion now working as a transvestite prostitute, a Jewish doctor, an aging Algerian Muslim carpet salesman, a Cameroonian fire-eater, and a Catholic French neighbor are among the many downtrodden who console or help Madame Rosa and Momo throughout the story.

At the novel's climax, when Momo's father, Youssef Kadir, unexpectedly arrives to claim his son, Madame Rosa offers him a Jewish boy instead, claiming the two had been unintentionally swapped. To Kadir, the shock is deadly. As his desperation mounts, he explodes, "I gave you an Arab son in due and proper form and I expect you to give me back an Arab son. I absolutely don't want a Jewish son, Madame. . . . I have nothing against the Jews, Madame, God forgive them. But I'm an Arab, a good Moslem, and I had a son of the same faith. Mohammed, Arab, Muslim. I entrusted him to you in good condition, and I expect you to give him back in the same condition." Madame Rosa's retort captures the novel's central thematic: "Oh well, he was an Arab, now he's slightly Jewish, but he's still your boy," and later, "Arab and Jew are all the same to us here."[190] When Madame Rosa finally dies, Momo hides her corpse, claiming to have sent her to live in Israel. Her Jewish doctor responds in amazement, "It's the first time an Arab has ever sent a Jew to Israel."[191]

Gary's heartwarming if macabre portrayal of the bond between the Jewish woman and the Muslim boy celebrates the humanity linking diverse peoples and, in many ways, serves as a call for such ends. Yet the novel also provides ample evidence of the tensions that had marked France's interethnic terrain. Momo's father's insistence on the return of his Arab son and Dr. Katz's shock at Momo's support for Madame Rosa's departure to Israel serve as crucial reminders of this history as do Momo's numerous references to Jewish and Arab terrorists, Algerian self-determination struggles, and Jewish experiences under the Nazis. While Momo and Madame Rosa transcend this history, their very insistence that "all men were equal when steeped in misery and shit, and if the Jews and Arabs clobber each other it's because whatever you may say to the contrary the Jews and the Arabs are no different from anybody else," reminds us that by 1975, few saw it that way.[192]

To read Gary in this way is to acknowledge how profoundly French public consciousness had come to see Muslim-Jewish divisions as the norm by the 1970s. If traditional chronologies have emphasized the Arab-Israeli wars of 1967 and 1973 as touchstone moments in this increasing ethnic polarization, they have overlooked the way political culture at the local and national level helped shape the ethnic landscape. On the one hand, the unpredictable alliance between radical leftists—many of them Jewish—Muslim students, and Palestinian representatives, bridged core ideological disagreements to bring the Palestinian plight to French public attention and to link the issue to immigrant politics. On the other hand, late 1960s radicalism pushed France's Jewish population—and particularly its high school and university students—away from traditional affiliations on the left and toward a more combative politics. The combustible result was a confrontational communal politics that linked Jews with Israel and North African Muslims with Palestinians in increasingly rigid ways.

The immediate impact of these events was limited. Most Jews and Muslims never came into direct conflict. Belleville's residents, for the most part, laid low during the riots. Membership in radical Jewish and Muslim student organizations was small. North African immigrants—if increasingly sympathetic to Palestinians—saw their own struggles as more pressing. Jewish and Muslim leaders urged moderation to ensure collective safety and prosperity. Moreover, the Jewish leadership continued to see the Muslim immigrant population as distinct from their spokesmen, asserting as late as 1976 that Fatah's impact on the immigrant milieu was limited.[193]

The radical energies of the late 1960s also soon dissipated due to the French government's ban of the Gauche prolétarienne in 1970 and the Ligue Communiste in 1973, the economic crisis that year, disagreements among different leftist currents, and the failures of various internationalist efforts. The MTA lost steam in response to opposition from the ADAE and other North African immigrant associations and the Ministry of the Interior, which imprisoned or expelled the organization's most active militants.[194] While it continued to pursue the Palestinian issue throughout its existence, by 1976 the MTA had dissolved.[195] Jewish gauchistes likewise began backing away from their most radical positions regarding Israel during the 1973 war, frustrated with the emotional and intellectual contradictions in their politics.[196] Jewish student reactionaries, always a small group, continued their activities but remained marginal to wider communal life.[197]

The brief life-span of these developments, however, does not diminish their decisive impact on Muslim-Jewish relations. First, as Gary's novel makes clear, the period's radicalism brought the story of Muslim-Jewish polarization into France's national conversation. While earlier developments had introduced a discourse of polarization in particular circles, 1968 and its aftermath made that story mainstream. Second, if the fusion between gauchisme, immigrant politicization, and Jewish radicalism was brief, the decade's themes were enduring. Ethnic tensions around the Middle East were henceforth presumed. Third, by the mid-1970s, Muslims and Jews had begun to see each other as competitors in the French public square. In the words of one Jewish commentator, "[O]ur only weapon is public opinion in this country where we number hardly 1% (less numerous than the Arabs, who do not have the right to vote, but ballots, alas, count for little, and they can strike, which we cannot)."[198] Although these remarks underscored the Jews' insider position as "citizens" against Arab foreignness, it portrayed them as pitted against each other in the court of public opinion. By the 1980s, as a new generation of French-born Muslim citizens came of age, such distinctions were increasingly meaningless. Yet as a new generation of Muslim activists strove to assert their place in the polity, equal access to all the benefits of French citizenship became a new domain of Muslim-Jewish contestation.

Particularism versus Pluriculturalism

The Birth and Death of the Anti-Racist Coalition

This chapter traces the rise and fall of a Muslim-Jewish alliance to fight racism in 1980s France. Two political shifts early in the decade allowed the joint anti-racist campaign to emerge. First was the coming of age of a new generation of French-born Muslim activists who began, often in religious or ethnic terms, to articulate a politics of resistance to their political and social exclusion. Reaching out to the isolated, economically excluded, and socially contained youth of the French *banlieue*, the so-called Beur Movement created momentum around a new identity politics.[1] The second development evolved from experiments in multiculturalism that followed François Mitterrand's victory in the 1981 presidential election on a platform that included calls for greater immigrant rights and decentralization. For the first time, the French political establishment recognized in law the nation's cultural and linguistic diversity, a shift that led to new forms of ethno-religious organization. For young Muslim and Jewish activists who took advantage of this legal recognition of difference, the public square was now open to unprecedented expressions of communal politics.

This shift in French political culture created two overlapping but ultimately competing approaches to ethno-religious participation in the French state, both with implications for Muslim-Jewish relations. The first was a particularistic vision that encouraged intergroup solidarity as a way of fighting for the individual community's needs. Evident in the Beur Movement's anti-racist demonstrations and in increasing Jewish political mobilization, the early 1980s saw a heightened focus on the specific needs of particular communities as distinct from the national collective. In the case of Muslim-Jewish relations, such identity politics could split, as representatives of both articulated priorities that at times placed them on opposite sides of domestic, or more often, international policy debates.

Yet if "particularistism" created opportunities for ethnic polarization, a second response to the legitimization of France's diverse landscape was a new "pluricultural" model of ethno-religious cooperation. The term "pluricultural"—as opposed to the more commonly deployed, "multicultural"—refers specifically to bridging differences in order to create a democratic and just public sphere. Most evident in the anti-racist movement that surged in the middle of the decade, "pluriculturalists" argued that whatever differences marked French citizens, they could work together to create a tolerant and just society. Driven by widespread media attention, the socialist machine, and the electoral growth of the far-right party, the Front nationale (FN), several organizations, including the newly established SOS racisme and the UEJF, worked together to ensure equal rights for all.[2] One highly celebrated aspect of this campaign was the effort to unite Muslim and Jewish citizens in a common struggle. Epitomized by SOS racisme's slogan, "We cannot solve the Israel-Palestinian problem on the banks of the Seine," activists sought to contain differences by stressing similar struggles.

These two approaches to ethno-politics, "particularist" and "pluricultural," both broke with French assimilatory traditions that subsumed ethnic and religious differences in the wider national culture, and in this sense shared a basic commitment to Mitterrand's "right to be different" policies. Such policies, however, never fully broke with republican assimilationist traditions or fully embraced a politics of multiculturalism, a reality that became starkly clear by decade's end when growing support for the FN led officials across the political spectrum to return to more conservative policies toward religious and cultural difference. "Integration" rather than the "right to be different" again became the watchword of the day, as officials and media outlets focused on Beur criminality, the "threat" of Islam, and "Arab" fanatacism as threats to civic life.[3] This mounting conservatism, while mostly directed at France's Muslim population, affected all religious minorities, particularly in 1989 when three girls were expelled from school for wearing the Islamic head scarf, launching a heated debate on religion in the public sphere.[4] While some Jewish figures defended particulalrism in the schools, others backed away from public connection to Muslims, asserting the fusion of Jewishness and Frenchness in contradistinction to Muslim foreignness.[5] Meanwhile, Muslim activists who had seen value in underscoring a common anti-racist agenda began reasserting the particularist nature of their own struggles. By decade's end, pluricultural cooperation had collapsed.

This chapter will argue that widespread excitement over the joint anti-racist campaign in the mid-1980s overlooked ongoing tensions between "particularistic" and "pluricultural" approaches to ethno-religious participation in the French state. Divisions over the Palestinian-Israeli conflict both prior to and during the 1991 Gulf War made these tensions evident as, once again, debates over the Middle East became a means of making sense of politics at home. Although calls for joint anti-racist campaigns never disappeared, by the end of the 1980s, those who articulated such appeals had backed away from a "pluricultural" model. While Muslims and Jews should work together, they argued, their perspectives and goals were necessarily divergent.

Identity Politics in the Early 1980s

Nineteen-eighties France saw an unprecedented rise of identity politics in a nation that had long subsumed cultural, linguistic, and religious diversity in the wider national project. Giving voice to many who had previously been excluded—particularly the so-called Beur generation— this shift provided opportunities for Muslims *and* Jews to articulate "unabashedly public forms of . . . political and religious engagement," an activism that encouraged communal representatives to debate domestic and international issues from the perspective of their "group."[6] Yet the establishment of a multicultural France also provided opportunities for joint endeavors. The spike in antisemitism and Islamophobia early in the decade provided one arena in which the tensions between "particularism" and "pluriculturalism" played out, raising questions over what linked different forms of exclusion. While early 1980s identity politics stressed their unique characteristics, a counterdiscourse emphasized commonalities.[7]

Racism against Muslims began surging in the mid-1970s after the 1973 oil crisis and the U.S. decision to untie the dollar from gold created stresses on the French economy.[8] By 1974, unemployment was widespread. Although France's immigrant populations were hit hardest—introducing a cycle of poverty that was often pushed onto their children—anger at decreasing opportunities and fear for the nation's prosperity led to a rise in xenophobic attacks and a tightening of national immigration policies beginning with the *circulaire Fontanet* in 1972, limiting immigrant mobility, and culminating with the 1974 decision to close national borders to new immigrants (although family reunification policies still allowed newcomers to migrate to France).[9] With attention deflected from new immigrants, however, public interest soon shifted to the residentially, culturally, and politically isolated "second generation," particularly as the latter began expressing their frustrations in clashes with local police. Most notably, the Lyons "rodeos" in July and August 1981—during which 250 cars were burned, seven policemen wounded, and over twenty young Muslims arrested— received widespread media coverage. In these portrayals, North African (read "foreign") "delinquents" were seen as pitted against the forces of order. After the Iranian Revolution, fears of spreading Islamic fundamentalism exacerbated such concerns, as media outlets speculated whether aimless banlieu youth would join global jihad movements.[10] Over these years, then, fears that immigrants were taking jobs evolved into broader concerns that "Muslims" were failing to integrate into the nation or even threatening it with violence.

The spectacular rise of the FN, the far-right nationalist party founded in 1972 by Jean-Marie Le Pen, emerged in response to these developments, obtaining its first victories in the muncipal elections of spring 1983.[11] The June 1984 European elections, which brought Le Pen's group 11 percent of the vote, increased the party's visibility. FN candidates then won 9 percent and 10 percent during cantonal, legislative, and regional elections in 1985 and 1986. While the party's appeal was not limited to its xenophobia, Le Pen and his followers adopted the defense of French national identity as a central motif, arguing that non-European immigration endangered the nation's Christian values and its national community.[12] Although this rhetoric positioned Le Pen against both Jewish and Islamic minorities, the FN's longer trajectory indicated a move away from earlier antisemitic outbursts toward an increasing focus on Muslims as its primary target.[13]

Racism surged in this environment. From 1980 until 1994, 26 Muslims were killed and another 351 injured in racist incidents, while anti-Muslim tracts and graffiti increased significantly.[14] Antisemitic grafitti and violence increased as well, suggesting a wider anti-minority animosity, as several synagogues and cemeteries were desecrated and as bombs targeted the chief rabbi's home, a kosher cafeteria, and the rue Copernic synagogue.[15]

The spike in violence raised new questions about the place of ethno-religious minorities in France. For some, what seemed most striking was their shared marginalization. Already in the mid-1970s, groups that had long taken note of shared aspects of racism—such as the pre–World War II organizations established to fight antisemitism, the Mouvement contre le racisme, l'antisémitisme et pour la paix (MRAP), the Ligue international contre le racisme et l'antisémitisme (LICA), and the Ligue des droits de l'homme—placed a new focus on these commonalities.[16] As one Jewish representative in Marseille noted in the mid-1970s, "[W]hen we see anti-Arab campaigns developing, we must condemn them for we know that racism is never directed against only one minority. . . . Anti-Arab racism can very easily be transformed into anti-Jewish racism."[17] In February 1978, the magazine L'Arche published a screed against contemporary racism that drew direct links with prewar antisemitism.[18] That December, Roger Ascot also warned that anti-Arabism was only one step removed from antisemitism.[19] Most notably, in 1979 the CRIF condemned the murder of two African workers following a series of synagogue fires and Jewish cemetery desecrations by declaring itself "in solidarity with all immigrant workers no matter their origin."[20] By placing synagogue desecrations in the same context as xenophobia, the CRIF went a long way to bridging the distance that had appeared in its earlier anti-racist proclamations. Some French Muslims also drew parallels between the way Jews and Muslims had been targeted in French society. As Houria, an Algerian-born resident from Lyons explained, "we are the Jews of immigration, and I'm afraid yes, afraid that some day the French will do to us what they did to the Jews during the last war."[21]

In the late 1970s, however, there was little infrastructure to promote Muslim-Jewish cooperation around fighting racism or much else. New organizations, such as Identité et Dialogue, founded in 1976 by André Azoulay, a Moroccan-born Jewish newspaper editor and public relations professional, emphasized cultural connections between Muslims and Jews.[22] Seeking to unite North African migrants regardless of their religious beliefs, Azoulay and fellow travelers hoped to highlight a common heritage "at a moment when political discourse is infective."[23] Such efforts remained marginal, however, with identity politics on the ascendancy.

Indeed, despite a flurry of interest in the commonalities among all forms of racism, by 1980 both Jewish and Muslim activists were most interested in their own struggles. Among Jews, the rise in antisemitic attacks raised the specter of their own dark history in Europe.[24] Articles in the Jewish press focused heavily on foreign terrorists (Palestinians or Arabs) and neo-Nazis, thereby highlighting the particularity of anti-Jewish aggression and even portraying Arabs as perpetrators rather than as fellow victims of violence.[25] Even those calling for joint anti-racist activism tended to emphasize differences. In 1980, for example, Jacquot Grunewald urged readers of *Tribune juive* to fight anti-Arab racism as follows:

> I know that most immigrant workers . . . are Arab citizens from North Africa; they support the Arab *ummah* and have a perspective on Israel that is intolerable from our perspective. But, would it not be possible, with men, women, and children who suffer from so many difficulties, for us, the Jews of France, who identify with the Jews of Israel, to open a dialogue that is artificially forbidden by the leaders of the Arab world?[26]

Moreover, while the CRIF continued to express "solidarity and sympathy" with victims of racism, its appeals called on Jewish citizens to aid immigrant foreigners and hence downplayed similarities between French-born Muslims and Jews.[27] CRIF officials were also quick to note that racism had crystallized around "Arabs" while far smaller numbers expressed dislike for Jews.[28] Countering such formulations, the philosopher and political sociologist Shmuel Trigano warned Jews not to believe that anti-Muslim racism could shield them from what was, in fact, indirect racism toward Jews. Hardly calling for a joint anti-racist struggle, however, Trigano warned that "in the worsening crisis, the Arabs are more powerful than the Jews" as a way to push the latter to mobilize on their own.[29]

The emerging Muslim anti-racist movement was also inwardly directed.[30] Originating from the "Beur generation," anti-racism came in two forms that both underscored the distinctive exclusion facing Muslims.[31] The first were peaceful demonstrations that called for greater inclusion in French society, most famously the October–November 1983 Marche pour l'égalité et contre le racisme (and two follow-up marches in 1984 and 1985). Second were retributive protests aimed at police and symbols of economic exclusion, including approximately 250 "rodeos" such as those described above.

Articulated in the context of Mitterrand's presidential victory, the Beur Movement helped usher in recognition of a multicultural French public sphere. Having campaigned on the right to be different (*droit à la différence*) as a fundamental human right, Mitterrand quickly implemented policies that supported minority cultural development and linguistic diversity, such as the option of teaching local languages in public schools. This opening of the public space to a broader range of cultural practices had an impact on all ethnic and religious minorities. For example, in summer 1981, when Mitterrand overturned the 1938 legislation prohibiting immigrant associations and increased funding for local rehabilitation programs and education reform, hundreds of "second-generation" cultural, political, and social associations emerged.

This context also created space for unprecedented Jewish organizational and political development.[32] The Jewish response to the October 1980 bombing of the rue Copernic synagogue illustrated well the shift, as large numbers of Jews poured into the streets to protest. While the 1960s and 1970s had seen large pro-Israel demonstrations, the fight against antisemitism had been largely an institutional affair.[33] In addition, changes in laws on state funding of private schools sent increasing numbers of Jewish students to these institutions, while the 1980s embrace of multicultural politics saw efforts to channel a Jewish vote in a nation where special-interest lobbies and ethnic political organization had been an anathema.[34]

The 1982 Israeli invasion of Lebanon, which like prior Middle Eastern wars exacerbated political divisions between France's Muslim and Jewish populations, took place in this context of heightened identity politics. While French Jews were uncharacteristically divided over Israeli actions, support for Palestinians increased substantially among Beur activists,[35] and anti-war rallies saw some donning keffiahs and crying, "Jewish assassins," particularly after the Sabra and Shatila massacre, when Israeli soldiers were accused of enabling Christian Phalangist militia massacres of two Palestinian refugee camps.[36] As one Algerian-born Muslim commented when dismissing her connection to her home country, "I feel much more involved over the Palestinian problem."[37] Following earlier patterns, Algerian, Moroccan, and Tunisian organizations worked with the Comité Palestine de France to organize protests, fund-raise, and collect medical supplies.[38] In Strasbourg, for example, the Union nationale des étudiants marocains raised 35,000 francs from the city's North African, Iranian, and Turkish populations as well as from those on the far left.[39]

This visible pro-Palestinian sentiment among Muslim youth frightened Jewish residents who accused demonstrators of chanting "death to Jews" at pro-Palestinian rallies.[40] Indeed, if in the early 1970s, Jewish communal leaders feared that Muslims *might* turn against their Jewish neighbors, in 1982, various Jewish representatives asserted that this eventuality had come to pass, and some Jewish communities even organized internal security measures to protect against retributive attacks.[41] According to one Tunisian Jewish communist working in Marseille's banlieues, antisemitism among Beurs was commonly expressed: "[T]he *yids* [*youpins*] have the power and the money. It's the Jews who are in charge, dirty *yids*."[42] In a moment of high scandal, the left-leaning *Libération* published a letter to the editor by a J. P. Kapel threatening vengeance against all Jews for Middle East bloodshed: "The Arabs of France and our friends will not stand with arms crossed. The blood of martyrs calls for vengeance. There will be no quarter. To us Belleville and Sentier, to us Montmartre and Saint-Paul and even Sarcelles."[43] Le Monde's report on a letter denying the Holocaust in the Moroccan newspaper, L'Opinion (organ of Istiqlal), added to fears that Muslim antisemitism was coming closer to home.[44]

For young Muslims (identified with Palestinians as symbols of their own struggle) and young Jews (trying to balance support for Israel with a growing criticism of Israel at home) the Lebanese invasion had local meaning. As one Beur told Le Matin the next winter, linking murders of French Muslim youth to the Palestinian plight: "We are going through a quiet Sabra and [S]hatila."[45] Such formulations left little room for cross-ethnic cooperation, particularly when many Jews were feeling singled out. In the words of one French Jewish youth, "Someone or something always reminds you that you're Jewish, a spit in the face that in the world's eyes you are a dirty Jew. . . . And you do nothing primarily because you are alone."[46] This construction of Jewish isolation in the face of mounting hostility underscored concerns—bolstered during the 1982 invasion of Lebanon—that Muslim immigrants were themselves antisemitic.[47] However, the new identity politics also created opportunities for cooperation. Three responses in L'Arche to the first Marche pour l'égalité point to these contradictions. Highly critical of various aspects of the march, Annie Kriegel expressed dismay that Beur activists wore kaffiyehs in solidarity with Palestinians.[48] An editorial in the same edition titled, "Pluricultural France?" stressed the difficulties of peaceful cohabitation within a diverse nation while nevertheless calling for respect for all.[49] Seven months later, an article titled, "We are all Maghrebins" underscored the dangers Jean-Marie Le Pen posed for all minorities.[50] Such constructions became the basis of SOS racisme's pluricultural anti-racist agenda, which both built on and challenged the particularistic focus of the previous few years.

SOS Racisme and the Invention of Pluriculturalism

SOS racisme was born in fall 1984 to celebrate and defend interethnic France. The Socialist party, eager to capitalize on the energy of the Beur Movement, encouraged the creation of associations that would connect with its own bodies and attract potential voters. Under its tutelage, former Trotskyist activists Julien Dray, Didier François, and Harlem Désir created SOS racisme to extend "second-generation" youth politics to a wider public around the notion of an all-embracing and enlightened France.[51] Like all anti-racist groups, SOS racisme denounced racist crimes and called for open policies toward immigrants and their children, but it did so by distancing itself from the Beur Movement by embracing a multicultural perspective. According to one of its organizers, "it was necessary for the anti-racist movement not to be linked directly to any one community, which had been the Beur movement's weakness."[52] Known best for its hand-shaped yellow badge that read *"Touche pas à mon pote"* (Hands off my friend), SOS racisme was quickly a media sensation. Selling 1.5 million badges in 1985 alone, the term "pote" symbolized a new figure that was neither entirely French nor foreign. Désir, the offspring of an Antillesian father and an Alsatian mother, seemed emblematic of this emerging multiracial society. Engaging in highly symbolic actions, SOS racisme invested its energies in huge concerts, poster campaigns, and television appearances, seeking to win adherents among celebrities, intellectuals, and youth. With 500,000 attendees at the first concert on 15 June 1985 at the Place de la Concorde, SOS racisme surged on the energy of a generation of young voters attracted to multiculturalism and leftist politics.[53] As one of its more prominent supporters noted, "This is a youth movement, foreign to prior political cleavages and based on positive values."[54] Or as another supporter asserted, "SOS Racisme is radically different: it does not represent the desires of immigrants but of the majority of French citizens."[55]

Key, then, to SOS racisme's struggle was the assertion that a truly multicultural France could transcend ethno-religious divisions to constitute a united civil society. As evidence, the organizers pointed to the numerous Jews and Muslims who worked together in its activities. While Désir was president, and many "second-generation" Muslims helped run the organization, Dray—an Algerian Jew from Oran—was one of the its primary animators, and Eric Ghébali, president of the Union des étudiants juifs de France [UEJF], was its secretary general. Moreover, in February 1985, SOS racisme won the sponsorship of prominent Jewish intellectuals Bernard-Henri Lévy and Marek Halter, who created a news agency to disseminate information on its activities. Their appearance in a UEJF-sponsored anti-racist demonstration in Paris on the theme, " 'I am not a racist but . . . ' There is no 'but'!" provided SOS racisme with its initial media prominence.[56] Thus while Muslim-Jewish cooperation was only one aspect of the association's activities, interethnic alliance quickly became linked with its central mission.

In order to justify the alliance, supporters made a range of arguments that stressed profound similarities between Muslim and Jewish experiences in France. As one speaker at the UEJF event argued, "I protest against absurd assertions that say that two million unemployed are two million immigrants too many. That reminds me of another assertion that 600,000 Jews were 600,000 unemployed."[57] Eric Ghébali similarly pointed to the shared immigrant past: "Our history has taught us to be wary of hatred of the stranger, we who, as the Bible tells us, were strangers in Egypt, we who today are almost all children or grandchildren of immigrants."[58] In another interview, he went further, arguing that young Jews had to participate in a struggle that "affects all *basanes* [slang for dark-skinned people]."[59] Such racial linkages expressly connected the two minorities in contradistinction to white European society. For Marc Bitton, another leader of the student organization, Jewish participation in the anti-racist movement was justified by a shared commitment to French society—"each and everyone's business" and "NECESSARILY pluricommunal." Jewish participation would thus broaden anti-racist activities that had been driven by the Beur movement's particularistic concerns.[60]

The UEJF's visible connection to SOS racisme defined the student organization's identity for the next several years. Having entered a period of dormancy in the mid-1970s due to divisions between those favoring an aggressive pro-Israeli migration policy and those favoring stabilization of local structures, membership dropped from 15,000 to 1,500 by 1980.[61] The bombing at rue Copernic, coupled with a rise in Holocaust denial, early calls for multiculturalism, and the increasing youth-centered political culture, however, energized Jewish students—called *feujs* in the *verlan* of the day—as it had their Beur peers.[62] By 1982, two thousand students had joined its ranks, and by 1985, membership had risen to ten thousand.[63] Three years later, fifteen sections throughout Paris and the provinces had fifteen thousand members.[64]

Support for Israel remained central to the UEJF's agenda.[65] The pro-Zionist position, however, coexisted with a commitment to a vibrant Diaspora and a critical stance toward the French government.[66] The three hundred attendees at the 1980 national congress, for example, condemned France's reception of PLO representatives and called on all Jewish citizens "to express their disapproval of national policies by all democratic means" even at the risk of alienating Jewish communal bodies.[67] This readiness to criticize a range of domestic and international policies opened the door to the UEJF's participation in the anti-racist movement.

The primary force driving the UEJF's affiliation with SOS racisme was Eric Ghébali, its president from January 1983 until May 1986. Ghébali, a former member of the Strasbourg chapter and a student of economics in Paris, used the early years of his presidency to rebuild the UEJF's membership and strengthen its Zionism.[68] In his initial election, however, Ghébali also made "Judeo-Arab reconciliation" part of his agenda.[69] This interest in reaching across ethno-religious lines combined with a commitment to fighting antisemitism encouraged Ghébali—and the UEJF with him—to help build SOS racisme.

It was only in March 1985, however, that the UEJF/SOS racisme alliance took center stage. On 21 March, two men murdered a twenty-eight-year-old Moroccan immigrant in Menton explaining, "We don't like Arabs." The following Friday, a bomb exploded at a Parisian Jewish film festival wounding twenty-six, and the next day, eighteen-year-old Noureddine Daouadji was killed on the outskirts of Marseille. An SOS racisme demonstration on 6 April and another the next day in front of the bombed theater saw protesters cry, "Arabs in Menton, Jews in Paris, they are killing our friends [potes]." According to news reports this was "the first time representatives of Jewish movements and Arab immigrant organizations find themselves shoulder to shoulder." Désir was quick to underscore the importance of this development: "Usually when Jews and Arabs share common cause, it's in political corridors [*salons politiques*]. . . . This is the first time it's on the streets of Paris." While the minister of justice, Robert Badinter, blamed the theater bombing on international terrorism, SOS racisme and many of the reporters who covered its activities saw more local origins.[70] In the words of one Jewish representative from SOS racisme, "In terms of racist threats, we are second in line, just behind the Arabs."[71] Jacquot Gruenwald wrote in the *Tribune juive*, "[T]he development in France of an often murderous racism, even if it does not directly target the Jewish community, is intolerable. Racism cannot be divided. Jews who only yesterday were its privileged victims feel directly attacked."[72] Writing in *Le Monde*, Daniel Schneidermann asserted that the two murders and the bombing had "in the course of one weekend begun to weaken the substantial mental barriers between Arabs and Jews in France."[73] Still other reports focused on several Algerian Jews who "had rallied behind Arab immigrants."[74] Even Serge July's 1 April editorial in *Libération*, which argued that diminishing antisemitism could not be compared to the daily rejection of North African immigrants, celebrated new cooperative efforts, noting, "[F]or the first time Arab intellectuals in France also signed a petition denouncing the attack against the cinema Rivioli."[75]

As July's statement suggested, Muslim and Jewish intellectuals encouraged new cooperative endeavors. The writers Marek Halter and Tahar Ben Jelloun, for example, were interviewed together for *Libération* in a story subtitled "Arabs and Jews side by side." In the piece, Ben Jelloun underscored that "racism is not selective. One cannot be anti-Jewish and like Arabs or anti-Black and like Jews." For both, SOS racisme marked a new stage in interethnic exchange.[76]

This new cooperation was most evident in May when a group of prominent Muslim intellectuals publically criticized President Regan's visit to Bitburg, Germany, to lay a wreath at the graves of German soldiers, including forty-nine SS troops. Protesting the "insult to the memory of the victims," the signatories, which included the editorial team of the Beur newspaper, *Sans frontières*, activists such as Souad Bennani and Saliha Amara, the sociologist Adil Jazouli, members of the Association des Marocains en France, and writers Tahar Ben Jelloun and Leïla Sebbar, argued that victims of racism must unite.[77] SOS racisme similarly took part in a UEJF-sponsored protest at Bitburg. As SOS racisme's Dahmane Abderrahmane commented on the Beur presence, "We have put our political differences aside: the Middle East is one thing, the struggle against racism another. We came to demonstrate at the side of our Jewish friends. I hope they will do the same for us when it's necessary."[78]

As Abderrahmane hoped, such cooperative activities occurred several more times over the next few months. When Gorbachev went to Paris, for example, SOS racisme helped organize rallies on behalf of Soviet Jews, and Marek Halter used SOS racisme's banner to declare, "Hey Gorbachev, Soviet Jews are also our friends [*potes*]!"[79] In June 1985, two Muslim members of SOS racisme's governing board participated in a UEJF-sponsored trip to Majdanek and Auschwitz, and in October, the UEJF joined SOS racisme in commemorating Algerians killed in Paris in 1961.[80] Moreover, other groups embraced the new cooperative spirit. In June 1985 the École Central, for example, held a Jewish-Muslim cultural evening in which speakers addressed the need to fight racism together by first combating racism *between* them.[81] In addition, the Jeunes Arabes de Lyon et banlieue (JALB) criticized the Organisation nationale maghrebine for initiating a boycott against Jewish businesses in response to the Israeli bombing of PLO headquarters in Tunis. Rejecting calls for solidarity with Palestinians, one member remarked, "being anti-racist means, of course, not being antisemitic."[82]

These much-fêted cross-ethnic endeavors were, however, always shadowed by the decade's particularistic politics, creating challenges that required Jewish and Beur leaders to test the parameters of their alliance.[83] As one young Muslim told a reporter, SOS racisme was "for the *feujs*, not for us."[84] One dramatic example of such criticism came in December 1984 when the UEJF organized a panel on Middle East peace at Jussieu campus. When the 250 students arrived to hear presentations from Marek Halter and the cultural attaché for the Israeli embassy, they were greeted by 200–300 protestors from different Tunisian, Lebanese, and Moroccan associations screaming, "Zionists, fascists, out of Jussieu." "For us," said one protestor, "this is a racist meeting," and the UEJF, "which walks hand in hand with SOS racisme," is a Zionist front.[85] Similarly, the organization "Palestine vaincra" distributed brochures at metro stations claiming that Zionists had infiltrated anti-racist movements.[86] Marche des Beurs organizers also expressed doubts over SOS racisme's links to the UEJF. Most notably, Christian Delorme, the Protestant minister from Lyons who helped organize the 1983 march, wrote to Harlem Désir in April 1985 criticizing the UEJF's predominance and SOS racisme's efforts to supplant Beur anti-racist associations.[87]

Meanwhile, Jewish critics also expressed doubts about pluriculturalism. While left-leaning organizations, such as Judaïsme et socialisme, Association des Juifs de gauche, and the Cercle Bernard Lazare, publicly supported SOS racisme as did the two Jewish publications *Tribune juive* and *L'Arche* (the latter of which published SOS racisme's small yellow badge on its April 1985 cover), many spokesmen proved suspicious.[88] Remembering cries of "death to the Jews" in summer 1982, Jewish leaders felt no affection for the Beur Movement and its kaffiyeh-wearing demonstrators.[89] As Jean-Pierre Bloch, president of the Ligue internationale contre le racisme et l'antisémitisme (LICRA) remarked, "it would be interesting to know the position of the youth of 'Hands off my friend' toward the abominable UN resolution: Zionism = Racism."[90] Others criticized the UEJF/Beur alliance for ignoring clashing views on Israel.[91] While "a natural link exists between us and we face the same danger," penned Richard Liscia in *L'Arche*, "the Middle East crisis separates us." Skeptical of the optimism around

SOS racisme he noted, "not only do few Arabs feel concerned by the attack against the Jewish cinema, but even fewer would be ready to condemn Islamic Jihad if they confirmed that it originated the attack." Muslims, in his view, unlike Jews, were not yet willing to divide their perspectives on the Middle East from a universalist anti-racism: "I do not even ask them to accept Israel, only to be capable of separating things. To know that there is a struggle that we can carry out together despite all who oppose us."[92] Others embraced SOS racisme's anti-racist charge while questioning its ability to bridge real differences. CRIF president, Théo Klein, for example, displayed the SOS racisme badge on his desk and celebrated the fact that "Jewish and Arab intellectuals are working hand in hand," but explained its popularity as a fad.[93] Jean-Paul Elkan, president of the Consistoire de France, embraced SOS racisme's anti-racist charge while undermining its pluricultural message. When speaking to the Consistoire's Assemblée Générale in June, he reminded his audience that racism against North African immigrants was on the rise and insisted that a history of suffering led Jews to fight for human rights for all. His focus on racism, however, quickly brought him to Zionism since Israel served as the "best line of defense against anti-Semitism in the world."[94]

In light of such particularistic challenges, SOS racisme continued to sharpen its pluricultural approach. Meetings in spring 1985 between the UEJF and prominent members of the Beur Movement tackled thorny questions such as, "Racism and anti-Semitism in France: Is Solidarity Possible between Jews and Arabs?"[95] At one such "cards on the table" meeting, Jewish and Muslim participants tackled their differences around the Middle East. While UEJF representatives unapologetically asserted their Zionism, they agreed with Beur representatives that the Middle Eastern conflict was irrelevant to forging a cohesive anti-racist movement. Attendees left the meeting citing the slogan, "We cannot solve the Israel/Palestinian problem on the banks of the Seine" and agreeing that they shared more than divided them. As Ghébali underscored, "[W]e now have a common cultural heritage between us, we are beginning to get to know each other better."[96] Marek Halter summarized the meeting's significance as follows: "There was someone during the discussion who said: 'If they touch Israel, it's as if they have torn out a piece of my flesh, but in France, if they touch an immigrant—an Arab, a Portuguese—it's the same thing, they tear out a piece of my flesh. That is why I'm committed to SOS Racisme.' Much has changed. Such a speech would have been impossible ten years ago and would had been rejected by young Moroccans, Tunisians, Algerians."[97]

If the vow of silence regarding the Middle East conflict preserved alliances within SOS racisme, supporters of particularistic and pluricultural approaches to the anti-racist struggle still clashed.[98] The following autumn, for example, two anti-racist marches left Bordeaux for Paris after negotiations to unite them failed, the first sponsored by Beur associations and the second by SOS racisme. While the former emphasized the necessity of giving Beurs a political voice,[99]

SOS racisme sought to demonstrate that "French citizens of Jewish origin, Arab origin, etc. constitute a piece of the pluricultural Europe of the future."[100]

Such tensions were likewise evident in a December 1985 *Libération* interview with Julien Dray and Mejid Daboussi Ammar, a Tunisian-born French journalist and founder of *Sans frontières*. While both remained committed to Muslim-Jewish cooperation and both denounced Reagan's visit to Bittburg, Ammar repeatedly stressed the differences facing the two populations. Dray, in contrast, emphasized how theirs was a generation "of mixtures [*mélanges*]" all facing the same question: how to create a society where communities with different histories but with some commonalities can coexist. "Ammar and I have things in common. Our pasts are different but we share a common future." Ammar rejected such formulations, or rather, he noted that French Muslims could not yet embrace "mixture" while still fighting for basic rights: "You, Julien, assert that you are more at ease with 'mixture' and I would like to be able to say the same thing. Except I come from a devestated community that has never had the floor. I cannot afford that luxury. You can have it because you have an organized community that can defend itself." "Before calling for mixture or pluri-culturalism," Ammar continued, "we must establish a certain equality between communities."[101]

Ammar's insistence on his own community's needs was echoed by certain Jewish spokemen who worried about the impact of comparing Muslims and Jews in French society. André Wormser, for example, director of the Centre d'études et de recherches sur l'antisémitisme contemporain (CERAC), wrote to CRIF president, Théo Klein, on the one hand of the "useful" new contacts that young Jews had established with Muslims, while on the other hand warning that some of their initiatives "are inopportune and could take the community down a dangerous path." What exactly was the danger for Wormser? Given Jewish visibility in the anti-racist movement, the press and public opinion were beginning to see Jews as outsiders:

> It is often with the best of intentions that newspapers, *Le Monde* in particular, links all the victims of ordinary racism (immigrants, Jews, Arabs, or blacks), xenophobia, and anti-Semitism, making it seem as if Jews are foreigners to the French nation. We stand in solidarity with and are fraternally concerned by the attacks perpetrated against immigrants. I agree with all of our declarations in this sense and my own commitment to Muslims speaks for itself. However, in these linkages there is, on the one hand, historical error and, on the other, the enclosure of the community in a category where it does not belong. These are distinctions on which we must insist.[102]

Wormser's distinctions between Muslim "immigrants" and Jewish "citizens" was an implicit rejection of pluriculturalism (and a blatant if popular distortion of Beur national status). Given that elsewhere Wormser had argued that Muslims shared a "collective sense of belonging to France," his perspective is particularly revealing of how even sympathetic fellow travelers within the Jewish establishment remained wary of pluriculturalism.[103]

One of the most vociferous opponents of linking Muslims and Jews was Annie Kriegel. In several articles in *L'Arche* she lambasted efforts to create such parallels, arguing that the two groups differed in terms of their history, size, transnational affiliations, leadership, and integrative possibilities. While Jews, she argued, constituted a *community*, which is to say, a voluntary and religiously based group, Muslims constituted a *minority*, and thus the two were incomparable.[104] Dismissing those who emphasized the threat of the FN to Muslims and Jews alike, Kriegel stressed successful Jewish integration and insisted that the real danger came from conflating the Muslim and Jewish experience.[105] Many Jews are "ready to renounce their civic status in order to better share the status and torments of the immigrant condition." Instead, Jews should reflect alongside all citizens on how France could preserve its cohesion and educate newcomers on their rights and duties.[106] Such formulations insisted on profound distinctions between Muslims and Jews, linking Jews fully with the French nation and casting Muslims as perennial outsiders.

Other depictions went further in underscoring Muslim foreignness while also highlighting significant polarization between Muslims and Jews. In a long piece entitled, "*L'Islam contemporain et les juifs*" published by the Comité d'initiative pour Israël, Michel Gurfinkiel argued that although antisemitism had diminished in the West, Muslim immigrants were importing a Koran-based anti-Jewish propaganda with them. Gurfinkiel particularly highlighted anti-Jewish sentiment among Muslims in France:

> In fact, it is 'because of the Jews' that many Muslims refuse to integrate into the French nation where they believe that their efforts are doomed to fail. The presence in France of what [the Muslims] perceive to be a powerful and well organized Jewish community, with positions in politics, business, and even the Church, seems to them an almost insurmountable obstacle in their ambiguous desires for integration. . . . If the effort to enter into a secularized Christian system leads to the de facto submission to a social authority exercised by Jews, the effort is judged impossible. Such responses are found in all Muslim immigrant circles, even the most peripheral or the most integrated to French culture.[107]

Bolstering such fears, in February 1987, LICRA accused an Islamic bookstore in Belleville of selling the *Protocols of the Elders of Zion*, the fraudulent text describing a Jewish plan to achieve global domination.[108] Likewise, the bulletin of the association Décider agir avec vigilance pour Israël et la diaspora (DAVID) warned against antisemitic diatribes on Islamic radio stations seeking to "turn French 'Beurs' against the Jews."[109]

Certainly, not all French Jews accepted such a stark representation of Muslim-Jewish relations, with some even defending SOS racisme as a sign of

Beur integration.[110] Nevertheless, debates between particularlistic and pluricultural approaches to ethno-religious cooperation continued to plague the anti-racist movement throughout the mid-1980s. They gathered steam as France's evolving political landscape shifted the agenda to those emphasizing particularistic priorities.

Cohabitation, Integration, and the End of Pluriculturalism

The 1986 parliamentary elections proved a repudiation of Mitterrand's socialist hold over the French political establishment, ushering in a period with a president from one party (Mitterrand) and a prime minister from another (Jacques Chirac). While Mitterrand won reelection in 1988, bringing back a leftist majority, from 1986 to 1988 the balance of power had shifted. Moreover, the FN continued to win electoral victories, earning 9.7 percent of the vote or thirty-five seats in the 1986 parliamentary elections and, more shocking to many, 14 percent, or nearly 4.5 million of those cast in the first round of the May 1988 presidential elections.[111] In response, Chirac's government ushered in a period of stricter controls on immigration—a touchstone issue for FN voters—reviving financial inducements for immigrants to return home, tightening entry restrictions, and launching debates over the nationality code. The latter, in particular, created widespread debate as conservatives proposed to modify citizenship laws for the children of foreigners.[112] Although the proposal foundered due in part to widespread opposition by anti-racist organizations, by 1988 all parties were emphasizing cultural amalgam over multiculturalism as a means to ensure social stability. If the Right focused on threats to French security and the Left on integration, both saw "immigration" as a "problem" to be solved.[113] For the Socialists, such shifts led to efforts to isolate the Beur Movement from the larger immigrant community. Fearing the movement's collective strength and the development of sectarian religious and ethnic groupings, officials sought to define the boundaries of Beur activism by co-opting the leadership and limiting funding and logistical support to programs that supported the state's integrative interests. Such efforts succeeded in weakening the Beur Movement considerably.[114]

It was in the midst of these shifts that the first intifada broke out in Israel in December 1987. The eruption of yet another Middle Eastern conflict created new tensions within the French anti-racist movement as Beur and Jewish representatives split along pro-Israel or pro-Palestinian lines. To understand debates around the intifada as purely the transplantation of the Middle East conflict to France, however, overlooks the way national conversations on immigration and diversity shaped the outlook of Beurs, Jews, and the wider anti-racist movement. As France's political establishment and media began reemphasizing integration, divisions were exacerbated within and among these groups that

undermined pluricultural experiments. Such shifts did not immediately interfere with cooperative Muslim-Jewish anti-racist campaigns, but the nature of
those campaigns became transformed. Rather than focusing on the formation
of a pluricultural public sphere, Muslim and Jewish activists began stressing
"dialogue." Although a subtle shift, this new framework highlighted divisions
rather than shared struggles.

In this context, a second anti-racist organization, France plus, founded in
1985 by Arezki Dahmani, played a significant role. France plus brought together children of harkis and "second-generation" French Muslims with the
goal of encouraging integration through the exercise of civic rights and responsibilities. The organization thus emphasized voter registration and the election
of Muslim candidates.[115] Like SOS racisme, France plus promoted a multiracial and multi-ethnic society. Unlike SOS racisme, however, France plus, the
considerably smaller of the two organizations, placed far greater emphasis on
Beur politics.[116] If SOS racisme was dedicated to creating minority unity, France
plus was founded on the principle of ethnic political organization.[117] Dahmani
was thus less interested in working *with* Jews than in mirroring their political
strategies. After the outbreak of the first intifada, however, it was France plus—
rather than SOS racisme—that forged a successful alliance with the UEJF, an
alliance that stressed dialogue as the only means of sustaining a unified anti-
racist struggle.

Israel's response to the Palestinian uprising in December 1987 sparked
strong reactions across France's left-leaning Beur organizations.[118] Protesters,
including Hayet Boudjemaa (SOS racisme), Nacer Kettane (Radio Beur), and
Arezki Dahmani (France plus) visited the Israeli embassy, and pro-Palestinian
empathy increased "on the ground."[119] As one Muslim student told a reporter,
"The guys fighting the Zionists are the same age as us. They were born in camps;
we have known the *cités de transit* and the bidonvilles. We put ourselves in their
place." Others articulated an intensifying Arab unity: "North Africans, Egyp-
tians, Palestinians, we all have the same blood."[120]

Such reactions did not, however, fully capture the range of responses to
events in the Middle East. As the president of Sans frontières, Farid Aïchoune,
editorialized in *Le Monde*, if many Beurs identified with the Palestinians, most
did *not* imagine themselves as part of a wider Arab political struggle but as
French: "We *Beurs* do not dream of an I-don't-know-what Arab Revolution
that the Palestinians would spearhead. Myths of this kind are finished for us.
Beurs do not want to scream 'Death to Israel,' even if sometimes we are angered
by certain images."[121] Likewise, according to Khaled Melhaa, secretary general
of Radio Beur, while the station had received some angry calls from listeners,
few expressed the passions of 1973. As one Beur told a reporter, "Frankly, Palestine is kind of far away. . . . What I want first is to find a job. After, we'll see."
Or according to another, "We live in France not in Palestine or another Arab
country. . . . For us, what is happening now is primarily a problem of justice

and human rights." If the Beurs identified with the Palestinians, he continued, it was based on a shared experience of marginalization: "Of course Palestinians are my brothers, I am completely in solidarity with them, and at the same time, we are not 100% Arab."[122]

If Beurs articulated a range of views on the intifada, Jews were equally divided. Media representations portrayed the Jewish population as "in disarray" and "traumatized" over aggressive Israeli responses to the violence.[123] As one reporter noted, "throughout the French Jewish community we find a malaise, an internal rupture between a visceral fidelity to Israel and these painful images."[124] Some well-known Jewish figures—echoing Jewish leftists of past decades—publically criticized Israeli actions, while others were silent, and still others remained loyal to Israel despite mounting discomfort.[125] This diversity of responses created space for Muslims and Jews to issue joint appeals for Middle Eastern peace that echoed the decade's pluricultural themes.[126]

In a context that repeatedly underscored the difficulties of immigrant and Beur integration, however, pluriculturalism was beginning to founder. According to Kaïssa Titous, a member of SOS racisme's steering committee and a Beur activist, "For many Beurs, there has been a rupture with the Jewish community which, in their eyes, does not sufficiently support the anti-racist struggle even if it has taken steps in that direction."[127] As Titous's remarks make clear, while Jews and Muslims sometimes clashed over Middle Eastern policy, domestic issues were also a source of tension. As one young Beur told a reporter, he had distanced himself from his best friend (Jewish) because he refused to admit the "ideological imperialism" that the "Jewish lobby exercised in all areas of society."[128]

This conflation of the international and French identity politics led in the words of the UEJF's Arié Bensemhoun to "a sort of explosion inside the [anti-racist] movement."[129] In March 1988, the UEJF announced it was considering dissolving ties with SOS racisme in response to "anti-Israel initiatives" taken by some provincial committees and, in particular, the distribution of anti-UEJF tracts.[130] Harlem Désir's call for direct Israeli negotiations with the PLO, which most Jewish organizations considered a terrorist organization, also angered those who insisted that SOS racisme remain neutral on Israel/Palestine. "We are first and foremost Zionist activists," declared the new UEJF president, Marc Bitton. "We must take into account the concerns of our community."[131] The shift from pluricultural to particularistic politics was clear.

At SOS racisme's congress the following April, Jewish and Muslim members spent hours trying to bridge the impasse. On the one hand, Eric Ghebali demanded that the organization recognize *both* Israeli and Palestinian rights, while, on the other, Kaïssa Titous called for a condemnation of the repression, insistence on Israeli military retreat, and recognition of Palestinian national rights. The three hundred delegates finally settled on a compromise that affirmed their "solidarity with the victims of repression in the occupied

territories," while also stating the necessity for Palestinians and Israelis to recognize the other's legitimate existence. Ten members nevertheless abstained
because the declaration did not go far enough.[132]

The declaration allowed the UEJF and the SOS racisme to reconfirm their
link, a timely move given Le Pen's strong showing in the May presidential elections.[133] In its June-July newsletter, the UEJF thus re-embraced its pluriculturalism, stating that, "racism, xenophobia, and anti-Semitism cannot be fought
from a ghetto." Yet, the same article set limits on Beur activism: "It might seem
natural for a young Beur to feel close to a young Palestinian, but to fight for the
integration of *immigrants* while brandishing the Palestinian flag is nonsensi-
cal." Without acknowledging the double standard, the UEJF, which was vocally
pro-Israel, criticized double allegiances among the Beurs and highlighted their
foreign origins (by definition Beurs were not immigrants), implicitly underscoring differences from their *French* Jewish peers.[134]

The UEJF's reemphasis of particularism while holding firm to its anti-racism
was mirrored by France plus, which called for dialogue across ethno-religious
lines as a means of strengthening the anti-racist coalition. The call for "dialogue," while seemingly overlapping with SOS racisme's pluriculturalism, differed in significant ways. Like the leaders of SOS racisme, Dahmani understood
that certain commonalities linked Muslims and Jews. For him, however, political differences were paramount and he stressed "dialogue" as a way to surmount
them. As such, unlike SOS racisme, which had remained neutral on the Middle
East, France plus actively supported the Palestinians *while* formally recognizing Israel (becoming the first "Franco-Maghrebin" organization to do so), and
in February 1988, launched a committee "Shalom-Salem" for all "French of
Maghrebian origin." During a press conference announcing the new organization, Dahmani underscored the importance of dialogue.[135] While disagreeing
about the Middle East, Muslims and Jews agreed on a minimum program of
past (shared North African heritage), present (anti-racism and inclusion for all
in French society), and future (Middle East peace).[136] According to Dahmani:
"If in our collective memory, these two youth—'Beurs and Feujs'—are linked,
one thing separates them: the Israeli-Palestinian conflict. For France plus, the
construction of a democratic anti-racist front necessarily must pass through
the settlement of the conflict."[137]

Dahmani took part in numerous public "dialogues" to facilitate this end.[138] In
July 1988, for example, Arié Bensemhoun, the UEJF's new president, and Arezki
Dahmani published a debate on the Middle East facilitated by historian Benjamin Stora. All three of North African origin (Bensemhoun born in Morocco,
Dahmani and Stora in Algeria) and all three highly educated—Bensemhoun
was a doctoral dental surgeon, Dahmani and Stora assistant professors—they
came to the Middle Eastern conflict with similar investments in intercommunal cooperation but also cognizant of deep divisions. As Bensemhoun said
later, "While we were inevitably brought together in the anti-racist struggle,

events in the Middle East caused a deep rift to develop between young Jews and young Arabs."[139] A close look at the discussion, however, shows the way disagreements over Israel-Palestine underscored other divisions. Dahmani, for example, distinguished between the racism facing Muslims and Jews even if both shared a common enemy in Le Pen: "For French-Maghrebians, racism is experienced daily, linked to their disadvantaged social status. They face the racism of the 'ground floor.'" For Jews, he argued, whose social status was considerably higher, racism was largely encountered in history and memory. For Bensemhoun, the problem was not structural. Rather he focused on the conflation of anti-Zionism and antisemitism among French Muslims: "There were demonstrations in France because of events in the territories. In the streets, I saw people with whom we have typically fought racism. They were screaming: 'Zionists, fascists, assassins!' and other slogans that sounded more like antisemitism than simple support for the Palestinian cause." Thus while Dahmani accused the anti-racist movement of crumbling around Jews' unwillingness to challenge Israeli racism (versus Beurs who condemned racism everywhere), Bensemhoun accused Beurs of their own form of racism. When asked if Jewish-Arab cooperation was over, Bensemhoun remarked, "Quite. Too often we spout off about Jewish-Arab dialogue. We say: 'Oh! If we could just have dialogue that would fix all the problems in France and the Middle East.' This is insufficient. We have always had dialogue. Jews and Arabs have lived together for centuries. This is not new."[140]

While Bensemhoun was correct that Muslims and Jews had been interacting for centuries, the commitment to "dialogue" as a political strategy *was* new, and both the UEJF and France plus asserted the importance of confronting differences as a way to find common ground. Most notably, on 11 October 1988, five hundred participants came together in what was billed as the "first encounter between Arabs and Jews in France." Organized by the Jewish monthly *Passages*, the event brought the UEJF and France plus together with other activists to discuss "Is Jewish-Arab dialogue possible for tomorrow's France?"[141] Notably absent was SOS racisme, whose pluricultural approach was losing ground in the strident French identity politics of the late 1980s.[142] As Eric Ghébali—still secretary general of SOS racisme but long since replaced as UEJF president—responded to the event,[143] "We obviously favor anything that encourages Israeli-Arab dialogue. But we want to address a whole generation without distinctions. The identity stance taken by l'UEJF and France plus seems like a regression to us. Why emphasize differences and position themselves against each other?"[144]

Ghébali was not the only detractor.[145] Hamadi Essid, head of the Arab League's mission in Paris, criticized the event for leaving out Middle Eastern representatives in what was really a "Franco-French" debate. Here, Essid was right. Held in the National Assembly, symbolic site of political inclusion, the event moved well beyond the Middle East to a range of minority issues. According to Rabeh Touïsi, vice president of France plus, "We will stay in strictly

Franco-French terrain. We are young Jews and Arabs in France. We were born here. We have grown up together, attended the same schools, confronted the same problems. But, alas, too often there are tensions. I have seen them enough myself to speak of them. These are the tensions we must eliminate, and for that, we must begin by speaking frankly together."[146]

Despite such hopes, divisions surfaced throughout the day. While the audience was mixed, Jews and Muslims each sat with their own.[147] Panels were also highly charged, particularly one on the Middle East in which Arié Bensemhoun's passionate pro-Israel presentation led some to yell angrily, "We are not in the Knesset!" Although one Jewish leftist reminded all, "You are no more Palestinian than I am an Israeli citizen," the angry tone permeated other panels as well.[148] In one session, for example, a Muslim attendee circulated a document that read, "What should we think of the *Protocols of the Elders of Zion*—slander or truth—when we see how much of the world finances are concentrated in the hands of the American Jewish lobby and its Judeo-Nazi comportment in Israel, the occupied territories, Lebanon and elsewhere." In the session on racism, UEJF representatives cautioned Beur attendees not to compare the Holocaust to murders in Algeria, while the latter reminded Jewish peers, "In colonial Algeria, the Jewish community chose the occupier over the occupied!" Not to be outdone, their interlocutors retorted, "Jewish blood ran in the synagogues; I don't think that it ran in the mosques." Here, references to colonial Algeria were quickly entangled with the particularist politics of contemporary France. As one Beur complained, "We are the primary victims of racism in France. Maghrebians provide a barrier for the Jews." While Bitton countered, "We are all in the same sack!" another responded, "The Jews are often overvalued: they do everything better. In contrast, Arabs are undervalued: nothing."[149] By the end of the day, Jewish participants were complaining that no Muslims had denounced anti-Jewish activities in Egypt, Syria, and Iraq, while Muslims were attacking the pro-French attitude of the Jews during decolonization, and the lack of recognition of Muslim aid to French Jews during the Holocaust. This reference to decolonization and World War II underscored the multiple layers to identity politics in late 1980s France. Ostensibly a fight about Israelis and Palestinians, the exchange was very much a "Franco-French" debate in which tensions around history, memory, and immigration politics were paramount.[150]

Subsequent debates between Dahmani and Bensemhoun continued to emphasize differences between Muslims and Jews. For Dahmani, the primary challenge facing Muslims was integration into French society. Rather than pursuing the "right to be different," so significant at the beginning of the decade, Beurs required the "right to indifference."[151] Bensemhoun, in contrast, underscored that "Jews have no problem with integration. Jews were in France even before France was France! Even if antisemitism is on the increase, it is difficult to compare the situation of the Jews and the Beurs. The Beurs are still working for their integration." On this Dahmani agreed, "We can not really compare ourselves with the Jewish community."[152] Elsewhere, Bensemhoun went further, "We must differentiate the Jewish community in France from that of the Arab community. While the former has successfully integrated, if not without difficulties, the latter is seeking its place." Here too Dahmani agreed: "[T]he Jewish community is better integrated than the Arab community. . . . What I ask of our Jewish friends is that they draw on their experience to help us succeed with our integration."[153]

In such depictions particularistic concerns overwhelmed pluricultural celebrations, a perspective the UEJF's Marc Rochman emphasized when explaining his organization's relationship with France plus. While the UEJF had co-founded SOS racisme in 1985, the latter's turn to Beur integration had taken it in a different direction, which "if commendable is not our own." The response of certain leaders to the intifada had chilled the collaboration further. Instead, Rochman noted, "we now dialogue with the young Beurs of France plus. Each defends his own ideas on the basis of a fraternal dialogue."[154] What is interesting about this portrayal is that France plus was actually both more openly pro-Palestinian and more vocally committed to Beur integration than SOS racisme.[155] The appeal of France plus was rather its call for "dialogue," which assumed essential differences rather than celebrating similarities, providing the UEJF with the freedom to do the same.

Ironically, this emphasis on difference came at a moment when Jews and Muslims were more the "same" than they had ever been, sharing the status of ethno-religious minority citizens within the French state. Despite this shared "positionality"—or maybe even because of it—Jewish and Muslim activists began to distance themselves from each other. This shift was, necessarily, incomplete, which meant that pluricultural and particularistic approaches to minority integration continued to coexist. Even the CRIF, which had long avoided pluricultural politics, showed greater appreciation for shared minority struggle under its new president Jean Kahn. In fall 1989, for example, Kahn increased contacts with Muslim authorities, arguing, "We must not forget that we live side by side with 3,000,000 Muslims in France, of whom 800,000 are citizens like us who face common problems."[156]

As French political culture took a turn to the right, attempting to solve the "immigration problem" with more forceful calls for integration, however, Jewish links to Muslims appeared increasingly dangerous. In response, some communal leaders stressed fundamental differences between Jews and Muslims.[157] The latter similarly backed away from alliances with a group that seemed to represent all they hoped to achieve but also the limitations on their own integration. For both, it was the particular and not the pluricultural that resonated. Three episodes—two domestic and one international—at the end of the decade cemented this shift.

The Head Scarf, Carpentras, the Gulf War and the
End of Pluriculturalism

Three seemingly unconnected social crises at the end of the 1980s rang the
death knell on pluriculturalism. The Islamic head-scarf controversy in October
1989, the desecration of the Jewish cemetery in Carpentras in May 1990, and
the outbreak of the first Gulf War in January 1991 each in their own way underscored the particular struggles facing Muslim and Jewish French citizens.
While each theoretically provided an opportunity for joint activism, the late
1980s shift to an intensified identity politics meant that few such appeals resonated. With the new decade, the UEJF dissolved its ties with SOS racisme, symbolically closing the door both organizations helped open in 1984.

On 3 October 1989 three Muslim girls were expelled from a middle school in
Creil (thirty miles from Paris) for refusing to remove their head scarves, expulsions the principal justified on the grounds that the girls were breaking one of
the central pillars of republican universalism—*laïcité* or French secularism—by
violating the law on the separation of church and state and making religious
difference a public rather than private matter. The media frenzy that followed (echoed in similar controversies in 1994 and 2003) can be understood
as a response to fears that the public school—the central institution of French
republicanism—was under assault and as an indication of the country's increasing
discomfort with Islam.[158] Despite the decade's vocal anti-racist campaigns, the
end of the 1980s saw mounting fears over terrorism, international Islam, and
Arab militancy in response to terrorist attacks in France in 1986, the intifiada,
and the 1989 Iranian fatwa against Salman Rushdie. In particular, fears focused
on "second generation" French Muslims whose marginalization made them seem
ripe for fundamentalist outreach.[159] The seemingly insignificant expulsion of two
girls from high school thus soon evolved into a national debate on Islam and minority integration. The debates around *l'affaire foulard*, when coupled with those
around the Jewish cemetery desecration in 1990 in Carpentras and the 1991 Gulf
War, continued to emphasize Muslim and Jewish difference in ways that brought
SOS racisme's pluricultural model to a breaking point.

For Jews, *l'affaire foulard* proved disconcerting, since discussions of the
Muslim head scarf seemed to lend themselves to easy comparisons with the
Jewish yarmulke.[160] If Islam posed a fundamental challenge to the French public
sphere, could the same be said of Judaism? And if so, would the comparisons
raise the same kinds of questions about Jewish integration that plagued French
Muslims? The answers to these questions reflected the range of pluricultural
and particularistic agendas that had coexisted uneasily for much of the decade.
The UEJF, for example, criticized "fundamentalist secularism" and stressed the
importance of protecting universities, at the very least, as open to all particularistic expressions.[161] Likewise, Chief Rabbi Sitruk joined a group of Catholic
and Protestant clerics in arguing for religious tolerance in schools. For him,

defending the head scarf was equivalent to defending the yarmulke (although no Jews were forced to remove head coverings during the head-scarf affair). While hardly a "pluriculturalist" (Sitruk's position grew out of deeply particularistic perspectives), his call for religious tolerance necessarily stressed shared concerns between France's two largest religious minorities. More moderate rabbis disagreed. Gilles Bernheim, for example, argued that because Jews had successfully integrated into French society, they "should serve as models for the Muslim community" in remaining faithful to French republicanism. Since very few Muslim women actually wore head scarves (14 percent), Bernheim's position can be understood as stressing differences as a way to legitimize Jewish "Frenchness."[162] Likewise, the CRIF, while never taking a strong stand, promoted state secularism as a way of celebrating Jewish integration, while certain Jewish intellectuals such as Alain Finkielkraut denounced the "holy alliance of clergies" for their attack on public schools.[163] Others adopted a more strident position, drawing decisive lines between Jews and Muslims in response to troubling conflations that seemed to raise doubts about Jewish integration. Richard Liscia, for example, wrote in L'Arche that donning the head scarf was a fundamentalist provocation that differed profoundly from the yarmulke, which only sought to distinguish Jews from other people, and the cross, which served as a national unifying symbol.[164] Such rhetoric, which emphasized Jewish Frenchness in contradistinction to Muslim foreignness, built on the discourse of difference that had emerged over previous years, with some even blaming SOS racisme for the blurring of such distinctions.[165] Shmuel Trigano thus argued that "the brainless policies of certain Jewish institutions like the UEJF" drew equivalencies between Jewish and Muslim assimilation, "giving birth to SOS racisme," and raising new questions about the Jewish community's place in French society.[166]

This emphasis on difference gathered steam in May 1990 when a body was exhumed from a Jewish cemetery in Carpentras. While there had been many desecrations in the preceding period, the impalement of Félix Germont's body on an umbrella created unprecedented public outrage. A huge CRIF-sponsored protest in Paris on 14 May brought out hundreds of thousands, including President Mitterrand and representatives from across the political spectrum. The collective support nevertheless reaffirmed Jewish distinctiveness since the media and official representations generally framed the attack as directed against a unified "community."[167] Moreover, a concerted journalistic and political focus on the "return of antisemitism" had the effect of distinguishing it from other forms of racism.[168]

The massive support for Jews highlighted for many Muslims the differences facing the two populations. In response, France plus made another effort to protect the anti-racist alliance, this time organizing a symposium with the CRIF on Muslim-Jewish dialogue.[169] CRIF president Jean Kahn likewise told Prime Minister Rocard that the Jewish community hoped to increase discussions with

SOS racisme and France plus.[170] His address six months later to SOS racisme's annual congress stressed pluricultural themes: "We feel each attack against a North African as an attack against ourselves, it makes us ache and anxious. . . . Alone you cannot fight racism. Alone we cannot fight anti-Semitism. . . . All is linked."[171] Nevertheless, the very distinction between "racism" and "antisemitism" was itself a kind of particularistic discourse that revealed the limits of the speaker's pluriculturalist vision. Marc Rochman's speech at the same event similarly paid lip service to collective anti-racist struggles while focusing primarily on the particularlistic issues of Holocaust education and antisemitism in France and Eastern Europe.[172]

The first Gulf War dealt the final blow to pluriculturalism. Iraq's August 1990 invasion of Kuwait touched off a storm of controversy, as discussions over the nation's engagements in the Middle East and the prospect of war created fears that Muslims would reject French positions in favor of "Arab" solidarity.[173] Indeed, although French Muslims took diverse positions on the Gulf conflict, mirroring disagreements throughout the Arab world, media outlets and public commentators assumed the worst.[174] According to Charles Rebois in the *Figaro*, "If war breaks out, what side will they be on? . . . No matter what one does or says, the Beur from Seine-Saint-Denis will always feel close to his brothers who jeer France in the streets of Algiers and Tunis." Three national polls from the end of January 1991 showed over 80 percent of the French believing that terrorism would increase, and over 70 percent claiming that war would provoke "serious incidents" within France's Muslim population.[175] International events, such as massive anti-French, pro-Iraqi demonstrations in North Africa, Saddam Hussein's call for jihad, and the Iraqi leader's decision to fire missiles at Israel once war broke out, exacerbated such fears. According to one Marseille resident, "We buy sugar, the Arabs buy bullets." Or, in the words of another, "if [war] explodes, the police and army won't be able to do anything here."[176] In fact, the racist attacks went in the other direction; from Christmas 1990 to the beginning of 1991, anti-immigrant incidents were recorded in the Midi, Béziers, Nimes, Martigues, Istres, Paris, and the Haut-Rhin probably due to the rising heated rhetoric around "Arabs" in France.

Responding to mounting concerns, the Ministry of the Interior implemented the "Plan Vigipirate" in early January, increasing surveillance of airports, official buildings, public gathering places, mosques, and immigrant neighborhoods.[177] Systematic identity checks of North African Muslims facilitated greater connections in the public eye between Beurs and Saddam Hussein. Pro-Iraqi newspapers were banned, several suspected immigrant sympathizers were expelled, and three North African workers were removed from areas around Ain's nuclear power station to prevent sabotage. While President Mitterrand and other officials insisted that law-abiding Muslim residents had nothing to fear, such measures continued to draw negative attention to France's Muslim population.[178]

In this atmosphere, media outlets began predicting a clash between Jewish and Muslim communities, often portrayed as two well-organized bodies preparing to mobilize.[179] According to Marseille's chief rabbi, "an army of journalists invaded the city. . . . expect[ing] a violent confrontation between Arabs and Jews," while in Lyons, *L'Autre journal* told of "an abyss . . . widening between communities."[180] Muslim and Jewish religious leaders echoed these concerns, holding several ecumenical prayer services to stave off interethnic conflict,[181] while the UEJF augmented security in all chapters, and Marseille's Consistoire requested permission to arm key communal figures.[182] Meanwhile, imams used the last Friday before the UN withdrawal deadline of 15 January to call for calm, as did the Conseil national des français d'origine arabe.[183] "All our work to bring the communities together risks being wasted," lamented the French Algerian comedian Smaïn.[184]

The greatest casualty of the tense environment was the joint anti-racist coalition. Despite disagreements, SOS racisme and the UEJF had remained linked throughout the decade.[185] In 1991, however, the UEJF accused SOS racisme of breaking its "neutrality" agreement on the Middle East when the latter began participating in the anti-war movement.[186] In response, several Jewish patrons of the organization quit, including Bernard-Henri Lévy.[187] The UEJF, which had spent the late 1980s defending Israel on college campuses, formally resigned from SOS racisme after Iraq's scud attack on Israel.[188] While both organizations condemned the attack, SOS racisme stressed the importance of avoiding escalation, while the UEJF harshly criticized nations that compelled Israel to remain passive before an evident threat. In addition, the UEJF accused SOS racisme of "facilitating the identification of young French citizens of Maghrebian origin with Saddam Hussein," creating "major risks for intercommunal co-habitation and integration into French society."[189] As the UEJF president replied when asked if he believed that SOS racisme was responsible for the Beurs' attachment to Hussein: "They are not the only ones responsible, but they contributed." Noting that, "young French citizens of Arabic origins are mature and fully enough part of the French democratic universe to resist falling for the incitement of a dictator," he simultaneously implied that those who supported Hussein were not real democrats and hence not fully French.[190] By February, the UEJF was heavily engaged in a pro-Israel campaign, the publicity for which read, "We love Israel like we love liberty, democracy, courage, peace, or even France."[191] Here French citizenship and love for Israel were entangled, an implicit suggestion that to be pro-Arab and fully French was impossible.

The Gulf War, then, sounded the death knell of pluriculturalism. Following the head-scarf affair and the Carpentras cemetery desecration, Gulf War political posturing emphasized the distinctive paths of Muslims and Jews in French society. With SOS racisme and the UEJF having backed into opposing corners and with assertions of interethnic conflict dominating the media, cooperative anti-racist campaigns gave way to the decade's particularistic politics.

A similar process was evident "on the ground" as Muslim citizens were re-minded that despite the decade's lip service to pluriculturalism, they faced dis-tinctive challenges not shared by their Jewish neighbors. Once again, Marseille provides an excellent example of this wider phenomenon. The weeks around the Gulf War witnessed increasingly widespread fears of intercommunal vio-lence and intermittent aggression by some Muslim and Jewish residents, in-cluding one imam's threat that it was necessary to "persecute [Jews] until they disappear," and an unknown Zionist organization's claim to have detonated an explosion at an immigrant workers' hostel. Yet, as I have argued elsewhere, numerous communal spokesmen reminded their co-religionists that such ac-tions were marginal provocations in an otherwise peaceful city.[192] To under-score the point, the chief rabbi and several Islamic leaders took an active role in Marseille-Espérance, a multiconfessional and multiethnic body created in 1990 by Mayor Robert Vigouroux (elected after Defferre's death in 1986).[193] This organization's appeals for calm symbolically demonstrated that peaceful coex-istence was possible even in the most trying times, while the affiliation with the mayor's office opened lines of communication from the municipality to a wide range of religious and ethnic leaders, a distinct change from Defferre's one-sided wooing of Marseille's Jewish community.

Yet if such appeals contributed to the lack of violence in Marseille in winter 1991, they could not prevent Muslim residents' sense of betrayal during the Gulf War, often felt through direct comparison of their own experiences with those of their Jewish neighbors. Indeed, although Marseille's Jews expressed deep pain when Iraq dropped scud missiles on Tel Aviv, widespread Western support and France's decision to join the coalition and condemn the attack sug-gested that French and Jewish concerns were coinciding, easing fears among Jews who had long criticized France's "pro-Arab" policies.[194] Muslims felt no such sense of security. A poll in late January thus reported 58 percent voicing fears for their future and 73 percent fearing a rise in racism.[195] In Marseille, this insecurity manifested itself by a marked decrease in street life, a 60 percent drop in market activity, and low attendance at religious gatherings. Several ex-pulsions of Iraqi, Moroccan, Algerian, and Lebanese activists increased fears, as did the ongoing Vigipirate regulations. As police noted, "the expulsions' psy-chological impact are much greater than one might have imagined. . . . [I]t is thus a sense of fear and an attitude of discretion that dominates."[196]

Thus if in the months prior to the war both Muslims and Jews feared the war's potential ramifications in France, by March, Jewish fears had diminished. For Muslims, in contrast, increased surveillance raised fears that their future was in peril. For many, the 1980s had seen rapid political integration;[197] the sense of rejection that came with 1991 was thus all the more profound. As a prominent Muslim spokesman commented bitterly in a February interview in Le Méridional, there was a gap between the inclusive message being promoted by national leaders and its "every day transcription, lived poorly by Muslims."[198] Likewise police reported that Muslims in Marseille were "disappointed" with authorities, believing they had earned greater trust and "the official removal of all ambiguity regarding their citizenship."[199]

While the sense of insecurity engendered by the war explains the root of this alienation, comparisons with their Jewish neighbors played a part. By early March, police thus reported bitterness among Marseille's Muslims at having been considered "citizens of a second order . . . sacrificed to the Jewish community that had the benefit of a reassuring public discourse."[200] Indeed, during the war, Jewish connections to Israel were rarely questioned as authorities seemingly embraced the nation's Jewish minority.[201] For Muslims, in contrast, accusations of double loyalties emerged in force. These differences underscored the different positions of Muslims and Jews in contemporary France, further undermining the assertions of "sameness" that undergirded pluriculturalism.

Conclusion

The high-profile split between SOS racisme and the UEJF, and the erosion of Muslim-Jewish relations during the Gulf War meant that by the end of 1991 particularism had triumphed over pluriculturalism.[202] Among Beur activists, the pluricultural vision—insofar as it had ever been attractive—had become untenable. Due to the machinations of socialist politics, the Beur Movement was in crisis as associations disappeared and as the leadership retreated into professional careers away from the urban enclaves of their youth.[203] For the generation that followed, the urban landscape eroded even further. More disconnected from their countries of origin, this new generation—which adopted the verlan appellation of *rabeus* (an inversion of Beurs)—proved more politically apathetic and disenchanted with collective organization. In their eyes, the politics of pluriculturalism had failed. In its place, the rabeus turned to local affiliations around housing projects or joined transnational ethnic and religious social movements based in Berberist or Islamist politics, both of which rejected calls for integration.[204]

Jews also ended the decade disillusioned with pluriculturalism. Like the "rabeus," many children of North African Jewish immigrants drew into themselves, distancing themselves both from French and Muslim peers.[205] The UEJF, as we have seen, rejected pluricultural formulations. Its 1992 campaign, "I have two loves," featured posters of a baguette holding up an Israeli and French flag, proudly embracing the "dual loyalty" label for which Jews had so often been criticized. While making the mainstream Jewish leadership uncomfortable, the campaign shows how dramatically the student organization had moved away from pluricultural models.[206] Although the 1993 Oslo Accords brought the

UEJF into discussions with Peace Now, France plus, and even the PLO, leading to a publicity campaign that seemingly returned to pluricultural ideals in its celebration of tolerance and pluralism, the focus was entirely on the Middle East; minority politics in France were no longer part of the discussion.[207] After September 2000, when the UEJF once again allied with SOS racisme in an effort to restore peaceful interethnic relations after the outbreak of the second intifada, the two organizations would find themselves trying to undo a polarized landscape they themselves had helped to create.[208]

Conclusion

We end where we began in October 2000, when six Molotov cocktails thrown at a synagogue in Villepinte unleashed in France the violence some had feared would become a regular feature of interethnic relations following the Belleville riots in 1968. Annual statistics and detailed studies have subsequently confirmed mounting antisemitism among French Muslim youth, particularly in the urban banlieus where stereotypes of powerful and wealthy Jews circulate widely.[1] While analysts disagree as to the cause of this hostility, all agree that the year 2000 marked a turning point of significant consequence in which the forces that had previously kept violence at bay gave way to a new, more aggressive ethno-religious landscape.

For many the cause was self-evident. Increasing links between young French Muslims and their co-religionists in Palestine had brought the Middle Eastern conflict to France. Given that violence has increased significantly during moments of Middle East unrest, such as the outbreak of the second intifada, the battle in Jenin in April 2002, and the second Gulf War, such analyses made some intuitive sense. As we have seen, well before 2000, French Muslim youth had begun identifying with the Palestinian cause as a way to express their own social frustrations.[2] For those who feel marginalized and disenfranchised in France's poor urban neighborhoods, the Palestinian struggle for recognition has taken on symbolic meaning, allowing anger at Israel to become increasingly entangled with anti-Jewish stereotypes.[3] In a setting in which, as Esther Benbassa has argued, transnational identifications have taken on greater significance for *both* Muslims and Jews, interethnic relationships have become increasingly fraught.[4] Indeed, as more recent scholarship reminds us, Muslims and Jews have *both* moved away from republican models of cultural integration. Less interested in transnational affiliations, such work has emphasized the way shifts in French identity politics has led to more vocal and politicized minority expression, challenging republican norms in place since the Revolution.[5]

As the previous pages make clear, however, the origins of recent Muslim-Jewish tensions predate the year 2000 by several decades and are more mutual than a focus on the "new Judophobia" suggests.[6] The arguments here have been threefold. First, I have suggested that to understand fully the way Muslim-Jewish political conversations have evolved in France, we must begin in North

Africa in the decade and a half after World War II as France first tried to hold on to and then extricate itself from the region. Throughout the decolonization period, various political actors, including colonial administrators, international Jewish representatives, and indigenous nationalist leaders began singling out a "Jewish story" that emphasized a growing split from their Muslim neighbors. Given the diversity of the region and of the Muslim and Jewish populations therein, this focus on conflict necessarily oversimplified a landscape in which many Muslims and Jews cohabited with ease and even convivially. The emerging focus on a cross-regional Jewish problem just as independent states were breaking away from French colonial control, however, worked to create the very conflict it purported to describe by directing significant attention to the most highly politicized sectors of both populations and shaping conversations about Muslim-Jewish polarization long into the future. While bitterness over Jewish departures or Muslim aggression were not the *only* memories of ethnic relations to take root in France—nostalgic references to harmonious religious exchanges, cultural and linguistic affinities, and neighborly affections also remained a part of Muslim-Jewish life particularly in shared urban spaces following their initial arrival in France—the sense of rupture was profound. During moments of conflict, activists from both populations were easily drawn to this history with Jewish spokesmen reminding their co-religionists of Muslim aggression and their Muslim counterparts referring to Jewish affection for colonial oppressors.[7]

Moreover—and perhaps more importantly—the inequities of colonial administration in North Africa were replicated on French soil. While Muslim immigrants were trapped in a cycle of poverty passed on to their children, Jewish migrants experienced a much more rapid social ascent aided, in part, by a more favorable welcome by French authorities, such as was evident in Marseille. These differences meant that encounters between French Muslims and Jews never happened on an even playing field, helping to shape political choices thereafter, such as in the 1980s when joint anti-racist efforts collapsed in part over a sense that whatever Muslim and Jewish French citizens shared, their struggles were necessarily divergent.

This reference to French minority politics points to a second argument weaving through this text: disagreements over Middle Eastern war and the Israeli-Palestinian struggle cannot in and of themselves explain the evolution of Muslim-Jewish political conversations in France over the last fifty years. To be sure, the Middle East proved highly divisive. Beginning in 1948, when Zionist and Arab nationalist activists sparred in Marseille or in 1968 when Belleville was torn apart at the anniversary of the 1967 war, or in 1982 when the outbreak of the first Palestinian intifada led demonstrators in France to don kaffiyehs, disagreements over Israel sparked confrontations among highly politicized sectors of France's Muslim and Jewish populations. As I have argued, however, these conflicts were often about more than the Middle East, becoming a way of talking about inequities at home. Moreover, if "transnational diaspora affiliations" helped spur conflict since 2000, they were not the inevitable outcome of Israel's birth in 1948 or a necessary result of the encounter between Muslims and Jews in France. Rather, as the chapters on decolonization, 1968 French radical politics, and the 1980s experiments in multiculturalism make clear, the Arab-Israeli conflict often grew in local significance thanks to shifts in *French* political culture that shaped the choices of a wide range of social actors, including police charged with maintaining the social order; media personnel; self-appointed communal spokesmen; political militants on the French far left; international Jewish representatives; Algerian, Moroccan, and Tunisian nationalists; anti-racist activists; and so on. This diverse cast of characters established the parameters of Muslim-Jewish relations in France over several decades and out of a series of developments that were global but also national and local. Indeed, the continued focus on interethnic relations in Marseille has served to remind us of the local dimensions to an issue that is so often framed in terms of an inevitable sparring between "Arabs" and "Jews" wherever they reside. In Marseille, Muslim-Jewish relations were as much a reflection of political culture in the municipality; urban development programs; the struggle over limited resources; city geography; and entangled interethnic commercial networks as they were a reflection of developments in the Middle East. And when disagreements over Israel took center stage, they often served as a proxy for wider Muslim and Jewish political negotiations with the French state.

Lastly, I have stressed the powerful ways in which binary constructions of Muslim-Jewish interaction have worked to erase the more complex social terrain in which Muslims and Jews have interacted in late twentieth-century France. Here too, a brief return to Marseille helps illustrate this point. As numbers of Jews and Muslims grew in the port city in the 1950s and 1960s, their daily interactions were more diverse than a focus on polarization suggests. Just two years prior to the Gulf War and its widespread predictions of interethnic disturbances, local police described convivial relations between neighbors: "In Marseille, 90% of Jewish merchants are found in a quarter with a large percentage of North African [Muslims] and for many years, there have been good relations between these two communities."[8] One controversy from the period shows just how misleading language of political polarization can be. In 1988 and 1989, at the very moment pluriculturalism was collapsing as a rallying cry, a schism *within* Marseille's Jewish community led two synagogues and three kosher butchers to break away from consistorial control. In response, the consistorial leadership, which under French law controls the granting of kosher status to all vendors, revoked the butchers' certification. To get around the ban, the "dissidents" turned to Muslim slaughterers whose ritual techniques are similar to those of religious Jews and whose authorization was governed by Marseille's prefectorial authorities. A local imam even provided one shohet with a card authorizing him to slaughter and sell ritual meat.[9]

This temporary religious alliance between Muslims and Jews in response to an intercommunal conflict among Jews points to the weaknesses of "polarization" as a model for understanding Muslim-Jewish relations in France. Nevertheless, two years later, media outlets, local police, and communal spokesmen from both Muslim and Jewish organizations were predicting violent conflict if war broke out in the Middle East. In this construct, disagreements over possible outcomes in Kuwait overshadowed a longer history in which settlement patterns, relations to the municipality, economic inequities, colonial histories, religious traditions, and shared anti-racist struggles shaped the way peoples from different origins met and lived together.[10] Repeatedly, then, a reductionist-charged narrative of polarization has hidden a more complex set of social interactions, a phenomenon that helps explain why, despite all of the dire predictions, the city of Marseille never manifested the interethnic conflict that so many social commentators feared.

In tracing the way "Muslim-Jewish" has become shorthand for a rigid opposition politics that has obscured a more complex interethnic landscape, *Muslims and Jews in France* has thus sought to trace both the multifaceted origins of the charged political landscape and to underscore its powerful impact. While language of "conflict" may not accurately describe the daily interactions of most Muslims and Jews throughout the period under study, the emergence of this political landscape shaped the parameters of public discourse and narrowed the range of choices available to those representing communal life. The marked rise in anti-Jewish violence in 2000 emerged from this history of narrowing political categories and also helped solidify them, meaning that whatever the diversity of social life on the ground, Muslim-Jewish conflict is likely to remain a salient feature of French political life for the foreseeable future.

ABBREVIATIONS

Archives

AJDC	American Jewish Joint Distribution Committee
AIU	Alliance israélite universelle
AJC	American Jewish Committee
AN	Archives nationale
APP	Archives du Prefecture de police de Paris
BdR	Archives départementales des Bouches-du-Rhône
CAC	Centre des archives contemporaines
CC	Consistoire centrale
CJDC	Centre de documentation juive contemporaine
MAE	Archives diplomatiques, Ministère des affaires étrangères
UEJF	Union des étudiants juifs de France

Abbreviations in Notes

AE	*Algérien en Europe*
ADAM	Archives de la délégation de l'AIU au Maroc
AL	1944–59 Afrique-Levant, 1944–1959
BIL	*Bulletin d'information et de liaison du Comité de coordination des organisations juives de France*
FJL	Fonds Jacques Lazarus
IPFL 1	944–65 Inventaire provisoire du fonds Levant 1944–1965
GILR	Groupe d'information et de liaison régional, région de Provence-Côte d'Azur
MAMT	Ministre des affaires marocaines et tunisiennes
MI	Ministère de l'intérieur
ME	Ministère des affaires étrangères
Préfet des BdR	Préfet des Bouches-du-Rhône
RG	Renseignements généraux (all references to the Service départemental des renseignements généraux, the Direction des renseignements généraux, or the Direction centrale des renseignements généraux, will be designated RG).
SEAA	Secrétariat d'état aux affaires algériennes
SG/1948	Séries géographiques après 1948

NOTES

Introduction

1. Although of mixed-ethnic origin, the gang that murdered Halimi was led by Parisian-born Youssouf Fofana and reportedly read Koranic verses while torturing their victim. For a recent study of growing Jewish racism, see Kimberly Arkin, "'It's the French and the Arabs against the Jews': Identity Politics and the Construction of Adolescent Jewishness in France" (Ph.D. diss., University of Chicago, 2008).

2. Citation is from Raphaël Draï, *Sous le signe de Sion: L'antisémitisme nouveau est arrivé* (Paris: Éditions Michalon, 2001), p. 14.

3. Those who make the case for a new form of antisemitism include, Michael Berenbaum ed. *Not Your Father's Antisemitism: Hatred of the Jews in the Twenty-first Century* (St. Paul, Minn.: Paragon House, 2008); Alain Finkielkraut, *Au nom de l'autre: Réflexions sur l'antisémitisme qui vient* (Paris: Gallimard, 2003); Raphael Israeli, *Muslim Anti-Semitism in Christian Europe* (New Brunswick: Transaction Publishers, 2009); Pierre-André Taguieff, *La nouvelle judéophobie* (Paris: Mille et une nuits, 2002); and Shmuel Trigano, *La démission de la République: Juifs et Musulmans en France* (Paris: Presses universitaires de France, 2003). In contrast are those who question both the "newness" of recent anti-Jewish violence and the level of threat it poses. See, for example, Anthony Lerman, "Sense on Antisemitism," in *A New Antisemitism? Debating Judeophobia in 21st Century Britain*, eds. Paul Iganski and Barry Kosmin (London: Institute for Jewish Policy Research, 2003): 54–67 and Amikam Nachmani, "'The Triangle': Europeans, Muslims, Jews," in *Muslim Attitudes to Jews and Israel: The Ambivalences of Rejection, Antagonism, Tolerance and Cooperation*, ed., Moshe Ma'oz (Portland: Sussex Academic Press 2010): 264–84. Matti Bunzl, *Anti-Semitism and Islamophobia: Hatreds Old and New in Europe* (Prickly Paradigm Press, 2007), provides a helpful critique of this debate.

4. For the former, see Esther Benbassa, *La République face à ses minorités: Les Juifs hier, les Musulmans aujourd'hui* (Paris: Mille et une nuits, 2004). For the latter, see Jean-Marc Dreyfus and Jonathan Laurence, "Anti-Semitism in France," *U.S.-France Analysis*, 14 May 2002; Jonathan Laurence and Justin Vaisse, *Integrating Islam: Political and Religious Challenges in Contemporary France* (Washington, D.C.: Brookings Institution Press, 2006), pp. 222–43; Denis Sieffert, *Israël-Palestine, une passion française: La France dans le miroir du conflit israélo-palestinien* (Paris: Éditions la Découverte, 2004), pp. 212–30. For Jews, Arkin "'It's the French and the Arabs against the Jews.'"

5. More nuanced analyses include Michel Wieviorka's, *La tentation antisémite: Haine des Juifs dans la France d'aujourd'hui* (Paris: Robert Laffont, 2005), which debunks the link between Islam and antisemitism and posits that antagonism will recede with the alleviation of socioeconomic inequities, and Ethan Katz, "Jews and Muslims in

the Shadow of Marianne: Conflicting Identities and Republican Culture in France (1914–1975)" (Ph.D. diss., University of Wisconsin–Madison, 2009), which explores the long and rich historical connections between Muslims and Jews in France.

6. French law prohibits census takers from distinguishing among citizens based on religion, meaning estimates of the Jewish and Muslim populations vary widely. In the early 1980s, Doris Bensimon and Sergio Della Pergola, *La population juive de France: Socio-démographie et identité* (Jerusalem, The Institute of Contemporary Jewry, Hebrew University, 1984), p. 25, put the number of Jews at 535,000. Erik H. Cohen, *The Jews of France Today: Identity and Values* (Leiden and Boston: Brill, 2011), pp. 59–63, estimates the number today at 500,000–550,000. For lower estimates on Muslims, see Michèle Tribalat, "Counting France's Numbers—Deflating the Numbers Inflation," *The Social Contract Journal* 14, 2 (Winter 2003–2004), http://www.thesocialcontract.com/artman2/publish/tsc1402/article_1210.shtml (last accessed 2 January 2013). In 2000, the French Ministry of the Interior, *L'Islam dans la République* (Haut conseil à l'intégration, November 2000), p. 26, claimed 4.1 million. Politicians on the far right claim as many as 6–8 million. See Laurence and Vaïsse, *Integrating Islam*, 17–22, who settle on 5 million, for more on this debate.

7. For linguistic and cultural similarities, see Arkin, "'It's the French and the Arabs against the Jews,'" 171. For comparisons of Muslim and Jewish integration into French society, see Martine Cohen, "Juifs et Musulmans en France: Le modèle républicain d'intégration en question," *Sociétés contemporaines* 37 (2000): 89–120; "Laïcité et intégration des vagues migratoires juives et musulmanes en France: Du cadre national à la mondialisation," in *Politiques de la laïcité au XXe siècle*, ed. Patrick Weil (Paris: Presses universitaires de France, 2007): 571–89; "Jews and Muslims in France: Changing Responses to Cultural and Religious Diversity," in *Legal Practice and Cultural Diversity*, ed. Ralph Grillo (London: Ashgate, 2009): 219–36; Rémy Leveau and Dominique Schnapper, *Religion et politique: Juifs et Musulmans maghrébins en France* (Paris: Association française de science politique and the Centre d'études et de recherches internationales, 1987); and William Safran, "Ethnoreligious Politics in France: Jews and Muslims," *West European Politics* 27, 3 (May 2004): 423–51. Shmuel Trigano challenges the legitimacy of such comparisons in "Les logiques perverses de la politique française," *Observatoire du monde juif*, November 2000, pp. 22–28 and elsewhere. For links between antisemitism and other forms of racism in France, see Gérard Noiriel, *Immigration, antisémitisme et racisme en France (XIX–XX siècle): Discours publics, humiliations privées* (Paris: Fayard, 2007). Yvan Gastaut, *L'Immigration et l'opinion en France sous la Ve République* (Paris: Éditions du Seuil, 2000), insists, in contrast, on the singularity of anti-Muslim attitudes in France.

8. As Ethan Katz, "Jews and Muslims," 44–235, has convincingly argued, colonialism, nationalism, and French minority policies began shaping the contours of Muslim-Jewish relations by World War I. My focus on a later period, however, reflects my sense of the seismic impact of decolonization on subsequent Muslim-Jewish politics in the metropole.

9. Joëlle Bahloul, *The Architecture of Memory: A Jewish-Muslim Household in Colonial Algeria, 1936–1962*, trans. Catherine du Peloux Ménagé (Cambridge University Press, 1996), p. 85.

10. A Middle-Eastern focus is common. For example, according to Henry Weinberg, "French Jewry: Trauma and Renewal," *Midstream* (December 1982), p. 12: "In the end, the place of Jews in French society will to a large extent be determined in a region distant from France's boundaries." Doris Bensimon, *Les Juifs de France et leurs relations avec Israël, 1945–1988* (Paris: Éditions l'Harmattan, 1989), p. 237, asserts that Jews and Muslims were "too implicated" in the Israeli-Arab conflict to establish a legitimate dialogue.

11. For the significance of North African history to the postcolonial migrant experience, see Sayad Abdelmalek, *La double absence: Des illusions de l'émigré aux souffrances de l'immigré* (Paris: Seuil, "Liber", 1999), p. 56.

12. Patrick Weil, *La France et ses étrangers: L'aventure d'une politique de l'immigration de 1938 à nos jours*, 1st ed. (Paris: Calmann-Lévy, 1991), pp. 41–128. By 1975, newcomers made up 6.5 percent of the French population. Noiriel, *Immigration, antisémitisme et racisme*, 484.

13. Figures come from Neil MacMaster, *Colonial Migrants and Racism: Algerians in France, 1900–62* (New York: St. Martin's Press, 1997), pp. 3, 189, and Benjamin Stora, *Ils venaient d'Algérie: L'immigration en France (1912–1992)* (Paris: Fayard, 1992), pp. 94, 401. The citation is from Belkacem Hifi, *L'immigration algérienne en France: Origines et perspectives de non-retour* (Paris: l'Harmattan CIEM, 1985), p. 171.

14. Noiriel, *Immigration, antisémitisme et racisme*, 543.

15. Bensimon and Della Pergola, *La population juive de France*, 36. Also see Jacques Taïeb, "Immigrés d'Afrique du Nord: Combien? quand? pourquoi?" in *Terre d'exil terre d'asile: Migrations juives en France aux XIXe et XXe siècles*, ed. Colette Zytnicki (Paris: Éditions de l'Éclat): 149–54.

16. Véronique Poirier, *Ashkénazes et Séfarades: Une étude comparée de leurs relations en France et en Israël* (Paris: Cerf, 1998); Sarah Sussman, "Changing Lands, Changing Identities: The Migration of Algerian Jewry to France, 1954–1967" (Ph.D. diss., Stanford University, 2003), pp. 321–64.

17. Pierre Baillet, "Les rapatriés d'Algérie en France," *Notes et études documentaires*, No. 4275–76 (29 March 1976), pp. 46–57. As Clifford Rosenberg, *Policing Paris: The Origins of Modern Immigration Control Between the Wars* (Ithaca: Cornell University Press 2006), makes clear, if inequities toward Muslims were embedded throughout the colonial project, they were not only "imported" to France but also emerged out of metropolitan efforts to define citizenship and belonging under the Third Republic.

18. For Morocco, see Jonathan Wyrtzen, "Constructing Morocco: Colonial Struggle to Define the Nation, 1912–1956" (PhD. diss., Georgetown University, 2009), pp. 39–83. For Tunisia, see Richard C. Parks, "Hygiene, Regeneration, and Citizenship: Jews in the Tunisian Protectorate" (Ph.D. diss., University of Minnesota, 2012). For the power of French ethnic constructions in Algeria, see Paul Silverstein, *Algeria in France: Transpolitics, Race, and Nation* (Bloomington: Indiana University Press, 2004), pp. 35–67, and Patricia Lorcin, *Imperial Identities: Stereotyping, Prejudice and Race in Colonial Algeria* (London: I. B. Tauris, 1995) and *Kabyles, Arabes, Français: Identités coloniales* (Limoges: Presses universitaires de Limoges, 2005).

19. Joshua Schreier, *Arabs of the Jewish Faith: The Civilizing Mission in Colonial Algeria* (Piscataway, N.J.: Rutgers University Press, 2010) argues that Jewish "worthiness" for emancipation was used to exclude Muslims who were seen as comparatively less able to become French.

20. Arkin, "It's the French and the Arabs," chap. 1, nicely synthesizes this history while underscoring the blocks preventing complete Jewish integration into French colonial society. Pathways to citizenship existed for certain Jews, particularly in Tunisia where several thousand were naturalized primarily in the 1920s and early 1930s despite French colonial administrators' opposition to blanket naturalization. See Parks, "Hygiene, Regeneration, and Citizenship," 34–37, 98–100. Fayçel Cherif, "Jewish-Muslim Relations in Tunisia during World War II: Propaganda, Stereotypes, and Attitudes, 1939–1943," in *Jewish Culture and Society in North Africa*, eds. Emily Benichou Gotreich and Daniel Schroeter (Bloomington: Indiana University Press, 2011), p. 314, reports 7,160 Jewish naturalizations from 1911 to 1940. In Morocco, the rules against naturalization were tighter. André Chouraqui, *Histoire des Juifs en Afrique du Nord: Le retour en orient* (Monaco: Éditions du Rocher, 1998), p. 39.

21. Citation from Noiriel, *Immigration, antisémitisme, et racisme*, 537. For ongoing administrative limitations on Algerians, see Abdelmalek Sayad, Jean-Jacques Jordi, and Émile Témime, *Le Choc de la décolonisation (1945–1990)*, vol. 4 of *Migrance: Histoire des migrations à Marseille*, ed. Émile Témime (Aix-en-Provence: Éditions Jeanne Laffitte, 1991), pp. 48, 187–78, and Emmanuel Blanchard, *La police parisienne et les Algériens (1944–1962)* (Paris: Nouveau monde éditions, 2010). Amelia Lyons, "Invisible Immigrants: Algerian Families and the French Welfare State in the Era of Decolonization (1947–1974)" (Ph.D. diss., University of California–Irvine, 2004), pp. 9, 40–49, argues that prior to 1962, welfare institutions did seek to incorporate Algerian Muslims into French society.

22. Todd Shepard, *The Invention of Decolonization: The Algerian War and the Remaking of France* (Ithaca/London: Cornell University Press, 2006), pp. 39–43, 172–73.

23. For Algerian Jewish settlement, see Sussman, "Changing Lands, Changing Identities," 188–89. Alexis Spire, *Étrangers à la carte: L'administration de l'immigration en France (1945–1975)* (Paris: Grasset, 2005), pp. 189–222, shows how even Muslim repatriates who had fought for the French army were treated as administratively distinct from "European" repatriates. Fatima Besnaci-Lancou and Gilles Manceron eds., *Les harkis: Dans la colonisation et ses suites* (Paris: Les Éditions de l'Atelier, 2008), pp. 30–31, 112. Tom Charbit, *Les harkis* (Paris: La Découverte, 2006), pp. 60–61. For aid to repatriates, see Jean Jacques Jordi, *De l'exode à l'exil: Rapatriés et pieds-noirs en France* (Paris: Éditions l'Harmattan, 1993) and *1962, L'Arrivée des pieds-noirs* (Paris: Autrement, 1995).

24. Robert Lever, "Finding the Promised Land," *Present Tense*, January–February 1989, pp. 33–35. Martin Messika, "L'accueil des Juifs marocains en France," in *Terre d'exil, terre d'asile*, 175–78.

25. Maud Mandel, *In the Aftermath of Genocide: Armenians and Jews in Twentieth-Century France* (Durham: Duke University Press, 2003).

26. Mônica Raisa Schpun, "Les premiers migrants Juifs d'Afrique du Nord dans la France de l'après guerre: Une découverte pour les services sociaux," and Laura Hobson Faure, "Le travail social dans les organisations juives françaises après la Shoah: Création made in France ou importation Américaine," *Archives juives* 42, 1 (2012): 43–73; Colette Zytnicki, "A immigration d'un nouveau type, réponses nouvelles: Les organisations communautaires et l'exodes des Juifs d'Afrique du Nord," in *Terre d'exil, terre d'asile*, 155–70. Conflict between incoming North African Jews and their

French Jewish co-religionists is documented in Poirier, *Ashkénazes et Séfarades*; Sussman, "Changing Lands," 321–64. For organizational efforts to fight antisemitism, see Samuel Ghiles-Meilhac, "From an Unsolvable Dispute to a Unifying Compromise: Zionism at the Heart of the Debates Underlying the Creation of the French Jewish Umbrella Organization, the CRIF," *Bulletin du centre de recherche français à Jérusalem*, 20 (2009), http://bcrfj.revues.org/6196 (last accessed on 26 June 2012).

27. Stora, *Ils venaient d'Algérie*.

28. The inclusion of Arabic sources would likely enhance the picture of how Muslim discourses on Jews shifted over time and place, particularly in chapter 2, which deals with North African decolonization. However, given my focus on discourses of conflict in mainland France (where very few Arabic archival sources were produced), the absence is less significant than it would be for a study rooted in North Africa.

29. For the shifting Jewish economic and professional profile, see Cohen *The Jews of France Today*, 67–72.

30. Noiriel, *Immigration, antisémitisme et racisme en France*, 622–24.

31. Joan Scott, *Politics of the Veil* (Princeton: Princeton University Press, 2007), pp. 1–2.

32. Arkin, "It's the French and the Arabs," 207–17; Pierre Birnbaum, *Jewish Destinies: Citizenship, State and Community in Modern France*, trans. Arthur Goldhammer (New York: Hill and Wang, 2000), pp. 191–213.

33. For divisions before the war, see Nancy Green, *The Pletzl of Paris: Jewish Immigrant Workers in the Belle Époque* (New York: Holmes and Meier, 1986); Paula Hyman, *From Dreyfus to Vichy: The Remaking of French Jewry, 1906–1939* (New York: Columbia University Press, 1979); and David H. Weinberg, *A Community on Trial: The Jews of Paris in the 1930s* (Chicago: University of Chicago Press, 1977). Nadia Malinovich, *French and Jewish: Culture and the Politics of Identity in Early Twentieth-Century France* (Oxford: Littman Library of Jewish Civilization, 2008), pp. 5–6, 109–14, argues that such divisions have been too starkly drawn. As noted, Poirier, *Ashkénazes et Séfarades* and Sussman, "Changing Lands," 321–64, document tensions between Jews settled in France and those incoming in the 1950s–1970s.

34. Laurence and Vaïsse, *Integrating Islam*, 7, 15–48.

35. Silverstein, *Algeria in France*, 130.

36. The majority of initial Algerian migrants were Kabyles, a mountain-dwelling people of Berber descent. When more Algerian Arabs began arriving in the interwar years, tensions emerged between them and their predecessors, as did tensions between Algerians and those from other North African countries. Macmaster, *Colonial Migrants*, passim, and Stora, *Ils venaient d'Algérie*, 13–74.

37. Abdellali Hajjat, "Les usages politiques de l'héritage colonial," in *Immigrances: L'immigration en France au XXème siècle*, ed., Émile Temime (Paris: Hachette littératures, 2007), pp. 198–99.

38. Laurence and Vaïsse, *Integrating Islam*, 16. Benjamin Stora, *Ils venaient d'Algérie*, 117–18, reminds us that Arabic and Islam also created bridges.

39. Dominique Schnapper, Chantal Bordes-Benayoun, and Freddy Raphaël, *Jewish Citizenship in France: The Temptation of Being among One's Own*, trans., Catherine Temerson (New Brunswick and London: Transaction Publishers, 2010), pp. 13–16, 111, argue that although many French Jews still speak of Ashkenazic and Sephardic divisions, modes of identity and political expression do not differ substantially between those identifying with either group.

40. Joyce Dalsheim, "On Demonized Muslims and Vilified Jews: Between Theory and Politics," *Comparative Studies in Society and History* 52, 3 (2010), p. 586, n. 11. Thanks to Ethan Katz for directing me to this article.

41. Naomi Davidson, *Only Muslim: Embodying Islam in Twentieth-Century France* (Ithaca and London: Cornell University Press, 2012), p. 4 and passim.

42. Shepard, *The Invention of Decolonization*, 238. Shepard and Davidson disagree as to the timing of this process, with Davidson emphasizing the interwar and World War II period, and Shepard emphasizing the Algerian war.

43. Mandel, *In the Aftermath of Genocide*, 151–77.

44. Blanchard, *La police parisienne et les Algériens* 36–40.

45. For the stereotypes associated with the label "Arab," see Gastaut, *L'Immigration et l'opinion*, 109. For North African Muslim attraction to Arab political causes, see Rabah Aissaoui, *Immigration and National Identity: North African Political Movements in Colonial and Postcolonial France* (London and New York: Tauris Academic Studies, 2009) and Abdellali Hajjat, "Les Comités Palestine (1970–1972): Aux origines du soutien de la cause palestinienne en France," *Revue d'études palestiniennes*, 98 (Winter 2006): 74–92, and "L'expérience politique du mouvement des travailleurs arabes," *Contretemps* 16 (May 2006): 76–85. For a combined revision of these two articles see "Des Comités Palestine au Mouvement des travailleurs arabes (1970–1976)," in Ahmed Boubeker and Abdellali Hajjat, eds., *Histoire politique des immigrations (post) coloniales: France, 1920–2008* (Paris: Éditions Amsterdam, 2008): 145–56.

46. Silverstein, *Algeria in France*, 106, 108; Noiriel, *Immigration, antisémitisme et racisme*, 611–13; Gastaut, *L'immigration et l'opinion*, 478–512.

47. Demographers, sociologists, and historians have suggested that the saliency of Islam among those of North African Muslim heritage has intensified in recent decades. For a summary of this literature, see "Muslims in the EU: Cities Report, Preliminary Research Report and Literature Survey, France" (Grenoble: Open Society Institute EU Monitoring and Advocacy Program, 2007), pp. 19–27.

48. The first figure comes from Marie Attard-Maraninchi and Émile Témime, *Le cosmopolitisme de l'entre-deux-guerres (1919–1945)*, vol. 3 of *Migrance: Histoire des migrations à Marseille*, ed., Émile Témime (Aix-en-Provence: Édisud, 1990), p. 160. The latter come from Sayad, Jordi, and Témime, *Le Choc*, 8, 61–64, 89–98.

49. Jean-Jacques Jordi, "L'été 62 à Marseille: Tensions et incompréhensions," in *Marseille et le choc des décolonisations: Les rapatriements, 1954–1964*, eds., Jean-Jacques Jordi and Émile Témime (Aix-en-Provence: Édisud, 1996), p. 73. Émile Témime, *Histoire de Marseille de la Révolution à nos jours* (Perrin 1999), p. 330. Algerians made up 30,190 of the 35,860 Muslims in 1968. By 1974, they were still the majority, but the number of Tunisians and Moroccans had grown. Institut national d'études démographiques, Universités de Lyon II et III, Aix-Marseille I et Poitiers, *Immigrés du Maghreb: Études sur l'adaptation en milieu urbain* (Paris: Presses universitaires de France, 1977), pp. 10, 13. Sayad, Jordi, and Témime, *Le Choc*, 121, claim 44,000 Muslims in Marseille in 1975.

50. Statistics from 1945 come from Roland Avitol, "Marseille," *L'Arche* (March/April, 1968): 19–20, and from Donna F. Ryan, *The Holocaust & the Jews of Marseille: The Enforcement of Anti-Semitic Policies in Vichy France* (Urbana and Chicago: University of Illinois Press, 1996), p. 13. The figure of 12,000 comes from the FSJU and is included in Julian Breen to Boris Sapir, 15 February 1963, 309, AJDC. Avitol put the figure at 15,000 as did Jacques Sabbath, "Communauté vivante," *L'Arche*, November

1962, pp. 2–4. The city's Jewish demographics in the late 1950s are documented in an untitled report, November 1964, 346, AJDC.

51. Préfet de la région de Provence to RG, "La communauté juive de Marseille," 17 January 1972, 135W57, BdR, claimed 75,000 Jews in Marseille by the early 1970s. However, Bensimon-Donath, *L'intégration des Juifs,* 55, reports 65,000 in 1966. Some reports put the population as high as 100,000 in 1967, perhaps due to transients. R.G., Mle, "Milieux juifs," 30 May 1967, 137W363, BdR. For Algerian Jewish repatriation, see, Sussman, "Changing Lands," 188–245.

52. Yvan Gastaut, "Marseille cosmopolite après les décolonisations: Un enjeu identitaire," *Cahiers de la Méditerranée* 67 (2003), http://cdlm.revues.org/index134.html#bodyftn17 (last accessed 6 August 2012).

53. For the impact of Marseille's urban development pattern on ethnic collectivities, see Cesari, *Être musulman en France,* 71, and Katharyne Mitchell, "Marseille's Not for Burning: Comparative Networks of Integration and Exclusion in Two French Cities," *Annals of the Association of American Geographers* 101, 2 (2011), p. 414.

54. Témime, *Histoire de Marseille,* 366–67; INED, *Immigrés du Maghreb,* 17–19.

55. Émile Témime, *Marseille transit: Les passagers de Belsunce* (Paris: Éditions Autrement, 1995), p. 19; Mitchell, "Marseille's Not for Burning," 412–13.

56. Jean André Carreno, Alain Hayot, and Francis Lesme, *Le quartier de la porte d'Aix à Marseille: Ethnologie d'un centre urbain* (Aix-en-Provence: Université de Provence, 1974), p. 15, make clear that notwithstanding the large numbers of immigrants in these neighborhoods, the majority were "French." Jocelyne Cesari, Alain Moreau, and Alexandra Schleyer-Lindenmann, *"Plus marseillais que moi, tu meurs!" Migrations, identités et territoires à Marseille* (Paris: L'Harmattan, 2001), pp. 20–21, 121, argue that while economic and social cleavages divide northern sectors to this day, all residents consider themselves part of the city and have spent considerable time in its center.

57. Sayad, Jordi, and Témime, *Le Choc,* 11, 124.

58. Témime, *Marseille transit,* 12. For Belleville, see Patrick Simon and Claude Tapia, *Le Belleville des Juifs tunisiens* (Paris: Éditions Autrement, 1998).

59. Francis Lesme, *Provence, Bulletin de l'association des anciens élèves,* Marseille, n. 4, May 1972, cited in Gastaut, "Marseille cosmopolite après les décolonisations." Gastaut makes clear that despite its image of convivial cosmopolitan intermingling, the city experienced plenty of racist extremism.

60. Mitchell, "Marseille's Not for Burning," links the city's ethnically networked capitalist system with its urban development to help explain the relatively peaceful ethnic landscape.

61. Claire Berlinski, "The Hope of Marseille," *Azure* 19 (Winter 5765/2005), p. 38.

Chapter 1. Colonial Policies, Middle Eastern War, and City Spaces: Marseille in 1948

1. Telegram, Cairo to Département de Levant, 14 June 1948, IPFL 1944–65, 401, MAE. The source in this instance refers to "North African dockworkers" and not "Muslims" as such. See the Introduction for clarification of my use of terminology.

2. RG, Mle, "L'affaire palestinienne," 28 January 1949, 148W185, BdR.

3. Idith Zertal, *From Catastrophe to Power: Holocaust Survivors and the Emergence of Israel* (Berkeley: University of California Press, 1998), pp. 52–53. Émile Témime, *Histoire de Marseille de la Révolution à nos jours* (Perrin 1999), p. 329, puts the number at 15,000.

4. By 1954, Algerian Muslims numbered 210,000 throughout the country, mostly in Paris. Abdelmalek Sayad, Jean-Jacques Jordi, and Émile Témime, *Le choc de la décolonisation (1945–1990)*, vol. 4 of *Migrance: Histoire des migrations à Marseille*, ed. Émile Témime (Aix-en-Provence: Éditions Jeanne Laffitte, 1991), p. 49; Benjamin Stora, *Ils venaient d'Algérie: L'immigration en France (1912–1992)* (Paris: Fayard, 1992), p. 143.

5. Sayad, Jordi, and Témime, *Le Choc*, 40; 48, 187–88, and Todd Shepard, *The Invention of Decolonization: The Algerian War and the Remaking of France* (Ithaca and London: Cornell University Press, 2006), pp. 39–43.

6. RG, Mle, 6 September 1950, 148W191, BdR. As Sayad, Jordi, and Témime, *Le Choc*, 70–71, make clear, Marseille was never the center of Algerian political mobilization in France thanks to the size and transience of its Algerian Muslim population.

7. Although on record for backing Jewish national ambitions after the 1917 Balfour Declaration, French diplomats had, since the 1920s, expressed concern that support for Zionism would alienate their Muslim subjects and promote Arab nationalism. Tsilla Herscho, *Entre Paris et Jérusalem: La France, le Sionisme et la création de l'État d'Israël, 1945–1949*, trans. from Hebrew by Claire Darmon (Paris: Honoré Champion, 2003), p. 16; Catherine Nicault, *La France et le Sionisme, 1897–1948* (Paris: Calmann-Lévy, 1992), pp. 158–72; Denis Sieffert, *Israël-Palestine: Une passion française* (Paris: La Découverte, 2004), pp. 56–57. Jonathan Wyrtzen, "Constructing Morocco: Colonial Struggle to Define the Nation, 1912–1956" (Ph.D. diss., Georgetown University, 2009), pp. 39–83, 224, 231, 234–38, traces these fears in Morocco.

8. Zertal, *From Catastrophe to Power*, 52–92. Herscho, *Entre Paris et Jérusalem*, 31–32 notes that some foreign ministry officials favored moderate migration to Palestine (and elsewhere) to encourage Jewish departures from France.

9. "Le problème palestinien: La fin éventuelle du mandat et les intérêts français" (1947), IPFL 1944–65, 373, L.72.1, MAE.

10. Examples of such concerns include Gabriel Puaux to Monsieur le Général d'armée, "Émigration juive vers la Palestine," 8 November 1944, IPFL 1944–65; "Note sur l'attitude française à l'égard de la Déclaration Balfour et du Sionisme," 13 July 1946, IPFL 1944–65, 373, L.72.1; Note pour le ministre, "Installation en France d'un gouvernement exilé de la Palestine hébraïque," no date, IPFL 1944–65, 23, K.13.7, MAE.

11. "Note pour le ministre," 8 April 1947, 30, G3, MAE.

12. Tsilla Herschco, "France and the Partition Plan: 1947–8," *Israel Affairs*, 14, 3 (July 2008): 486–98.

13. Jacques Dalloz, *Georges Bidault: Biographie politique* (Éditions l'Harmattan, 1992), p. 273.

14. "Question étrangères," and "Entrée clandestine en France de Juifs en provenance de camps de concentration allemands," Direction générale de la sûreté nationale, 13 September 1946, f/1a/3368, AN; RG, Mle, "Activité du service social de la Fédération des sociétés juives de France à Marseille," 13 May 1947, 148W185, BdR; Zertal, *From Catastrophe to Power*, 52–92; Herscho, *Entre Paris et Jerusalem*, 20–44, 59–62, 69–70.

15. Direction d'Afrique-Levant to Direction des conventions administratives et sociales, "Émigration clandestine vers la Palestine et activité en France d'organisations sionistes," no date, IPFL 1944-65, 376, L.72.2, MAE.

16. Ambassadeur de France en Grande Bretagne to Bidault, "Camp d'entraînement pour combattants juifs en France," 5 July 1948, IPFL 1944–65, 401, MAE. As Mônica Raisa Schpun, "Les premières migrants juifs d'Afrique du Nord dans la France de l'après-guerre: Une découverte pour les services sociaux," *Archives juives* 45, 1 (2012): 61–73, makes clear, a significant percentage of North African Jews who went to Israel returned home and some who went were already living in France.

17. Yves Chataigneau to MI, "Sionisme," 2 November 1946, AL 1944–59, 5, K.38.2, MAE; RG, Mle, "Activité des Juifs d'Algérie en faveur des Sionistes," 10 June 1948, 148W185, BdR; E. de Beauverger to ME, "Départs israélites pour la Palestine, via France," 3 February (1948?), IPFL 1944–65, 376, 72.2, MAE.

18. Paula Hyman, *The Jews of Modern France* (Berkeley: University of California Press, 1998), p. 137.

19. Neil MacMaster, *Colonial Migrants and Racism: Algerians in France, 1900–1962* (New York: St. Martin's Press, 1997), p. 223.

20. Esther Benbassa, *Jews of France: A History from Antiquity to the Present*, trans. M. B. DeBevoise (Princeton: Princeton University Press, 1999), p. 149.

21. Ethan Katz, "Tracing the Shadow of Palestine: The Zionist-Arab Conflict and Jewish-Muslim Relations in France, 1914–1945," in *Israeli-Palestinian Conflict in the Francophone World*, ed., Nathalie Debrauwere-Miller (Routledge, 2009): 25–40.

22. Unless otherwise noted, discussion of the period prior to and during World War II is drawn from Ethan Katz, "Jews and Muslims in the Shadow of Marianne: Conflicting Identities and Republican Culture in France, 1914–1975" (Ph.D. diss., University of Wisconsin, 2008), pp. 44–235.

23. For Jewish life after World War II, see Mandel, *In the Aftermath of Genocide*.

24. Blanchard, *La police parisienne*, 17–18.

25. Patrick Weil, *Qu'est-ce qu'un Français? Histoire de la nationalité française depuis la Révolution* (Paris: Bernard Grasset: 2002), p. 243.

26. Sayad, Jordi, and Témime, *Le Choc*, 40, 48, 187–88. Shepard, *The Invention of Decolonization*, 39–43, argues that while the category *citoyens français musulmans d'Algérie* emerges from 1944–46, it was not given a legally binding definition until 1956. Also see Blanchard, *La police parisienne*, 20–27.

27. Accounts of French Zionism vary between those who stress its initial institutional weakness and those who underscore its long-term impact on ethnic cohesion. For the former, see Nicault, *La France et le Sionisme*. For the latter, see Michel Abitbol, *Les deux terres promises: Les Juifs de France et le Sionisme, 1897–1945* (Paris: Orban, 1989); Paula Hyman, *From Dreyfus to Vichy: The Remaking of French Jewry, 1906–1939* (New York: Columbia University Press 1979), chap. 6; Nadia Malinovich, *French and Jewish: Culture and the Politics of Identity in early Twentieth-Century France* (Oxford: Litmann Library of Jewish Civilization, 2007), pp. 57–67; Aron Rodrigue, "Rearticulations of French Jewish Identities after the Dreyfus Affair," *Jewish Social Studies* 2, 3 (1996): 1–24.

28. For French Zionism after World War II, see Mandel, *In the Aftermath of Genocide*, 134–48; Hershco, *Entre Paris et Jérusalem*, pp. 21–22, 57–74; Nicault, *La France et le*

Sionisme, 207–230; Renée Poznanski, "Le Sionisme en France pendant la deuxième guerre mondiale: Développements institutionnels et impact idéologique," in *Les Juifs de France, le sionisme et l'État d'Israël*, eds., Doris Bensimon and Benjamin Pinkus (Paris: Publications Langues'O, 1989), p. 212.

29. Poznanski, "Le Sionisme en France," pp. 212, 265–70; Samuel Ghiles-Meilhac, "From an Unsolvable Dispute to a Unifying Compromise: Zionism at the Heart of the Debates Underlying the Creation of the French Jewish Umbrella Organization, the CRIF," *Bulletin du Centre de recherche français à Jérusalem*, 20 (2009), put online 10 March 2010, consulted on 26 June 2012, URL: http://bcrfj.revues.org/6196. Jewish communists, guided by Soviet instructions, initially supported Israel's establishment. By the late 1950s, however, disenchantment with Soviet antisemitism had raised doubts about communism, and by the Suez crisis, many Jewish communists (and former communists) actively supported Israel. See Jacques Frémontier, *L'étoile rouge de David: Les Juifs communistes en France* (Paris: Fayard, 2002), passim, and Benjamin Pinkus, "La campagne de Suez et son impact sur les Juifs de France," in *Les Juifs de France*, 357–60.

30. "La propagande antibritannique dans les milieux juifs de Paris," 11 July 1946, Palestine—Zionism, f/1a/3368, AN.

31. Minutes, Comité d'études questions juives, 28 April 1945, IPFL 1944–65, 23, K.13.14, MAE.

32. Hershco's assessment in *Entre Paris et Jérusalem* that French Jews went from "opposition to indifference" understates sympathy for the movement, but is correct in that most believed Zionism was a solution for Eastern European Jewish refugees and not applicable to them.

33. Benjamin Stora and Emile Témime, *Immigrances: L'immigration en France au XXe siècle* (Paris: Hachette littératures 2007), p. 37; Abdellali Hajjat, "L'expérience politique du Mouvement des travailleurs arabes," *Contretemps* (16 May 2006), p. 79; Hajjat, "Les Comités Palestine (1970–1972): Aux origines du soutien de la cause palestinienne en France," *Revue d'études palestiniennes*, 98 (Winter 2006), p. 75. For Algerian Muslim migrants' engagment as citizens, see Amelia Lyons, "Invisible Immigrants: Algerian Families and the French Welfare State in the Era of Decolonization (1947–1974)" (Ph.D. diss., University of California–Irvine, 2004), p. 260. According to Catherine Wihtol de Wenden, *Les immigrés et la politique: Cent cinquante ans d'évolution* (Paris: Presses de la Fondation nationale des sciences politiques, 1988), pp. 155–80, France's Muslim population became politically active in domestic affairs in 1968. See also Daniel A. Gordon, *Immigrants and Intellectuals: May '68 and the Rise of Anti-Racism in France* (Merlin Press, 2012).

34. Chef de la brigade du quartier de la bourse to Commissaire central à Marseille, "Population musulmane," 13 June 1949, 148W191, BdR. Gordon, *Immigrants and Intellectuals*, makes clear that French police consistently downplayed immigrant political activities.

35. Stora, *Ils venaient d'Algérie*, 93–119, 163.

36. Rabah Aissaoui, *Immigration and National Identity: North African Political Movements in Colonial and Postcolonial France* (London and New York: Tauris Academic Studies, 2009), pp. 118–21; Katz, "Jews and Muslims," 245–46.

37. Stora, *Ils venaient d'Algérie*, 107–10. See Paul Silverstein, *Algeria in France: Transpolitics, Race, and Nation* (Bloomington and Indianapolis: Indiana University Press,

2004), pp. 68–70, for a challenge to the binaries associated with the so-called Berber crisis. Sieffert, *Israël-Palestine*, 101, suggests with scant evidence that most French Muslim Algerians shared the pro-Palestinian sentiment of certain nationalist leaders in the 1950s.

38. For more on this meeting see Katz, "Tracing the Shadow of Palestine," 25–40.

39. K. Hakki to ME, 30 October 1944, IPFL 1944–65, 373, L.72, MAE.

40. For the re-bonding of French Jews with the republic after World War II, see Mandel, *In the Aftermath of Genocide*, passim.

41. Herscho, *Entre Paris et Jérusalem*, 45–53, 95–99, 113–23; Dalloz, *Georges Bidault*, 269–77. Herscho argues that because Arab representatives were officially recognized state actors, they had an initial advantage, since Jewish Agency representatives lacked similar access to the Quai d'Orsay. She overlooks, however, the way well-placed French Jews—even those not fully convinced of the need for a Jewish state—sought to promote Jewish refugee settlement in Palestine or to defend Jewish interests on the international stage.

42. "La Propagande du Sionisme en France," *Al Afif*, 12 September 1948.

43. Association des amis de la Palestine arabe to ME, 18 February 1947, IPFL 1944–65, 373, L.72.1, MAE; Herscho, *Entre Paris et Jérusalem*, 83–88.

44. AIU officials, for example, protested to the Foreign Ministry that British policies "would encourage already developing tendencies towards unity and autonomy across the Arab world." René Cassin to Bidault, 4 July 1946, IPFL 1944–65, 373, L.72.1, MAE; (René Mayer and Jules Braunschvig to ME), no date, N° 30 G3, MAE. Nicault, *La France et le Sionisme*, 215, notes that AIU representatives were more comfortable demanding liberal immigration policies in Palestine than asserting long-term political solutions.

45. CRIF meeting, 15 May 1945, MDI 1–55, CDJC.

46. "La propagande du Sionisme en France," *Al afif*, 12 September 1948.

47. "Activité des Sionistes en France," 14 January 1948, BA 2315 Communauté juif, PPA.

48. RG, Afrique du Nord, "Activité du parti du peuple algérien," 2 February 1948, 5 Activités nationalistes, K.38.3, MAE.

49. Clipping from *Franc-Tireur*, 14 April 1948 in CRIF meeting, 27 July 1948, MDI 1–55, CDJC. The paper defined protestors as "Arabs," a catch-all phrase often used by the press to describe North African Muslim laborers. For the conflation of these terms, see Yvan Gastaut, *L'immigration et l'opinion en France sous la Ve République* (Paris: Éditions du Seuil, 2000), p. 109.

50. Nicault, *La France et le Sionisme*, 214, 258; Doris Bensimon, *Les Juifs de France et leurs relations avec Israël, 1945–1988* (Paris: Éditions l'Harmattan, 1989); Bernard Wasserstein, *Vanishing Diaspora: The Jews in Europe since 1945* (Cambridge, Mass.: Harvard University Press, 1996), pp. 85–102. Laura Hobson Faure, "Un 'Plan Marshall juif': La présence juive américaine en France après la Shoah, 1944–54" (Ph.D. diss., École des hautes études en sciences sociales, 2009), p. 361, notes that French Jews raised 200 million francs for Israel in 1948.

51. Flyer, "Grand meeting," LICRA and MNCR, Dossier 43-d, Antisémitisme 1948, CC.

52. Témime, *Histoire de Marseille*, 296; Marie Attard-Maraninchi and Émile Témime, *Le cosmopolitisme de l'entre-deux-guerres (1919–1945)*, vol. 3 of *Migrance: Histoire des migrations à Marseille*, ed. Émile Témime (Aix-en-Provence: Édisud, 1990), pp. 159–60.

53. Émile Témime and Nathalie Deguigné, *Le camp du Grand Arénas Marseille, 1944–1966* (Paris: Éditions Autrement, 2001), pp. 17–19.

54. Sayad, Jordi, and Témime, *Le Choc*, 18–26, note that a weak economy from 1945 through 1954 lowered immigration when compared to elsewhere in France.

55. Témime and Deguigné, *Le camp du Grand Arénas*, 20.

56. The practice of lodging Muslims in camps began during the war, particularly after the Allied invasion of North Africa trapped thousands in France, and grew thereafter. Attard-Maraninchi and Témime, *Le cosmopolitisme*, 150–53; Sayad, Jordi, and Témime, *Le Choc*, 48; Témime, *Histoire de Marseille*, 330; Témime and Deguigné, *Le camp du Grand Arénas*, 21. Minutes, Bureau des affaires musulmanes nord-africaines de Marseille, 24 October 1944, 150W170, BdR.

57. For the immigrant roots of this neighborhood, see Émile Témime, *Marseille transit: Les passagers de Belsunce* (Paris: Éditions Autrement, 1995).

58. MI to Direction Afrique Levant, "Egypte: Émission radiophonique 'En Algérie: Arabophobie et pro-Sionisme de la France,'" 17 September 1947, AL 1944–59, K.38.2, MAE.

59. Attard-Maraninchi and Témime, *Le cosmopolitisme*, 131–60. The actual tally was probably higher due to those in hiding, seeking passage out of the country, or incarcerated in internment camps. Florence Berceot, "Renouvellement socio-démographique des Juifs de Marseille 1901–1937," *Provence historique* 175 (1994), 39–40, 44, and Donna F. Ryan, *The Holocaust & the Jews of Marseille: The Enforcement of Anti-Semitic Policies in Vichy France* (Urbana and Chicago: University of Illinois Press, 1996), p. 13, offer slightly different numbers of Jews from Turkey, Greece, and the Maghreb in the late 1930s.

60. Figure comes from Pascal le Pautremat, *La politique musulmane de la France au XXe siècle: De l'hexagone aux terres d'Islam. Espoirs, réussites, échecs* (Paris: Maisonneuve & Larose, 2003), pp. 302–303, who lists fifteen thousand in Marseille in 1934 and seventeen thousand in the Bouches-du-Rhône and Le Gard in 1938.

61. "État d'esprit de Musulmans algériens de Marseille," 13 December 1941, 76W205, BdR. Thanks to Ethan Katz for sharing this document.

62. Katz, "Jews and Muslims," 181–88, 200, 221–22, 225–30; Charles-Robert Ageron, "Les populations du Maghreb face à la propagande allemande," *Revue d'histoire de la Deuxième Guerre Mondiale*, 114 (April 1979): 1–39.

63. Mandel, *In the Aftermath of Genocide*, 52–85.

64. Roland Avitol, "Marseille," *L'Arche* (March/April, 1968): 19–20; Ryan, *The Holocaust & the Jews of Marseille*, 13.

65. While Jews lived in all areas of the city in 1941, 62 percent lived within 1.5 kilometers of the Old Port. Given that this area was hardest hit during the war, the remaining Jewish population was necessarily dispersed. For this and for the ethnic and class distinctions that marked Jewish life before the war, see Ryan, *The Holocaust*, 13–18, 176–93.

66. Interview with Silvio Benveniste, cited in Sarah Sussman, "Changing Lands, Changing Identities: The Migration of Algerian Jewry to France, 1954–1967" (Ph.D. diss., Stanford University, 2003), p. 350.

67. Frederick Cooper, *Decolonization and African Society: The Labor Question in French and British Africa* (Cambridge: Cambridge University Press, 1996); Eric T. Jennings, *Vichy in the Tropics: Pétain's National Revolution in Madagascar, Guadeloupe, and Indochina, 1940–1944* (Stanford: Stanford University Press, 2001).

68. Shepard, *The Invention of Decolonization*, 39–43.
69. MI to Commissaires de la République and préfets, "Carte d'identité des français Musulmans d'Algérie," 20 February 1946; Préfecture des Bouches-du-Rhône to Chef de service des étrangers, 25 July 1947, 150W170, BdR.
70. Blanchard, *La police parisienne*, 36–40, shows how police consistently ignored Algerian Muslim citizenship even after the 1947 statute formally changed their status.
71. The poverty and difficulties facing Muslim migrants are detailed in Préfet to Ministre du travail et de la sécurité sociale, "Commission consultative pour la main-d'œuvre nord-africain," 13 June 1947, 150W170, BdR. High crime rates testify to the difficulties many faced making ends meet. Chef de la brigade du quartier de la bourse to Commissaire central à Marseille, "Population musulmane," 13 June 1949, 148W191, BdR.
72. Although police noted that Muslim factory workers would not cross picket lines, Sayad, Jordi, and Témime, *Le Choc*, 21, argue otherwise. For CGT efforts to win Muslim adherents, see documents in 148W191, BdR. Statistics on Muslim voters comes from Chef de la brigade du quartier de la bourse to Commissaire central à Marseille, "Population musulmane," 13 June 1949, same file. For North African political engagement, see Jocelyne Cesari, *Être musulman en France: Associations, militants, et mosquées* (Paris: Éditions Karthala et Iremam, 1994), 30–31; Wihtol de Wenden, *Les immigrés et la politique*, passim.
73. Aissaoui, *Immigration and National Identity*, 129.
74. Cabinet du préfet, "Les renseignements généraux communiquent," 10 October 1946; Direction général de la sureté nationale to Préfet des Bouches-du-Rhône (BdR), "Note d'information," 11 October 1946; Direction générale de la sureté nationale to Préfet BdR, "Thèmes essentiels développés dans les divers discours prononcés à l'occasion du passage de Messali Hadj," 10 October 1946; Chef de cabinet to Préfet des BdR, "Réunion tenue à la 'Cassa d'Italia,' par le leader nord africain Messali Hadj," 10 October 1946, 150W170, BdR.
75. Préfet to Commissaire principal, "Activité déployé à Marseille par les nationalistes algériens," 24 October 1947, 150W170; Commissaire de police, "Population musulmane," 13 June 1949, 148W191, BdR.
76. RG, Mle, "Réaction dans les milieux musulmans de Marseille après la réception de leurs représentants par M. le Préfet des Bouches-du-Rhône," 5 January 1950, 148W191, BdR. Michel Renard, "Aperçu sur l'histoire de l'Islam à Marseille, 1813–1962: Pratiques religieuses et encadrements des Nord-Africains," *Revue française d'histoire d'outre-mer* 90 (2003): 269–96.
77. RG, Mle, "Présence des Nord Africains à la manifestation de CGT du 1er Mai à Marseille," 2 May 1950, 148W146, BdR.
78. RG, Mle, "Compte rendu du meeting MTLD de Marseille organisé au cinéma St. Lazare à 10h, le 7.5.1950," 9 May 1950, 148W191, BdR.
79. Inspecteur de la brigade de la bourse to Commissaire de police, 13 May 1950; RG, Mle (Untitled), 6 September 1950, 148W191, BdR. Police were still describing most of Marseille's laboring Muslim population as apolitical at this time and "shocked by the separatists' outrageous tone." Furthermore, it is worth noting a diversity of Algerian Muslim positions on independence. See Ethan Katz "Jews and Muslims," 281–82.
80. *L'Émigré* 2, no date, in Directeur départemental des services de police to Préfet BdR, "A/S Journal du PPA, *L'Émigré*," 19 December 1947, 150W170, BdR.
81. RG, Mle, 6 May 1950, 148W146, BdR.

82. "Note," 6 May 1948, 148W185, BdR.
83. Telegram to MI, "Attitude des milieux musulmans à l'égard des Israélites," 9 June 1948, 148W185, BdR.
84. RG, 9 June 1948, 148W185, BdR.
85. Robert Assaraf, *Une certaine histoire des Juifs du Maroc: 1860–1999* (Paris: Jean-Claude Gawsewitch, 2005), 522–25; Mohammed Kenbib, *Juifs et Musulmans au Maroc, 1859–1948* (Rabat: Publications de la faculté des lettres et des sciences humaines, Université Mohammed V, 1994): 677–87; Michael Laskier, *North African Jewry in the Twentieth Century: The Jews of Morocco, Tunisia, and Algeria* (New York: New York University Press, 1994), pp. 5–19, 94–101, Yaron Tsur, *Ḳehilah ḳeru'ah: Yehude Maroḳo yeha-le'umiyut, 1943–1954* (Tel Aviv: Universiṭat Tel Aviv, ha-'Amutah le-ḥeḳer ma'arkhot ha-ha'palah 'a. sh. Sha'ul Avigur: 'Am 'oved, 2001), pp. 84–91; Wyrtzen, "Constructing Morocco, 271–74.
86. While some have argued the violence was a spontaneous outbreak of war tension, most see the events as preplanned by nationalists. Norman A. Stillman, *Jews of Arab Lands in Modern Times* (Philadelphia: The Jewish Publication Society, 2003), p. 152, for example, calls the riot in Oujda a response to Arab failures to demolish Israel. Tsur, *Kehilah keru'ah*, 87–89, points out the difficulty of knowing whether events were spontaneous or preplanned while stressing anti-Zionist sentiment and nationalist activities. Benbib, *Juifs et Musulmans*, 677–87, places considerable emphasis on the role of the French administration and Israeli agents. For conflicting interpretations, see Laskier *North African Jewry*, 94–101, who emphasizes Moroccan nationalist agitation.
87. Telegram, A. Juin, Rabat, 18 June 1948, SG/1948, 75 (ex 29), MAE. Officials also noted temporary alliances between Communist activists and Moroccan nationalists. Ministre plénipotentiaire to Schuman, "Situation politique intérieure au Maroc: Attitude du parti communiste et du parti nationaliste l'Istiqlal," 29 July 1948; Brunel to Résident général, 19 June 1948, same file.
88. Paroles personnelles par M. Obadia, 12 June 1948, ADAM, 425, AIU.
89. "Extrait d'une lettre de M. Pinhas Eshkénazi, instituteur à Oujda," 7 July 1948, ADAM, 425, AIU.
90. Tajouri to président de l'Alliance israélite, June 1948, ADAM, 425, AIU. In Djérada, he argues, perpetrators were not nationalists but Muslims who worked with Jews in the mines.
91. Tsur, *Kehilah keru'ah*, 87, notes that because many illegal Jewish immigrants collected in the town, all others were viewed as potential migrants.
92. Assaraf, *Une certaine histoire*, 271–72.
93. Juin, in contrast, reported that violence began when a Muslim customer stabbed a Jewish shopkeeper. Telegram from Juin, Rabat, 8 June 1948, SG/ 1948, 75 (ex 29), MAE.
94. Brunel to Résident général, 19 June 1948, SG/1948, 75 (ex 29), MAE.
95. Telegram from Juin, 10 June 1948, SG/1948, 75 (ex 29), MAE. Subsequently, he emphasized the role of the Parti populaire algérien and nationalists more generally. Telegram, A. Juin, 17 and 18 June 1948, same file. Months later, he linked nationalist agitation and clandestine departures again. Juin to Schuman, "Règlement des incidents d'Oujda," 21 October 1948, same file.
96. Circulaire N° 157-IP, ME, Service d'information et de presse, "Des incidents entre Arabes et Juifs à Oujda et Djérada," 10 June 1948, SG/1948, 75 (ex 29), MAE. By

the early 1950s, Francis Lacoste, the resident general, described clandestine migration as the spark in Oujda. Lacoste to MAMT, 17 December 1954, SG/1948, 96 (ex 22c), MAE.

97. RG du port, "État d'esprit des travailleurs arabes dans le port," 9 June 1948, 148W185, BdR.

98. RG du port, "A/S incidents judéo-arabes," 9 June 1948, 148W185, BdR.

99. Telegram to MI, "Attitude des milieux musulmans à l'égard des Israélites," 9 June 1948; RG du port, "État d'esprit des travailleurs arabes dans le port," 9 June 1948, 148W185, BdR.

100. RG, Mle, "La guerre en Palestine—Projection de films jugés provocateurs par les Arabes de Marseille," 10 June 1948, 148W185, BdR. Police shut down the film in response. Commissaire de police to Commissaire divisionnaire, 12 June 1948, same file.

101. Préfecture BdR, "Note pour monsieur le préfet: Circulation et transit des Musulmans français d'Algérie dans le sens Afrique du Nord, métropole et vice versa," 16 August 1948; "Situation dans le département des Bouches-du-Rhône au regard de la présence de l'accueil et du rapatriement des Nord Africains," 22 July 1948, 148W191, BdR.

102. RG, Mle, "Attitude des divers milieux arabes de Marseille et du département envers les Juifs de Marseille et de la région," 9 June 1948, 148W185, BdR.

103. Unless otherwise noted, the discussion of Zionist activities in Marseille is drawn from Témime and Deguigné, *Le camp du Grand Arénas*, 56–69, and Sayad, Jordi, and Témime, *Le Choc*, 35–37.

104. Témime and Deguigné, *Le camp du Grand Arénas*, 66–68.

105. RG, Mle, "Activité de la Ligue française pour la Palestine libre," 24 May 1947, 148W185, BdR. Arrests of Irgun arms smugglers are recorded in F715292, AN. For the Marseille link, see "Après l'affaire du camion de la rue Marx Dormoy la police opère à Marseille: Onze tonnes d'armes onze arrestations," *Populaires*, 9 March 1948. RG, Mle, "Existence éventuelle d'une filiale de l'Irgun à Marseille," 23 October 1947, 148W185, BdR; Sayad, Jordi, and Témime, *Le Choc*, 35. More information on Irgun activities in France is located in "Terrorisme juif, 1946–1950," IPFL 1944–65, 376, L.72.3, MAE.

106. Foreigners only became a majority in this neighborhood in the 1970s. In the 1980s, Algerian Muslims made up 40 percent of the total. Témime, *Marseille transit*, 38–39, 42–43.

107. Having been shut in November 1942, the postwar Fédération relied on aid from the Joint and the UNRRA. RG, Mle, "État critique de la situation financière de la FSJF," 25 June 1947, 148W185, BdR.

108. Laura Margolis to Henrietta Buchman, 31 December 1948, 316, AJDC.

109. The Zionist youth organization, Hechaloutz, and the religious organization, Bahad, created their own camps housing 3,500–4,000 in 1950, and 35,000 by the middle of the decade. RG, Section frontières, "Le mouvement de transmigration des Israélites: La question israélienne," June 1950, F7/15589, AN.

110. RG, Mle, "Attitude des divers milieux arabes de Marseille et du département envers les Juifs de Marseille et de la région," 9 June 1948; RG, Mle, "Activité de groupements israélites à Marseille," 30 June 1948, 148W185, BdR.

111. Cabinet du Préfet BdR, no date, 148W185, BdR.

112. RG, Mle, "Réaction des milieux arabes de Marseille à la suite de la trêve en Palestine," 16 June 1948, 148W185, BdR.

113. RG, Mle, "A.S du navire Altalena amarré à Martigues par l'armement des Juifs," 15 June 1948, 148W185, BdR.

114. 11 June 1948, 148W185, BdR; RG, Mle, "L'ordre de trêve en Palestine," 12 June 1948, 148W185, BdR. According to historian Saul Friedländer, *When Memory Comes*, trans. Helen R. Lane (New York: Farrar, Straus, and Giroux, Inc., 1979), p. 179, who was sailing to Israel on the boat, the French army and many passengers loaded it.

115. RG, Mle, "Attitude des divers milieux arabes de Marseille et du département envers les Juifs de Marseille et de la région," 9 June 1948; RG, Mle, "Activité de groupements israélites à Marseille," 30 June 1948, 148W185, BdR.

116. RG, "Activité de groupements israélites à Marseille," 30 June 1948; RG, Mle, "Propagande du PPA en faveur des armée arabes en Palestine," 16 June 1948; RG, Mle, "L'Office d'immigration de l'État d'Israël," 19 June 1948, 148W185, BdR.

117. RG, Mle, "Incidents entre Juifs et Arabes au centre d'accueil du Grand Arénas à Mazargues," 14 June 1948, 148W185, BdR. While the report is not explicit as to who forced the lost Algerian Muslim laborer to work in the canteen, the implication is that Jewish residents detained him.

118. Commissaire de police du quartier de St. Giniez to Commissaire divisionnaire, Mle, 27 June 1948, 148W185, BdR.

119. This organization, formerly the Congrès musulman algérien de Marseille, was established in November 1944 to create links between "French Muslims from Algeria and their French brothers in the metropole." Mohamed Seghir Talmoudi to Préfet, 29 November 1944; RG, Mle, "A/S de l'Association des Musulmans algériens de Marseille," 26 March 1945, 150W170, BdR.

120. RG, Mle, "Incidents entre Juifs et Arabes au centre d'accueil du Grand Arénas à Mazargues," 14 Juin 1948; RG, Mle, "Incidents entre Juifs et Musulmans au camp du Grand Arénas à Mazargues," 30 June 1948, 148W185, BdR.

121. Vernet, Directeur départemental du travail et de la main-d'œuvre, to Préfet BdR, "Hébergement de réfugiés israélites au centre de transit du Grand Arénas," 25 October 1948, 148W141, BdR.

122. Commissaire divisionnaire to Directeur départemental des services de police-préfecture, "Tension judéo-arabe," 11, 12, and 14 June 1948, 148W185, BdR.

123. Local Muslims nevertheless complained that the truce was partial to Israel. RG, Mle, "A/S de la cessation des combats en Palestine," 21 July 1948. Anger mounted again when a training camp for Jewish pilots was found outside Algiers, forty of whom escaped to Palestine via Marseille. RG, Mle, "Pilotes juifs venant d'Alger, à destination de la Palestine," 8 October 1948, 148W185, BdR.

124. RG, Mle, "La guerre de Palestine jugé par les divers milieux arabes de Marseille," 7 January 1949, 148W185, BdR.

125. RG, Mle, "L'affaire Palestinienne," 28 January 1949; RG, Mle, "A/S de la guerre de Palestine," 4 February 1949, 148W185, BdR.

126. RG, Mle, "La position du gouvernement français vis à vis du nouvel état d'Israël vu par la colonie de Marseille," 21 June 1948, 148W185, BdR.

127. Témime and Deguigné, *Le camp du Grand Arénas*, 68–69.

128. Note for Préfet, 18 October 1948; Note for Préfet, 29 November 1948, 148W185, BdR.

129. Directeur départemental des services de police to Commissaire central (pour éducation), 14 May 1949; Directeur départemental des services de police to M. Thau, 14 May 1949; Commissaire principal to Directeur départemental des services de police, 11 May 1949, 148W141, BdR.

130. Joan Wolf, *Harnessing the Holocaust: The Politics of Memory in France* (Stanford: Stanford University Press, 2004), pp. 28–29, points out that Jewish publications were more devoted to Israel than to any other issue. For institutional support, see Phyllis Albert, "French Jewry and the Centrality of the State of Israel: The Public Debate, 1968–1988," *From Ancient Israel to Modern Judaism: Intellect in Quest of Understanding, Essays in Honor of Marvin Fox*, vol. 4, eds. Ernest Frerichs and Jacob Neusner (Atlanta: Scholars Press, 1989), pp. 207–209.

131. Emile Touati, "Profil d'une jeunesse indécise," *La revue du FSJU*, 13 (1955), pp. 16–17.

132. Raymond Aron, *Mémoires* (Paris: Julliard, 1983), pp. 502–505. For the reticence of Jewish intellectuals to embrace Israel, see Maurice Szafran, *Les Juifs dans la politique française: De 1945 à nos jours* (Paris: Flammarion, 1990), pp. 83–92.

133. Sylvie Korcaz, *Les Juifs de France et l'État d'Israël* (Paris: Éditions Denoël, 1969), p. 78, explains this gap by arguing that American-style fund-raising was less valued in France as a sign of social prestige.

Chapter 2. Decolonization and Migration: Constructing the North African Jew

1. Norman A. Stillman, *Jews of Arab Lands in Modern Times* (Philadelphia: The Jewish Publication Society, 2003), pp. 71–72. Général de corps d'armée de Latour to MDMT, "Émigration des Juifs nord-africains en Israël," 24 January 1955, SG/1948, 96 (ex 22c), MAE; Michael Laskier, *North African Jewry in the Twentieth Century: The Jews of Morocco, Tunisia, and Algeria* (New York: New York University Press, 1994), p. 274.

2. Claude Tapia, *Les Juifs sépharades en France (1965–1985)* (Paris: L'Harmattan, 1986), p. 27. Jacques Taïeb, "Immigrés d'Afrique du Nord: Combien? Quand? Pourquoi?" in *Terre d'exil terre d'asile: Migrations juives en France aux XIXe et XXe siècles*, ed. Collette Zytnicki (Paris: Éditions de l'Éclat): 150, puts the number at a much lower twelve thousand. Jewish departures in the 1950s were statistically proportionate to that of other French citizens. Doris Bensimon and S. Della Pergolla, *La population juive de France: Socio-démographie et identité* (Jerusalem: Hebrew University of Jerusalem and CNRS, 1984), p. 50; Sarah Sussman, "Changing Lands, Changing Identities: The Migration of Algerian Jewry to France, 1954–1967" (Ph.D. diss. Stanford University, 2002), p. 174.

3. Esther Benbassa, *Jews of France: A History from Antiquity to the Present* (Princeton: Princeton University Press, 1999), p. 186. While 90 percent of Moroccan Jews settled in Israel, French citizenship brought a similar percentage of Algerian Jews to the metropole. About half of Tunisian Jews went to France and half to Israel.

4. For a discussion of the complex factors pushing departures, see Taïeb, "Immigrés d'Afrique du Nord," 149–54.

5. According to Jonathan Wyrtzen, "Constructing Morocco: Colonial Struggle to Define the Nation, 1912–1956" (Ph.D. diss. Georgetown University, 2009), pp. 232–38, such concerns dated from early in the century when Zionism first emerged in Morocco.

6. Todd Shepard, *The Invention of Decolonization: The Algerian War and the Remaking of France* (Ithaca and London: Cornell University Press, 2006). Kimberly Arkin, " 'It's the French and the Arabs against the Jews': Identity Politics and the Construction of Adolescent Jewishness in France" (Ph.D. diss., University of Chicago, 2008), chap. 1, and Elizabeth Friedman, *Colonialism and After: An Algerian Jewish Community* (South Hadley, Mass.: Bergin and Garvey Publishers, Inc., 1988), make clear that "Frenchification" was not as successful on the ground as legal categories suggest.

7. Michael M. Laskier, *The Alliance Israélite Universelle and the Jewish Communities of Morocco, 1862–1962* (Albany: State University of New York Press, 1983).

8. Yaron Tsur, "L'AIU et le Judaïsme marocain en 1949: L'émergence d'une nouvelle démarche politique," *Archives juives* 34, 1 (2001): 54–73.

9. For international Jewish aid in Tunisia, see Claude Nataf, "Les mutations du Judaïsme tunisien après la seconde guerre mondiale," *Archives juives* 30, 1 (2006): 125–36.

10. As Tsur, "L'AIU et le Judaïsme marocain en 1949," shows, Jewish organizations pursued both Zionist *and* assimilationist goals.

11. For a useful discussion of how even ostensibly inclusive, universalizing nationalist thought can function to delineate ethnic categories, see Jonathan Glassman, *War of Words, War of Stones: Racial Thought and Violence in Colonial Zanzibar* (Bloomington: Indiana University Press, 2011).

12. For example, Muslims and Jews worked closely together in the Communist party, particularly in Tunisia and Morocco, providing an alternative political vision to the one I am describing here.

13. Recent scholarship has rightly stressed the differences among Moroccan, Algerian, and Tunisian Jews following a wider historiographical move to challenge colonial frameworks that collapsed "North Africa" into one unvarigated analytic construct. My decision to tell a cross-national story seeks not to rehomogenize the North African landscape. However, as the sources traced here make clear, many of the actors under study spoke of Jewish life in cross-regional terms. The goal of this chapter is to understand the political consequences of such homogenization.

14. Martin Thomas, "From French North Africa to Maghreb Independence: Decolonization in Morocco, Tunisia and Algeria from 1945 to 1956," in *Crisis of Empire: Decolonization and Europe's Imperial States, 1918–1975* (London: Hodder Education, Part of Hachette Livre UK), pp. 209–27.

15. Lacoste to MDMT, "Départ pour la Palestine d'Israélites marocaines," 16 December 1954; Lacoste to Embassy in Tel Aviv, 13 May 1955, SG/1948, 96 (ex 22c), MAE.

16. Note pour la Direction des affaires administratives et sociales from Direction générale des affaires politiques (Afrique-Levant), "Émigration des Juifs nord-africains vers Israël" (September 1955), SG/1948, 96 (ex 22c), MAE.

17. Stillman, *Jews of Arab Lands*, 166. Of these 28,781 were from Morocco (about 10 percent of the population). According to Yaron Tsur, *Ḳehilah ḳeru'ah: Yehude Maroḳo*

yeha-le'umiyut, 1943–1954 (Tel Aviv: Universiṭat Tel Aviv, ha-'Amutah le-ḥeḳer ma'arkhot ha-ha'palah 'a. sh. Sha'ul Avigur: 'Am 'oved, 2001), pp. 93–96, although Zionism increased in Morocco after 1948, support actually waned in response to the poor treatment of Moroccan immigrants in Israel. According to Haïm Saadoun, "L'influence du sionisme sur les relations judéo-musulmanes en Tunisie," in *Juifs et Musulmans en Tunisie: Fraternité et déchirements*, ed., Sonia Fellous (Paris: Somogy, 2003), p. 228, in Tunisia, the movement's emphasis was not on migration but on expressing ethnic belonging.

18. MI to ME, Direction Afrique-Levant, "Emigration des Israélites marocains," 28 February 1949, IPFL 1944–65, 376, L.72.2, MAE.
19. Note pour le Ministre from Direction d'Afrique Levant, sous-direction des protectorats, "Emigration à destination de la Palestine d'Israélites originaires de l'Afrique du Nord," 5 March 1949, IPFL 1944–65, 376, L.72.2, MAE.
20. Others objected to migration on the grounds that Morocco and Tunisia would be deprived of loyal Jewish subjects. ME, Direction d'Afrique–Levant to Rabat, Tunis, Tanger, and Tétouan, "Émigration à destination de la Palestine d'Israélites originaires de l'Afrique du Nord," 6 April 1949; Telegram, ME, direction d'Afrique–Levant to Parodi, Clappier, de Sourbon, and Busset, 30 May 1949, IPFL 1944–65, 376, L.72.2, MAE. Some Ministry of Interior officials *did* support Jewish migration based on the principle of self-determination and on hopes it would facilitate relations with Israel. RG, "Le mouvement de transmigration des Israélites: La question israélienne," June 1950, F7/15589, AN.
21. Those claiming refugee status, in this view, were European Zionists who had traveled clandestinely to Algeria to push the issue. AE, Direction des conventions administratives et sociales, "Note: Israélites d'Afrique du Nord," 23 March 1949, SG/1948, 93 (ex 30), MAE. Direction des conventions administratives et sociales to Ministre plénipotentiaire, Tanger, "Émigration juive vers Israël," 11 April 1949, IPFL 1944–65, 376, L.72.2, MAE.
22. Telegram from Juin, 8 April 1949, SG/1948, 93 (ex 30), MAE.
23. The one exception was Tunisia, where resident general, Jean Mons, reported difficulties were receding. Mons to Schuman, "Départs de Juifs tunisiens pour la métropole," 21 December 1948, F716088, AN; Mons to Schuman, "Départ des Israélites de Tunisie pour la Palestine," 29 March 1949, IPFL 1944–65, 376, L.72.2, MAE. Saadoun, "L'influence du Sionisme," 22, confirms little hostility to Jewish migration in Tunisia from Neo-Destour, despite some sensitivity "on the ground."
24. M. Ernst to MI, "Situation d'Israélites marocains arrivés en Algérie," January 1949, F716088, AN.
25. E. de Beauverger, Ministre plénipotentiaire, Tanger, to ME, "Activité pro-Sioniste des milieux israélites tangérois" and "Émigration juive vers Israël," 8 and 19 March 1949, IPFL 1944–65, 376, L.72.2, MAE.
26. Concerns over numbers are recorded in ME to Résident général, Rabat, "Émigration des Juifs marocains à destination d'Israël," 12 January 1953, and Direction général des affaires politiques, "Note pour la direction des affaires administratives et sociales," 17 August 1953, SG/1948, 94 (ex 22a), MAE. Others sought to limit migration because Jews represented a source of social stability who "assimilate to Western customs more easily than the Muslims." Note pour le secrétaire général, "M. Jarblum de l'Agence juive," 20 February 1954, SG/1948, 95 (ex 22b), M.9.3, MAE. By early

1953, Israeli officials were predicting that American Jewish aid, French efforts to stabilize living conditions, and poor economic horizons in Israel would encourage Jews to stay. Yves Debroise, Chargé d'affaires de France A.I. en Israël to Bidault, "L'immigration des Juifs nord-africains," 11 February 1953, SG/1948, 94 (ex 22a), MAE; Consul général de France, Jerusalem, to ME, direction Afrique-Levant, 18 February 1953, same file.

27. ME to MAMT, "Immigration des Juifs nord-africains en Israël," 13 November 1954, SG/1948, 96 (ex 22c), MAE.

28. Résident général Rabat to Martuni, 14 September 1954, SG/1948, 96 (ex 22c), MAE.

29. While many administrators blamed Zionist propaganda for Jewish flight, others, such as Lacoste to MAMT, 17 December 1954, SG/1948, 96 (ex 22c), MAE, faulted widespread poverty.

30. Ironically, the push to *legalize* migration to Israel grew out of such fears, as some argued that regularized policies would alleviate pressures that came from *illegal* migration. Francis Lacoste, Minister Plenipotentiary and delegate to the resident general in Morocco, for example, one of the fiercest opponents of Jewish migration as late as September 1948 made this case. Lacoste to Schuman, "Émigration juive marocaine vers l'État d'Israël," 3 June 1949, IPFL 1944–19, 376, L.72.2, MAE. Numerous documents in the MAE attest that by the 1950s, while French administrators were still worried about their interests in North Africa, they also feared offending Israel.

31. "Après les pogroms de Petitjean (Maroc): La situation des Juifs, noyés dans une masse arabe fanatisée, devient chaque jour plus tragique," *La Terre retrouvée*, 1 October 1954.

32. Board of Deputies of British Jews, "Memorandum: Safeguards for Jews in Morocco and Tunisia," November 1954, SG/1948, 95 (ex 22b), MAE.

33. Jonathan Wyrtzen, "Constructing Morocco: Colonial Struggle to Define the Nation, 1912–1956" (Ph.D. diss., Georgetown University, 2009), p. 268.

34. Telegram from Bonnet, 22 June 1948, SG/1948, 93 (ex 30), MAE.

35. Cited in Robert Assaraf, *Une certaine histoire des Juifs du Maroc: 1860–1999* (Paris: Jean-Claude Gawsewitch, 2005), p. 526.

36. Laskier, *North African Jewry*, 168–69. Henri Bonnet to Schuman, "Attitude du World Jewish Congress concernant les problèmes de l'Afrique du Nord," 8 August 1952, SG/1948, 94 (ex 22a), MAE.

37. Yaron Tsur, "Les dirigeants du Judaïsme marocain et l'indépendance: Le problème de l'intégration et l'influence des organisations juives internationales," in Michel Abibol, ed., *Relations judéo-musulmanes au Maroc: Perceptions et réalités* (Paris: Éditions Stavit, 1997): 225–36.

38. Roger Vaurs, Directeur du service de presse et d'information de l'Ambassade de France to Henri Bonnet, Ambassadeur de France, "World Jewish Council conférence du Dr. Perlzweig sur la politique française en Afrique du Nord," 15 September 1954, SG/1948, 95 (ex 22b), MAE.

39. "Les organisations israélites américaines et l'Istilqlal," 20 June 1955, SG/1948, 95 (ex 22b), MAE.

40. An August 1955 Istiqlal press release insisted that accusations of Muslim antisemitism came from French efforts to discredit the movement. Muslims and Jews had a shared past and a common enemy; independent Morocco would guarantee equality

for all. Ahmed Balafrej, Sec. Gen., Istiqlal Party of Morocco, "Moroccan Jews" 12 August 1955, SG/1948, 95 (ex 22b), MAE.

41. Maurice Couve de Murville, Ambassadeur de France aux États-Unis to Antoine Pinay, ME (Direction d'Afrique–Levant), 22 September 1955; Murville to Pinay, "Contacts entre le Congrès juif mondial et l'Istiqlal," 18 November 1955, SG/1948, 95 (ex 22b), MAE.

42. Murville to Pinay, 22 September 1955, SG/1948, 95 (ex 22b), MAE. For the WJC's efforts to avoid irritating both sides, see Laskier, *North African Jewry*, 169–70.

43. "Meeting of the Administration Committee of the Joint Distribution Committee," 5 April 1955, 55/64 # [45/64#114], AJDC.

44. Benjamin B. Goldman, "Information on North Africa and Other Moslem Lands," 11 October 1949, 45/54 #6, AJDC.

45. "Notes of the New York JDC Staff Meeting No. 2–49," 17 January 1949, 45/54 #6, AJDC. Motivating many Joint officials was the hope that Jews of Arab lands would serve as a "resource for the upbuilding [*sic*] of the Jewish people" after the Holocaust. "Notes of the New York JDC Staff Meeting No. 2–49," 17 January 1949, same file.

46. "Memorandum on visit to North Africa by Rabbi Shapiro from December 7th to December 28th, 1949," 45/54 #5, AJDC.

47. "Minutes of meeting held at 2, rue de Cygne," 19 October 1948, 45/54 #6, AJDC.

48. Hélène Cazes-Benatar, "Report on the Political Situation in North Africa," October 1950, 45/54 #5, AJDC.

49. "Meeting of the Administration Committee of the Joint Distribution Committee," 5 April 1955, 55/64 # [45/64#114], AJDC.

50. Haber's comments on poverty are documented in Samuel L. Haber, "Dir. 593," 30 December 1954, 45/54 #9, AJDC. His call for migration is cited in Laskier, *North African Jewry*, 168.

51. André Blumel to Comité d'action sioniste, 24 August 1955, MDI 69, CDJC.

52. Interestingly, migration was also not obvious to many Moroccan, Tunisian, and Algerian Jewish leaders who expressed exasperation at the "excessive zeal" of American Jewish organizations. Such outsiders, they feared, were *creating* disruption through their visits and calls to action without paying adequate attention to local Jewish concerns. Indeed, in the early 1950s, indigenous Jewish leaders often feared that migration would hurt communal vitality and diminish chances for improving local conditions even if they favored modest migration for Morocco's poorest Jews. "Israélites d'Afrique du Nord," Paris, 8 July 1955, SG/1948, 95 (ex 22b); Lacoste to MAMT, 17 December 1954, SG/1948, 96 (ex 22c), MAE. Algerian Jewish organizations also begged international Jewish agencies not to do anything that could backfire. Jacques Lazarus, "Rapport sur la situation des Juifs en Algérie au début de l'année 1958," Assises du Judaïsme algérien, 12–13 March 1958, republished in *Archives juives: Revue d'histoire des Juifs de France* 29, 1 (1ère semestre 1996), p. 59.

53. Tsur, *Ḳehilah ḳeru'ah*, 112–27; Tsur, "L'AIU et le Judaïsme marocain en 1949," 54–73. Léon Meiss to Olivier Marin, 11 October 1948, SG/1948, 75 (ex 29); S.M. le Sultan, Secrétariat particulier to René Cassin, 18 May 1949, SG/1948, 93 (ex 30), M.9.3, MAE and ADAM, 237, AIU

54. For Morocco, see Wyrtzen, "Constructing Morocco, 264–77; Tsur, "Les dirigeants du Judaïsme marocain et l'indépendance," 225–36; Joseph Levy, "Témoignage d'un militant Juif marocain," in *Juif du Maroc: Identité et dialogue*, Actes du colloque

international sur la communauté juive marocaine (Paris, 1980). For Tunisia, see Nataf, "Les mutations du Judaïsme tunisien," 125–36. For Algeria, see numerous citations in part 3 of this chapter.

55. Jacques Dalloz, *Georges Bidault: Biographie politique* (Éditions l'Harmattan, 1992), p. 273. For Neo Destour on Zionism, see Haïm Saadoun, "L'influence du Sionisme sur les relations judéo-musulmanes en Tunisie," in *Juifs et Musulmans en Tunisie: Fraternité et déchirements,* ed., Sonia Fellous (Paris: Somogy, 2003): 219–29. For Morocco, see Wyrtzen, "Constructing Morocco, 264–77. For Algeria, see part 3 of chapter.

56. For example, in 1955 the Tunisian Resident General only allowed Jews to depart in small groups so they would not stand out from other travelers. Général de corps d'armée de Latour, res. gen. de France en Tunisie to MAMT, "Émigration des Juifs nord-africains en Israël," 24 January 1955, SG/1948, 96 (ex 22c), MAE.

57. For example, in December 1954, the Egyptian radio station, *La voix des Arabes,* protested migrations (not particularly surprising coming from Nasser's international mouthpiece). Lacoste to MAMT, 17 December 1954, SG/1948, 96 (ex 22c); "Traduction d'une émission radiophonique de langue arabe, Radio Damas du 15/2/55," SG/1948, 95 (ex 22b), MAE.

58. Lacoste to MAMT, "Émigration juive vers Israël," 13 May 1955, SG/1948, 96 (ex 22c), MAE.

59. MAMT to ME, "Émigration vers Israël des Juifs nord-africains," 8 July 1955, SG/1948, 96 (ex 22c), MAE.

60. Gilbert to ME, "Immigration marocaine en Israël," 25 September 1955, SG/1948, 96 (ex 22c), MAE.

61. Maurice J. Goldbloom, André Zaoui, and Henry Levy, "Foreign Countries: North Africa," *American Jewish Year Book* 58 (1957), p. 356.

62. Saadoun, "L'influence du Sionisme," 226.

63. More came in the after that point. Taïeb, "Immigrés d'Afrique du Nord," 149–51.

64. Jewish figure is from Sussman, *Changing Lands,* 1 (Taïeb, "Immigrés d'Afrique du Nord," 150, puts the figure of Algerian Jews at 120,000). The wider figure is from Jacques Fremeaux, "Le reflux des Français d'Afrique du Nord 1956–1962," in *Marseille et le choc des décolonisations,* eds., Jean-Jacques Jordi and Emile Temime (Aix-en-Provence: Édisud, 1996), p. 15. The number of harkis includes 85,000 who participated in the military's supplemental units (families included) and 55,000 notables, functionaries or career military men who adopted a pro-French position during the war. Tom Charbit, *Les harkis* (Paris: La Découvert, 2006), pp. 9, 21–23, 62, 71.

65. Shepard, *The Invention of Decolonization,* 182. Sussman, "Changing Lands," 162, argues that Jewish and pieds noirs destinies converged while still asserting that "[Algerian Jews] represent the only Jews in history to migrate en masse not because they suffered discrimination as Jews." Also see, Jacques Frémontier, *L'étoile rouge de David: Les Juifs communistes en France* (Paris: Fayard, 2002), p. 56.

66. Arkin, "'It's the French and the Arabs against the Jews,'" 129–30; Chantal Benayoun, "Juifs, pieds-noirs, séfarades ou les trois termes d'une citoyenneté," in *Marseille et le choc des décolonisations,* 125–32; Ethan Katz, "Jews and Muslims in the Shadow of Marianne: Conflicting Identities and Republican Culture in France, 1914–1975"

(Ph.D. diss., University of Wisconsin, 2008), pp. 263–66; Albert Memmi, "The Colonized Jew," *Jews and Arabs*, trans. Eleanor Levieux (Chicago: J. Philip O'Hara, Inc., 1975), pp. 38–45; Benjamin Stora, *Les trois exils: Juifs d'Algérie* (Paris: Stock, 2006), p. 144; and Sussman, "Changing Lands," 87–186.

67. Max Lapides, "An Algerian Odyssey," 3 May 1961, 55/64 # [45/64#28], AJDC. For Jewish support for the FLN, see Jean Laloum, "Portrait d'un Juif du FLN," in *Archives juives: Revue d'histoire des Juifs de France* 29, 1 (1ère semestre 1996): 65–71, and Frémontier, *L'étoile rouge de David*: 250–53. For diverse Algerian and French Jewish positions on the war, see Katz, "Jews and Muslims," 263–81. For generational diversity, see David Cohen, "Le Comité juif algérien d'études sociales dans le débat idéologique pendant la guerre d'Algérie (1954–1961)," *Archives juives* 29, 1 (1ère semestre 1996), pp. 37.

68. Ethan Katz, "Between Emancipation and Persecution: Algerian Jewish Memory in the *Longue durée*," *Journal of North African Studies* 17, 5 (November 2012): 793–820, argues convincingly that Algerian Jews began articulating a "violence and vulnerability narrative" following the 1934 Muslim-Jewish riots in Constantine, which served as a powerful counter to long-standing narratives focused on the progress and patriotism of Algerian Jews. This "violence and vulnerability narrative" then fed into a more regional narrative following World War II and at the beginning of the French decolonization process when a wide range of social actors began speaking of Jewish victimization throughout Algeria, Tunisia, and Morocco.

69. Phrase used by Jewish representatives visiting Paul Delouvrier, Délégué général du gouvernement en Algérie, Note d'information de Jacques Lazarus, "Algérie," 23 October 1959, III, FJL, AIU.

70. According to Stillman, *Jews of Arab Lands in Modern Times*, 170–71, Algerian Jews were "caught in the cross fire," unable to "identify with either side." See also Richard Ayoun, "Les Juifs d'Algérie pendant la guerre d'indépendance," *Archives juives* 29, 1 (1996): 15–29; Sussman, *Changing Lands*; Shepard, *The Invention of Decolonization*, 170; Mylène Sultan, "La synthèse impossible, 1954–1962," in Jean Laloun and Jean Luc Allouche eds, *Les Juifs d'Algérie: Textes et images* (Paris 1987) pp. 42–48; Stora, *Les trois exils*, 140, and "L'impossible neutralité des Juifs d'Algérie," in Mohammed Harbi and Benjamin Stora, *La guerre d'Algérie* (Paris: Hachette, 2005), pp. 287–316. Katz, "Jews and Muslims," 236–310, in contrast (and more convincingly), traces a shift in Jewish responses over time.

71. For some, French control was framed as pro-Muslim. Georges Zerapha thus wrote to Jacques Lazarus, 19 May 1960, XVI, FJL, AIU, that the only way "to draw the Arabs from their destitution and duress" was under French rule. Katz, "Jews and Muslims," 265, discusses Jewish sympathy for Muslim political aspirations.

72. Cited in Felix Allouche, "Il y a dix ans: Les Juifs d'Algérie quittèrent ce pays," *Information juive*, 1 August 1972. Also see Henri Chemouilli, "La grande peur des Juifs d'Algérie," *L'Arche*, 8–9 (August–September 1957), pp. 20–22.

73. Procès-Verbal du CJAES, 2 November 1954, FJL, AIU. For the CJAES position, see Cohen, "Comité juif algérien d'études sociales," pp. 30–50.

74. Cited in Lazarus, "Rapport sur la situation des Juifs," 59–60. Published as "Une déclaration du Comité juif algérien d'études sociale," *Information juive* 82 (November 1956).

75. Note d'information de Jacques Lazarus, "Algérie," 23 October 1959, III, FJL, AIU. Sussman, "Changing Lands," 112, and Stora, *Les trois exils*, 147, note that Jewish "neutrality" was often a smoke screen for more partisan views.

76. Hélène Cazes-Benatar, "Report on the Political Situation in North Africa," October 1950, 45/54 #5, AJDC.

77. Congrès juif mondial, Bureau nord-africain, "Note concernant le séjour en Afrique du Nord de M. Emmanuel Celler et le séjour à Tunis de MM. Perlzweig et Lazarus," 25 November 1954, XVI, FJL, AIU.

78. André Chouraqui, Louis D. Horowitz and Hélène Cazes-Benatar, "Foreign Countries: North Africa," *American Jewish Year Book* 54 (1953), p. 372.

79. For "European" reactions to decolonization, see Yann Scioldo-Zürcher, *Devenir métropolitain: Politique d'intégration et parcours de rapatriés d'Algérie en métropole (1954-2005)* (Paris: Éditions de l'École des hautes études en sciences sociales, 2010).

80. Stillman, *Jews of Arab Lands in Modern Times*, 172-75.

81. Claude Martin, *Histoire de l'Algérie française 1830-1962* (Paris: Éditions des Quatre fils Aymon, 1963), p. 467; Cohen, "Le Comité juif," 36.

82. For examples, see, "Rien ne doit altérer les sentiments de fraternité qui existent entre Israélites et Musulmans," and "En marge des événements du Moyen Orient," *Information juive*, November 1956.

83. Stora, *Les Trois Exils*, 151-52; Bahloul's informants in *The Architecture of Memory: A Jewish-Muslim Household in Colonial Algeria, 1937-1962*, trans. Catherine de Peloux Ménagé (Cambridge: Cambridge University Press, 1996), p. 119, claimed first becoming nervous during the Suez crisis.

84. RG, Mle, "Étrangers-Égyptiens. Brimades exercées par le gouvernement égyptien envers les ressortissants égyptiens juifs," 9 February 1952, 148W141, BdR; "La masse musulmane algérienne saura-t-elle toujours distinguer entre Israélites et Israéliens?" *Le Monde*, 2 November 1956, p. 7; "Un article déplacé" *Information juive*, November 1956.

85. Elie Gozlan to Mr. Haber, 9 July 1955, 55/64# [45/74#28, 86], AJDC.

86. Malka to Lazarus, 6 October 1962, I, FJL, AIU.

87. The AJDC's Stanley Abromovitch, touring Algeria that June, blamed French police for paying Jewish informants to expose Algerian nationalists. The Tunisian nationalist paper, *L'Action*, 15 October 1956, also asserted that Jews spied for payment. For alternative explanations, see Gilbert Meynier, *Histoire intérieure du FLN, 1954-1962* (Paris: Fayard, 2002), p. 255, and Laskier, *North African Jewry*, 319-21 who, like, Stora, *Les trois exils*, 152-54, assert that unbeknownst to the French or FLN, Israeli military emissaries aided these efforts.

88. Cited in Moses Leavitt to Charles H. Jordan, 19 April 1957, 55/64# [45/74#28, 86], AJDC.

89. Jacques Attal to Lazarus, 14 April 1957, XVI, FJL, AIU.

90. In Jean-David Attal's interview in Robert I. Weiner and Richard E. Sharpless, eds. *An Uncertain Future: Voices of a French Jewish Community, 1940-2012* (Toronto: University of Toronto Press, 2012), pp. 246-55, for example, he notes that his father, while angered by the Algerian nationalists' extremism, did not feel victimized as a Jew but as a French citizen. For a similar assessment, see "Le FLN algérien menace les Juifs" *Notre drapeau*, 25 October 1956, pp. 1-2. According to Jacques Mosel,

"Parcours algérien," *L'Arche* 2, 15 (March 1958), pp. 14–15, a sense of Jewish specificity differed according to location.

91. S. Cohen to Lazarus, "Rapport sur les attentats terroristes au quartier juif d'Oran les samedi 27 et dimanche 28 juillet 1957," 1 August 1957, I, FJL, AIU. Henri Chemoulli, "Le Judaïsme français change de visage," *Évidences*, September 1962, pp. 2–5, likewise noted that victims were not necessarily killed as Jews.

92. Armand Barmon, Communauté israélite de Boghari, "Note d'information sur la situation locale avant et après l'attentat du 29 septembre 1958," I, FJL, AIU.

93. Samuel Lévis to Sidney Nelson and Marits Souget, 20 December 1960, 55/64# [45/74#28, 86], AJDC. For examples of neighborly outreach, see untitled document accompanying "Photos publiées dans mois de juin 1992," *Information juive*, III, FJL; Sussman, "Changing Lands," 108; Ayoun, "Les Juifs d'Algérie," 25.

94. Henri Chemouilli, "La grande peur des Juifs d'Algérie," *L'Arche*, 8–9 (August–September 1957), pp. 20–22.

95. Sciodo-Zürcher, *Devenir métropolitain*, 55, argues that all "Europeans" fled out of fear.

96. See, for example, Sussman, "Changing Lands," 107–109, and Katz, "Jews and Muslims," 300. For Stora, *Les trois exils*, 135, the crucial moment came with the murder of Jewish musician Raymond Leyris, famous for his mastery of Arabo-Andalusian music and deep connections with all religious communities.

97. Cohen, "Le Comité juif," 40.

98. Stora, *Les trois exils*, 132, argues that in the mid-1950s, Jews—like most Algerian French citizens—believed themselves safe. Katz, "Jews and Muslims," 266, and Sussman, "Changing Lands," 89–105, point to the building of new Jewish institutions throughout the late 1950s as an indication of communal leaders' belief in an Algerian Jewish future. Yves C. Aouate, "Note et observations sur une histoire en construction," *Archives juives: Revue d'histoire des Juifs de France* 29, 1 (1e semestre 1996,) p. 8, concurs while positing a transition from "confidence to fear" from 1954 to 1958.

99. Daniel Timsit, *Algérie, récit anachronique* (Paris: Bouchène, 1999), cited in Stora, *Les trois exils*, 133.

100. Jean Bensimon, "Être juif en Algérie: Une illusion perdue?" *Kadimah*, December 1962.

101. "Moslem Countries," 14 January 1958, 55/64# [45/74#28, 86], AJDC. The Hebrew Immigrant Aid Society (HIAS) initially failed to establish an office to help Jews leave due to lack of interest. AJC, "North African Jews on the Move," January 1962, 55/64 # [45/64 #27], AJDC. Discussions about bringing HIAS to Algeria appear in Réunion du conseil du CJAES, 3 December 1955, XVI, FJL, AIU.

102. Frederick Fried to Louis Horowitz, 28 January 1956, 55/64# [45/74#28, 86], AJDC.

103. Some posited a class dimension to migration in these years, with wealthier Jews preparing for possible migration, while employees, workers, and others waited. Lévis to Nelson and Souget, 20 December 1960, 55/64# [45/74#28, 86], AJDC. Max Lapides made similar observations.

104. Fried to Horowitz, 28 January 1956, 55/64# [45/74#28, 86], AJDC.

105. Abromovitch, "Memorandum: Report on Algeria," 11 June 1956, 55/64# [45/74#28, 86], AJDC.

106. Ibid.
107. Réunion du conseil du CJAES, 19 June 1957, XVI, FJL, AIU.
108. Abromovitch, "Memorandum: Report on Algeria," 11 June 1956, 55/64#, [45/74#28, 86], AJDC.
109. Lazarus, "Rapport sur la situation des Juifs," 54.
110. Jacques Lazarus, "Foreign Countries: North Africa," *American Jewish Year Book* 61 (1960), 332; "Moslem Countries," 6 October 1959, 55/64# [45/74#28, 86], AJDC; Katz, "Jews and Muslims," 267–68.
111. Charles-Robert Ageron, *La décolonisation française* (Paris: Armand Colin, 1991), p. 158. Sciodo-Zürcher, *Devenir métropolitain*, 63, 78, argues French Algerians experienced a "collective catharsis" after de Gaulle's return to power. His declaration to support autodetermination, however, alienated many.
112. Rabbi Abraham Sellem (Bou Sadda) to Lazarus, 16 October 1959, I, FJL, AIU.
113. Henry Levy, "Foreign Countries: North Africa," *American Jewish Year Book* 60 (1959), p. 277.
114. Réunion du conseil du CJAES, 19 June 1957, XVI, FJL, AIU.
115. Lazarus to Nehemiah Robinson, 17 June 1957, III, FJL, AIU.
116. Sussman, "Changing Lands," 95–97.
117. Press clippings are in I, FJL, AIU. Lazarus also asked Léon Elbaz, 23 September 1958, I, FJL, AIU, to be updated on "all incidents affecting our co-religionists in your area particularly with regard to security."
118. Lazarus to Perlzweig, 14 January 1957, III, FJL, AIU.
119. Lazarus, "Rapport sur la situation des Juifs," 52.
120. For Jewish efforts to prove their "Frenchness," see Shepard, *The Invention of Decolonization*, 169–82.
121. Sussman, "Changing Lands," 115; Ayoun, "Les Juifs d'Algérie," 21. This claim was particularly important for the FLN's efforts to win international legitimacy. Mathew Connelly, *A Diplomatic Revolution: Algeria's Fight for Independence and the Origins of the Post–Cold War Era* (Oxford: Oxford University Press, 2002). According to Stora, *Les trois exils*, 160, the FLN's failure to win over Algerian Jews played a role in its "ideological hardening."
122. See Frémontier, *L'étoile rouge de David*, 252, for the story of an FLN request to one Jewish member to establish a group of Jewish supporters for which only five expressed interest.
123. Charbit, *Les harkis*.
124. Scholars disagree on the penetration of Algerian nationalism in the 1950s. Meynier, *Histoire intérieure*, 153–57, posits that by summer 1955 most Algerians had embraced the FLN's struggle. Benjamin Stora, *La gangrène et l'oubli: La mémoire de la guerre d'Algérie* (Paris: Découverte, 1991), pp. 161–71, and Paul Silverstein, *Algeria in France: Transpolitics, Race, and Nation* (Bloomington: Indiana University Press, 2004), 39–40, argue that colonial policies had strengthened ethnic distinctions among Algerian Muslims, limiting nationalist penetration. Katz, "Jews and Muslims," 255–57, makes clear that in the 1950s, many Muslims still believed in French republicanism while Shepard, *The Invention of Decolonization*, passim, shows how decolonization itself created "Algerians."
125. Many scholars have posited, in contrast, that FLN activists did not believe their own rhetoric on Jewish belonging to the nation and have thus deemphasized the

FLN's hardening views *in response* to Jewish politics. See Charles-Robert Ageron, "Une guerre religieuse, *"Archives juives: Revue d'histoire des Juifs de France* 29, 1 (1e semestre 1996): 11–14; Ayoun, "Les Juifs d'Algérie," 24; Sussman, "Changing Lands," 128.

126. "La parole du peuple" in the PPA newspaper *L'Émigré*, for example, called for universal suffrage for all Algerians, no matter their race or confession. Excerpt in Directeur départemental des services de police to Préfet des BdR, "A/S Journal du PPA, *L'Émigré*," 19 December 1947, 150W170, BdR.

127. Cited in Cohen, "Le Comité juif," 31.

128. *Al Istiqlal*, June 1956, cited in Ayoun, "Les Juifs d'Algérie," 21.

129. On the Congress, see Meynier, *Histoire intérieure*, 191–200, who suggests that most Algerians never embraced the idea of a non-Muslim state. For the Congress's implications for Jews, see, Ayoun, "Les Juifs d'Algérie," 22; Cohen, "Le Comité juif," 31–32; Katz, "Jews and Muslims," 258–61; and Stora, *Les trois exils*, 142–43.

130. "Lettre aux Israélites d'Algérie," in *El Moudjahid* 3 (September 1956), p. 52.

131. "Le FLN et les Israélites algériens," *France observatoire*, 18 October 1956.

132. Sussman, "Changing Lands," 123–25, and Ayoun, "Les Juifs d'Algérie," 23, argue that following de Gaulle's September 1959 declaration proclaiming the value of self-determination, nationalist appeals to Jews diminished.

133. "La communauté juive d'Algérie," Twelth Session of the General Assembly of the United Nations, No date, XVI, FJL, AIU.

134. "Executive Meeting," 14 January 1958, 55/64# [45/64#28, 86], AJDC. For rising violence, see Katz, "Jews and Muslims," 262. Meynier, *Histoire intérieure*, 255, notes that blackmail attempts were concentrated in the country's southern regions.

135. "Les Juifs d'Algérie dans le combat pour l'indépendance nationale," *Le Monde*, 19 February 1960. For a discussion of this piece and the original proclamation by the FLN, see Cohen, "Le Comité juif," 32–33.

136. The comment was made in an interview with Guy Mollet, secretary general of the SFIO and member of de Gaulle's cabinet. "Le général de Gaulle m'a dit: Ma solution pour l'Algérie, un état fédéral," *Le Monde*, 18 February 1960.

137. Cohen, "Le Comité juif," 40–45, covers this history from the CJAES's perspective and Shepard, 170–73, from the French government's perspective.

138. Lazarus to Easterman, 13 June 1960, III and IV, FJL, AIU.

139. Maître Benizri, "Mémoire: Inspiré par les préoccupations des Israélites français d'Algérie à la suite de la politique dite des communautés," 1961, SEAA, 121 bis, MAE.

140. Extract from "Jewish Chronicle, Features," 16 March 1960 in "Menaces du FLN contre les Juifs d'Algérie," 17 March 1960, MDI 87, CDJC; "FLN warns Algerian Jewry," *Jewish Telegraphic Agency*, 25 July 1960, Bulletin No. 194, p. 4, in XVI, FJL, AIU.

141. "Le FLN condamne l'antisémitisme," 16 January 1961, MDI 89, CDJC; Ayoun, "Les Juifs d'Algérie," 24. Meynier, *Histoire intérieure*, 255, argues that FLN literature was only rarely antisemitic, and then only in nonmainstream texts from the southern regions.

142. Cited in Cohen, "Le Comité juif," 34. Demonstrations calling for "Muslim Algeria" rather than "Algerian Algeria" during de Gaulle's December 1960 visit suggest that the revolution was changing course.

143. WJC, Information Department, "Antisemitism in Algeria" (excerpts from a letter by A. Chanderli, Permanent representative of the Algerian Front of National Liberation), 7 March 1961, XVI, FJL, AIU.

144. RG Alger, "FLN Documents intitulés 'Les Juifs d'Algérie dans le combat pour l'indépendance nationale,' " 14 March 1961, SEAA, 121 bis, MAE; "Les tentatives du FLN auprès des communautés israélites d'Algérie," Écho d'Alger, 16 March 1961, XVI, FJL, AIU.

145. AJC to Moses Leavitt, "Conference with M. Chanderli on March 27," 25 April 1961, 55/64 # [45/64 #28], AJDC.

146. Lazarus to Louis Joxe, "Algérie," March 1961, III, FJL, AIU. Lazarus and the CJAES demanded the same right of autodetermination that Muslim Algerians sought for themselves. "Mémoire sur le Judaïsme algérien, présenté par le Comité juif algérien d'études sociales et la fédération des communautés israélites d'Algérie," Alger, 1 March 1961, II, FJL, AIU. For the CJAES response, see Cohen, "Le Comité juif," 35.

147. Moses A. Leavitt to Mr. Philip Soskie, 30 December 1960, 55/64 # [45/64#28, 86], AJDC. Emphasis mine.

148. AJC, "Memorandum to Foreign Affairs Department," 8 June 1961, 55/64 #, [45/64 #28], AJDC.

149. Lapides, "An Algerian Odyssey," 3 May 1961, 55/64 # [45/64 #28], AJDC, claimed that while most Algerian Jews, stressed the necessity of departure, there was a great deal of "indecision, hesitation and confusion" around the issue. HIAS finally established an Algerian office in March 1961.

150. "Droits égaux en Algérie," L'Observateur du Moyen Orient, 13 September 1957. GPRA spokesmen cited in Kalef, "Conversations algériennes," L'Arche, August–September 1961, p. 34. Also see Ayoun, "Les Juifs d'Algérie," 24.

151. For Algerian relations with Israel, see Michael Laskier, "Israel and Algeria and French Colonialism and the Arab-Israeli Conflict, 1954–1978," Israel Studies 6, 2 (2001): 1–32, and Stora, Les trois exils, 154–55.

152. The WJC and Jewish Agency denied encouraging such departures. Jean Morin, Délégué général en Algérie, to Ministre d'état, Chargé des affaires algériennes, "Activité des missions israéliennes en Algérie," 24 March 1961, SEAA, 121 bis, MAE. For Israeli efforts in Algeria, also see Shepard, The Invention of Decolonization, 174–77. "Memorandum: Report on Algeria," 11 June 1956, 55/64# [45/64 #28, 86], AJDC, discusses nationalist irritation at Israeli agents' training of Jewish self-defense groups.

153. AJC to Moses Leavitt, "Conference with M. Chanderli on March 27," 25 April 1961, 55/64 # [45/64 #28] AJDC.

154. Henri Chemouilli, "Un an après: Lettres à un ami d'Algérie," L'Arche 78 (July 1963): 22–26.

155. Claude Estier, "Les journées de décembre," Droit et liberté, January 1961.

156. A French deputy, Chibi actively pushed for peace. "End of War Called For," Herald Tribune, 21 July 1959. The written exchange occurred via a Jewish teacher in Bône, Charles Levy, 12 March; 24 March; 6 April 1961; and letter from Lazarus to Chibi, 20 March 1961, II, FJL, AIU.

157. France soir and France observateur reported Algerian accusations that Jews had instigated the violence, while Le Monde and Algerian Jewish sources insisted that

such claims were a pretext for the destruction. Note à l'attention de M. le Grand Rabbin J. Kaplan, "Sac de la synagogue de la Casbah à Alger," 11 December 1960, MDI 87, CDJC.

158. In June 1961, Algerian Jewish personalities met again to reaffirm their French citizenship. RG, Alger, "Communauté juive," 4 July 1961, 121 bis, MAE.

159. *Le Monde diplomatique*, July 1961, cited in Ayoun, "Les Juifs d'Algérie," 24. See also Sussman, "Changing Lands," 130. The AJC and Lazarus also reported on this shift. "North African Jews on the Move," January 1962, 55/64 # [45/64 #27], AJDC; Note d'information de Jacques Lazarus, "Algérie," 28 February 1962, Entretien entre le Délégué général en Algérie M. Jean Morin et MM. Jaques Lazarus et André Narboni, III, FJL, AIU.

160. Shepard, *The Invention of Decolonization*, 168–82.

161. Samuel Lévis to Herbert Katzki, 20 October 1961, 55/64 # [45/64 #28], AJDC.

162. Abe Karlikow, Untitled, 19 June 1962, 55/64 # [45/64# 27], AJDC.

163. Katz, "Jews and Muslims," 300, counts over 130 attacks against Jews or Jewish establishments from January 1961 until April 1962.

164. Délégation générale en Algérie, Direction générale des affaires politiques et de l'information, "Note sur les réactions de la communauté israélite d'Algérie face à l'évolution du problème algérien," 24 January 1962, 121 bis, MAE.

165. Paul Sebag, *Histoire des Juifs de Tunisie: Des origines à nos jours* (Paris: Éditions l'Harmattan, 1991), pp. 296–98; Laskier, *North African Jewry*, 299–302; Taïeb, "Immigrés d'Afrique du Nord," 151–52.

166. Abe Karlikow, Untitled, 19 June 1962, 55/64# [45/64 #27], AJDC.

167. AJC, "North African Jews on the Move," January 1962, 55/64# [45/64 #27], AJDC.

168. Stora, *Les trois exils*, 161; "Meeting on Algeria" 9 November 1961, 55/64# [45/64 #28]; AJC, "North African Jews on the Move," January 1962, 55/64# [45/64 #27], AJDC. Léo Palacio, "Violents incidents à Oran entre Musulmans et Israélites," *Le Monde*, 13 September 1961, p. 3.

169. Gilbert Cohen-Tanugi, Victor Malka, and Arnold Mandel, "Foreign Countries: North Africa, South Africa," *American Jewish Year Book* 64 (1963) 405–406; RG, "Communauté juive," September 1961, 121 bis, MAE. For FLN efforts to curb interethnic violence, see M. Souget to Charles H. Jordan, "Algeria," 9 January 1962, 55/64 # [45/64 #27], AJDC. CJAES discussions are in Réunion du conseil du Comité juif algérien d'études sociales, 13 September 1961, XVI, FJL, AIU.

170. AJC, "North African Jews on the Move," January 1962, 55/64 #, [45/64 #27], AJDC.

171. "Tunis en Arabe," 11 September 1961, 121 bis, MEA.

172. Cohen, "Le Comité juif," 37 and Henri Chemouilli, *Une diaspora méconnue: Les Juifs d'Algérie* (Paris: 1976), p. 390, blame the OAS for this attack. Jewish fears are documented in Délégation générale en Algérie, Direction générale des affaires politiques et de l'information, "Note sur les réactions de la communauté israélite d'Algérie face à l'évolution du problème algérien," 24 January 1962, 121 bis, MAE; Eugène Mannoni, "Juifs et Musulmans à leur tour à Oran," *Le Monde*, 14 September 1961, p. 2.

173. Herbert Katzki to Moses Leavitt, "Situation in Algeria," 15 November 1961, 55/64 # [45/64 #28], AJDC.

174. RG, "État d'esprit de la communauté israélite," 7–10 October 1961, 121 bis, MAE.

175. Délégation générale en Algérie, Direction générale des affaires politiques et de l'information, "Note sur les réactions de la communauté israélite d'Algérie face à l'évolution du problème algérien," 24 January 1962, 121 bis, MAE.

176. RG, "État d'esprit de la communauté israélite," 7–10 October 1961, 121 bis, MAE.

177. James Rice to members of the United HIAS Service Board of Directors and National Council, 13 July 1962, 55/64 # [45/64 #27], AJDC; "La communauté israélite d'Algérie," 19 October 1962, 121 bis, MAE.

178. Joseph Barry, "Algeria: Again the Cruel Dilemma," *The ADL Bulletin*, December 1961.

179. M. Souget to Charles H. Jordan, "Algeria," 9 January 1962; AJC, "North African Jews on the Move," January 1962, 55/64 # [45/64 #27], AJDC; Stora, *Les trois exils*, 166–69.

180. M. Souget to Charles H. Jordan, "Algeria," 9 January 1962, 55/64 # [45/64 #27], AJDC, predicted 40–50 percent would remain.

181. Stora, *Les trois exils*, 164–65, and AJC, "North African Jews on the Move," January 1962, 55/64 # [45/64 #27], AJDC, explain how Jewish OAS members reconciled themselves to their choice.

182. Ayoun, "Les Juifs d'Algérie," 28; Cohen "Le Comité juif," 37.

183. Stora, *Les trois exils*, 165, and Sussman, "Changing Lands," 133, argue that Jewish support for French Algeria could be confused with support for the OAS. For an example of Jewish opposition to the OAS, see Cathie Busidan's testimony in *An Uncertain Future*, 23–33, and Bensimon, "Être juif en Algérie."

184. Délégation générale en Algérie, Direction générale des affaires politiques et de l'information, "Note sur les réactions de la communauté israélite d'Algérie face à l'évolution du problème algérien," 24 January 1962, 121 bis, MAE.

185. Shepard, *The Invention of Decolonization*, 174, 177–80.

186. Stora, *Les trois exils*, 135, describes a wave of panic from December 1961 through June 1962.

187. AJC, "North African Jews on the Move," January 1962, 55/64 # [45/64 #27], AJDC. Those who supported the FLN, according to the AJC, had changed their minds or had found it better to stay silent. "Half of Jews in Algeria Reported to Have Fled," *New York Times*, 26 June 1962, also reported "deep complicity" between Jews and the OAS, while pointing largely to Oran.

188. "Meeting on Algeria" 9 November 1961, 55/64 # [45/64 #28], AJDC.

189. Bureau du 22 décembre 1961, MDI 1–55, CDJC. CRIF debates are from meetings on 18 July 1961, and 18 and 25 January 1962, same microfilm. For OAS outreach to Jews, see Katz, "Jews and Muslims ," 302–305; Shepard, *The Invention of Decolonization*, 178–80; and Sussman, "Changing Lands," 135–36. OAS, "Appel aux Israélites d'Algérie," No date, II, FJL, AIU.

190. AJC, "North African Jews on the Move," January 1962, 55/64 # [45/64 #27], AJDC. M. Souget to Charles H. Jordan, "Algeria," 9 January 1962, same folder, makes the same point. Joint officials were threatened with assassination for helping "deserters" leave the country, and wealthy Jewish businessmen paid large sums to protect themselves against OAS threats. "Moslem Countries: Algeria," 21 November 1961, 55/64 # [45/64 #28], AJDC.

191. JTA Daily News Bulletin, "French Underground in Algiers Warns Jews against Leaving Country," 17 January 1962. For OAS assassinations of Jews, see Ayoun,

"Les Juifs d'Algérie," 27, and Stora, *Les trois exils*, 162–63. Despite its opposition to emigration, the OAS never blocked departures to Israel, which Jewish sources explained by noting that to the OAS, "Israel is something of a 'hero state,' being considered the only country that 'really knows how to deal with Arabs.'" AJC, "North African Jews on the Move," January 1962, 55/64 # [45/64 #27], AJDC.

192. "Memorandum of discussions between Mr. Warburg, Mr. Leavitt, Mr. Jordan," 20–21, November 1961, 55/64 # [45/64 #28], AJDC. Samuel Lévis to Herbert Katzki, 20 October 1961; Herbert Katzki to Moses Leavitt, "Situation in Algeria," 15 November 1961, same file.

193. "La communauté israélite d'Algérie," 19 October 1962, 121 bis, MEA.

194. Souget to AJDC, Geneva—Attn. H. Katzki, 28 February 1962, 55/64 # [45/64 #27], AJDC.

195. Administrative Meeting, 12 March 1962, 55/64 # [45/64 #27], AJDC.

196. Christian Mouly, "L'exode des familles israélites d'Algérie est particulièrement sensible à Constantine," *Le Monde*, 17 February 1962, p. 2, posited that departure rates increased after children got out of school.

197. Shepard, *The Invention of Decolonization*, 180. Juridically Shepard is correct that the Frenchness of Jewish migrants mattered over their ethnic affiliations.

198. AJC, "North African Jews on the Move," January 1962, 55/64 # [45/64 #27], AJDC. Per one reporter: "It is conceivable, the Algerian Jews believe themselves to be too deeply compromised to remain. The chances of a clash with Algerian Arab nationalism seem to them too great for safety." "The Jews of Algeria—Extrait d'un article de Aaron Secal in *The Spectator*, 23 February 1962," MDI 88, CDJC.

199. Sussman "Changing Lands," 144.

200. Note d'information de Jacques Lazarus, "Algérie," 28 February 1962; "Entretien entre le Délégué général en Algérie M. Jean Morin et MM. Jaques Lazarus et André Narboni," III, FJL, AIU.

201. "Appeal to Jews to Remain," *The Jewish Chronicle*, 13 April 1962.

202. Citation and threat from Abe Karlikow, Untitled, 19 June 1962, 55/64 # [45/64 # 27], AJDC.

203. Sussman, "Changing Lands,"185. For departures, see pp. 143–85.

204. Bensimon, "Être juif en Algérie."

205. Cited in Frémontier, *L'étoile rouge de David*, 250.

206. Stora, *Les trois exils*, 154–55, and Laskier, "Israel and Algeria and French Colonialism and the Arab-Israeli Conflict," 16–17. In summer 1961, the WJC ended negotiations with the FLN due to its stance on Israel. "Le Congrès juif mondial parle de l'Algérie," 25 August 1961, in XVI, FJL, AIU.

207. Laskier, "Israel and Algeria and French Colonialism and the Arab-Israeli Conflict," 12.

208. Bensimon, "Être juif en Algérie."

209. Stora, *Les trois exils*, 175. Also see Friedman, *Colonialism and After*, 33; Frémontier, *L'étoile rouge de David*, 37–42; and Denis Sieffert, *Israël-Palestine: Une passion française* (Paris: La Découverte, 2004), pp. 60–61.

210. Bensimon, "Être juif en Algérie."

Chapter 3. Encounters in the Metropole: The Impact of Decolonization on Muslim-Jewish Life in France in the 1950s and 1960s

1. CRIF meetings, 6 and 20 January 1948, MDI 1–55, CJDC.
2. Delegates asked about basic matters of communal composition and religious practice, demonstrating how little was known about Moroccan Jews. CRIF meeting, 6 January 1948 and 6 April 1948, MDI 1–55, CJDC.
3. CRIF meeting, 8 June and 6 October 1948, Joseph Fischer to Schuman, 30 November 1949, in CRIF meeting, 6 December 1949; MDI 1–55, CJDC; Meiss to Marin, 11 October 1948, SG/1948, 75 (ex 29), MAE. The CRIF also held periodic discussions of Moroccan Jewish difficulties migrating to Israel. CRIF meeting, 8 June 1948; Meiss to Olivier Marin, 11 October 1948, in CRIF meeting, 6 October 1948; CRIF meeting, 4 and 26 April 1949; Note d'information, 9 May and 2 June 1949; MDI 1–55, CDJC.
4. "Résolutions votées au 20ème congrès de la FSJF, le 8 novembre 1948," 13 November 1948, BA 2315 Communauté juive, APP.
5. Minutes, CRIF meeting, 20 October 1948, MDI 1–55, CDJC. Fédération des sociétés juives de France, Organisation sioniste de France, Congrès juif mondiale, 9 November 1949, BA 2315 Communauté juive, APP. For Iraqi Jews, see Esther Meir-Glitzenstein, *Zionism in an Arab Country: Jews in Iraq in the 1940s* (London and New York: Routledge, 2004).
6. CRIF meeting, 8 November and 6 December 1949, MDI 1–55, CDJC. Representatives disagreed on how publicly to make their case, agreeing finally to a behind-the-scenes approach. Links between Nazism and Iraqi persecutions are evident in Joseph Fischer to Robert Schuman, 30 November 1949; CRIF meetings 8 May 1951 and 5 February 1952, same reel.
7. CRIF meetings 20 October 1948 and 8 November 1949, MDI 1–55, CDJC. Joel Beinin, *The Dispersion of Egyptian Jewry: Culture, Politics, and the Formation of a Modern Diaspora* (Berkeley: University of California Press, 1998), pp. 19–21.
8. For the problem with migration statistics, see Beinin, *The Dispersion*, 288, note 83. For French Jewish responses, see Alexandre De Aranjo, "L'accueil des réfugiés d'Egypte en France et leur réinstallation en région parisienne, 1956–1960," in *Terre d'exil, terre d'asile: Migrations juives en France aux XIXe et XXe siècles*, ed. Colette Zytnicki (Paris: Éditions de l'Éclat, 2010), p. 133, and Benjamin Pinkus, "La campagne de Suez et son impact sur les Juifs de France," trans. from Hebrew by Jules Danan, in *Les Juifs de France, le Sionisme et l'État d'Israël*, vol. 2, eds., Doris Bensimon and Benjamin Pinkus (Paris: Publications Langues'O, 1987), pp. 357–60.
9. Mandel, "In the Aftermath of Genocide," chap. 8.
10. Jacques Piette, "Meeting de solidarité avec les combattants et l'État d'Israël, organisé par l'Association des anciens combattants et engagés volontaires juifs 1939–1945," 20 November 1956, BA 2315 Communauté juive, APP.
11. This linkage was also embedded in the French press. Denis Sieffert, *Israël-Palestine: Une passion française* (Paris: La Découverte, 2004), p. 106.
12. "Meeting organisé par l'Association indépendante des anciens déportés et internés de France et le Concours d'organisations juives, le 17/12/1956," 18 December 1956, MDI 69, CDJC.

13. One Egyptian Jewish lawyer, for example, downplayed public antisemitism and blamed the government. Assemblée plénière du 6 décembre 1956, MDI 1–55, CDJC. Jacques Baulin, "Le Caire nouvelle Mecque de l'antisémitisme," *L'Arche*, January 1960, pp. 23, 59.

14. Allocution de M. le Baron Alain de Rothschild to Conférence inter-organisations juives sur l'Égypte, 21 January 1957, MDI 1–55, CDJC. Conference documentation can be found in CRIF meeting, 25 January 1957; Bureau du CRIF, 8 January 1957, MDI 1–55 CDJC.

15. CRIF meeting, 6 January 1948, MDI 1–55, CDJC. For Jewish reluctance to criticize French policies in Algeria, see Ethan Katz, "Jews and Muslims in the Shadow of Marianne: Conflicting Identities and Republican Culture in France (1914-1975)" (Ph.D. diss., University of Wisconsin–Madison, 2009), pp. 270–71.

16. Most discussions focused on how to manage and pay for Jewish arrivals. See Mandel, "In the Aftermath of Genocide," chap. 8, and Sarah Sussman, "Changing Lands, Changing Identities: The Migration of Algerian Jewry to France, 1954–1967" (Ph.D. diss., Stanford University, 2002), pp. 252–319. The CRIF did protest the Petitjean murders. CRIF meeting, 4 October 1954, MDI 1–55, CDJC.

17. Bureau du CRIF, 4 November 1954, MDI 1–55, CDJC.

18. For the former, see "Après les pogroms de Petitjean (Maroc): La situation des Juifs, noyés dans une masse arabe fanatisée, devient chaque jour plus tragique," *La Terre retrouvée*, 1 October 1954. For the latter, see André Blumel, president, Fédération sioniste de France to Comité d'action sioniste, 24 August 1955, MDI 69, CDJC.

19. Philippe Boukara, "La gauche juive en France et la guerre d'Algérie," *Archives juives: Revue d'histoire des Juifs de France* 29, 1 (1ère semestre 1996): 72–81.

20. "CRIF" in "Press survey du WJC," 15 September 1954, MDI 68, CJDC.

21. Bureau du CRIF, 29 September 1955; CRIF meeting, 13 October 1955, MDI 1–55, CDJC.

22. For an in depth analysis of French Jewish responses to the Algerian war, see Katz, "Jews and Muslims," 269–76. Also see, Doris Bensimon, *Les Juifs de France et leurs relations avec Israël: 1945-1988* (Paris: Éditions l'Harmattan, 1989), pp. 236–37; Boukara, "La gauche juive en France et la guerre d'Algérie," 72–81; Benjamin Stora, *Les trois exils: Juifs d'Algérie* (Paris: Éditions Stock, 2006), pp. 157–60.

23. For mobilization protests, see Benjamin Stora, *Histoire de la guerre d'Algérie, 1954–1962*, 4th ed. (Paris: Éditions La Découverte & Syros, 2006), pp. 18–19.

24. CRIF delegates believed that political circumstances made intervention "inopportune." Bureau du CRIF, 4 November 1955; CRIF meeting, 23 December 1955, MDI 1–55; V. Modiano to l'Union des étudiants juifs de France, 9 December 1955, MDI 57, CDJC. The disagreement was as much over process as politics, since the UEJF had issued its statement without CRIF approval. Nevertheless, a year later CRIF delegates still proved hesitant to express their views on Algeria, arguing that they did not represent Algerian Jews. CRIF meeting, 18 October 1956, MDI 1–55, CDJC.

25. Raymond Aron, "Israël face à la tragédie," *Le Figaro littéraire*, 12–18 June 1967, for example, notoriously distanced his pro-independence position from his Jewish roots.

26. W. Rabi, "Nos frères: Au coeur du drame algérien," *L'Arche*, June 1959, pp. 28, 59.

27. Cited in Yair Auron, *Les Juifs d'extrême gauche en Mai 68: Une génération révolutionnaire marquée par la Shoah*, translated from Hebrew by Katherine Werchowski (Paris: Albin Michel 1998), pp. 62–63.

28. Cited in Lionel Cohn, "Réflexions d'un étudiant juif religieux sur le problème algérien," *Kadimah*, December 1960–January 1961, p. 1.
29. Cited in Auron, *Les Juifs d'extrême gauche*, 64.
30. Benjamin Hyman, "'The Hospitality of Your Columns': French Jewish and Muslim Student Press and the Rhetorical Construction of 'Dialogue,' 1957–1969," undergraduate paper, Brown University, fall 2010. I would like to thank Ben for allowing me to develop upon his insights in the following pages.
31. Henry Pohoryles, "1940–1955: Résurrection et évolution des mouvements de jeunes," *La Revue FSJU*, October 1955, Bibliothèque, UEJF. Roger Berg, "Studieuse et grave jeunesse," *L'Arche*, February 1957, p. 44, claimed two thousand members. Also see Lucine Lazare, "Student Movements, Jewish-France," *Encyclopaedia Judaica*, eds., Michael Berenbaum and Fred Skolnik, 2nd ed., vol. 19 (Detroit: Macmillan Reference, 2007), pp. 265–69.
32. While the UEJF supported Jewish independence in Palestine, it also favored Muslim-Jewish cooperation. "Union des étudiants juifs de France," F715292, AN.
33. Henri Atlan, "Rapport du conseil d'administration," 9ème congrès de l'UEJF, January 1963, II, FJL, AIU. This position caused a rift between the UEJF and their Algerian counterparts. "A nos camarades d'Algérie," *Kadimah*, December 1962. Atlan, while remaining committed to his prior position, acknowledged later, "it is true that I was not with them on site." Cited in Jean-Luc Allouche, "Algérie: Le vent de l'histoire," *L'Arche* December 1979, p. 36.
34. For more on Kateb, see Katz, "Jews and Muslims," 282–84.
35. Yacine Kateb, "Les rapports judéo-arabes," *Kadimah*, June/July 1957, p. 10ff.
36. "La paix israélo-arabe est-elle possible?" *L'Arche*, March 1958, p. 19. Memmi nevertheless remained committed to dialogue "because it is the only way."
37. Lionel Cohn, "Réflexions d'un étudiant juif religieux sur le problème algérien," *Kadimah*, December 1960–January 1961.
38. "Mohammed Ben Bachir, "Un étudiant musulman nous répond," *Kadimah*, April/May 1961, p. 1ff.
39. "La paix israélo-arabe est-elle possible?" in *L'Arche*, March 1958, p. 18. While acknowledging the inaccuracy of the term "antisemitism," the editors adopted it nonetheless.
40. Interestingly, most questionnaire respondents did not reflect the editorial biases, downplaying anti-Jewish animosity in the Muslim world while agreeing that relations had deteriorated. "Lettre aux lecteurs," *L'Arche*, March 1958, p. 5.
41. Jacques Mosel, "Parcours algérien," *L'Arche*, March 1958, p. 14. For more measured discussions of Muslim-Jewish relations in North Africa, see "Le Judaïsme nord-africain s'interroge sur son avenir," *L'Arche*, February 1957, pp. 10–11; Henri Chemouilli, "La grande peur des Juifs d'Algérie," *L'Arche*, August–September 1957, pp. 20–22; Albert Memmi, "Une tragédie si quotidienne," *L'Arche* February 1961, pp. 18–23. As should be clear from earlier citations, Memmi's views vacillated somewhat.
42. Perhaps unsurprisingly, French Zionist publications remained consistently pessimistic, as in "La chronique politique de J. Ariel: La mise en demeure du FLN," *La Terre retrouvée*, 15 May 1960, which warned that an FLN victory would mean "the end of Algerian Judaism" or "Le FLN algérien menace les Juifs," *Notre drapeau*, 25 October 1956, pp. 1–2.

43. Emile Touati, "Avec un dinar en poche: Après Bizerte, le problème des réfugiés d'Afrique du Nord se pose encore d'une manière plus aiguë. Notre communauté saura-t-elle y faire face?" *L'Arche*, October 1961, p. 34. This depiction can be contrasted to "La communauté juive menacée," *Les Écoutés*, 31 August 1961, in MDI 89, CDJC, that described anti-Jewish sentiment as emerging from the political establishment rather than from the wider population.

44. "Menaces de pogrom à Oran," 1 June 1962, MDI 88, CDJC.

45. While written in English this piece by Joseph Barry, "Algeria: Again the Cruel Dilemma," *The ADL Bulletin*, December 1961, in Notes d'information, 1961, MDI 88, CDJC, was part of the CRIF's clippings collection.

46. Robert Buchard, "Des élèves musulmans passent à tabac des Israélites," *Paris presse*, 20 November 1961, MDI 89, CDJC.

47. "Un tract OAS juive," *Le Figaro*, 13 March 1961, in MDI 89, CDJC.

48. The CRIF's left-leaning member organizations called for a condemnation of OAS violence in May 1961, unleashing a debate over whether the OAS was antisemitic (given FLN attacks against Jews), whether CRIF involvement would harm Algerian Jews, and whether the CRIF should speak out on French political questions. CRIF meetings, 8 May and 8 December 1961; Bureau du CRIF, 22 December 1961, MDI 1–55, CDJC.

49. Marcel Liebman, "Les Juifs devant le problème algérien," *Les Temps modernes*, 18 April 1961, pp. 1328–42.

50. The CRIF's final statement (which passed with several abstentions) was decidedly apolitical, condemning violence and Nazi-inspired tactics with no mention of Jews, Muslims, the OAS, the FLN, or French policy. CRIF meetings, 18 and 25 January 1962, MDI 1–55, CDJC. On Jewish leftists and the Algerian crisis, see Bensimon, *Les Juifs de France*, 236–37; Boukara, "La gauche juive en France, 72–81, and Stora, *Les trois exiles,* 157–60.

51. Jim House and Neil MacMaster, *Paris 1961: Algerians, State Terror, and Memory* (Oxford: Oxford University Press, 2006).

52. Elio Boublil to Vidal Modiano, 6 November 1961, MDI 73B; "Meeting juif contre le racisme musulman," 24 November 1961, MDI 89, CDJC.

53. Boukara, "La gauche juive," 78–79.

54. Isi Blum and Dr. Danovski to Docteur Modiano 25 October 1961, MDI 73B, CDJC.

55. Bureau du 27 novembre 1961; Assemblée plénière du 8 décembre 1961, MDI 1–55, CDJC.

56. *La Terre retrouvée*, 15 November 1961, cited in Boukara, "La gauche juive," 79. For republicanism and Jewish responses to the Algerian war, see Katz, "Jews and Muslims," 269–98.

57. Citation comes from Robert Sommer, Jewish author and founder of Fondation sepher and Bureau du Chabbat, to Jacques Lazarus, 14 March 1961, XVI, FJL, AIU. Lazarus's infuriated response is in the same file. Information on the protest can be found in Raph. Feigelson, Sec Gen. Comité juif d'action anti-fasciste, 25 June 1962, MDI 71, CDJC. Signatories included: Amicale des anciens déportés juifs; Amicale des Juifs anciens résistants; Cercle Bernard Lazare; Cercle Mishmar; Fédération générale et industriels, Artisans et façonniers juifs; Union des engagés volontaires et anciens combattants juifs; Union des Juifs pour la résistance et l'entraide; Union des sociétés juives de France, and the Cercle d'études juives Beth Hakerem.

58. M. Moch à l'attention de M. Jacques Meyer, "Note sur la situation de la communauté juive d'Algérie et l'exode massif de Juifs en France," 4 January 1963, MDI 83, CDJC. For another example, see André Nehar, "Dans le feu de l'épreuve," *L'Arche*, March 1963, p. 29.

59. Gérard Israel, "Éléments pour un portrait-robot du rapatrié," *L'Arche*, March 1963, pp. 52–53.

60. Arab attempts in 1964 to boycott French companies with contracts in Israel exacerbated this view. Relevant CRIF discussions can be found MDI 1–55; MDI 84; MDI 85; MDI 91, and MDI 93, CJDC. Also see Kassir and Mardam-Bey, *Itinéraires de Paris à Jerusalem*, 16–17.

61. One exception was Pierre Vidal-Naquet, "La guerre révolutionnaire et la tragédie des harkis," *Le Monde*, 11–12 November 1962, who condemned the treatment of Muslim immigrants. Most Jewish journalists paid little attention to incoming Muslims. See, for example, T.C. "Le FSJU face au problème social des Juifs nord-africains," *La revue du FSJU*, December 1953, p. 9, which comments that Jewish arrivals were "often submerged in the mass of Muslim immigrants of the same origin," but never again mentioned the latter. Emile Touati's article discussed below is another exception.

62. Chouchana Boukhobza, "Exil, quand tu nous tiens," *Communauté nouvelle*, No. 23, February–March 1985.

63. Paul Hyman, *The Jews of Modern France* (Berkeley: University of California Press, 1998), p. 195. Paris held 175,000 Jews and 126,000 Muslims by the late 1950s. Katz, "Jews and Muslims," 248.

64. Kimberly Arkin, "'It's the French and the Arabs against the Jews': Identity Politics and the Construction of Adolescent Jewishness in France" (Ph.D. diss., University of Chicago, 2008), pp. 170–71; Doris Bensimon and Sergio Della Pergolla, *La population juive de France: Socio-démographie et identité* (Jerusalem: Institute of Contemporary Jewry of Hebrew University and Centre national de la recherche scientifique, Paris, 1984), pp. 250, 253, 286–87, have shown, traditional Jewish neighborhoods in Paris actually included both Muslims and Jews. For Marseille, see René Duchac, "Facteurs urbains de l'adaptation des immigrés maghrébins: Étude comparative de trois quartiers de Marseille," in *Les immigrés du Maghreb: Études sur l'adaptation en milieux urbain, travaux et documents* 79 (Paris: Presses universitaires de France, 1977), pp. 14–15; Sussman, "Changing Lands," 235–36.

65. Numbers of Arabic speakers differed according to country and region of origin. Doris Bensimon, *L'intégration des Juifs nord-africains en France* (La Haye: Mouton, 1971), p. 22–23.

66. Interview cited in Jacques Frémontier, *L'étoile rouge de David: Les Juifs communiste en France* (Paris: Fayard, 2002), p. 197. The interviewee was a communist and a member of the FLN during the Algerian War.

67. Katz, "Jews and Muslims," 249–54, 287–94.

68. Pierre Baillet, "Les rapatriés d'Algérie en France," *Notes et études documentaires*, No. 4275–76 (29 March 1976), pp. 46–57.

69. Gérard Noiriel, *Immigration, antisémitisme et racisme en France (XIXe–XXe siècle): Discours publics, humiliations privées* (Paris: Fayard, 2007), p. 537. Amelia Lyons, "Invisible Immigrants: Algerian Families and the French Welfare State in the Era of

Decolonization (1947–1974)" (Ph.D. diss., University of California, Irvine 2004), pp. 9, 40–49, argues that prior to 1962, welfare institutions did seek to incorporate Algerian Muslims into French society.

70. Even Jewish refugees often benefited from a welcoming administrative structure. See Aranjo, "L'accueil des réfugiés d'Egypte en France," 141, for example, for governmental attitudes toward arriving Jews.

71. "Sources of Financing for the Principal Relief and Rehabilitation Programs in France in 1962," Julian Breen, 29 July 1963, 309, AJDC; Sussman, "Changing Lands," 188–89.

72. For distinctions between Jewish and Muslim Algerians, see Todd Shepard, *The Invention of Decolonization: The Algerian War and the Remaking of France* (Ithaca/London: Cornell University Press, 2006), pp. 172–73. Alexis Spire, *Étrangers à la carte: L'administration de l'immigration en France (1945–1975)* (Paris: Grasset, 2005), pp. 189–222, shows how even Muslim repatriates who had fought for the French army were treated as administratively distinct from "European" repatriates. Fatima Besnaci-Lancou and Gilles Manceron eds., *Les harkis: Dans la colonisation et ses suites* (Paris: Les Éditions de l'Atelier, 2008), pp. 30–31, 112. Tom Charbit, *Les harkis* (Paris: La Découvert, 2006), pp. 60–61. For aid to repatriates, see Jean Jacques Jordi, *De l'exode à l'exil: Rapatriés et pieds-noirs en France* (Paris: Éditions l'Harmattan, 1993) and *1962, L'arrivée des pieds-noirs* (Paris: Autrement, 1995). For aid to Morrocan Jewish immigrants, see Martin Messika, "L'accueil des Juifs marocains en France," *Terre d'exil terre d'asile: Migrations juives en France aux XIXe et XXe siècles*, ed., Colette Zytnicki (Paris: Éditions de l'Éclat, 2010), pp 175–78.

73. While more immigrants and pieds noirs went to Paris, they made up a smaller percentage of the city's population. Abdelmalek Sayad, Jean-Jacques Jordi, and Émile Témime, *Le choc de la décolonisation (1945–1990)* vol. 4 of *Migrance: Histoire des migrations à Marseille*, ed. Émile Témime (Aix-en-Provence: Éditions Jeanne Laffitte, 1991), pp. 8, 58–59, 61–64.

74. Préfet des Bouches-du-Rhône, "Exposé sur l'état actuel de la question sociale nord-africaine dans le département des Bouches-du-Rhône et la 9e région militaire," 20 July 1953, 148W193, BdR. While another report put the number at 30,000, or nearly 4 percent of Marseille's total population (Commissaire de police de la sureté to Commissaire principal, "Délinquance nord-africaine et délinquance d'ensemble comparées," 2 January 1953, same file), most others reported 11,000 in Marseille with 3,000–4,000 in the surrounding towns. The numbers of Moroccan and Tunisians Muslims numbered 600 and 550, respectively, in October 1953. André Pelabon to Ministre de l'Intérieur, "Enquête sociale sur la situation des Musulmans originaires d'Algérie résidant en métropole, Département des Bouches-du-Rhône," 26 October 1953, same file. The 1959 figure comes from Sayad, Jordi, and Témime, *Le Choc*, 67.

75. Sayad, Jordi, and Témime, *Le Choc*, 10, 51, 68–89; Émile Témime, *Histoire de Marseille de la Révolution à nos jours* (Paris: Perrin, 1999), p. 334. Only in 1974 did family unification become the primary migratory source. Alain Gillette and Abdelmalek Sayad, *L'immigration algérienne en France*, 2nd ed. (Paris: Éditions entente, 1984), p. 61; Lyons, *Invisible Immigrants*; André Michel, *Les travailleurs algériens en France* (Paris: Éditions du CNRS, 1956); Jacques Simon, ed., *L'immigration algérienne en France: De 1962 à nos jours* (Paris: L'Harmattan, 2002), pp. 16–26, 37, 42–44; Benjamin Stora, *Ils venaient d'Algérie: L'immigration en France (1912–1992)* (Paris: Fayard, 1992), p. 400.

76. From 1949 to June 1950, about seventy thousand traveled through the city, although many were from Eastern Europe. RG, Section frontières, "Le mouvement de trans-migration des Israélites: La question israélienne," June 1950, F7/15589, AN.

77. For Grand Arénas, see Émile Témime and Nathalie Deguigné, *Le camp du Grand Arénas Marseille, 1944–1966* (Paris: Éditions Autrement, 2001), pp. 76–136. For Egyptian Jews in Marseille, see Aranjo, "L'accueil des réfugiés d'Egypte en France," 142.

78. Roland Avitol, "Marseille," *L'Arche* (March/April, 1968), pp. 19–20; statistics compiled by the FSJU and included in a letter from Julian Breen to Boris Sapir, 15 February 1963, 309, AJDC.

79. Sayad, Jordi, and Témime, *Le Choc*, 69–70.

80. A. H. Boullet, Sec. Gen., Association des foyers nord-africains de Provence to Préfet, 23 August 1952, 148W193, BdR.

81. André Pelabon to MI, "Enquête sociale sur la situation des Musulmans originaires d'Algérie résidant en métropole, Département des Bouches-du-Rhône," 26 October 1953, 148w193, BdR.

82. Cited in Témime and Deguigné, *Le camp du Grand Arénas*, 99.

83. Ibid., 115–16, 117–18.

84. Ibid., 117.

85. Jean André Carreno, Alain Hayot and Francis Lesme, *Le quartier de la porte d'Aix à Marseille: Ethnologie d'un centre urbain* (Aix-en-Provence: Université de Provence, 1974), pp. 39–41.

86. Cited in Sayad, Jordi, and Témime, *Le Choc*, 159–60.

87. Jocelyne Cesari, Alain Moreau, and Alexandra Schleyer-Lindenmann, *"Plus marseillais que moi, tu meurs!" Migrations, identités et territoires à Marseille* (Paris: L'Harmattan, 2001), pp. 20–21, 121.

88. Bensimon, *Les Juifs de France*, 237. Katz, "Jews and Muslims," 250, 253, 286–87.

89. Algerian Jews attended European public schools while Moroccan and Tunisian Jews attended AIU schools. For rates of Jewish immigrant education in France, see Bensimon and Della Pergola, *La population juive de France*, 167. Simon, *Immigration algérienne en France*, 95, notes that by the 1980s, Algerian Muslim families had embraced education as the key to success.

90. North African Jews of varying socioeconomic backgrounds experienced rapid social mobility in France. Bensimon and Della Pergola, *La population juive de France*, 179–220; Hyman, *The Jews of Modern France*, 196–97; Véronique Poirier, *Ashkénazes et Séfarades: Une étude comparée de leurs relations en France et en Israël (années 1950–1990)*, pp. 92–94, 137–401; Claude Tapia, *Les Juifs sépharades en France (1965–1985): Études psychosociologiques et historiques* (Paris: Éditions l'Harmattan, 1986), p. 221.

91. Simon, *L'immigration algérienne en France*, 20. The cultural and scholarly level of the migrants improved over time. Gillette and Sayad, *L'immigration algérienne en France*, 210.

92. M.S. "Témoignages: Les Juifs nord-africains de St-Fons." *L'Arche* (December 1953), p. 121.

93. Émile Touati, "Analyse de l'immigration nord-africaine," *L'Arche* (March 1956), pp. 36–38. Katz, "Jews and Muslims," 273–74, notes that although Touati's portrayal reflected some truth, it also served to highlight differences between Jewish citizens and Muslim "outsiders."

94. Simon, *L'immigration algérienne en France*, 211-12; Gilette and Sayed, *L'immigration algérienne*, 62–63. According to Catherine Wihtol de Wenden, *Les immigrés et la politique: Cent cinquant ans d'évolution* (Paris: Presses de la Fondation nationale des sciences politiques, 1988,) pp. 175–76, Tunisian Muslim migrants were more urban and educated than those from Morocco and Algeria.

95. Mandel, *In the Aftermath of Genocide*, 167–77; "Philanthropy or Cultural Imperialism? The Impact of American Jewish Aid in Post-Holocaust France," *Jewish Social Studies*, 9, 1 (Fall 2002): 53–94; and Laura Hobson Faure, "Un 'Plan Marshall juif': La présence juive américaine en France après la Shoah, 1944–54" (Ph.D. diss., École des hautes études en sciences sociales, Paris, 2009).

96. Aranjo, "L'accueil des réfugiés d'Egypte en France," 142–44; Julien Samuel, "Rapport moral: Regard sur 10 années d'activité du Fonds social juif unifié," in *Assemblée générale du Xe anniversaire du Fonds social juif unifié* (Paris: 1960), p. 5. Mônica Riasa Schpun, "Les premiers migrants juifs d'Afrique du Nord dans la France de l'après-guerre: Une découverte pour les services sociaux," *Archives juives* 45, 1 (2012): 61–73.

97. "Integration of Algerian Jews in France: Report from Paris Office, American Jewish Committee," Meeting of the External Affairs Committee, 13 November 1962, Anglo-Jewish Association Papers, AJ95/1/31, Parkes Library.

98. Encounters between native French Jews and their incoming North African co-religionists could also be conflictual. See Mandel, "In the Aftermath of Genocide," chap. 8; Poirier, *Ashkénazes et Séfarades*, 66–69, 70–74; Sussman, "Changing Lands," chaps. 4 and 5.

99. Israel Salzer to Germaine Haguenau, 28 May 1956, Juifs et Afrique du Nord, Archives Mlle Haguenau, CC.

100. "Table ronde du FSJU: La communauté et l'intégration des Juifs nord-africains," *L'Arche*, 15 (March 1956), p. 34.

101. RG, Mle, "Propagande anti-française dans les milieux NA de Marseille," 13 September 1951, 148W191, BdR. The small numbers of Moroccan and Tunisian Muslim migrants limited their participation in separatist movements. RG, Mle, "Nord Africains: Réactions des N.A. à l'occasion des événements du Moyen-Orient," 2 November 1951, same file. Témime, *Histoire de Marseille*, 331.

102. Émile Témime, *Marseille transit: Les passagers de Belsunce* (Paris: Éditions Autrement, 1995), pp. 70–71.

103. "Place Jules-Guesde: Plastique devant un bar exploité par un Nord-Africain," *Le Méridional*, 12 January 1962; E.R., "A Marseille: Les bandes musulmanes rivales règlent leurs comptes au plastique," *Le Méridional*, 22 January 1962; Sayad, Jordi and Témime, *Le Choc*, 74–77, Témime, *Histoire de Marseille*, 333–34.

104. The cités de transit were designed as way stations to ease "poorly adjusted" immigrants into European society. Residence, however, often became permanent. While not all inhabitants were immigrants, new arrivals and their descendants made up the majority. Marie-Claude Blanc-Chaléard, "Les immigrés et le logement en France depuis le XIXe siècle: Une histoire paradoxale," in Benjamin Stora and Emile Témime, eds., *Immigrances: L'immigration en France au XXe siècle* (Paris: Hachette littératures, 2007), pp. 67–96; Richard Derderian, *North Africans in Contemporary France* (New York: Palgrave Macmillian, 2004), pp. 8–9; Yvan Gastaut, *L'immigration et l'opinion en France sous la Ve république* (Paris: Éditions du Seuil,

2000), pp. 71–72, 77–93, 262–64; Sayad, Jordi and Témime, *Le Choc*, 79, 135–39; Témime, *Histoire de Marseille*, 334–35, 368–72; Simon, *L'immigration algérienne en France*, 81–91, notes that biases against Muslim residents often prevented their settlement in the HLMs.

105. Abed Guendouz to Maire de Marseille, 24 February 1960, 138W73, BdR. Thanks to Ethan Katz for sharing this source.

106. Préfet de la région de Provence to Préfet, "La communauté juive de Marseille," 17 January 1972, 135W57, BdR, counted 75,000 Jews in Marseille by the early 1970s. However, Bensimon-Donath, *L'intégration des Juifs nord-africains*, 55, documents 65,000 in 1966. Reports in 1967 numbered the population as high as 100,000, perhaps due to transients. RG, Mle., "Milieux juifs," 30 May 1967, 137W363, BdR.

107. "A Marseille quand arrive le bateau d'Algérie," *Al Djazaïri*, 4 February 1965, pp. 4–5.

108. INED, *Les immigrés du Maghreb: Études sur l'adaptation en milieu urbain* (Paris: Presses universitaires de France, 1977), pp. 13, 16–17. Sayad, Jordi, and Témime, *Le Choc*, 107–8, 121, claim 44,000 Muslims in Marseille in 1975.

109. Jean-Jacques Jordi, "L'été 62" and Guy Pervillé, "Les conditions de départ: L'Algérie," in *Marseille et le choc des décolonisations: Les rapatriements 1954–1964*, ed., Jean-Jaques Jordi and Emile Temime (Aix-en-Provence: Édisud, 1996), pp. 54–74. Sayad, Jordi, and Témime, *Le Choc*, 89–98. Citation and statistics are from Témime, *Histoire de Marseille*, 338–39.

110. Between 1952 and 1964 more than eighty thousand new housing units were built. Témime, *Histoire de Marseille*, 369.

111. Irving (Dickman) to Moe (Moses Leavitt), 7 June 1962, 328, AJDC.

112. Eighty percent of Jewish repatriates entered through Marseille where Jewish organizations, in particular the FSJU, directed those seeking aid to relevant agencies. Sidney Nelson to Charles Jordan, "Summary Report," 25 April 1963, 309, AJDC. Louis Hackett, "It's 1945 All Over Again," press release, no date, 328, AJDC. Sussman, "Changing Lands," 351–52. "A l'œuvre: Le Fonds social juif unifié," *Le Provençal*, 30 May 1962; "Le Fonds social juif unifié a fait le bilan de l'année écoulée," *Le Méridional*, 1 April 1963. For the FSJU's local efforts, see Avitol, "Marseille," 19–20. For Jewish responses to arriving Algerian Jews more generally, see Colette Zytnicki, "A immigration d'un nouveau type, réponses nouvelles: Les organizations communautaires et l'exodes des Juifs d'Afrique du Nord, in *Terre d'exil, terre d'asile: Migrations juives en France aux XIXe et XXe siècles*, ed. Colette Zytnicki (Paris: Éditions de l'Éclat): 155–70.

113. F. de Muizon, "Les Juifs de Marseille: La 'révolution' des pieds-noirs," *Regard*, no date (1976?), MDI 159, CDJC.

114. Avitol, "Marseille," 19.

115. As Michel Wieviorka, "The Changing French Jewish Identity," in *Contemporary Jewries: Convergence and Divergence*, eds., Eliezer Ben-Rafael, Yosef Gorney, and Yaacov Ro'i (Leiden: Koninklijke: Brill NV, 2003): p. 255, reminds us, although North African Jewish arrivals shared some characteristics, they nowhere constituted a homogeneous community.

116. R. Musnik and L. Cohn, "Visit to Marseilles," 14–15 May 1961, 346, AJDC. While downtown Marseille still held most of the French Jewish population, the newcomers generally lived in HLM structures eight or ten kilometers away. Moreover, unlike Paris and Lyon, Marseille had no communal structure in the city center and

no "Jewish quarter." Deborah Miller, "Visit to Marseilles," 17–19 May 1961; Untitled Report on Marseille, November 1964, 346, AJDC. De Muizon, "Les Juifs de Marseille."

117. Jordi, *De l'exode*, 218–19.

118. Préfet de la région de Provence to Directeur central de RG, "La communauté juive de Marseille," 17 January 1972, 135W57, BdR. Muizon, "Les Juifs de Marseille." W. Rabi, "Le 'boom' de Marseille: La vague des rapatriés d'Afrique du Nord disloquera-t-elle la seconde communauté de France ou lui donnera-t-elle un nouvel essor?" *L'Arche* 60 (January 1962), pp. 41–45, 67, and De Muizon, "Les Juifs de Marseille."

119. Sussman, "Changing Lands," 350; Richard Ayoun and Bernard Cohen, *Les Juifs d'Algérie: Deux mille ans d'histoire* (Paris: Jean-Claude Lattès, 1982), p. 198; Jacques Sabbath, "Communauté vivante," *L'Arche*, November 1962, pp. 2–4.

120. Untitled Report on Marseille, November 1964; R. Musnik and L. Cohn, "Visit to Marseilles," 14–15 May 1961, 346, AJDC.

121. Cited in Rabi, "Le 'boom' de Marseille," 44–45. Deborah Miller, "Visit to Marseilles," 17–19 May 1961, 346, AJDC.

122. Whatever the divisions, as Sussman, "Changing Lands," 350–63, argues the Consistoire worked hard to bridge differences. "Outlook Much Brighter Now," *Jewish Chronicle*, 9 August 1963, in "La situation des réfugies Juifs à Marseille," 4/9/63, MDI 83; "La communauté israélite de Marseille 70,000 membres" (May/June 1967), MDI 159, CJDC.

123. The term "harkis," which comes from the Arabic *harka*, applies strictly to soldiers in auxiliary units who fought with the French army against Algerian nationalists in 1954–62. Once in France, however, the term came to refer to all Algerian Muslims who fought for the French or adopted a pro-French position and hence left quickly after independence. The number 140,000 includes 85,000 who participated in the military's supplemental units (families included) and 55,000 notables, functionaries, or career military. While those with some status (such as the notables and upper level military personnel integrated into French society relatively rapidly, those in the supplemental units struggled to be accepted. Charbit, *Les harkis*, 9, 21–23, 62, 71. For the different types of *Français musulmans rapatriés*, see Mohand Hamoumou, "L'histoire des harkis et Français musulmans: La fin d'un tabou?" in Benjamin Stora and Mohammed Harbi, *La guerre d'Algérie* (Paris: Éditions Robert Laffont, 2004), pp. 317–23.

124. As Charbit, *Les harkis*, 29–35, points out, while often accused of treason, the mostly rural army recruits had little ideological or political affiliation with the French.

125. For numbers, see Sayad, Jordi, and Témime, *Le Choc*, 90, 106, 122, and Katz, "Jews and Muslims," 331. For citation, see Baillet, "Les rapatriés d'Algérie en France," 46, 52. Private associations sometimes stepped in to fill this administrative gap. See Hamoumou, "L'histoire des harkis," 334–35. For more on intra-Algerian Muslim tensions, see Charbit, *Les harkis*, 82–83, and Abderahmen Moumen, "Du camp de transit à la cité d'accueil: Saint-Maurice-l'Ardoise: 1962–1976" in Besnaci-Lancou and Manceron, *Les harkis*, 13–40.

126. Émile Touati, "Avec un dinar en poche: Après Bizerte, le problème des réfugiés d'Afrique du Nord se pose encore d'une manière plus aiguë. Notre communauté saura-t-elle y faire face?" *L'Arche* 57 (October 1961), p. 32.

127. René Sussan, "Les grandes vacances des Juifs d'Algérie: Un témoignage de René Sussan," *L'Arche* 66 (July 1962), p. 16. One thousand Jews, it should be noted, sought aid from the *Service des affaires musulmanes* (SAM). Katz, "Jews and Muslims," 330–31; Sussman, "Changing Lands," 172–73.

128. Charbit, *Les harkis*, 58–59, 75–83; Hamoumou, *L'histoire des harkis*, 337–38. Also see essays by Giulia Fabiano, Abdel Kader Hamadi, Abderahmen Moumen, and the Introduction of Besnaci-Lancou and Manceron, *Les harkis*, 31–32, 118–45. For the move from seeing *harkis* as citizens to refugees, see Todd D. Shepard, "Excluding the *Harkis* from Repatriate Status, Excluding Muslim Algerians from French Identity." *Transnational Spaces and Identities in the Francophone World*, eds., Hafid Gafaïti, Patricia M. E. Lorcin, and David G. Troyansky (Lincoln: University of Nebraska Press, 2009): 94–114.

129. Sayad, Jordi, and Témime, *Le Choc*, 190.

130. Sussman, "Changing Lands," 235–36, 350; INED, *Immigrés du Maghreb*, 13, 16–17; Sayad, Jordi, and Témime, *Le Choc*, 122–25; Duchac, "Facteurs urbains de l'adaptation des immigrés maghrébins," 14–15. According to Sussman, a 1992 FSJU study of Jewish poor in Marseille claimed that 15 percent of the Jewish population remained in the city's poor northern quarters.

131. INED, *Immigrés du Maghreb*, 17–19. By the early 1970s, 8,000–9,000 immigrant laborers lived in bidonvilles; 15,000–18,000 lived in HLM housing units owned and managed by the Société nationale de construction de logements pour les travailleurs (Sonacotra), and about 2,000 lived in four transit camps (cité de transit).

132. Shepard, *The Invention of Decolonization*, chap. 9.

133. Direction générale de la police nationale, "Étude sur la communauté juive des Bouches-du-Rhône," 16 October 1989, 1693W233, BdR.

134. De Muizon, "Les Juifs de Marseille."

135. Préfet de la région de Provence to Directeur central de RG, "La communauté juive de Marseille," 17 January 1972, 135W5; Direction générale de la police nationale, "Étude sur la communauté juive des Bouches-du-Rhône," 16 October 1989, 1693W233, BdR.

136. Gaston Defferre, "Israël et l'Algérie," *Le Monde*, 1 June 1962. Laskier, "Israel and Algeria and French Colonialism and the Arab-Israeli Conflict, 1954–1978," *Israel Studies* 6, 2 (2001), p.15 (Laskier incorrectly cites Defferre's piece as from 31 May).

137. For Defferre's views on Algerian independence, see Isabelle Rambaud, "Le fonds Gaston-Defferre aux archives de Marseille," in Jordi and Temime, *Marseille et le choc*, 184–89.

138. The Israeli consul general and other Jewish organizations held numerous events to support the young state. "Le gala du comité de jumelage Marseille-Haïfa a été une grande réussite," *Le Méridional*, 22 January 1962; "Les conférences: 'Vers le deuxième million d'immigrants en Israël,'" *Le Méridional*, 24 January 1962; "La chanteuse israélienne Rika Zarai à la nuitée des étudiants juifs," *Le Méridional*, 2 March 1962.

139. "Note," 24 April 1950; "Note" for Préfet des Bouches-du-Rhône, 22 May 1950; RG, Mle., "Étrangers juifs: Campagne d'aide à Israël, 1952," 19 February 1952, 148W141, BdR. "Immense succès des fêtes du 14ème anniversaire de l'indépendance d'Israël," *Le Provençal*, 21 May 1962.

140. Gaston Defferre, "Impressions sur Israël," *Le Provençal*, 29–30 May, 1 June 1962.

141. "Marseille et Haïfa officiellement jumelles," *Le Méridional*, 18 May 1962. Haifa built a cultural center in Defferre's honor after his death. "Posé d'une première pierre à Haïfa: Le ciel, le vent, la mer et Gaston Defferre" and "Coup de cœur pour Jérusalem: Impression du voyage," *Haboné*, January 1989; RG, "Numéro spécial de la revue *Haboné* imprimé par le Consistoire à l'issue du voyage de M. Jean Claude Gaudin en Israël, 20 February 1989, 1693W233, BdR. Message de Théo Klein (December 1988), MDI 188 CJDC.

142. "Inauguration de l'exposition de dessins d'enfants d'Israël et de Marseille," *Le Provençal*, 26 June 1962.

143. "Quarante jeunes Israéliens en visite à Marseille," *Le Méridional*, 30 April 1963; "Une exposition sur Israël au palais de la Bourse," *Le Provençal*, 1 April 1967.

144. A counterexample saw vandals set fire to Jewish Agency offices on 20 March 1960. While police never determined the arsonists, efforts to undermine the Jewish Agency's mission were presumably at work. ME to MI, "Au sujet d'un incendie criminel à l'Agence juive pour Israël," 21 March 1960, 137W236, BdR.

145. Rabi, "Le 'boom' de Marseille," 41.

146. The rare conflicts that did occur, such as on 27 May 1963 when a fight broke out between two dozen Muslim and Jewish youth on the rue Sainte-Antoine in Paris, captured media attention, thereby calling attention to atypical antagonism rather than to daily neighborly exchanges. "A Paris, violente bagarre entre Algériens et Israélites à la sortie d'un bal," *Le Méridional*, 27 May 1963.

Chapter 4. The 1967 War and the Forging of Political Community

1. Citation from Paula Hyman, *The Jews of Modern France* (Berkeley: University of California Press, 1998), p. 203. Abdellali Hajjat's pathbreaking work on Muslim activism around the Palestinian issue has focused primarily on the 1970s. See "Les Comités Palestine (1970–1972): Aux origines du soutien de la cause palestinienne en France," *Revue des études palestinienes* 8 (Winter 2006): 74–92 and "Des comité Palestine au Mouvement des travailleurs arabes (1970–1976)," in Amhed Boubeker and Abdellali Hajjat, eds., *Histoire politique des immigrations (post) coloniales, France, 1920-2008* (Paris: Éditions Amsterdam, 2008): 145–56. Ethan Katz's work has focused more fully on this issue in "Tracing the Shadow of Palestine: The Zionist-Arab Conflict and Jewish-Muslim Relations in France, 1914–1945," in Nathalie Debrauwere-Miller, ed., *Israeli-Palestinian Conflict in the Francophone World* (New York: Routledge, 2010): 25–44, and "Jews and Muslims in the Shadow of Marianne: Conflicting Identities and Republican Culture in France, 1914–1975" (Ph.D. diss., University of Wisconsin, 2008).

2. Dominique Schnapper, *Jewish Identities in France: An Analysis of Contemporary French Jewry*, trans. Arthur Goldhammer (Chicago: University of Chicago Press, 1984), pp. xlvi–lxvii.

3. For an overview, see Michel Winock, *La France et les Juifs: De 1789 à nos jours* (Paris: Éditions du Seuil, 2004), pp. 307–16. Samir Kassir and Farouk Mardam-Bey, *Itinéraires de Paris à Jerusalem: La France et le conflit israélo-arabe*, vol. 2: 1958–91

(Paris: Revue d'études palestiniennes, 1993), pp. 52–90, argue that emphases on a "rupture" in French/Israeli relations in 1967 is exaggerated, since diplomatic relations were never cut off.

4. The Jewish press expressed concerns about changing French Middle Eastern policies as early as 1962. See, for example, Michael Salomon, "Le Judaïsme français à l'heure des révisions déchirantes? Un entretien avec Guy de Rothschild," *L'Arche*, April 1962, pp. 24–33, 65, and "Renversement des alliances au Moyen Orient? La reprise des relations avec le monde-arabe est-elle compatible avec le maintien de l'amitié franco-israélienne?" May 1962, *L'Arche*, pp. 28–33, 63. For Jewish reponses to the shifting political terrain in 1967, see Doris Bensimon, *Les Juifs de France et leurs relations avec Israël: 1945–1988* (Paris: Éditions l'Harmattan, 1989), pp. 154–62; Hyman, *The Jews of Modern France*, 200–205. Denis Sieffert, *Israël-Palestine: Une passion française* (Paris: La Découverte, 2004), p. 117, and Kassir and Mardam-Bey, *Itinéraires de Paris à Jerusalem*, 11, 127–31, argue that the media remained staunchly behind Israel during the conflict if becoming more critical with the occupation of new territories. Nevertheless, Jewish representatives watched the press closely for "misleading information." Moch to Pierre Kaufmann, 2 June 1967, MDI 65C, CDJC.

5. Kassir and Mardem-Bey, *Itinéraires de Paris*, 131; Winock, *La France et les Juifs*, 317; Joan Wolf, *Harnessing the Holocaust: The Politics of Memory in France* (Stanford: Stanford University Press, 2004), pp. 36–37.

6. Michel Winock, *Chronique des années soixante* (Paris: Éditions du Seuil, 1987), pp. 200–202.

7. *BIL*, N° 7, 11 June 1967, MDI 98, CDJC.

8. Sieffert, *Israël-Palestine*, 151–59.

9. Articles in the Jewish press complained of contradictions in leftist positions toward Israel. See, for example, "La gauche française contre Israël?" *L'Arche*, February 1957, p. 23; Jean Daniel, "Israël avait épuisé toutes les possibilités de négociation," *L'Arche*, February 1957, p. 24; Ephraïm Tari, "Une certaine gauche toujours prisonnière des mythes," *L'Arche*, February 1963, pp. 13–17. Jewish organizations also criticized one another for leftist-inspired anti-Israeli politics. In 1957, for example, the FSJF excluded groups whose attitude toward Israel was questionable. Réunion, Fédération stes. juives de France, 18 March 1957, MDI 69, CDJC.

10. See, for example, H. Smolarski, "Suis-je le gardien de mon frère?" *Bulletin de nos communautés*, 26 May 1967.

11. Daniel Mayer, "La guerre des six jours a-t-elle modifié la conscience juive en France?" *L'Arche*, March/April 1968, p. 39.

12. Wolf, *Harnessing the Holocaust*, 34–35, notes that while some of the traditional Jewish leadership conceded only slight disappointment with de Gaulle and called for restrained communal responses, they were out of step with most French Jews. The massive popular backing for Israel also helps explain why Jewish leaders proved so willing to criticize national policies. As one declared on 4 June to a meeting of fellow activists, "The majority of the French are with us. . . . Judaism (and with it, French opinion) will not weaken, no matter how diplomacy evolves." *BIL*, N° 5, 7 June 1967, MDI 98, CDJC. Numerous letters to the Consistoire (Moyen Orient/Guerre de 6 jours, 1967–68, FCC) document non-Jewish support for Israel.

13. Joëlle Allouche-Benayoun and Doris Bensimon, *Juifs d'Algérie, hier et aujourd'hui, mémoires et identité* (Toulouse: Privat, 1989), pp. 173, 216, 228; Doris

Bensimon-Donath, *L'intégration des Juifs nord-africains en France* (Paris: Mouton, 1971), pp. 216–35; Claude Tapia, "Religion et politique: Interférence dans le Judaïsme français après l'immigration judéo-maghrébine," in Lasry and Tapia, eds., *Les Juifs du Maghreb* (1989), pp. 207–23 ; and Michel Wieviorka, "The Changing French Jewish Identity," in *Contemporary Jewries: Convergence and Divergence*, eds., Eliezer Ben-Rafael, Yosef Gorney, and Yaacov Ro'i (Leiden: Koninklijke: Brill NV, 2003), pp. 257.

14. The Jewish establishment followed these developments closely, as is clear in documents found in MDI 1–55, MDI 65C, MDI 98, and MDI 100. For articles in the Jewish press, see Cohen Tanougi, "Les otages: 600,000 Juifs ont fusillé les pays arabes mais 110,000 demeurent encore," *L'Arche*, July 1962, pp. 42–43; "Judas pas mort!" *Carrefour*, 21 June 1967.

15. Cited by Annette Wieviorka, "Les Juifs en France depuis la guerre des Six Jours," in *Les Juifs de France de la Révolution à nos jours*, eds., Jean-Jacques Becker et al. (Paris: L. Levi, 1998), p. 377.

16. Wolf, *Harnessing the Holocaust*, 31. Kassir and Mardam-Bey, *Itinéraires de Paris*, 131–35, note that links between Nasser and Hitler, and concerns about a second genocide saturated the press as a whole.

17. Police report, 7 June 1967, 19980547, art. 13 (Israël), CAC.

18. Cited in *BIL*, N° 3, 4 June 1967, MDI 98, CDJC.

19. Alain Seviram to Jacob Kaplan, 22 May 1967, Moyen Orient/Guerre de 6 jours, 1967–68, CC.

20. Direction des renseignements généraux et des jeux, "La communauté juive dans la région parisienne," 1970, 19900353, Art 10 (liasse 1); Préfecture de police, 21 January 1969, 19990426, art. 15 (liasse 6), CAC.

21. Report, 29 May 1967, BA 2315, Fédération des sociétés juives de France, APP; 26 Congrès national de la LICRA, Banquet de clôture, 28 May (29/5/67), MDI 72, CDJC. H. Smolarski, "Suis-je le gardien de mon frère?"; André Neher, "Comme Israël, comme solidarité," *Bulletin de nos communautés*, 26 May 1967; Motion arrêteé par le Comité de rédaction, désigné par l'assemblée plénière, 26/5/67, MDI 65C; Assemblée plénière du 26 mai 1967-procès-verbal, MDI 1–55, CDJC.

22. Report, 7 June 1967, BA 2315, Fédération des sociétés juives de France, APP; Direction des renseignements généraux et des jeux, "La communauté juive dans la région parisienne," 1970, 19900353, Art 10 (liasse 1); Préfecture de police, 21 January 1969, 19990426, art. 15 (liasse 6), CAC.

23. Report, "La crise du Proche-Orient, réactions d'ensemble en France," 31 May 1967, 19980547, art. 13 (Israël), CAC.

24. "La situation en Israël," *Information rabbiniques*, 25 May 1967, Moyen Orient/Guerre de 6 jours, 1967–68, CC.

25. Déclaration adoptée à l'issue de la réunion constitutive du Comité de coordination des organisations juives de France, "La communauté juive de France solidaire d'Israël en péril," *Journal des communautés*, 18e année, Supplément au N° 395, (2 June 1967); *BIL*, N° 2, 29 May 1967, MDI 98, CDJC. While the Fédération sioniste de France joined forces with this new committee, the impetus was consciously handed to others so as to provide the new body with more legitimacy. Joseph Weinberg, Org. sioniste de France to Grand Rabbin Kaplan, 24 May 1967, Moyen Orient/Guerre de 6 jours, 1967–68, CC.

26. *BIL*, N° 2, 29 May 1967, MDI 98, CDJC.
27. *BIL*, N° 2, 29 May 1967, N° 3, 4 June 1967, and N° 7, 11 June 1967, MDI 98, CDJC. MDI 98, CDJC; Michel Salomon, "Israël vivra!" *L'Arche*, June 1967, p. 3. For examples of individual initiatives, see Gisele Rutman to l'ambassadeur d'Israël, 12 June 1967 and Docteur Paul Kossowski to Monsieur le Rabbin, 26 May 1967, Moyen Orient/Guerre de 6 jours, 1967–68, CC. For an example of the Comité de coordination's attempt to maintain control over pro-Israel efforts, see Alain de Rothschild to Monsieur le Rabin Samuel Cohen, 6 July 1967, Moyen Orient/Guerre de 6 jours, 1967–68, CC.
28. While the community's public face was united, divisions were ongoing. In Marseille, for example, the city's traditional leadership clashed with newcomers over appropriate responses to the war. Numerous documents in MDI 159, CJDC, document the rift.
29. Flyer, Comité de coordination des organisations juives de France, MDI 98, CDJC; *BIL*, N° 3, 4 June 1967, same microfilm; Moch to Jean-Pierre Gerschel, 4 January 1968, MDI 65C, CDJC. For an example of how a local committee formed, see Report, Comité local de la Drôme et de l'Ardèche, Moyen Orient/Guerre de 6 jours, 1967–68, CC.
30. *BIL*, N° 5, 7 June 1967, MDI 98, CDJC.
31. Speeches from the Conférence extraordinaire du Comité de coordination, 4 June 1967, are reprinted in *BIL*, N° 5, 7 June 1967, MDI 98, CDJC.
32. "Après l'application de la décision française d'embargo sur les arme destinées à Israël: Déclaration de M. le Grand Rabbin Kaplan," no date, MDI 1–55, CDJC. The CRIF remained reticent to criticize the government publicly. Bureau du CRIF, 3 July 1967, MDI 1–55, CDJC.
33. "Allocation prononcée par M. Guy de Rothschild, président du Comité de coordination, à l'occasion de la Conférence extraordinaire des communautés et organisations juives de France," 4 June 1967, *BIL*, N° 6, 8 June 1967, MDI 98, CDJC. Reprinted as "Nous nous identifions à Israël pour le droit à la vie," *L'Arche*, June 1967, p. 4.
34. André Neher, "Nous sommes l'arrière: Israël est le front!" reprinted in *BIL*, N° 5, 7 June 1967, MDI 98, CDJC.
35. Emphasis in text. "Le peuple juif premier allié d'Israël: Une interview de Claude Kelman, vice-président du Comité national de coordination," *L'Arche*, June 1967, p. 6. Also see Yair Auron, *Les Juifs d'extrême gauche en Mai 68*, translated from Hebrew by Katherine Werchowski (Paris: Albin Michel, 1998), p. 168. While Wolf, *Harnessing the Holocaust*, 34–36, argues that Rothschild and Kelman represented contrasting responses to the war with Rothschild articulating a more traditional perspective on Franco-Jewish solidarity, even Rothschild was more critical of the government than had been typical.
36. "Allocation prononcée par M. Guy de Rothschild, président du Comité de coordination, à l'occasion de la Conférence extraordinaire des communautés et organisations juives de France," 4 June 1967, *BIL*, N° 6, 8 June 1967, MDI 98, CDJC.
37. Cited in Maurice Szafran, *Les Juifs dans la politique française: De 1945 à nos jours* (Paris: Flammarion, 1990), p. 154.
38. Flyer, Comité de coordination des organisations juives de France (section de Nice), Moyen Orient/Guerre de 6 jours, 1967–68, CC.

39. Appeal from Association cultuelle israélite Dantibes—Juan-les-Pins, "Premier jour de la guerre en Israël," Moyen Orient/Guerre de 6 jours, 1967–68, CC.

40. "Un appel de M. Alain de Rothschild," *Journal des communautés*, 2 June 1967; *BIL*, N° 5, 7 June 1967, MDI 98, CDJC.

41. Jacques Frémontier, *L'étoile rouge de David: Les Juifs communiste en France* (Paris: Fayard, 2002), pp. 150, 282–83.

42. *BIL*, N° 2, 29 May 1967 and N° 3, 4 June 1967, MDI 98, CDJC. According to at least one French Jew, the moment for building synagogues in France was over; all efforts now had to be directed to rebuilding the Temple in Jerusalem. Monique Karsenky to M. le Grand Rabbin de France, June 1967, Moyen Orient/Guerre de 6 jours, 1967–68, CC.

43. *BIL*, N° 8, 16 June 1967, MDI 98, CDJC.

44. Sylvie Korcaz, *Les Juifs de France et l'État d'Israël, essai* (Paris: Denoël, 1969), pp. 78, 146. Numbers dropped the subsequent year. "Le peuple juif premier allié d'Israël: Une interview de Claude Kelman, vice-président du Comité national de coordination," *L'Arche*, June 1967, p. 6.

45. S. Castro to A. Loss, "Évolution de la situation générale," 17 June 1967, MDI 159, CJDC.

46. Arnold Mandel, "France," *American Jewish Yearbook*, 1967, p. 313.

47. Patrick Wajsman, "Notre jeunesse retrouve son âme," *L'Arche*, June 1967, pp. 21–22, cited in Samuel Moyn, *A Holocaust Controversy: The Treblinka Affair in Post-War France* (Waltham, Mass.: Brandeis University Press; Hanover: University Press of New England, 2005), p. 163.

48. Cited in Szafran, *Les Juifs dans les politiques française*, 154.

49. Interview with Françoise Tenenbaum in Robert I. Weiner and Richard E. Sharpless, eds. *An Uncertain Future: Voices of a French Jewish Community, 1940–2012* (Toronto: University of Toronto Press, 2012), p. 67.

50. Interview with Cathie Busidan in *An Uncertain World*, p. 25.

51. Police report, 7 June 1967, 19980547, art. 13 (Israël), CAC.

52. Ibid., 29 June 1967, 19980547, art. 13 (Israël), CAC.

53. Two hundred departed from Marseille's Gare St. Charles on 12 June. Préfet to Ministre de l'intérieur, "Manifestation organisée à Marseille par le Comité de soutien à Israël," 1 June 1967; Commissariat central de Marseille, "Départ de volontaires pour Israël," 12 June 1967, 137W363, BdR. "Plusieurs centaines de Marseillais ont signé leur engagement pour Israël," *Le Méridional*, 6 June 1967. Details of the Comité de coordination's civil service program can be found in *BIL*, N°s 3, 7, and 8, 4, 11, and 16 June 1967, MDI 98, CDJC.

54. Police report, "La crise du Proche-Orient, réactions d'ensemble en France," May 31 1967, 19980547, art. 13 (Israël), CAC.

55. Direction des renseignements généraux et des jeux, "La communauté juive dans la région parisienne," 1970, 19900353, Art 10 (liasse 1), CAC.

56. Bensimon, *Les Juifs de France*, 171.

57. According to Korcaz, *Les Juifs de France*, 85–92, Jewish emigration patterns mirrored that of other citizens. Schnapper, *French Jewish Identities*, 44, notes that North African Jews with strong pro-Israel sensibilities often remained in France.

58. Interview with Rabbi Simon Sibony in *An Uncertain Future*, p. 10.

59. Direction des renseignements généraux et des jeux, "La communauté juive dans la région parisienne," 1970, 19900353, Art 10 (liasse 1), CAC.

60. "Le peuple juif premier allié d'Israël: Une interview de Claude Kelman," *L'Arche*, June 1967, p. 6. "La guerre des six jours a-t-elle modifié la conscience juive en France?" *L'Arche*, March/April 1968, pp. 38–42, argued that pro-Israeli sentiment had been a long-standing if latent force in communal life.

61. S. Castro to A. Loss, "Évolution de la situation générale," 17 June 1967, MDI 159, CJDC.

62. *BIL*, N° 7, 11 June 1967, and N° 8, 16 June 1967, MDI 98; Moch to Jean-Pierre Gerschel, 4 January 1968, MDI 65C, CDJC.

63. Untitled statement by a Jewish organization (summer 1967), Moyen Orient/Guerre de 6 jours, 1967–68, CC.

64. Claude Kelman to Messiers, 22 March 1968, MDI 72, CDJC.

65. For example, a Jewish student protested at a debate in Aix-en-Provence over treatment of Palestinian refugees. Commissariat central d'Aix en Provence, "Un groupe de professeurs a organisé hier soir une réunion sur le problème israélien," 8 June 1967, 135W57, BdR.

66. For previous divisions, see Frémontier, *L'étoile rouge de David*, last chapter, and 279–83; Faure, "Un 'Plan Marshall juif,'" 450–73. Paris housed three Yiddish dailies, which W. Rabinovitch (Rabi), *Anatomie du Judaïsme français* (Paris: Éditions de Minuit, 1962), p. 173, estimated at a circulation of three thousand each.

67. Frémontier, *L'étoile rouge de David*, 150. In March 1968, the immigrant Jewish left formed the Fédération des organisations et des sociétés juives de France, which united the traditionally anti-Communist with those that had cut ties with the party during the 1967 war. Report, 25 March 1968, BA 2315 Communauté juive, APP.

68. Daniel Cohn-Bendit, *Le grand bazar* (Paris: P. Belfond, 1975), p. 11, cited in Auron, *Les Juifs d'extrême gauche*, 173–74.

69. For MRAP, see Frémontier, *L'étoile rouge de David*, 271–72. For an example of MRAP's anti-racism commitment, see "Courrier de l'émigration," *L'Algérien en Europe*, 1 June 1967, p. 2 (hereafter referred to as *AE*). According to Kassir and Mardam-Bey, *Itinéraires de Paris*, 141, the MRAP was the only anti-racist organization to protest intensifying anti-Arab sentiment. The Ligue internationale contre le racisme et l'antisémitisme, which was associated with more centrist political parties, increasingly supported Israel. According to Gérard Noiriel, *Immigration, antisémitisme et racisme en France (XIXe–XXe siècle): Discours publics, humiliations privées* (Paris: Fayard, 2007), pp. 486–89, the League des droits de l'homme ignored anti-Arab racism when Zionists were involved.

70. Yvan Gastaut, *L'immigration et l'opinion en France sous la Ve république* (Paris: Éditions du Seuil, 2000), p. 155; Hervé Hamnon and Patrick Rotman, *Génération*, vol. 2, *Les années de poudre* (Paris: Seuil, 1988), pp. 90–94.

71. "Aucun Arabe se trouvant au-delà du Jourdain ne sera autorisé à venir dans le secteur 'israélien,'" *Le Monde*, 15 June 1967, p. 3, and Gastaut, *L'immigration et l'opinion*, 277–78. Kassir and Mardam-Bey, *Itinéraires de Paris*, 142, nevertheless conclude that most intellectuals were "totally blind" to the excesses of pro-Israeli propaganda.

72. Wolf, *Harnessing the Holocaust*, 33–34, 48–49. For a contemporary overview of Jewish political responses to the war, see Rabi, "Israël: Une passion lucide," *L'Arche*, February/March, 1968, pp. 34–35, 63. For criticism of the Left's treatment of Israel,

see Robert Misrahi, "La gauche irresponsable," *L'Arche*, November–December 1967, p. 31, and Albert Memmi, "La libération du peuple juif tout entier," *L'Arche*, March/April, 1968, p. 40.

73. Frémontier, *L'étoile rouge de David*, 271, 278–83, 99. Frémontier joins Auron, *Les Juifs d'extrême gauche*, 166–77, and Schnapper *Jewish Identities*, 95, 154, in noting that those who distanced themselves from the wider Zionist consensus were also not fully in sync with the communist left on Israel.

74. Bureau du CRIF, 18 September, 6 November, and 21 December 1967, MDI 1–55, CDJC. By January 1968, dissent had diminished and the CRIF tabled the discussion.

75. Rabi, "Israël: Une passion lucide," *L'Arche*, February/March, 1968, p. 34, discusses diverging Jewish opinions following the war. For Raymond Aron, "Pas d'unité politique," *L'Arche*, December/January, 1967–68, pp. 36–37, such diversity made a unified communal politics impossible. Wolf, *Harnessing the Holocaust*, 48–49, analyzes divergence over the nature of Jewish identity in the war's aftermath.

76. Korcaz, *Les Juifs de France*, 77–83, 128, 145–50.

77. Yehouda Cohen to "Chère madame; cher monsieur," 10 April 1968, MDI 159, CJDC. The Préfecture de police drew similar conclusions, noting a "crisis of recruitment" in the major Zionist organizations (while noting the cultural renaissance that Zionism had inspired). Direction des renseignements généraux et des jeux, "La communauté juive dans la région parisienne" (1970?), 19900353, art. 10 (liasse 1, Israël), CAC. In 1971, CRIF officials also bemoaned French Jewish apathy toward Israel. Journées nationales du CRIF, 24 October 1971, MDI 136, CJDC.

78. Schnapper *Jewish Identities*, 95, 154.

79. Kassir and Mardam-Bey, *Itinéraires de Paris*, 131, 135–40.

80. Gastaut, *L'immigration et l'opinion*, 275–82, and Kassir and Mardam-Bey, *Itinéraires de Paris*, 140–41. Auron, *Les Juifs d'extrême gauche*, 168, notes in contrast that others see French neutrality in 1967 and de Gaulle's policies toward Israel as providing entrée for a renewed antisemitism silenced following World War II.

81. Cited in Gastaut, *L'immigration et l'opinion*, 113.

82. Small and underfunded, the UGEP joined other groups, such as the Comité de défense de la révolution arabe, a self-proclaimed representative of the Arab left, in condemning Israeli actions in 1967. Police report, 19 June 1967, 19980547, art. 13 (Israël), CAC.

83. In explaining the origins of the pro-Palestinian movement, Hajjat, "Les Comités Palestine (1970–1972)," overlooks the ADAE's earlier interest.

84. For the Amicale, see Alain Gillette and Abdelmalek Sayad, *L'immigration algérienne en France*, 2nd ed. (Paris: Éditions Entente, 1984), pp. 200–205; Jacques Simon, ed. *L'immigration algérienne en France: De 1962 à nos jours* (Paris: L'Harmattan, 2002), pp. 22–23; Benjamin Stora, *Ils venaient d'Algérie: L'immigration algérienne en France* (Paris: Fayard, 1992), pp. 418–19; Catherine Wihtol de Wenden, *Les immigrés et la politique: Cent cinquante ans d'évolution* (Paris: Presses de la Fondation nationale des sciences politiques, 1988), p. 174.

85. Préfecture de police, "L'Amicale des Algériens en Europe," 21 October 1968, Algériens–Activités politiques: Divers (1966–76), 19960311, art. 4, CAC.

86. Simon, ed., *L'immigration algérienne*, 22–23.

87. "Bilan de l'activité de l'Amicale des Algériens en Europe," 22 November 1967, and Préfecture de police, "L'Amicale des Algériens en Europe," 21 October 1968,

19960311, art. 4, CAC. Katz, "Jews and Muslims," 320, cites fifteen thousand as the French assessment of ADAE membership. The discrepancy undoubtedly reflects the authorities' poor grasp of the ADAE's internal workings.

88. Préfecture de police, "L'Amicale des Algériens en Europe," 21 October 1968, and Préfet de police to Ministre de l'intérieur, 15 October 1968, Algériens—Activités politiques: Divers (1966–76); ME, sous-direction Algérie, to MI, direction de la réglementation, "Activités de l'Amicale des Algériens en Europe," 3 October 1967, 19960311, art. 4, CAC. Gillette and Sayad, L'immigration algérienne, 200–201, explore the links between the FLN and the Amicale.

89. Emphasis mine. Police report, 12 July 1967, Amicale des Algériens en Europe, Notes relatives à l'organisation (1966–1969), 19850087, art. 37, CAC.

90. MI to ME, 21 September 1967; "Activités de l'Amicale des Algériens en Europe," Algériens—Activités politiques: Divers (1966–76), 19960311, art. 4, CAC.

91. Police report, Untitled, 12 July 1967, Amicale des Algériens en Europe, Notes relatives à l'organisation (1966–1969), 19850087, art. 37, CAC.

92. AE, 15 June 1967.

93. "L'émigration algérienne continue de s'organiser," AE, 15 July 1967, p. 6.

94. RG, Mle, "Les milieux algériens et la tension au Moyen-Orient," 6 June 1967, 137W363, BdR.

95. MI to ME, "Activités de l'Amicale des Algériens en Europe," 21 September 1967, 19960311, art. 4, CAC.

96. Yezid Sayigh, Armed Struggle and the Search for State: The Palestinian National Movement, 1949–1993 (Oxford: Oxford University Press, 1997), pp. 102, 126, 182.

97. "Solidarité avec le peuple palestinien," Al Djazaïri, 29 February 1964, p. 4.

98. "Journée de solidarité avec les travailleurs palestiniens," Al Djazaïri, 30 May 1964, p. 5.

99. "Les Palestiniens ne pleurent plus," El Moudjahid, 9–17 March 1967.

100. "Proche-Orient: Au delà de l'état d'alerte," AE, 1 June 1967, p. 18.

101. "A l'occasion du 19 juin réaffirmation de nos principes révolutionnaires," AE, 30 June 1967, pp. 4–5; "L'Algérie en état de guerre," AE, 15 July 1967, p. 7; Gerard Viratelle, "Des milliers d'Algériens ont manifesté aux cris de 'Nasser, trahison!'"; "Les trois pays du Maghreb se sont diversement engagés dans le conflit," Le Monde, 11–12 June 1967, p. 5; "Vaincre or mourir: Des dizaines de milliers d'Algériens manifestent dans les rues de la capitale," El Moudjahid, 10 June 1967, p. 1. Dozens of articles in El Moudjahid in late May and early June document the FLN's support for the Palestinian resistance.

102. Police report, Untitled, 12 July 1967, Amicale des Algériens en Europe, Notes relatives à l'organisation (1966–69), 19850087, art. 37, CAC.

103. Ahmed Ibrahim, "Une enquête sur le Moyen-Orient," AE, 15 May 1968, p. 21.

104. For examples of this link, see "L'impunité de l'agresseur: Un défi à la paix," AE, 15 July 1967, p. 3, and "13e anniversaire," AE, 1 November 1967, p. 2.

105. Every edition of AE devoted space to promoting Arab unity, lambasting Israeli aggression, and protesting anti-Arab racism.

106. Police report, 12 July 1967, 19850087, art. 37, CAC.

107. ME, Direction des affaires politiques (sous-direction Algérie), "Activités de l'Amicale des Algériens en Europe" (Sept. 1967), 19960311, art. 4, CAC.

108. Authorities nevertheless remained suspicious. Préfecture de police to Commissaire principal, Direction des RG, "Pour information," 14 December 1967, 19850087, art. 37, CAC.

109. "Le courrier de l'émigration," *AE*, 30 June 1967, p. 2. Katz, "Jews and Muslims," 353–54; 356–67, reports large numbers of Algerian Muslims in France becoming engaged after Israel's attack on 5 June, but ultimately agrees that most Muslim immigrants were unmoved by the pro-Palestinian campaign.

110. Stora, *Ils venaient d'Algérie*, 163–38.

111. Préfet de l'essonne to MI, "Activité de l'Amicale des Algériens en Europe," 4 September 1967, 19960311, art. 4, CAC.

112. Police report, Untitled, 12 July 1967, 19850087, art. 37, CAC.

113. Préfecture de police, "L'Amicale des Algériens en Europe," 21 October 1968, Algériens—Activités politiques: Divers (1966–76), 19960311, art. 4, CAC. Wihtol de Wenden, *Les immigrés et la politique*, 174, and Gillette and Sayad, *L'immigration algérienne*, 200–205, argue that most Algerian Muslim migrants distrusted the Amicale's links to the Algerian government.

114. RG, "Le rôle d'éléments algériens dans le terrorisme international," Algériens—Activités politiques: Divers (1966–76), 19960311, art. 4, CAC.

115. "Tous les Juifs ne sont pas sionistes," *AE*, 30 June 1967, pp. 12–13, 22–23. For a similar assertion the next year, see A. Zehraoui, "Palestine: L'injustice d'il y a 20 ans," *AE*, 15 May 1968. The ADAE had declared itself anti-racist and anti-antisemitic as reported in, "Aux journées contre le racisme à l'U.N.E.S.C.O, 'Nous sommes par définition contre le racisme,' déclare le porte parole de l'Amicale," *Al Djazaïri*, 30 May 1964, p. 9; and "8 Mai: Journée nationale contre le racisme et l'antisémitisme," *AE*, 20 April to 5 May, 1966, p.6. Such rhetoric did not, however, prevent the ADAE from recirculating antisemitic themes. As one tract argued, Israel's birth and the Suez Crisis had inaugurated a new form of Western imperialism that covered the "dreams of conquest and domination of European Jews." Police report, Untitled, 12 July 1967, Amicale des Algériens en Europe, Notes relatives à l'organisation (1966–69), 19850087, art. 37, CAC.

116. RG, Mle, "Comité de soutien à Israël-rassemblement de la jeunesse," 8 June 1967, 137W363, BdR.

117. Flyer, MDI 98, CDJC. Certain writers and intellectuals also emphasized commonality over discord, such as Raymond Aron who lamented in"Israël face à la tragédie," *Le Figaro littéraire*, 12–18 June 1967: "How much time will it take for Jews and Muslims, Israelis and Arabs, who believe in the same God, to begin to understand each other?"

118. The demographics in the piece were inaccurate. Guy Porte, "La quatrième guerre: En marge du conflit-à Marseille, Juifs et Arabes ont su éviter les pièges du racisme," 25 October 1973, *Le Monde*, p. 4. Porte's portrayal, written several years later, nevertheless downplayed racism.

119. "Important cortège de la Canebière à la Préfecture," *Le Méridional*, 1 June 1967, numbered protestors at eight thousand, while *Le Provençal*, 1 June, reported fifteen thousand. Appel unifié pour Israël and Comité de soutien à Israël à Marseille to Monsieur le Préfet, 27 May 1967; RG, "Milieu juif et israélien," 29 May 1967; Préfet to MI, 31 May 1967; RG, Mle, "Milieux juifs," 1 June 1967,137W363, BdR. *BIL*, N° 2,

2 June 1967, MDI 159, CJDC. Flyer, Le Comité de coordination de la jeunesse juive de France, 137W363, BdR.

120. The Comité unifié de soutien à Israël later joined forces with the Comité de coordination in Paris. Robert Ifrah to Pres. du Comité de coordination des organisations juives de France, no date; *BIL*, N° 2, 2 June 1967, MDI 159, CJDC. "Réunion et motion du Comité de soutien à Israël," 1 June 1967, 137W363, BdR.

121. Mandel "France," 450; "Informations du S.F. Israël," *Le Méridional*, 5 June 1967.

122. "Magnifique élan de solidarité de la population en faveur d'Israël: A partir de ce matin, collecte du sang," clipping with no paper or date, MDI 159, CJDC; Commissariat central de Marseille, "Note," 7 June 1967, 137W363, BdR.

123. Préfet, Région Provence to MI, 31 May 1967, 137W363, BdR. "Le conflit israélo-arabe a soulevé une vive émotion à Marseille," *Le Méridional*, 6 June 1967. "Pour une paix et une justice qui ne soient pas aux dépens de l'État d'Israël," *Le Méridional*, 2 June 1967.

124. A survey of *Le Méridional* for May and June 1967 shows a largely pro-Israel Marseille, with three pages of calls for and reports on demonstrations appearing daily in the first week of June. At least one such article follows every day until 21 June.

125. "Magnifique élan de solidarité de la population en faveur d'Israël: A partir de ce matin, collecte du sang," clipping with no paper or date, MDI 159, CJDC.

126. René Andrieu, "Regarde la vérité en face," *Marseillaise*, 31 May 1967. Préfet to MI, "Manifestation organisée à Marseille par le Comité de soutien à Israël," 1 June 1967, 137W363, BdR.

127. Mandel "France," 450. When the editor refused to change his stance, Frédéric Thau threatened the withdrawal of all Jewish advertisements. RG, Mle, "Milieux juifs," 2 June 1967, 137W363, BdR.

128. Since the Socialist Party never held an absolute majority in Marseille, Defferre kept the city's large Communist Party in check by forming a centrist coalition with those on the non-Gaullist right. Émile Témime, *Histoire de Marseille de la Révolution à nos jours* (Perrin, 1999), pp. 354–56; Abdelmalek Sayad, Jean-Jacques Jordi, and Émile Témime, *Le choc de la décolonisation (1945–1990)*, vol. 4 of *Migrance: Histoire des migrations à Marseille*, ed., Émile Témime (Aix-en-Provence: Éditions Jeanne Laffitte, 1991), p. 100.

129. "Crise au Moyen-Orient," Bouches-du-Rhône-Marseille, 3 June 1967, 137W363, BdR.

130. RG, Mle, "Comité de soutien à Israël," 3 June 1967, 137W363, BdR.

131. "Conflit israélo-arabe," 6 June 1967, 137W363, BdR. "Le Comité de soutien à Israël a constitué son bureau et voté une motion condamnant l'agression égyptienne," *Le Provençal*, 4 June 1967.

132. RG, Mle, "Comité de soutien à Israël," 5 June, 1967, 137W363, BdR.

133. S. Castro to A. Loss, "Évolution de la situation générale," 17 June 1967, MDI 159, CJDC.

134. "Conflit israélo-arabe," 6 June 1967; Commissariat central de Marseille, "Affichage sur la voie publique pour la paix au Moyen-Orient," 7 June 1967, 137W363, BdR.

135. RG, Mle, "Comité de soutien à Israël-rassemblement de la jeunesse," 8 June 1967, 137W363, BdR.

136. RG, Mle, "Conflit israélo-arabe: Prise de position en faveur d'Israël," 8 June 1967, 137W363, BdR.

137. Commissariat central de Marseille, "Note," 7 June 1967; "Objet réunion publique pour le soutien à Israël," 12 June 1967; Commissariat central de Marseille, "Réunion publique en faveur du soutien français à Israël," 13 June 1967, 137W363, BdR. "Les orateurs du Comité de soutien à Israël longuement acclamés," 13 June 1967, *Le Provençal*, p. 3.

138. Police were nevertheless out in force on 29 May to ensure the city's interethnic harmony. RG, Mle, "Milieux juifs," 30 May 1967; Commissariat central de police, "Manifestation pour le soutien de la paix en Israël," 31 May 1967; RG, Mle, "Les milieux algériens et la tension au Moyen-Orient," 3 June 1967, 137W363, BdR.

139. Préfet to MI, "Manifestation organisée à Marseille par le Comité de soutien à Israël," 1 June 1967; RG, Mle, "Les milieux algériens et la tension au Moyen Orient," 3 June 1967, 137W363, BdR.

140. RG, Mle, "Les milieux algériens et la tension au Moyen-Orient," 6 June 1967, 137W363, BdR.

141. "J'Accuse," Mouvement d'action politique du Betar, RG, Mle, "Diffusion des tracts juifs en milieux étudiants," 29 May 1967, 137W363, BdR. Police claimed the tract was Betar's first foray into Marseille, although as we saw, during the 1948 war, the Irgun (Betar's parent organization), maintained a local presence.

142. For more on the AJOA, see Sussman, "Changing Lands," 351–52.

143. RG, Mle, "Conflit israélo-arabe: Prise de position en faveur d'Israël," 8 June 1967, 137W363, BdR.

144. The Consistoire request, which paralleled requests from other key synagogues, can be found in Préfecture des Bouches-du-Rhône, Communication téléphoniques, 5 June 1967, 135W57, BdR. The citation is from "État d'esprit des populations d'origine algérienne dans le département des Bouches-du-Rhône," 28 June 1967, 19960311, art. 4, CAC.

145. Jewish voters repaid Defferre for his support. While their electoral patterns mirrored the country's spread in the 1974, 1978, and 1981 national elections, in municipal elections, they stood collectively behind Defferre and his party, breaking away only after his death. Direction générale de la police nationale, "Étude sur la communauté juive des Bouches-du-Rhône," 16 October 1989; RG, "Communauté juive des BDR," 23 September 1986; "L'élection présidentielle et la communauté juive de Marseille," 26 February 1988, 1693W233, BdR.

146. Gaston Defferre, "De Gaulle et l'antisémitisme," *Le Provençal*, 8 January 1968.

147. The Comité de coordination requested a meeting with the regional prefect to express their anger at de Gaulle's pronouncement. The prefect never responded. Robert Ifrah to M. le Préfet régional de Marseille, 6 December 1967; Compte rendu de la réunion de l'exécutif du Comité coordination, 8 January 196(8), MDI 159, CJDC.

148. R.O., "Marseille 'porte israélienne' de l'Europe pour une conquête du marché agricole occidental," *Le Méridional*, 20 April 1968.

149. Cited in Témime, *Histoire de Marseille*, 341.

150. "Solidarité et paix thème du meeting de soutien à Israël," press clipping, no date or title, 135W57, BdR. Defferre reached out to the pieds-noirs, delegating a special adjunct for repatriate issues and supporting the indemnification and amnesty of all repatriates. "Importante réunion consacrée aux problèmes des rapatriés en présence du colonel Battesti, président national de l'ANFANOMA," and "En direct," 20 February and 4 March 1967, *Le Provençal*.

151. Préfet de la région Provence to MI, 7 February 1969, 135W57, BdR. "Solidarité et paix thème du meeting de soutien à Israël," press clipping, no date or title, 135W57, BdR.

152. Lucien Pucciarelli, "Étrange rassemblement," *Le Marseillais*, 7 February 1969, 135W57, BdR.

153. Although integrated relatively quickly into Marseille's economic structure, pieds noirs believed themselves abandoned by French authorities and the settled population. Jean-Jacques Jordi, *De l'exode: Rapatriés et pieds-noirs en France: L'exemple marseillais, 1954–1992* (Paris: L'Éditions l'Harmattan, 1993), pp. 216–17; Témime, *Histoire de Marseille*, 340; Sayad, Jordi, and Témime, *Le Choc*, 97–99, 101–105; Jean-Jacques Jordi, "L'été 62 à Marseille: Tensions et incompréhensions," in Jordi and Émile Témime, eds., *Marseille et le choc des décolonisations: Les rapatriements, 1954–1964* (Aix-en-Provence: Édisud, 1996), pp. 72–73.

154. Rabi, "Le 'boom' de Marseille," 43.

155. Sayad, Jordi, and Témime, *Le Choc*, 108–109, remind that "Manichean simplifications" of interethnic relations in Marseille can overemphasize tensions in often convivial neighborhoods. Moreover, the pieds noirs were not uniformly attracted to the far right, but spread out across the political spectrum.

156. "Débats et réunions," *Le Monde*, 24 May 1966, p. 8.

157. "Au cours d'une réunion à la Mutualité: Des organisations estudiantines arabes dénoncent la confusion entre le problème de l'antisémitisme et celui du conflit palestinien," *Le Monde*, 28 May 1966, p. 4.

158. Eric Rouleau, "Des organisations juives s'élèvent contre une récente réunion d'étudiants arabes à Paris," 13 July 1966, *Le Monde*, p. 4.

159. While Wolf, *Harnessing the Holocaust*, points to 1967 as the origin of such Holocaust imagery, by the mid-1960s, Nazi oppression was a common reference for those on both sides of the Israel-Palestine issue. The article, "Le racisme: Les travailleurs français et émigrés face au fléau," *AE*, 1–15 May 1966, pp. 14–15, for example, addressed the mistreatment of immigrant workers in France with a picture of a swastika captioned, "Nazism is not dead. Hunger and racism. Three million immigrant workers." See Moyn, *A Holocaust Controversy*, 149, for a critique of Wolf's focus on 1967 as a turning point.

160. Michel Salomon, "Opération bonne conscience: La gauche française et la propagande arabe," *L'Arche*, July 1966, pp. 8–9. Solomon focused his ire primarily on Claude Glayman, Maxime Rodinson, and French leftists.

161. "Correspondance: Les Juifs, les Arabes et le MRAP," *Le Monde*, 6 July 1966, p. 4.

162. "Résolution adopté à la journée du MRAP," 16 May 1965, MDI 71, CDJC, and Journée nationale contre le racisme, l'antisémitisme et pour la paix, same file.

163. Un colloque de l'union mondiale des étudiants, 14/10/65, MDI 71, CDJC.

164. MM 23/11/65, MDI 72, CDJC.

165. Michel Salomon, "Opération bonne conscience: La gauche française et la propagande arabe," *L'Arche*, July 1966, pp. 8–9.

166. V. Modiano to Alain Peyrefitte, Ministre de l'éducation nationale, 8 May 1967; Alain Peyrefitte to Modiano, 20 July 1967, MDI 65C, CDJC. The Minister of Education claimed fears over the escalation of a tense environment and not Arab student pressure had driven the decision to cancel.

167. "Journée internationale de la Palestine à Paris," *El Moudjahid*, 20 May 1967, p. 8.

168. Cited in Jocelyne Cesari, *Être musulman en France: Associations, militants, et mosquées* (Paris: Éditions Karthala et Iremam, 1994), p. 174.
169. Les étudiants arabes en France dénoncent la collusion de l'impérialisme anglo-américaine avec les sionistes," *El Moudjahid*, 8 June 1967, p. 5.
170. Commissariat central d'Aix en Provence, "Un groupe de professeurs a organisé hier soir une réunion sur le problème israélien," 8 June 1967, 135W57, BdR.
171. "Dans les universités," *Bulletin de nos communautés*, 26 May 1967.
172. MI to Préfet des Bouches-du-Rhône, 30 May 1967; RG, Mle, "Diffusion des tracts juifs en milieux étudiants," 29 May 1967, 137W363, BdR.
173. Police report, 27 May 1967, 19980547, art. 13 (Israël), CAC.
174. Victor Malka, "Incertitude jeunesse," *L'Arche*, December 1964, reported ongoing UEJF efforts to establish contacts with Arab student organizations in France.
175. *BIL*, N° 3, 4 June 1967 and N° 5, 7 June 1967, MDI 98, CDJC.

Chapter 5. Palestine in France: Radical Politics and Hardening Ethnic Allegiances, 1968–72

1. Most studies of postwar French Jewish life have ignored or brushed over the role of 1968 in shaping Jewish political life. For notable exceptions, see Yair Auron, *Les Juifs d'extrême gauche en Mai 68*, translated from Hebrew by Katherine Werchowski (Paris: Albin Michel 1998); Judith Friedlander, *Vilna on the Seine: Jewish Intellectuals in France since 1968* (New Haven: Yale University Press, 1990); Jonathan Judaken, "'To Be or Not to Be French': *Soixante-Huitard* Reflections on '*La question juive*,'" *Journal of Modern Jewish Studies* 1, 1 (2002): 3–21. For discussion of the impact of 1968 radicalism on North African Muslims in France, see Abdellali Hajjat, "Les Comités Palestine (1970–1972): Aux origines du soutien de la cause palestinienne en France," *Revue d'études palestiniennes*," 98 (Winter 2006): 74–92, and "L'expérience politique du Mouvement des travailleurs arabes," *Contretemps* 16 (May 2006): 76–85. A combined revision of these two articles has been published as "Des Comités Palestine au Mouvement des travailleurs arabes (1970–1976)," in Ahmed Boubeker and Abdellali Hajjat eds., *Histoire politique des immigrations (post) coloniales: France, 1920–2008* (Paris: Éditions Amsterdam, 2008): 145–56. Ethan Katz, "Jews and Muslims in the Shadow of Marianne: Conflicting Identities and Republican Culture in France, 1914–1975" (Ph.D. diss., University of Wisconsin, 2008), pp. 311–82, also addresses this issue.
2. Debates over the transformative power of 1968 emerged immediately thereafter. Michael Seidman's *The Imaginary Revolution: Parisian Students and Workers in 1968* (New York: Berghahn Books, 2004), for example, insists on its limited impact. All agree, however, that various social issues won wider public hearing. For important discussions of May 1968 and its impact, see Kristin Ross, *May '68 and Its Afterlives* (Chicago: University of Chicago Press, 2002) and Julian Jackson, *May 68 : Rethinking France's Last Revolution* (New York: Palgrave Macmillan, 2011).
3. Samir Kassir and Farouk Mardam-Bey, *Itinéraires de Paris à Jérusalem: La France et le conflit israélo-arabe*, vol. 2: 1958–91 (Paris: Revue d'études palestiniennes, 1993), pp. 162–64, mark 1967 as the birth of French awareness of the Palestinian struggle,

despite support for Israel. Subsequently, ADAE and the Parisian office of the Arab League continued to push the issue, as did individual politicians and journalists. See, for example, the April 1968 edition of *L'Algérien en Europe*. Untitled report, Préfecture de police, 2 April 1968, 19960311, art. 4; RG, "Les activités du bureau de la Ligue arabe à Paris," June 1972, 19990260, art. 23, CAC.

4. For differences among Maoists, Trotskyists, Anarchists, and other groups, see Hervé Bourges, *The French Student Revolt: The Leaders Speak* (New York: Hill and Wang, 1968).

5. Poster cited in letter to CRIF, 3 November 1969, MDI 147, CJDC.

6. "Les étudiants français dénoncent l'agression impérialo-sioniste," *El Moudjahid*, 9–10 July 1967, p. 6.

7. Direction de la réglementation, 14 September 1971, 19960311, art. 1, CAC; Kassir and Mardam-Bey, *Itinéraires de Paris à Jérusalem*, 164–65, 167; Auron, *Les Juifs d'extrême gauche*, 139–40; "France," *American Jewish Yearbook* (1969), p. 332.

8. Yezid Sayigh, *Armed Struggle and the Search for a State: The Palestinian National Movement, 1949–1993* (Oxford: Oxford University Press, 1997), p. 173.

9. Kassir and Mardam-Bey, *Itinéraires de Paris à Jérusalem*, 105.

10. Auron, *Les Juifs d'extrême gauche*, passim; Maurice Szafran, *Les Juifs dans la politique française: De 1945 à nos jours* (Paris: Flammarion, 1990), pp. 181–88; Joan Wolf, *Harnessing the Holocaust: The Politics of Memory in France* (Stanford: Stanford University Press, 2004), pp. 57–58.

11. For the riot, see Daniel Gordon, "Immigrants and the New Left in France, 1968–1971" (Ph.D. diss., University of Sussex, 2001), pp. 164–91, and "Acteurs transméditerranéens dans un quartier cosmopolite: Juifs et Musulmans, entre tolérance et conflit, à Belleville (Paris XXe)," *Cahiers de la Méditerranée* (December 2003); Katz, "Jews and Muslims" (Ph.D. diss., University of Wisconsin, 2008), pp. 311–12, 360–66; and Patrick Simon and Claude Tapia, *Le Belleville des Juifs tunisiens* (Paris: Éditions Autrement, 1998), pp. 168–73. For the riot's impact, see Yvan Gastaut, *L'immigration et l'opinion sous la Ve république* (Paris: Éditions du Seuil, 2000), pp. 47–51. My discussion also draws and from "Les échauffourées de Belleville," *Le Monde juif: La revue du centre documentation juive contemporaine*, 50 (1968).

12. Tapia and Simon, *Le Belleville des Juifs tunisiens*, 170, note that most residents hid at home.

13. Michel Legris, "Après les vifs incidents de Belleville: Les représentants de la communauté israélite et des diplomates maghrébins interviennent pour obtenir le retour au calme," *Le Monde*, 5 June 1968, p. 18; Untitled report, 14 January 1970, La Fédération des sociétés juives de France, BA 2315, APP; "Après les bagarres des deux derniers jours: A Belleville, un tract arabe appelle à la 'guerre sainte' contre les Juifs," *Le Figaro*, 5 June 1968, p. 2. Tensions persisted for weeks. Jean Farkas to Rabbi Chouchena, 21 July 1968, 1967–68, CC.

14. For competing theories on the origins, see Gastaut, *L'immigration et l'opinion*, 37–51. Gordon, "Immigrants," 164–91, convincingly critiques four of the most prevelant explanations without offering a new one.

15. Material on Belleville is from Katz, "Jews and Muslims," 336–40; Simon and Tapia, *Le Belleville des Juifs tunisiens*, 161–67; and Claude Tapia, *Les Juifs sépharades en France (1965–1985): Études psychosociologiques et historiques* (Paris: L'Harmattan, 1986), pp. 109–45.

16. Simon and Tapia, *Le Belleville des Juifs tunisiens*, 89, number 82 percent of Belleville's Jewish population as Tunisian in 1970.
17. *La jeune Afrique*, 1–7 July 1968, p. 25, cited in Gordon, "Immigrants," 171.
18. Simon and Tapia, *Le Belleville des Juifs tunisiens*, 168–69.
19. Katz, "Jews and Muslims," 365.
20. "Une déclaration de l'ambassadeur d'Algérie," *Le Figaro*, 5 June 1968, p. 2; "Après les incidents de Belleville: Appels au calme adressés aux communautés musulmane et israélite," *Le Figaro*, 6 June 1968, p. 2; "Les échauffourées de Belleville"; "Le grand rabbin de France s'adresse aux populations Israélites et Musulmanes du quartier de Belleville," 7 June 1968, 1967–68, CC; Bureau du CRIF, 5 June 1968, MDI 1–55, CDJC.
21. For the ADAE's statement, see Untitled, *AE*, 15 June 1968, p. 2. F. Abdelali, "Violences sionistes à Paris," and "Bagarres à Paris entre Algériens et groupe armés sionistes," *El Moudjahid*, 4 June 1968, p. 1, 3. An example of Jewish efforts to blame anti-Israeli agitators appears in Moch to Monica Blum, Anti-Defamation League of B'nai Brith, 21 June 1968, MDI 65C, CDJC. "Après les bagarres des deux derniers jours," 2, refers to the call for Holy War.
22. "Jeunes Juifs de la révolte," *L'Arche*, June–July 1968, p. 77.
23. Front des étudiants juifs to CRIF, "Le FEJ," 9 August 1974, MDI 146 B, CJDC.
24. Norman Stillman, *Jews of Arab Lands in Modern Times* (Philadelphia: The Jewish Publication Society, 1991), pp. 173–74; Michael M. Laskier, *North African Jewry in the Twentieth Century: The Jews of Morocco, Tunisia, and Algeria* (New York: New York University Press, 1994), pp. 308–9.
25. Simon and Tapia, *Le Belleville des Juifs tunisiens*, 35–41, 168.
26. "Jeunes Juifs de la révolte," 77.
27. Scholars debate the level of foreign participation during May 1968. See, for example, Gastaut, *L'immigration et l'opinion*, 38–39, 43, and Gordon, "Immigrants," passim.
28. Cited in Simon and Tapia, *Le Belleville des Juifs tunisiens*, 168–69, 173.
29. Scholarship has largely overlooked these events. Simon and Tapia, *Le Belleville des Juifs tunisiens*, 172, for example, claim that the 1968 riot, "inconceivable and unexpected . . . did not recur." Katz, "Jews and Muslims," 370–74, is a notable exception. Coverage of the riot included, "A Belleville (20ème): Flambée de violence entre Musulmans et Israélites: Une soixantaine de vitrines brisées," *Le Figaro*, 16 June 1970, p. 11; "Violents affrontements entre Israélites et Musulmans: 33 personnes interpellées," *Le Monde*, 17 June 1970, p. 17; "Après les incidents de Belleville," *Le Monde*, 20 June 1970, p. 13; "France," *American Jewish Yearbook* (1970), p. 344.
30. "Belleville: L'agression d'Israël continue," *AE*, 25 June–9 July 1970, pp. 5, 20.
31. *AE*, 9–23 July 1970, p. 2.
32. "Après les incidents de Belleville," 13.
33. "A Belleville, contre les divisions et la haine," *Droite et liberté*, July–August 1970; "Seize personnes sont toujours en garde à vue après les incidents de Belleville," *Le Monde*, 18 June 1970, p. 12.
34. "CRIF communiqué," *Le Monde*, 21–22 June 1970, p. 14.
35. CRIF responses were drawn from meeting, 2 July 1970, MDI 1–55, CDJC; Bureau du CRIF, 22 June (1970), same reel.
36. "Seize personnes," 12; "Violents affrontements," 17.
37. For relationships between gauchistes and immigrants, see Gastaut, *L'immigration et l'opinion*, 37–51; Gordon, "Immigrants," passim; and Gérard Noiriel, *Immigration,*

antisémitisme et racisme en France, XIXe–XXe siècle: Discours publics, humiliations privées (Paris: Fayard, 2007), pp. 558–64. For Maoist and North African student collaboration, see Hajjat, "Les Comités palestine" and "L'expérience politique du Mouvement des travailleurs arabes." While Hajjat expertly covers the history of these organizations, his account downplays Fatah's role in the establishment of the Comités Palestine. My account seeks to correct this imbalance.

38. RG, "Les Organisations palestiniennes en France," 20 June 1972; RG, "El Fatah et les révolutionnaires français," 25 June 1969; RG, "Présence de la Palestine," June 1972, 19990260, art. 23; RG, "Campagne de l'Amicale des Algériens en faveur des Palestiniens," 17 November 1969, 19960311, art. 4; RG, "Association 'Présence de la Palestine,'" 27 May 1971, 19990426, art 176 (liasse 1 N° 454), CAC. Préfecture de police, 1 May 1971, T9 Terrenoire, APP. Kassir and Mardam-Bey, *Itinéraires de Paris à Jérusalem*, 105, 170.

39. See Gordon, "Immigrants," 175, for a face-off between pro-Palestinian supporters and left-wing Zionists on 4 June at the Sorbonne.

40. Notes d'information, 1968, MDI 95, CDJC; Sayigh, *Armed Struggle*, 190.

41. Police incorrectly dated the group's birth to 1969 (as noted, the Union first formed in 1965). Conflicting dates appear in Untitled Reports, Préfecture de police, 19 February 1970 and March 1972, 19870799, art. 20, N° 3383; "L'Union générale des étudiants palestiniens en France," June 1972, 19990260, art. 23, CAC.

42. RG, "Les comités de soutien au peuple palestinien," 29 January 1969, 19990426, art. 15 (liasse 6 N° 122); RG, "El Fatah et les mouvements révolutionnaires en France," 29 April 1969, 19990426, art. 15 (liasse 7 N° 140); RG, "Les activités politiques des Nord-Africains résidant en France," April 1970, 19850087, art. 39; RG, "Les activités du bureau de la Ligue arabe à Paris," June 1972, 19990260, art. 23, CAC. Hajjat, "Les Comités Palestine," 80, 84, claims these bodies were intermittently active in 1969.

43. RG, "El Fatah et les révolutionnaires français," 25 June 1969, 19990260, art. 23, CAC.

44. Préfecture de police, 23 January 1969, 19990426, art. 15 (liasse 6 N° 122), CAC.

45. "Prochaine création d'une association dite 'Section française du Mouvement contre le racisme anti-Arabe (M.R.A.A.),'" 18 November 1968, 19990426, art 15 (liasse 5 N° 74); RG, "El Fatah et les mouvements révolutionnaires en France," 29 April 1969, 19990426, art. 15 (liasse 7 N° 140); "Création à Paris d'un mouvement contre le racisme anti-Arabe," *AE*, 1 December 1968, p. 17.

46. "Rubrique: Antisionisme et anti-impérialisme [*sic*]," *Résistance populaire*, 15 May (1968), pp. 22–25.

47. Préfecture de police, 23 January 1969, 19990426, art. 15 (liasse 6 N° 122), CAC. Ideology could also divide. Fatah's commando actions proved particularly attractive to Maoists who believed that Third World liberation movements had revolutionary potential. Trotskyists were drawn to George Habash's Popular Front for the Liberation of Palestine (PFLP), a guerrilla movement that called for social and economic transformation as part of its nationalist revolution, and to Nayef Hawatmeh's Popular Democratic Front for the Liberation of Palestine (PDFLP), a more extreme left-wing break-away organization. RG, "El Fatah et les révolutionnaires français," 25 June 1969; RG, "Le rôle d'éléments algériens dans le terrorisme international," 26 June 1971; RG, "Les organisations palestiniennes en France," 20 June 1972, 19990260, art. 23; RG, "Nervosité chez les Algériens en France," 3 July 1969, 19960311, art. 4; CAC. According to Sayigh, *Armed Struggle*, 232–33, the PFLP's Marxism was "skin-deep."

Also see Auron, *Les Juifs d'extrême gauche*, 219, and Denis Sieffert, *Israël-Palestine, une passion française: La France dans le miroir du conflit israélo-palestinien* (Paris: Éditions la Découverte, 2004), p. 159.

48. Links between *gauchistes* and immigrant workers is drawn from Noiriel, *Immigration, antisémitisme et racism*, 558–64; Gastaut, *L'immigration et l'opinion*, 37–51, 149–67; Direction de la réglementation, "L'Immigration étrangère en France" (1970), 19960311, art. 1, CAC.

49. Préfecture de police, 6 October 1970, 19960311, art. 4; Note pour Monsieur le Ministre de l'Intérieur, 1 March 1971, 19900353, art. 14 (liasse 1); Direction de la réglementation, 14 September 1971, 19960311, art. 1, CAC.

50. Direction de la réglementation, "L'immigration étrangère en France" (1970), 19960311, art. 1, CAC.

51. "Création à Paris d'un mouvement contre le racisme anti-Arabe," 17; RG, "El Fatah et les mouvements révolutionnaires en France," 29 April 1969, 19990426, art. 15 (liasse 7 N° 140), CAC. It is worth noting that what is called "Islamophobia" in contemporary parlance was called anti-Arab racism in the 1960s, reflecting some of the dictional changes discussed in the Introduction.

52. "Rubrique: Unité des travailleurs arabes et français," *Résistance populaire*, 15 May (1968), pp. 26–28.

53. "Meeting contre le racisme à Paris," *AE*, 30 June–15 July 1971, p. 27; Posters, Semaine de la Palestine, 24–28 March 1969, 8 Fi 791/1, BdR.

54. Gastaut, *L'immigration et l'opinion*, 157, dates this interest to the fusion of numerous pro-Chinese groups around Vive la Révolution! and the Gauche prolétarienne in March 1969.

55. Unless noted, discussion of Jewish leftists is from Auron, *Les Juifs d'extrême gauche*.

56. RG, "El Fatah et les révolutionnaires français," 25 June 1969, 19990260, art. 23, CAC.

57. Dominique Schnapper, *Juifs et Israélites* (Paris: Gallimard, 1980), pp. 171–87. Auron, *Les Juifs d'extrême gauche* 71, 163–213, discusses Jewish leftists who refused radical anti-Zionism. Also see Wolf, *Harnessing the Holocaust*, 55–57.

58. In June 1967, Rodinson helped found the Groupe de recherches et d'action pour le règlement du problème palestinien, which declared itself a "defender of Judaism" and "hostile to Zionism." RG, "Groupe de recherches et d'action pour le règlement du problème palestinien GRAPP," June 1972, 19990260, art. 23, CAC.

59. Emmanuel Lévyne, "L'israélisation d'une communauté juive de la région parisienne," *AE*, 1 January 1970, pp. 26–27; A. Zehraoui, "Meeting sur la Palestine à la Mutualité," *AE*, 15 November 1969, p.4. Emmanuel Lévyne, *Judaïsme contre Sionisme* (Paris: Éditions Cujas, 1969).

60. RG, "El Fatah et les révolutionnaires français," 25 June 1969, 19990260, art. 23, CAC. Auron, *Les Juifs d'extrême gauche*, 191.

61. Rabah Aissaoui, *Immigration and National Identity: North African Political Movements in Colonial and Postcolonial France* (London and New York: Tauris Academic Studies, 2009), p. 214.

62. RG, "Les organisations palestiniennes en France," 20 June 1972, 19990260, art. 23, CAC. According to Auron, *Les Juifs d'extrême gauche*, 184. Jews were particularly drawn to Trotskyist organizations, which held less extreme views on Israel.

63. Poster cited in letter to CRIF, 3 November 1969, MDI 147, CDJC.

64. Szafran, *Les Juifs dans la politique française*, 58.

65. Auron, *Les Juifs d'extrême gauche* 60–63, 192–93. Like many Jewish radicals, both Levy and Geismar eventually backed away from their anti-Zionism.
66. Szafran, *Les Juifs dans la politique française*, 188–90.
67. Poster cited in letter to CRIF, 3 November 1969, MDI 147, CDJC.
68. According to Hajjat, "Les Comités Palestine," 75–81, subsequent Comités Palestine were more autonomous from the GP. Also see Aissaoui, *Immigration and National Identity,* 212–17; "L'expérience politique du Mouvement des travailleurs arabes," 78–79; Kassir and Mardam-Bey, *Itinéraires de Paris,* 105, 170, 173; Sieffert, *Israël-Palestine,* 138.
69. RG, "Les activités politiques des Nord-Africains résidant en France," April 1970; RG, "Les activités politiques des Nord-Africains résidant en France," April 1970, 19850087, art. 39, CAC. Hajjat, "Les Comités Palestine," 75–76. For prior activism among such students, see Guy Pervillé, *Les étudiants algériens de l'université française, 1880–1962* (Paris: Éditions du Centre national de la recherche scientifique, 1984).
70. The Croisssant-rouge palestinian was supported in part by the ADAE funds. Préfecture de police, "La situation actuelle de Jordanie révèle l'hostilité des pays arabes vis-à-vis du gouvernement du roi Hussein et déclenche dans la capitale un vaste mouvement humanitaire," 5 October 1970, T9 Terrenoire, APP. Additional ADAE pro-Palestinian activities are documented in RG, "Campagne de l'Amicale des Algériens en faveur des Palestiniens," 17 November 1969 and MI to ME, "Campagne de l'Amicale des Algériens en Europe en faveur des Palestiniens," 18 December 1969, 19960311, art. 4; RG, "El Fatah et les mouvements révolutionnaires en France," 29 April 1969, 19990426, art. 15 (liasse 7 Nᵒ 140); RG, "Les activités politiques des Nord-Africains résidant en France," April 1970, 19850087, art. 39; Préfecture de police, 25 November 1972, 19850087, art. 37, CAC. *L'Algérien en Europe* also regularly criticized Israel.
71. As members of Moroccan opposition groups, they could not return home. Untitled report, Préfecture de police, 30 December 1970, 19960311, art. 5 CAC. The Association des Marocains en France (AMF) also served as a meeting spot for pro-Palestinian Muslim leftists, as did the Association des étudiants musulmans d'Afrique du Nord's headquarters on boulevard Saint Michel. Hajjat, "Les Comités Palestine," 76–78.
72. In June 1971, the Popular Front for the Liberation of Palestine, a break-away guerrilla movement from Fatah, estimated that 80 percent of the group's membership was located in universities. RG, "Le rôle d'éléments algériens dans le terrorisme international," 26 June 1971, 19960311, art. 4, CAC. If, as Hajjat, "Les Comités Palestine," 77, and Aissaoui, *Immigration and National Identity,* 154, claim, Algerian students played a smaller role on the Comités Palestine than Moroccans and Tunisians, the Palestinian issue still made inroads among them. Untitled report, Préfecture de police, 17 September 1971, 19850087, art. 39, CAC.
73. Hajjat, "Les Comités Palestine," 84–86. Both the PFLP and the PDFLP also sought to link the anti-imperialist struggle with the problems facing immigrant workers in France via the Palestinian issue, although Hajjat (p. 80) notes that many North African students avoided Trotskyist organizations, which prioritized socialist revolution over national and anti-colonial struggles. Evidence of some North African participation in the PFLP can nevertheless be found in RG, "Le rôle d'éléments algériens

dans le terrorisme international," 26 June 1971, 19960311, art. 4; RG, "Les organisations palestiniennes en France," 20 June 1972, 19990260, art. 23, CAC.

74. Préfecture de police, "Propagande menée par des Musulmans en milieu ouvrier en faveur de la révolution palestinienne," 3 December 1970, 19900353, art. 14 (liasse 1), CAC.

75. RG, "Le rôle d'éléments algériens dans le terrorisme international," 26 June 1971, 19960311, art. 4, CAC. Aissaoui, *Immigration and National Identity*, 160–66, 174–80.

76. Préfecture de police, 19 November 1969 (1970), 19900353, art. 11 (liasse 1), CAC.

77. The ADAE worked closely with Fatah once the latter established a presence in France, raising money; providing security for pro-Palestinian rallies; distributing pro-Palestinian tracts; and even sending a representative to a PLO training camp. Direction centrale des renseignements généraux, "El Fatah et les mouvements révolutionnaires en France," 29 April 1969, 19990426, art. 15 (liasse 7 N° 140); Direction centrale des renseignements généraux, April 1970, "Les activités politiques des Nord-Africains residant en France," 19850087, art 39, CAC. In 1972, the ADAE dedicated funds raised during Ramadan to Palestinian relief efforts, mimicking FLN policies in Algeria where such donations were mandatory. Prefecture de police, 25 November 1972, 19850087, art. 37, CAC. Hajjat, "Les Comités Palestine," 77, notes that the ADAE often clashed with Muslim leftists.

78. RG, "Les comités de soutien au peuple palestinien," 29 January 1969; RG, "El Fatah et les mouvements révolutionnaires en France," 29 April 1969, 19990426, art. 15 (liasse 7 N° 140), CAC. Articles praising de Gaulle's pro-Arab stance can be found in *AE* on 1 December 1967, 15 February 1968, 15 January 1969, and 15 April 1969, although criticism of covert military aid to Israel appears in "Où en est l'embargo?" *AE*, 16 January 1970, p. 26.

79. Directeur central des RG to Directeur de la règlementation, 6ème bureau, "Renseignements sur l'Union générale des étudiants de Palestine," 18 August 1970, 19870799, art. 20, no. 3383; RG, "Les organisations palestiniennes en France," 20 June 1972, 19990260, art. 23, CAC; Sieffert, *Israël-Palestine*, 138–42.

80. RG, "El Fatah et les révolutionnaires français," 25 June 1969, 19990260, art. 23, CAC.

81. Sayigh, *Armed Struggle*, 196–200, discusses ideological tensions within Fatah's commitment to Arab unity. To quell concerns of supporters further to the left, the organization often adopted a moderate socialism. MI, Direction de la surveillance du territoire, "Note d'information: Projet d'installation d'un bureau de presse du Fatah à Paris. Évolution du Fatah," 1 September 1969, 19990260, art. 23, CAC. For an example of Fatah's more leftist efforts, see "Dans un communiqué publié à Alger: L'organisation palestinienne 'El Feth' s'engage a poursuivre la lutte jusqu'à la victoire," *El Moudjahid*, 4 May 1968, p. 7.

82. Directeur central des RG to Directeur de la règlementation, 6ème bureau, "Renseignements sur l'Union générale des étudiants de Palestine," 18 August 1970, 19870799, art. 20, N° 3383, CAC. Ideological divisions ultimately threatened the UGEP. Préfecture de police, 19 February 1970, 19870799, art. 20, N° 3383; "L'Union générale des étudiants palestiniens en France," June 1972, 19990260, art. 23, CAC.

83. Préfecture de police, 1 November 1972, 19870799, art. 20, N° 3383; Préfecture de police, 12 November 1972, 19990260, art. 23, CAC.

84. Cited in Auron, *Les Juifs d'extrême gauche*, 107–10.

85. Simon, *L'immigration algérienne en France*, 24–26.

86. Gastaut, *L'immigration et l'opinion*, 282–97, points to 1971–73 as the height of anti-Arab racism.

87. Wihtol de Wenden, *Les immigrés et la politique*, 155–79.

88. Aissaoui, *Immigration and National Identity*, 153–216, and Hajjat, "L'expérience politique du Mouvement des travailleurs arabes," 76–85.

89. The GP had been weakened in 1970 after a French government ban and a controversial decision to attack the Jordanian embassy as well as after 1972 disagreements over the Palestinian resistance organization Black September's kidnapping of Israeli athletes at the Munich Olympics, which some members (primarily the Jewish leadership) condemned. Auron, *Les Juifs d'extrême gauche*, 145–46, 227–40; Jocelyne Cesari, *Être musulman en France: Associations, militants, et mosquées* (Paris: Éditions Karthala et Iremam, 1994), p. 174; Szafran, *Les Juifs dans la politique*, 177–93.

90. Posters in Marseille prior to Golda Meir's 1973 visit to France, for example, linked anti-Zionism and the immigrant struggle. Commissariat central de Marseille to Préfet de la région, 12 January 1973; Commissariat central de Marseille, "Note," 12 January 1973; Commissariat de police de la Ciotat to Contrôleur général, "Diffusion d'un tract émanant de divers mouvements gauchistes et relatif à la visite en France de Mme Golda Meir," 12 January 1973, 135W57, BdR.

91. Cited in Gastaut, *L'immigration et l'opinion*, 161. For the centrality of Palestine, see Hajjat, "Les Comités Palestines," 90; Wihtol de Wenden, *Les immigrés et la politique*, 178. Aissaoui, *Immigration and National Identity*, 156–60, 212–17, notes that MTA activists took up all issues relevant to the Arab people.

92. Ministre des armes, Bureau emploi-renseignement, "Collecte en faveur des Palestiniens," 7 May 1973, 19980547, art. 17 (extrait: Palestine), CAC. For the MTA's ethno-national politics, see Aissaoui, *Immigration and National Identity*, 156–60.

93. Cited in Hajjat, "Les Comités Palestine," 90. Mauritians and Pakistanis broke away from the MTA in 1974 complaining of its over-involvement in the struggle against Zionism and North African regimes. RG, 22 June 1974, 19900353, Article 11 (liasse 1), CAC.

94. RG, "Nervosité chez les Algériens en France," 3 July 1969, 19960311, art. 4, CAC.

95. RG, "Les activités politiques des Nord-Africains résidant en France," April 1970, 19850087, art. 39, CAC.

96. Commissariat central de Marseille, "Note: Distribution de tracts aux Ets Coder," 7 October 1970; Directeur départemental des services de sécurité publique de Bouches-du-Rhône to Directeur central de la sécurité publique, Paris, "Pénétration du milieu des travailleurs immigrés par les gauchistes," 10 July 1970, 135W124, BdR.

97. GILR, Procès-verbal de la réunion du 16 mai 1970; Directeur départemental des services de sécurité publique de Bouches-du-Rhône to Directeur central de la sécurité publique, Paris, "Pénétration du milieu des travailleurs immigrés par les gauchistes," 10 July 1970, 135W124, BdR. By July, the GP's influence had been weakened by arrests and departures. GILR, Procès verbal de la réunion du 8 juillet 1970, same file.

98. Cited in Hajjat, "Les Comités Palestine," 84–86.

99. Préfet to ME and MI, "Association dite 'Bureau d'aide en France à la révolution palestinienne' B.A.R.P.," 14 September 1971, 19990426, art. 17 (liasse 1 N° 468); RG, "Le rôle d'éléments algériens dans le terrorisme international," 26 June 1971, 19960311, art. 4, CAC.

100. GILR, Procès verbal de la réunion du 20 octobre 1970; "Un responsable de l'ex-gauche prolétarienne, à Antony envisage de s'installer définitivement dans la région de Marseille," 7 October 1970, 135W124, BdR. Direction de la réglementation, 14 September 1971, 19960311, art. 1, CAC.

101. Commissariat central de Marseille, "Note," 27 March 1972, 135W57, BdR.

102. MI, "Marseille—Manifestation gauchiste du 12-12-72," 18 December 1972, 135W57, BdR.

103. Ibid.

104. Gordon, "Immigrants," 25.

105. Annexe 3 du rapport du Préfet du police du 23 août 1971, "Activité politique des principales colonies étrangères," 19900353, art. 11 (liasse 1); Direction de la réglementation, 14 September 1971, 19960311, art. 1, CAC.

106. Annexe 3 du rapport du Préfet du police du 23 août 1971, "Activité politique des principales colonies étrangères," 19900353, art. 11 (liasse 1), CAC.

107. Direction de la réglementation, 14 September 1971, 19960311, art. 1, CAC.

108. Préfecture de police, 19 November 1969, 19900353, art. 11 (liasse 1), CAC.

109. Hajjat, "Les Comités Palestine," 86.

110. RG, "Les organisations palestiniennes en France," 20 June 1972, 19990260, art. 23, CAC.

111. "L'Union générale des étudiants palestiniens en France," June 1972, 19990260, art. 23, CAC.

112. "Les travailleurs de Suresnes-Puteaux soutiennent la révolution palestinienne," Fedai (1972), in Commissariat central de Marseille, "Note," 27 March 1972, 135W57, BdR.

113. Police reported apathy among Muslim workers and students for the Palestinian cause as late as 1976. "Échec de la campagne gauchiste en faveur du Liban," 29 October 1976, 19900353, Article 11 (liasse 2), CAC.

114. Préfecture de police, 5 March 1970, 19990260, art. 23, CAC. Some Algerian immigrants blamed an explosion on 4 December 1969 at the mosqué de Paris on those tyring to punish its Algerian director for refusing to support the cause. Untitled Report, 14 January 1970, La Fédération des sociétés juives de France, BA 2315, APP. A. Selmi, "L'attentat contre la Mosquée de Paris ou le Nazisme nouvelle vague," AE, 15 December 1969, blamed Israelis.

115. Préfet des Vosges to MI, 8 September 1969, Algériens–Activités politiques: Divers (1966–76), 19960311, art. 4, CAC.

116. Préfecture de police, Direction des renseignements généraux et des jeux, "La communauté juive dans la région parisienne" (1970?), 19900353, art. 10 (liasse1), CAC. Roger Ascot, "Quinze mille jeunes," L'Arche, February 1969, pp. 17–21, claimed that 10–15 percent of Jewish youth participated in organized communal life.

117. Noiriel, Immigration, antisémitisme et racism, 558–64; Auron, Les Juifs d'extrême gauche, passim. For an example of divisions, see "Jeunes Juifs de la révolte," L'Arche, June–July 1968, pp. 33–36, 73–77.

118. Roger Ascot, "Le mal de la jeunesse," L'Arche, December 1968–January 1969; Wolf, Harnessing the Holocaust, 55–57.

119. Simmy Epstein and Meïr Waintrater, "Université: Les étudiants juif au pied du mur," L'Arche, February–March 1970, p. 40.

120. Meir Yoguev, "Les héritiers de mai 68," *L'Arche*, 25 May–25 June 1973, pp. 37–42. Also see Regina Rittel, "Les écoles juives et la crise de l'enseignement," pp. 43–46, 65, in same edition.

121. Meir Yoguev, "Les héritiers de mai 68," *L'Arche*, 25 May–25 June 1973, pp. 37–42. RG, "Les comités de soutien au peuple palestinien," 29 January 1969 19990426, art. 15 (liasse 6, N° 122), CAC.

122. He also credited the 1967 war. Lucien Poznanski, "L'UEJF aujourd'hui," *L'Arche*, February–March 1970, p. 63.

123. In May 1969, for example, Grenoble's UEJF protested an exposition on Palestinian resistance. RG, "El Fatah et les révolutionnaires français," 25 June 1969, 19990260, art. 23, CAC.

124. RG, "Les comités de soutien au peuple palestinien," 29 January 1969, 19990426, art. 15 (liasse 6 N° 122), CAC.

125. One Jewish communal leader remarked, "such people just deserve a pistol shot in the neck." M. P. Elkouby to M. A. Loss, "UEJF," 2 May 1972, MDI 159, CJDC.

126. Front des étudiants juifs to CRIF, "Le FEJ" (August 1974?) MDI 146 B, CDJC. For organizaing among Jewish high school students, see Auron, *Les Juifs d'extrême gauche*, 131–32.

127. Interview with Françoise Tenenbaum in Robert I. Weiner and Richard E. Sharpless, eds. *An Uncertain Future: Voices of a French Jewish Community, 1940-2012* (Toronto: University of Toronto Press, 2012), p. 68.

128. Letter to CRIF, 3 November 1969, MDI 147, CJDC.

129. Posters, Semaine de la Palestine, 24–28 March 1969, 8 Fi 791/1, BdR.

130. Untitled Report, 14 January 1970, La Fédération des sociétés juives de France, BA 2315, APP.

131. Front des étudiants juifs to CRIF, "Le FEJ" (August 1974?) MDI 146 B, CJDC. The source is a review of the FEJ's prior activities beginning in 1968.

132. RG, "El Fatah et les révolutionnaires français," 25 June 1969, 19990260, art. 23, CAC; Meir Yoguev, "Les héritiers de mai 68," *L'Arche*, 25 May–25 June 1973, pp. 37–42.

133. RG, "El Fatah et les révolutionnaires français," 25 June 1969, 19990260, art. 23, CAC.

134. Some blamed violence on antisemitic orators while others accused Betar of instigating the attack. The latter denied involvement. "Incidents antisémites au centre universitaire Censier," Bureau du CRIF, 4 February 1970, MDI 1–55; "Les incidents de Censier," 15 December 1969, MDI 66, CDJC; Préfecture de police, direction des renseignements généraux et des jeux, "La communauté juive dans la région parisienne" (1970?), 19900353, art. 10 (liasse 1, Israël), CAC; "Affrontement à Censier," *L'Aurore*, 11 December 1969, p. 3. Zionist student groups published their own account in "Des mouvements sionistes condamnent l'agression de Censier," *Le Monde*, 13 December 1969, p. 4.

135. "Incidents antisémites au centre universitaire Censier," Bureau du CRIF, 4 February 1970, MDI 1–55, CDJC; Préfecture de police, direction des renseignements généraux et des jeux, "La communauté juive dans la région parisienne" (1970?), 19900353, art. 10 (liasse 1, Israël), CAC.

136. MDI 146 B, CJDC.

137. Préfecture de police, 20 June 1970, 19850087, art 39, CAC.

138. A few days before, "the Irgoun's watching" had been scrawled on the building's door.

139. "Des mouvements sionistes," 4.

140. Préfecture de police, direction des renseignements généraux et des jeux, "La communauté juive dans la région parisienne" (1970?), 19900353, art. 10 (liasse 1, Israël), CAC.

141. "Des mouvements sionistes," 4.

142. "Incidents antisémites au centre universitaire Censier," Bureau du CRIF, 4 February 1970, MDI 1–55, CDJC.

143. CRIF meeting, 13 March 1970, MDI 146 B and MDI 1–55, CDJC.

144. CRIF meeting, 11 December 1969, MDI 1–55, CDJC.

145. Epstein and Meir, "Université," 39.

146. CRIF meeting, 24 January 1969, MDI 1–55, CDJC. Discussions of the "anti-Israel campaigns" and efforts to monitor pro-Palestinian activities can be found in Bureau du CRIF, 5 December 1969, MDI 1–55; "Solidarité avec les réfugiés palestiniens: L'association de solidarité franco-arabe vend des cartes de vœux au profit des réfugiés arabes de Palestine, qui passent un 22ème hiver en exil," 22 December 1969, MDI 326, CDJC.

147. CRIF meeting, 2 July 1970, MDI 1–55, CDJC. Fears of the conflation of anti-Zionism and antisemitism circulated widely. One such reference to the Comité Palestine can be found in Journées nationales du CRIF, in October 1971 MDI 136.

148. Préfecture de police, 23 June 1971, T9 Terrenoire, APP.

149. "A l'approche du 4ème anniversaire du conflit israélo-arabe, les Algériens de Paris craignent des provocations de la part des Israélites," 18 May 1971, Comité des étudiants juifs, BA 2315, APP. Préfecture de police, 26 May 1971, 19990260, art. 23, CAC.

150. Police report, 13 January 1972, 19990260, art. 23, CAC, blamed the FEJ and the Comité de soutien aux Juifs d'URSS.

151. Préfecture de police, 8 June 1972; Police report, 28 July 1972, 19900260, art. 23, CAC, made clear that while such tactics mirrored Meir Kahne's Jewish Defense League in New York City, the culprits had no plans to follow through.

152. In Marseille, posters accusing Israeli fascists of occupying Palestine illegally blamed deaths in Munich on German police and Israeli intransigence. Commissariat central de Marseille, "Note," 11 September 1972, 135W57, BdR. For disagreements on the far left, see Auron, Les Juifs d'extrême gauche, 227–40.

153. CRIF statement, 6 September 1972, MDI 146 B, CDJC.

154. Préfecture de police, 5 September 1972, 19990260, art. 23, CDAC.

155. Préfecture de police, 16 November 1972, 19990260, art. 23, CAC.

156. Threats came from the Jewish Defense League (JDL), via the FEJ. Préfecture de police, 25 November 1972, 19990260, art. 23; "Compte-rendu de la réunion de liaison consacré aux problèmes de terrorisme," 14 December 1972, 19890576, art 4 (liasse 1), CAC. ADAE accusations of JDL terrorism appear in, "Lâche attentat sioniste contre la librairie 'Palestine' à Paris," AE, 15 October 1972, p. 34. See documents in 19980547, Article 17 (extrait: Palestine), CAC, for Palestinian requests for police protection from Zionists.

157. Kassir and Mardam-Bey, Itinéraires de Paris à Jérusalem, 106; M.B., "Attentat sioniste contre le représentant de l'O.L.P. à Paris," AE, 16–30 December 1972, pp. 28–29; "Recrudescence du contre-terrorisme en France," 11 December 1972, 19990260,

art. 23, CAC; "La 2ème conférence des jeunes d'Europe et des pays arabes: Contre l'impérialisme et le Sionisme," *AE*, 16–30 December 1972, pp. 26–27; "Menaces et injures adressées à l'ambassade d'Algérie à Paris," *AE*, 16–29 November 1972, p. 22; Direction générale de la police nationale, "Compte-rendu de la réunion de liaison consacré aux problèmes de terrorisme," 14 December 1972, 19890576, art 4 (liasse 1), CAC.

158. In June 1971, the CRIF president warned that Paris had become "a hub of actions against Israel." CRIF meeting, 2 June 1971, MDI 1–55, CDJC. While skeptical that Jewish terrorists had bombed the Librarie Palestine, the CRIF criticized all provocateurs. CRIF meeting, 5 October 1972. Several pro-Palestinian and North African student groups called for protection from Israel's "vast liquidation campaign." MI from Union générale des étudiants de Palestine, Union nationale des étudiants du Maroc, Union général des étudiants libanais en France, Association des étudiants irakiens en France, 26 April 1973, 19990260, art. 23, CAC.

159. Meir Yoguev, "Université: Une nouvelle génération antisioniste," *L'Arche*, 26 January–25 February 1973, pp. 21–22.

160. CRIF meeting, 5 October 1972; Communiqué, 9 January 1973, MDI 146 B, CDJC.

161. "L'attentat contre l'Agence juive," *L'Arche*, January–February 1973, p. 30. For another example, see Philippe Ben's "La dernière contre offensive arabe," *L'Arche*, March–April 1973, pp. 19–20, in which the terms "Arab" and "Palestinian" are nearly always accompanied by the term "terrorism."

162. Préfecture de police, 15 December 1972, 19990260, art. 23, CAC.

163. "Le terrorisme sioniste," *AE*, 16–30 September 1972, p. 5. Rare references to Jews qua Jews included articles that compared anti-Muslim sentiment in France negatively to antisemitism in *AE*,1 December 1968; 1 November 1969; and 15 March 1968. *AE*, 1 March 1969, p. 3, accused the chief rabbi of blind support for Israel and unfair representations of Jewish life in Arab lands. Articles blurring lines between Zionists and Jews include, "À la limite de l'antisémitisme," *AE*, 1 July 1969, p. 2, and "Haro sur l'embargo," *AE*, 1 February 1969, p. 17, which provided a list of pro-Israel supporters and blamed the "pressure exercised by the Jewish milieu on French affairs" for the "hysteria" in the press after the January 1969 arms embargo on Israel. Other pieces argued that Jews controlled the media and promoted racist images of Arabs and Algerians. "Le Sionisme dans la presse française," *AE*, 14 July 1969, p. 31; "Sionisme et cie," *AE*, 14–28 May 1970, p. 31. Articles on the pro-Israel bias of the French media include: September 1969, 18 September 1969, 1 November 1969 (article about anti-Arab biases in French television), 1 December 1969, 15 December 1969, 16 January 1970, 9 April 1970, 4–17 September 1970, 1–7 October 1970, 6–21 February 1971. Préfecture de police, 12 November 1972, 19960311, art. 4, CAC.

164. MI, "Marseille—Manifestation gauchistes du 12-12-72," 18 December 1972, 135W57, BdR.

165. High schools, for example, reported frequent altercations between pro-Zionist and pro-Palestinian students. Arnold Mandel, "France," *American Jewish Yearbook* (1973), p. 399; Meir Yoguev, "L'antisionisme dans les lycées," *L'Arche*, 26 December–25 January 1973, pp. 41–45.

166. Direction de la réglementation, 22 February 1973, 19990260, art. 23, CAC.

167. Gastaut, *L'immigration et l'opinion*, 290–95.

168. Cited in Noiriel, *Immigration, antisémitisme et racism*, 567.
169. Jews were occasionally targeted as well. Vacationing Tunisian Jews in Juan-les Pins, for example, were attacked for speaking Arabic and for loitering in a local café. Arnold Mandel, "France," *American Jewish Yearbook* (1974–75), p. 427.
170. Hajjat, "L'expérience politique," 84.
171. "Maoïstes et travailleurs immigrés," 22 October 1976, 19960311, art. 4, CAC. (Comité des travailleurs algériens), December 1984; "Soutenez le CTA," 1693W234, BdR.
172. "Avant la manifestation du 14 septembre: Le gauchisme français et les travailleurs immigrés," 12 September 1973, 19960311, art. 4, CAC.
173. CRIF meeting, 8 November 1973, MDI 146 B; "Attentat ambassade d'Algerie," Marseille, no date, MDI 146, CDJC.
174. Organisation des ouvriers tunisiens, section de Toulouse, "La victoire est aux peuples arabes combattants," MDI 219; Anonymous letter to the CRIF, 21 October 1973, same reel, CJDC. The CRIF also monitored the gauchiste newspaper *Libération* (which it accused of Palestinian backing), for stories on French Jewish attacks against Muslims. Note de Service, "Comment *Libération* nourrit la campagne raciste en France," 10 October 1973; MDI 222, CJDC.
175. Interventions IIIe journée nationale du CRIF, MDI 145, CDJC.
176. These funds came from over half of the Jewish families in France. "French Jewish Leaders under Fire," no date, MDI 146, CDJC. Also see the *BIL* report on the CRIF's pro-Israel activities in MDI 146B and "Depuis le 6 October" (no date), MDI 144, CDJC. Jews on the far left, however, remained highly critical of Israeli actions.
177. Guy Porte, "La quatrième guerre: En marge du conflit-à Marseille, Juifs et Arabes ont su éviter les pièges du racisme," 25 October 1973, *Le Monde*, p. 4. Three thousand demonstrators participated. Commissariat central de Marseille, "Note," 8 October 1973, 135W57, BdR.
178. "Les organisations d'opposants algériens nuisent-elles aux bonnes relations gouvernementales entre la France et l'Algérie?" 3 November 1973, 19960311, art. 4, CAC.
179. Commissariat central de Marseille, "Note," 8 October 1973, 135 W 57.
180. Porte, "La quatrième guerre," 4.
181. "Avant la manifestation du 14 septembre: Le gauchisme français et les travailleurs immigrés," 12 September 1973, 19960311, art. 4, CAC.
182. Porte, "La quatrième guerre," 4.
183. Aissaoui, *Immigration and National Identity*, 177, 214. Porte, "La quatrième guerre," 4.
184. "Lettre aux jeunes," Service de la jeunesse en coopération avec les services culturel et de l'enseignement du FSJU, MDI 219, CJDC. Thirty Jewish volunteers left for Israel on 25 October. Secteur sud de la police de l'air et des frontières, "Note d'information," 26 October 1973, 135W57, BdR.
185. For the meeting, see D. Allen and A. Pijpers, eds., *European Foreign Policy-Making and the Arab-Israeli Conflict* (The Hague: Martinus Nijhoff Publishers, 1984), pp. 4–5, 15. Numerous articles in MDI 159, CJDC document Jewish outrage.
186. Appel du Comité de Marseille du Conseil représentatif des institutions juives de France, MDI 159, CJDC, printed in *Le Provençal*, 18 December 1974; G. L., "Les étudiants sionistes-socialistes et la situation au Moyen-Orient," *Le Provençal*, 3 December 1974.

187. Marseille's Jewish community organized the demonstration without support from the Parisian CRIF, which local leaders criticized for its silence. M. P. Elkouby to M. A. Loss, "Manifestation sur la Canebière contre la politique française au Proche Orient le 7 novembre 1974," 8 November 1974, MDI 159, CJDC.

188. "Les associations juives de Marseille ont manifesté contre la reconnaissance de l'OLP par la France," *Le Provençal*, 8 November 1974, MDI 159, CJDC.

189. Entretien accordé le 5 novembre 1974 à une délégation du Comité de coordination des associations juives de Marseille, 135W57, BdR.

190. Romain Gary (Émile Ajar) *The Life Before Us*, trans. Ralph Manheim (New York: A New Directions Book, 1986), pp. 128–31.

191. Gary, *The Life Before Us*, 167.

192. Ibid., 31.

193. "Projet de campagne d'information en faveur de l'image d'Israel," 1976, MDI 107, CDJC.

194. ADAE efforts to suppress the MTA are in "Réorganisation de l'Amicale des Algériens en Europe pour prémunir les travailleurs algériens contre la propagande de l'ex Ligue communiste et de l'ex 'Gauche Prolétarienne,'" 10 November 1973; "Les responsables de l'Amicale des Algériens en Europe multiplient les initiatives en vue d'une plus étroite collaboration avec les autorités françaises," 26 February 1975, 19960311, art. 4, CAC. Also see Aissaoui, *Immigrant and National Identity*, 206–208.

195. Hajjat, "L'experience politique du Mouvement des travailleurs arabes," 76–85. Étude, "Maoïstes et travailleurs immigrés," 22 October 1976, 19960311, art. 4, CAC. For diminishment in pro-immigrant political movements, see Gastaut, *L'immigration et l'opinion*, 164; Wihtol de Wenden, *Les immigrés et la politique*, 216–19.

196. Some Jewish leftists, however, criticized Israel's appropriation of Jewish identity. Auron, *Les Juifs d'extrême gauche*, 198–200.

197. In March 1976, for example, the Comité de soutien aux Juifs d'URSS attacked attendees of a pro-Palestinian meeting. RG, 1 April 1976, 19980547, Article 17 (extrait Palestine), CAC.

198. J. Ph Levy to Steg, no date, MDI 146, CDJC.

Chapter 6. Particularism versus Pluriculturalism: The Birth and Death of the Anti-Racist Coalition

1. Paul Silverstein, *Algeria in France: Transpolitics, Race, and Nation* (Bloomington: Indiana University Press, 2004), pp. 151–66. The term "Beur" marked "second-generation" marginalization linguistically. Using verlan—a form of slang that inverts syllables—to transform the term "Arab" (the misappelation of their parents who were usually of Berber origin) to "Beur," "second generation" Muslims created a new identity that was neither French nor North African.

2. Gérard Noiriel, *Immigration, antisémitisme et racisme en France (XIX–XX siècle): Discours publics, humiliations privées* (Paris: Fayard 2007), pp. 589–664.

3. Noiriel, *Immigration, antisémitisme et racisme en France*, 622–24; Judith E. Vichniac, "French Socialists and *Droit à la différence*: A Changing Dynamic," *French Politics & Society* 9, 1 (1991): 410–56.

4. Joan Scott, *Politics of the Veil* (Princeton: Princeton University Press, 2007), pp. 1–2.
5. Kimberly Arkin, "'It's the French and the Arabs against the Jews': Identity Politics and the Construction of Adolescent Jewishness in France" (Ph.D. diss., University of Chicago, 2008), pp. 207–17; Pierre Birnbaum, *Jewish Destinies: Citizenship, State and Community in Modern France*, trans. Arthur Goldhammer (New York: Hill and Wang, 2000), pp. 191–213; Judith E. Vichniac, "Jewish Identity Politics and the Scarf Affairs in France," *French Politics, Culture & Society* 26, 1 (2008): 111–28.
6. Arkin, "It's the French and Arabs," 160, makes this point specifically about Jewish activism but it could be made about Beur activism as well.
7. Scholars debate the relative virulence of antisemitism and Islamophobia in the 1980s. Yvan Gastaut, *Immigration et l'opinion en France sous la Ve république* (Paris: Seuil, 2000), pp. 276–82, for example, argues that anti-Jewish attitudes—on the decline since the end of World War II—were replaced by anti-Arab hostility. In contrast, Birnbaum, *Jewish Destinies*, 185–88, downplays the specificity of anti-Arab attitudes, placing them in a longer history of French xenophobia. He nevertheless agrees that antisemitism diminished significantly. Henry Weinberg, "French Jewry: Trauma and Renewal," *Midstream* (December 1982), p. 7, denies a decrease in antisemitism.
8. Nicholas Atkin, *The Fifth French Republic* (New York: Palgrave, 2005), pp. 128–29. For an overview of the rise in such racism, see Fausto Giudice, *Arabicides, une chronique française, 1970–1991* (Paris: La Découverte, 1992).
9. Gastaut, *L'immigration et l'opinion*, 298–338.
10. Silverstein, *Algeria in France*, 106, 108; Noiriel, *Immigration, antisémitisme et racisme*, 611–13; Gastaut, *L'immigration et l'opinion*, 478–512.
11. Noiriel, *Immigration, antisémitisme et racisme*, 625–27; Gastaut, *L'immigration et l'opinion*, 133–38.
12. Birnbaum, *Jewish Destinies*, 226–27.
13. Most Jews found the FN's xenophobia too close to traditional antisemitism to be comfortable. A tiny minority nevertheless were attracted to its targeting of Muslims. Jean Charles Bloch and Robert Hemmerdinger, Comité national des français juifs, no date, MDI 188, CJDC.
14. Birnbaum, *Jewish Destinies*, 184–85. Silverstein, *Algeria in France*, 159, notes that this new wave targeted children of immigrants rather than their parents.
15. Alain Chouraqui, "Note sommaire sur les agressions antisémites en France après mai 1981," December 1982, MDI 206b, *CJDC*, reported a 31 percent rise in anti-Jewish violence from 1975 to 1980. Birnbaum, *Jewish Destinies*, 236–39, provides a compendium of attacks between 1980 and 1994. Anti-Jewish violence surged again during the 1982 war in Lebanon, most famously, with the 9 August attack on Jo Goldenberg's delicatessen. Weinberg, "French Jewry," 7–12. While this violence often originated with far-right extremist groups, some—such as the bomb at rue Copernic—was carried out by organizations based in the Middle East. Michel Wieviorka, *La tentation antisémite: Haine des Juifs dans la France d'aujourd'hui* (Paris: Robert Laffont, 2005), p. 20.
16. The MRAP changed its name to the Mouvement contre le racisme et pour l'amitié entre les peuples, while in 1979, the LICA became LICRA (the "R" for "racisme" being added to the acronym), despite some reluctance against collapsing anti-Arab racism and antisemitism. Gastaut, *L'immigration et l'opinion*, 181–84.

17. Cited in F. de Muizon, "Les Juifs de Marseille: La 'révolution' des pieds noirs," *Regard*, in (1976), MDI 159, CJDC.
18. Martine Gozlan, "Le racisme de tous les jours," *L'Arche*, February 1978, pp. 32–35.
19. Roger Ascot, "Racisme: Fantômes et réalités," December 1978, pp. 24–26. Also see "Le petit racisme de tous les jours," *L'Arche*, August 1979, pp. 96–98.
20. "Communiqué: Le CRIF face au racisme," *Tribune juive*, 22–28 June 1979.
21. Tahar Ben Jelloun, *French Hospitality: Racism and French Hospitality*, trans. Barbara Bray (New York: Columbia University Press, 1999), p. 94.
22. Doris Bensimon, *Les Juifs de France et leurs relations avec Israël: 1945–1988* (Paris: Éditions l'Harmattan, 1989), pp. 237–38; Haim Zafrani, "Le patrimoine judéo-arabe et judéo-berbère," *Cultures de France*, 11 August 1979.
23. "Festival judéo-arabe de musique," *L'Arche*, August 1979, p. 40.
24. C.G., "Racisme: Danger," *L'Arche*, February 1979, pp. 61–62.
25. For examples of the former, see Weinberg, "French Jewry under the Mitterrand Presidency," 228–41, in MDI 187, CJDC and Richard Liscia, "Le temps des terroristes," *L'Arche*, May 1982, pp. 42–44. For the latter, see Alain Chouraqui, "Note sommaire sur les agressions antisémites en France après mai 1981," December 1982, MDI 206b, CJDC.
26. Jacquot Grunewald, "La nécessité de solidarité avec les travailleurs immigrés," *Tribune juive*, 6–12 March 1980, p. 4, cited in Arkin, "It's the French and the Arabs," 199.
27. "Meeting anti-raciste du Renouveau juif à la Mutualité," *ATJ*, 26 February 1981, MDI 181, CJDC.
28. Sabine Roitman, "France" no date, MDI 187, CJDC.
29. Shmuel Trigano, "Face à la montée des périls," *L'Arche*, August 1979, pp. 99–101.
30. As Rabah Aissaoui, *Immigration and National Identity: North African Political Movements in Colonial and Postcolonial France* (London and New York: Tauris Academic Studies, 2009), pp. 181–91, makes clear, they explained bigotry as capitalism's reaction to Muslim immigrant mobilization in particular. Their approach, however, was also rooted in universalist values around class.
31. Unless noted, material on the Beur Movement is from Silverstein, *Algeria in France*, 151–66.
32. Arkin, "It's the French and Arabs," 160–217; Birnbaum, *Jewish Destinies*, 200.
33. Michel Wieviorka, "Une communauté insaisissable," *Passages*, MDI 188, CJDC.
34. By the late 1980s, 17,000 out of 100,000 Jewish school-age children (often of North African origin) were attending such schools. By 2002, the number had grown to 30,000, or one quarter of the school-age population. Arkin, "It's the French and the Arabs," 34; Birnbaum, *Jewish Destinies*, 190–94; Erik Cohen, *L'étude et l'éducation juive en France* (Paris: Le Cerf, 1991), pp. 25–27. For speculation on a Jewish vote prior to the 1980s, see *L'Arche*, January and February 1973, March 1978. Also see Sylvie Strudel, *Votes juifs: Itinéraires migratoires, religieux et politiques* (Paris: Presses de la Fondation nationale des sciences politiques, 1996).
35. As in 1967 and 1973, the CRIF proclaimed unwavering French Jewish support for Israel. Unlike previously, however, a vocal Jewish minority publicly condemned the invasion and the CRIF for claiming to speak for them. Institutional declarations of support for Israel, including the CRIF's, are found in MDI 223, CJDC. For Jewish criticism of the invasion, see "Un appel d'organisations juives progressistes pour une manifestation contre l'invasion," *Le Monde*, 15 June 1982; "Des intellectuels

juifs français dénoncent la politique de Jérusalem"; Paul Balta, "Devant l'ambassade d'Israël à Paris"; and Liliane Atlan, "Madame, c'est du poison que je voudrais," *Le Monde*, 17 June 1982, pp. 2–3. MDI 223, 224, and 225, CJDC include numerous documents attesting to the controversy. Also see Yair Auron, *Les Juifs d'extrême gauche en Mai 68*, translated from Hebrew by Katherine Werchowski (Paris: Albin Michel 1998), pp. 202–207.

36. Tahar Ben Jelloun called summer 1982 the moment Beur activists embraced the Palestinian cause in Annette Levy-Willard, "Dialogue d'en France: Marek Halter et Tahar Ben Jelloun," *Libération*, 15–16 June 1985. Also see Esther Benbassa, *La République face à ses minorités: Les Juifs hier, les Musulmans aujourd'hui* (Paris: Mille et une nuits, 2004), pp. 21–23; Jocelyne Cesari, *Être musulman en France: Associations, militants, et mosquées* (Paris: Éditions Karthala et Iremam, 1994), pp. 48–50; and Denis Sieffert, *Israël-Palestine, une passion française: La France dans le miroir du conflit israélo-palestinien* (Paris: Éditions la Decouverte, 2004), pp. 30–31.

37. Cited in Jelloun, *French Hospitality*, 93.

38. "Mobilisons-nous pour soutenir le peuple palestinien," Box Bibliothèque, UEJF. This file also holds documentation protesting Israeli actions from the Comité Liban de soutien à l'Association libanaise d'action populaire and the Centre international d'information sur les prisonniers, déportés et disparus palestiniens et libanais.

39. "Recrutement de volontaires et soutien aux Palestiniens," 7 July 1982; "Solidarité et manoeuvres frauduleuses," 9 July 1982; "Collecte de fonds et départs de volontaires," 19 July 1982 19980547, art. 17 (extrait: Palestine), CAC. Documentation of the pro-Palestinian groups that raised awareness that summer is located in Box Bibliothèque, UEJF.

40. "Motion pour la paix au proche-orient de la commnauté israélite de Belfort" (June 1982), MDI 223, CJDC. Various press accounts concurred, including "Manifestation 'contre l'agression israélienne au Liban': Les syndicats appellent à une solidarité active," *L'Est républicain*, 1 July 1982; and Luc Rosenzweig, "Les Feujs mettent la main à la pâte: Entraînée par ses étudiants, la communauté juive oublie le keffié des Beurs," *Libération*, 15–16 June 1985.

41. Appel, no date, MDI 223, CJDC.

42. Fernard I. cited in Jacques Frémontier, *L'étoile rouge de David: Les Juifs communistes en France* (Paris: Fayard, 2002), pp. 261–62.

43. J. P. Kapel, "Français, Arabe de France et fier de l'être," *Libération*, 31 July–1 August 1982. See Patrick Jarreau, "Les controverses sur la politique israélienne provoquent une crise au sein de la communauté juive française," *Le Monde*, 16–17 October 1983, for the fissures this incident created among Jews over the legitmacy of criticizing Israel.

44. "Une étrange conception du nazisme," *Le Monde*, 2 June 1982. Istiqlal denied links between the author's opinions and those of the party. Said Fatm, "Le Nazisme: Création du Sionisme," *L'Opinion*, 30 May 1982. "Non à l'amalgame," *L'Opinion*, 6 June 1982. Mhamed Douiri, Ministre du plan, de la formation des cadres, et de la formation professionnelle, Maroc, to André Azoulay, Identité et dialogue, 21 June 1982, MDI 182; Alain de Rothschild to Youssef Ben Abbes, Ambassadeur du Royaume du Maroc, 2 June 1982, MDI 182E, CJDC.

45. Brigitte Kantor, "Le 'Sabra et Chatila Tranquille' des 'Beurs,'" *Le Matin*, 4 December 1983.

46. Valeie Serfati, "Bilan antisémitisme," *Amphi J*, December 1981, Section de Strasbourg: Archives administratives/Toulouse, UEJF.

47. A focus on the links between antisemitism and anti-Zionism helped legitimize such views. See, for example, David Benizri, "L'antisionisme: Nouveau prétexte à l'antisemitisme?" *Amphi J*, December 1981.

48. Annie Kriegel, "Parler vrai," *L'Arche*, January 1984, pp. 79–83.

49. Adam Loss, "Une France pluriculturelle?" *L'Arche*, January 1984, p. 9.

50. Richard Liscia, "Nous sommes tous des Maghrébins," *L'Arche*, August–September 1984, pp. 52–53.

51. Romain Garbaie, *Getting into Local Power: The Politics of Ethnic Minorities in British and French Cities* (Malden, Mass.: Wiley-Blackwell, 2006), p. 77.

52. Cited in Eric Favereau, "SOS racisme au tournant: Des potes s'en mêlent," *Libération*, 10 May 1985.

53. Gastaut, *L'immigration et l'opinion*, 184–88.

54. Bernard-Henri Lévy as cited in Robert Solé, "SOS racisme victime de son succès: Touche pas à mon badge," *Le Monde*, 30 March 1985.

55. Cited in Annette Levy-Willard, "Dialogue d'en France: Marek Halter et Tahar Ben Jelloun," *Libération*, 15–16 June 1985.

56. Invitation, " 'Je ne suis pas raciste mais': Il n'y a pas de mais," MDI 207, CJDC. Claude Askolovitch, "Respecte l'étranger," *L'Arche*, April 1985, p. 48; Eric Favereau, "SOS racisme au tournant: des potes s'en mêlent," *Libération*, 10 May 1985. Lévy and Halter had years of involvement in French Jewish politics, and Halter had worked since the 1960s to promote dialogue between Israelis and Palestinians. Bensimon, *Les Juifs de France*, 237–38.

57. Michel Chemin, "Lifting pour l'antiracisme: SOS racisme, la dernière née des associations antiracistes veut démontrer que la société multiraciale existe," *Libération*, 20 February 1985; Roselyne Posnanski, "Racisme: SOS politique," *La Croix*, 23 February 1985.

58. Eric Ghébali, "Moi, je ne suis pas raciste mais, il n'y a pas de mais. On est raciste ou on ne l'est pas," reprinted in *Amphi J*, May–June 1985, p. 5.

59. Cited in Arkin, "It's the French and the Arabs," 172.

60. Marc Bitton, "Le sens d'un engagement," *Amphi J*, November 1985. Bitton's article was written to justify adhesion to SOS racisme for critics *within* the UEJF. The UEJF almost vetoed the iconic symbol of SOS racisme, which they found "too Beur" due to its invocation of the hand of Fatma, the palm-shaped amulet popular throughout the Middle East and North Africa as a defense against the evil eye. Eric Favereau, "La génération d'un Must," *Libération*, 13 June 1985.

61. D.J., "Étudiants juifs: Le congrès de la relance," XVIIème congrès national, Strasbourg 7–10 November 1980, UEJF. Juif en France, *Agence télégraphique juive*, 13 November 1980, XVIIème congrès national, Strasbourg 7–10 November 1980, UEJF.

62. "Exorciser la peur d'autres," no date, Section de Strasbourg, Archives administratives/Toulouse, UEJF.

63. The 1982 figure comes from "Interview avec Eric Sprung, président de UEJF," *Le Journal de l'UEJF*, March 1982, Section de Strasbourg: Archives administratives/Toulouse, UEJF. Eric Ghébali, "Ne touche pas à notre indépendance," *Amphi J*, May–June 1985, p. 2.

64. "Dossier sponsor et promotion publicitaire," Union des étudiants juifs de France, XIème congrès, Paris, 24–27 March 1988, Binder: Bitton, Marc I (06/05086-27/03/88), UEJF.

65. This commitment was clear in November 1980 at the first national congress since 1976. Motions, XVIIème congrès national, Strasbourg, 7–10 November 1980, UEJF.

66. D.J., "Étudiants juifs: Le congrès de la relance," XVIIème congrès national, Strasbourg, 7–10 November 1980, UJEF.

67. Materials in the UEJF archives point to the attack on the kosher restaurant in Paris as the impetus behind the new organizational strength. "De l'intérêt d'être syndiqué, Union générale des étudiants de Strasbourg," Section de Strasbourg: Archives administratives/Toulouse, UEJF. Materials on the first national congress come from, D.J., "Étudiants juifs: Le congrès de la relance," XVIIème congrès national, Strasbourg, 7–10 November 1980, UJEF.

68. Under his leadership, the organization held a conference on "Europe et Israël—Politique et culture" in December 1983 for eight hundred students from sixteen countries, demanded that the government denounce the PLO as a detriment to Middle East peace, and railed against Jewish passivity before rising antisemitism. Report, Colloque européen, Europe et Israël: Politique et culture, December 1983; "La France doit reconnaître le véritable visage de l'OLP," Dossier OLP, Box Ghébali; Colette Partoche, "La vie de l'UEJF: Antisémitisme," Amphi J, December 1983, Section de Strasbourg: Archives administratives/Toulouse, UEJF.

69. "Ghébali Président: Élections nationales de l'UEJF Ghébali: 17 voix," Le Journal de l'UEJF, February 1983, Box Ghébali, UEJF.

70. Katia D. Kaupp, "SOS racisme: La main magique, Le Nouvel observateur, 5 April 1985, pp. 21–22; "La France, est-elle vraiment raciste?" Le Point, 8 April 1985, p. 58.

71. Cited in Daniel Schneidermann, "Juifs et Arabes, même combat?" Le Monde, 4 April 1985, p. 8. The UEJF visually cemented this relationship on the cover of its journal in May/June 1985. The image, which carried the title, "Touche pas à mon pote," depicted the murder in Menton by showing a man holding a pistol to the head of a wounded Beur. The SOS racisme badge stood behind both, shot through with bullets and dripping blood. Chapters in the provinces similarly declared a commitment to the anti-racist agenda. Amphi J, May–June 1985; Charlie Bensemhoun, "Toulouse tient ses promesses," Amphi J, November 1985.

72. Jacquot Gruenwald, "De la rue Copernic en 1980 à la rue de Rivoli en 1985: Les étapes de l'espoir," Tribune juive, 5–11 April 1985, p. 17, cited in Arkin, "It's the French and the Arabs," 198.

73. Daniel Schneidermann, "Juifs et Arabes, même combat?" Le Monde, 4 April 1985, p. 8.

74. Robert Solé, "SOS racisme victime de son succès: Touche pas à mon badge," Le Monde, 30 March 1985.

75. Serge July, "L'antiracisme ne se partage pas," Libération, 1 April 1985.

76. Annette Levy-Willard, "Dialogue d'en France: Marek Halter et Tahar Ben Jelloun," Libération, 15–16 June 1985.

77. E.F., "Initiative spectaculaire dans un cadre précis: Des personnalités arabes appuient l'initiative anti-Bitburg de SOS racisme," Libération, 2 and 5 May 1985.

78. Cited in Agathe Logeart, "La marche des jeunes Juifs de France et de SOS racisme: 'Ni haine ni oubli,'" Le Monde, 2 May 1985.

79. Marek Halter, "Eh Gorbatchev, les Juifs d'URSS sont aussi nos potes!" *Amphi J*, November 1985. This article and several others defending Soviet Jews ran under the heading, "SOS racisme / Touche pas à mon pote."

80. SOS racisme to Mme Sabine Roitman, CRIF, 3 October (1985), MDI 207 CJDC; Philippe Bernard, "La main dans la main," *Le Monde*, 25 June 1985. Journalists documented large numbers of Jewish high school students selling SOS racisme's badge. Luc Rosenzweig, "Les Feujs mettent la main à la pâte: Entraînée par ses étudiants, la communauté juive oublie le keffié des Beurs," *Libération*, 15–16 June 1985.

81. Mylene Sebbah, "Le Juif et l'Arabe," *L'Arche*, July 1985, pp. 22–23.

82. Claude Regent, "La voix des jeunes arabes de Lyon," *Le Monde*, 2 December 1985.

83. Daniel Schneidermann, "Juifs et Arabes, même combat?" *Le Monde*, 4 April 1985, p. 8, Eric Favereau, "SOS racisme au tournant: Des potes s'en mêlent," *Libération*, 10 May 1985, and Philippe Bernard, "Une grande fête de SOS racisme le 15 Juin: La nuit de la Concorde," *Le Monde*, June 1985.

84. Cited in Eric Favereau, "Le soutien des associations juives," *Libération*, 6 December 1985.

85. Jean-Francois Moruzzi, "Incidents entre étudiants juifs et pro-palestiniens à Jussieu," *Quotidien de Paris*, clipping with no date; "Meeting de l'UEJF à la faculté de Jussieu," ATJ, 18 February 1985; "Jussieu: Des étudiants pro-palestiniens contre des étudiants juifs," *Libération*, clipping with no date, Box Amphi J, UEJF. Ongoing struggles between the UEJF and pro-Palestinian organizations on campus are documented in *Amphi J*, June/July 1988, Box Amphi J; Communiqué, 30 March 1990, Box Bensehoun, Arié, 27/3/88-00/01/90, UEJF.

86. "Racisme et Palestine vaincra," *Droit et vivre* (March 1986), MDI 211, CJDC.

87. Cited in Eric Favereau, "SOS racisme au tournant: Des potes s'en mêlent," *Libération*, 10 May 1985. Delorme also faulted SOS racisme for turning racial attacks into a media circus.

88. SIONA, B'nai Brith, Renouveau juif, Fédération des Juifs de France, Éclaireurs israélites de France, and Identité et dialogue, also offered support. Eric Favereau, "Le soutien des associations juives," *Libération*, 6 December 1985.

89. Claude Askolovitch, "Respecte l'étrangère," *L'Arche*, April 1985, p. 48.

90. Elvis Journo, "Est-ce bon pour nous?" *Journal de B'nai B'rith*, June–July 1985. Block was on record for asserting that the struggle against racism, whether targeted at Arabs or Jews was the same, although the organization directed most of its efforts to fighting antisemitism. Roger Ascot and Haïm Musicant, "Contre tous les racismes," *L'Arche*, August 1983, pp. 50–51.

91. Eric Favereau, "Le soutien des associations juives," *Libération*, 6 December 1985.

92. Richard Liscia, "Le racisme nous connaissons," *L'Arche*, May 1985, pp. 59–60.

93. Elvis Journo, "Est-ce bon pour nous?" *Journal de B'nai B'rith*, June–July 1985; Eric Favereau, "SOS racisme au tournant: Des potes s'en mêlent," *Libération*, 10 May 1985. In an October 1985 speech, Klein insisted that the Jews' experiences during World War II compelled them to fight for the rights and dignity of all, including particularly North African immigrants. Théo Klein, "Le droit de s'exprimer et la responsabilité de le faire," published in *CRIF Rencontres*, 19–20 November 1985, p. 11, MDI 133, CJDC.

94. Jean Paul Elkann, "Le Judaïsme! Une Mosaïque?" *Haboné*, August/September 1985, p. 31.

95. "Un débat sur la solidarité entre Juifs et Arabes," clipping with no title or date; "Appel judéo-arabe contre le racisme et l'antisémitisme," 9 June early 1980s, MDI 207, CJDC.

96. Elvis Journo, "Est-ce bon pour nous?" *Journal de B'nai B'rith*, June–July 1985; Eric Favereau, "Débat cartes sur table entre SOS racisme et les Beurs," *Libération*, 13 May 1985; Luc Rosenzweig, "Les Feujs mettent la main à la pâte: Entraînée par ses étudiants, la communauté juive oublie le keffié des Beurs," *Libération*, 15–16 June 1985.

97. Annette Levy-Willard, "Dialogue d'en France: Marek Halter et Tahar Ben Jelloun," *Libération*, 15–16 June 1985.

98. Philippe Bernard, "La main dans la main," *Le Monde*, 25 June 1985. Disagreements within SOS racisme nevertheless emerged, such as when Kaïssa Titous criticized Bernard-Herni Lévy—both prominent members of SOS racisme—for arguing that anti-Zionism rendered antisemitism acceptable. "Antisémitisme," *Droit et vivre* (March 1986), MDI 211, CJDC.

99. Eric Favereau, "'Divergences 85' pour les deux marches de l'anti-racisme," *Libération*, 18 October 1985. For divisions *within* the Beur Movement, see Eric Favereau and Nicolas Beau, "Loin de SOS, la marche des Beurs implose," *Libération*, 30 October 1985.

100. Eric Landal, "Julien Dray: 'SOS racisme' veut s'appuyer sur toutes les communautés," *Libération*, 22 October 1985. In late November, representatives from SOS racisme and the Beur Movement agreed to march together to the Place de la Concorde. Didier François, "Beurs et potes bras dessus bras dessous," *Libération*, 22 November 1985.

101. Eric Favereau, "Le dialogue de deux exils," *Libération*, 6 December 1985.

102. André Wormser to Théo Klein, 10 April 1985, MDI 211, CJDC. See also Jean Yves Camus, "Contre tous les racismes: Le C.E.R.A.C., la crise et la montée des périls," *L'Arche*, May 1985, p. 60.

103. A. Wormser, Centre d'études et de recherches sur l'antisémitisme contemporain, N° 9, September–October 1986, MDI 211, CJDC. The CERAC's increasing interest in France's North African population and its attitudes toward fundamentalism, Jews, and the Middle East is documented in MDI 212, CJDC, particularly André Wormser and Nelly Hansson to Cher(e) Ami(e), 4 June 1986. The CRIF also started paying closer attention to France's Muslim population, evident in numerous clippings on Islam, Muslim politics, and Beur radio stations in MDI 182, CJDC.

104. Annie Kriegel, "Juifs et Musulmans," *L'Arche*, March 1987, pp. 28–31.

105. See, for example, Ivan Levaï, "Les dessous du je: Raciste, antisémite"; and Pierre Birnbaum, "Rétro: National-populisme et antisémitisme," *L'Arche*, October 1987, pp. 22–23, 44–45.

106. Annie Kriegel, "Le vrai danger," *L'Arche*, November 1987, pp. 28–30.

107. Michel Gurfinkiel, "L'Islam contemporain et les Juifs" (Paris: Comité d'initiative pour Israël, [1987]), MDI 182, CJDC.

108. "Antisémitisme, faits et analyse" (1988), MDI 270, CJDC. An Islamic bookstore in Lyon also carried copies. "Intégrisme islamique et antisémitisme," *Le Monde*, 8 February 1987.

109. "Beurs-Feujs: Garre aux excès," *Lettre d'information: David*, September 1988. In "Le silence des intellectuels arabes," *Le Nouvel observateur*, 11 February 1985, Jean

Daniel, editor of *Nouvel obvsevateur* and of Algerian Jewish origin, spoke of radio propaganda seeking to raise questions for Arab immigrants about the Holocaust's veracity.

110. Pierre Birnbaum, "Les Beurs et la République," *L'Arche*, December 1987, pp. 84–85.

111. Gastaut, *L'immigration et l'opinion*, 133–35.

112. Ibid., 545–61. See Miriam Feldblum, *Reconstructing Citizenship: The Politics of Nationality Reform and Immigration in Contemporary France* (Albany: State University of New York Press, 1999), for the roots of this process.

113. Scott, *The Politics of the Veil*, 22–23, Silverstein, *Algeria in France*, 132–33, 139–42; Patrick Weil, *La France et ses étrangers: L'aventure d'une politique de l'immigration, 1938–1991* (Paris: Calmann-Lévy, 1991), p. 287; Noiriel, *Immigration, antisémitisme et racisme*, 628.

114. Silverstein, *Algeria in France*, 165–73.

115. *La Lettre de France plus*, 1 February 1989, MDI 181, CJDC.

116. Gastaut, *Immigration et l'opinion*, 184–88.

117. Alec G. Hargreaves, *Immigration, Race, and Ethnicity in Contemporary France* (London; New York: Routledge, 1995), pp. 144–48. Hargreaves makes clear that despite fighting for opportunities for North Africans who suffered from discrimination, France plus did not expect its political candidates to pursue an ethnic agenda and instead supported "integration." Also see, Garbaie, *Getting into Local Power*, 77.

118. "Répression en Palestine des organisations girondines réagissent," *Sud-Ouest*, 31 December 1987.

119. Farid Aïchoune, "La logique des sourds," *Le Monde*, January 1988, MDI 181, CJDC.

120. "Les Beurs de France, les Arabes de Palestine," *Libération*, 3 March 1988.

121. Farid Aïchoune, "La logique des sourds," *Le Monde*, January 1988, MDI 181, CJDC.

122. "Les Beurs de France, les Arabes de Palestine," *Libération*, 3 March 1988.

123. Jean-Michel Caradech, "Juifs de France: Le désarroi. Une communauté troublée par les images de la violence, même si la fidélité à Israël ne se discute pas," *L'Express*, 19–25 February 1988.

124. Dominique Audibert, "Juifs français: La déchirure," *Le Point*, 18 February 1988. For other examples, see Jean-Moise Brattberg, "France: Une communauté partagée entre le désarroi et l'amertume," *Quotidien de Paris*, 14 January 1988; "Juifs: Le grand désarroi," *Le Nouvel observateur*, 19–25 February 1988; "Les Juifs français face au drame israélien," *L'Événement*, 3–10 February 1988. Théo Klein, "Un peu de modération et de justice," *Le Monde*, 12 January 1988, p. 2, expressed frustration over media portrayals of Israel. While not fully condoning Israeli policies, Klein emphasized multiple "guilty parties."

125. For criticisms, see "Appel de Juifs pour la défense des droit de l'homme dans les territoires occupés et en Israël," *Le Monde*, 20 January 1988, p. 11.

126. "Appel: Arabes et Juifs pour la paix," *Le Monde*, 22 February 1988.

127. Alain Léauthier, "Palestine: Poussée de fièvre chez les Beurs," *Libération*, clipping with no date, MDI 181, CJDC.

128. "Les Beurs de France, les Arabes de Palestine," *Libération*, 3 March 1988.

129. "Bensemhoun-Dahmani: Attention aux dérapages!" *L'Express*, July 1988, reprinted in *Amphi J*, June–July 1988.

130. Alain Léauthier, "Palestine: Poussée de fièvre chez les Beurs," *Libération*, clipping with no date, MDI 181, CJDC.

131. Cited in "Désapprouvant une prise de position sur le Proche-Orient: L'Union des étudiants juifs va reconsidérer; ses relations avec SOS racisme," *Le Monde*, 26 April 1988.

132. Rafaële Rivais, "A son deuxième congrès national: SOS racisme trouve un compromis entre Juifs et Arabes," *Le Monde*, 5 April 1988.

133. Monique Ayoun, "SOS racisme: Les Feujs et les Beurs," *L'Arche*, May 1988, pp. 63–64. Jewish fears of Le Pen spiked in spring 1988 as is evident in the numerous articles in *L'Arche*. While most focused on the meaning of Le Pen's showing for France and for Jews, Richard Liscia ("Le parti du malheur," pp. 69–70) called on Jews to defend Arabs.

134. Emphasis mine. "Congrès malgré," *Amphi J*, June–July 1988.

135. "Bensemhoun-Dahmani: Attention aux dérapages!" *L'Express*, July 1988 (Reprinted in *Amphi J*, June–July 1988). Alain Léauthier, "Palestine: Poussée de fièvre chez les Beurs," *Libération*, clipping with no date, MDI 181, CJDC. A.B., "Des Juifs et des Beurs appellent au dialogue," *Le Quotidien de Paris*, 11 February 1988; N.B. "Quand les Beurs rencontrent les Sépharades," *Politis, le citoyen*, 18 February 1988.

136. Etienne Gau, "La paix maintenant: Des Juifs et des Maghrébins de France ouvrent le dialogue," *La Croix*, 18 February 1988.

137. "Une France unie pour l'intégration," *La Lettre de France plus*, 1 February 1989, MDI 181, CJDC.

138. See, for example, Benjamin Stora's interview with Arezki Dahmani and Farid Aïchone in *Passages*, 1988 (MDI 181, CJDC). The pro-dialogue context also facilitated a public debate between Théo Klein, president of CRIF, and Hamadi Essid, head of the Arab League's mission in Paris, on the Israeli/ Palestinian conflict. Hamadi Essid and Théo Klein, *Deux vérités en face: Un dialogue* (Paris: Lieu commun, 1988), p. 7.

139. "Beurs-Feujs: La rencontre événement d'octobre," *Passages*, 17 October 1988.

140. "Bensemhoun-Dahmani: Attention aux dérapages!" *L'Express*, July 1988, reprinted in *Amphi J*, June–July 1988.

141. "Première rencontre entre Arabes et Juifs en France," MDI 182, CJDC. Tegouva, Département de la jeunesse et du Héhaloutz to Chers Amis, 19 November 1988, *Amphi J*, UEJF.

142. The organization continued to work with SOS racisme *and* France plus. Nevertheless, 1987/1988 saw a shift in the UEJF's willingness to submerge its interests in the wider anti-racist movement. "Beurs-Feujs: La rencontre événement d'octobre," *Passages*, 17 October 1988.

143. After his presidency, Ghébali had a falling-out with the UEJF, resulting in the removal of his title as honorary president (awarded to all former presidents). Marc Bitton to Tous les responsables de section and toutes les institutions juives de France, 17 March 1988, MDI 188, CJDC; "Chers amis," no date, Marc I (06/05/86-27/03/88), UEJF; "Les états généraux des étudiants juifs parisiens," no date, Binder Bitton, Marc I (06/05/86-27/03/88), UEJF; Arié Behsemhoun to Mme Sabine Roitman, 1 January 1988, MDI 188 CJDC.

144. "Dialogue difficile entre Beurs et Feujs à l'occasion du premier colloque judéo-arabe en France," *AFP*, 11 October 1988.

145. David Francés, "Des Juifs et les Beurs," *L'Arche*, November 1988, pp. 56–57, accused the event of being a publicity stunt and largely inconsequential.

146. Lionel Raux, "Le dialogue des 'Beurs' et 'Feujs,' " *L'Est républicain*, 6 October 1988. Elsewhere, Touïsi emphasized even stronger links with Jews: "I grew up with Jews. When I see them beside other French men and women, they are the ones most like me." Alain Léauthier, "Palestine: Poussée de fièvre chez les Beurs," *Libération*, clipping with no date, MDI 181, CJDC.

147. Valérie Colin, "Rencontre Beurs-Feujs: La démocratie à l'endroit," *Amphi J*, January–February 1989, p. 30.

148. François Devinat, "Dialogue à haut risque entre les Beurs et les Feujs," *Libération*, 12 October 1988; Robert Solé, "Une rencontre inédite à Paris, Arabes et Juifs face à face," *Le Monde*, 13 October 1988. See also Étienne Gau, "Rencontre judéo-arabe: Premières pierres d'un dialogue," *La Croix*, 14 October 1988.

149. François Devinat, "Dialogue à haut risque entre les Beurs et les Feujs," *Libération*, 12 October 1988.

150. "Dialogue difficile entre Beurs et Feujs à l'occasion du premier colloque judéo-arabe en France," *AFP*, 11 October 1988.

151. By late 1980s, SOS racisme had moved to a similar construction. Harlem Désir and SOS racisme, *SOS désirs* (Paris: Calmann Lévy, 1987).

152. "Beurs-Feujs: La rencontre événement d'octobre," *Passages*, 17 October 1988.

153. Jean-Moïse Braitberg, "Juifs-Arabes: Un premier dialogue, *Le Quotidien de Paris*, 11 October (circa 1988), clipping in MDI 182, CJDC.

154. Report, Marc Rochman, Binder Bitton, Marc I (circa 1988) (06/05/86-27/03/88), UEJF.

155. Albert Jorevitch, "La courte échelle," *L'Arche*, November 1988, p. 57, criticized this pro-Palestinian stance.

156. Jacqueline Keller, "Rapport moral et d'activités, présenté à l'assemblée générale du 19 novembre 1989," MDI 125, CJDC. In a communiqué, 18 August 1989, same file, Kahn also decried anti-Muslim activities.

157. Arkin, "It's the French and the Arabs," 197. See, for example, Annie Kriegel, "Ça compte pour du beurre?" *L'Arche*, November 1988, pp. 26–29.

158. Scott, *Politics of the Veil*, passim.

159. Gastaut, *Immigration et l'opinion*, 512–18.

160. Unless noted, discussion of Jewish responses to the head-scarf controversy comes from Birnbaum, *Jewish Destinies*, 200–13, and Vichniac, "Jewish Identity Politics and the Scarf Affairs in France," 111–28.

161. Discours de Marc Rochman, president de l'UEJF au troisième congrès de SOS racisme, le 30 avril 1990 à Longjumeau, Rochman, M., Correspondances, 1990 (Janv.–Juin I), UEJF.

162. Annie Kriegel, "La marginalisation," *L'Arche*, December 1989, pp. 21–22, also criticized Rabbi Sitruck for drawing unsubstantiated equivalencies. Figure comes from Scott, *The Politics of the Veil*, 3.

163. The CRIF's rather equivocal position emphasized the organization's commitment to state secularism while also calling for greater compromise around individual religious commitment. Déclaration du président du CRIF, 23 October 1989; Jean Kahn, Adresse au premier ministre, 18 November 1989; Jacqueline Keller, Rapport moral et d'activités, présenté à l'assemblée générale du 19 novembre 1989, MDI 125, CJDC.

164. Richard Liscia, "De la liberté," *L'Arche*, December 1989, p. 43.

165. For a Jewish focus on Muslim "foreignness," see Arkin, "It's the French and the Arabs," 209–21.

166. Shmuel Trigano, "Notre continuité," *L'Arche*, January 1990, pp. 75–76. In the same edition, Kriegel again challenged comparisons between Arab-Muslims and Jews in France.

167. Birnbaum, *Jewish Destinies*, 231–50.

168. Noiriel, *Immigration, antisémitisme et racisme*, 323.

169. Benjamin Stora, "Dialoguer," *L'Express*, 13 October 1989.

170. "Racisme: M. Rocard a reçu le président du CRIF," *Le Monde*, 12 October 1989.

171. Discours de Monsieur Jean Kahn, président du CRIF au troisième congrès de SOS racisme, 28, 29 30 avril 1990 à Longjumeau, MDI 208, CJDC. Some of Kahn's efforts to fight racism are documented in Jacqueline Keller, directrice de CRIF, to Cher Monsieur, Chère Madame, 24 January 1990, Rochman (1990/91)—Institutions juives; Institutions publiques I, UEJF. Arezki Dahmani to CRIF, 5 April 1990; Jean Kahn to Arezki Dahmani, 23 April 1990, MDI 182; Déclaration de M. Jean Kahn, président du CRIF, 27 March 1990, MDI 208, CJDC.

172. Discours de Marc Rochman, président de l'UEJF au troisième congrès de SOS racisme, le 30 avril 1990 à Longjumeau, Rochman, M., Correspondances, 1990 (Janv.–Juin I), UEJF.

173. Pierre Birnbaum, "Les Juifs, nouveaux boucs émissaires," *L'Arche*, November 1990, p. 60, claimed that antisemitism increased as well while Annie Kriegel, "Notre après-guerre," *L'Arche*, March 1990, pp. 21–22, argued that the French public supported Israel and the Jews.

174. For French Muslim diversity on the war, see Gastaut, *L'immigration et l'opinion*, 441.

175. Gastaut, *L'immigration et l'opinion*, 436–42; Noiriel, *Immigration, antisémitisme et racisme*, 624–25.

176. "Crise du Golfe—État de l'opinion publique des Bouches-du-Rhône," 16 January 1991, 1693W239, BDR.

177. Articles by Dominique le Guilledoux, *Le Monde*, 16, 17, and 24 January 1991. See Silverstein, *Algeria in France*, 130–35, for the Plan Vigipirate's role in criminalizing Muslims later in the decade.

178. "L'entretien télévisé du chef de l'état," *Le Monde*, 22 January 1991, p. 13.

179. Gastaut, *L'immigration et l'opinion*, 438.

180. First citation from Robert P. Vigouroux and Jacques Ouaknin, *Laïcité + religions: Marseille-Espérance* (Marseille: Transbordeurs, 2004), p. 41. *L'Autre journal*, 9 February 1991, cited in Gastaut, *L'immigration et l'opinion*, 438.

181. The chief rabbi also cosigned a petition with the rector of the Mosquée de Paris calling for intercommunal calm. H.T., "Veillées de prières en France," *Le Monde*, 16 January 1991, p. 10.

182. Marc Rochman to tous les responsables, 21 January 1991, Rochman (1991)—17/10/91, Correspondances, UEJF. "Crise dans le Golfe persique: Réactions de l'opinion publique des Bouches-du-Rhône," 14 December 1990; "Réactions de l'opinion publique des Bouches-du-Rhône à la tension dans le Golfe persique et aux perspectives de guerre," 8 January 1991; "Crise du Golfe—État de l'opinion publique des Bouches-du-Rhône," 16 January 1991, 1693W239, BdR.

183. "État d'esprit de la communauté musulmane à l'approche de l'expiration de l'ultimatum du 15/1/91," 14 January 1991; "Crise du Golfe—État de l'opinion publique des Bouches-du-Rhône," 16 January 1991, 1693W239, BdR.

184. Cited in Bernard Philippe, "Les Beurs entre la fierté et la crainte," *Le Monde*, 17 January 1991, p. 9.

185. As documents in Bensehoun, Arié, 27/3/88-00/01/90 and Rochman M., Corre-spondances, 1990 (Janv.—Juin I), UEJF, attest, the UEJF and SOS racisme created an Observatoire de l'antisémitisme in 1989, and published a brochure on the Ho-locaust for secondary schools and universities in 1990. However, they clashed in May 1989 when President Mitterrand officially welcomed Yassir Arafat to Paris. See Benjamin Stora, "Dialoguer," *L'Express*, 13 October 1989. XXIème congres, 24–31 December 1989, Box Bensemoun, Arié, 27/3/88-00/01/90; UEJF.

186. SOS racisme et Fédération indépendante et démocratique lycéenne (FIDL), "Ar-rêtez la guerre," 21 January 1991, Rochman, M. Correspondances 1990 (Juillet–Dec.) II, UEJF. Muslim-Jewish links in SOS racisme were further undermined in 1990 when Serge Malik, one early leader, accused SOS racisme's top leadership of encouraging UEJF participation in order to marginalize Beur activists. In Malik's version, SOS racisme capitalized on Muslim-Jewish tensions as a way to seem in-clusive while pushing aside those who might interfere with the leadership's ambi-tions. Although Malik's text was dismissed as the ramblings of a bitter man, the organization's image as a space in which Muslims and Jews could work together had been further compromised. Serge Malik, *L'histoire secrète de SOS racisme* (Paris: Éditions Albin Michel, 1990), p. 89. The UEJF's dismissal of Malik's analysis is evident in Alain Kisermann, "Résumé de l'histoire secrète de SOS racisme,'" no date, Rochman, M. Correspondances 1990 (Juillet–Décembre) II, UEJF.

187. Bernard Philippe, "Le recentrage de SOS-racisme," *Le Monde*, 2 February 1991, p. 7. Eric Ghébali and Marek Halter stayed affiliated while expressing anger at Désir's position.

188. The UEJF's relationship with Israel intensified at the end of the 1980s as docu-ments in Bensehoun, Arié, 27/3/88-00/01/90; Rochman, M. Correspondances, 1990 (Janv.—Juin I); and Rochman (1991)—17/10/91, Correspondances, UEJF, make clear.

189. SOS racisme, Communiqué, 18 January 1991; UEJF, "Communiqué no. 1," 18 Janu-ary 1991, Rochman (1991)—17/10/91, Correspondances, UEJF.

190. "Les potes penchent vers le pacifisme et perdent leurs parrains," *Actualité juive*, 21 January 1991.

191. Minutes, 3 February 1991; Marc Rochman to tous les présidents de section, 22 February 1991; Belaich, Président villetaneuse to Cher ami, 11 March 1991; Serge Vatine, Responsable national de la collecte to tous les présidents, 12 March 1991; Rochman to Jean Kahn, 17 April 1991; Marc Rochman to Raphy Bensimon, Di-recteur general du l'AUJF, 16 July 1991, Rochman (1991)—17/10/91, Correspon-dances, UEJF. Invitation, Rochman, M., J'aime Israël, Paris le 14 Avril 1991, UEJF.

192. "Premier bilan de la confrontation armée dans le Golfe pour la communauté mu-sulmane," 6 March 1991; "Crise du Golfe—Réactions de l'opinion publique des Bouches-du-Rhône," 28 January 1991, 1693W239, BdR; Maud Mandel, "The War Comes Home: Muslim/Jewish Relations in Marseille during the 1991 Gulf War," in *Israeli-Palestinian Conflict in the Francophone World*, ed. Nathalie Debrauwere-Miller (New York: Routledge, 2010): 163–79.

193. "Crise du Golfe—État de l'opinion publique des Bouches-du-Rhône," 15 January 1991; Vigouroux and Ouaknin, *Laïcité + religions*.

194. "Conflit du Golfe—Réactions de l'opinion publique des Bouches-du-Rhône," 18 January 1991; "Conflit dans le Golfe—Réactions de la communauté juive dans

la région Provence, Alpes, Côte d'Azur," 19 January 1991; "Conflit du Golfe—Réactions de l'opinion publique de la région Provence-Alpes-Côte d'Azur," 21 January 1991, 1693W239, BdR.

195. Gastaut, *Immigration et opinion*, 441; Henri Tincq, "Selon un sondage de l'IFOP incertitude et peur chez les Musulmans en France," *Le Monde*, 30 January 1991, p. 9.

196. "Crise du Golfe—Réactions de la communauté musulmane," 26 January 1991, 1693W239, BdR.

197. Jocelyne Cesari, "Les modes d'action collective des Musulmans en France: Le cas particulier de Marseille," in Bruno Étienne, ed., *L'Islam en France: Islam, état et société* (Paris: Éditions du Centre national de la recherche scientifique, 1991): 282–94.

198. "Communauté islamique de Marseille: État d'esprit des responsables associatifs," 25 February 1991, 1693W239, BdR.

199. "Premier bilan de la confrontation armée dans le Golfe pour la communauté musulmane," 6 March 1991, 1693W239, BdR.

200. "Premier bilan de la confrontation armée dans le Golfe pour la communauté musulmane," 6 March 1991, 1693W239, BdR.

201. Annie Kriegel, "Notre après-guerre," *L'Arche*, March 1991, pp. 21–22, even attributed Muslims' relatively muted response to the war to an understanding that France stood with Jews and Israel.

202. During the Gulf War, the rare pluricultural appeal was still heard. See, for example, "Juifs et Arabes retrouvent une mémoire commune," *Libération*, 23–24 February 1991.

203. Garbaie, *Getting into Local Power*, 77.

204. Silverstein, *Algeria in France*, 173–74.

205. Arkin, "It's the French and the Arabs," passim.

206. Relevant documents in 1992, Vive émotion dans la communauté juive; Cohen, Francis 1992: Correspondances I, UEJF.

207. Documents in Pinto S. 05/1993-09/1993 and Pinto S. 03/1993-04/1993; *Entre nous*, 1 October 1993, Pinto S. 10/1993-11/1993, UEJF. Controversy surrounded the conference, but the debate was internal, focusing on the legitimacy of Jewish criticism of Israel.

208. Manifs (July 1999–June 2001), UEJF. The file "Subvention 1999" makes clear the UEJF began thinking of these issues prior to the violence in September 2000. After 2000, SOS racisme rejoined the struggle against antisemitism. Wieviorka, *La tentation antisémite*, 29.

Conclusion

1. Michel Wieviorka's, *La tentation antisémite: Haine des Juifs dans la France d'aujourd'hui* (Paris: Robert Lafont, 2005).

2. Jacques Tarnero, "Les territoires occupés de l'imaginaire Beur," *Observatoire du monde juif*, Bulletin No.1, November 2001, pp. 39–40, cited in Pierre-André Taguieff, *La nouvelle judéophobie* (Paris: Mille et une nuits, 2002), pp. 178-79, discusses a 1997/1998 survey in which French-born Muslim youth made these links.

3. Denis Sieffert, *Israël-Palestine, une passion française: La France dans le miroir du conflit israélo palestinien* (Paris: Éditions la Decouverte 2004), pp. 212–15.

4. Esther Benbassa, *La République face à ses minorités: Les Juifs hier, les Musulmans aujourd'hui* (Paris: Mille et une nuits, 2004).
5. Kimberly Arkin, "'It's the French and the Arabs against the Jews': Identity Politics and the Construction of Adolescent Jewishness in France" (Ph.D. diss., University of Chicago, 2008). Sieffert, *Israël-Palestine*, 217–30, discusses the way the fight against antisemitism has itself served to polarize.
6. Taguieff's focus in *La nouvelle judéophobie* and other work on fusions between radical Islam and third-worldism is useful for understanding a discursive shift in anti-Jewish thought. It is limited, however, in explaining transitions in social practice. Nor does such a framework help explain evolving Jewish positions on Muslims.
7. Benjamin Stora, *Les trois exils: Juifs d'Algérie* (Paris: Éditions Stock, 2006), pp. 177–81, makes a similar point.
8. "Réactions des responsables de la communauté juive des Bouches-du-Rhône, après l'attentat par explosif d'un foyer Sonacotra à Cagnes-sur Mer et sa revendication par un 'groupe Massada,'" 22 December 1988, 1693W233, BdR.
9. Alain Goldman to Monsieur le Grand Rabbin Haik, Toulouse, 19 April 1989; Alain Goldman to Fernand Tarraube, Directeur abattoire municipale, St Gaudens; Monsieur Fuzere, Vétérinaire abattoir municipal, St Gaudens, 19 April 1989; "Dissensions au sein de la communauté juive dans les Bouches-du-Rhône," 16 June 1989; "La communauté juive dans les Bouches-du-Rhône," 17 November 1989,1693W233, BdR.
10. In 2000, as Paris and other large French cities saw Muslim youth lash out against their Jewish neighbors, Marseille also experienced its share of violence, including the March 2002 arson of the Or Aviv synagogue. Unlike elsewhere in France, however, such attacks diminished rapidly, and Marseille saw very little social unrest in 2005 when banlieues throughout France were burning. Claire Berlinski, "The Hope of Marseille," *Azure* 19 (Winter 5765/2005), p. 33–34. Social commentators and scholars have disagreed over the cause for the relative calm in Marseille, focusing on everything from its sunny weather to its cohesive urban geography. For the range of explanations, see Jocelyne Cesari, Alain Moreau and Alexandra Schleyer-Lindenmann, *"Plus marseillais que moi, tu meurs!" Migrations identités et territoires à Marseille* (Paris: L'Harmattan, 2001), p. 11–26. For a recent analysis, see Katharyne Mitchell, "Marseille's Not for Burning: Comparative Networks of Integration and Exclusion in Two French Cities," *Annals of the Association of American Geographers* 101, 2 (2011): 404–23, who argues that Marseille's ethnically networked capitalist system combined with the city's urban development help explain its relatively peaceful ethnic landscape.

CPSIA information can be obtained
at www.ICGtesting.com
Printed in the USA
BVOW08s0500131017
497568BV00002B/40/P